THIS BOOK BELONGS TO:
Park to Close!
Park to Close!
Daily Safari

Bonkers
An original concept by author Cath Jones

Illustrated by Chris Jevons
MAVERICK ARTS PUBLISHING LTD
Studio 3A, City Business Centre, 6 Brighton Road, Horsham, West Sussex, RH13 5BB
 +44 (0)1403 256941

First Published in the UK in 2017 by **MAVERICK ARTS PUBLISHING LTD**
under the title *Bonkers About Beetroot*

Maverick children's books

Studio 3A, City Business Centre, 6 Brighton Road,
Horsham, West Sussex, RH13 5BB

+44 (0)1403 256941

distributed by Lerner

American edition published in 2018 by Maverick Arts Publishing, distributed in the United States and Canada by Lerner Publishing Group Inc., 241 First Avenue North, Minneapolis, MN 55401 USA

ISBN 978-1-84886-310-1

BONKERS

written by
Cath Jones

illustrated by
Chris Jevons

It was another quiet day at Sunset Safari Park.

“Good evening Penguin!” called Zebra.

But Penguin scowled.

"Are you **BONKERS**?" he said.

"How can it be a *good* evening? Nobody visited the park today. Our home is doomed!"

Zebra called a meeting.

"We have to find more visitors," he said, "We need to save our park."

"You're wasting your time," Penguin said. "Nobody comes because we're boring."

But Zebra tried anyway.

The animals hunted for the missing visitors.

Suddenly, Zebra let out a yell...

“BEETS!”

"Beets?" Penguin asked.

Zebra nodded. "People are crazy about beets. We must grow the biggest beets in the world."

"BONKERS!" said Penguin. "No one will visit a BEETS safari park."

But Zebra tried anyway.

He made a list of everything they would need.

So the animals built a **mighty** manure mountain.

"STOP!" shouted Penguin. "That's a **BONKERS** manure heap."

The animals

planted the seeds.

They watered.

The seeds began to grow.

One plant grew bigger than the rest...

"WOW-EE!" said Zebra.
"What a whopper!"

"When will that **BONKERS** beet stop growing?" Penguin asked.

Zebra wasn't sure.

The beet **grew** and **grew**...

Hundreds of visitors came to see the **giant** beet!

But the beet kept on growing...

RUMBLE
SQUELCH
RUSTLE
This vegetable is out of control, I have to stop it!

It grew **BIGGER** and **BIGGER**.

Soon there was no room for visitors!

MONSTER BEET
TAKES OVER PARK

Zebra began to **EAT** the giant beet.

"Are you **BONKERS**?" said Penguin.
"You can't eat all that."

But Zebra tried anyway.

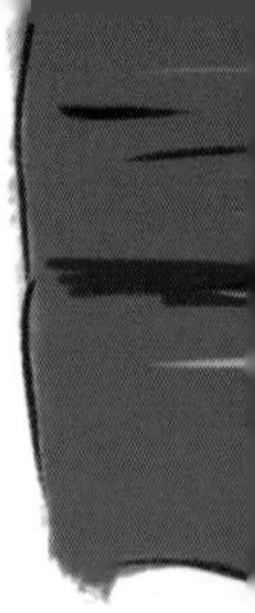

MUNCH
CRUNCH
SLURP

"AAGGHHH, OWWWW

WWWOOOOOO," moaned Zebra.

"HELP!" cried the animals, "Zebra is sick."
"Zebra's not sick," said Penguin. "But he's...

...turned **PURPLE**!"

Thousands of visitors arrived to see the only purple zebra in the world!

"Hooray for Zebra!" cheered the animals.

"He's saved our home."

And Penguin said...

"BONKERS!"

The End.

PURPLE ZEBRA
SAVES SAFARI PARK

Typo-
DESIGN
GRAPHic

FOREWORD BY KIT HINRICHS

DESIGN BY DAVID BRIER

This book is printed in four-color process. A few of the designs reproduced here may appear to be slightly different than in their original reproduction.

ISBN 0-942604-23-7

PRODUCTION CREDITS

Designer: David Brier

Design Associate: Denise M. Anderson

Editorial Associate: Marlene Hamerling

Administrative Associates:
Joelle Pastor
Chris Fuller

Computer Typography:
Bonnie Cohen
Paul Wohlstetter

Black & White Photography:
Stan Schnier

Cover Typography and Handlettering
David Brier

Library of Congress Catalog Card Number 91-066763

Distributors to the trade in the United States and Canada:
Madison Square Press
10 East 23rd Street
New York, NY 10010

Distributed throughout the rest of the world by:
Hearst Books International
1350 Avenue of the Americas
New York, NY 10019

Publisher:
Madison Square Press
10 East 23rd Street
New York, NY 10010

Printed in Hong Kong

ACKNOWLEDGMENTS

The following are acknowledged for their selfless assistance and persistence, which made this project possible:

Denise M. Anderson
Marlene Hamerling
Joelle Pastor
Chris Fuller
Bonnie Cohen
Paul Wohlstetter
Harvey Hirsch
Paul Pullara
Vicki Felix
Scott Harvin
Jerry McConnell
Steven M. Brier
Joyce Reis
New Type
Fox River Paper
Bell Press

My deepest thanks also go to the many other individuals who provided support along the way and, without whom, this volume would not exist.

. . . .

DEDICATION

This book is dedicated to the late, great Herb Lubalin, who provided me my first inspiration as to what could possibly be achieved with design and typography.

David Brier

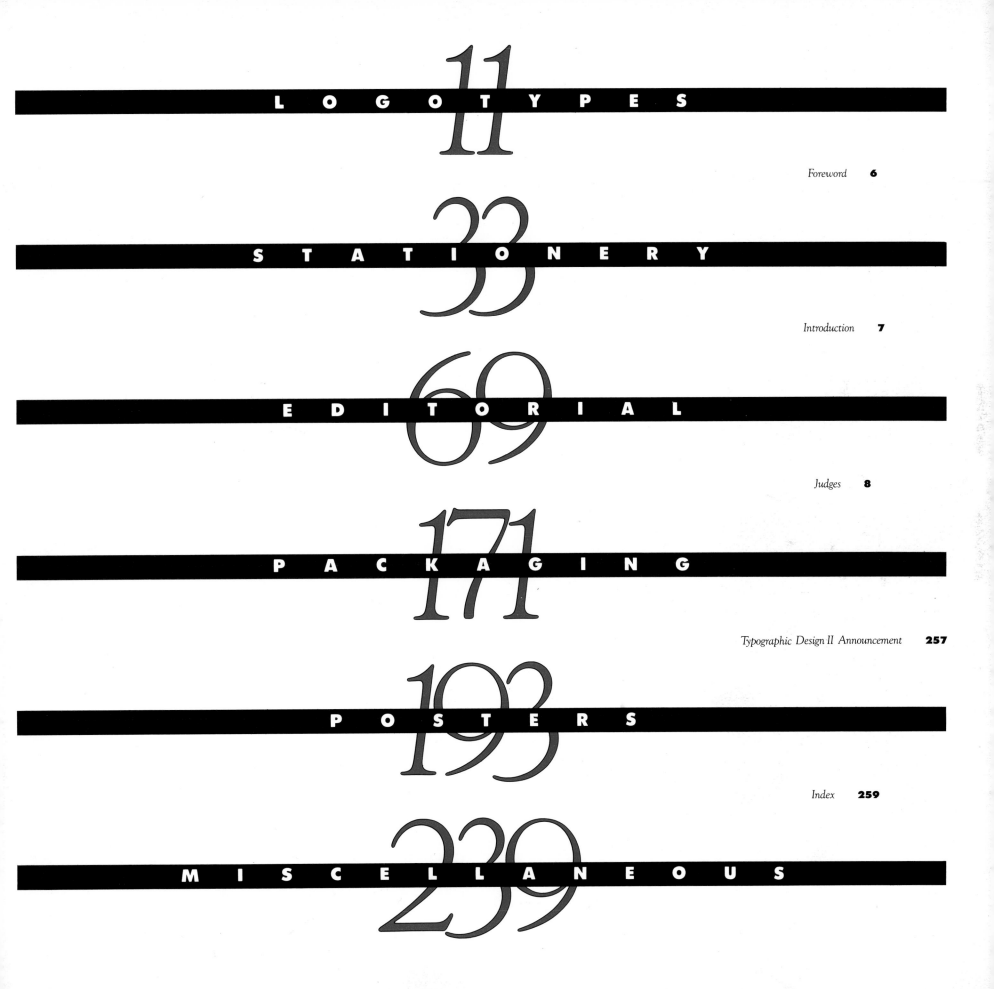

KIT HINRICHS
Partner
Pentagram

Typography, appropriately used, is one of the most effective means of communicating ideas with mood, style and emotion. Although ubiquitous in nearly every scrap of printed communications and electronic messages, typography continues to be a challenge to the master and novice alike.

Rapid technological changes over the past 10 years have had a profound effect on the character of typography within our profession. The 'coming of age' of the computer has created on one hand, a reinvestigation of traditional hand-set type, while on the other, a complete abandonment of typographic standards, leading to grotesque distortion of classic typographic forms, and everywhere in between.

Typographic Design may be the single document to chronicle, in detail, the typographic revolution of the editorial, promotional, corporate and advertising design of the 80's.

Kit Hinrichs

INTRODUCTION

Typographic Design is the result of 14 months of orchestrating, administering, and designing this international collection of what we feel are the best designs done from 1980 through 1990 — selected from more than 7,000 entries. The judges with whom I was honored to share the panel were Kit Hinrichs, Partner in Pentagram; Richard Wilde, Chairman of the School of Visual Arts Design and Advertising Department; and Fred Woodward, Art Director of Rolling Stone.

The work is presented in chronological order within each section. Because the book covers a decade, you may note trends that, while not 'today's look' are, nonetheless, completely valid and classically timeless.

In this age of computer-generated typography, sound typrographic standards become even more necessary. Typographic Design hopes to provide these standards as well as be a source of inspiration to typographers and design professionals everywhere.

DAVID BRIER
Chairperson of Typographic Design
President & Creative Director
DBD International, Ltd.

DAVID BRIER
KIT HINRICHS

RICHARD WILDE
FRED WOODWARD

LOGOTYPES

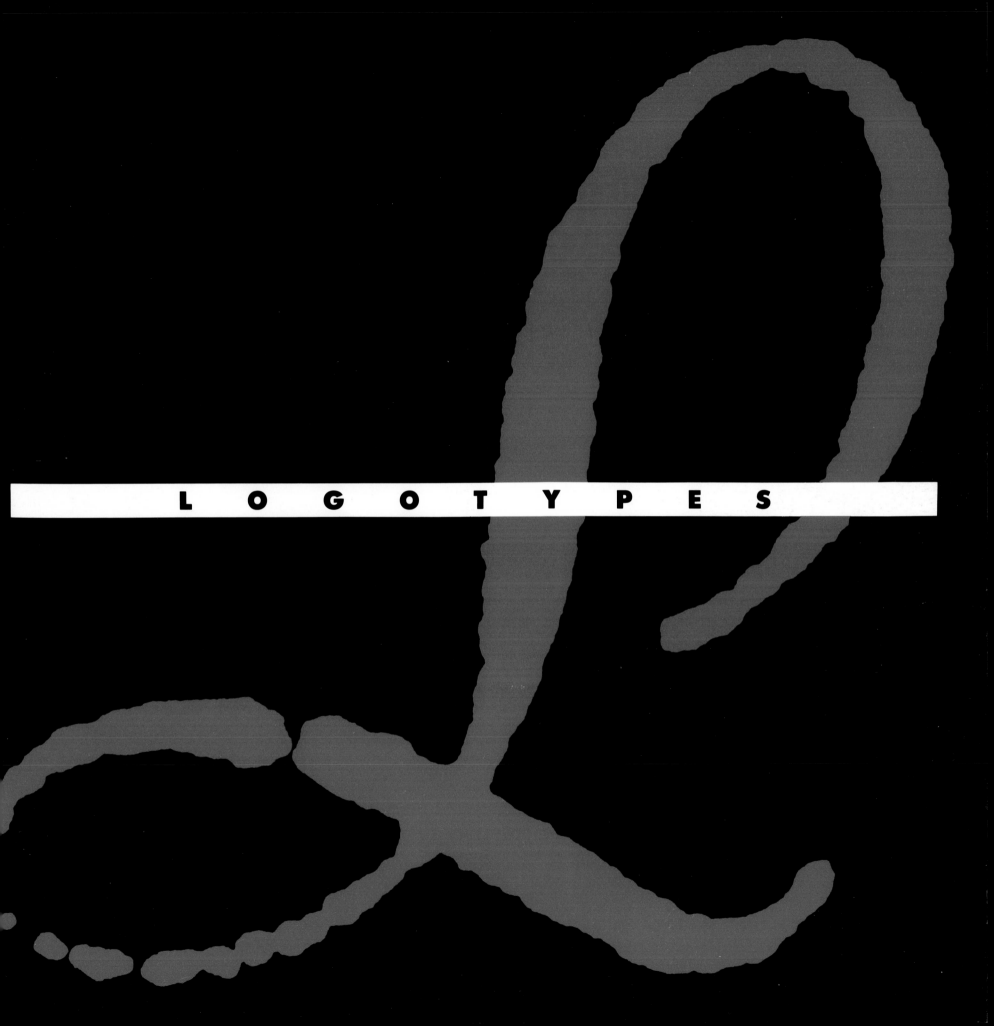

1
DESIGN FIRM: *Michael Doret, Inc.*
DESIGNER: *Michael Doret*
LETTERER: *Michael Doret*
HEADLINE TYPEFACE: *Handlettering*
CLIENT: *Graphic Artists Guild*

2
DESIGN FIRM: *Rousso & Associates*
DESIGNER: *Steven Rousso*
HEADLINE TYPEFACE: *Avant Garde*
CLIENT: *Rainbow Tree*

3
DESIGN FIRM: *Peter Nguyen*
DESIGNER: *Peter Nguyen*
HEADLINE TYPEFACE: *Helvetica Extra Compressed*
CLIENT: *New Hope MultiCultural Center*

4
DESIGN FIRM: *Pat Taylor, Inc.*
DESIGNER: *Pat Taylor*
LETTERER: *Pat Taylor*
CLIENT: *Miller Electric Company*

5
DESIGN FIRM: *Peterson & Company*
DESIGNER: *Bryan L. Peterson*
CLIENT: *Williams Pianos and Organs*

6
DESIGN FIRM: *Pat Taylor Inc.*
DESIGNER: *Pat Taylor*
LETTERER: *Pat Taylor*
CLIENT: *Hypertension Center*

1

2

3

4

5

6

8

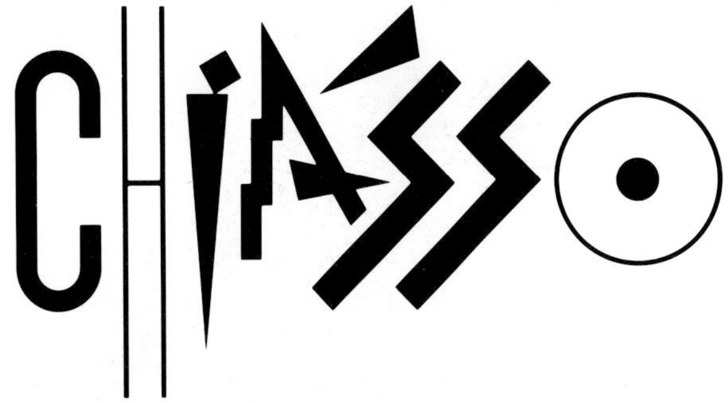

7

10

9

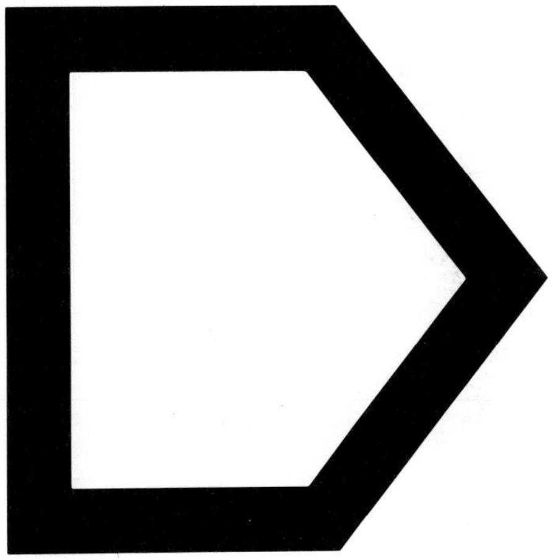

11

12

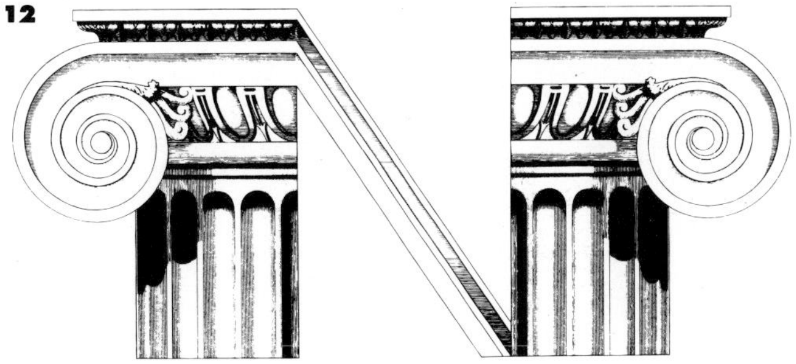

7
DESIGN FIRM: *Reactor Art & Design*
DESIGNER: *Louis Fishauf and Karen Cheeseman*
LETTERER: *Karen Cheeseman*
CLIENT: *Reactor Art & Design*

8
DESIGN FIRM: *Barnes Design Office*
DESIGNER: *Jeff Barnes*
LETTERER: *Jeff Barnes*
CLIENT: *Chiasso*

9
DESIGN FIRM: *Knape & Knape*
DESIGNER: *Willie Baronet*
CLIENT: *Dallas Advertising Softball League*

10
DESIGN FIRM: *Galarneau & Sinn, Ltd.*
DESIGNER: *Paul Sinn*
LETTERER: *Paul Sinn*
CLIENT: *Santa Cruz Hotel Bar & Grill*

11
DESIGN FIRM: *Peterson & Company*
DESIGNER: *Scott Paramski*
CLIENT: *Mountain Fuels Corporation*

12
DESIGN FIRM: *Neville Smith Graphic Design*
DESIGNER: *Neville Smith*
LETTERER: *Neville Smith*
CLIENT: *Novara Holdings Inc.*

13
DESIGN FIRM: *Peterson & Company*
DESIGNER: *Scott Paramski*
CLIENT: *Jim North*

14
DESIGN FIRM: *David Brier Design Works, Inc.*
DESIGNER: *David Brier*
LETTERER: *David Brier*
HEADLINE TYPEFACE: *Handlettering*
TEXT TYPEFACE: *Modified Garamond*
CLIENT: *David Brier Design Works, Inc.*

15
DESIGN FIRM: *Richards Brock Miller Mitchell and Associates*
DESIGNER: *Ken Shafer*
LETTERER: *Ken Shafer*
CLIENT: *Centennial*

16
DESIGN FIRM: *Eisenberg*
DESIGNER: *Scott Ray*
CLIENT: *Texas Hospice*

17
DESIGN FIRM: *Dennard Creative, Inc.*
DESIGNER: *Ken Koester*
LETTERER: *Ken Koester*
CLIENT: *Three Architectural Firm*

13

14

15

16

17

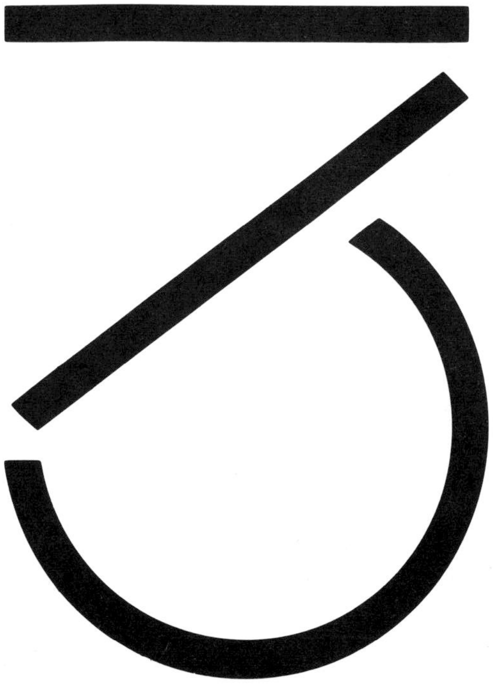

18

19

20

21

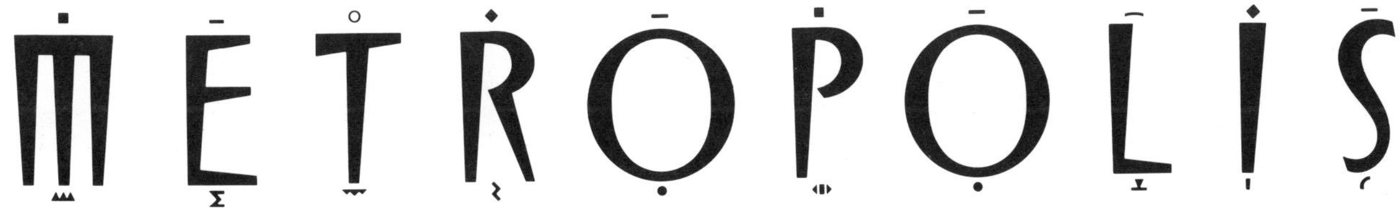

22

23

18
DESIGN FIRM: *The Duffy Design Group*
DESIGNER: *Charles S. Anderson*
LETTERER: *Charles S. Anderson*
HEADLINE TYPEFACE: *Garamond and Handlettering*
CLIENT: *Chaps-Ralph Lauren*

19
DESIGN FIRM: *The Duffy Design Group*
DESIGNER: *Charles S. Anderson*
LETTERER: *Charles S. Anderson and Lynn Schulte*
HEADLINE TYPEFACE: *Handlettering*
CLIENT: *Aura Editions*

20
DESIGN FIRM: *Daniel Pelavin*
DESIGNER: *Daniel Pelavin*
LETTERER: *Daniel Pelavin*
HEADLINE TYPEFACE: *Handlettering*
CLIENT: *Daniel Pelavin*

21
DESIGN FIRM: *Tim Girvin Design, Inc.*
DESIGNER: *Tim Girvin*
LETTERER: *Tim Girvin*
CLIENT: *Nordstrom*

22
DESIGN FIRM: *Tim Girvin Design, Inc.*
DESIGNER: *Tim Girvin*
LETTERER: *Tim Girvin*
CLIENT: *Bloomingdale's*

23
DESIGN FIRM: *Petro Graphic Design Associates*
DESIGNER: *Nancy Bero Petro*
LETTERER: *Nancy Bero Petro*
CLIENT: *Rocky River Board of Education*

24
DESIGN FIRM: *Petro Graphic Design Associates*
DESIGNER: *Nancy Bero Petro*
LETTERER: *Nancy Bero Petro*
CLIENT: *Visconsi Development Corporation*

25
DESIGN FIRM: *Pat Taylor, Inc.*
DESIGNER: *Pat Taylor*
CLIENT: *Marvelous Books Inc.*

26
DESIGN FIRM: *Hallmark Cards, Inc.*
DESIGNER: *Barb Mizik*
HEADLINE TYPEFACE: *Empire*
CLIENT: *Hallmark Cards, Inc.*

27
DESIGN FIRM: *Richards Brock Miller Mitchell and Associates*
DESIGNER: *Scott Paramski*
CLIENT: *Texas & Northern Industries*

28
DESIGN FIRM: *Peterson & Company*
DESIGNER: *Scott Ray*
CLIENT: *Phillip Cook*

24

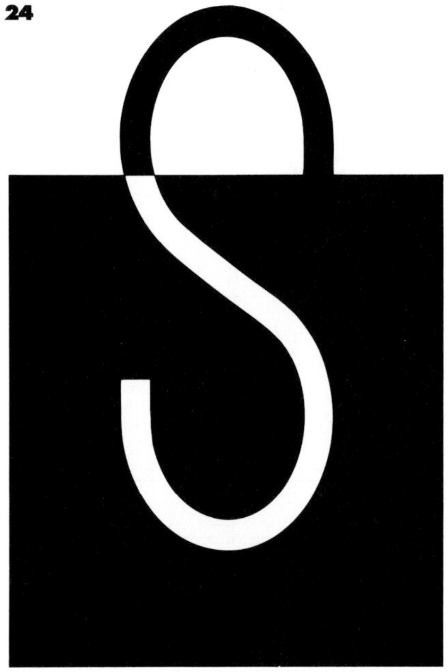

25

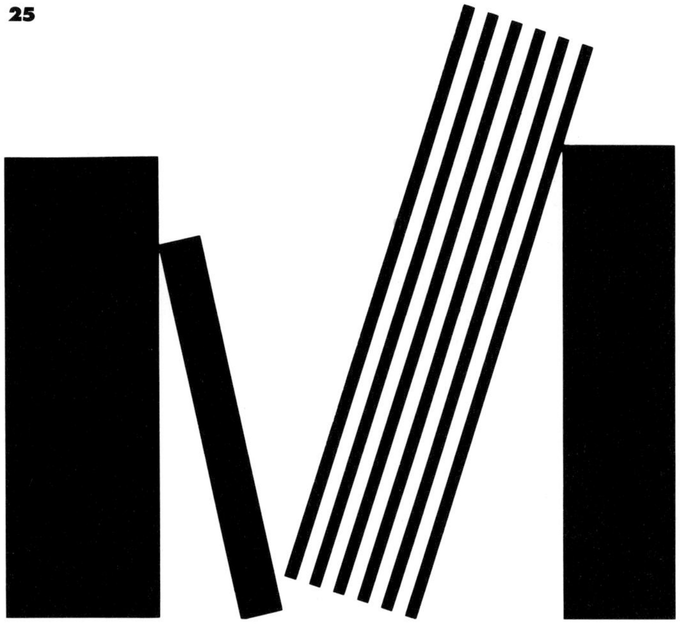

26

27

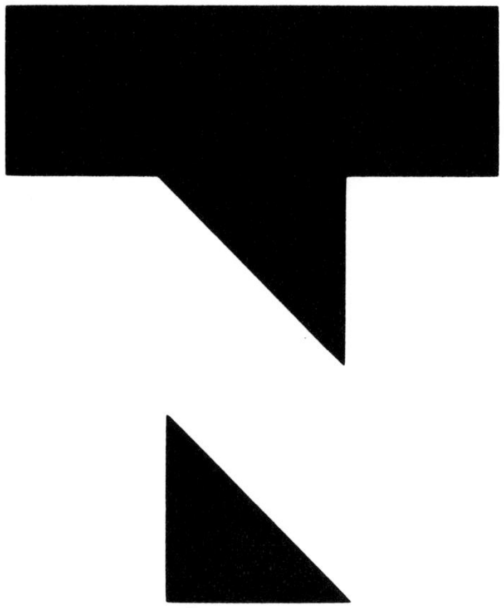

28

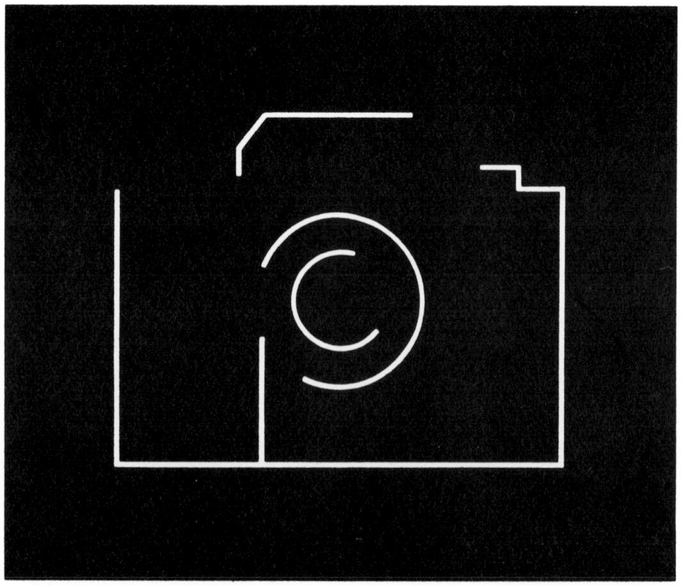

29

30

31

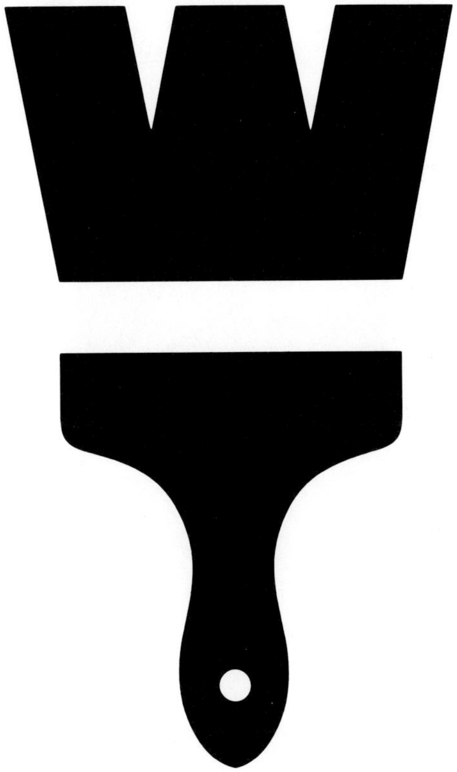

32

33

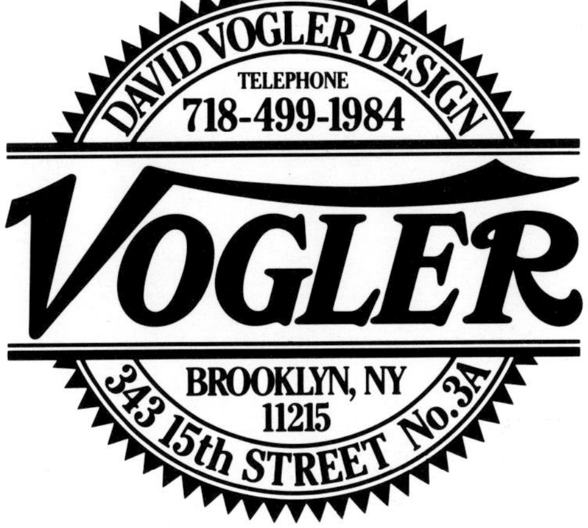

34

29
DESIGN FIRM: *The Duffy Design Group*
DESIGNER: *Joe Duffy and Sharon Werner*
HEADLINE TYPEFACE: *Cheltenham Book Italic, Helvetica Bold and Handlettering*
CLIENT: *Dickson's Inc.*

30
DESIGN FIRM: *The Duffy Design Group*
DESIGNER: *Charles S. Anderson*
LETTERER: *Lynn Schulte and Charles S. Anderson*
HEADLINE TYPEFACE: *Handlettering*
CLIENT: *French Paper Company*

31
DESIGN FIRM: *RBMM/The Richards Group*
DESIGNER: *D.C. Stipp*
CLIENT: *Willis Painting Contractors*

32
DESIGN FIRM: *Morla Design*
DESIGNER: *Jennifer Morla*
HEADLINE TYPEFACE: *Futura Bold*
CLIENT: *Levi Strauss & Company*

33
DESIGN FIRM: *David Vogler Design*
DESIGNER: *David Vogler*
LETTERER: *Ray Barber*
HEADLINE TYPEFACE: *Handlettering*
TEXT TYPEFACE: *Cheltenham Book Condensed ITC*
CLIENT: *David Vogler Design*

34
DESIGN FIRM: *Foster & Associates Design*
DESIGNER: *Jerry Foster*
LETTERER: *Jerry Foster*
CLIENT: *InterGlobe Financial*

35

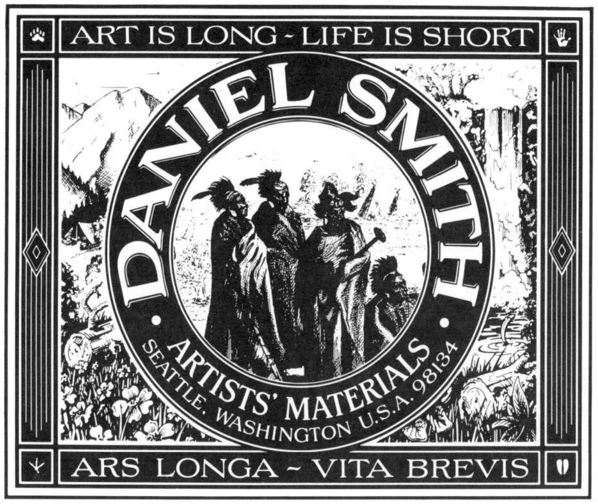

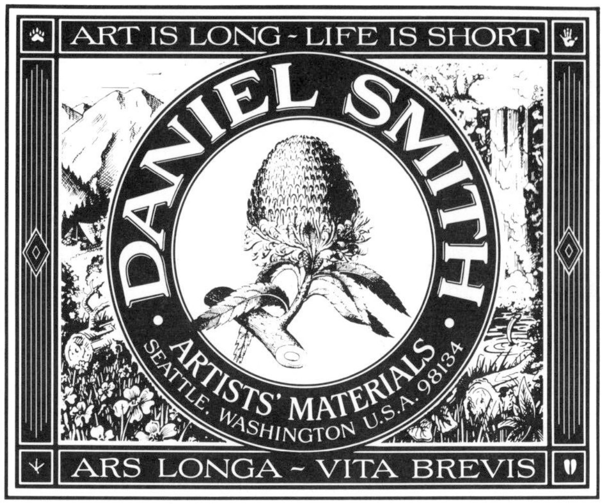

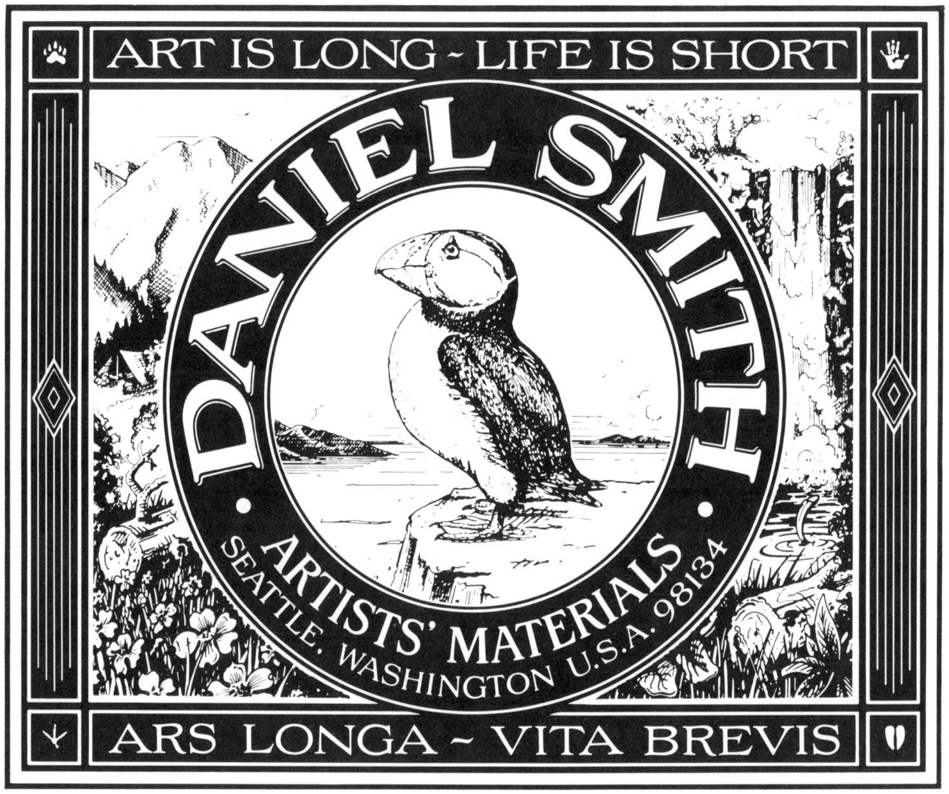

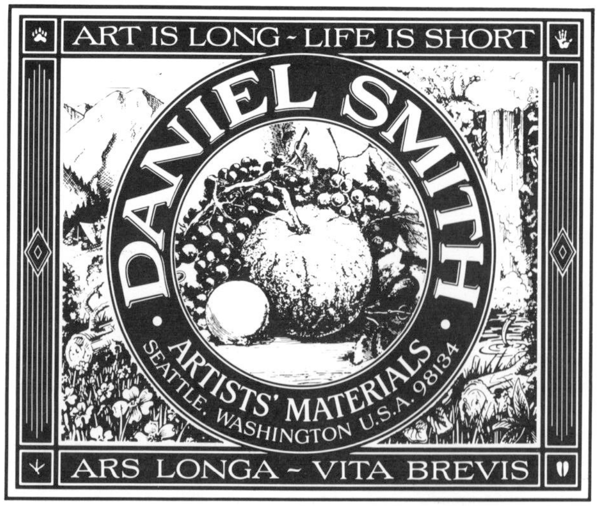

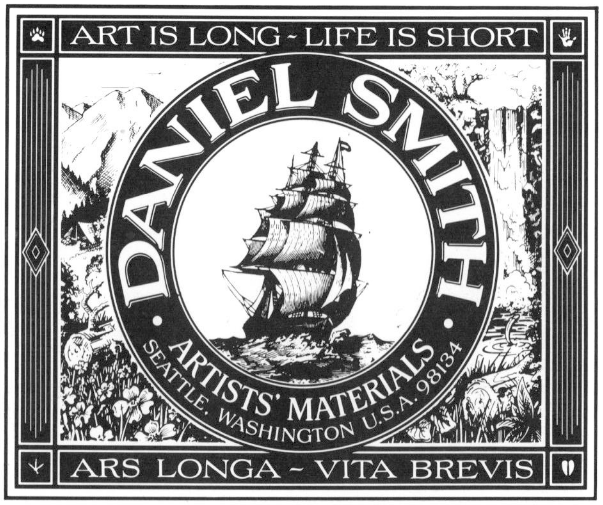

35
DESIGN FIRM: *Bruce Hale Design Studio*
DESIGNER: *Bruce Hale*
LETTERER: *Bruce Hale*
HEADLINE TYPEFACE: *Handlettering*
CLIENT: *Daniel Smith, Inc.*

36

37

39

38

40

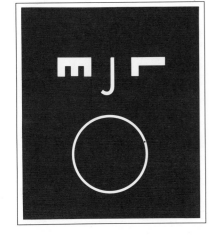

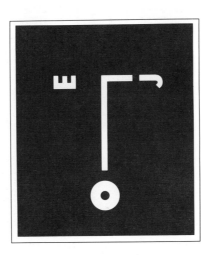

36
DESIGN FIRM: *The Duffy Design Group*
DESIGNER: *Sara Ledgard*
HEADLINE TYPEFACE: Onyx and Helvetica Bold
CLIENT: *Typeshooters*

37
DESIGN FIRM: *Principia Graphica*
DESIGNER: *Robin Rickabaugh and Paul Mort*
LETTERER: *Paul Mort*
CLIENT: *Oregon State University*

38
DESIGN FIRM: *Foster & Associates Design*
DESIGNER: *Jerry Foster*
LETTERER: *Jerry Foster*
CLIENT: *Hermes Ventures, Ltd.*

39
DESIGN FIRM: *Pentagram Design*
DESIGNER: *Peter Harrison and Susan Hochbaum*
TEXT TYPEFACE: *Univers*
CLIENT: *Elektra Entertainment*

40
DESIGN FIRM: H.M. + E. *Incorporated*
DESIGNER: *Paul Haslip*
HEADLINE TYPEFACE: *Futura*
TEXT TYPEFACE: *New Baskerville Bold and Italic*
CLIENT: *Joël Bénard Photography*

41
DESIGN FIRM: *Joseph Rattan Design*
DESIGNER: *Alan Colvin*
LETTERER: *Alan Colvin*
CLIENT: *David Baldwin Landscape Architect*

42
DESIGN FIRM: *Bruce E. Morgan Graphic Design*
DESIGNER: *Bruce E. Morgan*
LETTERER: *Bruce E. Morgan*
CLIENT: *Scherer & Sutherland Productions*

43
DESIGN FIRM: *Margo Chase Design*
DESIGNER: *Margo Chase and Lorna Stovall*
LETTERER: *Margo Chase*
HEADLINE TYPEFACE: *Handlettering*
CLIENT: *Gelinas*

44
DESIGN FIRM: *Supon Design Group, Inc.*
DESIGNER: *Supon Phornirunlit*
HEADLINE TYPEFACE: *Baby Teeth*
CLIENT: *Steven T. Bunn, DDS*

45
DESIGN FIRM: *Joseph Rattan Design*
DESIGNER: *Alan Colvin*
LETTERER: *Alan Colvin*
CLIENT: *Dr. David Dale*

46

47

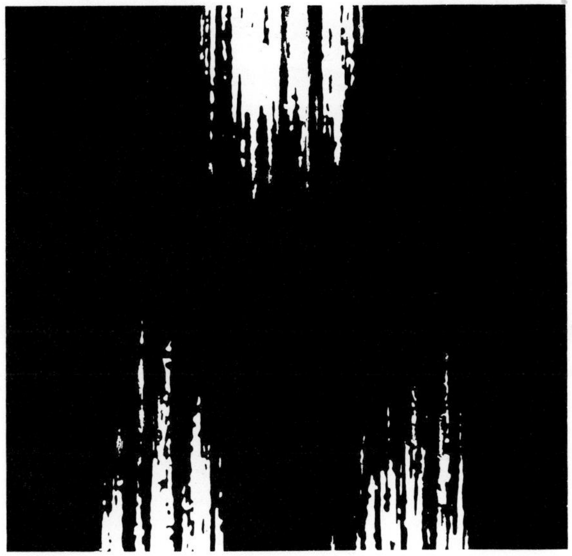

48

49

50

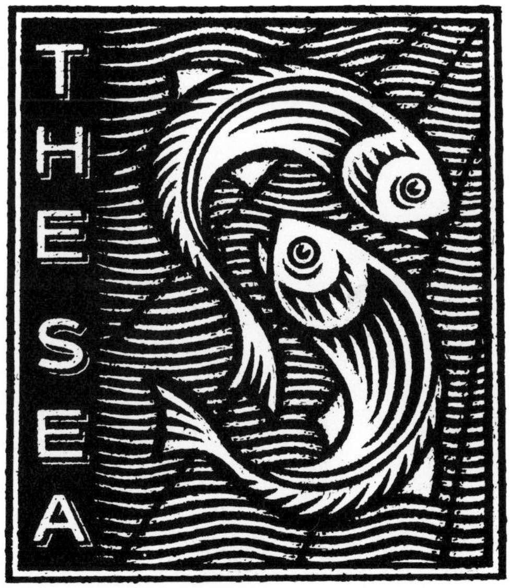

46
DESIGN FIRM: *Joseph Rattan Design*
DESIGNER: *Joe Rattan*
CLIENT: *Becky Wade*

47
DESIGN FIRM: *Minoru Morita Graphic Design*
DESIGNER: *Minoru Morita*
LETTERER: *Minoru Morita*
TEXT TYPEFACE: *Futura Book*
CLIENT: *Minoru Morita Graphic Design*

48
DESIGN FIRM: *Margo Chase Design*
DESIGNER: *Margo Chase*
LETTERER: *Margo Chase*
HEADLINE TYPEFACE: *Handlettering*
CLIENT: *Warner Brothers*

49
DESIGN FIRM: *The Duffy Design Group*
DESIGNER: *Haley Johnson*
LETTERER: *Sharon Werner*
HEADLINE TYPEFACE: *Handlettering*
CLIENT: *D'Amico & Partners*

50
DESIGN FIRM: *The Duffy Design Group*
DESIGNER: *Joe Duffy*
LETTERER: *Lynn Schulte and Joe Duffy*
HEADLINE TYPEFACE: *Handlettering*
CLIENT: *Essex & Sussex*

51

52

53

54

55

51
DESIGN FIRM: *The Duffy Design Group*
DESIGNER: *Haley Johnson*
LETTERER: *Haley Johnson and Lynn Schulte*
HEADLINE TYPEFACE: *Handlettering*
CLIENT: *Williamson Printing*

52
DESIGN FIRM: *The Duffy Design Group*
DESIGNER: *Sharon Werner*
LETTERER: *Sharon Werner and Lynn Schulte*
HEADLINE TYPEFACE: *Handlettering*
CLIENT: *Fox River Paper Company*

53
DESIGN FIRM: *Kilfoy Design*
DESIGNER: *Michael Kilfoy*
LETTERER: *Michael Kilfoy*
CLIENT: *Poster Poems*

54
DESIGN FIRM: *The Duffy Design Group*
DESIGNER: *Sharon Werner*
LETTERER: *Sharon Werner and Lynn Schulte*
HEADLINE TYPEFACE: *Handlettering*
CLIENT: *Lee Jeans*

55
DESIGN FIRM: *Peterson & Company*
DESIGNER: *Scott Ray*
CLIENT: *Dallas Repertory Theatre*

56

57

58

59

60

56
DESIGN FIRM: *RBMM/The Richards Group*
DESIGNER: *David Beck*
HEADLINE TYPEFACE: *Handlettering*
CLIENT: *Promotivators*

57
DESIGN FIRM: *The Pushpin Group*
DESIGNER: *Greg Simpson*
LETTERER: *Greg Simpson*
CLIENT: *Solo Editions*

58
DESIGN FIRM: *Margo Chase Design*
DESIGNER: *Margo Chase*
LETTERER: *Margo Chase*
HEADLINE TYPEFACE: *Handlettering*
CLIENT: *Warner Brothers*

59
DESIGN FIRM: *The Duffy Design Group*
DESIGNER: *Sharon Werner*
LETTERER: *Sharon Werner*
HEADLINE TYPEFACE: *Bodoni Italic and Handlettering*
CLIENT: *The Duffy Design Group/ Michael Peters Group*

60
DESIGN FIRM: *Jeffrey Halcro*
DESIGNER: *Jeffrey Halcro*
HEADLINE TYPEFACE: *Handlettering*
CLIENT: *Jeffrey Halcro*

61
DESIGN FIRM: *Margo Chase Design*
DESIGNER: *Margo Chase*
LETTERER: *Margo Chase*
HEADLINE TYPEFACE: *Handlettering*
CLIENT: *Sidney Cooper*

62
DESIGN FIRM: *Joseph Rattan Design*
DESIGNER: *Alan Colvin*
CLIENT: *Gallier Wittenberg/MEPC*

63
DESIGN FIRM: *Joseph Rattan Design*
DESIGNER: *Joe Rattan*
LETTERER: *Joe Rattan*
CLIENT: *Dallas Institute for Vocal Arts*

64
DESIGN FIRM: *Pat Taylor, Inc.*
DESIGNER: *Pat Taylor*
LETTERER: *Pat Taylor*
CLIENT: *Wisconsin Star Publishers*

65
DESIGN FIRM: *Adobe Systems, Incorporated*
DESIGNER: *Min Wang*
CLIENT: *Adobe Systems, Incorporated*

61

62

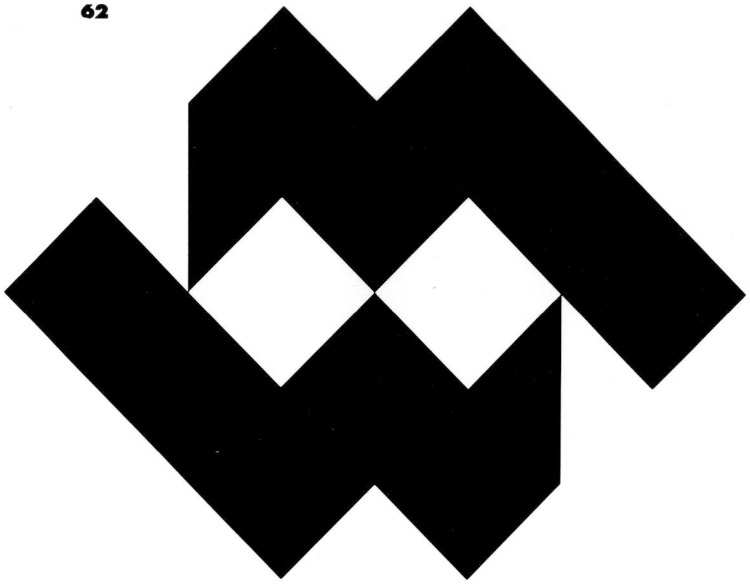

63

64

65

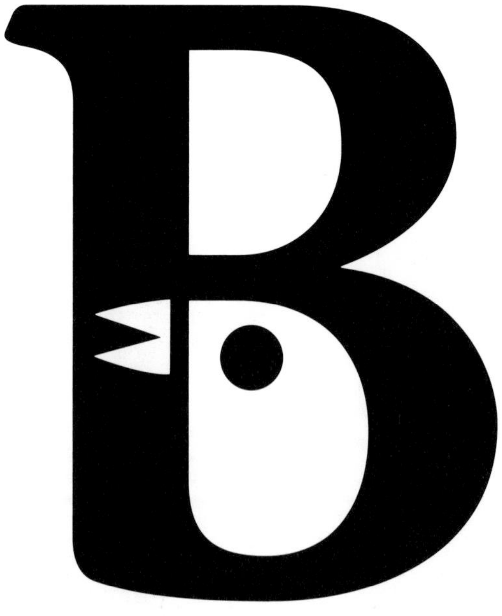

66

67

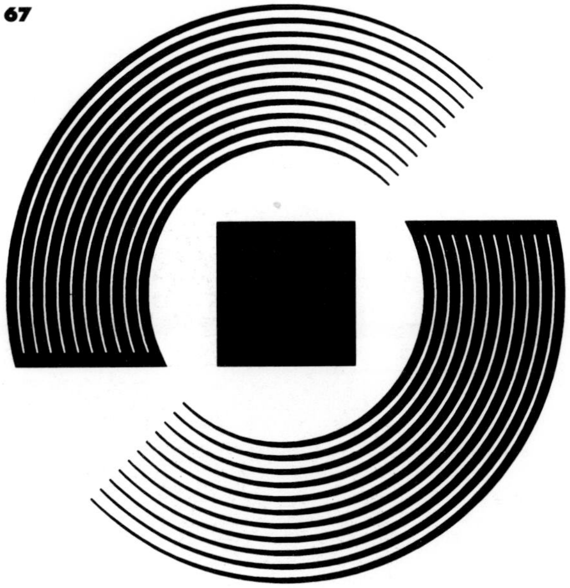

68

69

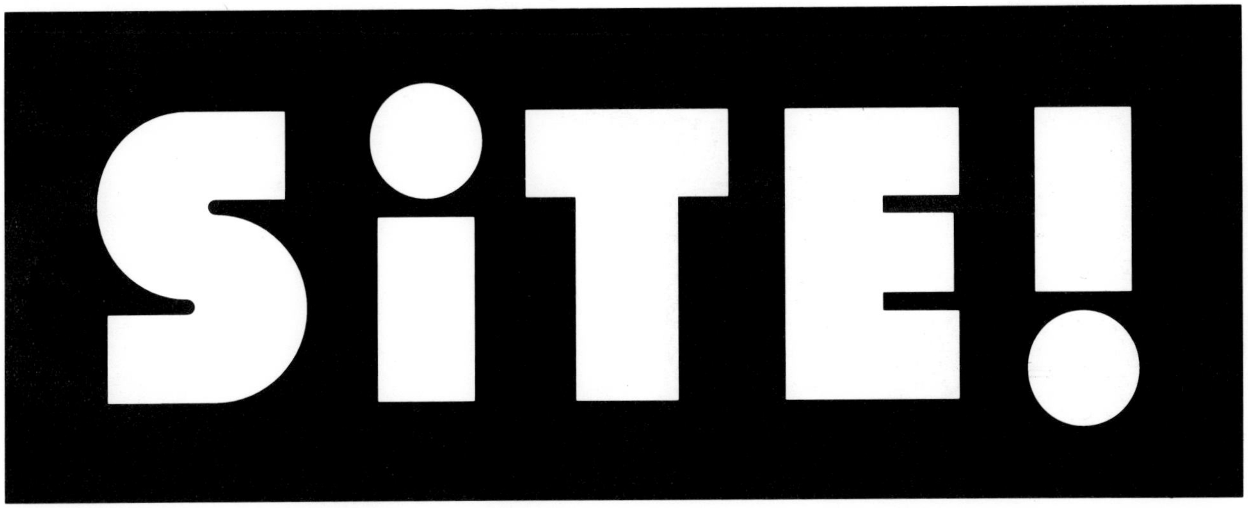

66
DESIGN FIRM: *Pentagram Design*
DESIGNER: *Susan Hochbaum and Woody Pirtle*
LETTERER: *Susan Hochbaum*
HEADLINE TYPEFACE: *Bodoni*
TEXT TYPEFACE: *Bodoni*
CLIENT: *Museum of Contemporary Art, Chicago*

67
DESIGN FIRM: *Knape & Knape*
DESIGNER: *Michael Connors*
CLIENT: *Strategic Telecom*

68
DESIGN FIRM: *Bennett Peji Design*
DESIGNER: *Bennett Peji*
LETTERER: *Bennett Peji*
HEADLINE TYPEFACE: *Handlettering*
CLIENT: *In to Ink-San Diego*

69
DESIGN FIRM: *Knape & Knape*
DESIGNER: *Allen Weaver*
LETTERER: *Allen Weaver and Michael Connors*
CLIENT: *City of Garland*

70

70
DESIGN FIRM: *Casa De'ideas*
DESIGNER: *Oswaldo Miranda*
LETTERER: *Oswaldo Miranda*
HEADLINE TYPEFACE: *Handlettering and Futura*
CLIENT: *Digital*

71

72

73

74

75

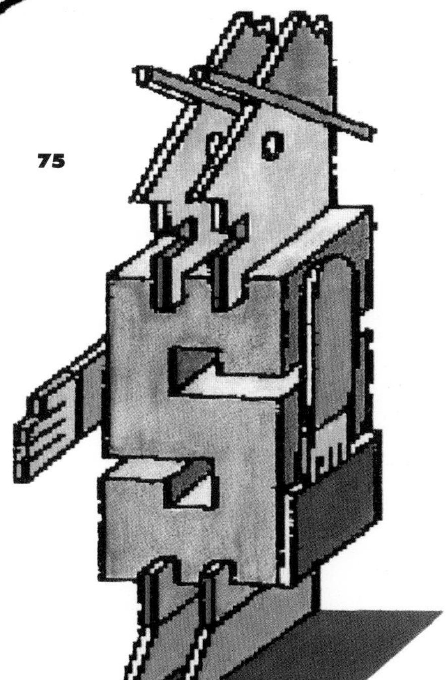

71
DESIGN FIRM: *Kan Tai-keung Design and Associates*
DESIGNER: *Kan Tai-keung and Vico Wong*
HEADLINE TYPEFACE: *Handlettering*
CLIENT: *Jade Pavilion Restaurant*

72
DESIGN FIRM: *Emerson, Wajdowicz Studios*
DESIGNER: *Jurek Wajkowicz*
HEADLINE TYPEFACE: *American Typewriter Condensed ITC*
CLIENT: *Grand Passage, S.A.*

73
DESIGN FIRM: *Kan Tai-keung Design & Associates, Ltd.*
DESIGNER: *Kan Tai-keung*
HEADLINE TYPEFACE: *English Calligraphy*
CLIENT: *LIS Forms & Printing (HK) Ltd.*

74
DESIGN FIRM: *Kan Tai-keung Design & Associates, Ltd.*
DESIGNER: *Kan Tai-keung Design & Associates, Ltd.*
LETTERER: *Kan Tai-keung and Freeman Lau Sin-hong*
HEADLINE TYPEFACE: *Chinese Calligraphy*
CLIENT: *Dragon Holdings Limited*

75
DESIGN FIRM: *Sullivan Perkins*
DESIGNER: *Art Garcia*
LETTERER: *Art Garcia*
CLIENT: *Sullivan Perkins*

76
DESIGN FIRM: *Gerard Huerta Design, Inc.*
DESIGNER: *Gerard Huerta*
LETTERER: *Gerard Huerta*
HEADLINE TYPEFACE: *Handlettering*
CLIENT: *CBS/Lou Dorfsman*

77
DESIGN FIRM: *The Duffy Design Group*
DESIGNER: *Sara Ledgard*
HEADLINE TYPEFACE: *Futura Bold*
CLIENT: *World Trade Center*

78
DESIGN FIRM: *Primo Angeli, Inc.*
DESIGNER: *Primo Angeli*
LETTERER: *Mark Jones*
CLIENT: *Lucca Delicatessens*

76

77

78

79

80

79
DESIGN FIRM: *Michael Doret, Inc.*
DESIGNER: *Michael Doret*
LETTERER: *Michael Doret*
HEADLINE TYPEFACE: *Handlettering*
CLIENT: *Margarethe Hubauer GmbH*

80
DESIGN FIRM: *Primo Angeli, Inc.*
DESIGNER: *Primo Angeli, Vicki Cero, Ray Honda, and Mark Jones*
LETTERER: *Mark Jones*
CLIENT: *Treesweet Products, Inc.*

81

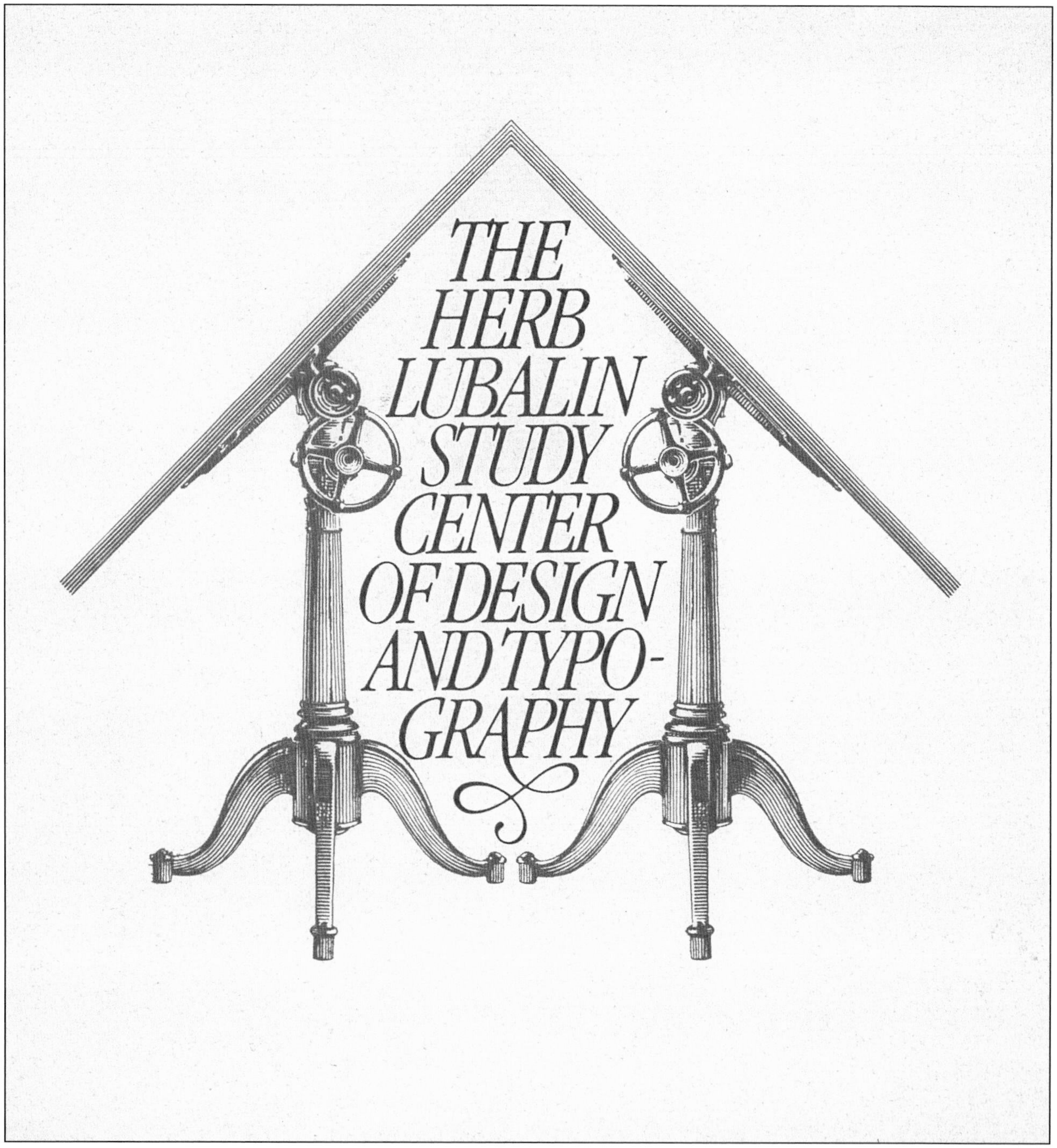

81
DESIGN FIRM: *Peckolick & Partners*
DESIGNER: *Tony Di Spigna*
LETTERER: *Tony Di Spigna*
HEADLINE TYPEFACE: *ITC Garamond Light Italic*
CLIENT: *Herb Lubalin Study Center*

82

83

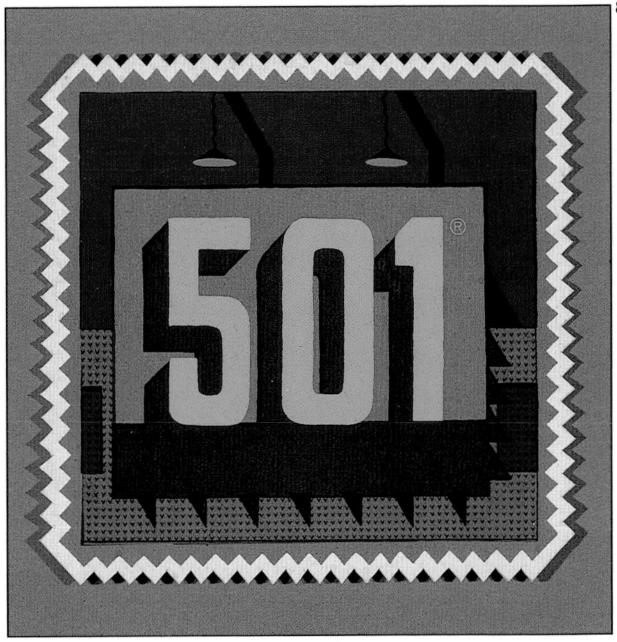

84

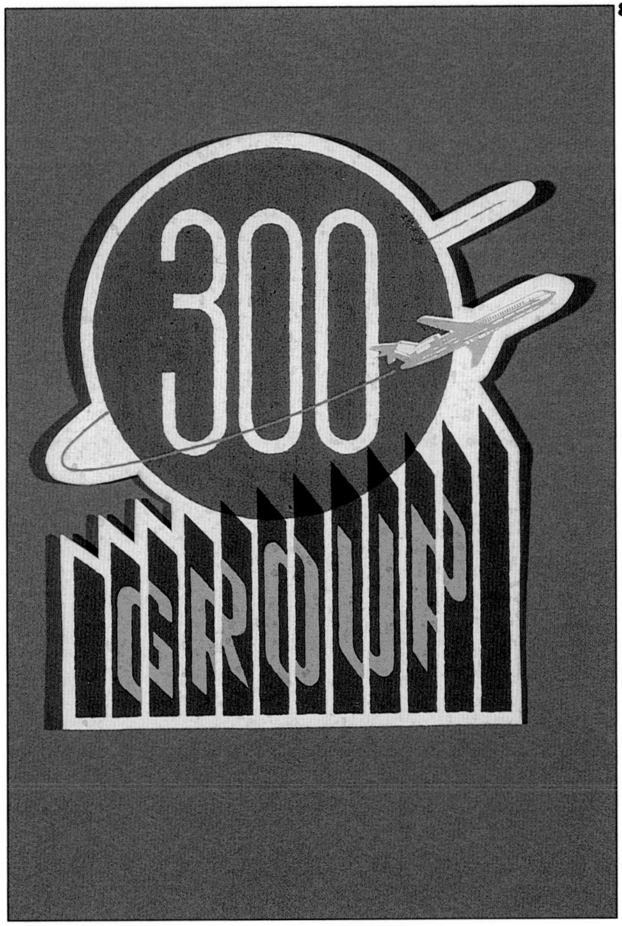

85

82
DESIGN FIRM: *Zimmermann Crowe Design*
DESIGNER: *Neal Zimmermann*
LETTERER: *Neal Zimmermann*
CLIENT: *Levi Strauss & Company*

83
DESIGN FIRM: *Zimmermann Crowe Design*
DESIGNER: *Neal Zimmermann*
LETTERER: *Neal Zimmermann*
CLIENT: *Levi Strauss & Company*

84
DESIGN FIRM: *Zimmermann Crowe Design*
DESIGNER: *Neal Zimmermann*
LETTERER: *Neal Zimmerman*
CLIENT: *Levi Strauss & Company*

85
DESIGN FIRM: *McCool & Company*
DESIGNER: *Deb Miner*
LETTERER: *Deb Miner*
HEADLINE TYPEFACE: *Modula and Futura*
TEXT TYPEFACE: *Modula and Futura*
CLIENT: *DataCard Corporation*

S T A T I O N E R Y

1

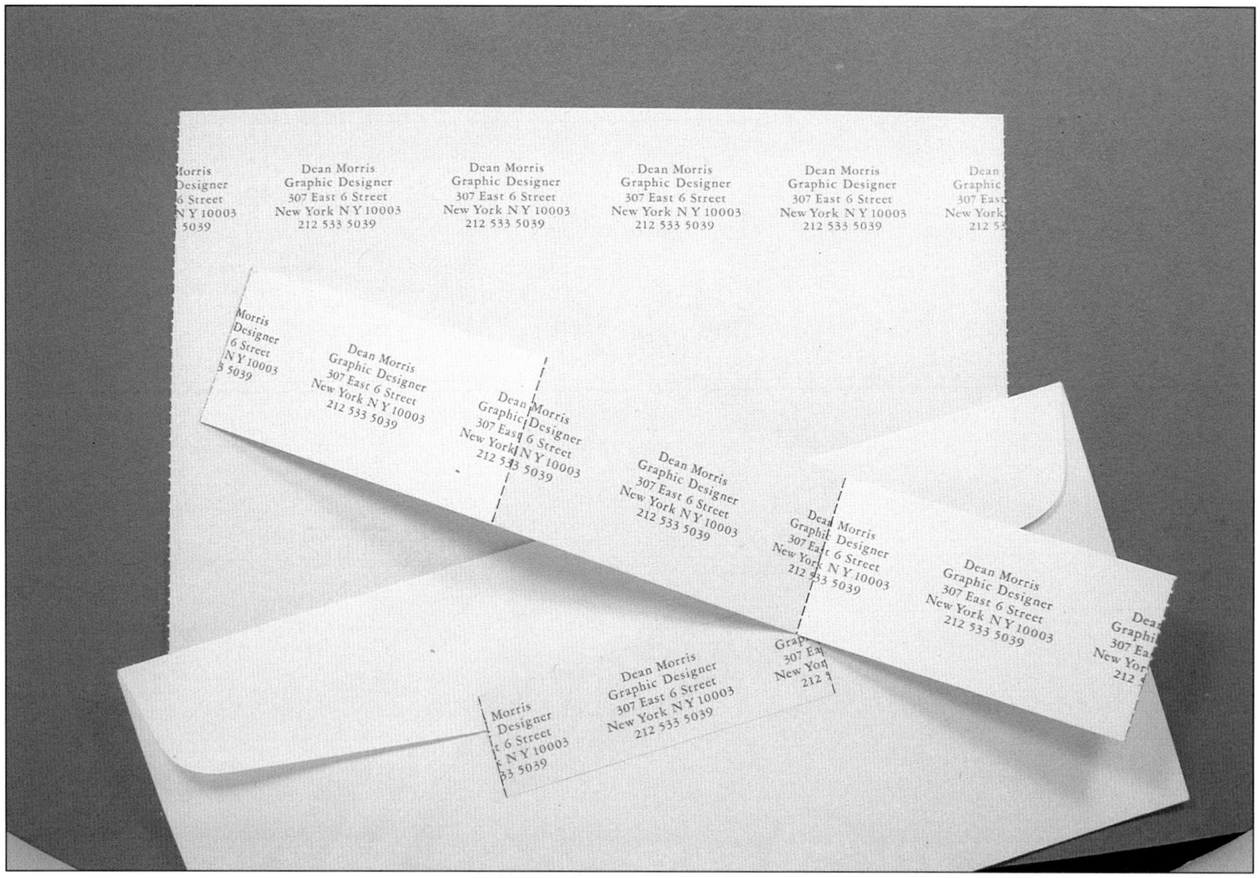

2

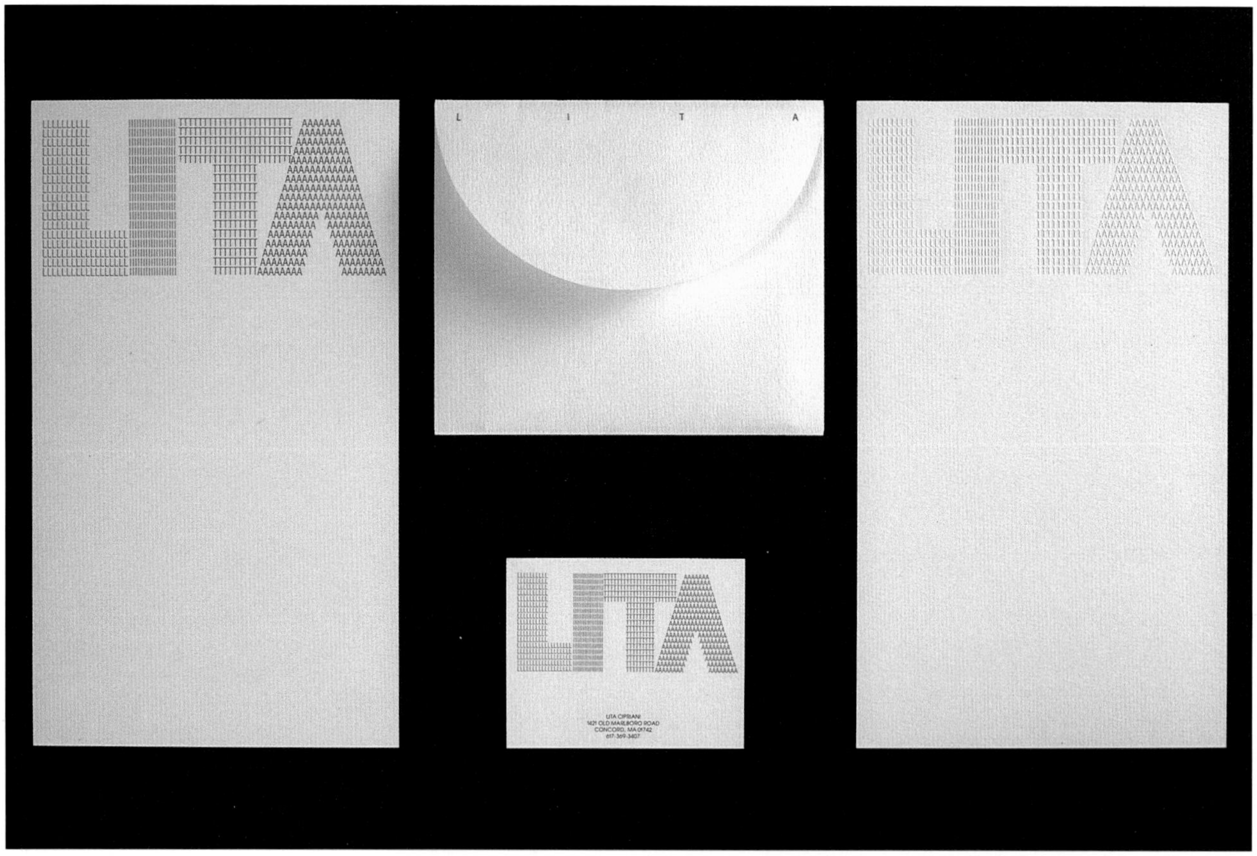

1
DESIGN FIRM: *Stylism*
DESIGNER: *Dean Morris*
HEADLINE TYPEFACE: *Garamond*
CLIENT: *Dean Morris Graphic Design*

2
DESIGN FIRM: *Cipriani Kremer Designs*
DESIGNER: *Robert Cipriani*
HEADLINE TYPEFACE: *News Gothic Condensed*
CLIENT: *Lita Cipriani*

3

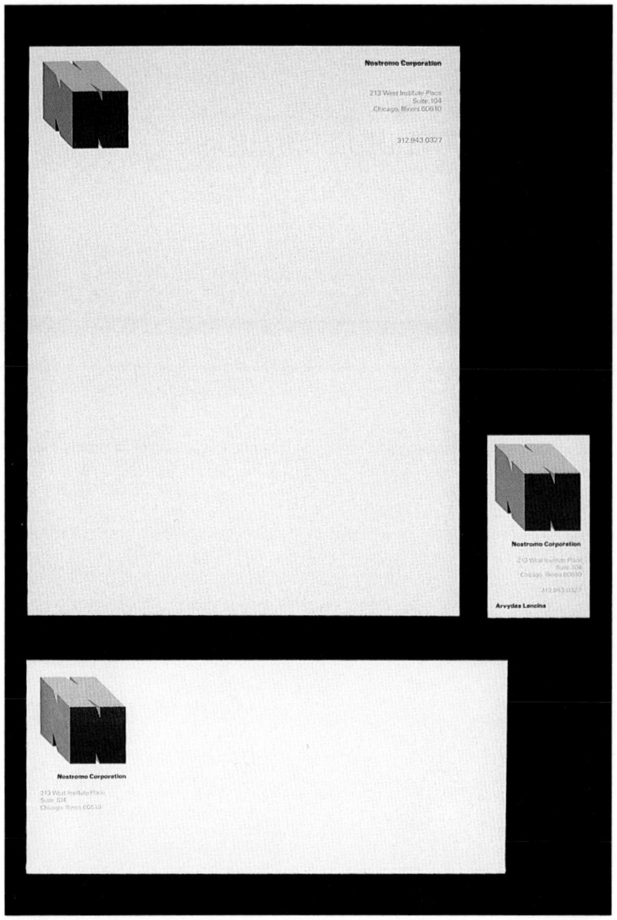

4

5

6

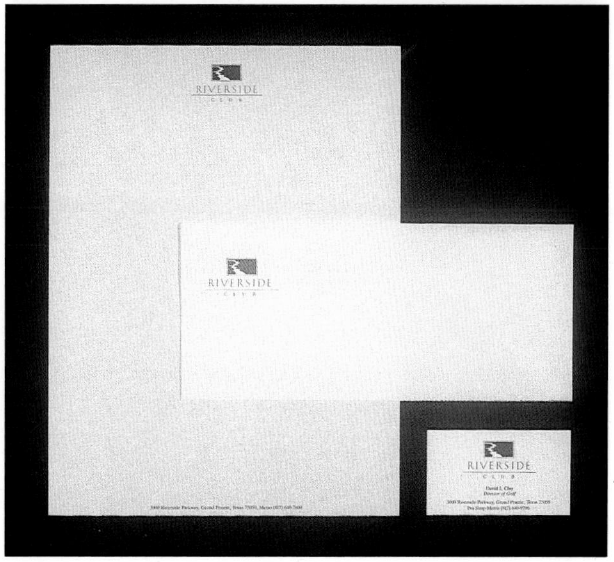

3
DESIGN FIRM: *Essex Two*
DESIGNER: *Joseph Michael-Essex*
LETTERER: *Joseph Michael-Essex*
TEXT TYPEFACE: *Univers 45*
CLIENT: *Nostromo Corporation*

4
DESIGN FIRM: *Essex Two*
DESIGNER: *Joseph Michael-Essex*
LETTERER: *Joseph Michael-Essex*
TEXT TYPEFACE: *Martin Gothic*
CLIENT: *Horwitz-Matthews*

5
DESIGN FIRM: *Neville Smith Graphic Design*
DESIGNER: *Neville Smith*
LETTERER: *Neville Smith*
HEADLINE TYPEFACE: *Handlettering*
CLIENT: *Black Cat Cafe*

6
DESIGN FIRM: *Dennard Creative, Inc.*
DESIGNER: *Bob Dennard*
HEADLINE TYPEFACE: *Bauer Text*
TEXT TYPEFACE: *Times Roman*
CLIENT: *Riverside Country Club*

7

7
DESIGN FIRM: *Kampa Design*
DESIGNER: *David Kampa*
LETTERER: *David Kampa*
TEXT TYPEFACE: *Frutiger Bold*
CLIENT: *Ellen Schuster*

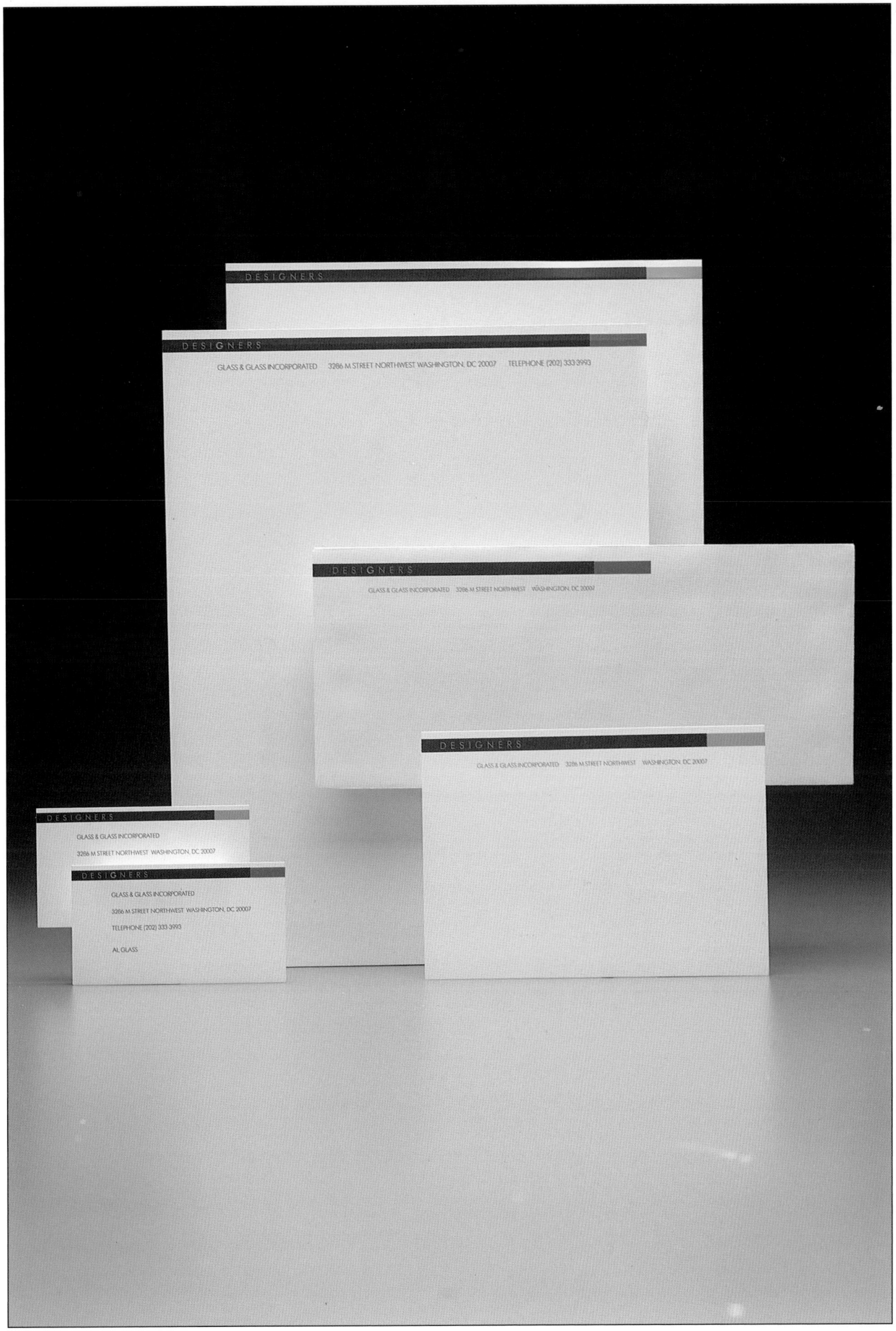

8

8
DESIGN FIRM: *Glass & Glass, Inc.*
DESIGNER: *Al Glass*
TEXT TYPEFACE: *Futura*
CLIENT: *Glass & Glass, Inc.*

9

10

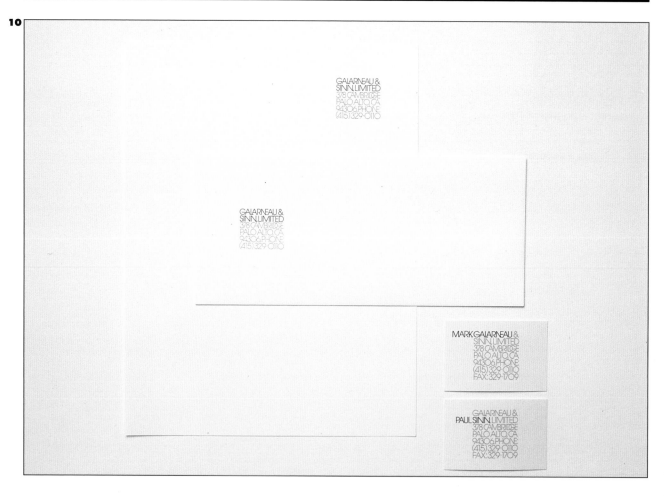

9
DESIGN FIRM: *DBD International, Ltd.*
DESIGNER: *David Brier*
LETTERER: *David Brier*
TEXT TYPEFACE: *Modified Garamondia*
CLIENT: *David Brier Design Works, Inc.*

10
DESIGN FIRM: *Galarneau & Sinn, Ltd.*
DESIGNER: *Mark Galarneau*
LETTERER: *Mark Galarneau*
HEADLINE TYPEFACE: *ITC Avant Garde*
CLIENT: *Galarneau & Sinn, Ltd..*

11

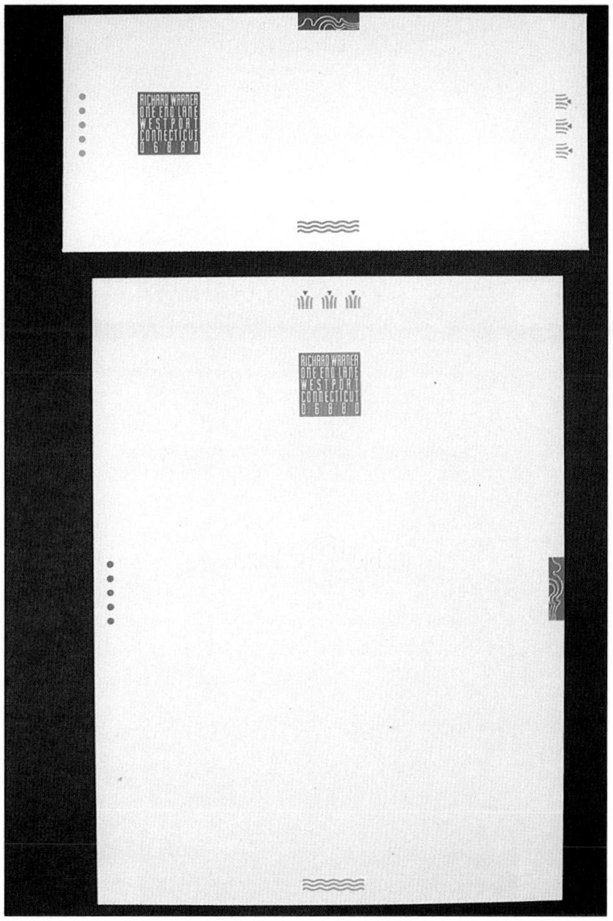

12

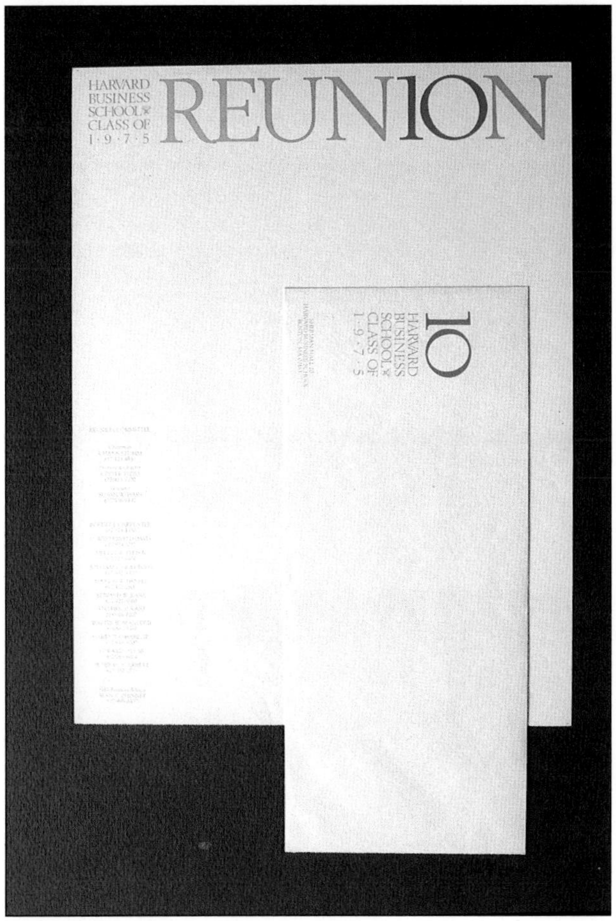

13

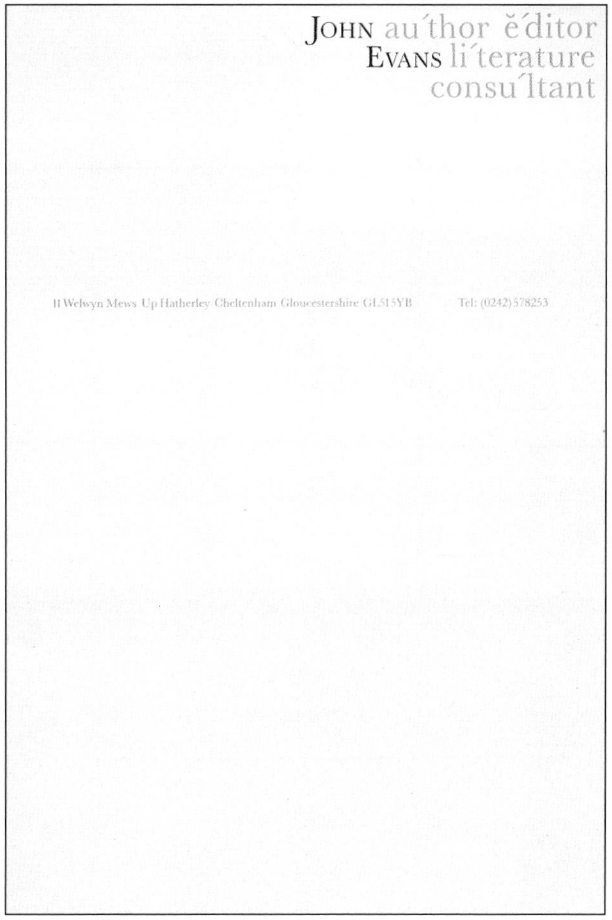

14

11
DESIGN FIRM: *The Duffy Design Group*
DESIGNER: *Charles S. Anderson*
HEADLINE TYPEFACE: *Futura Bold and Times Italic*
CLIENT: *Brooks Athletic Shoes*

12
DESIGN FIRM: *Daniel Pelavin*
DESIGNER: *Daniel Pelavin*
LETTERER: *Daniel Pelavin*
HEADLINE TYPEFACE: *Handlettering*
CLIENT: *Richard Warner*

13
DESIGN FIRM: *Rizzo, Simons, Cohn*
DESIGNER: *Rosemary Conroy*
HEADLINE TYPEFACE: *Goudy*
TEXT TYPEFACE: *Goudy*
CLIENT: *Harvard Business School*

14
DESIGN FIRM: *Richard Downer, Ltd.*
DESIGNER: *Richard Downer*
HEADLINE TYPEFACE: *Baskerville*
TEXT TYPEFACE: *Baskerville*
CLIENT: *John Evans*

15

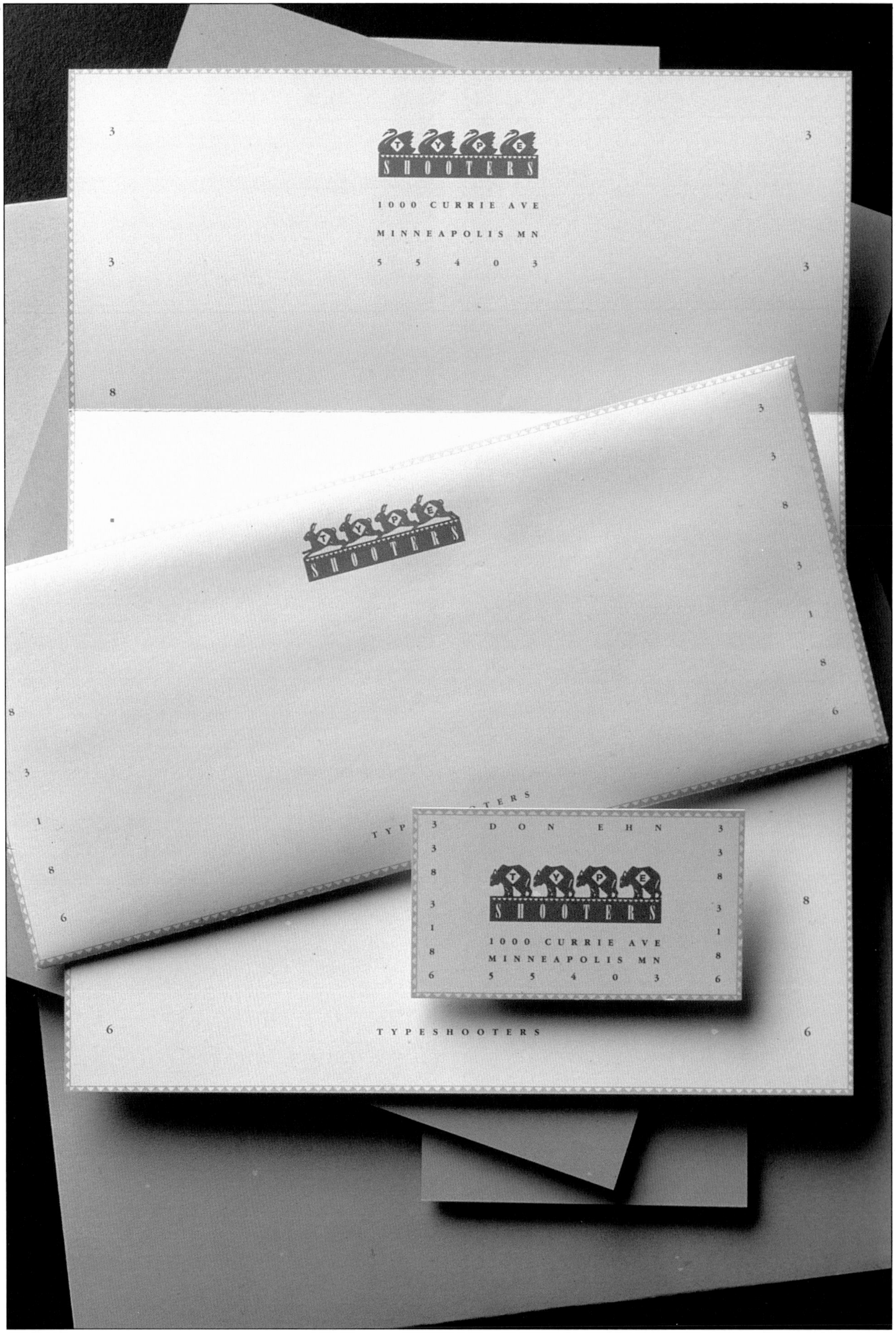

15
DESIGN FIRM: *The Duffy Design Group*
DESIGNER: *Sara Ledgard*
HEADLINE TYPEFACE: *Helvetica Bold and Garamond*
CLIENT: *TypeShooters*

16

16
DESIGN FIRM: *Sayles Design*
DESIGNER: *John Sayles*
LETTERER: *John Sayles*
HEADLINE TYPEFACE: *Handlettering*
TEXT TYPEFACE: *Garamond*
CLIENT: *Mid-America Student Loan Company*

17

17
DESIGN FIRM: *The Duffy Design Group*
DESIGNER: *Charles S. Anderson and Sharon Werner*
HEADLINE TYPEFACE: *Franklin Gothic*
CLIENT: *Medical Innovation Capital*

18

19

20

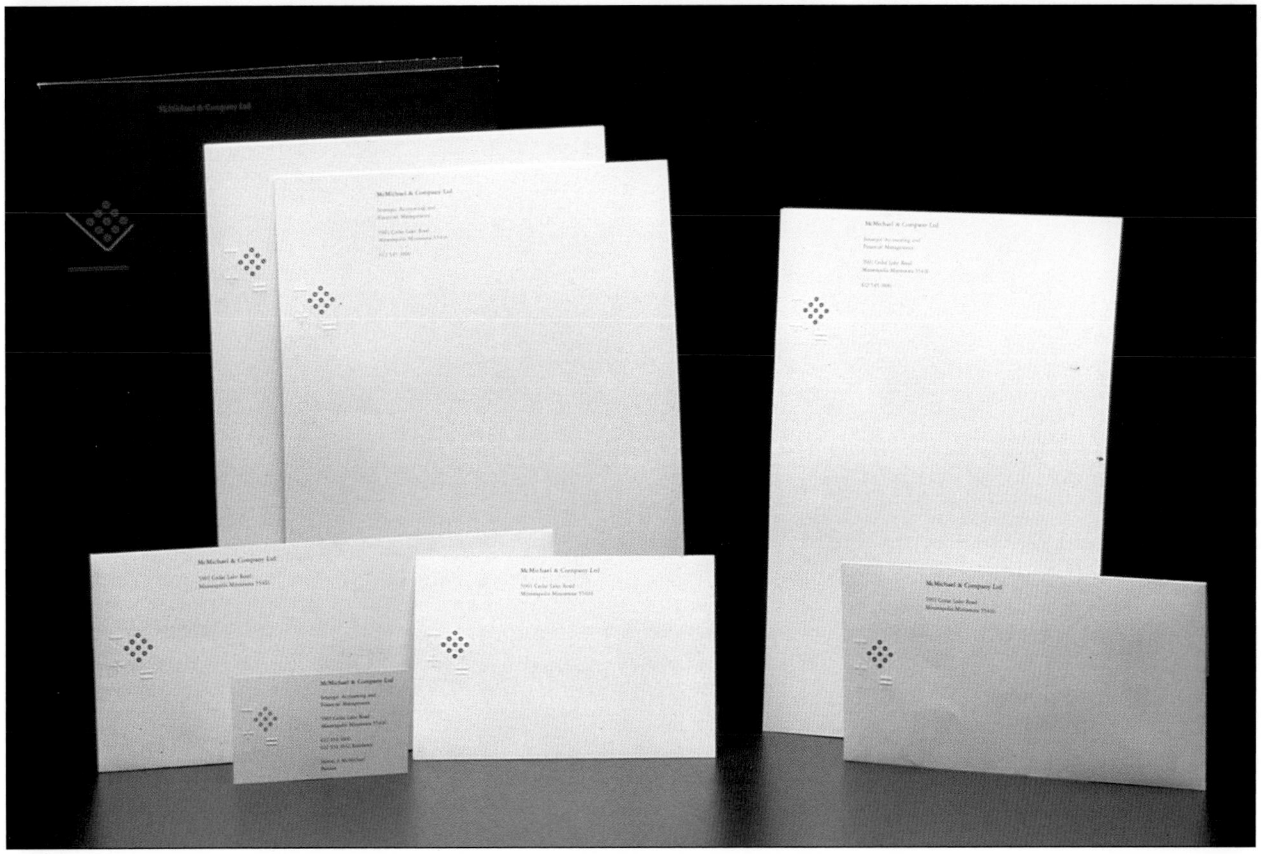
21

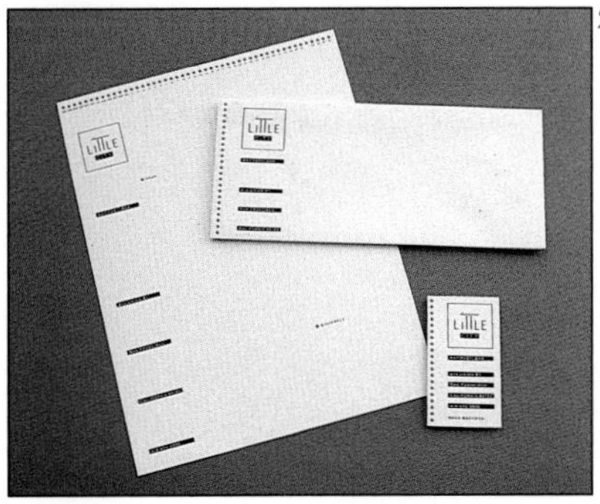
22

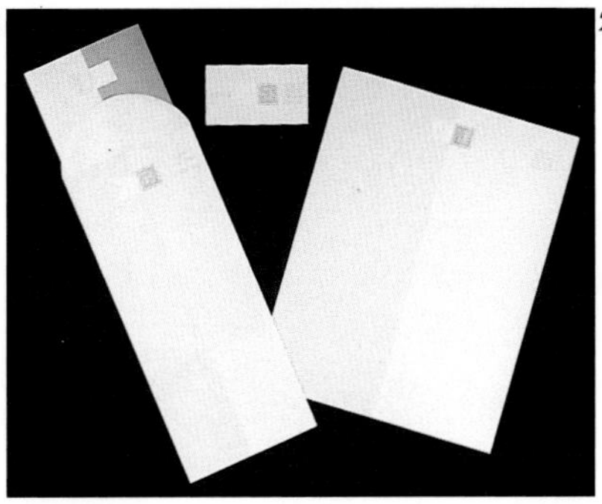
23

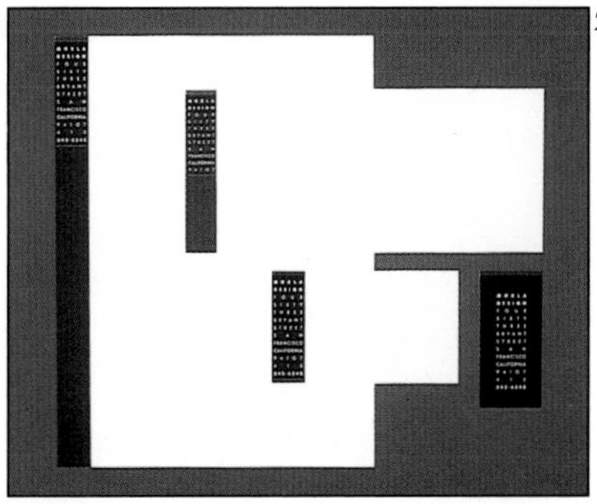
24

18
DESIGN FIRM: *The Duffy Design Group*
DESIGNER: *Sharon Werner*
HEADLINE TYPEFACE: *Century Schoolbook Italic*
CLIENT: *Dickson's Inc.*

19
DESIGN FIRM: *Neville Smith Graphic Design*
DESIGNER: *Neville Smith*
LETTERER: *Neville Smith*
HEADLINE TYPEFACE: *Handlettering*
TEXT TYPEFACE: *Berthhold Script Medium and McCanorma*
CLIENT: *Moda Hair Design*

20
DESIGN FIRM: *Muller & Company*
DESIGNER: *Patrice Eilts*
LETTERER: *Patrice Eilts*
HEADLINE TYPEFACE: *Univers 39*
TEXT TYPEFACE: *Garamond Lite Condensed*
CLIENT: *Spontaneous Combustion*

21
DESIGN FIRM: *McCool & Company*
DESIGNER: *Jo Davison Strand*
TEXT TYPEFACE: *Garamond 3*
CLIENT: *McMichael*

22
DESIGN FIRM: *Bruce Yelaska Design*
DESIGNER: *Bruce Yelaska*
LETTERER: *Bruce Yelaska*
TEXT TYPEFACE: *Copperplate Gothic*
CLIENT: *Little City Restaurant & Anti Pasta Bar*

23
DESIGN FIRM: *Muller & Company*
DESIGNER: *Patrice Eilts*
LETTERER: *Patrice Eilts*
HEADLINE TYPEFACE: *Univers 39*
TEXT TYPEFACE: *Univers 39*
CLIENT: *NIC Print*

24
DESIGN FIRM: *Morla Design*
DESIGNER: *Jennifer Morla*
HEADLINE TYPEFACE: *Futura Medium*
CLIENT: *Morla Design*

25

26

25
DESIGN FIRM: *Schafer Design*
DESIGNER: *Vickie Schafer*
LETTERER: *Vickie Schafer*
TEXT TYPEFACE: *Michaelangelo*
CLIENT: *Mac Arthur Construction Company*

26
DESIGN FIRM: *Merten Design Group*
DESIGNER: *Barry A. Merten and Roland Hill*
HEADLINE TYPEFACE: *Caslon*
TEXT TYPEFACE: *Futura Condensed*
CLIENT: *Typographic Arts*

27
DESIGN FIRM: *The Duffy Design Group*
DESIGNER: *Sara Ledgard*
HEADLINE TYPEFACE: *Helvetica Bold Extra Condensed*
TEXT TYPEFACE: *Helvetica Bold*
CLIENT: *Lennon and Bausman*

28
DESIGN FIRM: *Margo Chase Design*
DESIGNER: *Margo Chase*
LETTERER: *Margo Chase*
CLIENT: *Margo Chase Design*

29

DESIGN FIRM: *Ian Brignell Lettering Design*
DESIGNER: *Ian Brignell*
LETTERER: *Ian Brignell*
HEADLINE TYPEFACE: *Handlettering*
TEXT TYPEFACE: *Bodoni*
CLIENT: *Ian Brignell*

30

DESIGN FIRM: *Foster & Associates, Design*
DESIGNER: *Jerry Foster*
LETTERER: *Jerry Foster*
HEADLINE TYPEFACE: *Garth Regular*
TEXT TYPEFACE: *Garth Regular*
CLIENT: *Interglobe Financial*

29

30

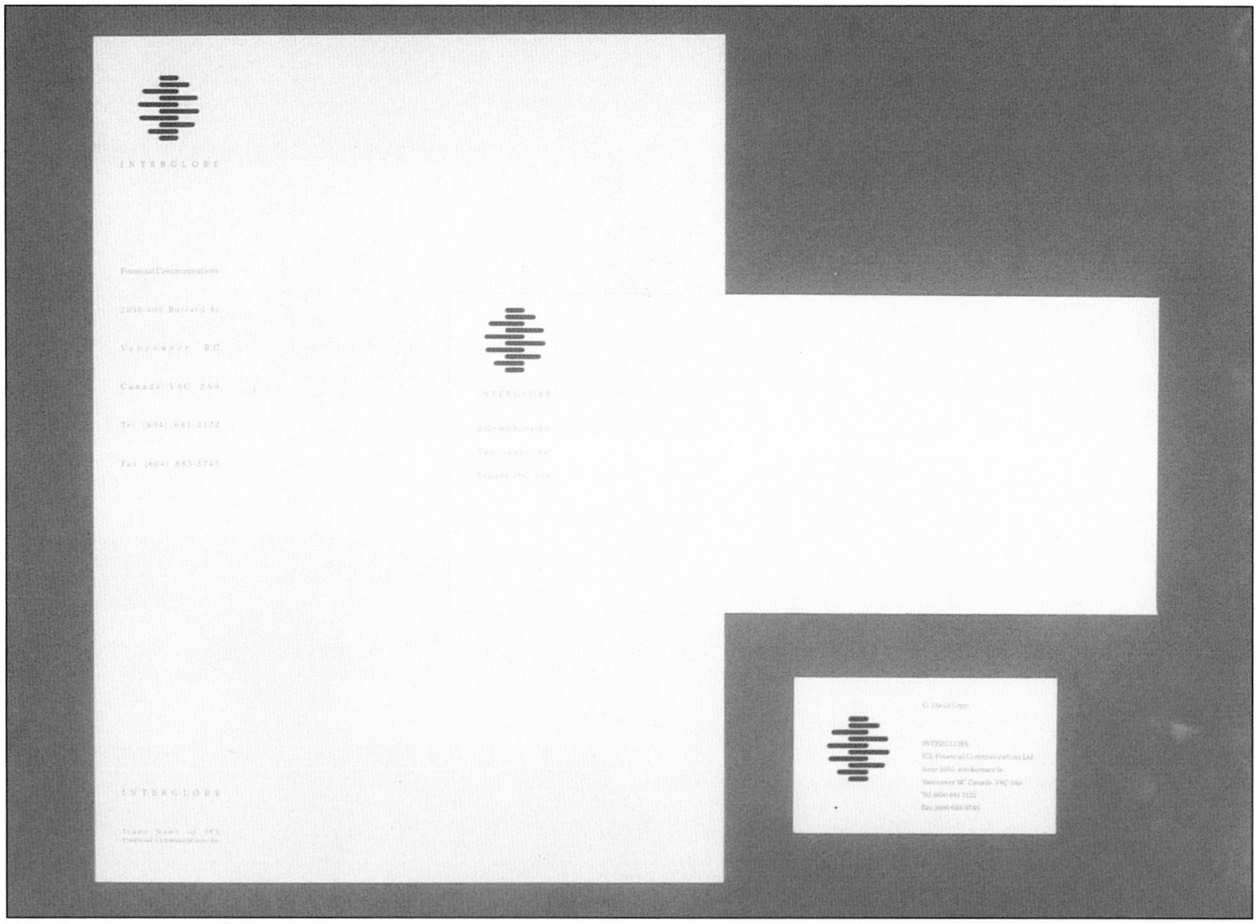

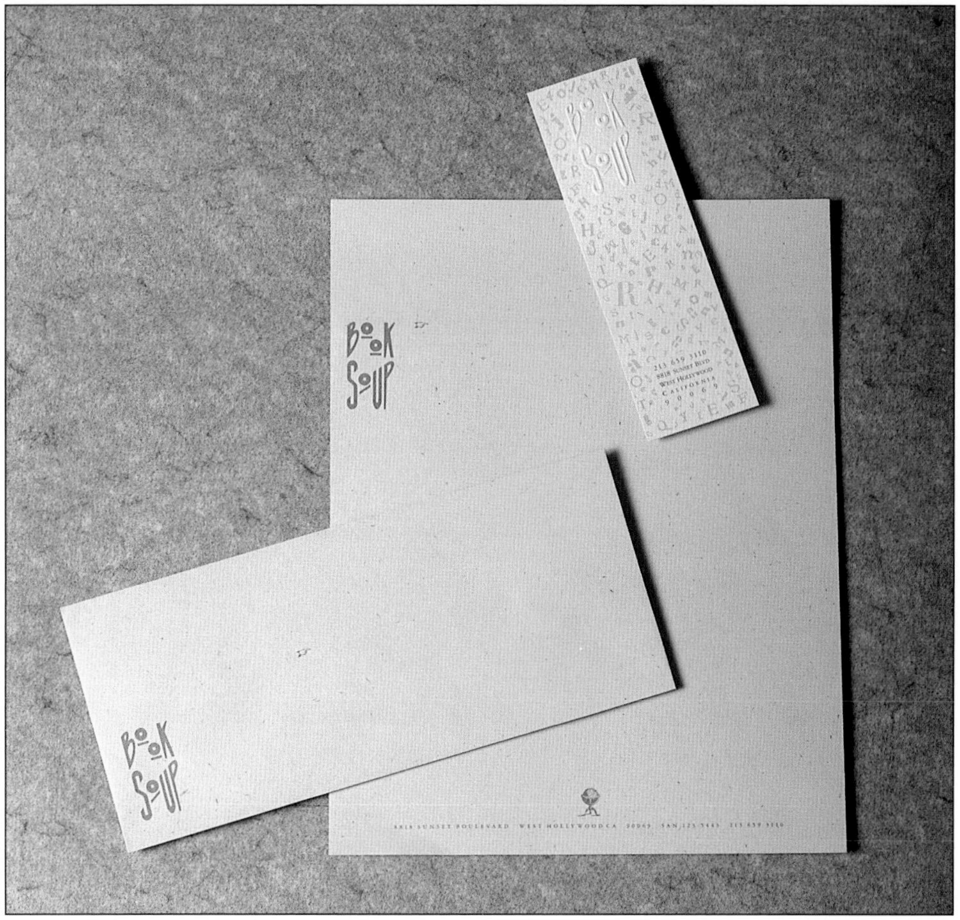

31

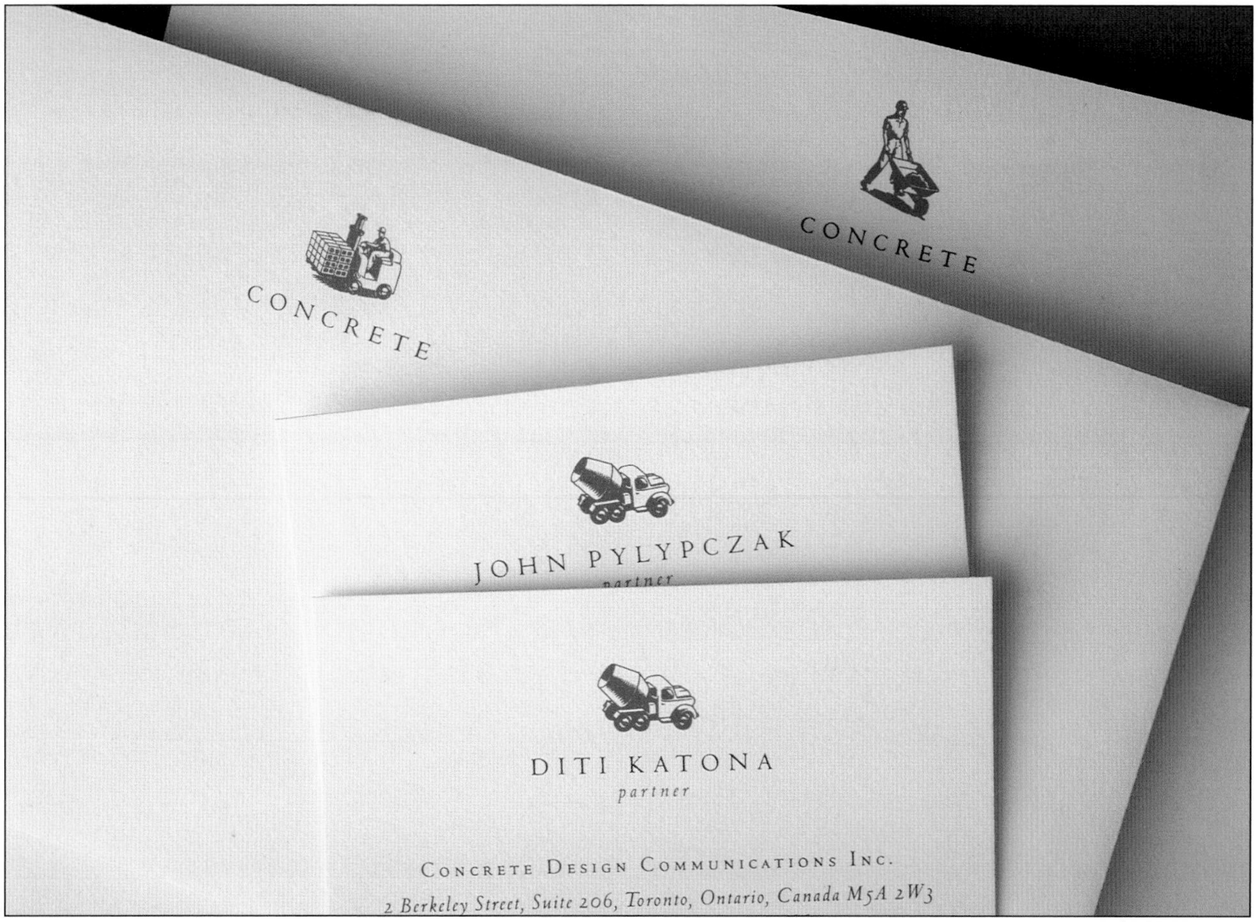

32

31
DESIGN FIRM: *Sarajo Frieden Studio*
DESIGNER: *Sarajo Frieden*
LETTERER: *Sarajo Frieden*
TEXT TYPEFACE: *Garamond*
CLIENT: *Glenn Goldman/Booksoup*

32
DESIGN FIRM: *Concrete Design Communications, Incorporated*
DESIGNER: *Diti Katona and John Pylypczak*
HEADLINE TYPEFACE: *Centaur*
CLIENT: *Concrete Design Communications, Incorporated*

33

33
DESIGN FIRM: *The Duffy Design Group*
DESIGNER: *Charles S. Anderson*
LETTERER: *Lynn Schulte and Charles S. Anderson*
HEADLINE TYPEFACE: *Futura Bold Condensed and Handlettering*
CLIENT: *French Paper Company*

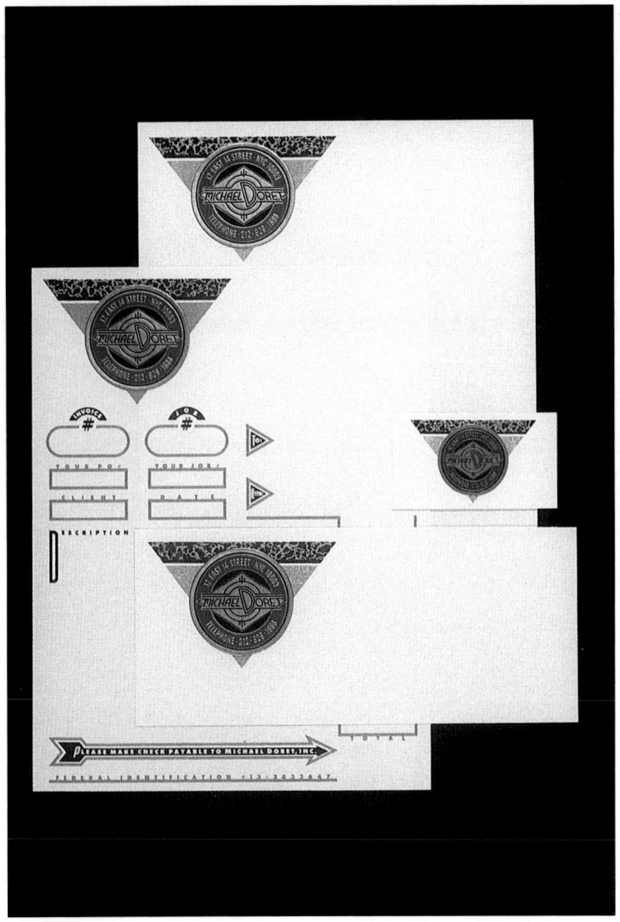

34

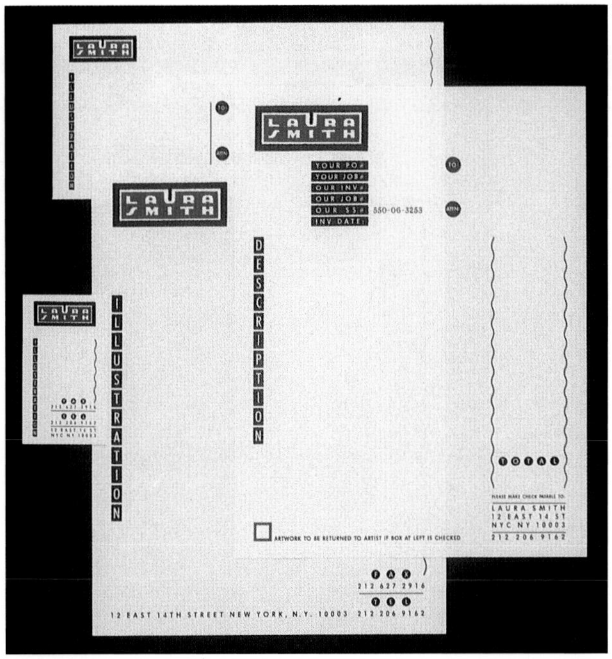

35

36

37

34
DESIGN FIRM: *Michael Doret, Inc.*
DESIGNER: *Michael Doret*
LETTERER: *Michael Doret*
HEADLINE TYPEFACE: *Handlettering*
TEXT TYPEFACE: *Futura Extra Black*
CLIENT: *Michael Doret, Inc.*

35
DESIGN FIRM: *Michael Doret, Inc.*
DESIGNER: *Michael Doret*
LETTERER: *Michael Doret*
HEADLINE TYPEFACE: *Handlettering*
TEXT TYPEFACE: *Futura Heavy and Bold Condensed*
CLIENT: *Laura Smith Illustration*

36
DESIGN FIRM: *The Duffy Design Group*
DESIGNER: *Haley Johnson*
LETTERER: *Haley Johnson and Lynn Schulte*
HEADLINE TYPEFACE: *Handlettering*
TEXT TYPEFACE: *Futura Bold Condensed*
CLIENT: *The Calhoun Beach Club*

37
DESIGN FIRM: *Summerford Design, Inc.*
DESIGNER: *Jack Summerford*
HEADLINE TYPEFACE: *Franklin Gothic Condensed*
TEXT TYPEFACE: *Century Light Condensed*
CLIENT: *Gary McCoy Photography*

38

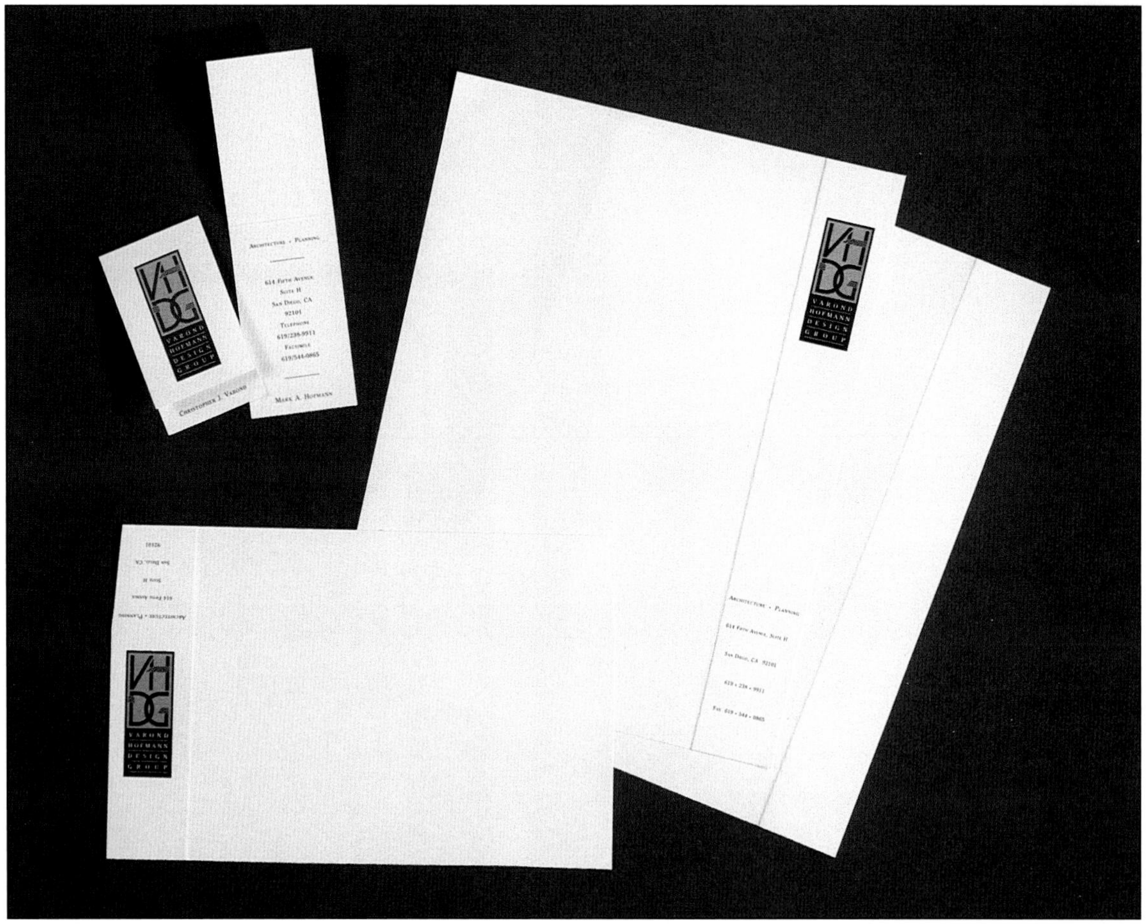

39

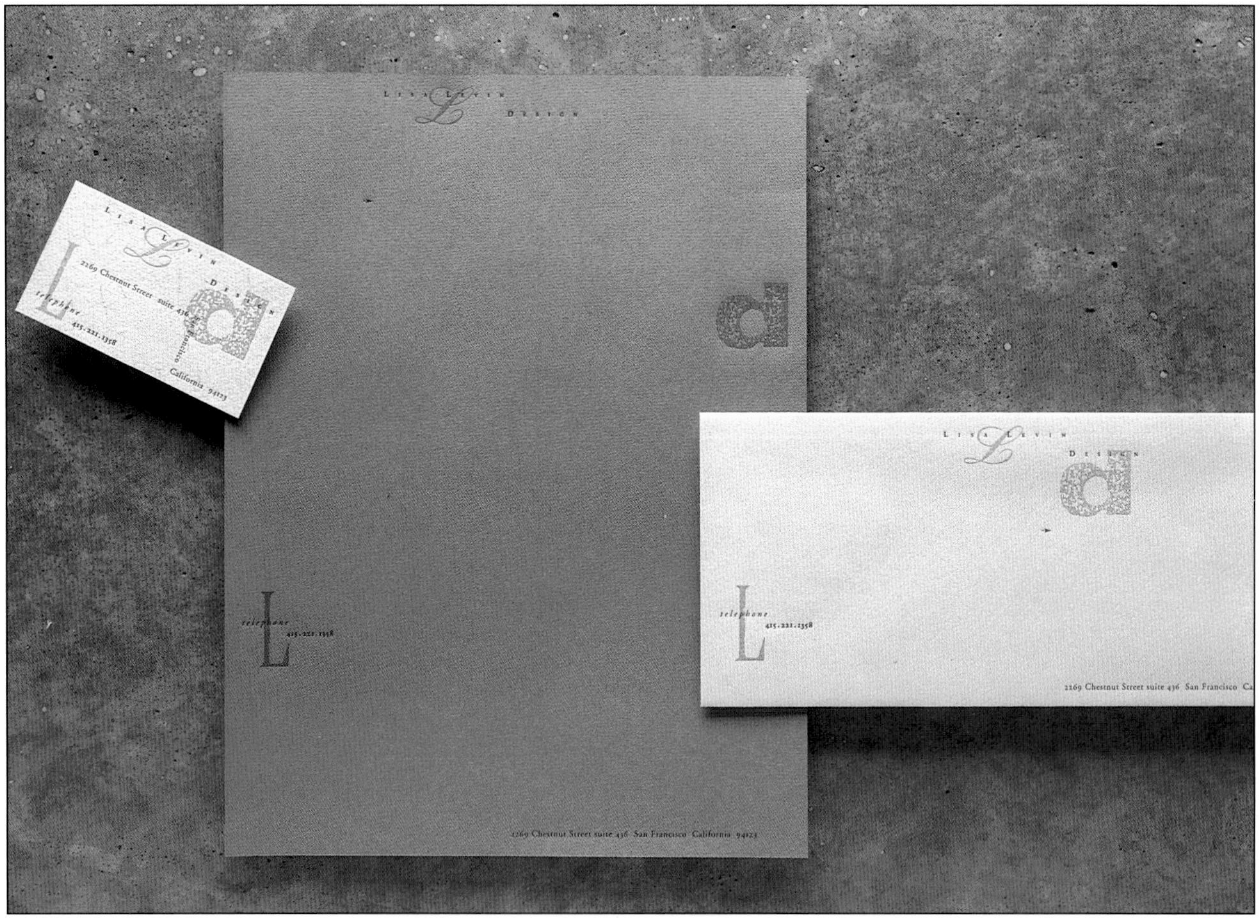

38
DESIGN FIRM: *Laura Coe Design Associates*
DESIGNER: *Laura J. Coe and Charlene Temple*
LETTERER: *Laura J. Coe and Charlene Temple*
HEADLINE TYPEFACE: *Handlettering*
TEXT TYPEFACE: *Cheltenham*
CLIENT: *Varond Hofmann Design Group*

39
DESIGN FIRM: *Lisa Levin Design*
DESIGNER: *Lisa Levin*
TEXT TYPEFACE: *Adobe Garamond*
CLIENT: *Lisa Levin Design*

40

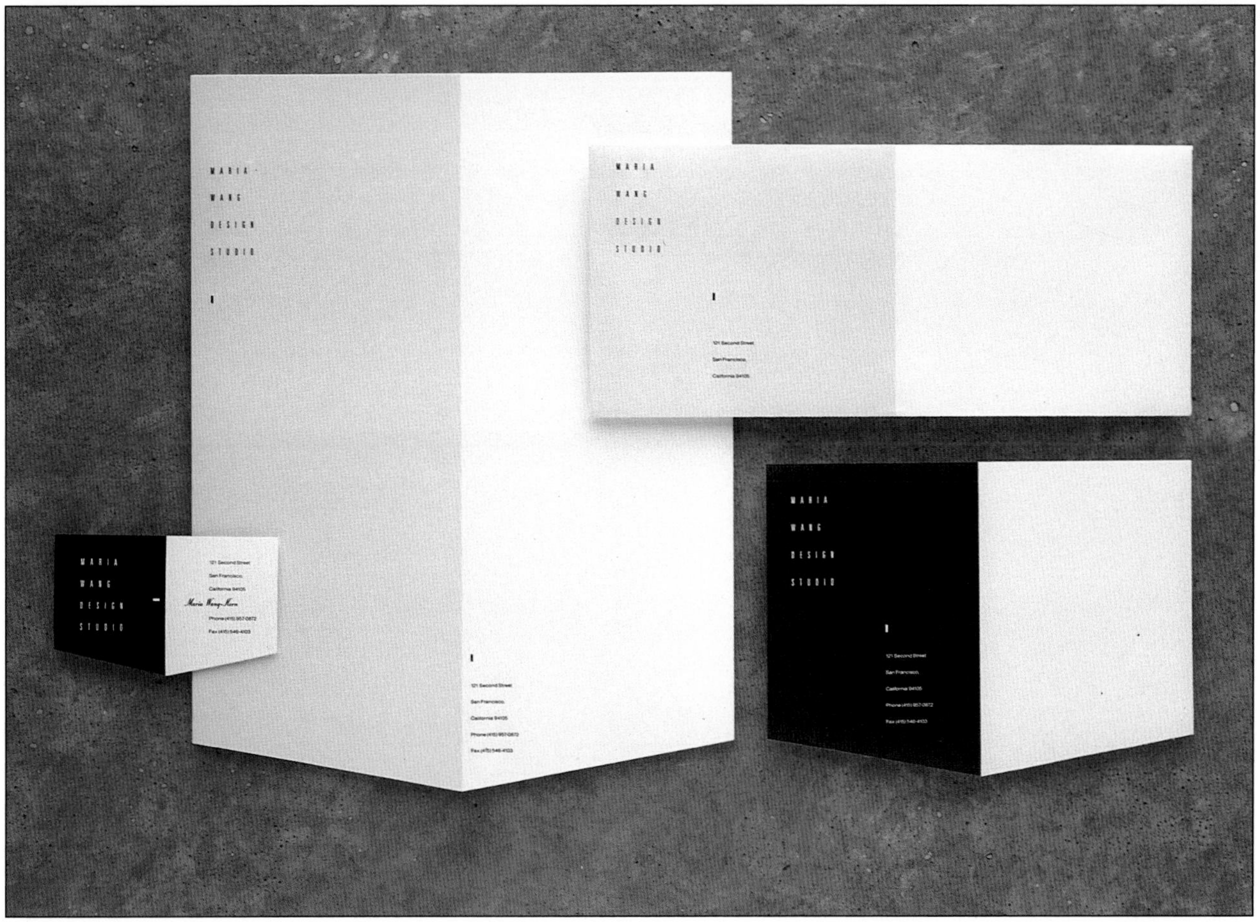

41

40
DESIGN FIRM: *Merten Design Group*
DESIGNER: *Barry A. Merten and Roland Hill*
HEADLINE TYPEFACE: *Fenice*
TEXT TYPEFACE: *Fenice*
CLIENT: *Jay Dickman Photography*

41
DESIGN FIRM: *Maria Wang Design Studio*
DESIGNER: *Sue Hutner*
HEADLINE TYPEFACE: *Universe 49 Bold*
TEXT TYPEFACE: *Univers Extended*
CLIENT: *Maria Wang Design Studio*

42

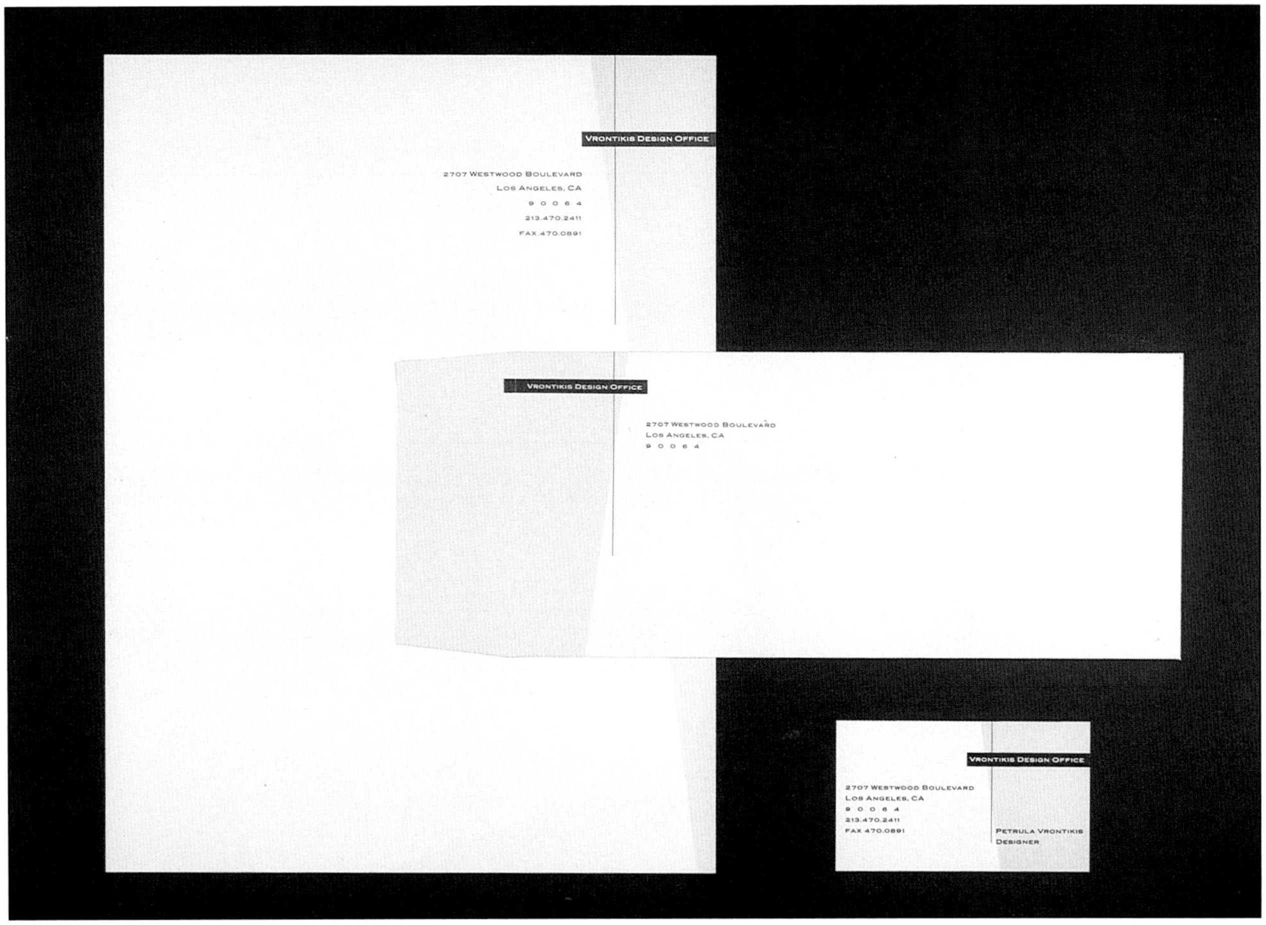

42
DESIGN FIRM: *Vrontikis Design Office*
DESIGNER: *Petrula Vrontikis*
HEADLINE TYPEFACE: *Copperplate*
CLIENT: *Vrontikis Design Office*

43

43
DESIGN FIRM: *Sarajo Frieden Studio*
DESIGNER: *Sarajo Frieden*
TEXT TYPEFACE: *Futura and Sabon Antiqua*
CLIENT: *Dayton Faris Inc.*

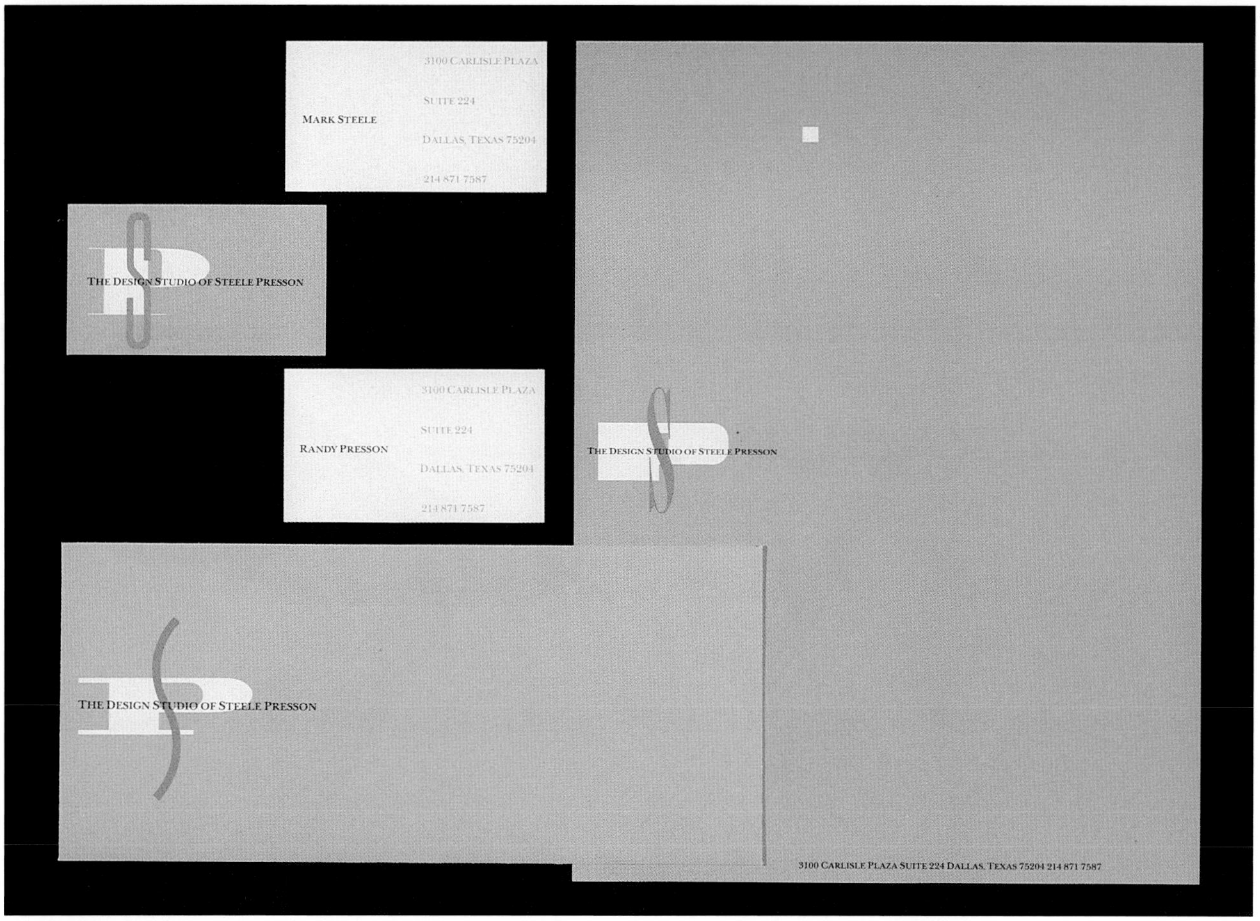

44

DESIGN FIRM: *Design Studio of Steele Presson*
DESIGNER: *Mark Steele*
TEXT TYPEFACE: *ITC New Baskerville*
CLIENT: *Design Studio of Steele Presson*

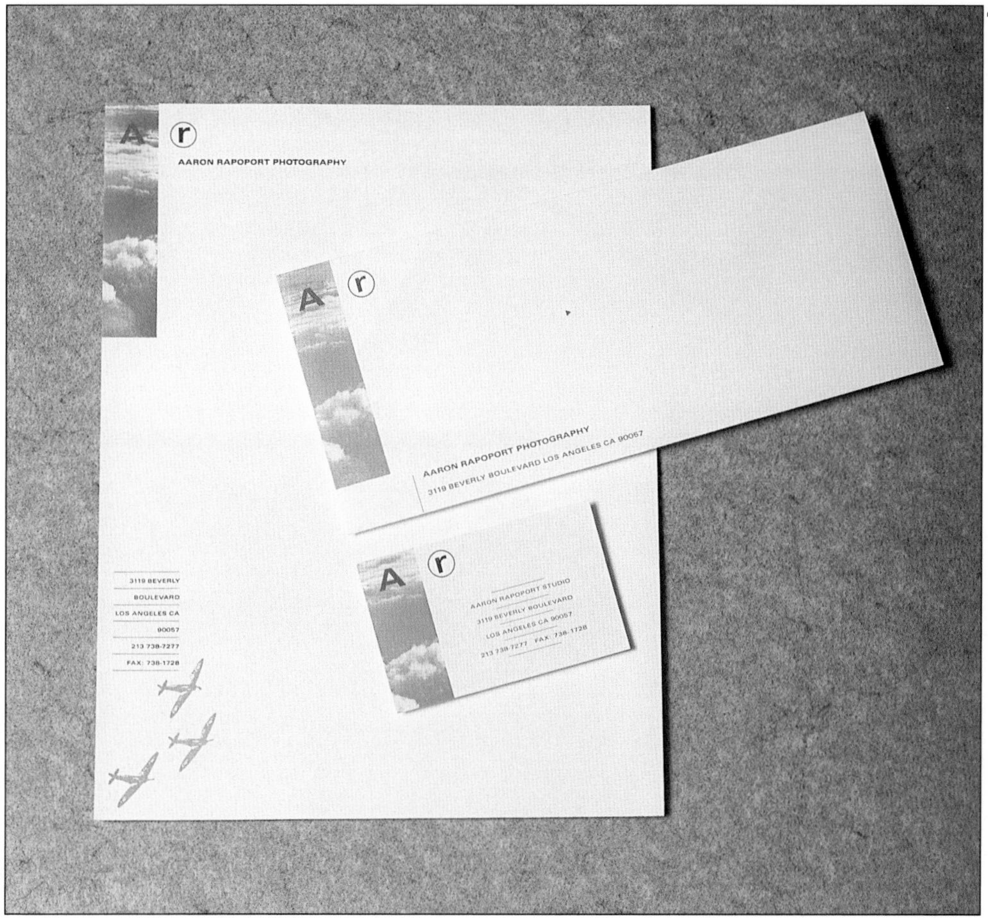

45

DESIGN FIRM: *Sarajo Frieden Studio*
DESIGNER: *Sarajo Frieden*
TEXT TYPEFACE: *Univers*
CLIENT: *Aaron Rapoport Photography*

46

46
DESIGN FIRM: *Merten Design Group*
DESIGNER: *Beth Parker and Barry A. Merten*
HEADLINE TYPEFACE: *Garamond Condensed*
TEXT TYPEFACE: *Futura Condensed Bold*
CLIENT: *Advertising Display Company*

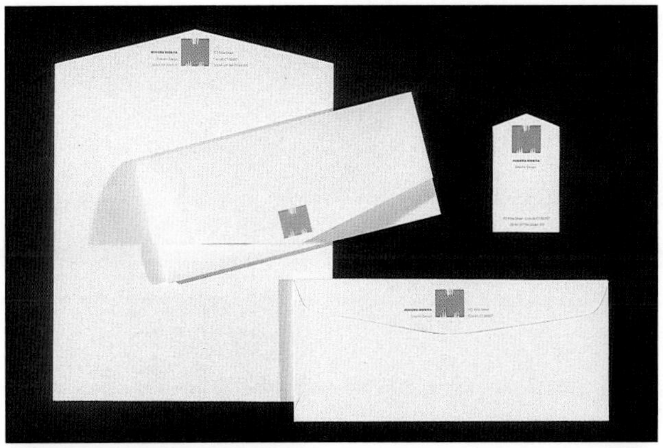

47

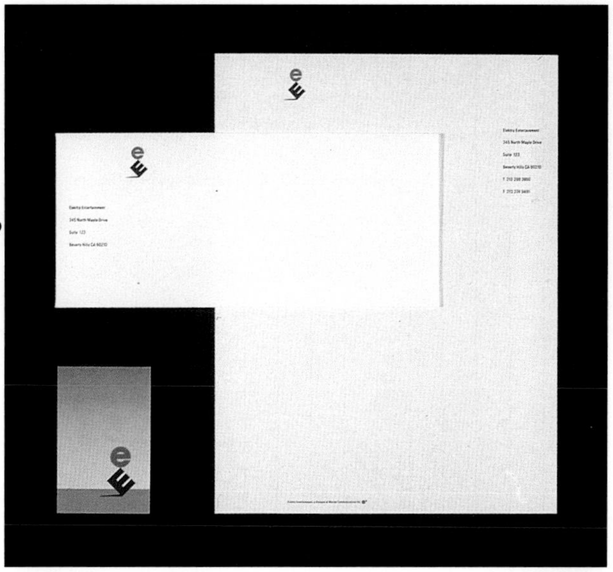

48

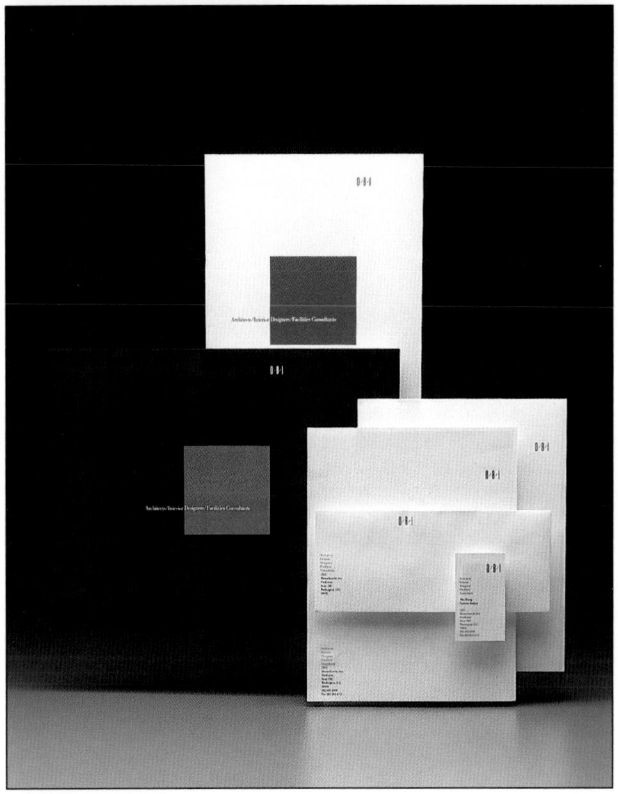

49

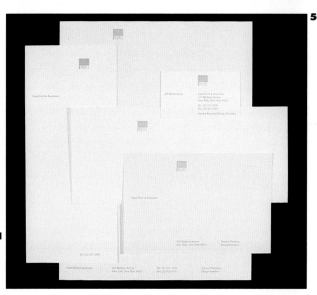

50

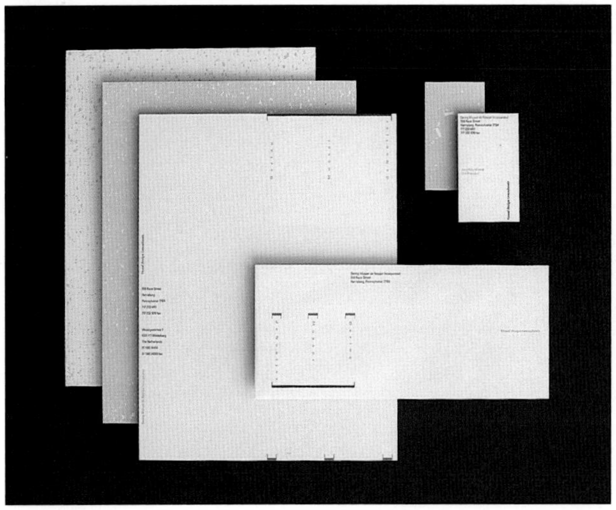

51

47
DESIGN FIRM: *Minoru Morita Graphic Design*
DESIGNER: *Minoru Morita*
LETTERER: *Minoru Morita*
TEXT TYPEFACE: *Futura Book*
CLIENT: *Minoru Morita Graphic Design*

48
DESIGN FIRM: *Pentagram Design*
DESIGNER: *Peter Hanson and Susan Hochbaum*
TEXT TYPEFACE: *Univers*
CLIENT: *Elektra Entertainment*

49
DESIGN FIRM: *Glass & Glass, Inc.*
DESIGNER: *Marianne Michalakis*
HEADLINE TYPEFACE: *Title Gothic Extra Condensed 12*
TEXT TYPEFACE: *Bodoni*
CLIENT: *DBI*

50
DESIGN FIRM: *Donovan & Green*
DESIGNER: *Nancye Green and Clint Morgan*
HEADLINE TYPEFACE: *Helvetica Compressed*
TEXT TYPEFACE: *Garamond 3*
CLIENT: *Carol Groh and Associates*

51
DESIGN FIRM: *Musser Design*
DESIGNER: *Jerry King Musser*
HEADLINE TYPEFACE: *Univers*
TEXT TYPEFACE: *Univers*
CLIENT: *Dering Musser deNooijer*

52

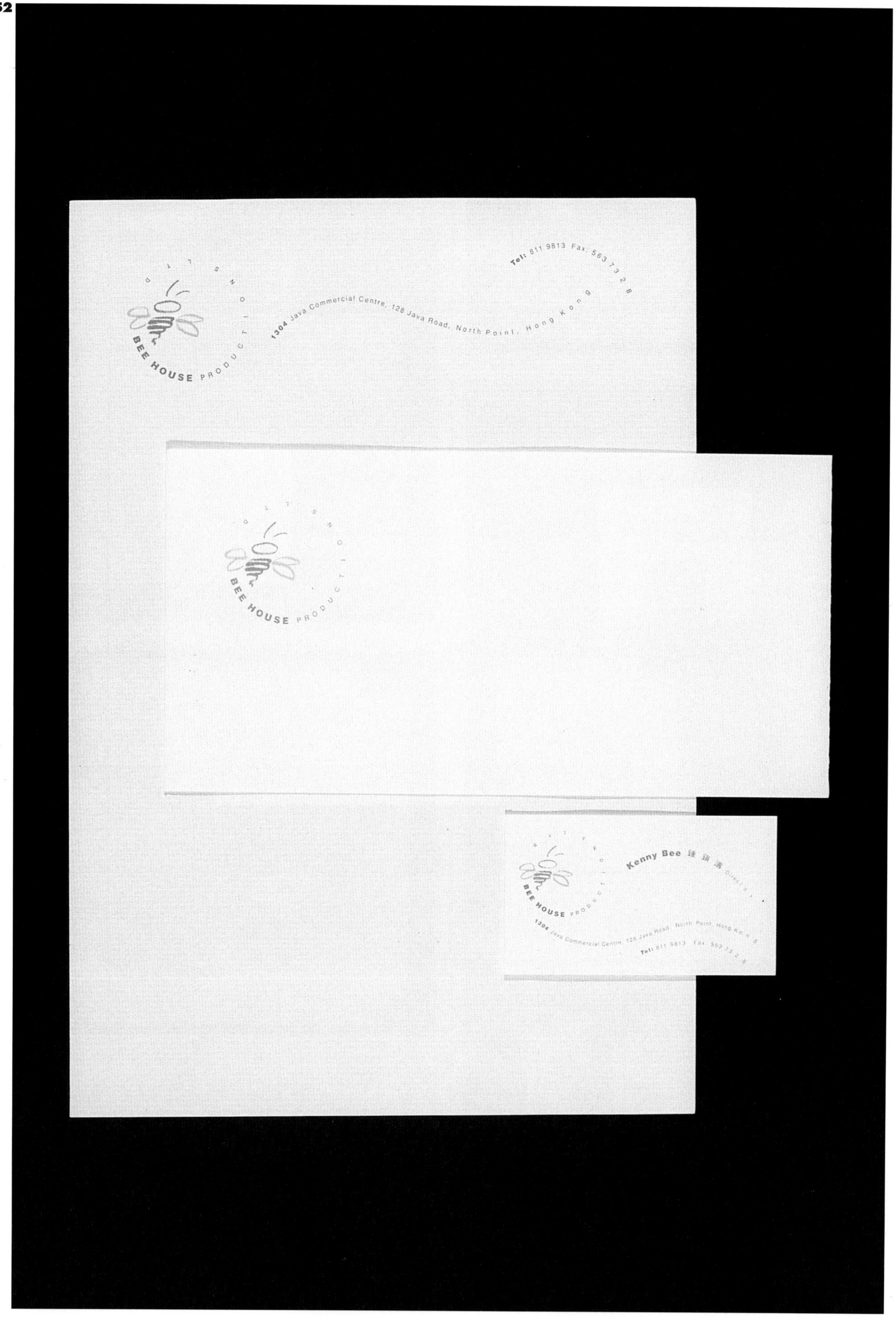

52
DESIGN FIRM: *Kan Tai-keung Design & Associates Ltd.*
DESIGNER: *Kan Tai-keung*
HEADLINE TYPEFACE: *Helvetica*
TEXT TYPEFACE: *Helvetica*
CLIENT: *Bee House Productions, Ltd.*

53

53
DESIGN FIRM: *H.M. &E. Incorporated*
DESIGNER: *Paul Haslip*
HEADLINE TYPEFACE: *Futura*
TEXT TYPEFACE: *New Baskerville Bold italic*
CLIENT: *Joel Bernard Photography*

54

54

DESIGN FIRM: *Hornall Anderson Design Works*

DESIGNER: *Jack Anderson and Julia LaPine*

HEADLINE TYPEFACE: *Modern*

TEXT TYPEFACE: *Bodoni Italic*

CLIENT: *Italia*

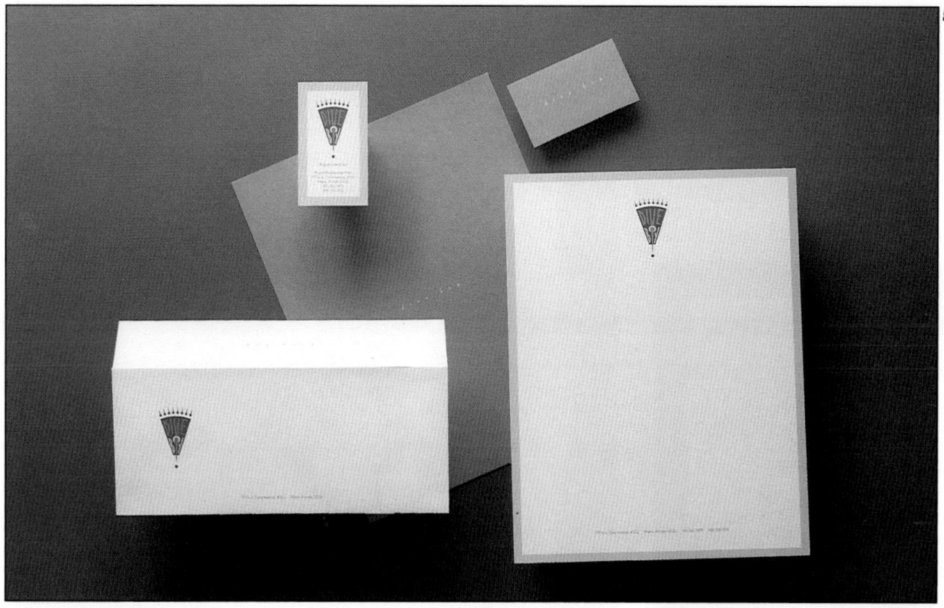

55

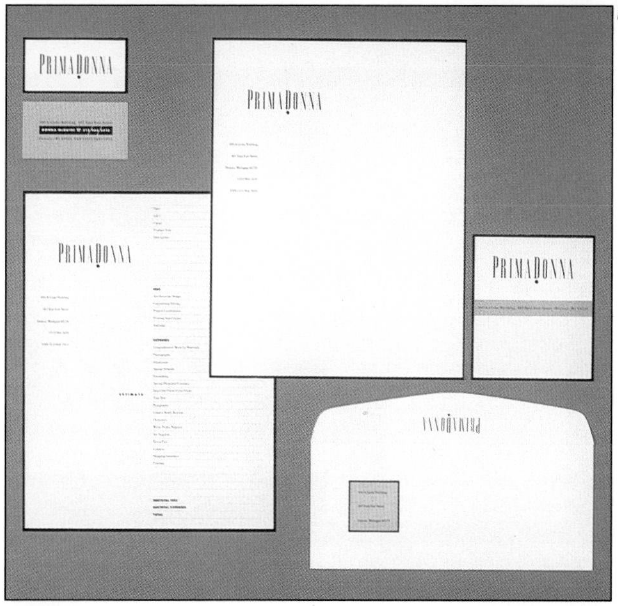

56

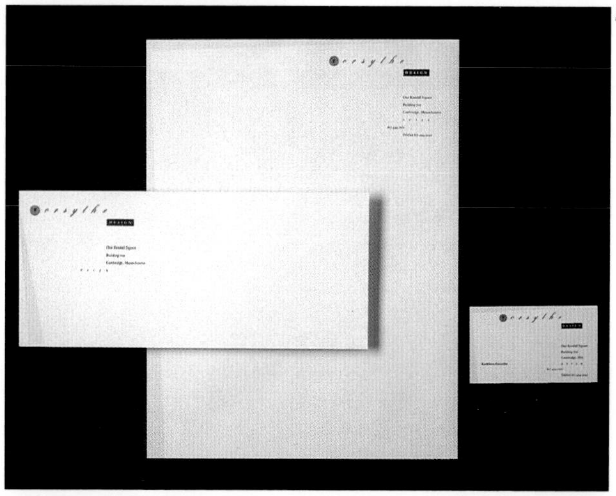

57

58

59

55
DESIGN FIRM: *Siquis. Ltd.*
DESIGNER: *Vickie Schafer*
LETTERER: *Vickie Schafer*
TEXT TYPEFACE: *Gill Sans Light and Bernhard Modern*
CLIENT: *Dive Boy Swimwear*

56
DESIGNER: *Donna McGuire*
HEADLINE TYPEFACE: *Raymundo Shaded*
TEXT TYPEFACE: *Bodoni*
CLIENT: *Prima Donna*

57
DESIGN FIRM: *Forsythe Design*
DESIGNER: *Julie Steinhilber*
HEADLINE TYPEFACE: *Bankscript and Serifa*
TEXT TYPEFACE: *Bembo*
CLIENT: *Forsythe Design*

58
DESIGN FIRM: *Stan Everson*
DESIGNER: *Stan Everson*
LETTERER: *Stan Everson*
CLIENT: *Stan Everson*

59
DESIGN FIRM: *Pentagram Design*
DESIGNER: *Woody Pirtle and Jennifer Long*
TEXT TYPEFACE: *Univers*
CLIENT: *Corgan Associates Architects*

60
DESIGN FIRM: *Porter/Matjasich & Associates*
DESIGNER: *Robert Rausch*
HEADLINE TYPEFACE: *Modified American Typewriter, Magnificat and Folio Bold*
TEXT TYPEFACE: *Folio Regular*
CLIENT: *Victoria Frigo*

61
DESIGN FIRM: *Studio Guarnaccia*
DESIGNER: *Steven Guarnaccia*
LETTERER: *Steven Guarnaccia*
CLIENT: *Studio Guarnaccia*

62
DESIGN FIRM: *Corey McPherson Nash*
DESIGNER: *Tim Nihofe*
HEADLINE TYPEFACE: *Bernhard Gothic*
TEXT TYPEFACE: *Futura*
CLIENT: *Smash Advertising*

63
DESIGN FIRM: *Muller & Company*
DESIGNER: *Patrice Eilts*
LETTERER: *Patrice Eilts*
HEADLINE TYPEFACE: *Handlettering*
TEXT TYPEFACE: *Kabel*
CLIENT: *Michael Weaver*

64
DESIGN FIRM: *Sage Design*
TEXT TYPEFACE: *Helvetica*
CLIENT: *Kim Sage*

65
DESIGN FIRM: *Sage Design*
HEADLINE TYPEFACE: *Metropolis*
TEXT TYPEFACE: *Cochin*
CLIENT: *Jonathan Luria*

61

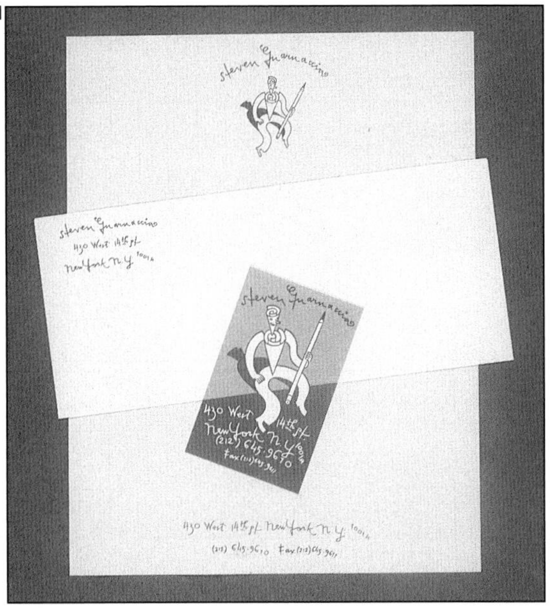

60

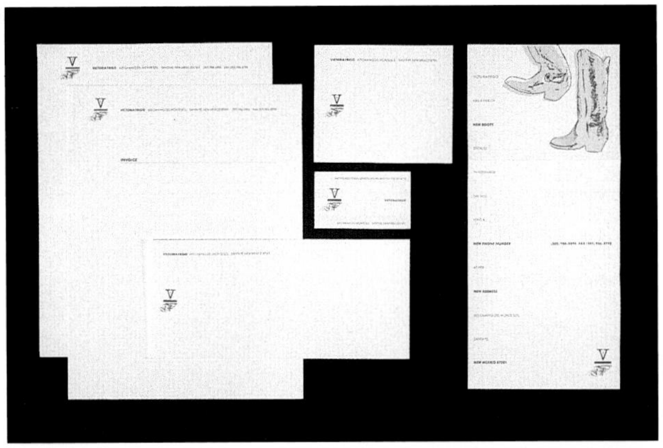

62

63

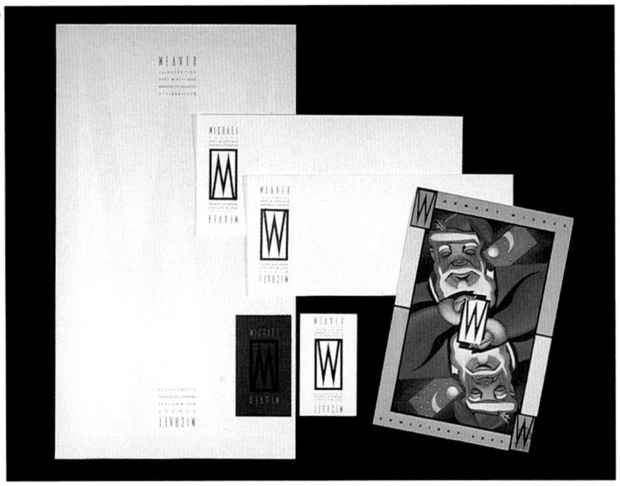

64

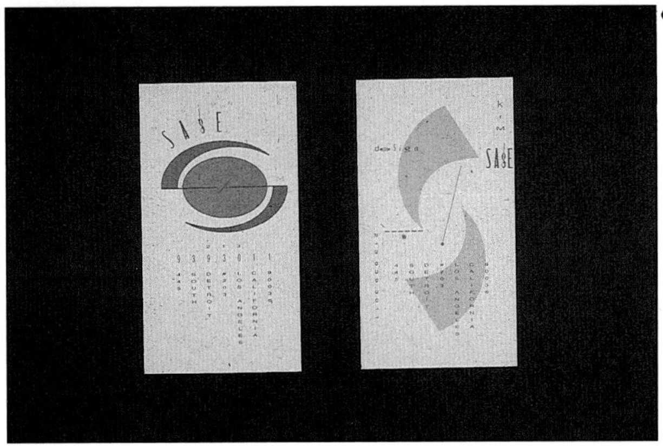

65

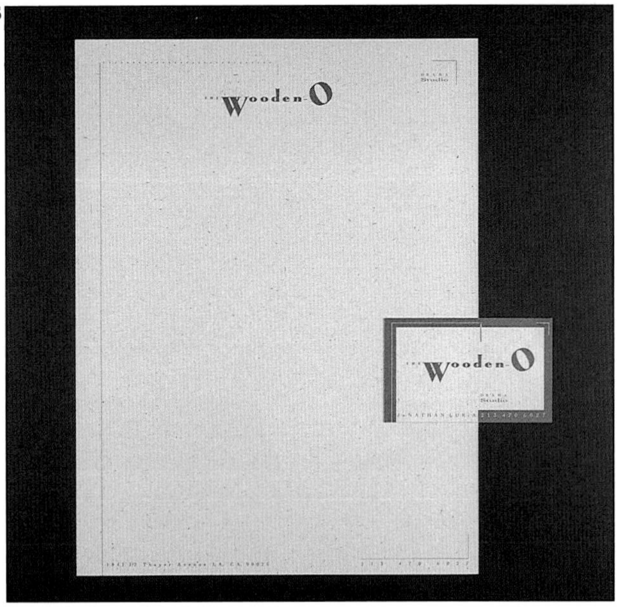

66

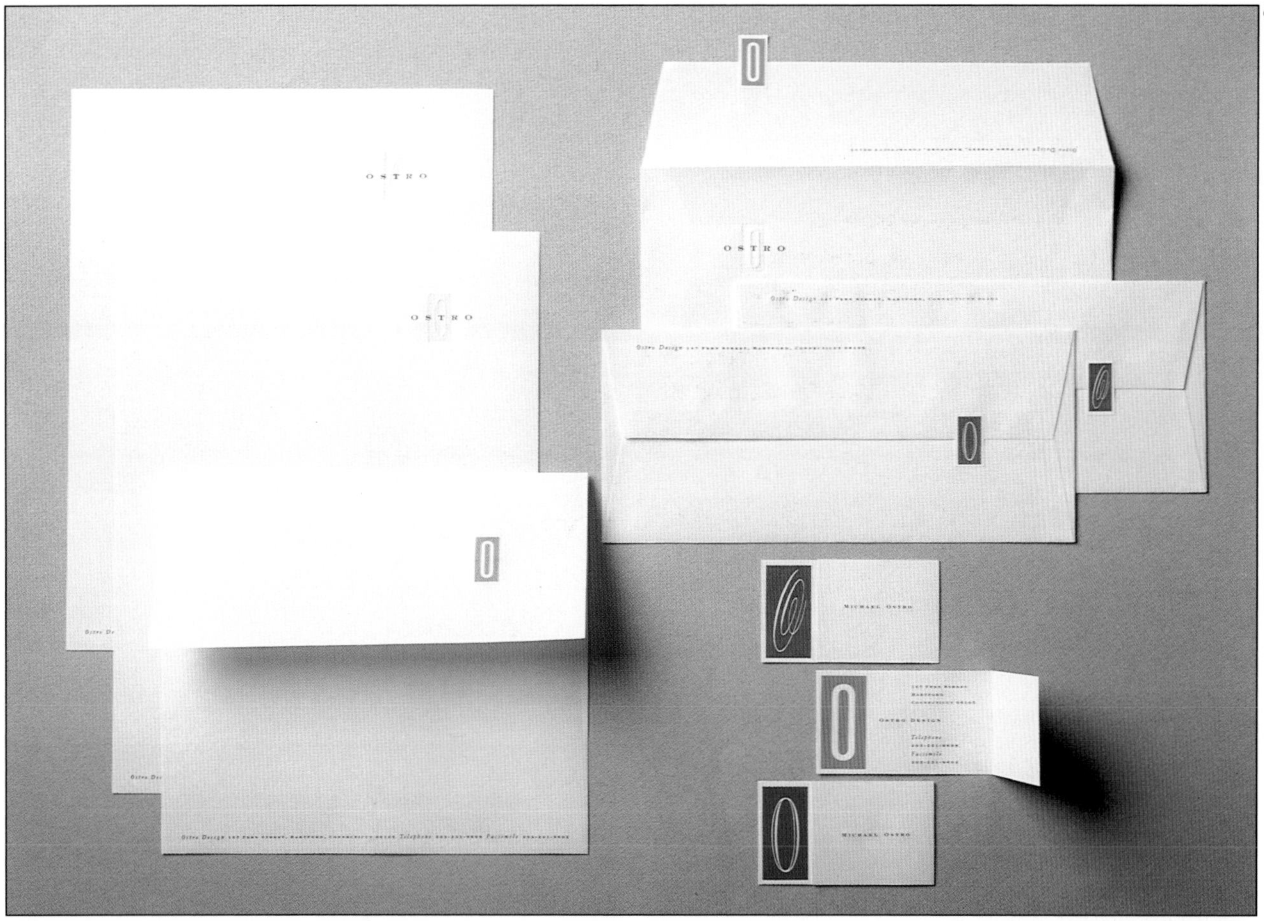

67

66
DESIGN FIRM: *Ostro Design*
DESIGNER: *Michael Ostro*
HEADLINE TYPEFACE: *Continental Script, Antique Open, and Univers 49*
TEXT TYPEFACE: *Engravers Boldface 9 B/C*
CLIENT: *Ostro Design*

67
DESIGN FIRM: *Pinhaus Design Corporation*
DESIGNER: *Ralf Schuetz*
LETTERER: *Ralf Schuetz*
HEADLINE TYPEFACE: *Handlettering*
TEXT TYPEFACE: *Matrix Wide and Park Avenue*
CLIENT: *Steve Miller/Rex Three, Inc.*

68
DESIGN FIRM: *Pentagram Design*
DESIGNER: *Woody Pirtle and Jennifer Long*
HEADLINE TYPEFACE: *Arrow, Helvetica and Garamond 3*
TEXT TYPEFACE: *Helvetica Bold and Garamond 3*
CLIENT: *ICOS Corporation*

69
DESIGN FIRM: *Pentagram Design*
DESIGNER: *Susan Hochbaum and Woody Pirtle*
LETTERER: *Susan Hochbaum*
HEADLINE TYPEFACE: *Bodoni*
TEXT TYPEFACE: *Bodoni*
CLIENT: *Museum of Contemporary Art, Chicago*

70
DESIGN FIRM: *Pentagram Design*
DESIGNER: *Woody Pirtle and Jennifer Long*
TEXT TYPEFACE: *Univers*
CLIENT: *Corgan Associates Architects*

71
DESIGN FIRM: *Pentagram Design*
DESIGNER: *Woody Pirtle and Leslie Pirtle*
TEXT TYPEFACE: *Garamond 3*
CLIENT: *Mary & Jonathan Alexander*

72
DESIGN FIRM: *Lisa Levin Design*
DESIGNER: *Lisa Levin*
HEADLINE TYPEFACE: *Boulevard*
TEXT TYPEFACE: *Roman Shaded*
CLIENT: *Esmeralda*

69
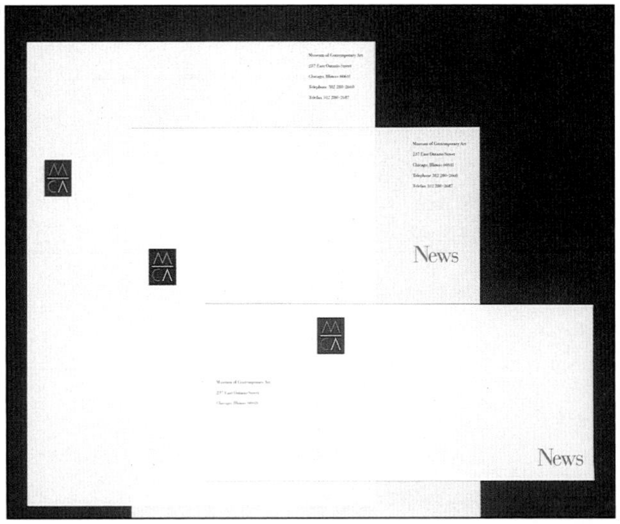

68
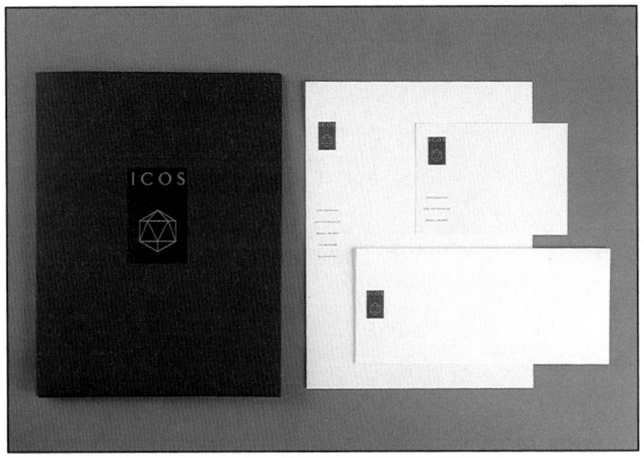

71
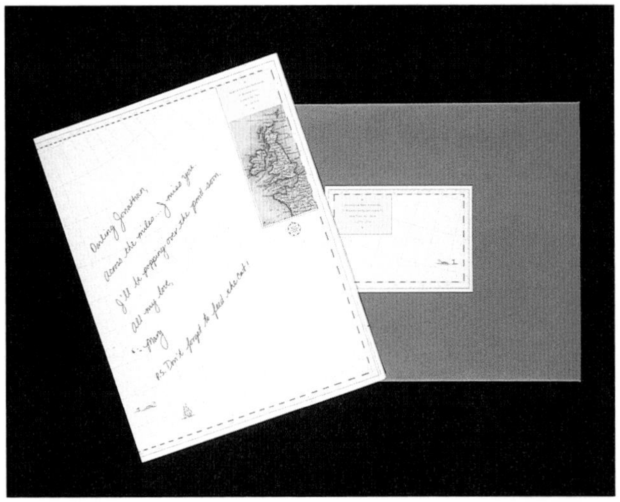

70
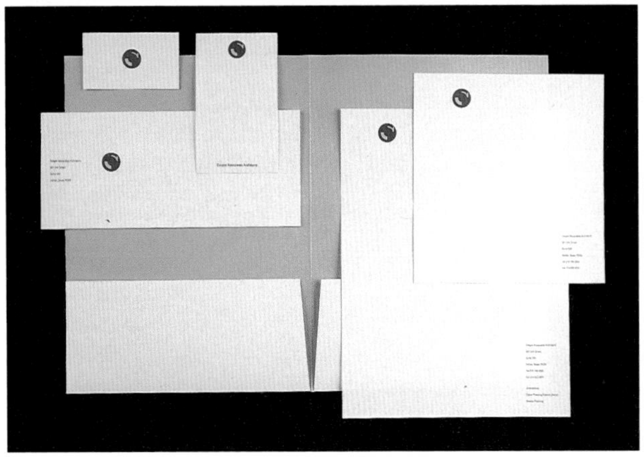

72
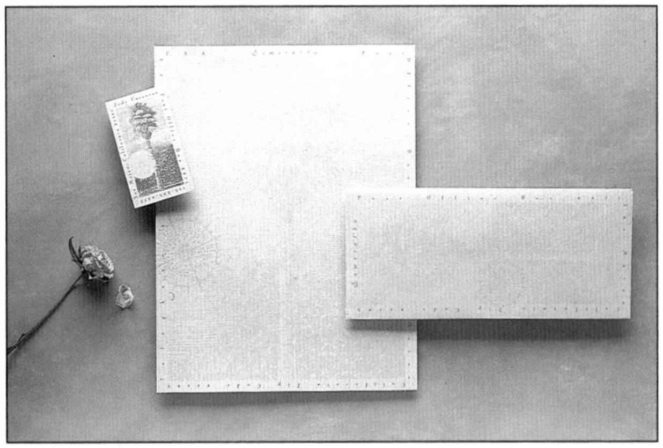

73

73
DESIGN FIRM: *Lisa Levin Design*
DESIGNER: *Lisa Levin*
HEADLINE TYPEFACE: *Boulevard*
TEXT TYPEFACE: *Roman Shaded*
CLIENT: *Esmeralda*

78

78
DESIGN FIRM: *The Duffy Design Group*
DESIGNER: *Sharon Werner*
LETTERER: *Sharon Werner and Lynn Schulte*
HEADLINE TYPEFACE: *Spartan Medium*
CLIENT: *D'Amico & Partners*

79

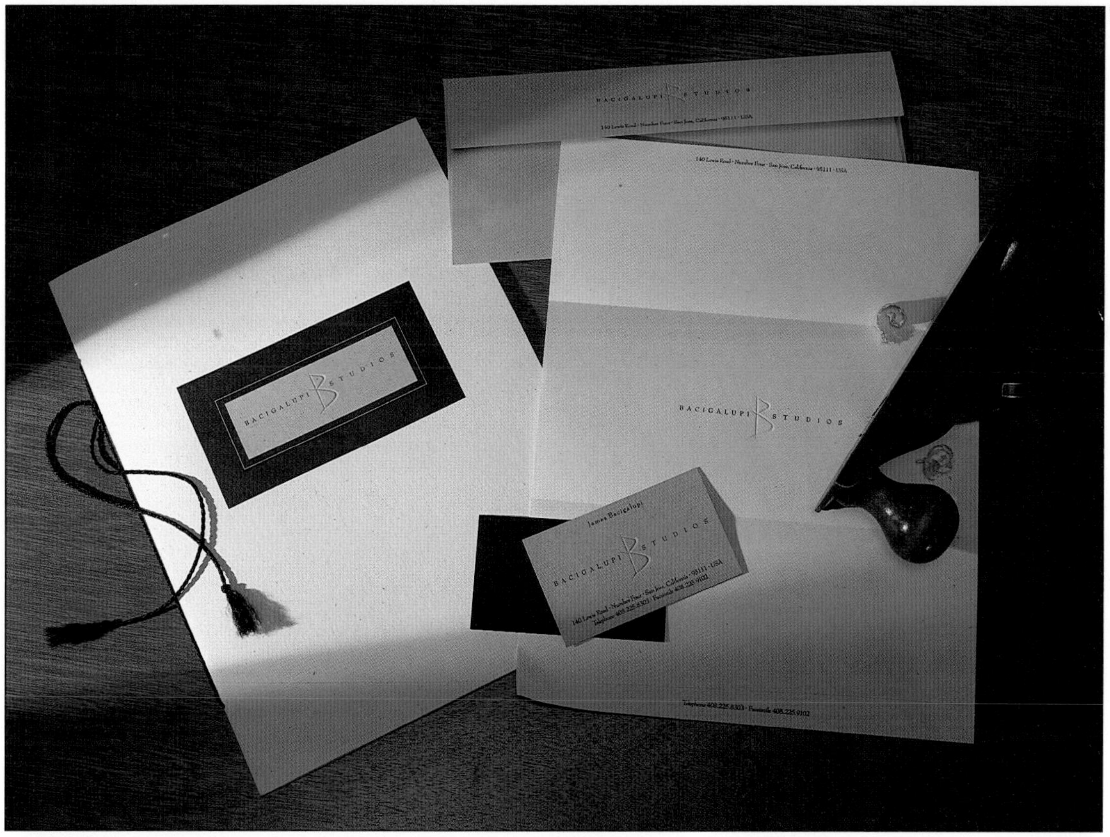

80

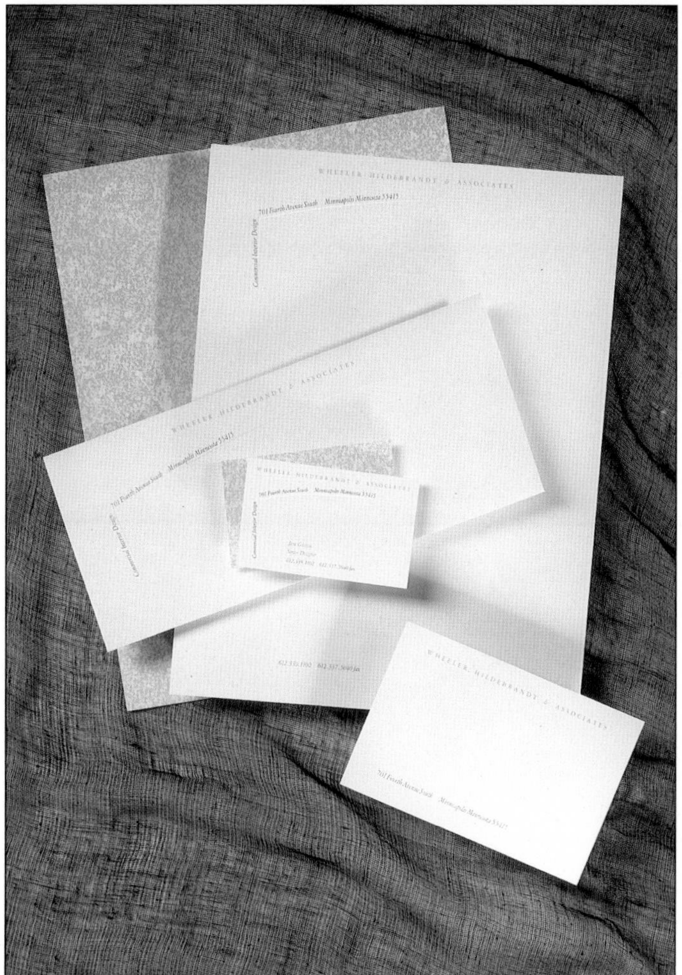

81

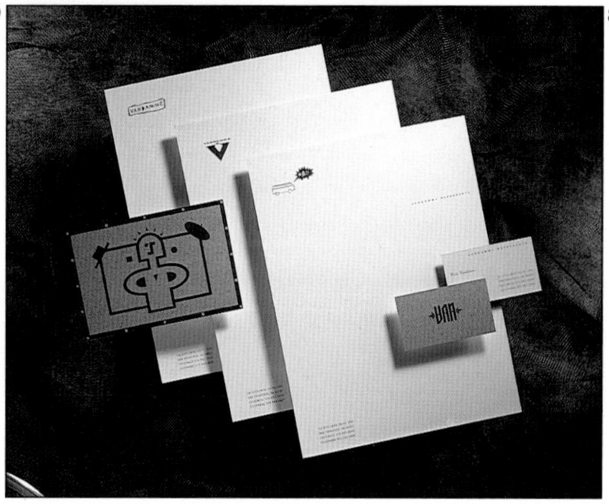

79
DESIGN FIRM: *Tharp Did It*
DESIGNER: *Rick Tharp and Jana Heer*
HEADLINE TYPEFACE: *Bernhard Modern*
TEXT TYPEFACE: *Bernhard Modern*
CLIENT: *Bacigalupi Studis*

80
DESIGN FIRM: *McCool & Company*
DESIGNER: *Jo Davison Strand*
TEXT TYPEFACE: *Garamond 3*
CLIENT: *Wheeler Hildebrandt*

81
DESIGN FIRM: *Zimmermann Crowe Design*
DESIGNER: *Dennis Crowe, John Pappas and Neal Zimmermann*
LETTERER: *Dennis Crowe, John Pappas and Neal Zimmermann*
HEADLINE TYPEFACE: *Eurotype*
TEXT TYPEFACE: *Eurotype*
CLIENT: *Vicki Vandamme: Artist's Representatives*

E D I T O R I A L

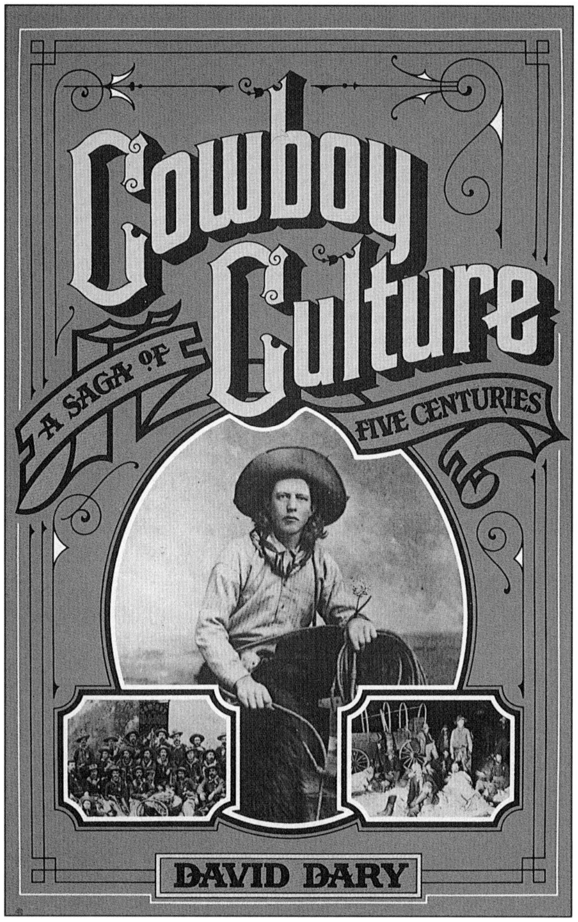

1
DESIGN FIRM: *Gerald Huerta Design, Inc.*
DESIGNER: *Gerard Huerta*
LETTERER: *Gerard Huerta*
HEADLINE TYPEFACE: *Handlettering*
TEXT TYPEFACE: *Handlettering*
CLIENT: *Knopf/Lydia Ferrara*

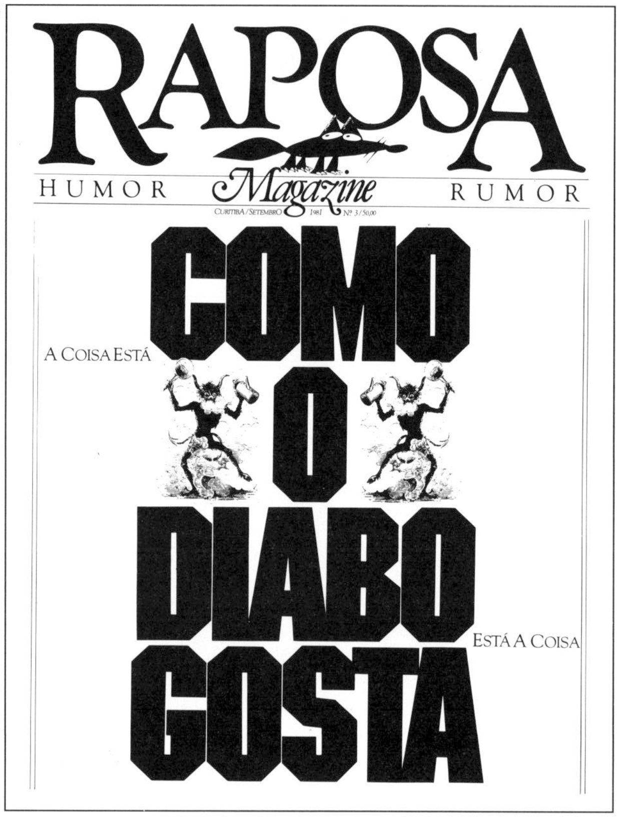

2
DESIGN FIRM: *Casa De Idéias*
DESIGNER: *Oswaldo Miranda*
HEADLINE TYPEFACE: *Machine*
TEXT TYPEFACE: *Goudy*
CLIENT: *Raposa/Diário, PR/Newspaper*

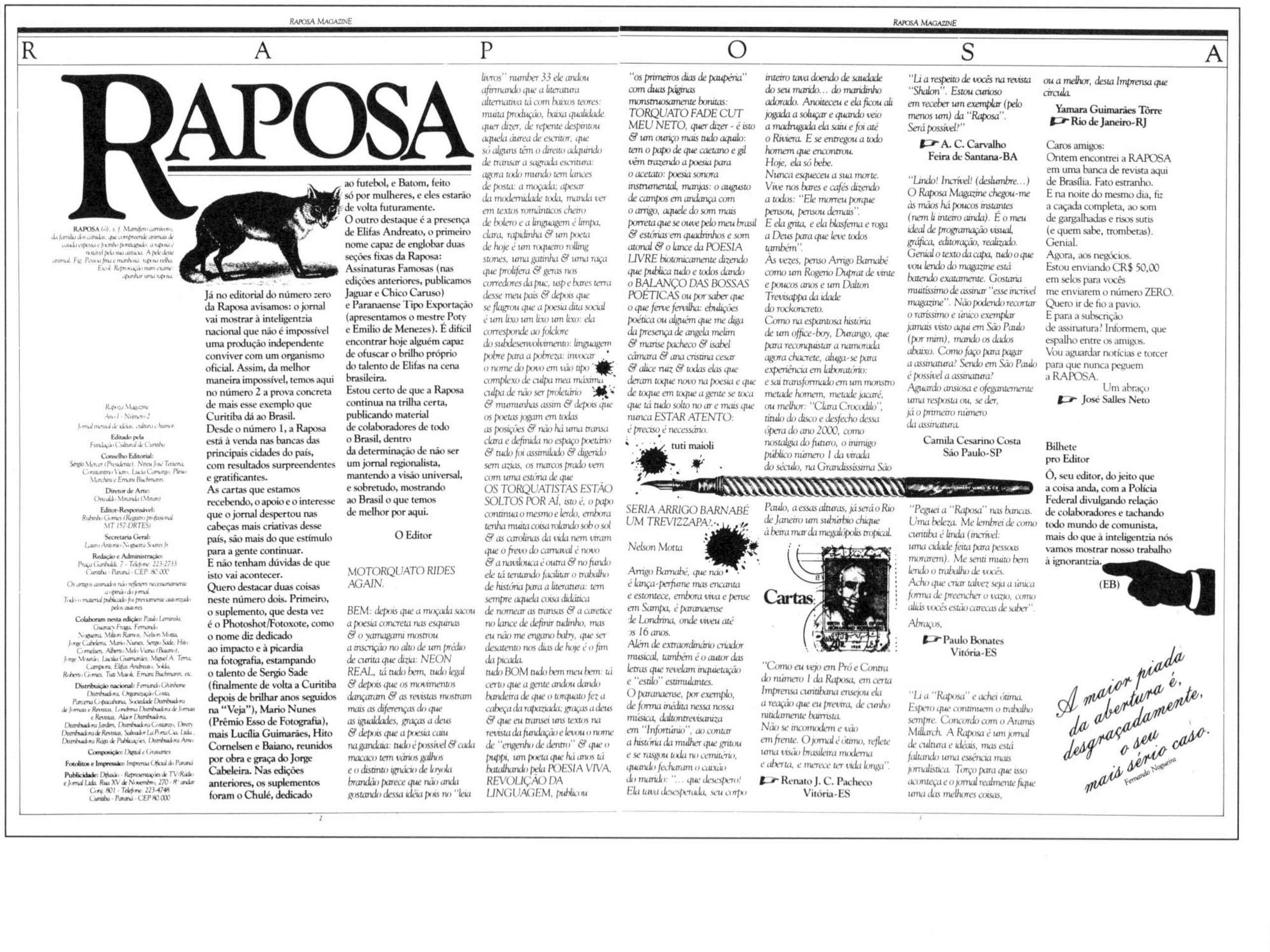

RAPOSA MAGAZINE

R A P O S A

RAPOSA

RAPOSA (ô), s. f. Mamífero carnívoro, da família dos canídas, que compreende animais de cauda espessa e focinho pontiagudo: a raposa é notável pela sua astúcia. A pele deste animal. Fig. Pessoa fina e manhosa: raposa velha. Escol. Reprovação num exame: apanhar uma raposa.

Já no editorial do número zero da Raposa avisamos: o jornal vai mostrar à inteligentzia nacional que não é impossível uma produção independente conviver com um organismo oficial. Assim, da melhor maneira impossível, temos aqui no número 2 a prova concreta de mais esse exemplo que Curitiba dá ao Brasil.
Desde o número 1, a Raposa está à venda nas bancas das principais cidades do país, com resultados surpreendentes e gratificantes.
As cartas que estamos recebendo, o apoio e o interesse que o jornal despertou nas cabeças mais criativas desse país, são mais do que estímulo para a gente continuar.
E não tenham dúvidas de que isto vai acontecer.
Quero destacar duas coisas neste número dois. Primeiro, o suplemento, que desta vez é o Photoshot/Fotoxote, como o nome diz dedicado ao impacto e à picardia na fotografia, estampando o talento de Sergio Sade (finalmente de volta a Curitiba depois de brilhar anos seguidos na "Veja"), Mario Nunes (Prêmio Esso de Fotografia), mais Lucília Guimarães, Hito Cornelsen e Baiano, reunidos por obra e graça do Jorge Cabeleira. Nas edições anteriores, os suplementos foram o Chulé, dedicado ao futebol, e Batom, feito só por mulheres, e eles estarão de volta futuramente.
O outro destaque é a presença de Elifas Andreato, o primeiro nome capaz de englobar duas seções fixas da Raposa: Assinaturas Famosas (nas edições anteriores, publicamos Jaguar e Chico Caruso) e Paranaense Tipo Exportação (apresentamos o mestre Poty e Emilio de Menezes). É difícil encontrar hoje alguém capaz de ofuscar o brilho próprio do talento de Elifas na cena brasileira.
Estou certo de que a Raposa continua na trilha certa, publicando material de colaboradores de todo o Brasil, dentro da determinação de não ser um jornal regionalista, mantendo a visão universal, e sobretudo, mostrando ao Brasil o que temos de melhor por aqui.

O Editor

Raposa Magazine
Ano 1 - Número 2
Jornal mensal de idéias, cultura e humor.
Editado pela Fundação Cultural de Curitiba
Conselho Editorial: Sérgio Mercer (Presidente), Nireu José Teixeira, Constantino Viaro, Lucia Camargo, Plinio Marchini e Ennio Buchmann.
Diretor de Arte: Oswaldo Miranda (Miran)
Editor-Responsável: Rubinho Gomes (Registro profissional MT 157-DRTES)
Secretaria Geral: Lauro Antonio Nogueira Soares Jr.
Redação e Administração: Praça Garibaldi, 7 - Telefone: 223-2733 Curitiba - Paraná - CEP: 80.000
Os artigos assinados não refletem necessariamente a opinião do jornal.
Todo o material publicado foi previamente autorizado pelos autores.
Colaboram nesta edição: Paulo Leminski, Guaracy Fraga, Fernando Nogueira, Milton Ramos, Nelson Motta, Jorge Cabeleira, Mario Nunes, Sergio Sade, Hito Cornelsen, Alberto Melo Viana (Baiano), Jorge Mourão, Lucília Guimarães, Miguel A. Terra, Campana, Elifas Andreato, Solda, Roberto Gomes, Tuti Maioli, Ennio Buchmann, etc.
Distribuição nacional: Fernando Chinaglia Distribuidora, Organização Costa, Parceria Copacabana, Sociedade Distribuidora de Jornais e Revistas, Londrina Distribuidora de Jornais e Revistas, Alaor Distribuidora, Distribuidora Jardim, Distribuidora Costurazzo, Direty Distribuidora de Revistas, Salvador La Porta Cia. Ltda., Distribuidora Régis de Publicações, Distribuidora Amo.
Composição: Digital e Gravartex
Fotolitos e Impressão: Imprensa Oficial do Paraná
Publicidade: Difusão - Representações de TV/Rádio e Jornal Ltda. Rua XV de Novembro, 270 - 8º andar Conj. 801 - Telefone: 223-4748 Curitiba - Paraná - CEP 80.000

MOTORQUATO RIDES AGAIN.

BEM: depois que a moçada sacou a poesia concreta nas esquinas & o yamagami mostrou a inscrição no alto de um prédio de curita que dizia: NEON REAL, tá tudo bem, tudo legal & depois que os movimentos dançaram & as revistas mostram mais as diferenças do que as igualdades, graças a deus & depois que a poesia caiu na gandaia: tudo é possível & cada macaco tem vários galhos e o distinto ignácio de loyola brandão parece que não anda gostando dessa idéia pois no "leia livros" number 33 ele andou afirmando que a literatura alternativa tá com baixos teores: muita produção, baixa qualidade, quer dizer, de repente despintou aquela áurea de escritor, que só alguns têm o direito adquirido de transar a sagrada escritura: agora todo mundo tem lances de posta: a moçada; apesar da modernidade toda, manda ver em textos românticos cheiro de bolero e a linguagem é limpa, clara, rapidinha & um poeta de hoje é um roqueiro rolling stones, uma gatinha & uma raça que prolifera & geras nos corredores da puc, usp e bares terra desse meu país & depois que se flagrou que a poesia dita social é um lixo um lixo um lixo: ela corresponde ao folclore do subdesenvolvimento: linguagem pobre para a pobreza: invocar o nome do povo em vão tipo complexo de culpa mea máxima culpa de não ser proletário & mumunhas assim & depois que os poetas jogam em todas as posições & não há uma transa clara e definida no espaço poetário & tudo foi assimilado & digerido sem azias, os marcos prado vem com uma estória de que OS TORQUATISTAS ESTÃO SOLTOS POR AÍ, isto é, o papo continua o mesmo e lerdo, embora tenha muita coisa rolando sob o sol & as carolinas da vida nem viram que o frevo do carnaval é novo & a navilouca é outra & no fundo ele tá tentando facilitar o trabalho de história para a literatura: tem sempre aquela coisa didática de nomear as transas & a caretice no lance de definir tudinho, mas eu não me engano baby, que ser desatento nos dias de hoje é o fim da picada.
tudo BOM tudo bem meu bem: tá certo que a gente andou dando bandeira de que o torquato fez a cabeça da rapaziada; graças a deus & que eu transei uns textos na revista da fundação e levou o nome de "engenho de dentro" & que o puppi, um poeta que há anos tá batalhando pela POESIA VIVA, REVOLIÇÃO DA LINGUAGEM, publicou "os primeiros dias de paupéria" com duas páginas monstruosamente bonitas: TORQUATO FADE CUT MEU NETO, quer dizer - é isto & um ouriço mais tudo aquilo: tem o papo de que caetano e gil vêm trazendo a poesia para o acetato: poesia sonora instrumental, manjas: o augusto de campos em andança com o arrigo, aquele do som mais porreta que se ouve pelo meu brasil & estórias em quadrinhos e som atonal & o lance da POESIA LIVRE biotonicamente dizendo que publica tudo e todos dando o BALANÇO DAS BOSSAS POÉTICAS ou por saber que o que ferve fervilha: ebulições poética ou alguém que me diga da presença de angela melim & marise pacheco & isabel câmara & ana cristina cesar & alice ruiz & todas elas que deram toque novo na poesia e que de toque em toque a gente se toca que tá tudo solto no ar e mais que nunca ESTAR ATENTO: é preciso é necessário.

tuti maioli

SERIA ARRIGO BARNABÉ UM TREVIZZAPA?

Nelson Motta

Arrigo Barnabé, que não é lança-perfume mas encanta e estontece, embora viva e pense em Sampa, é paranaense de Londrina, onde viveu até os 16 anos.
Além de extraordinário criador musical, também é o autor das letras que revelam inquietação e "estilo" estimulantes.
O paranaense, por exemplo, de forma inédita nessa nossa música, daltontrevisaniza em "Infortúnio", ao contar a história da mulher que gritou e se rasgou toda no cemitério, quando fecharam o caixão do marido: "... que desespero! Ela tava desesperada, seu corpo inteiro tava doendo de saudade do seu marido... do maridinho adorado. Anoiteceu e ela ficou ali jogada a soluçar e quando veio a madrugada ela saiu e foi até o Riviera. E se entregou a todo homem que encontrou.
Hoje, ela só bebe.
Nunca esqueceu a sua morte.
Vive nos bares e cafés dizendo a todos: "Ele morreu porque pensou, pensou demais".
E ela grita, e ela blasfema e roga a Deus para que leve todos também".
Às vezes, penso Arrigo Barnabé como um Rogerio Duprat de vinte e poucos anos e um Dalton Trevisappa da idade do rockoncreto.
Como na espantosa história de um office-boy, Durango, que para reconquistar a namorada agora chacrete, aluga-se para experiência em laboratório: e sai transformado em um monstro metade homem, metade jacaré, ou melhor: "Clara Crocodilo", título do disco e desfecho dessa ópera do ano 2000, como nostalgia do futuro, o inimigo público número 1 da virada do século, na Grandississima São Paulo, a essas alturas, já será o Rio de Janeiro um subúrbio chique à beira mar da megalópolis tropical.

Cartas:

"Como eu vejo em Pró e Contra do número 1 da Raposa, em certa Imprensa curitibana ensejou ela a reação que eu previra, de cunho nitidamente bairrista.
Não se incomodem e vão em frente. O jornal é ótimo, reflete uma visão brasileira moderna e aberta, e merece ter vida longa".
Renato J. C. Pacheco
Vitória-ES

"Li a respeito de vocês na revista "Shalon". Estou curioso em receber um exemplar (pelo menos um) da "Raposa".
Será possível?"
A. C. Carvalho
Feira de Santana-BA

"Lindo! Incrível! (deslumbre...) O Raposa Magazine chegou-me às mãos há poucos instantes (nem li inteiro ainda). É o meu ideal de programação visual, gráfica, editoração, realizado.
Genial o texto da capa, tudo o que vou lendo do magazine está batendo exatamente. Gostaria muitíssimo de assinar "esse incrível magazine". Não podendo recortar o raríssimo e único exemplar jamais visto aqui em São Paulo (por mim), mando os dados abaixo. Como faço para pagar a assinatura? Sendo em São Paulo é possível a assinatura?
Aguardo ansiosa e ofegantemente uma resposta ou, se der, já o primeiro número da assinatura.
Camila Cesarino Costa
São Paulo-SP

"Peguei a "Raposa" nas bancas. Uma beleza. Me lembrei de como curitiba é linda (incrível: uma cidade feita para pessoas morarem). Me senti muito bem lendo o trabalho de vocês.
Acho que criar talvez seja a única forma de preencher o vazio, como aliás vocês estão carecas de saber".
Abraços,
Paulo Bonates
Vitória-ES

"Li a "Raposa" e achei ótima. Espero que continuem o trabalho sempre. Concordo com o Aramis Millarch. A Raposa é um jornal de cultura e idéais, mas está faltando uma essência mais jornalística. Torço para que isso aconteça e o jornal realmente fique uma das melhores coisas, ou a melhor, desta Imprensa que circula.
Yamara Guimarães Tôrre
Rio de Janeiro-RJ

Caros amigos:
Ontem encontrei a RAPOSA em uma banca de revista aqui de Brasília. Fato estranho.
E na noite do mesmo dia, fiz a caçada completa, ao som de gargalhadas e risos sutis (e quem sabe, trombetas).
Genial.
Agora, aos negócios.
Estou enviando CR$ 50,00 em selos para vocês me enviarem o número ZERO.
Quero ir de fio a pavio.
E para a subscrição de assinatura? Informem, que espalho entre os amigos.
Vou aguardar notícias e torcer para que nunca peguem a RAPOSA.
Um abraço
José Salles Neto

Bilhete pro Editor
Ô, seu editor, do jeito que a coisa anda, com a Polícia Federal divulgando relação de colaboradores e tachando todo mundo de comunista, mais do que à inteligentzia nós vamos mostrar nosso trabalho à ignorantzia.
(EB)

A maior piada da abertura é, desgraçadamente, o seu mais sério caso.
Fernando Nogueira

2 3

3
DESIGN FIRM: *Casa De Idéias*
DESIGNER: *Oswaldo Miranda*
HEADLINE TYPEFACE: *Goudy*
TEXT TYPEFACE: *Goudy*
CLIENT: *Raposa/Diário PR/Newspaper*

RAPOSA

HUMOR *Magazine* RUMOR

A raposa é um animal esperto isto é um animal que se faz de esperto mas não é tão esperto assim porque um animal tão esperto não ia ficar por aí dando a impressão a todo mundo que é um animal esperto quando todo mundo sabe que malandragem demais atrapalha e a raposa é esperta bastante para saber que a imagem é tudo mais que aquilo que aparenta e que quanto mais a gente fizer com que as pessoas achem graça mais as raposas vão se divertir de todos aqueles que acham graça nas raposas que apenas tentam achar um modo de sobreviver a um mundo sem graça onde o lugar que cabe às raposas é mínimo porque outros animais mais ferozes se dedicam a tirar a pouca graça que resta à vida das raposas e outros animais bem humorados como ela que passa a vida achando graça onde tantos acham apenas um saco viver num mundo onde tantos acham apenas um meio de sobreviver num mundo que é um saco dentro do qual cabem todas as coisas que deixam a raposa mais triste principalmente a falta de humor dos animais que caçam raposas que nada fizeram a não ser rir como hienas de todos os pedaços de um mundo que não merece mais do que uma risada coisa que a raposa toda raposa que se preza ensina a todas as raposas. Paulo Leminski.

João Saldanha, Verissimo e Fraga estrelam no suplemento Chulé.

Sonhos de Lennon: idéias que não morrem.

O Festival de Wight, pelo sobrevivente Antonio Bivar.

Poty, curitibano, universal, simplesmente.

4

5

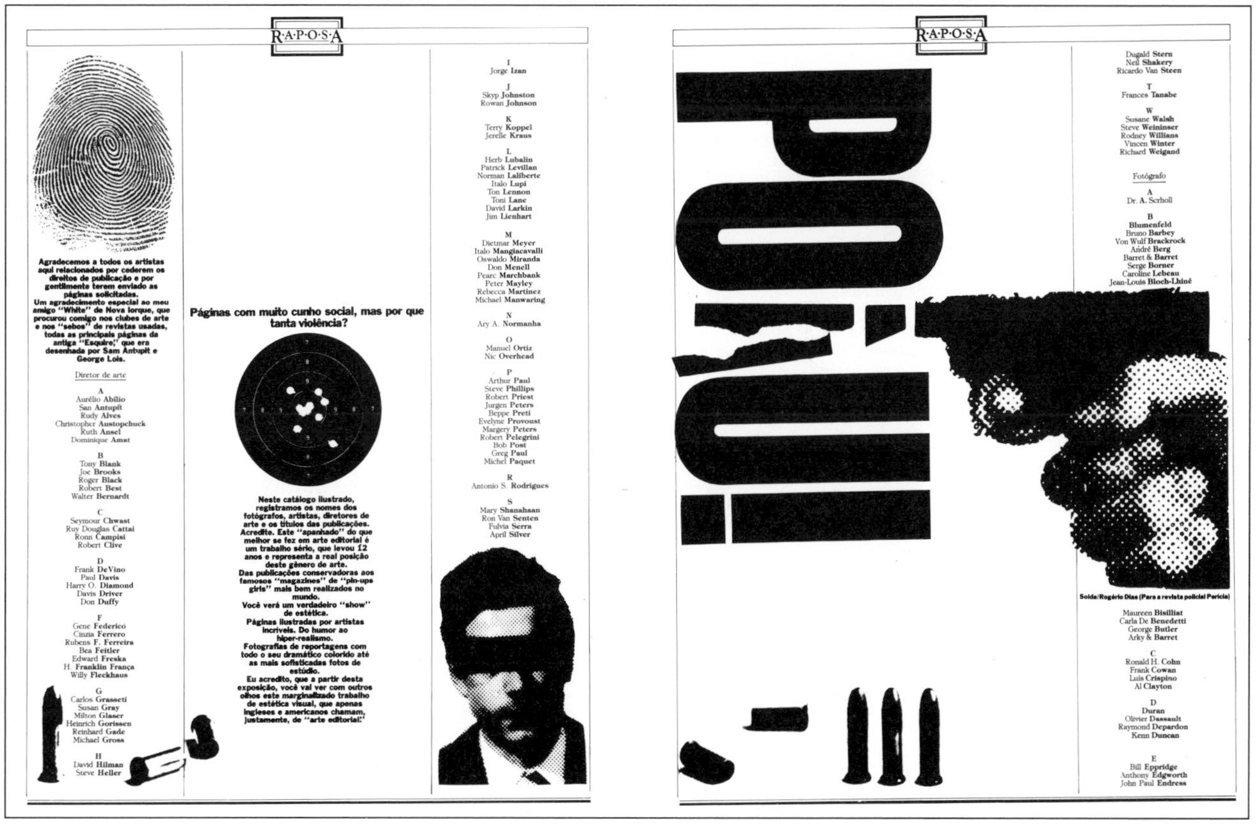

R·A·P·O·S·A

Agradecemos a todos os artistas aqui relacionados por cederem os direitos de publicação e por gentilmente terem enviado as páginas solicitadas.
Um agradecimento especial ao meu amigo "White" de Nova Iorque, que procurou comigo nos clubes de arte e nos "sebos" de revistas usadas, todas as principais páginas da antiga "Esquire," que era desenhada por Sam Antupit e George Lois.

Diretor de arte

A
Aurélio **Abílio**
San **Antupit**
Rudy **Alves**
Christopher **Austopchuck**
Ruth **Ansel**
Dominique **Amat**

B
Tony **Blank**
Joe **Brooks**
Roger **Black**
Robert **Best**
Walter **Bernardt**

C
Seymour **Chwast**
Ruy Douglas **Cattai**
Ronn **Campisi**
Robert **Clive**

D
Frank **DeVino**
Paul **Davis**
Harry O. **Diamond**
Davis **Driver**
Don **Duffy**

F
Gene **Federico**
Cinzia **Ferrero**
Rubens F. **Ferreira**
Bea **Feitler**
Edward **Freska**
H. **Franklin França**
Willy **Fleckhaus**

G
Carlos **Grasseti**
Susan **Gray**
Milton **Glaser**
Heinrich **Gorissen**
Reinhard **Gade**
Michael **Gross**

H
David **Hilman**
Steve **Heller**

Páginas com muito cunho social, mas por que tanta violência?

Neste catálogo ilustrado, registramos os nomes dos fotógrafos, artistas, diretores de arte e os títulos das publicações. Acredite. Este "apanhado" do que melhor se fez em arte editorial é um trabalho sério, que levou 12 anos e representa a real posição deste gênero de arte.
Das publicações conservadoras aos famosos "magazines" de "pin-ups girls" mais bem realizados no mundo.
Você verá um verdadeiro "show" de estética.
Páginas ilustradas por artistas incríveis. Do humor ao hiper-realismo.
Fotografias de reportagens com todo o seu dramático colorido até as mais sofisticadas fotos de estúdio.
Eu acredito, que a partir desta exposição, você vai ver com outros olhos este marginalizado trabalho de estética visual, que apenas ingleses e americanos chamam, justamente, de "arte editorial."

I
Jorge **Izan**

J
Skyp **Johnston**
Rowan **Johnson**

K
Terry **Koppel**
Jerelle **Kraus**

L
Herb **Lubalin**
Patrick **Levillan**
Norman **Laliberte**
Italo **Lupi**
Ton **Lennon**
Toni **Lane**
David **Larkin**
Jim **Lienhart**

M
Dietmar **Meyer**
Italo **Mangiacavalli**
Oswaldo **Miranda**
Don **Menell**
Pearc **Marchbank**
Peter **Mayley**
Rebecca **Martinez**
Michael **Manwaring**

N
Ary A. **Normanha**

O
Manuel **Ortiz**
Nic **Overhead**

P
Arthur **Paul**
Steve **Phillips**
Robert **Priest**
Jurgen **Peters**
Beppe **Preti**
Evelyne **Provoust**
Margery **Peters**
Robert **Pelegrini**
Bob **Post**
Greg **Paul**
Michel **Paquet**

R
Antonio S. **Rodrigues**

S
Mary **Shanahaan**
Ron Van **Senten**
Fulvia **Serra**
April **Silver**

R·A·P·O·S·A

Dugald **Stern**
Neil **Shakery**
Ricardo Van **Steen**

T
Frances **Tanabe**

W
Susane **Walsh**
Steve **Weininser**
Rodney **Willians**
Vincen **Winter**
Richard **Weigand**

Fotógrafo

A
Dr. **A.** Scrholl

B
Blumenfeld
Bruno **Barbey**
Von Wulf **Brackrock**
André **Berg**
Barret & **Barret**
Serge **Borner**
Caroline **Lebeau**
Jean-Louis **Bloch-Lhiné**

Solda/Rogério Dias (Para a revista policial Perícia)

Maureen **Bisilliat**
Carla De **Benedetti**
George **Butler**
Arky & **Barret**

C
Ronald H. **Cohn**
Frank **Cowan**
Luís **Crispino**
Al **Clayton**

D
Duran
Olivier **Dassault**
Raymond **Depardon**
Kenn **Duncan**

E
Bill **Eppridge**
Anthony **Edgworth**
John Paul **Endress**

6

4
DESIGN FIRM: *Casa De Idéias*
DESIGNER: *Oswaldo Miranda*
HEADLINE TYPEFACE: *Goudy and Franklin*
TEXT TYPEFACE: *Various*
CLIENT: *Raposa/Diário PR/Newspaper*

5
DESIGN FIRM: *Gerard Huerta Design, Inc.*
DESIGNER: *Gerard Huerta*
LETTERER: *Gerard Huerta*
HEADLINE TYPEFACE: *Handlettering*
TEXT TYPEFACE: *Handlettering*
CLIENT: *Newsweek-Ron Meyerson*

6
DESIGN FIRM: *Casa De Idéias*
DESIGNER: *Oswaldo Miranda*
HEADLINE TYPEFACE: *Helvetica Super*
TEXT TYPEFACE: *Tiffany and Franklin Bold*
CLIENT: *Raposa/Diário PR/Newspaper*

7
DESIGN FIRM: *Ronn Campisi Design*
DESIGNER: *Ronn Campisi*
HEADLINE TYPEFACE: *Garamond Oldstyle*
CLIENT: *The Boston Globe*

8
DESIGN FIRM: *Ronn Campisi Design*
DESIGNER: *Ronn Campisi*
HEADLINE TYPEFACE: *Anzeigen*
TEXT TYPEFACE: *Century Expanded*
CLIENT: *The Boston Globe*

9
DESIGN FIRM: *Drenttel Doyle Partners*
DESIGNER: *Rosemarie Turk*
HEADLINE TYPEFACE: *Modern 20*
TEXT TYPEFACE: *Modern 20*
CLIENT: *Rolling Stone Magazine*

7

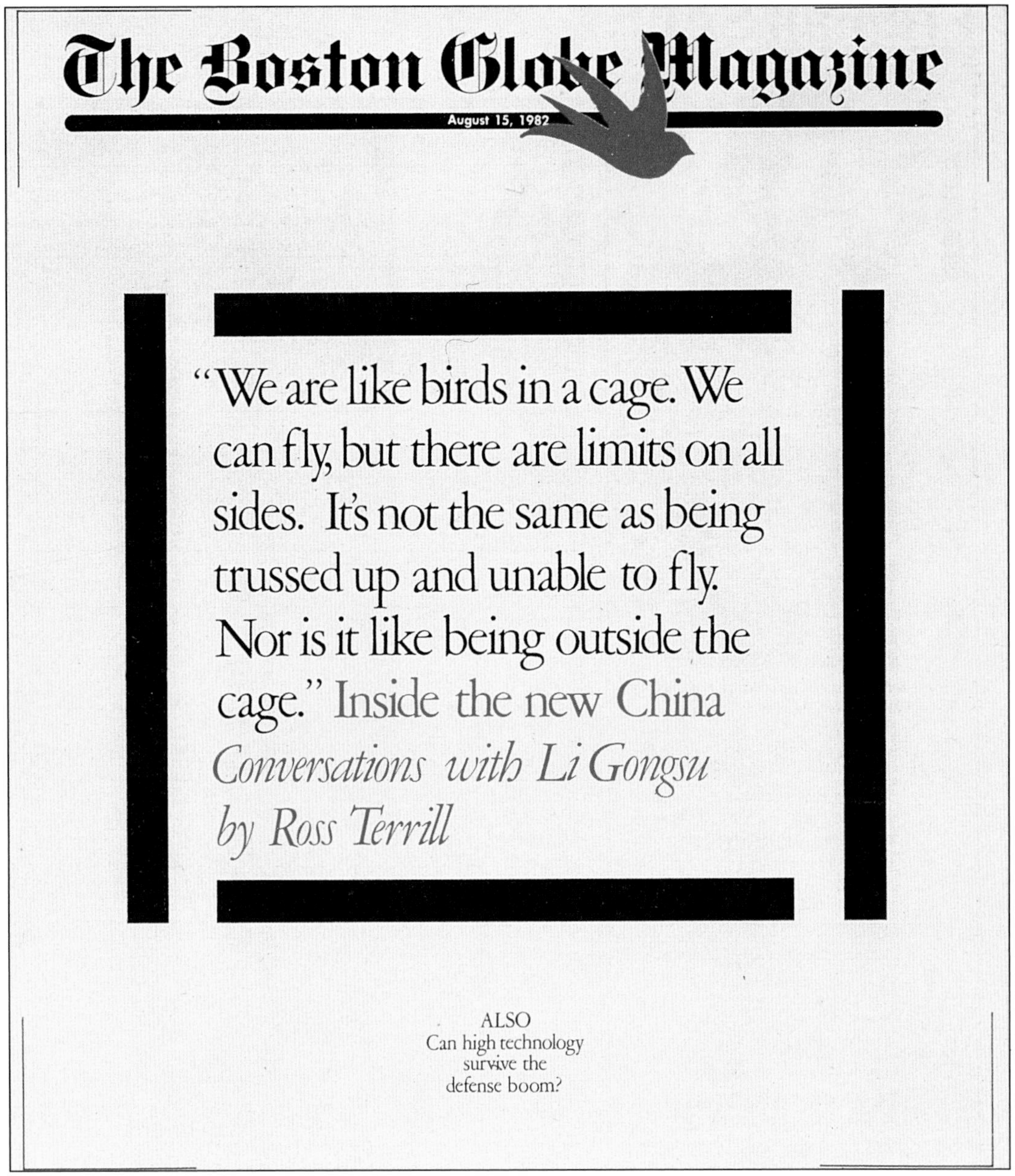

The Boston Globe Magazine

August 15, 1982

"We are like birds in a cage. We can fly, but there are limits on all sides. It's not the same as being trussed up and unable to fly. Nor is it like being outside the cage." Inside the new China

Conversations with Li Gongsu by Ross Terrill

ALSO
Can high technology survive the defense boom?

8

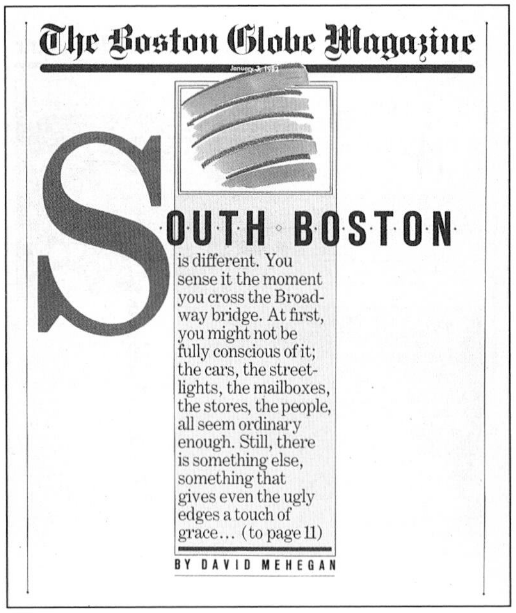

The Boston Globe Magazine

SOUTH BOSTON

is different. You sense it the moment you cross the Broadway bridge. At first, you might not be fully conscious of it; the cars, the streetlights, the mailboxes, the stores, the people, all seem ordinary enough. Still, there is something else, something that gives even the ugly edges a touch of grace... (to page 11)

BY DAVID MEHEGAN

9

When the Earthquake Hits Los Angeles

It will be the worst disaster in our history. There will be economic and social change as fundamental as that which followed the dust-bowl migrations. And no one is prepared.

BY MICHAEL ROGERS

If it happens at night, the sky over the Hollywood Hills will glow and a sound like 10,000 freight trains combined into one single subterranean voice will emerge. For millions of dozing Los Angeles residents, there will be that heart-stopping instant when they are awakened suddenly, unsure for a moment about just what has happened. And even as they wonder, the answer will be manifest in the shaking that will continue, violently, for one, two, perhaps three full minutes. Just as surely as the

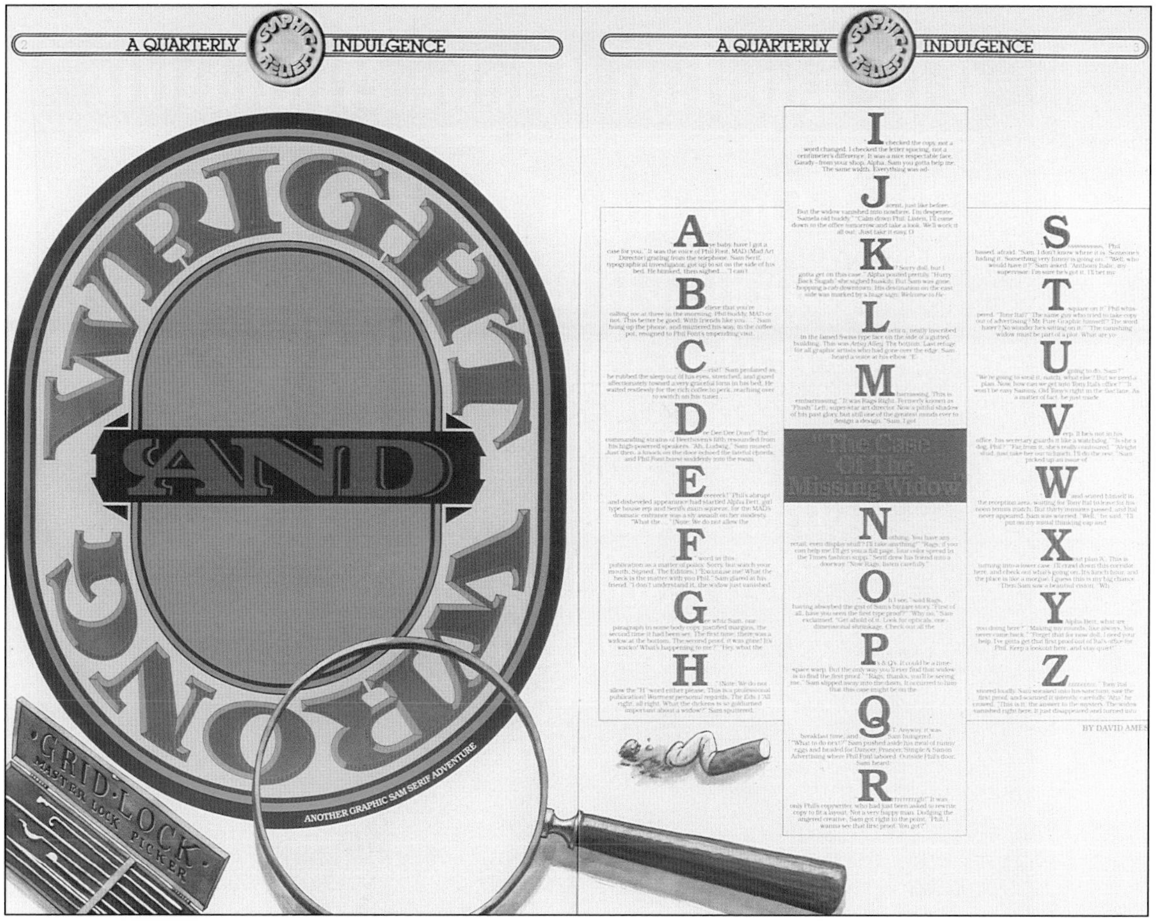

10

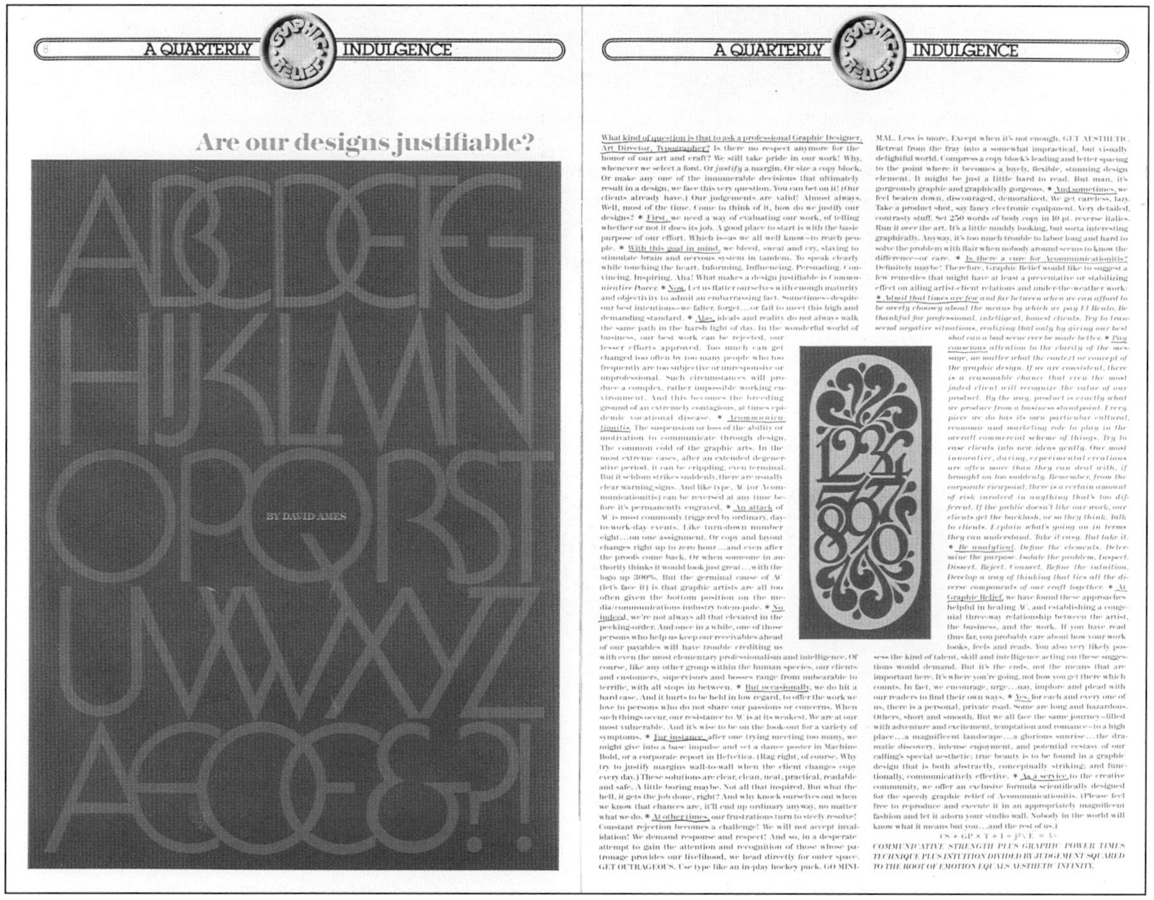

11

10

DESIGN FIRM: *David Brier Design Works, Incorporated*

DESIGNER: *David Brier*

LETTERER: *David Brier*

HEADLINE TYPEFACE: *ITC Bookman Bold*

TEXT TYPEFACE: *ITC Bookman*

CLIENT: *Graphic Relief*

11

DESIGN FIRM: *David Brier Design Works, Incorporated*

DESIGNER: *David Brier*

LETTERER: *David Brier*

HEADLINE TYPEFACE: *Handlettering and ITC Modern 216*

TEXT TYPEFACE: *ITC Modern 2156*

CLIENT: *Graphic Relief*

12
DESIGN FIRM: *Ronn Campisi Design*
DESIGNER: *Ronn Campisi*
HEADLINE TYPEFACE: *Century Expanded*
CLIENT: *The Boston Globe*

13
DESIGN FIRM: *Ronn Campisi Design*
DESIGNER: *Ronn Campisi*
HEADLINE TYPEFACE: *Century Expanded*
CLIENT: *The Boston Globe*

14
DESIGN FIRM: *Ronn Campisi*
DESIGNER: *Ronn Campisi*
HEADLINE TYPEFACE: *Onyx and Venus Extended*
CLIENT: *The Boston Globe*

12

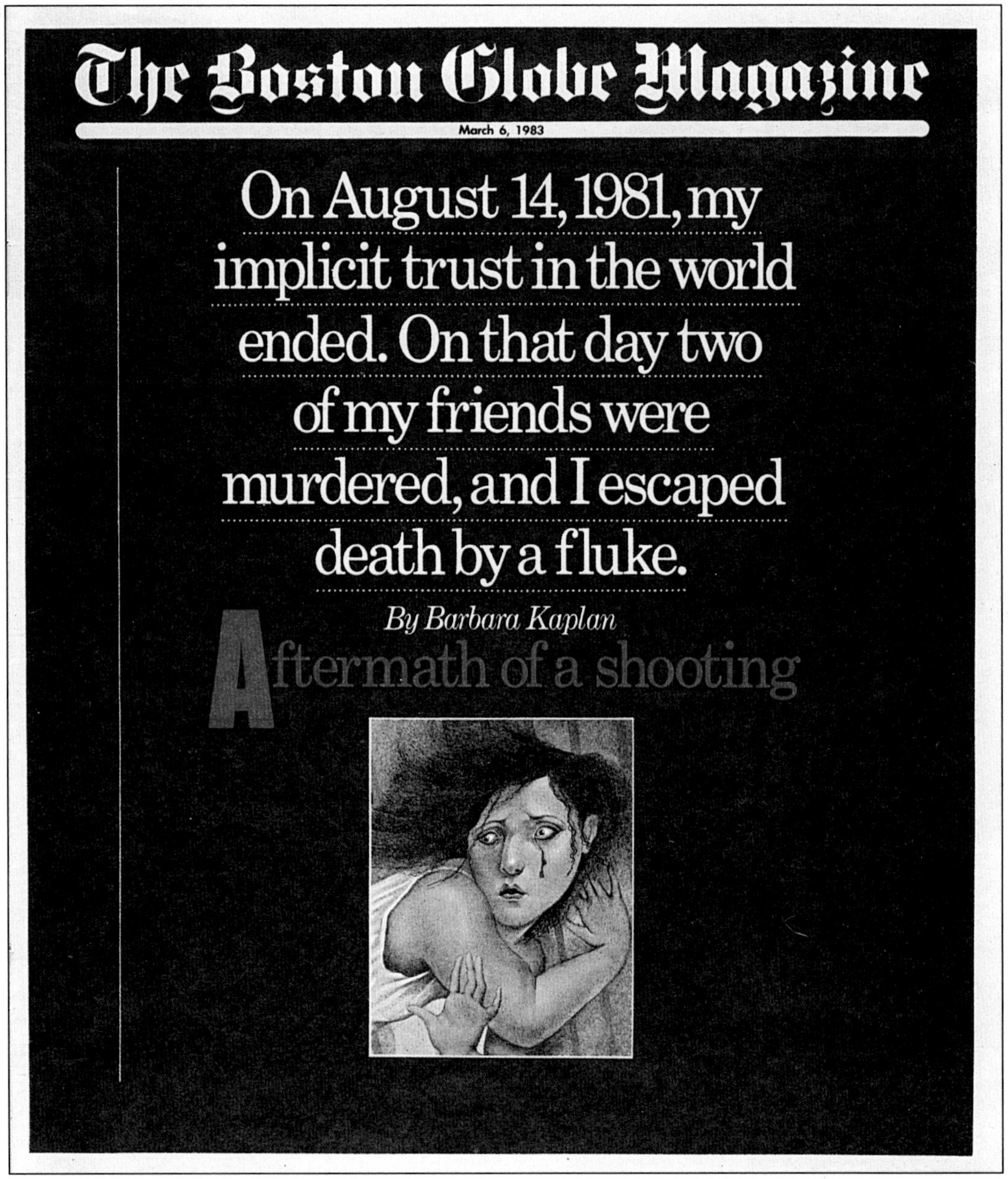

13

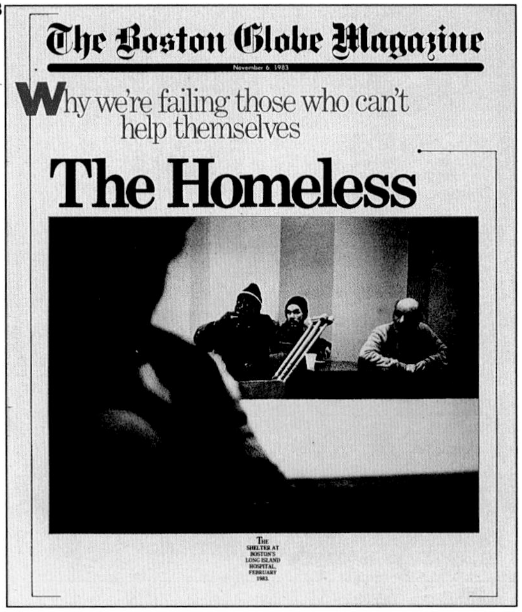

14

15

OCTOBER 1983
AMERICAN JOURNAL OF NURSING
AJN
ACUTE CARDIAC TAMPONADE: WHEN THE PRESSURE IS ON 1414
RESPITE CARE—WHAT IS IT AND WHO DOES IT? 1428
AGITATION AND AGGRESSION FOLLOWING HEAD INJURY 1408
SPEAKING UP
FOR
NURSING

15
DESIGN FIRM: *Jonson Pedersen Hinrichs & Shakery*
DESIGNER: *Daniel Pelavin*
LETTERER: *Daniel Pelavin*
HEADLINE TYPEFACE: *Handlettering*
TEXT TYPEFACE: *Futura*
CLIENT: *American Journal of Nursing*

16
DESIGN FIRM: *Lloyd Ziff Design Group, Inc.*
DESIGNER: *Lloyd Ziff*
HEADLINE TYPEFACE: *Hathaway*
TEXT TYPEFACE: *Radiant Goudy Oldstyle*
CLIENT: *Vanity Fair Magazine*

17
DESIGN FIRM: *Louise Fili, Ltd.*
DESIGNER: *Louise Fili*
LETTERER: *Craig de Camps*
CLIENT: *Pantheon Books*

18
DESIGN FIRM: *Daniel Pelavin*
DESIGNER: *Daniel Pelavin*
LETTERER: *Daniel Pelavin*
HEADLINE TYPEFACE: *Handlettering*
TEXT TYPEFACE: *Futura*
CLIENT: *Vintage Books*

16

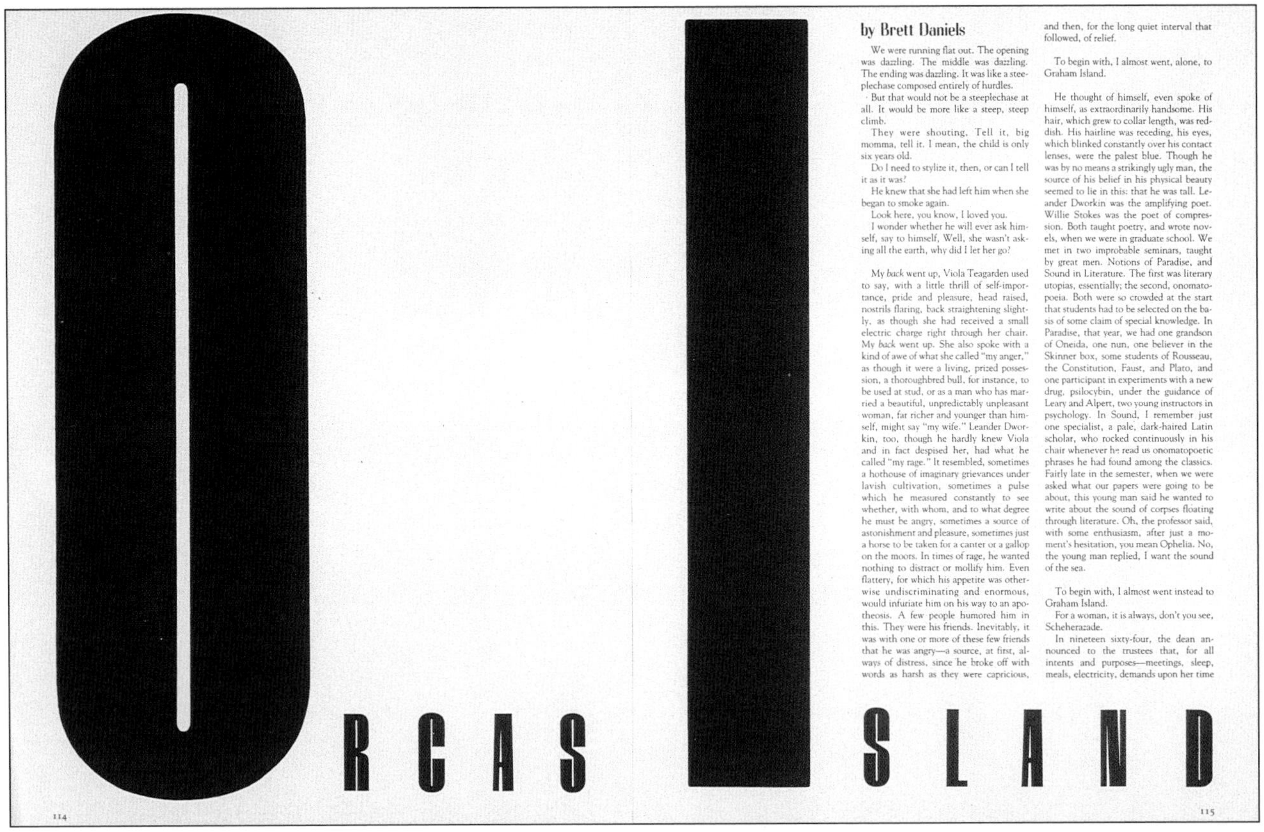

ORCAS ISLAND

by Brett Daniels

We were running flat out. The opening was dazzling. The middle was dazzling. The ending was dazzling. It was like a steeplechase composed entirely of hurdles.

But that would not be a steeplechase at all. It would be more like a steep, steep climb.

They were shouting, Tell it, big momma, tell it. I mean, the child is only six years old.

Do I need to stylize it, then, or can I tell it as it was?

He knew that she had left him when she began to smoke again.

Look here, you know, I loved you.

I wonder whether he will ever ask himself, say to himself, Well, she wasn't asking all the earth, why did I let her go?

My *back* went up, Viola Teagarden used to say, with a little thrill of self-importance, pride and pleasure, head raised, nostrils flaring, back straightening slightly, as though she had received a small electric charge right through her chair. My *back* went up. She also spoke with a kind of awe of what she called "my anger," as though it were a living, prized possession, a thoroughbred bull, for instance, to be used at stud, or as a man who has married a beautiful, unpredictably unpleasant woman, far richer and younger than himself, might say "my wife." Leander Dworkin, too, though he hardly knew Viola and in fact despised her, had what he called "my rage." It resembled, sometimes a hothouse of imaginary grievances under lavish cultivation, sometimes a pulse which he measured constantly to see whether, with whom, and to what degree he must be angry, sometimes a source of astonishment and pleasure, sometimes just a horse to be taken for a canter or a gallop on the moors. In times of rage, he wanted nothing to distract or mollify him. Even flattery, for which his appetite was otherwise undiscriminating and enormous, would infuriate him on his way to an apotheosis. A few people humored him in this. They were his friends. Inevitably, it was with one or more of these few friends that he was angry—a source, at first, always of distress, since he broke off with words as harsh as they were capricious, and then, for the long quiet interval that followed, of relief.

To begin with, I almost went, alone, to Graham Island.

He thought of himself, even spoke of himself, as extraordinarily handsome. His hair, which grew to collar length, was reddish. His hairline was receding, his eyes, which blinked constantly over his contact lenses, were the palest blue. Though he was by no means a strikingly ugly man, the source of his belief in his physical beauty seemed to lie in this: that he was tall. Leander Dworkin was the amplifying poet. Willie Stokes was the poet of compression. Both taught poetry, and wrote novels, when we were in graduate school. We met in two improbable seminars, taught by great men. Notions of Paradise, and Sound in Literature. The first was literary utopias, essentially; the second, onomatopoeia. Both were so crowded at the start that students had to be selected on the basis of some claim of special knowledge. In Paradise, that year, we had one grandson of Oneida, one nun, one believer in the Skinner box, some students of Rousseau, the Constitution, Faust, and Plato, and one participant in experiments with a new drug, psilocybin, under the guidance of Leary and Alpert, two young instructors in psychology. In Sound, I remember just one specialist, a pale, dark-haired Latin scholar, who rocked continuously in his chair whenever he read us onomatopoetic phrases he had found among the classics. Fairly late in the semester, when we were asked what our papers were going to be about, this young man said he wanted to write about the sound of corpses floating through literature. Oh, the professor said, with some enthusiasm, after just a moment's hesitation, you mean Ophelia. No, the young man replied, I want the sound of the sea.

To begin with, I almost went instead to Graham Island.

For a woman, it is always, don't you see, Scheherazade.

In nineteen sixty-four, the dean announced to the trustees that, for all intents and purposes—meetings, sleep, meals, electricity, demands upon her time

114

115

17

18

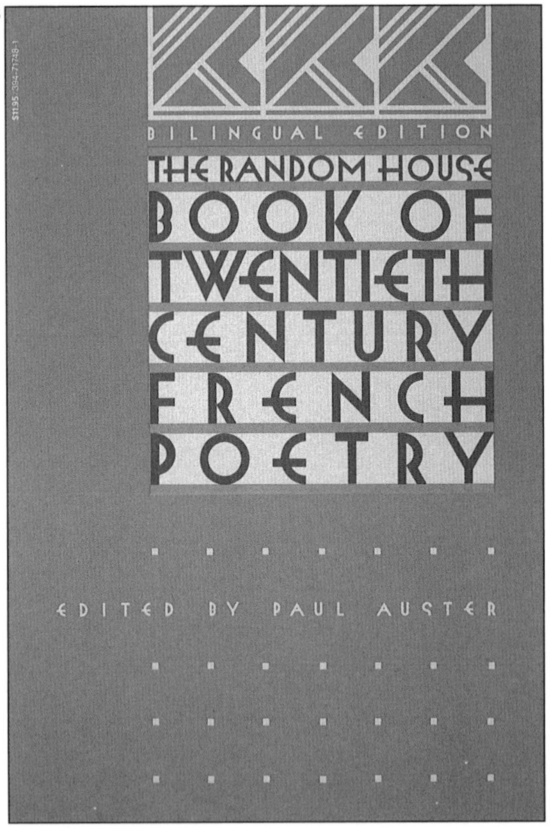

19

S U P E R
KIDS

SHOULD YOURS JOIN THE CLUB?

BY KERRY PECHTER

Super kids. When Linda Paul, a young mother from Haddonfield, New Jersey, saw a group of them for the first time, she thought she was in Lilliput. She found herself surrounded by a mob of precocious half-pints dressed in crazy lavender bib overalls, most of them no taller than her knees and all of them doing things that two- and three-year-olds ordinarily do not do. She saw an infant no older than seven months who could swim. She met a boy who could glance at a poster with a lot of red dots on it and tell her, without even counting, that there were 92 of them. And then there was the toddler, barely out of diapers, who could look at a card with the portrait of a 19th century composer on it and tell her, giggling, that his name

44 · SPRING · MAY · 1983

MAY · 1983 · SPRING · 45

20

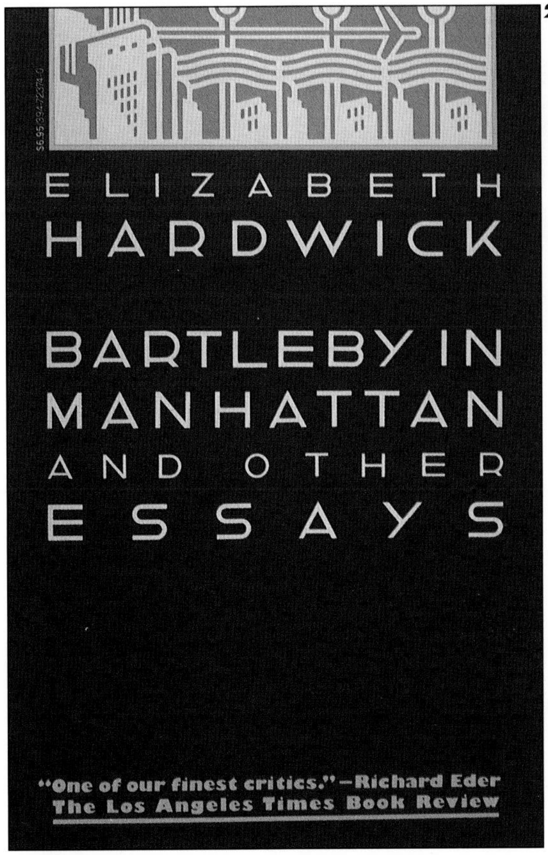

ELIZABETH
HARDWICK
BARTLEBY IN
MANHATTAN
AND OTHER
ESSAYS
"One of our finest critics."—Richard Eder
The Los Angeles Times Book Review

21

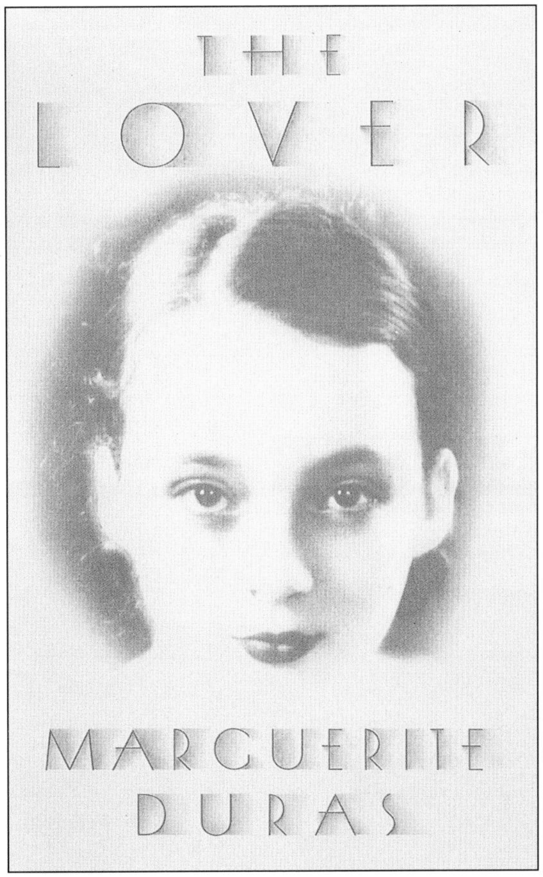

THE
LOVER
MARGUERITE
DURAS

19
DESIGN FIRM: *Tyler Smith Graphics, Inc.*
DESIGNER: *Joanne Dus-Zastron*
HEADLINE TYPEFACE: *Michaelangelo Titling*
TEXT TYPEFACE: *Horley Oldstyle*
CLIENT: *Rodale Press, Inc.*

20
DESIGN FIRM: *Daniel Pelavin*
DESIGNER: *Daniel Pelavin*
LETTERER: *Daniel Pelavin*
HEADLINE TYPEFACE: *Handlettering*
TEXT TYPEFACE: *Gill Sans*
CLIENT: *Vintage Books*

21
DESIGN FIRM: *Louise Fili, Ltd.*
DESIGNER: *Louise Fili*
LETTERER: *Louise Fili and Craig de Camps*
CLIENT: *Pantheon Books*

22
DESIGN FIRM: *Casa De Idéias*
DESIGNER: *Oswaldo Miranda*
CLIENT: *Grafica Magazine*

23
DESIGN FIRM: *Ronn Campisi Design*
DESIGNER: *Ronn Campisi*
HEADLINE TYPEFACE: *Grotesque 6 and Torino Italic*
CLIENT: *The Boston Globe*

24
DESIGN FIRM: *David Brier Design Works, Incorporated*
DESIGNER: *David Brier*
LETTERER: *David Brier*
HEADLINE TYPEFACE: *Handlettering*
TEXT TYPEFACE: *Franklin Gothic Condensed*
CLIENT: *Graphic Relief*

22

23

24

25

25
DESIGN FIRM: *Dennis Ortiz-Lopez*
DESIGNER: *Robert Best*
LETTERER: *Dennis Ortiz-Lopez*
HEADLINE TYPEFACE: *Handlettering*
CLIENT: *New York Magazine*

26
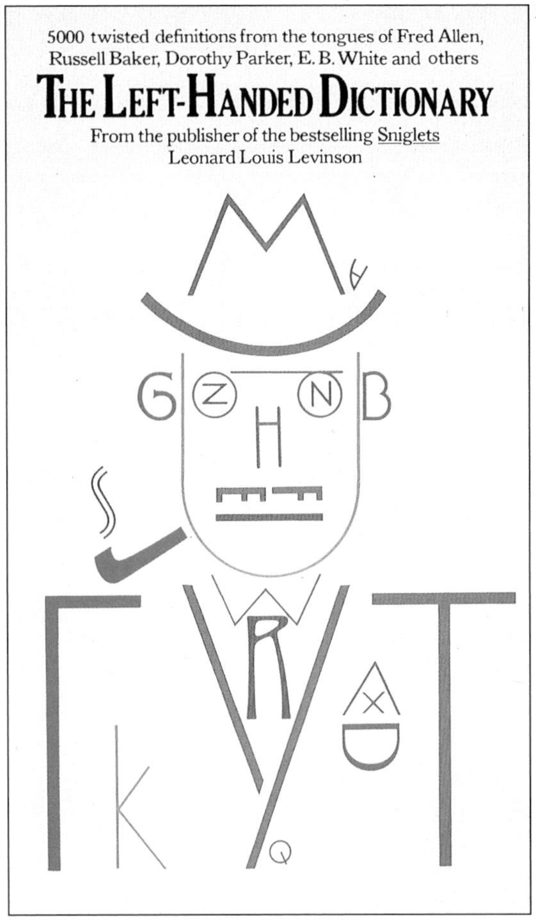

27
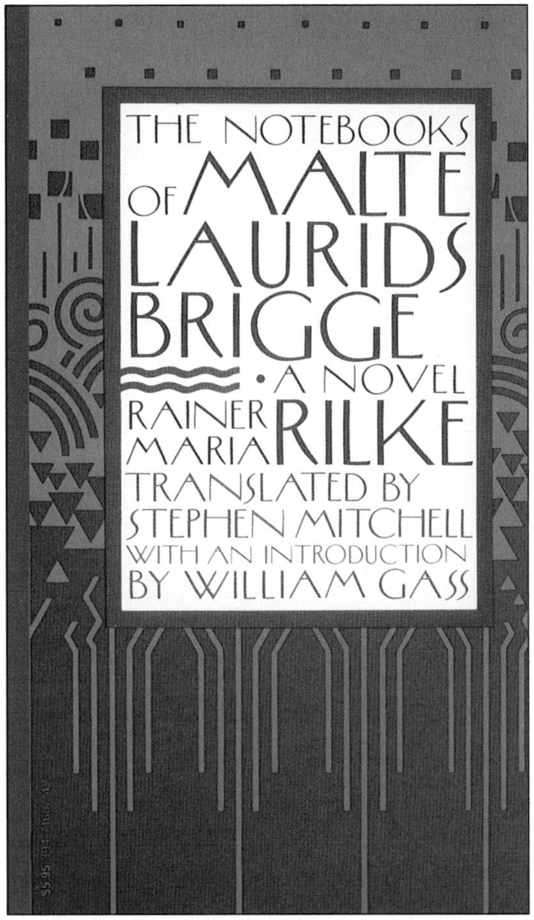

28
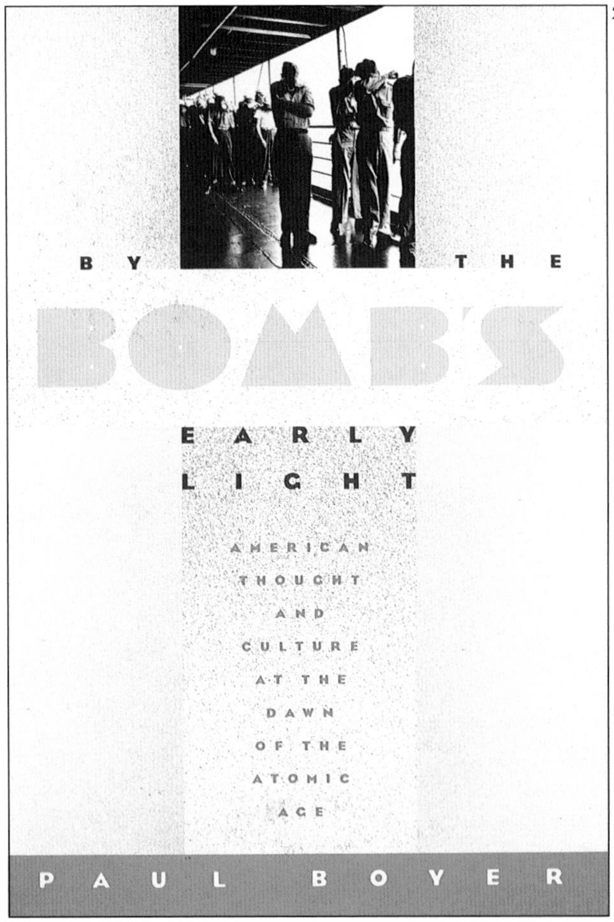

29
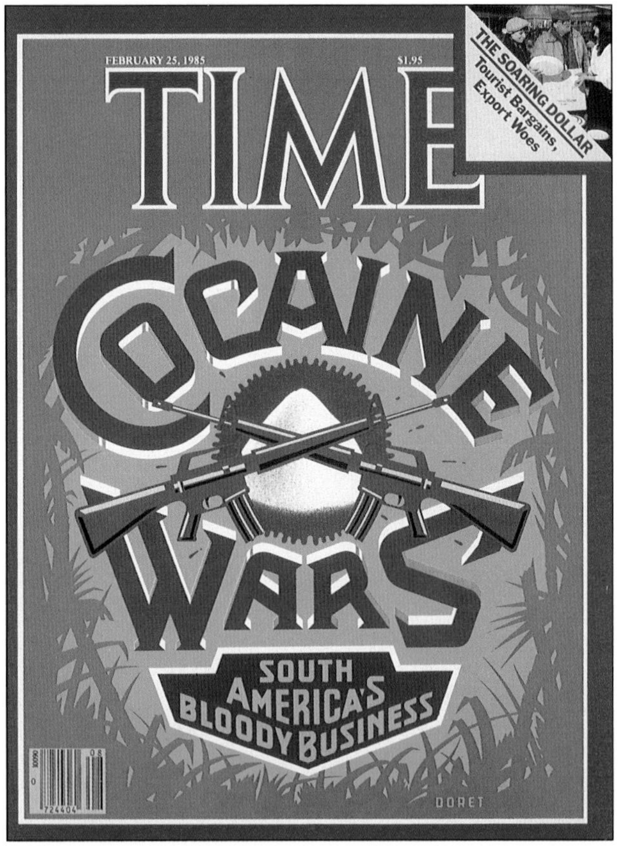

26
DESIGN FIRM: *Warner Books*
DESIGNER: *Seymour Chwast*
CLIENT: *Warner Books*

27
DESIGN FIRM: *Daniel Pelavin*
DESIGNER: *Daniel Pelavin*
LETTERER: *Daniel Pelavin*
HEADLINE TYPEFACE: *Handlettering*
TEXT TYPEFACE: *Kabel*
CLIENT: *Vintage Books*

28
DESIGN FIRM: *Louise Fili, Ltd.*
DESIGNER: *Louise Fili*
LETTERER: *Louise Fili*
HEADLINE TYPEFACE: *Handlettering*
TEXT TYPEFACE: *Eagle Bold*
CLIENT: *Pantheon Books*

29
DESIGN FIRM: *Michael Doret, Inc.*
DESIGNER: *Michael Doret*
LETTERER: *Michael Doret*
HEADLINE TYPEFACE: *Handlettering*
CLIENT: *TIME Magazine*

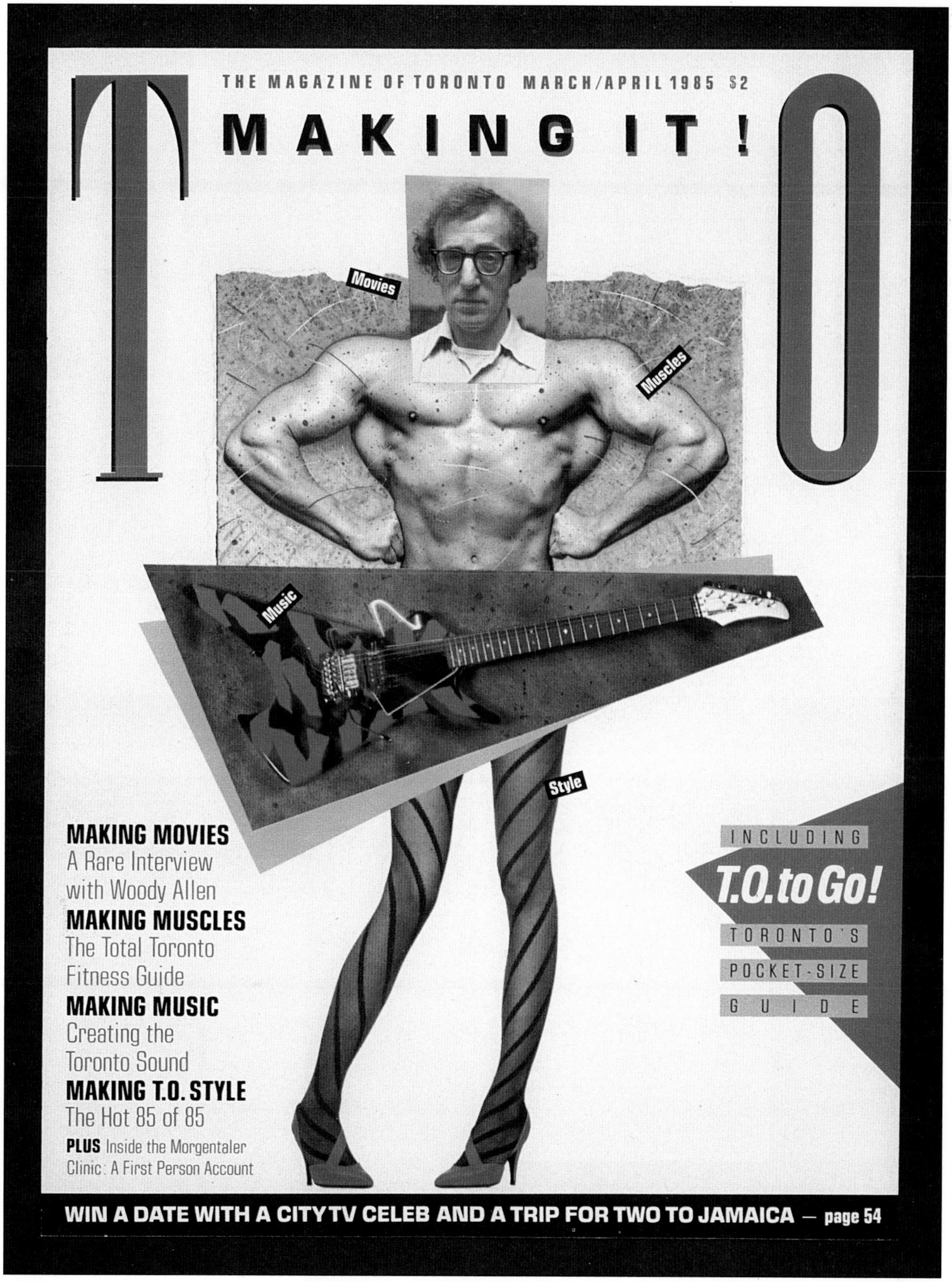

30

30
DESIGN FIRM: *Reactor Art & Design*
DESIGNER: *Louis Fishauf*
TEXT TYPEFACE: *Eurostile*
CLIENT: *T.O. Magazine*

10
A QUARTERLY
GRAPHIC RELIEF
INDULGENCE
A QUARTERLY
GRAPHIC RELIEF
INDULGENCE
11
Just When You Thought It Was Safe To Go Back Into The Office.
Business Ties
A GUIDE TO CORPORATE SEXUALITY AND WHAT KNOT TO DO.
WRITTEN BY DAVID KONIGSBERG
HIDDEN TIES
These two subjects broadcast a range of signals, none of them, shall we say, forthright? Feigning honesty (note the jackets flung open) they mask their true intentions—and hidden, can these intentions be anything close to honorable?…
TENTATIVE TIES
Heaven help the man or woman in the middle. Options left, options right, and they find themselves immobilized. Should they finish things with one? Take up with another? Check out a third? Check out, period? The choices seem too difficult to bear…
ALL-TOO-CLEAR-TIES
If ignorance is bliss, this pair should be ecstatic. Haven't they any notion that people read them like a book? In contractual negotiations, their hand is always showing. In social confrontations, they can't even put over a lie as simple as "I'm getting a separation."…
TENUOUS TIES
Casual to a fault, this couple signals a laid-back lifestyle that, socially and professionally, gets them nowhere fast. What we read is a lack of ambition, striking inefficiency, no attention to detail, and social liasons that come too easily—and evaporate a little too fast…
UNSTABLE TIES
Ambition (professional and sexual) knows no bounds for people like these. His down-slanting stripes betray false modesty; the breadth of the tie, a whopping ego; the protruding tie tail, a ninja's instinct for going for the jugular…
….Of course, they may simply have dripped gravey on their ties, in which case they possess a certain fashionable deftness in emergencies. Shall we give them the benefit of the doubt? Once, yes, but never twice. Keep an eye on them.
….Eventually, they'll learn, though, that juggling's the most difficult option of all. A single misstep—a slipped name, a vague reference, a forgotten excuse used last Thursday—and everything may slip through their fingers, leaving no ties but their neckties.
….It's not easy surviving ough and tumble world when your eyes, and lie, give everything away. Our advice is some counseling, and a little fashion advice. Both will toughen them up to play hardball, the socio-corporate national sport.
….Eventually, lack of accomplishment will seem unimpressive even to them. Without better ties, they will prove incapable of either true love or tangible success.
….Her strident, forked bowtie, meanwhile, seems at once lavacious and vicious. These two are made for each other. Tossed together, they may form a unit even more formidable than its parts—or a firey, kinetic mixture primed ultimately to self-destruct.

31
DESIGN FIRM: *David Brier Design Works, Incorporated*
DESIGNER: *David Brier*
LETTERER: *David Brier*
HEADLINE TYPEFACE: *Handlettering and Torino*
TEXT TYPEFACE: *Torino*
CLIENT: *Graphic Relief*

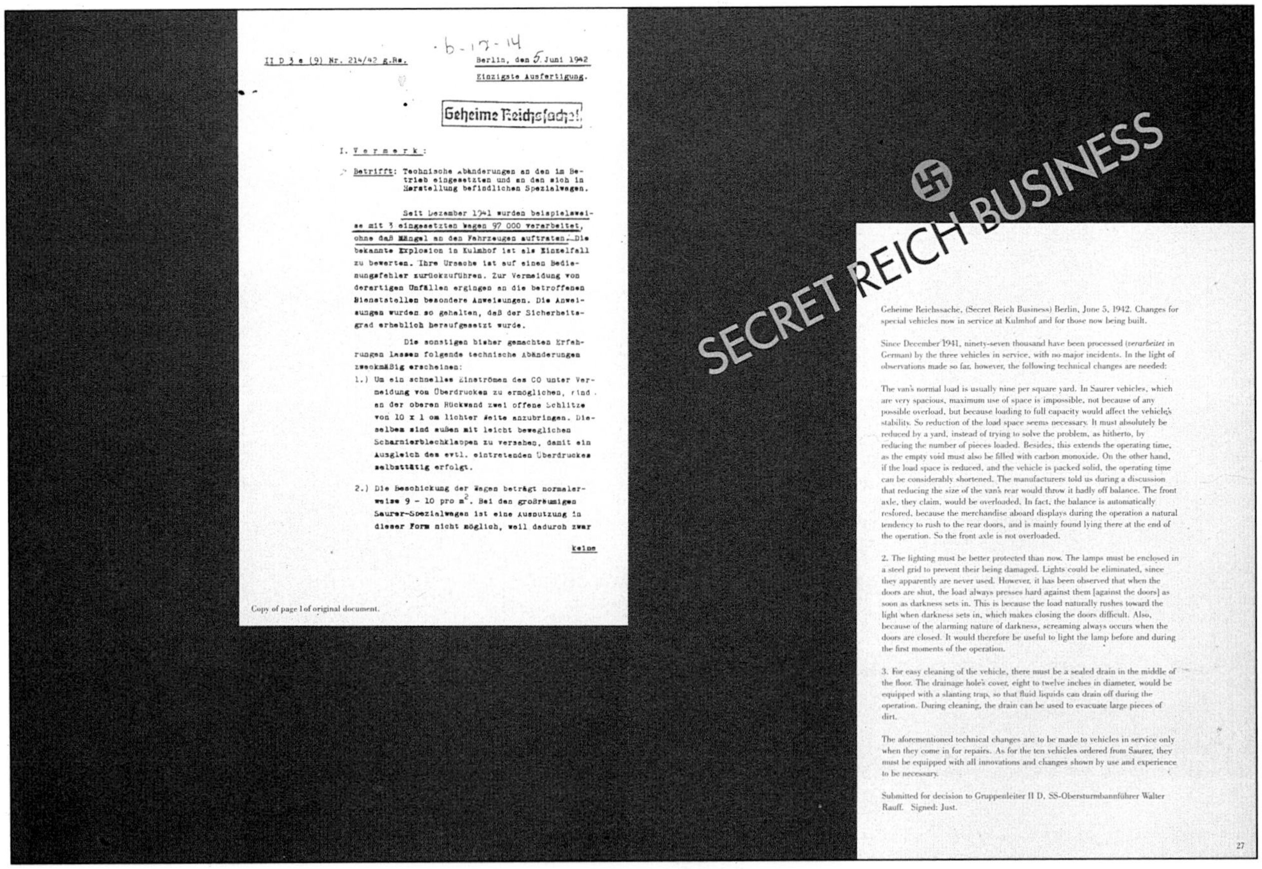

·6-17-14
II D 3 a (9) Nr. 214/42 g.Rs.
Berlin, den 5. Juni 1942
Einzigste Ausfertigung.
Geheime Reichssache!
I. Vermerk:
Betrifft: Technische Abänderungen an den im Betrieb eingesetzten und an den sich in Herstellung befindlichen Spezialwagen.
Seit Dezember 1941 wurden beispielsweise mit 3 eingesetzten Wagen 97 000 verarbeitet, ohne daß Mängel an den Fahrzeugen auftraten. Die bekannte Explosion in Kulmhof ist als Einzelfall zu bewerten. Ihre Ursache ist auf einen Bedienungsfehler zurückzuführen. Zur Vermeidung von derartigen Unfällen ergingen an die betroffenen Dienststellen besondere Anweisungen. Die Anweisungen wurden so gehalten, daß der Sicherheitsgrad erheblich heraufgesetzt wurde.
Die sonstigen bisher gemachten Erfahrungen lassen folgende technische Abänderungen zweckmäßig erscheinen:
1.) Um ein schnelles Einströmen des CO unter Vermeidung von Überdrucken zu ermöglichen, sind an der oberen Rückwand zwei offene Schlitze von 10 x 1 cm lichter Weite anzubringen. Dieselben sind außen mit leicht beweglichen Scharnierblechklappen zu versehen, damit ein Ausgleich des evtl. eintretenden Überdruckes selbsttätig erfolgt.
2.) Die Beschickung der Wagen beträgt normalerweise 9 - 10 pro m². Bei den großräumigen Saurer-Spezialwagen ist eine Ausnutzung in dieser Form nicht möglich, weil dadurch zwar
keine
Copy of page 1 of original document.
SECRET REICH BUSINESS
Geheime Reichssache, (Secret Reich Business) Berlin, June 5, 1942. Changes for special vehicles now in service at Kulmhof and for those now being built.
Since December 1941, ninety-seven thousand have been processed (verarbeitet in German) by the three vehicles in service, with no major incidents. In the light of observations made so far, however, the following technical changes are needed:
The van's normal load is usually nine per square yard. In Saurer vehicles, which are very spacious, maximum use of space is impossible, not because of any possible overload, but because loading to full capacity would affect the vehicle's stability. So reduction of the load space seems necessary. It must absolutely be reduced by a yard, instead of trying to solve the problem, as hitherto, by reducing the number of pieces loaded. Besides, this extends the operating time, as the empty void must also be filled with carbon monoxide. On the other hand, if the load space is reduced, and the vehicle is packed solid, the operating time can be considerably shortened. The manufacturers told us during a discussion that reducing the size of the van's rear would throw it badly off balance. The front axle, they claim, would be overloaded. In fact, the balance is automatically restored, because the merchandise aboard displays during the operation a natural tendency to rush to the rear doors, and is mainly found lying there at the end of the operation. So the front axle is not overloaded.
2. The lighting must be better protected than now. The lamps must be enclosed in a steel grid to prevent their being damaged. Lights could be eliminated, since they apparently are never used. However, it has been observed that when the doors are shut, the load always presses hard against them [against the doors] as soon as darkness sets in. This is because the load naturally rushes toward the light when darkness sets in, which makes closing the doors difficult. Also, because of the alarming nature of darkness, screaming always occurs when the doors are closed. It would therefore be useful to light the lamp before and during the first moments of the operation.
3. For easy cleaning of the vehicle, there must be a sealed drain in the middle of the floor. The drainage hole's cover, eight to twelve inches in diameter, would be equipped with a slanting trap, so that fluid liquids can drain off during the operation. During cleaning, the drain can be used to evacuate large pieces of dirt.
The aforementioned technical changes are to be made to vehicles in service only when they come in for repairs. As for the ten vehicles ordered from Saurer, they must be equipped with all innovations and changes shown by use and experience to be necessary.
Submitted for decision to Gruppenleiter II D, SS-Obersturmbannführer Walter Rauff. Signed: Just.
27

32
DESIGN FIRM: *Paul Davis Studio*
DESIGNER: *Paul Davis*
HEADLINE TYPEFACE: *Metro*
TEXT TYPEFACE: *Bodoni*
CLIENT: *Normal Magazine*

33

34

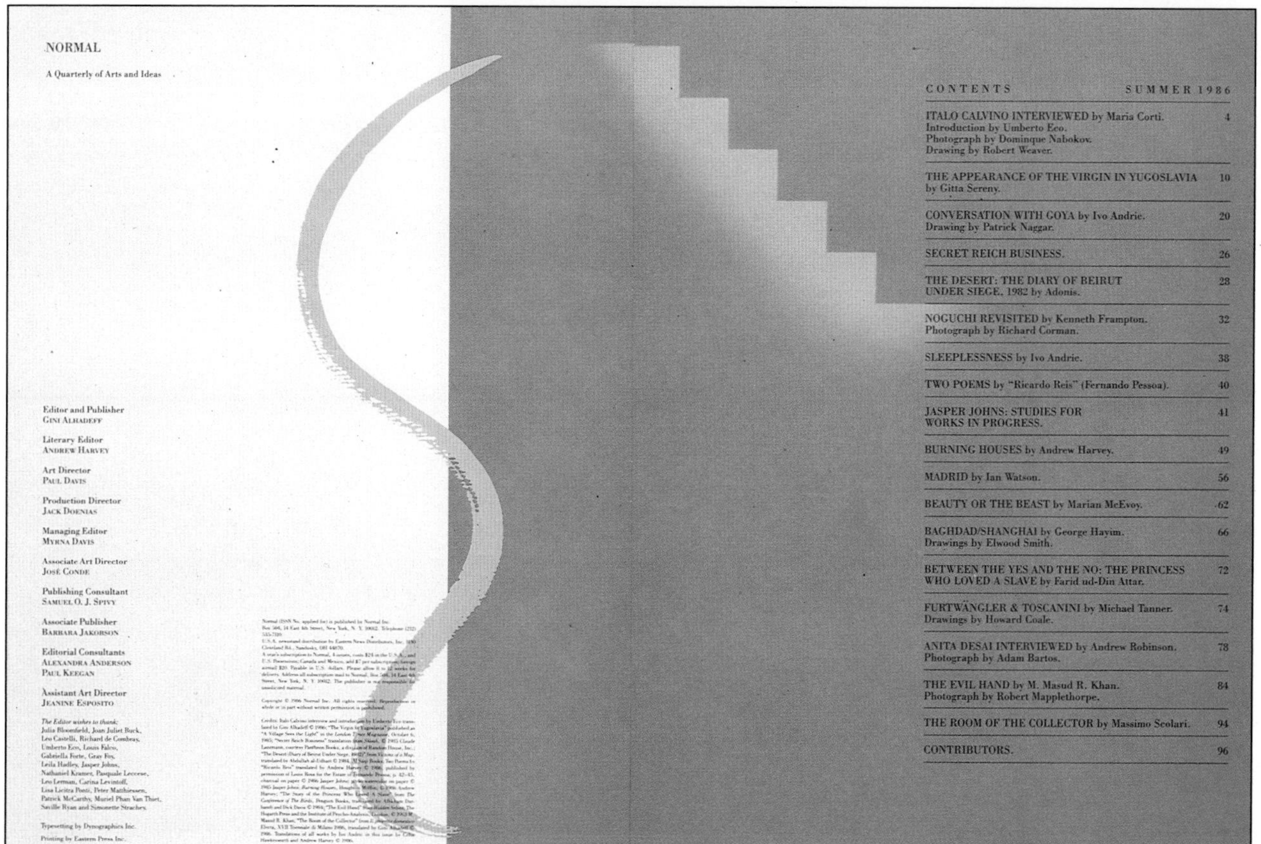

33
DESIGN FIRM: *Paul Davis Studio*
DESIGNER: *Paul Davis*
LETTERER: *Paul Davis*
HEADLINE TYPEFACE: *Collage and Handlettering*
TEXT TYPEFACE: *Futura*
CLIENT: *Normal Magazine*

34
DESIGN FIRM: *Paul Davis Studio*
DESIGNER: *Paul Davis and Jose Conde*
TEXT TYPEFACE: *Bodoni*
CLIENT: *Normal Magazine*

35
DESIGN FIRM: *Paul Davis Studio*
DESIGNER: *Paul Davis*
HEADLINE TYPEFACE: *Futura*
TEXT TYPEFACE: *Futura*
CLIENT: *Normal Magazine*

36
DESIGN FIRM: *Paul Davis Studio*
DESIGNER: *Jose Conde*
HEADLINE TYPEFACE: *Sabon*
TEXT TYPEFACE: *Sabon*
CLIENT: *Normal Magazine*

35

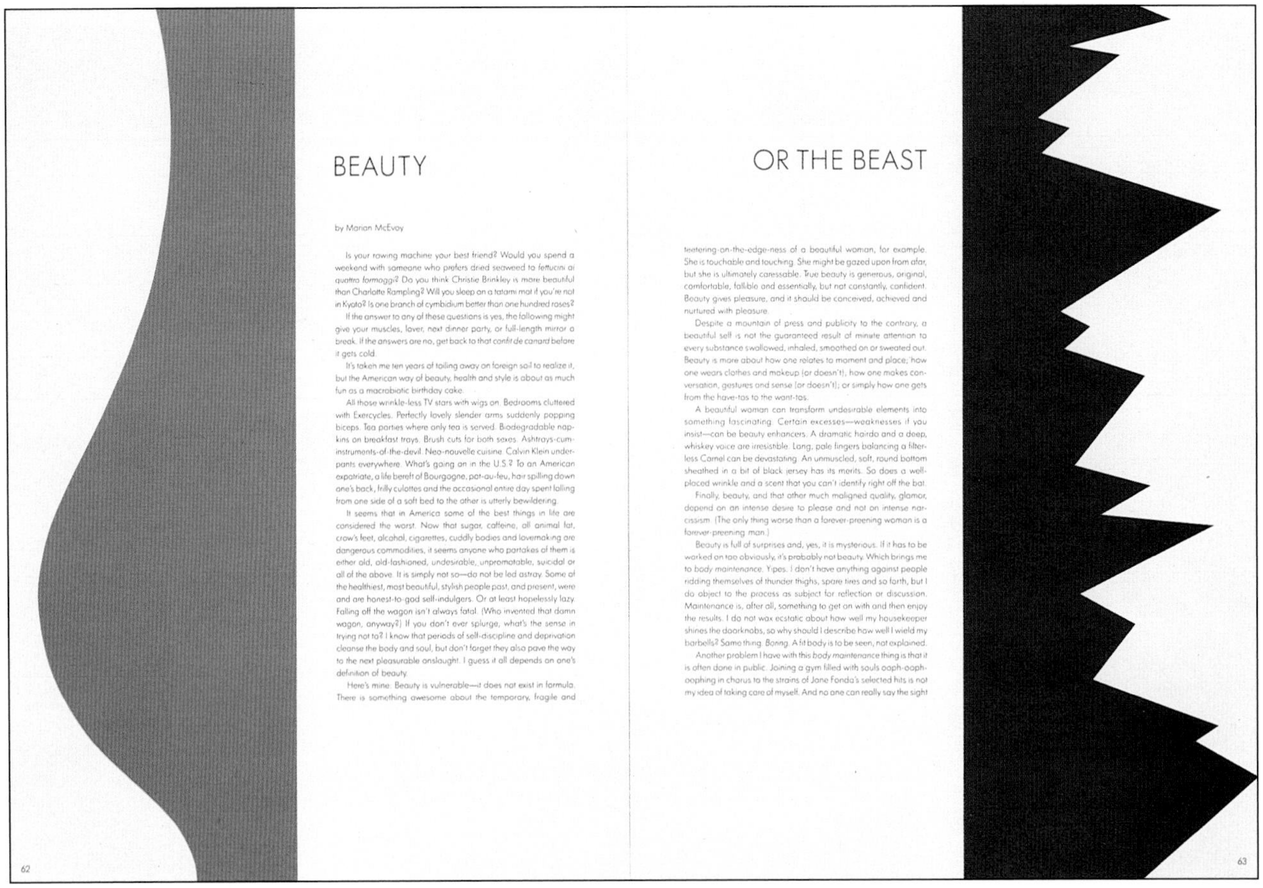

BEAUTY

OR THE BEAST

by Marian McEvoy

Is your rowing machine your best friend? Would you spend a weekend with someone who prefers dried seaweed to *fettucini ai quattro formaggi*? Do you think Christie Brinkley is more beautiful than Charlotte Rampling? Will you sleep on a tatami mat if you're not in Kyoto? Is one branch of cymbidium better than one hundred roses?

If the answer to any of these questions is yes, the following might give your muscles, lover, next dinner party, or full-length mirror a break. If the answers are no, get back to that *confit de canard* before it gets cold.

It's taken me ten years of toiling away on foreign soil to realize it, but the American way of beauty, health and style is about as much fun as a macrobiotic birthday cake.

All those wrinkle-less TV stars with wigs on. Bedrooms cluttered with Exercycles. Perfectly lovely slender arms suddenly popping biceps. Tea parties where only tea is served. Biodegradable napkins on breakfast trays. Brush cuts for both sexes. Ashtrays-cum-instruments-of-the-devil. Neo-nouvelle cuisine. Calvin Klein underpants everywhere. What's going on in the U.S.? To an American expatriate, a life bereft of Bourgogne, pot-au-feu, hair spilling down one's back, frilly culottes and the occasional entire day spent lolling from one side of a soft bed to the other is utterly bewildering.

It seems that in America some of the best things in life are considered the worst. Now that sugar, caffeine, all animal fat, crow's feet, alcohol, cigarettes, cuddly bodies and lovemaking are dangerous commodities, it seems anyone who partakes of them is either old, old-fashioned, undesirable, unpromotable, suicidal or all of the above. It is simply not so—do not be led astray. Some of the healthiest, most beautiful, stylish people past, and present, were and are honest-to-god self-indulgers. Or at least hopelessly lazy. Falling off the wagon isn't always fatal. (Who invented that damn wagon, anyway?) If you don't ever splurge, what's the sense in trying not to? I know that periods of self-discipline and deprivation cleanse the body and soul, but don't forget they also pave the way to the next pleasurable onslaught. I guess it all depends on one's definition of beauty.

Here's mine: Beauty is vulnerable—it does not exist in formula. There is something awesome about the temporary, fragile and teetering-on-the-edge-ness of a beautiful woman, for example. She is touchable and touching. She might be gazed upon from afar, but she is ultimately caressable. True beauty is generous, original, comfortable, fallible and essentially, but not constantly, confident. Beauty gives pleasure, and it should be conceived, achieved and nurtured with pleasure.

Despite a mountain of press and publicity to the contrary, a beautiful self is not the guaranteed result of minute attention to every substance swallowed, inhaled, smoothed on or sweated out. Beauty is more about how one relates to moment and place; how one wears clothes and makeup (or doesn't), how one makes conversation, gestures and sense (or doesn't); or simply how one gets from the have-tos to the want-tos.

A beautiful woman can transform undesirable elements into something fascinating. Certain excesses—weaknesses if you insist—can be beauty enhancers. A dramatic hairdo and a deep, whiskey voice are irresistible. Long, pale fingers balancing a filterless Camel can be devastating. An unmuscled, soft, round bottom sheathed in a bit of black jersey has its merits. So does a well-placed wrinkle and a scent that you can't identify right off the bat.

Finally, beauty, and that other much maligned quality, glamor, depend on an intense desire to please and not on intense narcissism. (The only thing worse than a forever-preening woman is a forever-preening man.)

Beauty is full of surprises and, yes, it is mysterious. If it has to be worked on too obviously, it's probably not beauty. Which brings me to *body maintenance*. Yipes. I don't have anything against people ridding themselves of thunder thighs, spare tires and so forth, but I do object to the *process* as subject for reflection or discussion. Maintenance is, after all, something to get on with and then enjoy the results. I do not wax ecstatic about how well my housekeeper shines the doorknobs, so why should I describe how well I wield my barbells? Same thing. *Boring*. A fit body is to be seen, not explained.

Another problem I have with this *body maintenance* thing is that it is often done in public. Joining a gym filled with souls ooph-ooph-oophing in chorus to the strains of Jane Fonda's selected hits is not my idea of taking care of myself. And no one can really say the sight

62

63

36

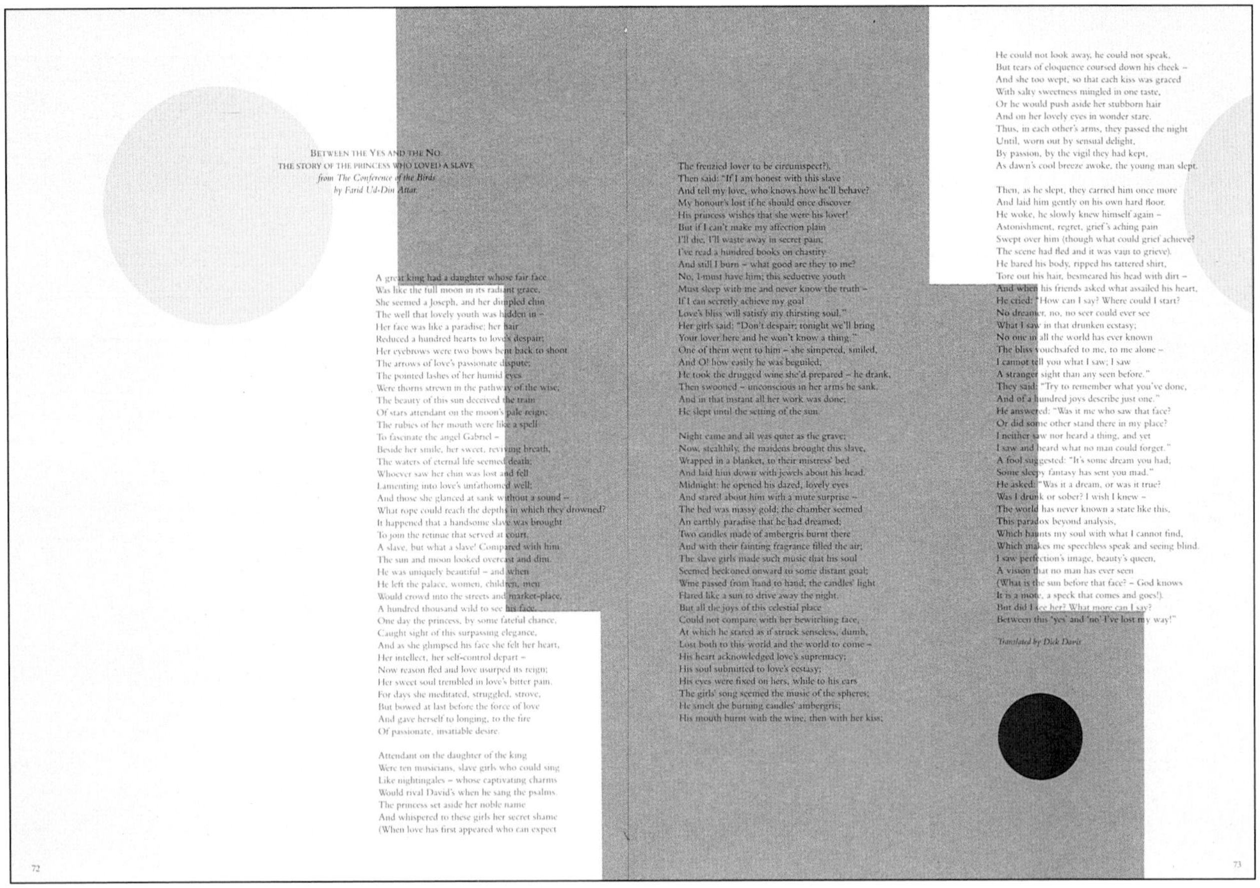

BETWEEN THE YES AND THE NO
THE STORY OF THE PRINCESS WHO LOVED A SLAVE
from The Conference of the Birds
by Farid Ud-Din Attar

A great king had a daughter whose fair face
Was like the full moon in its radiant grace,
She seemed a Joseph, and her dimpled chin
The well that lovely youth was hidden in –
Her face was like a paradise; her hair
Reduced a hundred hearts to love's despair;
Her eyebrows were two bows bent back to shoot
The arrows of love's passionate dispute;
The pointed lashes of her humid eyes
Were thorns strewn in the pathway of the wise;
The beauty of this sun deceived the train
Of stars attendant on the moon's pale reign;
The rubies of her mouth were like a spell
To fascinate the angel Gabriel –
Beside her smile, her sweet, reviving breath,
The waters of eternal life seemed death;
Whoever saw her chin was lost and fell
Lamenting into love's unfathomed well;
And those she glanced at sank without a sound –
What rope could reach the depths in which they drowned?
It happened that a handsome slave was brought
To join the retinue that served at court.
A slave, but what a slave! Compared with him
The sun and moon looked overcast and dim.
He was uniquely beautiful – and when
He left the palace, women, children, men
Would crowd into the streets and market-place,
A hundred thousand wild to see his face.
One day the princess, by some fateful chance,
Caught sight of this surpassing elegance,
And as she glimpsed his face she felt her heart,
Her intellect, her self-control depart –
Now reason fled and love usurped its reign;
Her sweet soul trembled in love's bitter pain.
For days she meditated, struggled, strove,
But bowed at last before the force of love
And gave herself to longing, to the fire
Of passionate, insatiable desire.

Attendant on the daughter of the king
Were ten musicians, slave girls who could sing
Like nightingales – whose captivating charms
Would rival David's when he sang the psalms.
The princess set aside her noble name
And whispered to these girls her secret shame
(When love has first appeared who can expect
The frenzied lover to be circumspect?),
Then said: "If I am honest with this slave
And tell my love, who knows how he'll behave?
My honour's lost if he should once discover
His princess wishes that she were his lover!
But if I can't make my affection plain
I'll die, I'll waste away in secret pain;
I've read a hundred books on chastity
And still I burn – what good are they to me?
No, I must have him; this seductive youth
Must sleep with me and never know the truth –
If I can secretly achieve my goal
Love's bliss will satisfy my thirsting soul."
Her girls said: "Don't despair; tonight we'll bring
Your lover here and he won't know a thing."
One of them went to him – she simpered, smiled,
And O! how easily he was beguiled;
He took the drugged wine she'd prepared – he drank,
Then swooned – unconscious in her arms he sank,
And in that instant all her work was done;
He slept until the setting of the sun.

Night came and all was quiet as the grave;
Now, stealthily, the maidens brought this slave,
Wrapped in a blanket, to their mistress' bed
And laid him down with jewels about his head.
Midnight: he opened his dazed, lovely eyes
And stared about him with a mute surprise –
The bed was massy gold; the chamber seemed
An earthly paradise that he had dreamed;
Two candles made of ambergris burnt there
And with their fainting fragrance filled the air;
The slave girls made such music that his soul
Seemed beckoned onward to some distant goal;
Wine passed from hand to hand; the candles' light
Flared like a sun to drive away the night.
But all the joys of this celestial place
Could not compare with her bewitching face,
At which he stared as if struck senseless, dumb,
Lost both to this world and the world to come –
His heart acknowledged love's supremacy;
His soul submitted to love's ecstasy;
His eyes were fixed on hers, while to his ears
The girls' song seemed the music of the spheres;
He smelt the burning candles' ambergris;
His mouth burnt with the wine, then with her kiss;
He could not look away, he could not speak,
But tears of eloquence coursed down his cheek –
And she too wept, so that each kiss was graced
With salty sweetness mingled in one taste,
Or he would push aside her stubborn hair
And on her lovely eyes in wonder stare.
Thus, in each other's arms, they passed the night
Until, worn out by sensual delight,
By passion, by the vigil they had kept,
As dawn's cool breeze awoke, the young man slept.

Then, as he slept, they carried him once more
And laid him gently on his own hard floor.
He woke, he slowly knew himself again –
Astonishment, regret, grief's aching pain
Swept over him (though what could grief achieve?
The scene had fled and it was vain to grieve).
He bared his body, ripped his tattered shirt,
Tore out his hair, besmeared his head with dirt –
And when his friends asked what assailed his heart,
He cried: "How can I say? Where could I start?
No dreamer, no, no seer could ever see
What I saw in that drunken ecstasy;
No one in all the world has ever known
The bliss vouchsafed to me, to me alone –
I cannot tell you what I saw; I saw
A stranger sight than any seen before."
They said: "Try to remember what you've done,
And of a hundred joys describe just one."
He answered: "Was it me who saw that face?
Or did some other stand there in my place?
I neither saw nor heard a thing, and yet
I saw and heard what no man could forget."
A fool suggested: "It's some dream you had;
Some sleepy fantasy has sent you mad."
He asked: "Was it a dream, or was it true?
Was I drunk or sober? I wish I knew –
The world has never known a state like this,
This paradox beyond analysis,
Which haunts my soul with what I cannot find,
Which makes me speechless speak and seeing blind.
I saw perfection's image, beauty's queen,
A vision that no man has ever seen
(What is the sun before that face? – God knows
It is a mote, a speck that comes and goes!).
But did I see her? What more can I say?
Between this 'yes' and 'no' I've lost my way!"

Translated by Dick Davis

72

73

37

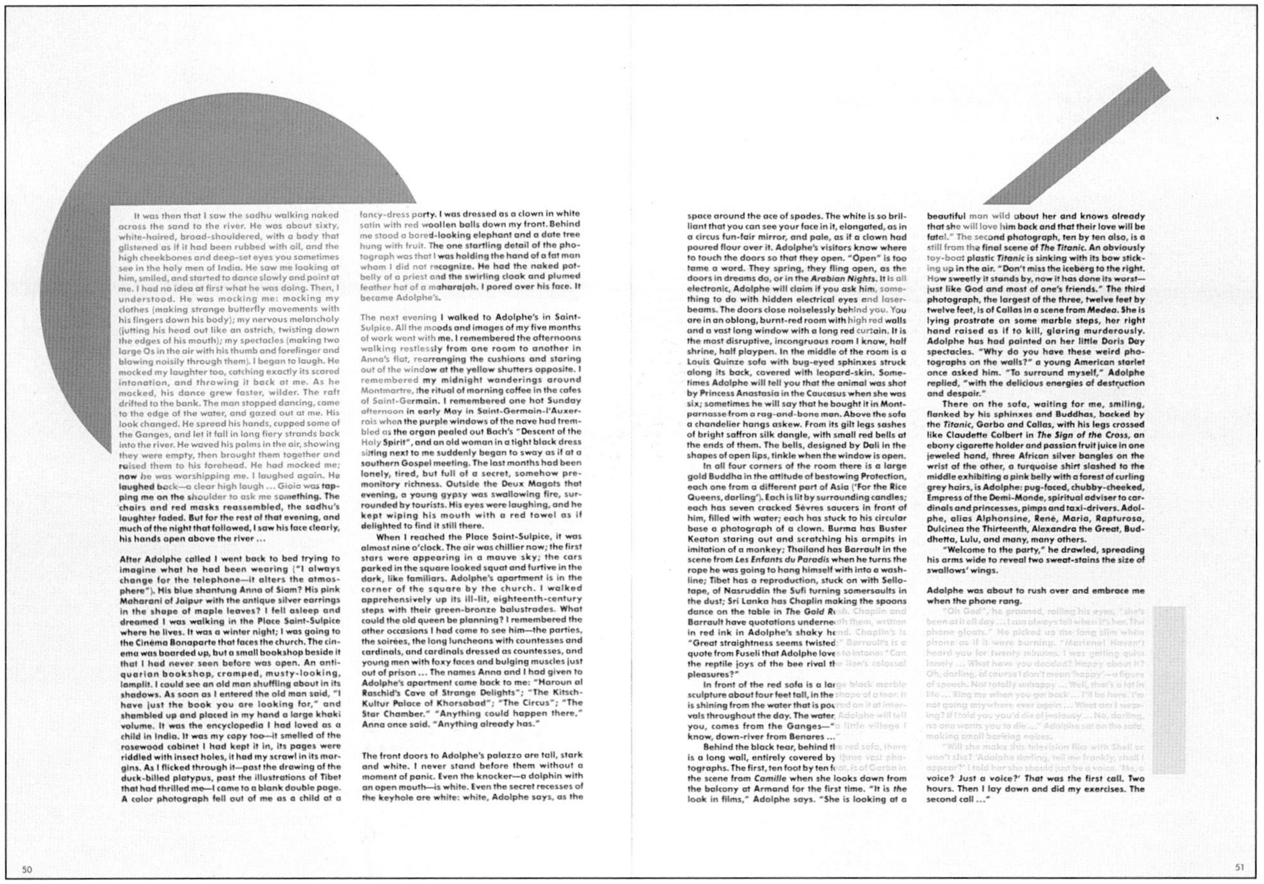

37

DESIGN FIRM: *Paul Davis Studio*

DESIGNER: *Paul Davis*

TEXT TYPEFACE: *Futura Bold*

CLIENT: *Normal Magazine*

38

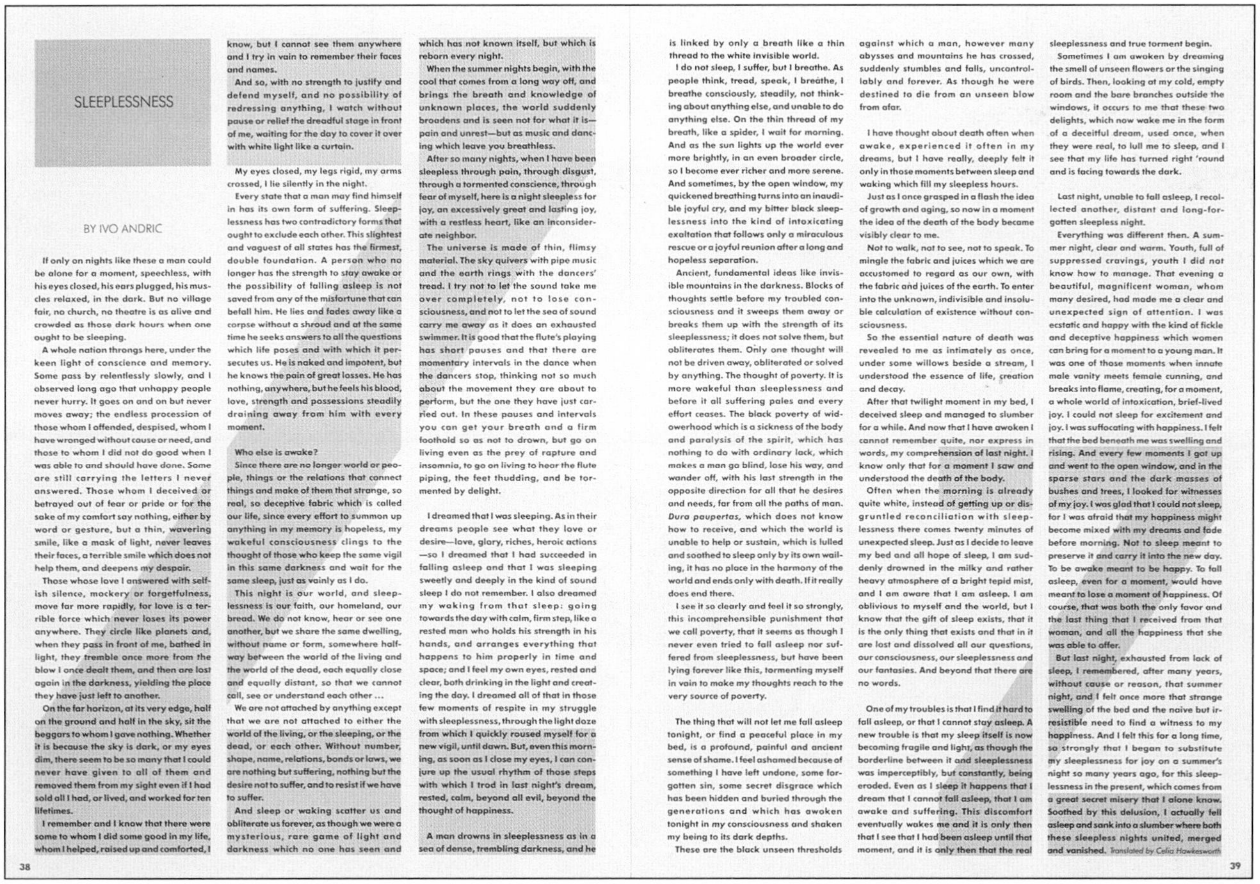

38

DESIGN FIRM: *Paul Davis Studio*

DESIGNER: *Paul Davis*

HEADLINE TYPEFACE: *Futura*

TEXT TYPEFACE: *Futura Bold*

CLIENT: *Normal Magazine*

39

40

41

39
DESIGN FIRM: *Paul Davis Studio*
DESIGNER: *Paul Davis*
TEXT TYPEFACE: *Futura*
CLIENT: *Normal Magazine*

40
DESIGN FIRM: *Paul Davis Studio*
DESIGNER: *Paul Davis*
HEADLINE TYPEFACE: *Metro*
CLIENT: *HOW Magazine*

41
DESIGN FIRM: *Michael Doret, Inc.*
DESIGNER: *Michael Doret*
LETTERER: *Michael Doret*
HEADLINE TYPEFACE: *Handlettering*
CLIENT: *The Graphic Artists Guild*

42

42
DESIGN FIRM: *Drentel Doyle Partners*
DESIGNER: *Rosemarie Turk*
HEADLINE TYPEFACE: *Metro Black and Grangon*
TEXT TYPEFACE: *Grangon*
CLIENT: *Spy Magazine*

43
DESIGN FIRM: *Drentel Doyle Partners*
DESIGNER: *Rosemarie Turk*
HEADLINE TYPEFACE: *Metro Black and Grangon*
TEXT TYPEFACE: *Grangon*
CLIENT: *Spy Magazine*

44
DESIGN FIRM: *Daniel Pelavin*
DESIGNER: *Daniel Pelavin*
LETTERER: *Daniel Pelavin*
HEADLINE TYPEFACE: *Handlettering*
TEXT TYPEFACE: *Kabel*
CLIENT: *Alfred A. Knopf*

45
DESIGN FIRM: *Louise Fili Ltd.*
DESIGNER: *Louise Fili*
LETTERER: *Louise Fili*
CLIENT: *Atlantic Monthly Press*

46
DESIGN FIRM: *Daniel Pelavin*
DESIGNER: *Daniel Pelavin*
LETTERER: *Daniel Pelavin*
HEADLINE TYPEFACE: *Handlettering*
TEXT TYPEFACE: *Kabel*
CLIENT: *Vintage Books*

43

44
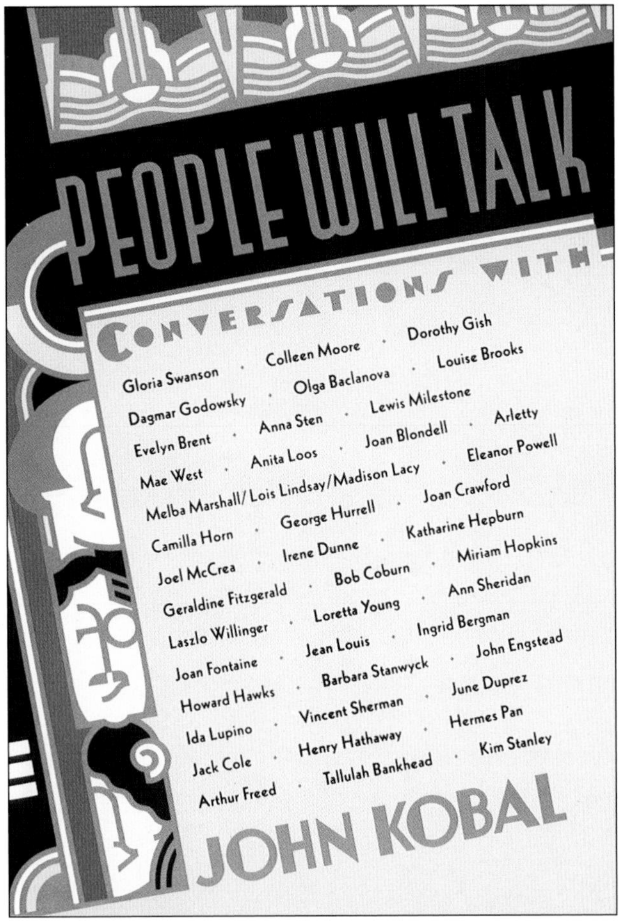

45
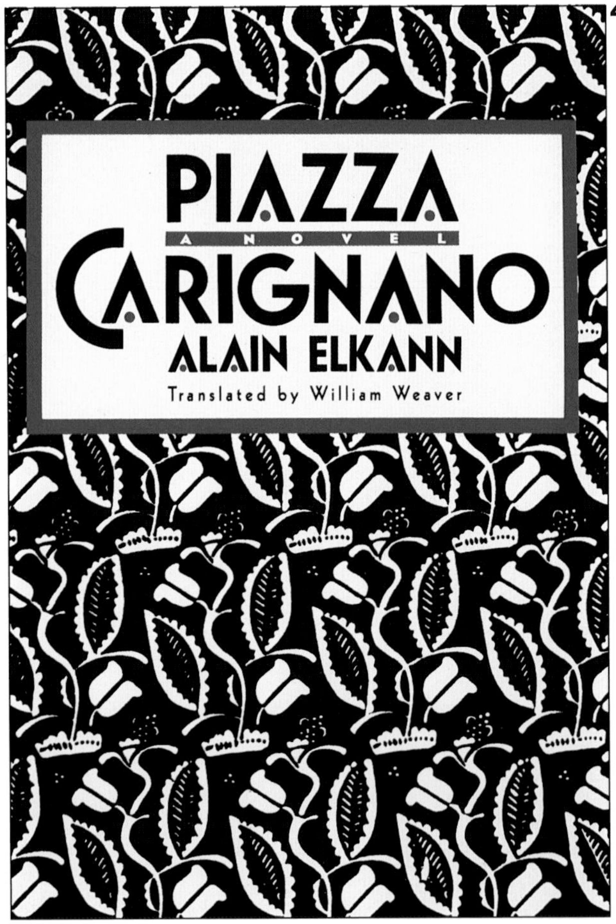

46
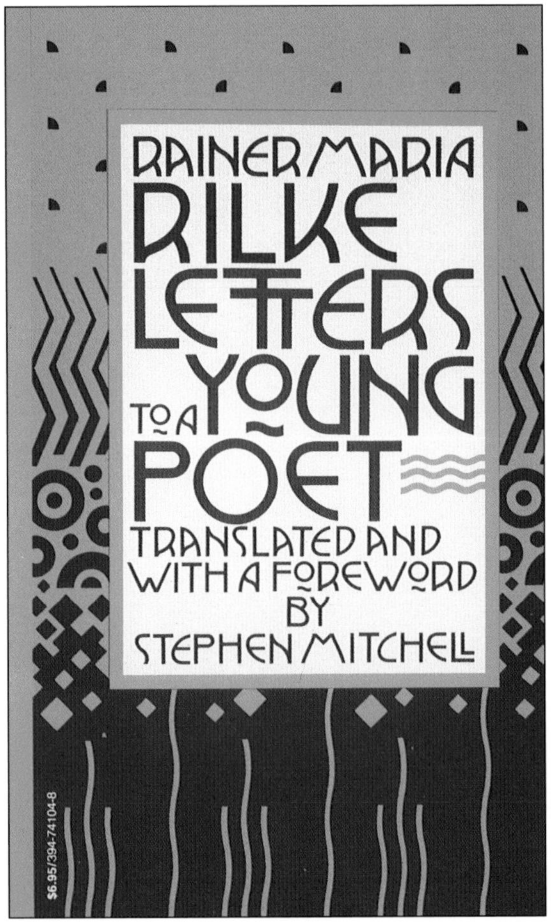

47

THE ROLLING STONE INTERVIEW BY DAVID BRESKIN

BONO

"Darling, I would love to take you by the hand, take you to some twilight land," sings the country songwriter, his voice wistful and cracked. He struggles through the verses, faltering a bit, forgetting, humming here and there, just pickin' his guitar and tappin' his foot gently in the corner of the darkened room. Finally, in a mood of wizened woe, he finishes the last chorus, "Am I left to burn and burn eternally? She's a mystery to me."

Now, what makes this particular moment in the history of tearful country ballads (a man, a guitar and PAIN!) a bit more fetching is that the lonesome critter over there in the corner, the sad-eyed young man who done wrote the song, who is sitting quietly at home in his modest castle – which is, in fact, an ancient seaside watchtower built with seven-foot-thick walls of granite and oxblood mortar to withstand shelling from hostile navies – happens to be the same fellow who usually spends his time fronting the world's most popular rock & roll band.

And when done crooning "She's a Mystery to Me," the strange and lovely song he's writing for Roy Orbison, he launches into "When Love Comes to Town," an uptempo chugger he figures might fit B.B. King. Barely pausing, he plunges into "Prisoner of Love," which features a handy doo-wop break in the chorus, and then assays his beloved ballad "Lucille," his first-ever country song, written way, way back in the spring of 1987. And so here we have Bono, at home outside Dublin, during a

PHOTOGRAPHS BY MATTHEW ROLSTON

47

DESIGN FIRM: *Rolling Stone Magazine In-house*
DESIGNER: *Fred Woodward*
HEADLINE TYPEFACE: *Grecian Woodtype Triple Condensed*
TEXT TYPEFACE: *Cloister Italic*
CLIENT: *Rolling Stone Magazine*

52
DESIGN FIRM: *Louise Fili Ltd.*
DESIGNER: *Louise Fili*
HEADLINE TYPEFACE: *Dainty*
CLIENT: *Simon & Schuster*

52

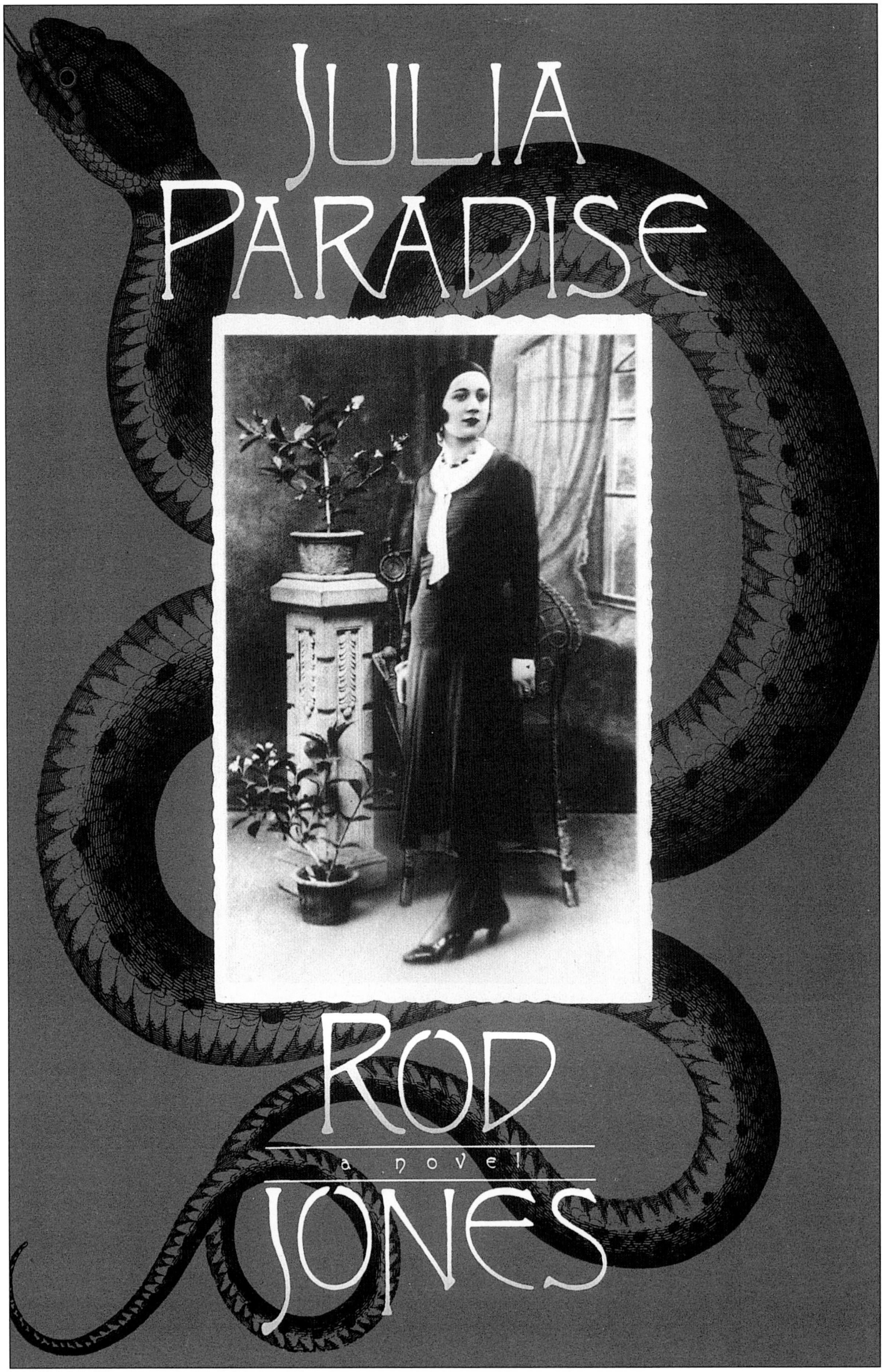

53

53
DESIGN FIRM: *Michael Doret, Inc.*
DESIGNER: *Michael Doret*
LETTERER: *Michael Doret*
HEADLINE TYPEFACE: *Handlettering*
CLIENT: *Reactor Design Ltd.*

54
DESIGN FIRM: *Michael Doret, Inc.*
DESIGNER: *Michael Doret*
LETTERER: *Michael Doret*
HEADLINE TYPEFACE: *Handlettering*
CLIENT: *TIME Magazine*

54

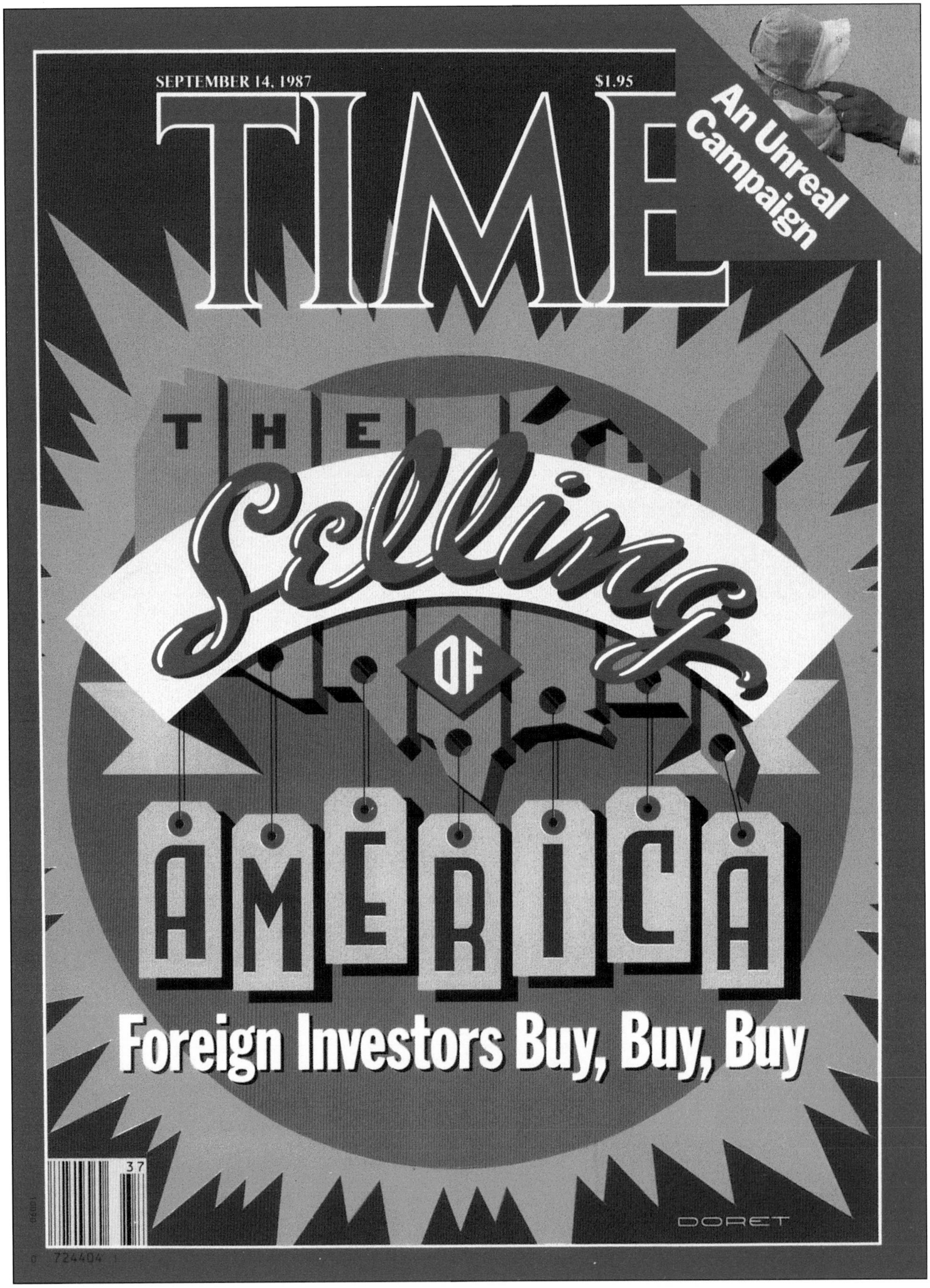

55

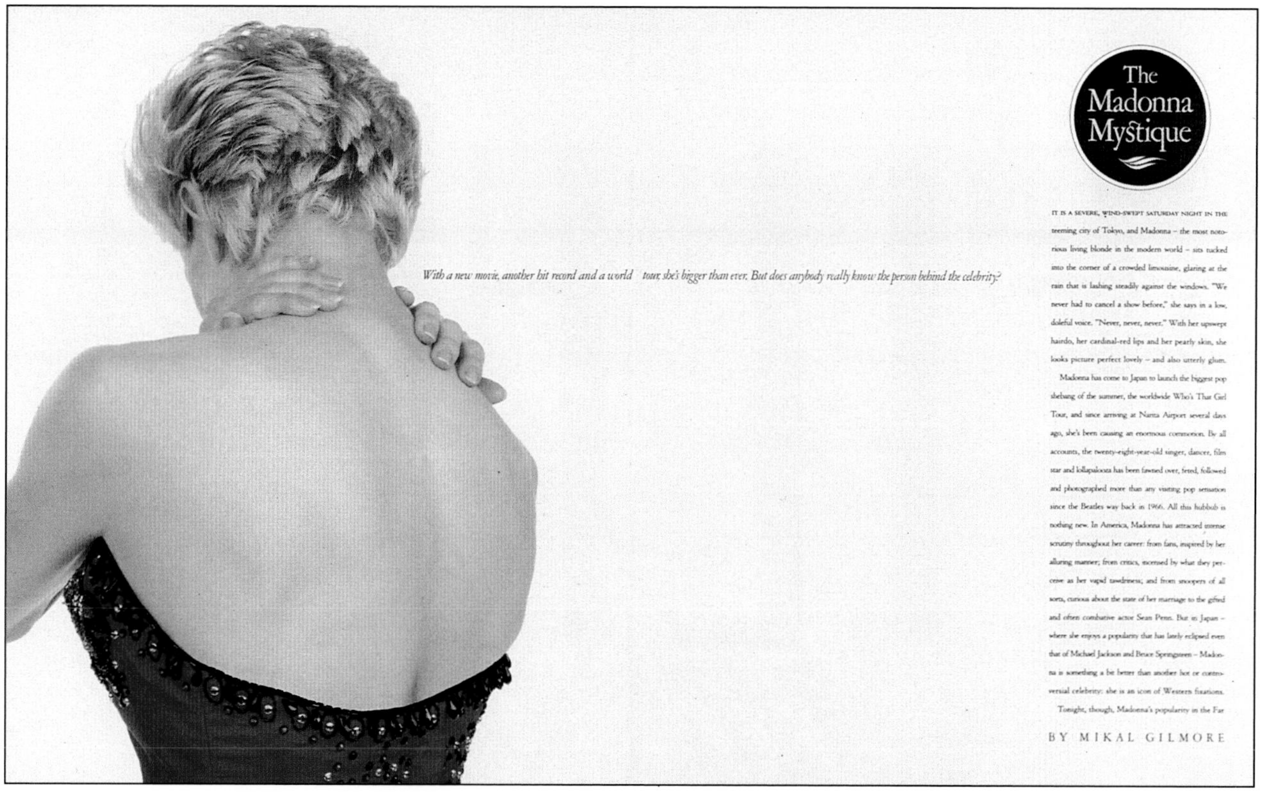

The Madonna Mystique

With a new movie, another hit record and a world tour, she's bigger than ever. But does anybody really know the person behind the celebrity?

IT IS A SEVERE, WIND-SWEPT SATURDAY NIGHT IN THE teeming city of Tokyo, and Madonna – the most notorious living blonde in the modern world – sits tucked into the corner of a crowded limousine, glaring at the rain that is lashing steadily against the windows. "We never had to cancel a show before," she says in a low, doleful voice. "Never, never, never." With her upswept hairdo, her cardinal-red lips and her pearly skin, she looks picture perfect lovely – and also utterly glum.

Madonna has come to Japan to launch the biggest pop shebang of the summer, the worldwide Who's That Girl Tour, and since arriving at Narita Airport several days ago, she's been causing an enormous commotion. By all accounts, the twenty-eight-year-old singer, dancer, film star and lollapalooza has been fawned over, feted, followed and photographed more than any visiting pop sensation since the Beatles way back in 1966. All this hubbub is nothing new. In America, Madonna has attracted intense scrutiny throughout her career: from fans, inspired by her alluring manner; from critics, incensed by what they perceive as her vapid tawdriness; and from snoopers of all sorts, curious about the state of her marriage to the gifted and often combative actor Sean Penn. But in Japan – where she enjoys a popularity that has lately eclipsed even that of Michael Jackson and Bruce Springsteen – Madonna is something a bit better than another hot or controversial celebrity: she is an icon of Western fixations.

Tonight, though, Madonna's popularity in the Far

BY MIKAL GILMORE

56

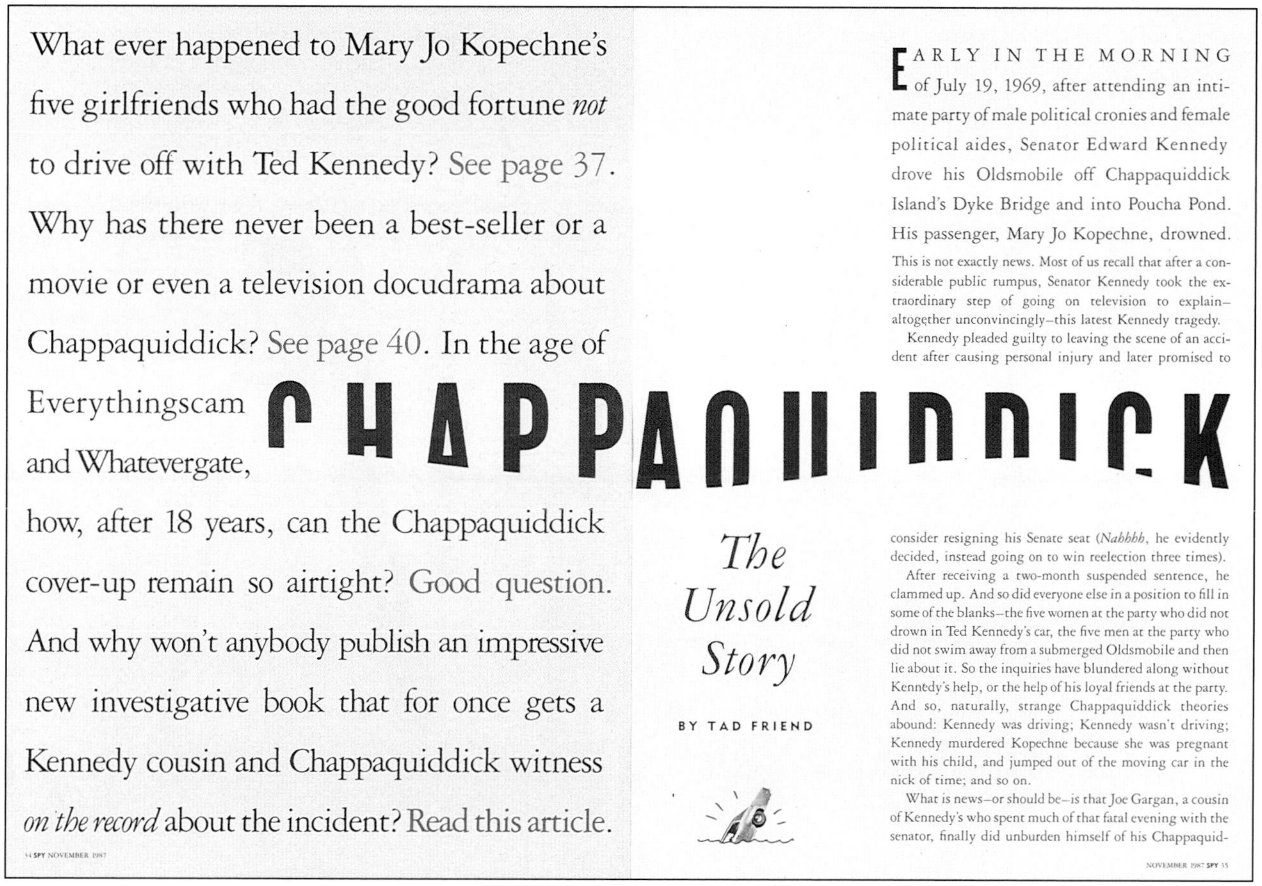

What ever happened to Mary Jo Kopechne's five girlfriends who had the good fortune *not* to drive off with Ted Kennedy? See page 37. Why has there never been a best-seller or a movie or even a television docudrama about Chappaquiddick? See page 40. In the age of Everythingscam and Whatevergate, how, after 18 years, can the Chappaquiddick cover-up remain so airtight? Good question. And why won't anybody publish an impressive new investigative book that for once gets a Kennedy cousin and Chappaquiddick witness *on the record* about the incident? Read this article.

54 SPY NOVEMBER 1987

CHAPPAQUIDDICK

The Unsold Story

BY TAD FRIEND

EARLY IN THE MORNING of July 19, 1969, after attending an intimate party of male political cronies and female political aides, Senator Edward Kennedy drove his Oldsmobile off Chappaquiddick Island's Dyke Bridge and into Poucha Pond. His passenger, Mary Jo Kopechne, drowned.

This is not exactly news. Most of us recall that after a considerable public rumpus, Senator Kennedy took the extraordinary step of going on television to explain—altogether unconvincingly—this latest Kennedy tragedy.

Kennedy pleaded guilty to leaving the scene of an accident after causing personal injury and later promised to consider resigning his Senate seat (*Nahhhh*, he evidently decided, instead going on to win reelection three times).

After receiving a two-month suspended sentence, he clammed up. And so did everyone else in a position to fill in some of the blanks—the five women at the party who did not drown in Ted Kennedy's car, the five men at the party who did not swim away from a submerged Oldsmobile and then lie about it. So the inquiries have blundered along without Kennedy's help, or the help of his loyal friends at the party. And so, naturally, strange Chappaquiddick theories abound: Kennedy was driving; Kennedy wasn't driving; Kennedy murdered Kopechne because she was pregnant with his child, and jumped out of the moving car in the nick of time; and so on.

What is news—or should be—is that Joe Gargan, a cousin of Kennedy's who spent much of that fatal evening with the senator, finally did unburden himself of his Chappaquid-

NOVEMBER 1987 SPY 55

55
DESIGN FIRM: *Rolling Stone Magazine In-house*
DESIGNER: *Fred Woodward*
HEADLINE TYPEFACE: *Garamond 3*
TEXT TYPEFACE: *Cloister*
CLIENT: *Rolling Stone Magazine*

56
DESIGN FIRM: *Spy Magazine In-house*
DESIGNER: *Alex Isley*
HEADLINE TYPEFACE: *Alternate Gothic*
TEXT TYPEFACE: *Garamond 3*
CLIENT: *Spy Corporation*

57

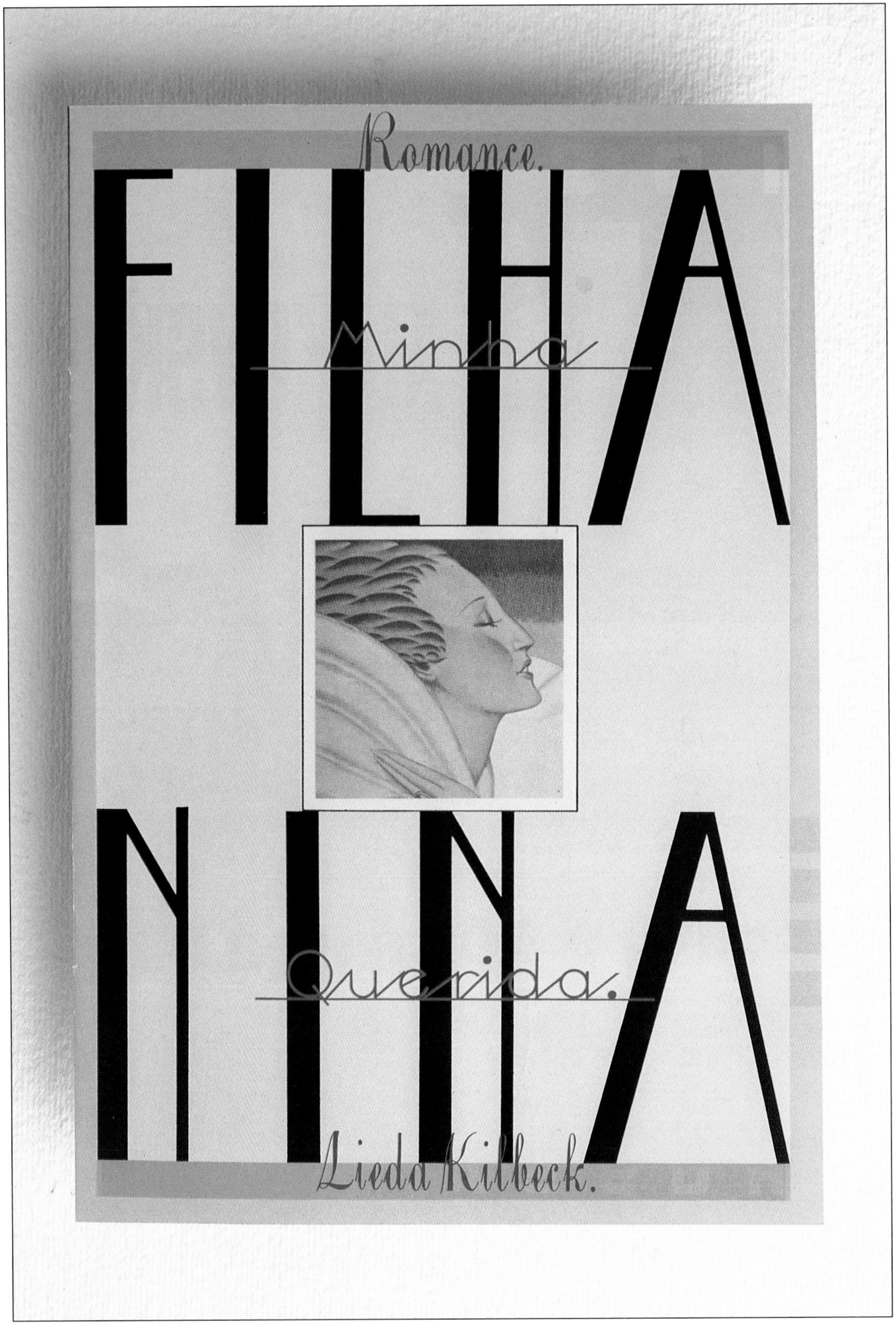

57
DESIGN FIRM: *Casa De Idéias*
DESIGNER: *Oswaldo Miranda*
HEADLINE TYPEFACE: *Art Deco Type*
CLIENT: *Library of Paraná State*

58

58
DESIGN FIRM: *Casa De Idéias*
DESIGNER: *Oswaldo Miranda*
HEADLINE TYPEFACE: *Art Deco Type*
CLIENT: *Library of Paraná State*

59

59
DESIGN FIRM: *The Duffy Design Group*
DESIGNER: *Joe Duffy*
LETTERER: *Lynn Schulte*
HEADLINE TYPEFACE: *Handlettering and Standard Condensed*
CLIENT: *Houghton Mifflin*

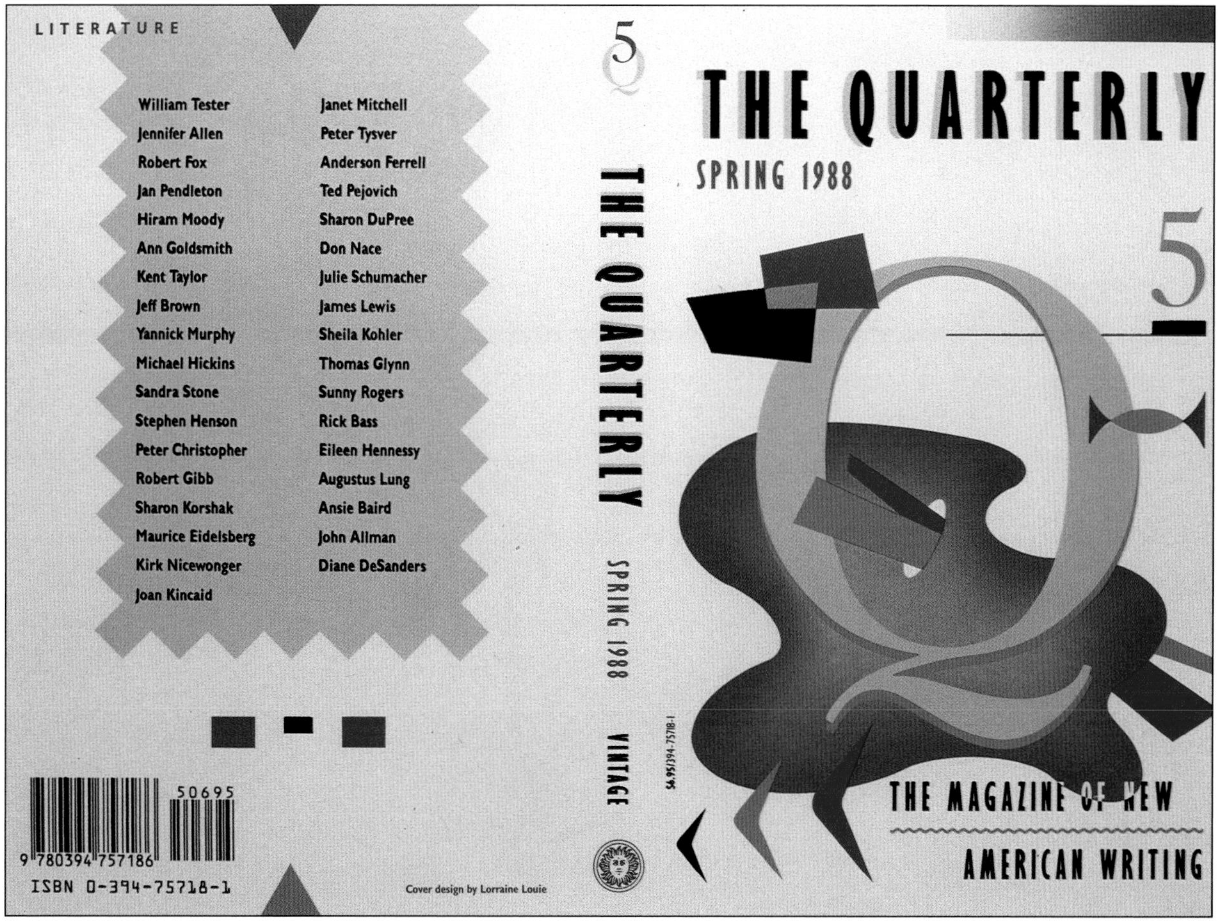

60

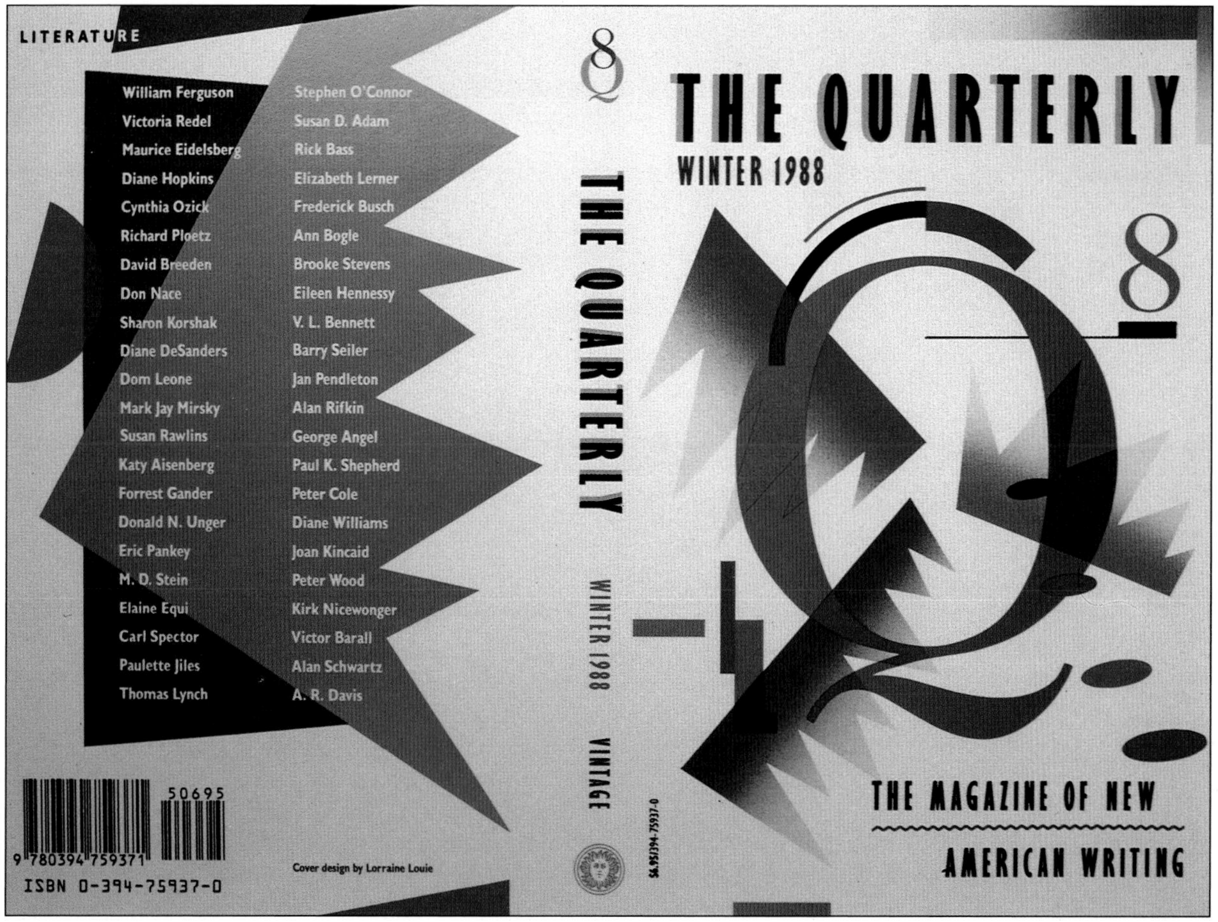

61

60
DESIGN FIRM: *Lorraine Louie Design*
DESIGNER: *Lorraine Louie*
HEADLINE TYPEFACE: *Gill Sans Extra Bold Condensed*
CLIENT: *Vintage Books, Random House*

61
DESIGN FIRM: *Lorraine Louie Design*
DESIGNER: *Lorraine Louie*
HEADLINE TYPEFACE: *Gill Sans Extra Bold Condensed*
CLIENT: *Vintage Books, Random House*

62

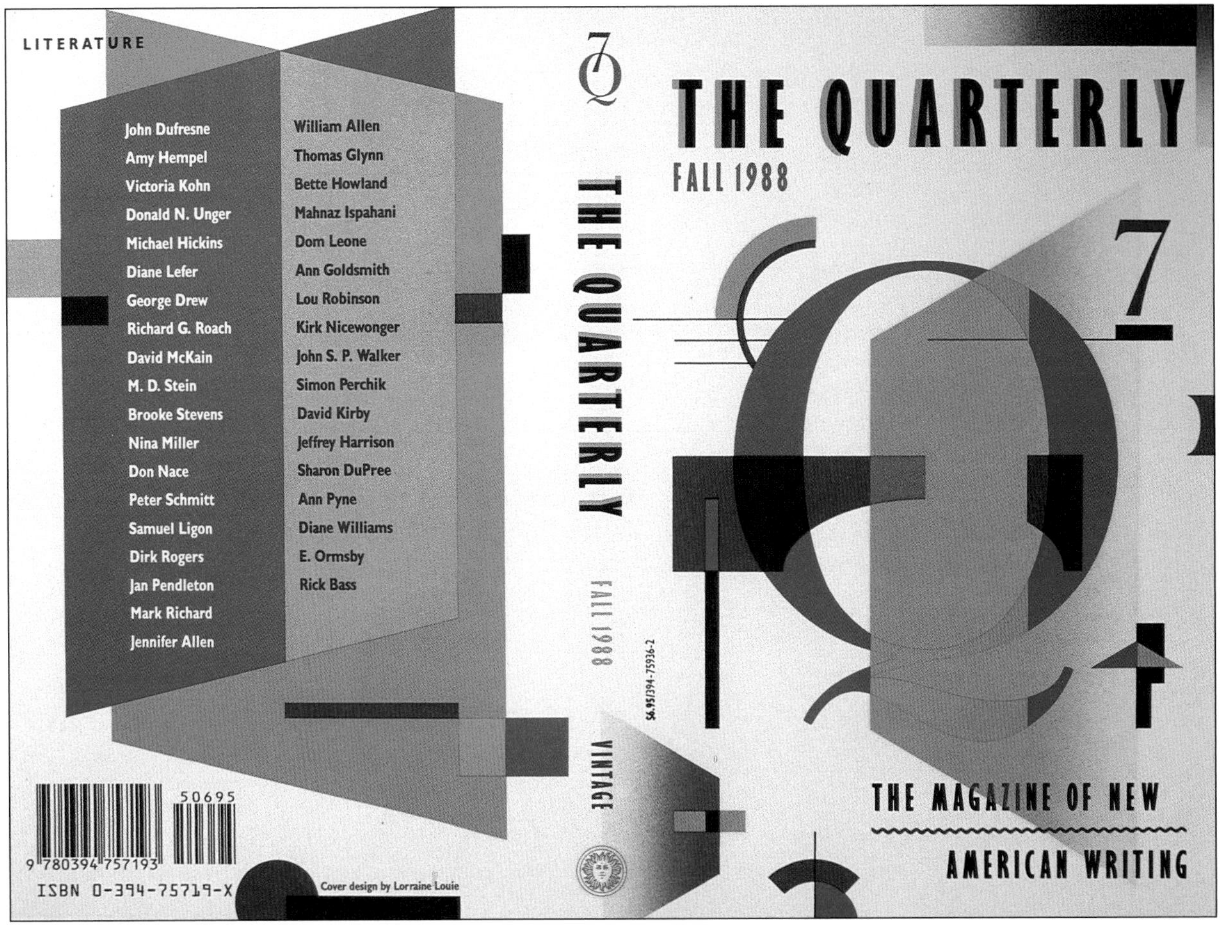

62
DESIGN FIRM: *Lorraine Louie Design*
DESIGNER: *Lorraine Louie*
HEADLINE TYPEFACE: *Gill Sans Extra Bold Condensed*
CLIENT: *Vintage Books, Random House*

63

63
DESIGN FIRM: *Shapiro Design Associates, Inc.*
DESIGNER: *Katsuichi Ito*
LETTERER: *Katsuichi Ito*
HEADLINE TYPEFACE: *ITC Symbol Book and ITC Novarese Book Italic*
TEXT TYPEFACE: *ITC Symbol Book*
CLIENT: *International Typeface Corporation*

64

64
DESIGN FIRM: *Pentagram Design*
DESIGNER: *Kit Hinrichs and Karen Boone*
HEADLINE TYPEFACE: *Futura Bold and Condensed*
TEXT TYPEFACE: *Bodoni Book*
CLIENT: *Art Center College of Design*

65
DESIGN FIRM: *Grauerholz Design, Inc.*
DESIGNER: *Cheryl Simon*
HEADLINE TYPEFACE: *Garamond Condensed*
TEXT TYPEFACE: *Sabon*
CLIENT: *Galerie Optica*

66
DESIGN FIRM: *Warner Books*
DESIGNER: *Carin Goldberg*
CLIENT: *Warner Books*

67
DESIGN FIRM: *Grauerholz Design, Inc.*
DESIGNER: *Cheryl Simon*
HEADLINE TYPEFACE: *Garamond Condensed*
TEXT TYPEFACE: *Sabon*
CLIENT: *Galerie Optica*

65

The Zone
of
Conventional Practice
and
Other Real Stories

66

"THE SORT OF BOOK THAT COULD START A REVOLUTION!" —Erica Jong, Vanity Fair
A LESSER LIFE
THE MYTH OF WOMEN'S LIBERATION IN AMERICA
"UTTERLY CONVINCING...Every American needs to think deeply about the questions Hewlett raises." —Washington Post Book World
SYLVIA ANN HEWLETT
WARNER BOOKS 39122 $12.95 U.S.A. (38512 $14.75 CAN.)

67

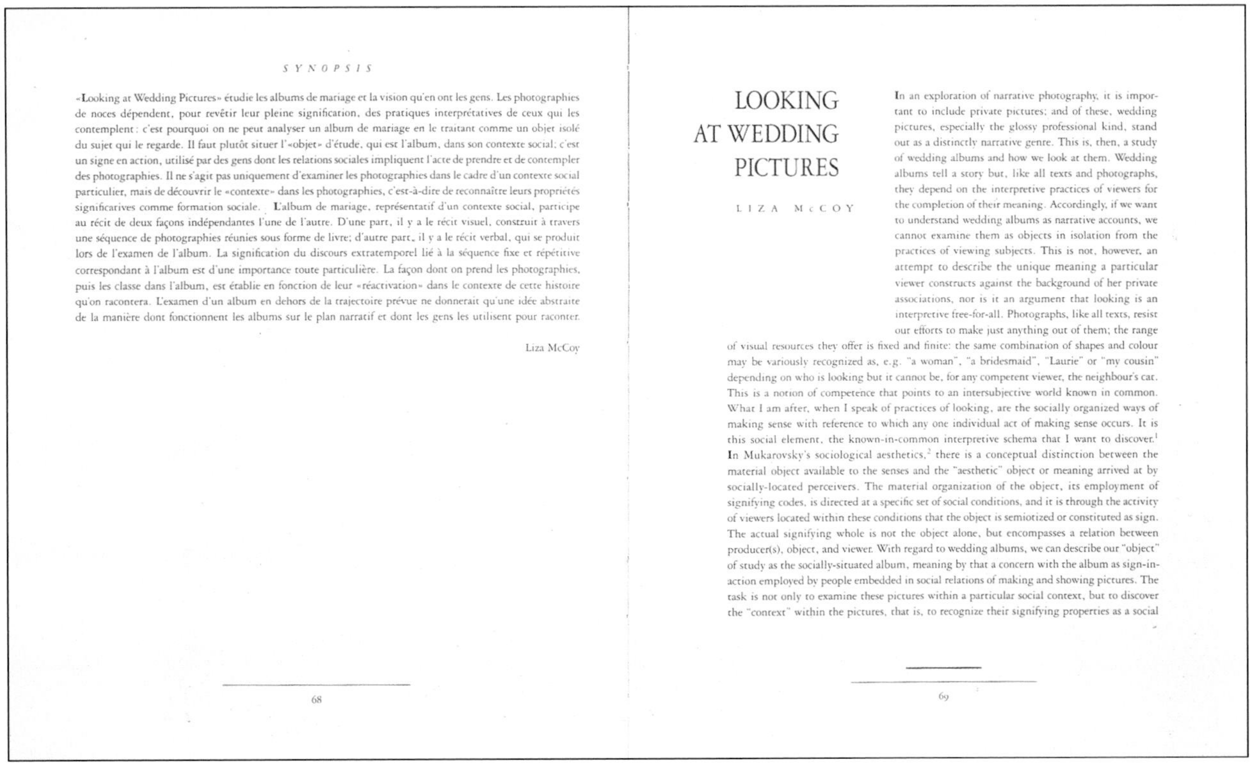

S Y N O P S I S

«Looking at Wedding Pictures» étudie les albums de mariage et la vision qu'en ont les gens. Les photographies de noces dépendent, pour revêtir leur pleine signification, des pratiques interprétatives de ceux qui les contemplent : c'est pourquoi on ne peut analyser un album de mariage en le traitant comme un objet isolé du sujet qui le regarde. Il faut plutôt situer l'«objet» d'étude, qui est l'album, dans son contexte social; c'est un signe en action, utilisé par des gens dont les relations sociales impliquent l'acte de prendre et de contempler des photographies. Il ne s'agit pas uniquement d'examiner les photographies dans le cadre d'un contexte social particulier, mais de découvrir le «contexte» dans les photographies, c'est-à-dire de reconnaître leurs propriétés significatives comme formation sociale. L'album de mariage, représentatif d'un contexte social, participe au récit de deux façons indépendantes l'une de l'autre. D'une part, il y a le récit visuel, construit à travers une séquence de photographies réunies sous forme de livre; d'autre part, il y a le récit verbal, qui se produit lors de l'examen de l'album. La signification du discours extratemporel lié à la séquence fixe et répétitive correspondant à l'album est d'une importance toute particulière. La façon dont on prend les photographies, puis les classe dans l'album, est établie en fonction de leur «réactivation» dans le contexte de cette histoire qu'on racontera. L'examen d'un album en dehors de la trajectoire prévue ne donnerait qu'une idée abstraite de la manière dont fonctionnent les albums sur le plan narratif et dont les gens les utilisent pour raconter.

Liza McCoy

68

LOOKING AT WEDDING PICTURES

L I Z A   M c C O Y

In an exploration of narrative photography, it is important to include private pictures; and of these, wedding pictures, especially the glossy professional kind, stand out as a distinctly narrative genre. This is, then, a study of wedding albums and how we look at them. Wedding albums tell a story but, like all texts and photographs, they depend on the interpretive practices of viewers for the completion of their meaning. Accordingly, if we want to understand wedding albums as narrative accounts, we cannot examine them as objects in isolation from the practices of viewing subjects. This is not, however, an attempt to describe the unique meaning a particular viewer constructs against the background of her private associations, nor is it an argument that looking is an interpretive free-for-all. Photographs, like all texts, resist our efforts to make just anything out of them; the range of visual resources they offer is fixed and finite: the same combination of shapes and colour may be variously recognized as, e.g. "a woman", "a bridesmaid", "Laurie" or "my cousin" depending on who is looking but it cannot be, for any competent viewer, the neighbour's cat. This is a notion of competence that points to an intersubjective world known in common. What I am after, when I speak of practices of looking, are the socially organized ways of making sense with reference to which any one individual act of making sense occurs. It is this social element, the known-in-common interpretive schema that I want to discover.[1] In Mukarovsky's sociological aesthetics,[2] there is a conceptual distinction between the material object available to the senses and the "aesthetic" object or meaning arrived at by socially-located perceivers. The material organization of the object, its employment of signifying codes, is directed at a specific set of social conditions, and it is through the activity of viewers located within these conditions that the object is semiotized or constituted as sign. The actual signifying whole is not the object alone, but encompasses a relation between producer(s), object, and viewer. With regard to wedding albums, we can describe our "object" of study as the socially-situated album, meaning by that a concern with the album as sign-in-action employed by people embedded in social relations of making and showing pictures. The task is not only to examine these pictures within a particular social context, but to discover the "context" within the pictures, that is, to recognize their signifying properties as a social

69

68

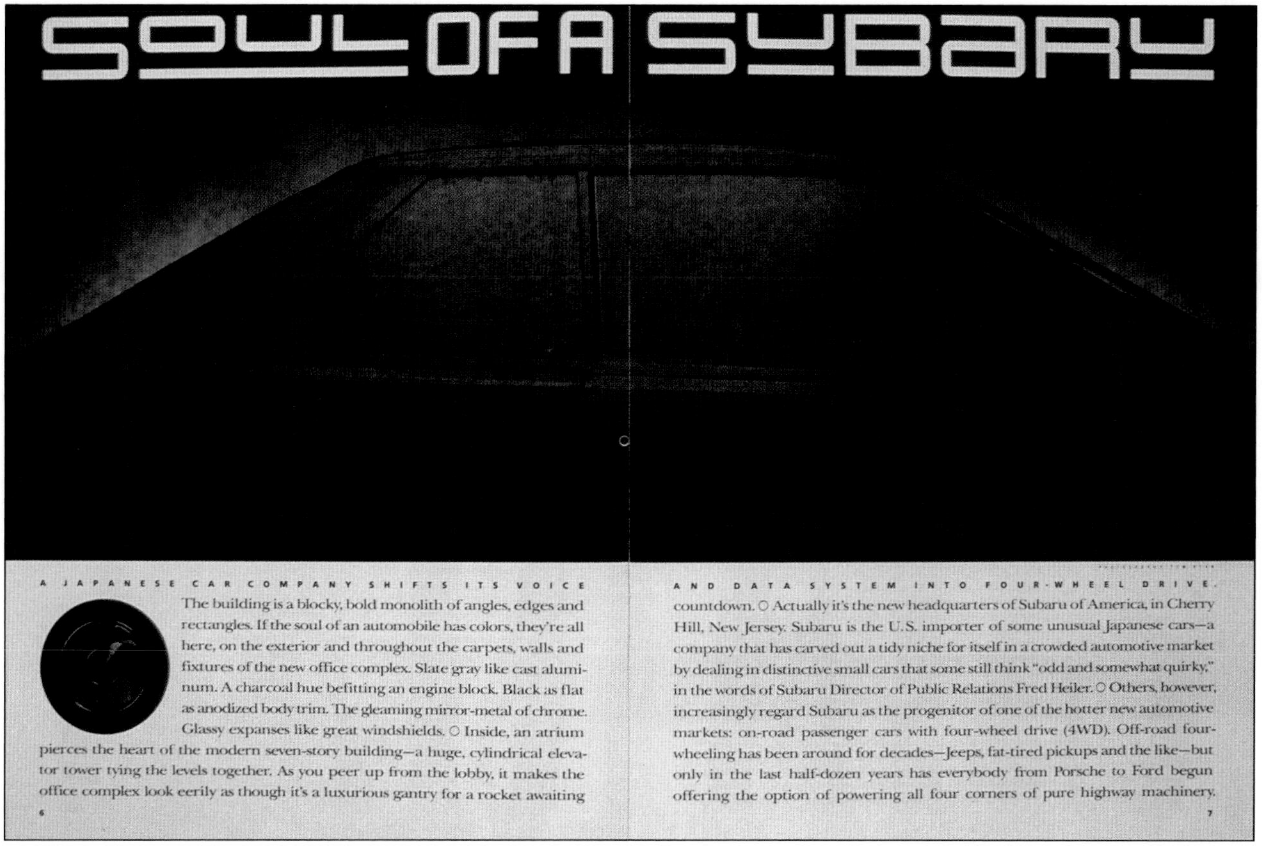

SOUL OF A SUBARU

A JAPANESE CAR COMPANY SHIFTS ITS VOICE AND DATA SYSTEM INTO FOUR-WHEEL DRIVE.

The building is a blocky, bold monolith of angles, edges and rectangles. If the soul of an automobile has colors, they're all here, on the exterior and throughout the carpets, walls and fixtures of the new office complex. Slate gray like cast aluminum. A charcoal hue befitting an engine block. Black as flat as anodized body trim. The gleaming mirror-metal of chrome. Glassy expanses like great windshields. ○ Inside, an atrium pierces the heart of the modern seven-story building—a huge, cylindrical elevator tower tying the levels together. As you peer up from the lobby, it makes the office complex look eerily as though it's a luxurious gantry for a rocket awaiting countdown. ○ Actually it's the new headquarters of Subaru of America, in Cherry Hill, New Jersey. Subaru is the U.S. importer of some unusual Japanese cars—a company that has carved out a tidy niche for itself in a crowded automotive market by dealing in distinctive small cars that some still think "odd and somewhat quirky," in the words of Subaru Director of Public Relations Fred Heiler. ○ Others, however, increasingly regard Subaru as the progenitor of one of the hotter new automotive markets: on-road passenger cars with four-wheel drive (4WD). Off-road four-wheeling has been around for decades—Jeeps, fat-tired pickups and the like—but only in the last half-dozen years has everybody from Porsche to Ford begun offering the option of powering all four corners of pure highway machinery.

6 7

69

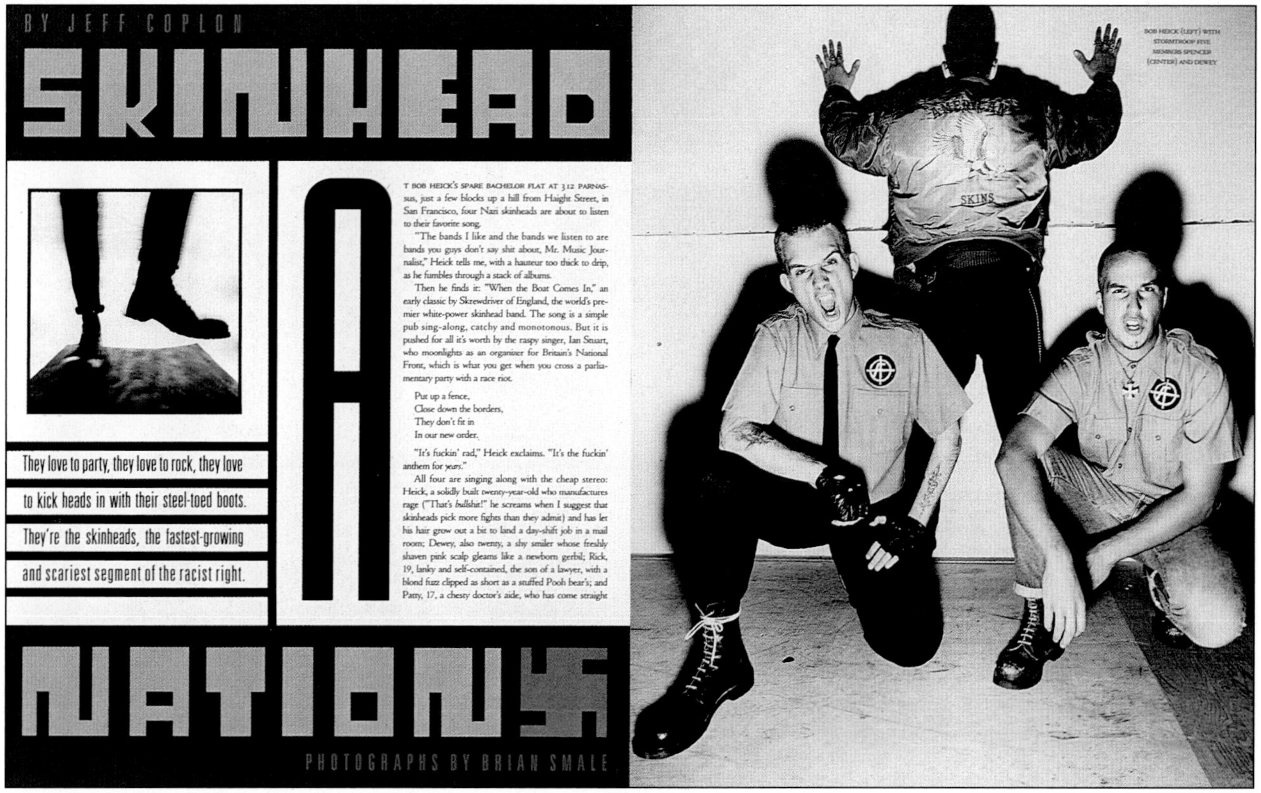

BY JEFF COPLON

SKINHEAD A NATION

They love to party, they love to rock, they love to kick heads in with their steel-toed boots. They're the skinheads, the fastest-growing and scariest segment of the racist right.

T BOB HEICK'S SPARE BACHELOR FLAT AT 312 PARNASSUS, just a few blocks up a hill from Haight Street, in San Francisco, four Nazi skinheads are about to listen to their favorite song.

"The bands I like and the bands we listen to are bands you guys don't say shit about, Mr. Music Journalist," Heick tells me, with a hauteur too thick to drip, as he fumbles through a stack of albums.

Then he finds it: "When the Boat Comes In," an early classic by Skrewdriver of England, the world's premier white-power skinhead band. The song is a simple pub sing-along, catchy and monotonous. But it is pushed for all it's worth by the raspy singer, Ian Stuart, who moonlights as an organizer for Britain's National Front, which is what you get when you cross a parliamentary party with a race riot.

Put up a fence,
Close down the borders,
They don't fit in
In our new order.

"It's fuckin' rad," Heick exclaims. "It's the fuckin' anthem for *years*."

All four are singing along with the cheap stereo: Heick, a solidly built twenty-year-old who manufactures rage ("That's *bullshit!*" he screams when I suggest that skinheads pick more fights than they admit) and has let his hair grow out a bit to land a day-shift job in a mail room; Dewey, also twenty, a shy smiler whose freshly shaven pink scalp gleams like a newborn gerbil; Rick, 19, lanky and self-contained, the son of a lawyer, with a blond fuzz clipped as short as a stuffed Pooh bear's; and Patty, 17, a chesty doctor's aide, who has come straight

BOB HEICK (LEFT) WITH STORMTROOP FIVE MEMBERS SPENCER (CENTER) AND DEWEY

PHOTOGRAPHS BY BRIAN SMALE

68
DESIGN FIRM: *Peterson & Company*
DESIGNER: *Bryan L. Peterson*
LETTERER: *Bryan L. Peterson*
HEADLINE TYPEFACE: *Handlettering*
TEXT TYPEFACE: *Baskerville and Frutiger*
CLIENT: *Northern Telecom*

69
DESIGN FIRM: *Rolling Stone Magazine In-house*
DESIGNER: *Gail Anderson*
LETTERER: *Dennis Ortiz-Lopez*
TEXT TYPEFACE: *Cloister*
CLIENT: *Rolling Stone Magazine*

70
DESIGN FIRM: *Carol Publishing Group*
DESIGNER: *Steven Brower*
LETTERER: *Steven Brower*
HEADLINE TYPEFACE: *Photolettering*
TEXT TYPEFACE: *Photolettering*
CLIENT: *Carol Publishing Group*

70

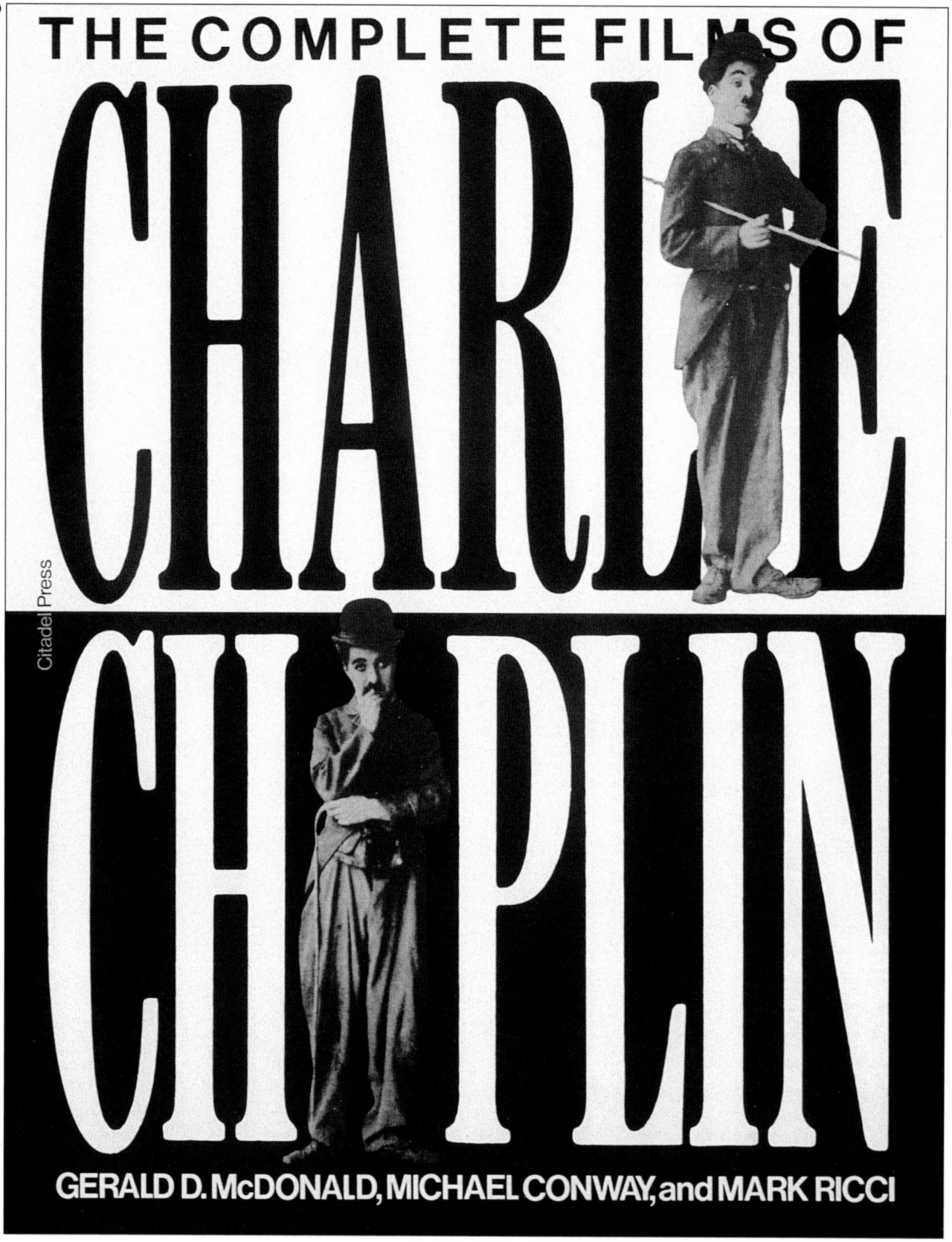

71

71
DESIGN FIRM: *Louie Fili, Ltd.*
DESIGNER: *Louise Fili*
LETTERER: *Louise Fili*
HEADLINE TYPEFACE: *Handlettering*
CLIENT: *Pantheon Books*

72

Mr.Big

Though he's past thirty and newly wed, Tom Hanks gets to feel like a kid again in his latest movie, 'Big'

OH, BACCHANALIA! TOM HANKS IS ABOUT TO DIVULGE details of his very recent bachelor party.

"You saw the film," he says. "Now live the reality."

So let's hear it. "I was on a sailboat with a bunch of guys," he says coyly, but not without promise. "We sailed to Catalina Island for the weekend. Seven guys on a boat. We left early Friday evening and got into Catalina by midnight. For two days, we just drifted around, ate a lot, jumped in the water, caught fish and got very, very sandy. We didn't shower or shave in seventy-two hours. It was a manly thing."

Yes. Fine. But what about the debauchery? Girls in baked goods. Donkeys in lingerie. Your basic fraternal

BY BILL ZEHME

PHOTOGRAPHS BY HERB RITTS

73

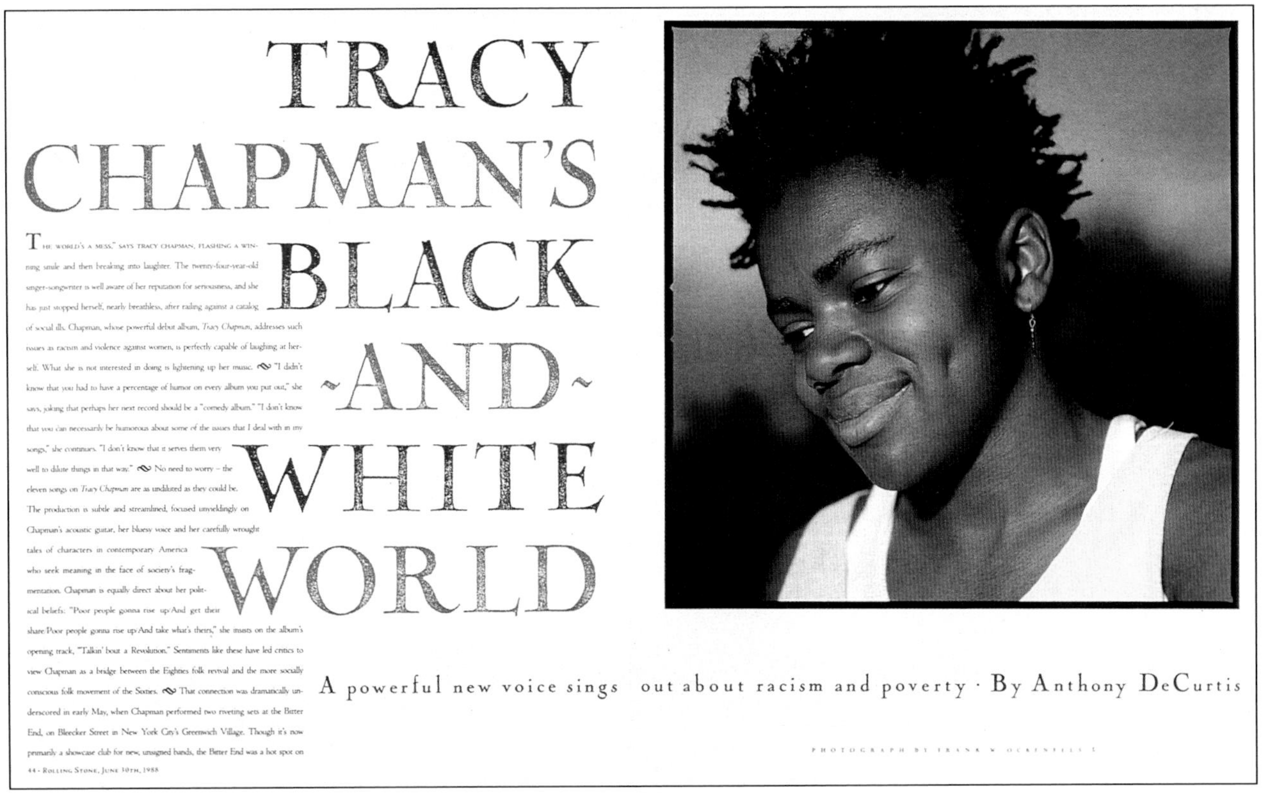

TRACY CHAPMAN'S BLACK ~AND~ WHITE WORLD

THE WORLD'S A MESS," SAYS TRACY CHAPMAN, FLASHING A WINNING smile and then breaking into laughter. The twenty-four-year-old singer-songwriter is well aware of her reputation for seriousness, and she has just stopped herself, nearly breathless, after railing against a catalog of social ills. Chapman, whose powerful debut album, *Tracy Chapman*, addresses such issues as racism and violence against women, is perfectly capable of laughing at herself. What she is not interested in doing is lightening up her music. "I didn't know that you had to have a percentage of humor on every album you put out," she says, joking that perhaps her next record should be a "comedy album." "I don't know that you can necessarily be humorous about some of the issues that I deal with in my songs," she continues. "I don't know that it serves them very well to dilute things in that way." No need to worry – the eleven songs on *Tracy Chapman* are as undiluted as they could be. The production is subtle and streamlined, focused unyieldingly on Chapman's acoustic guitar, her bluesy voice and her carefully wrought tales of characters in contemporary America who seek meaning in the face of society's fragmentation. Chapman is equally direct about her political beliefs: "Poor people gonna rise up/And get their share/Poor people gonna rise up/And take what's theirs," she insists on the album's opening track, "Talkin' bout a Revolution." Sentiments like these have led critics to view Chapman as a bridge between the Eighties folk revival and the more socially conscious folk movement of the Sixties. That connection was dramatically underscored in early May, when Chapman performed two riveting sets at the Bitter End, on Bleecker Street in New York City's Greenwich Village. Though it's now primarily a showcase club for new, unsigned bands, the Bitter End was a hot spot on

44 · ROLLING STONE, JUNE 30TH, 1988

A powerful new voice sings out about racism and poverty · By Anthony DeCurtis

72
DESIGN FIRM: *Rolling Stone Magazine In-house*
DESIGNER: *Gail Anderson*
LETTERER: *Dennis Ortiz-Lopez*
HEADLINE TYPEFACE: *Wood Type*
CLIENT: *Rolling Stone Magazine*

73
DESIGN FIRM: *Rolling Stone Magazine In-house*
DESIGNER: *Cathy Gilmore-Barnes*
HEADLINE TYPEFACE: *Nicholas Cochin*
TEXT TYPEFACE: *Cloister*
CLIENT: *Rolling Stone Magazine*

74

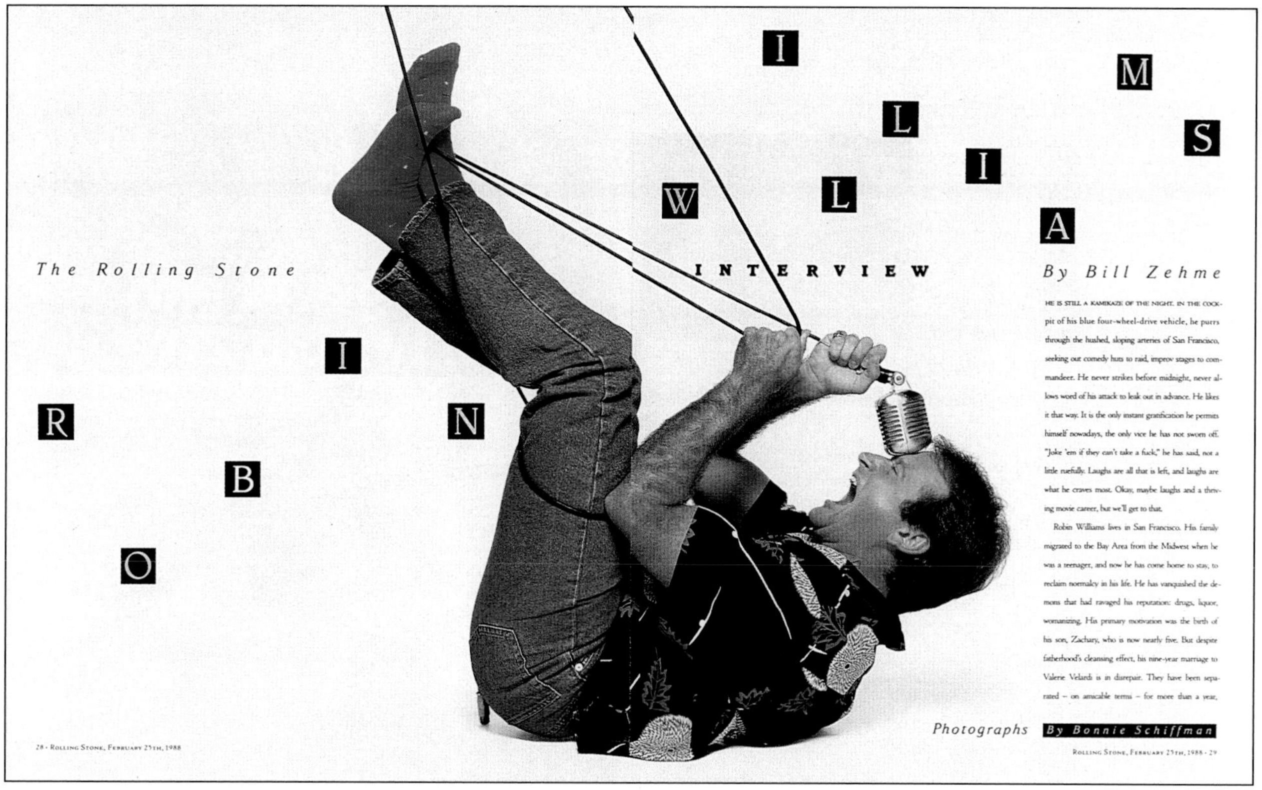

75

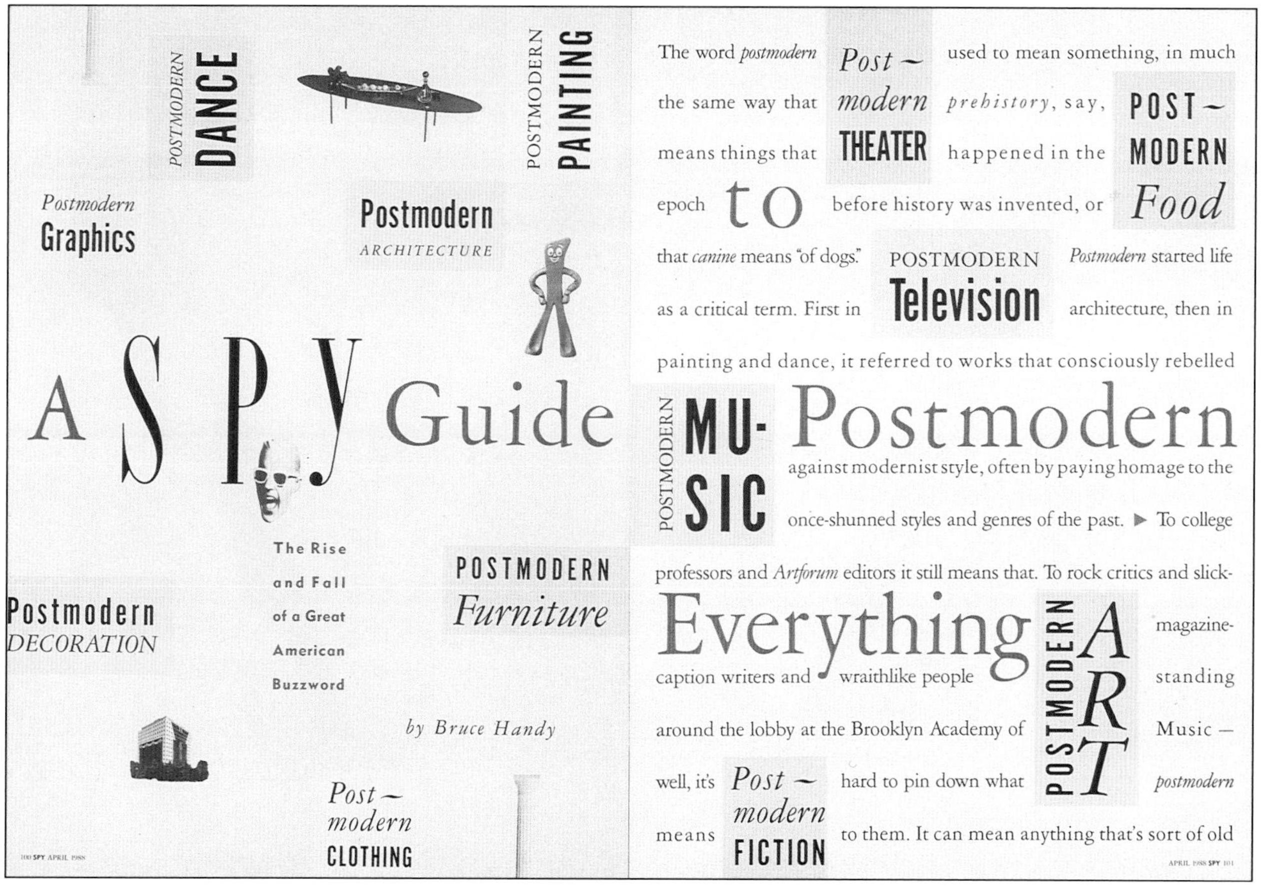

74
DESIGN FIRM: *Rolling Stone Magazine In-house*
DESIGNER: *Debra Bishop*
HEADLINE TYPEFACE: *Wood Type*
TEXT TYPEFACE: *Cloister*
CLIENT: *Rolling Stone Magazine*

75
DESIGN FIRM: *Spy Magazine In-house*
DESIGNER: *Alex Isley*
HEADLINE TYPEFACE: *Garamond 3 and Spire*
TEXT TYPEFACE: *Alternate Gothic and Garamond 3*
CLIENT: *Spy Corporation*

76
DESIGN FIRM: *Daniel Pelavin*
DESIGNER: *Daniel Pelavin*
LETTERER: *Daniel Pelavin*
HEADLINE TYPEFACE: *Handlettering*
TEXT TYPEFACE: *Kabel*
CLIENT: *Seven Days Magazine*

76

77

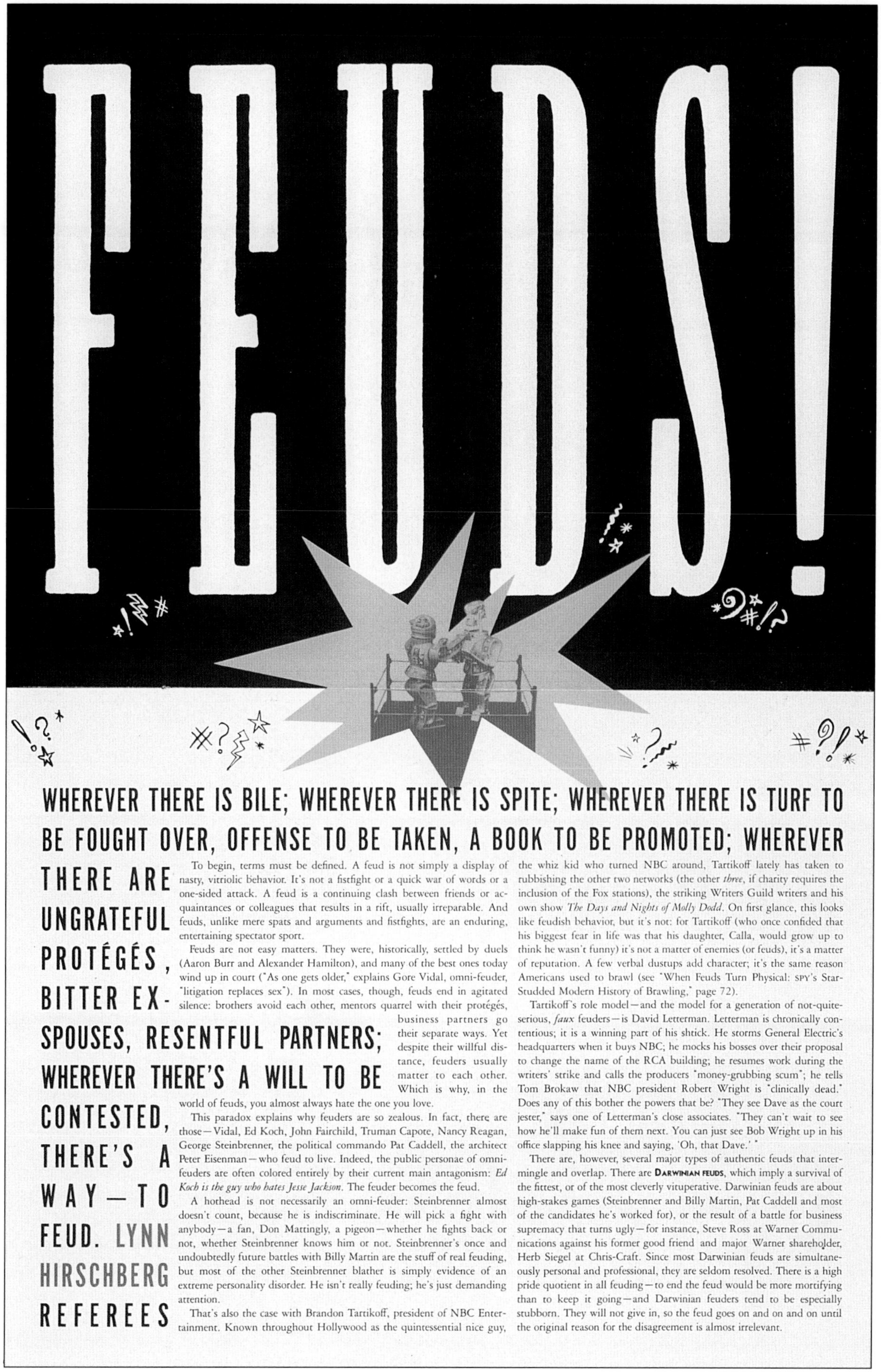

FEUDS!

WHEREVER THERE IS BILE; WHEREVER THERE IS SPITE; WHEREVER THERE IS TURF TO BE FOUGHT OVER, OFFENSE TO BE TAKEN, A BOOK TO BE PROMOTED; WHEREVER THERE ARE UNGRATEFUL PROTÉGÉS, BITTER EX-SPOUSES, RESENTFUL PARTNERS; WHEREVER THERE'S A WILL TO BE CONTESTED, THERE'S A WAY—TO FEUD. LYNN HIRSCHBERG REFEREES

To begin, terms must be defined. A feud is not simply a display of nasty, vitriolic behavior. It's not a fistfight or a quick war of words or a one-sided attack. A feud is a continuing clash between friends or acquaintances or colleagues that results in a rift, usually irreparable. And feuds, unlike mere spats and arguments and fistfights, are an enduring, entertaining spectator sport.

Feuds are not easy matters. They were, historically, settled by duels (Aaron Burr and Alexander Hamilton), and many of the best ones today wind up in court ("As one gets older," explains Gore Vidal, omni-feuder, "litigation replaces sex"). In most cases, though, feuds end in agitated silence: brothers avoid each other, mentors quarrel with their protégés, business partners go their separate ways. Yet despite their willful distance, feuders usually matter to each other. Which is why, in the world of feuds, you almost always hate the one you love.

This paradox explains why feuders are so zealous. In fact, there are those—Vidal, Ed Koch, John Fairchild, Truman Capote, Nancy Reagan, George Steinbrenner, the political commando Pat Caddell, the architect Peter Eisenman—who feud to live. Indeed, the public personae of omni-feuders are often colored entirely by their current main antagonism: *Ed Koch is the guy who hates Jesse Jackson*. The feuder becomes the feud.

A hothead is not necessarily an omni-feuder: Steinbrenner almost doesn't count, because he is indiscriminate. He will pick a fight with anybody—a fan, Don Mattingly, a pigeon—whether he fights back or not, whether Steinbrenner knows him or not. Steinbrenner's once and undoubtedly future battles with Billy Martin are the stuff of real feuding, but most of the other Steinbrenner blather is simply evidence of an extreme personality disorder. He isn't really feuding; he's just demanding attention.

That's also the case with Brandon Tartikoff, president of NBC Entertainment. Known throughout Hollywood as the quintessential nice guy, the whiz kid who turned NBC around, Tartikoff lately has taken to rubbishing the other two networks (the other *three*, if charity requires the inclusion of the Fox stations), the striking Writers Guild writers and his own show *The Days and Nights of Molly Dodd*. On first glance, this looks like feudish behavior, but it's not: for Tartikoff (who once confided that his biggest fear in life was that his daughter, Calla, would grow up to think he wasn't funny) it's not a matter of enemies (or feuds), it's a matter of reputation. A few verbal dustups add character; it's the same reason Americans used to brawl (see "When Feuds Turn Physical: SPY's Star-Studded Modern History of Brawling," page 72).

Tartikoff's role model—and the model for a generation of not-quite-serious, *faux* feuders—is David Letterman. Letterman is chronically contentious; it is a winning part of his shtick. He storms General Electric's headquarters when it buys NBC; he mocks his bosses over their proposal to change the name of the RCA building; he resumes work during the writers' strike and calls the producers "money-grubbing scum"; he tells Tom Brokaw that NBC president Robert Wright is "clinically dead." Does any of this bother the powers that be? "They see Dave as the court jester," says one of Letterman's close associates. "They can't wait to see how he'll make fun of them next. You can just see Bob Wright up in his office slapping his knee and saying, 'Oh, that Dave.' "

There are, however, several major types of authentic feuds that intermingle and overlap. There are **DARWINIAN FEUDS**, which imply a survival of the fittest, or of the most cleverly vituperative. Darwinian feuds are about high-stakes games (Steinbrenner and Billy Martin, Pat Caddell and most of the candidates he's worked for), or the result of a battle for business supremacy that turns ugly—for instance, Steve Ross at Warner Communications against his former good friend and major Warner shareholder, Herb Siegel at Chris-Craft. Since most Darwinian feuds are simultaneously personal and professional, they are seldom resolved. There is a high pride quotient in all feuding—to end the feud would be more mortifying than to keep it going—and Darwinian feuders tend to be especially stubborn. They will not give in, so the feud goes on and on and on until the original reason for the disagreement is almost irrelevant.

77
DESIGN FIRM: *Spy Magazine In-house*
DESIGNER: *B.W. Honeycutt*
HEADLINE TYPEFACE: *Antique Wood Type Triple Condensed and Alternate Gothic*
TEXT TYPEFACE: *Garamond 3*
CLIENT: *Spy Corporation*

78
DESIGN FIRM: *Peterson & Company*
DESIGNER: *Scott Ray*
LETTERER: *Scott Ray*
HEADLINE TYPEFACE: *Bodoni Book*
TEXT TYPEFACE: *Bodoni Book Italic*
CLIENT: *Maxus Energy Corporation*

79
DESIGN FIRM: *Spy Magazine In-house*
DESIGNER: *Alex Isley*
HEADLINE TYPEFACE: *Alternate Gothic and Metro Black*
TEXT TYPEFACE: *Commercial Script and Garamond 3*
CLIENT: *Spy Corporation*

78

INCREASING RESERVES

Seismic
Helps Maxus "See"
With Sound

LOOK-ing

FOR NEW PLAYS THROUGH NEW EYES

In today's environment, Maxus' value is measured in large part by its reserves: if the company replaces or finds reserves each year, it can increase value. In order to do so, however, we have to maximize the return from our exploration efforts. ¶ Helping us achieve that objective is a technology our company and others have been using for more than 50 years—seismic surveying. The contributions of seismic surveying continue to grow as its technology advances and as our markets and competitive environment change. ¶ Offshore seismic surveying—seeing with sound—has given Maxus new eyes with which to examine the rise and fall, dip and strike of ancient rock formations lying far below the ocean floor. For it is such changes in underlying rock formations that provide clues to the hiding places of oil and gas.

11

79

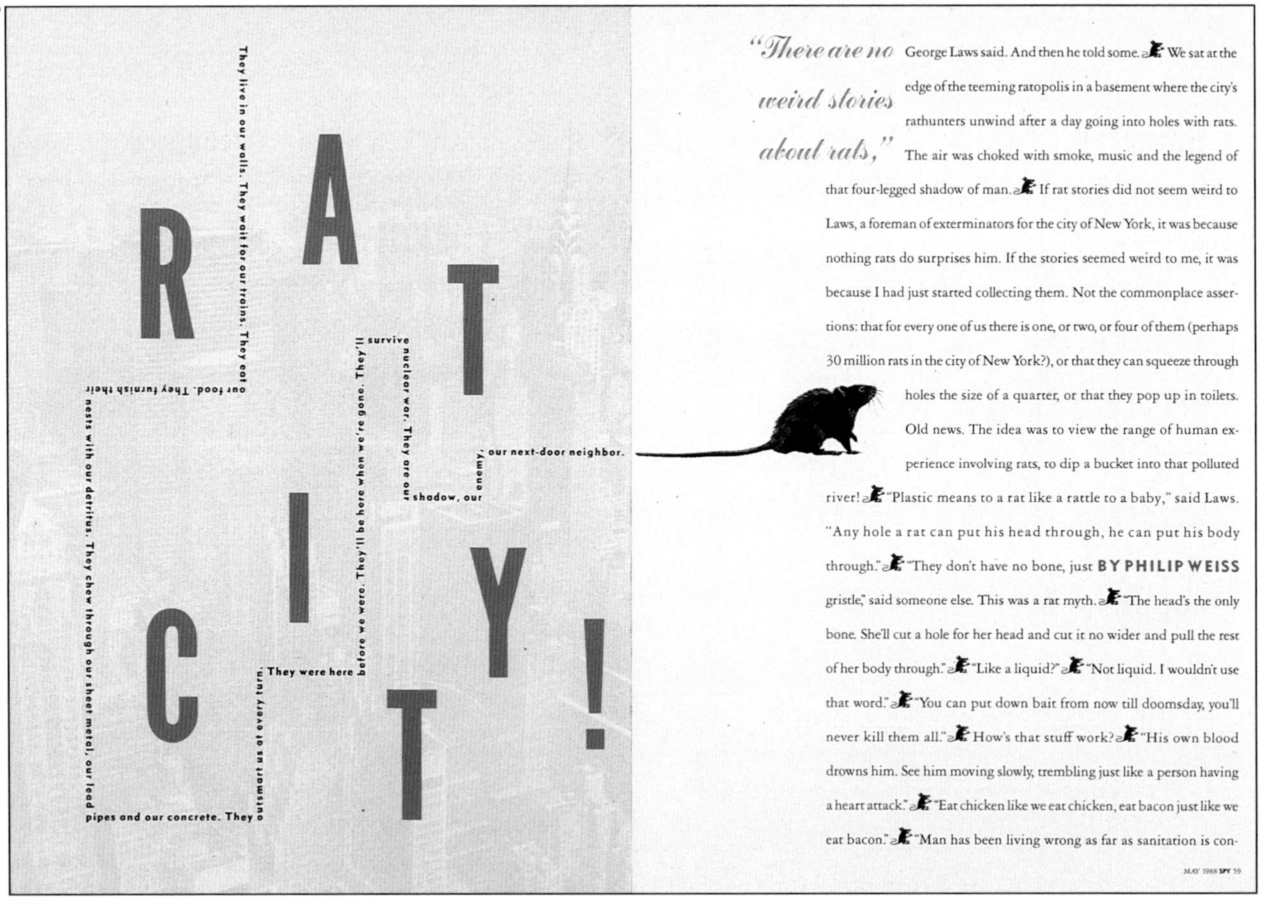
RAT CITY!

They live in our walls. They wait for our trains. They eat our food. They furnish their nests with our detritus. They chew through our sheet metal, our lead pipes and our concrete. They outsmart us at every turn. They were here before we were. They'll be here when we're gone. They'll survive nuclear war. They are our shadow, our enemy, our next-door neighbor.

"There are no weird stories about rats," George Laws said. And then he told some. We sat at the edge of the teeming ratopolis in a basement where the city's rathunters unwind after a day going into holes with rats. The air was choked with smoke, music and the legend of that four-legged shadow of man. If rat stories did not seem weird to Laws, a foreman of exterminators for the city of New York, it was because nothing rats do surprises him. If the stories seemed weird to me, it was because I had just started collecting them. Not the commonplace assertions: that for every one of us there is one, or two, or four of them (perhaps 30 million rats in the city of New York?), or that they can squeeze through holes the size of a quarter, or that they pop up in toilets. Old news. The idea was to view the range of human experience involving rats, to dip a bucket into that polluted river! "Plastic means to a rat like a rattle to a baby," said Laws. "Any hole a rat can put his head through, he can put his body through." "They don't have no bone, just gristle," said someone else. This was a rat myth. "The head's the only bone. She'll cut a hole for her head and cut it no wider and pull the rest of her body through." "Like a liquid?" "Not liquid. I wouldn't use that word." "You can put down bait from now till doomsday, you'll never kill them all." How's that stuff work? "His own blood drowns him. See him moving slowly, trembling just like a person having a heart attack." "Eat chicken like we eat chicken, eat bacon just like we eat bacon." "Man has been living wrong as far as sanitation is con-

BY PHILIP WEISS

MAY 1988 SPY 59

FIRE
THE HIGH COST OF KEEPING THE HIGH-RISE AT LOW RISK.

80

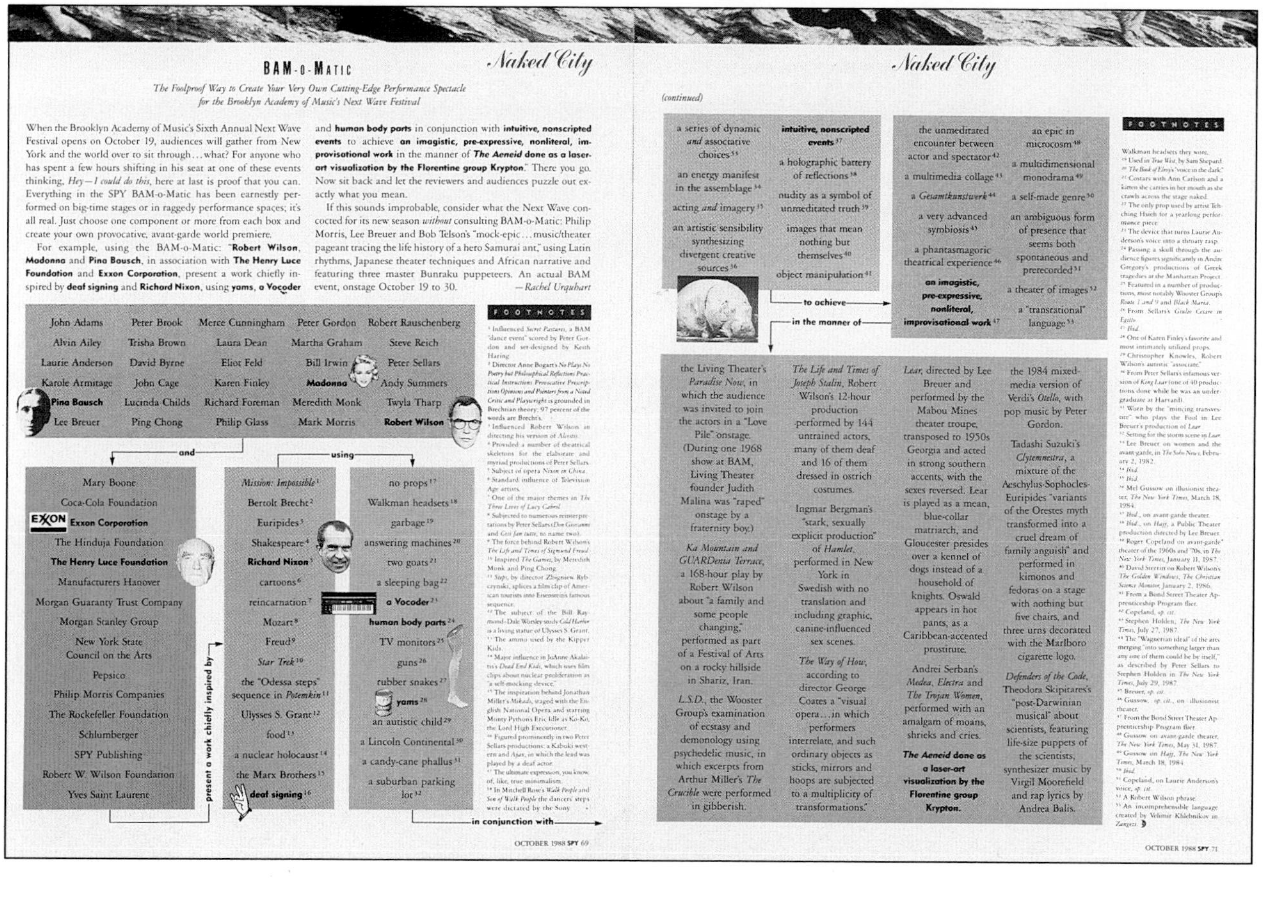

81

80
DESIGN FIRM: *Hess & Hess*
DESIGNER: *John Alcorn*
LETTERER: *John Alcorn*
CLIENT: *Edward S. Gordon Company, Inc.*

81
DESIGN FIRM: *Spy Magazine In-house*
DESIGNER: *B.W. Honeycutt*
HEADLINE TYPEFACE: *Alternate Gothic*
TEXT TYPEFACE: *Garamond 3 and Metro Black*
CLIENT: *Spy Corporation*

82
DESIGN FIRM: *Lance Anderson Design*
DESIGNER: *Lance Anderson*
LETTERER: *Lance Anderson*
CLIENT: *Chronicle Books*

82

83

DESIGN FIRM: *Carol Publishing Group*
DESIGNER: *Steven Brower*
LETTERER: *Dennis Potokar*
CLIENT: *Carol Publishing Group*

84
DESIGN FIRM: *Michael Doret, Inc.*
DESIGNER: *Michael Doret*
LETTERER: *Michael Doret*
HEADLINE TYPEFACE: *Handlettering*
CLIENT: *Scholastic, Inc.*

85
DESIGN FIRM: *Michael Doret, Inc.*
DESIGNER: *Michael Doret*
LETTERER: *Michael Doret*
HEADLINE TYPEFACE: *Handlettering*
CLIENT: *Pantheon Books*

86
DESIGN FIRM: *Michael Doret, Inc.*
DESIGNER: *Michael Doret*
LETTERER: *Michael Doret*
HEADLINE TYPEFACE: *Handlettering*
CLIENT: *Carol Communications*

87
DESIGN FIRM: *Spy Magazine In-house*
DESIGNER: *B.W. Honeycutt*
LETTERER: *B.W. Honeycutt*
HEADLINE TYPEFACE: *Thompson Triple Condensed and Spire*
TEXT TYPEFACE: *Alternate Gothic*
CLIENT: *Spy Corporation*

84

85
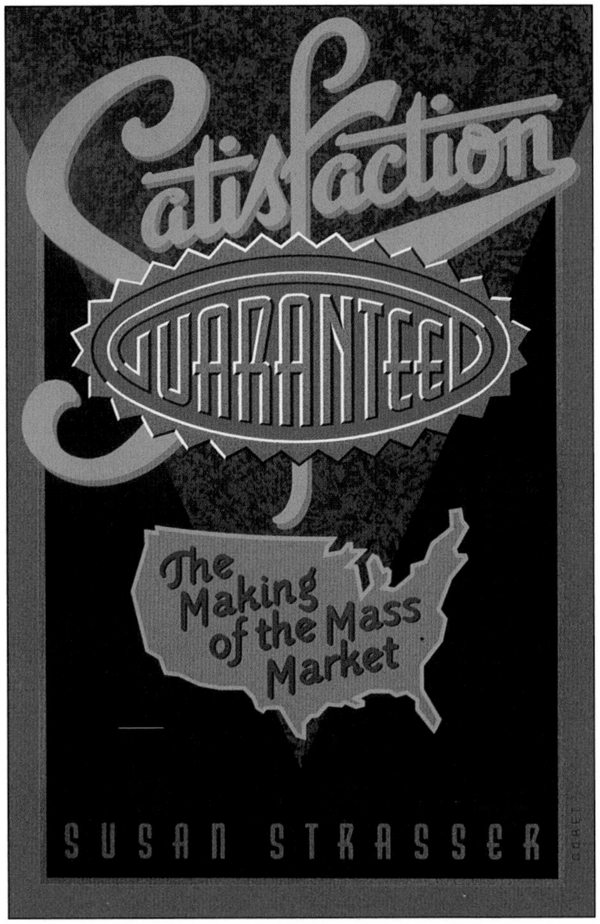

86
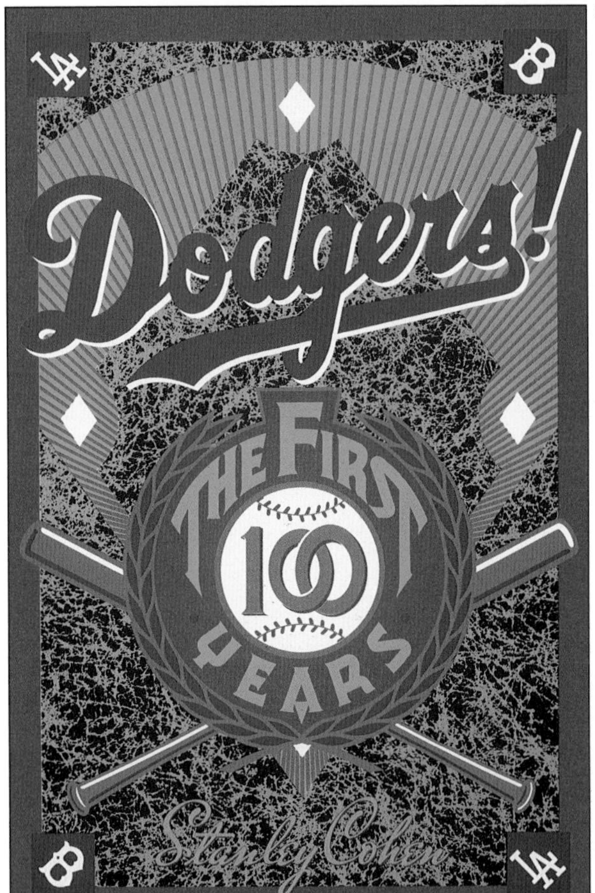

87

88

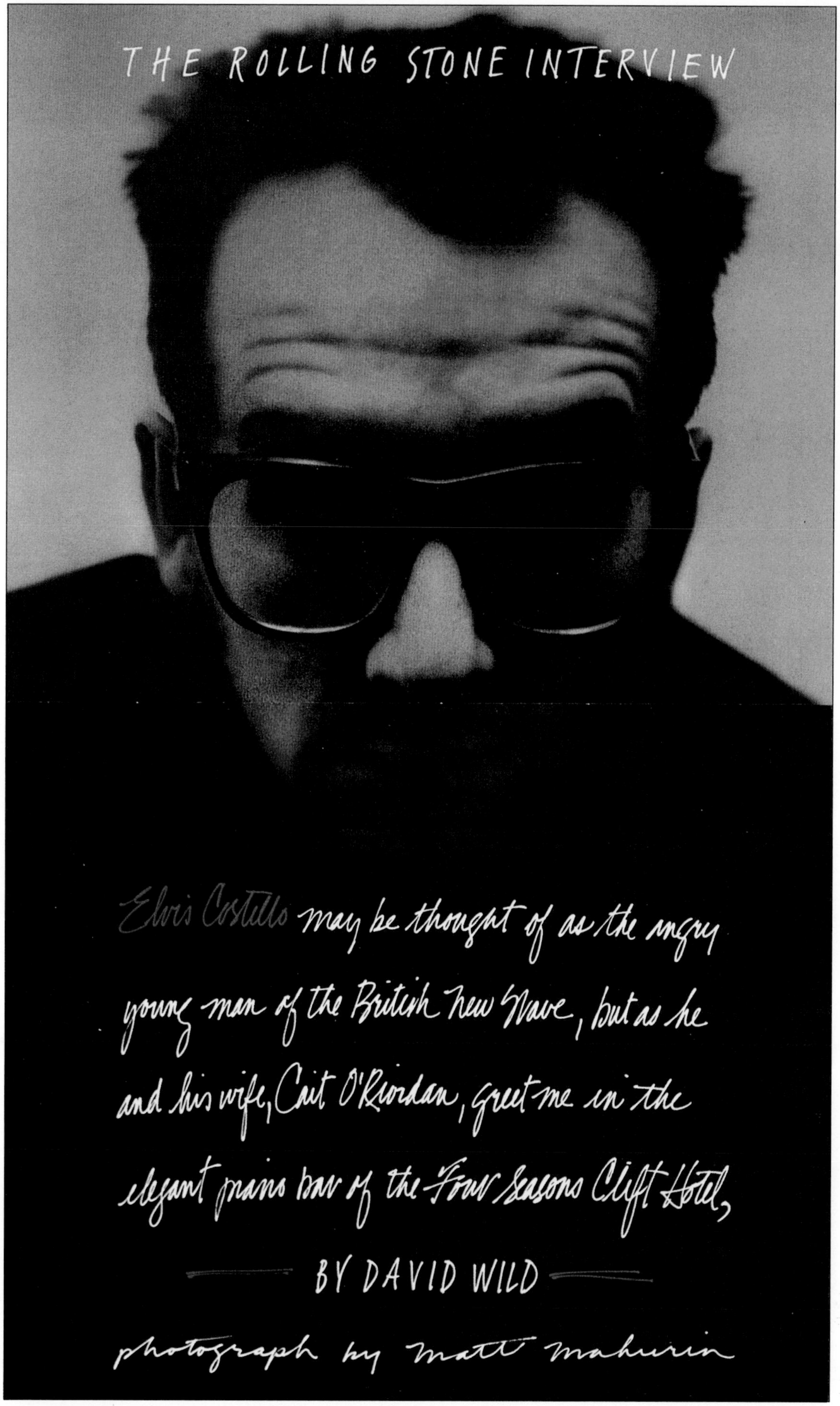
THE ROLLING STONE INTERVIEW
Elvis Costello may be thought of as the angry
young man of the British New Wave, but as he
and his wife, Cait O'Riordan, greet me in the
elegant piano bar of the Four Seasons Clift Hotel,
BY DAVID WILD
photograph by matt mahurin

88
DESIGN FIRM: *Rolling Stone Magazine In-house*
DESIGNER: *Jolene Cuyler*
LETTERER: *Jolene Cuyler*
HEADLINE TYPEFACE: *Handlettering*
CLIENT: *Rolling Stone Magazine*

89
DESIGN FIRM: *Pentagram Design*
DESIGNER: *Kit Hinrichs and Terri Driscoll*
HEADLINE TYPEFACE: *Futura Bold and Onyx*
TEXT TYPEFACE: *Bodoni Book*
CLIENT: *Art Center College of Design*

89

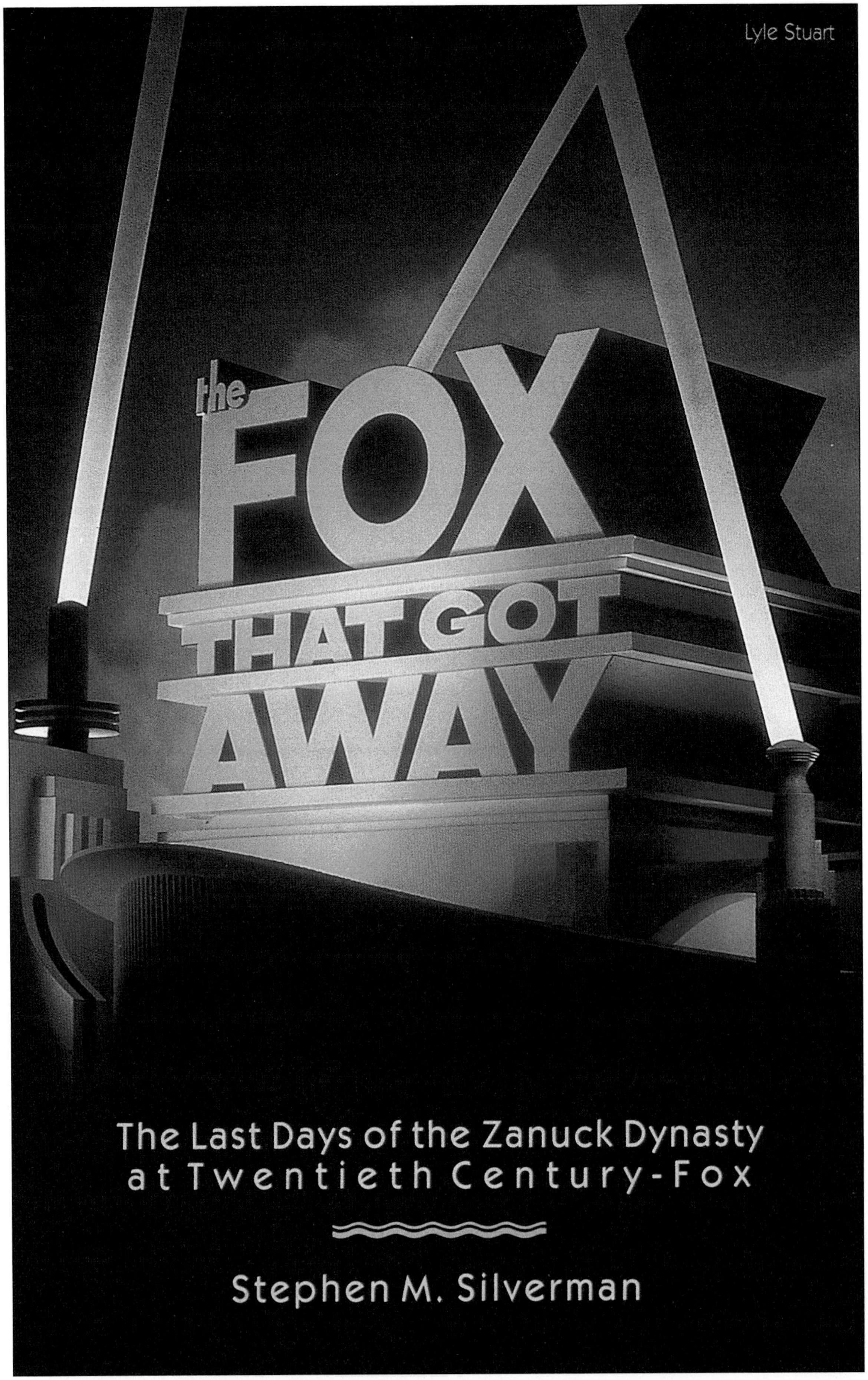

90

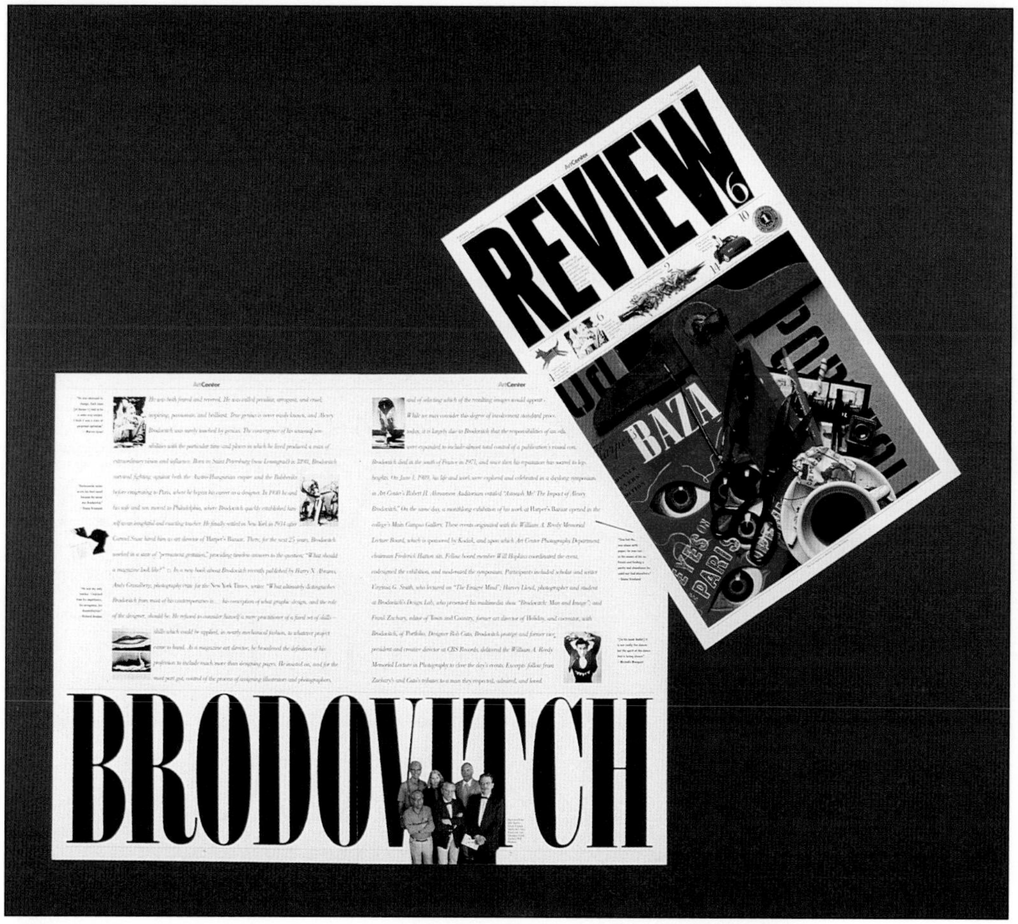

91

90
DESIGN FIRM: *Pentagram Design*
DESIGNER: *Kit Hinrichs and Terri Driscoll*
HEADLINE TYPEFACE: *Futura Bold and Onyx*
TEXT TYPEFACE: *Bodoni Book*
CLIENT: *Art Center College of Design*

91
DESIGN FIRM: *Pentagram Design*
DESIGNER: *Kit Hinrichs and Belle How*
HEADLINE TYPEFACE: *Bodoni and Univers 49*
TEXT TYPEFACE: *Bodoni*
CLIENT: *Pacific Telesis*

92

DESIGN FIRM: *Rolling Stone Magazine In-house*
DESIGNER: *Fred Woodward*
HEADLINE TYPEFACE: *Centaur Titling and Excelsior*
CLIENT: *Rolling Stone Magazine*

92

He hasn't CAN had a big hit album in years. The other Beatles are suing him. PAUL But with 'Flowers in the Dirt,' his strong new record, McCARTNEY and plans for his first world tour in more than a decade, the GET ex-Beatle is doing his best to toughen up his image and climb back BACK? to the top.
BY JAMES HENKE

93

DESIGN FIRM: *Rolling Stone Magazine In-house*
DESIGNER: *Debra Bishop*
HEADLINE TYPEFACE: *Will Bold Open*
TEXT TYPEFACE: *Cloister*
CLIENT: *Rolling Stone Magazine*

93

THE FOLLOWING EXCERPT IS FROM T. CORAGHESSAN BOYLE'S FORTHCOMING NOVEL 'EAST IS EAST,' WHICH WILL BE PUBLISHED IN 1990. BOYLE IS THE AUTHOR OF 'WORLD'S END,' 'IF THE RIVER WAS WHISKEY' AND OTHER FICTION. IN THIS PASSAGE, NEAR THE BEGINNING OF 'EAST IS EAST,' A COUPLE LOUNGING ON A BOAT OFF THE COAST OF GEORGIA ARE SURPRISED BY A VISITOR, WHO EMERGES FROM THE SEA.

"Shouldn't we have a light or something?"

"Hm?" His voice was a warm murmur at her throat. He was half-asleep.

"Running lights," Ruth said, her own voice pitched low, almost a whisper, " – isn't that what they call them?"

The boat rocked softly on the swells, serene and stable, rocked like a cradle, like the big lumpy bed with the Magic Fingers massage in the motel they'd stumbled across her first night in Georgia. There was a breeze too, salt and sweet at the same time, gentle, but just strong enough to keep the mosquitoes at bay. The only sound was of the water caressing the hull, soothing, rhythmic, a run and trickle that played in her head with the strains of a folk song she'd forgotten ten years ago. The stars were alive and conscious. The champagne was cold. He didn't answer.

Ruth Dershowitz was lying naked in the bow of Saxby Lights's eighteen-foot runabout. (Actually, the boat belonged to his mother, as did everything else in and attached to the big house on Tupelo Island.) Saxby was stretched out beside her, the drowsy flat of his cheek pressed to the swell of her breast. Each time the boat dipped beneath her, the friction of his fashionable stubble sent small fires burning all the way down to her toes. Five minutes earlier Saxby had knelt before her, adjusted her hips on the broad flat plank of the seat, stroked open her thighs and moved himself into her. Ten minutes before that she'd watched him grow hard in the dimming light as he sat across from her and tried, unsuccessfully, to inflate a plastic air mattress to cushion them. She'd watched him, bemused and excited, until finally she'd whispered, "Forget it, Sax – just come over here." Now he was asleep.

For a while she listened to the water and thought nothing. And then the image of Jane Shine, her enemy, rose up before her, and she banished it with a vision of her own inevitable triumph, her own inchoate stories jelling into art, conquering magazines and astonishing the world, and then she was thinking about the big house, thinking about her fellow writers, the sculptors and painters and the single walleyed composer whose music sounded like slow death in the metronome factory. She'd been among them for a week now, one week of an indefinite stay – a succession of months that came alive in her mind, months with little gremlin faces and hunched shoulders, leapfrogging into the glorious, limitless, sunlit and rent-free future. No more waitressing, no more hack work, no more restaurant reviews, *Parade* banalities or *Cosmo*

ILLUSTRATION BY TOM CURRY

126 • ROLLING STONE, OCTOBER 5TH, 1989

ROLLING STONE, OCTOBER 5TH, 1989 • 127

94

SKALD
VOL. 6 ISSUE 2
THE PUBLICATION FOR ROYAL VIKING LINE'S SKALD MEMBERS
FALL/WINTER 1989

94
DESIGN FIRM: *Pentagram Design*
DESIGNER: *Kit Hinrichs and Terri Driscoll*
HEADLINE TYPEFACE: *Bodoni Book*
TEXT TYPEFACE: *Century Expanded*
CLIENT: *Royal Viking Line*

95
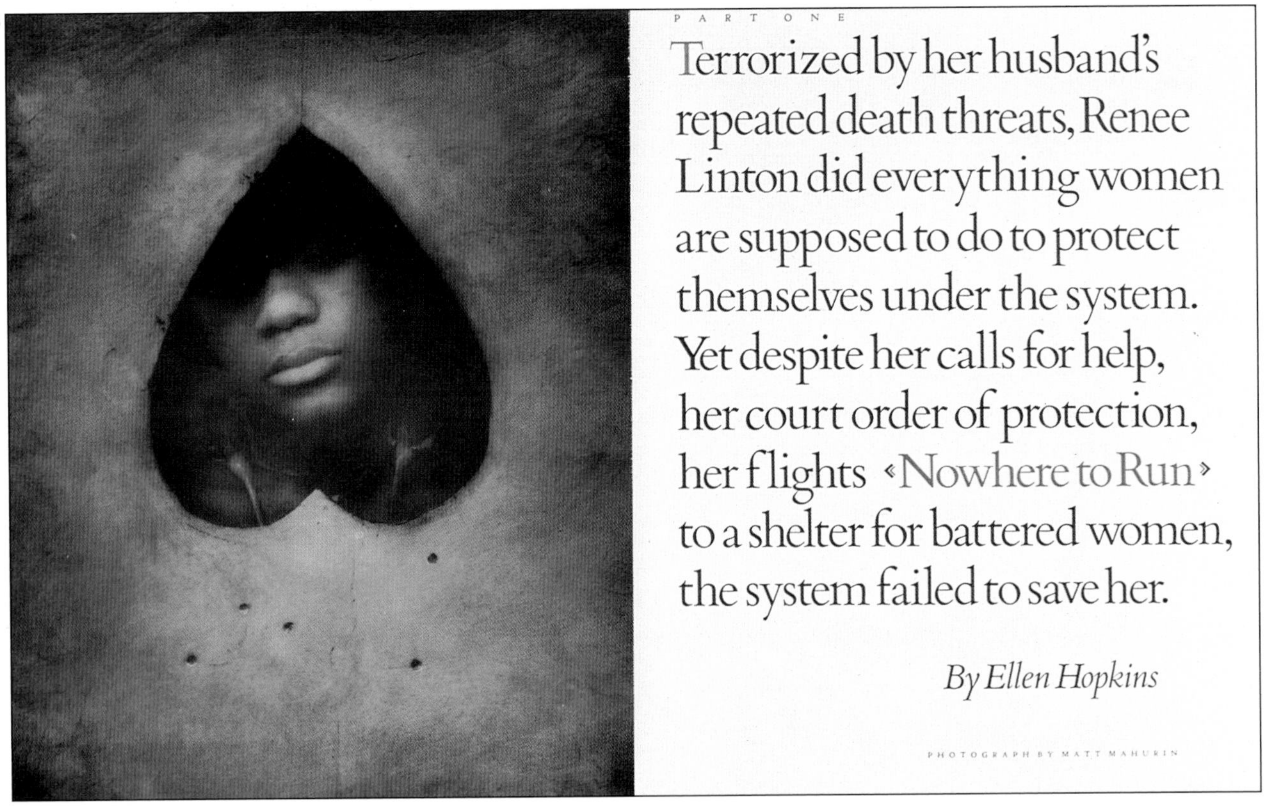

Terrorized by her husband's repeated death threats, Renee Linton did everything women are supposed to do to protect themselves under the system. Yet despite her calls for help, her court order of protection, her flights ‹Nowhere to Run› to a shelter for battered women, the system failed to save her.
By Ellen Hopkins

95
DESIGN FIRM: *Rolling Stone Magazine In-house*
DESIGNER: *Fred Woodward*
HEADLINE TYPEFACE: *Bembo Roman*
CLIENT: *Rolling Stone Magazine*

96

PART TWO: LIVING WITHOUT ENEMIES
Gorbachev wasn't just revolutionizing his own society; he was transforming ours as well. Since Stalin's day, the Soviets had played the perfect enemy. The evil Russian bear defined our national purpose and gave us a global mission. But here was Gorbachev declaring peace. Could we look at him and still see the face of the enemy? And what posed the greater threat, having an enemy or not having one? BY LAWRENCE WRIGHT
PEACE
54 • Rolling Stone, September 7th, 1989
ILLUSTRATIONS BY BRIAN CRONIN

96
DESIGN FIRM: *Rolling Stone Magazine In-house*
DESIGNER: *Fred Woodward*
HEADLINE TYPEFACE: *Bernhard Gothic Light*
TEXT TYPEFACE: *Bernhard Gothic Light*
CLIENT: *Rolling Stone Magazine*

97

HOLY ART!
THE REVEREND HOWARD FINSTER IS SPREADING GOD'S WORD AS FAST AS HE CAN PAINT, AND FOR GALLERY GOERS AND ROCK STARS ALIKE, SEEING IS BELIEVING
BY DAVID HANDELMAN
'TALKING HEADS VIEW THE WHOLE WORLD,' 1985
'THE ANGEL OF OUR CROSS PASSES OVER,' 1982
God's brushman can't get his sacred art finished 'cause the phone keeps a-ringing. He's got four paintings going—but there goes that phone again. "Somebody wantin' art!" exclaims Howard Finster. The wiry seventy-three-year-old retired minister picks up the receiver and settles into a lumpy, torn vinyl chair in his Summerville, Georgia, studio. A gas heater blazes in the corner, fermenting the room's musty, doggy smell.
PHOTOGRAPH BY DEBORAH FEINGOLD

98

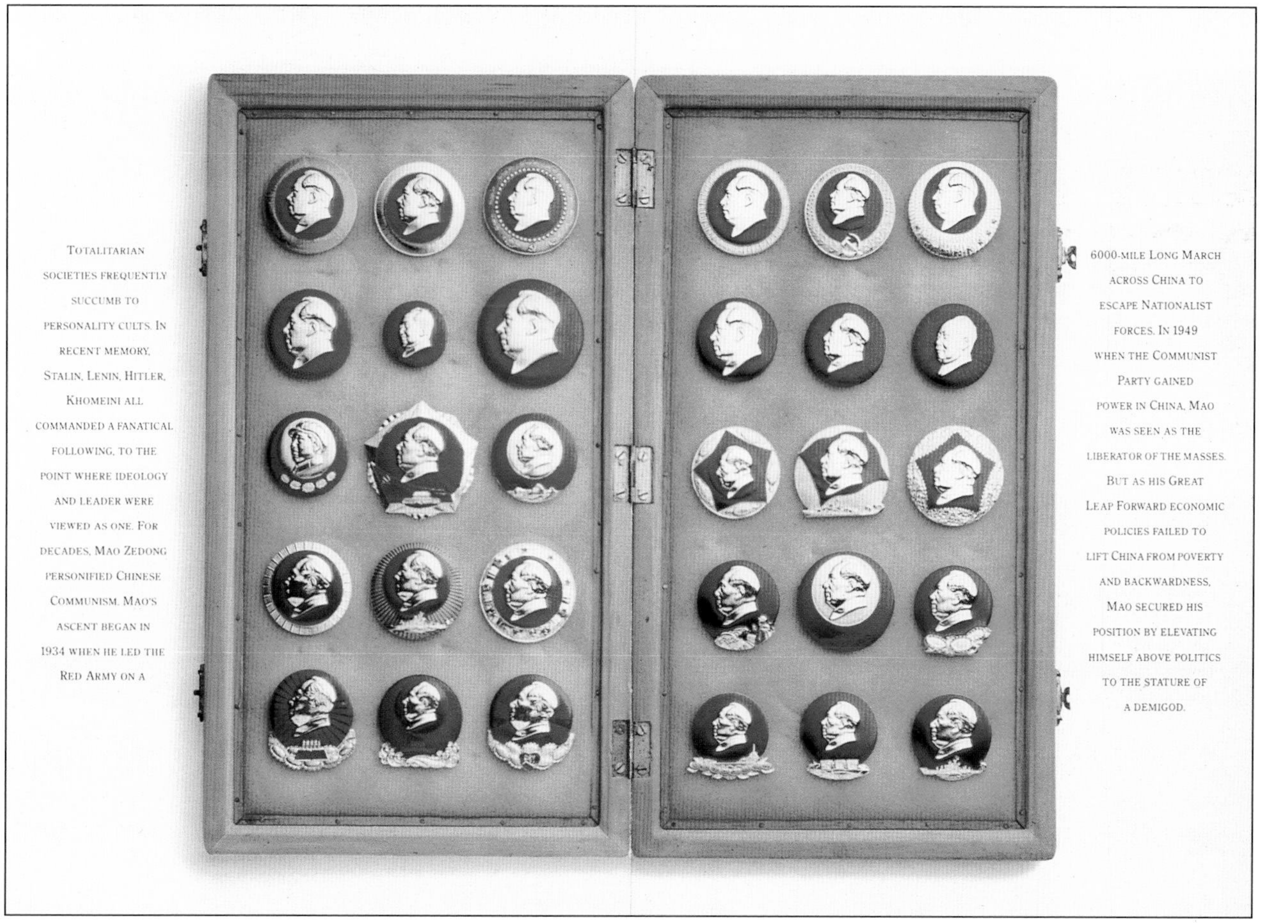

Totalitarian societies frequently succumb to personality cults. In recent memory, Stalin, Lenin, Hitler, Khomeini all commanded a fanatical following, to the point where ideology and leader were viewed as one. For decades, Mao Zedong personified Chinese Communism. Mao's ascent began in 1934 when he led the Red Army on a
6000-mile Long March across China to escape Nationalist forces. In 1949 when the Communist Party gained power in China, Mao was seen as the liberator of the masses. But as his Great Leap Forward economic policies failed to lift China from poverty and backwardness, Mao secured his position by elevating himself above politics to the stature of a demigod.

97
DESIGN FIRM: *Rolling Stone Magazine In-house*
DESIGNER: *Gail Anderson*
LETTERER: *Gail Anderson*
HEADLINE TYPEFACE: *Handpainting*
TEXT TYPEFACE: *Handpainting*
CLIENT: *Rolling Stone Magazine*

98
DESIGN FIRM: *Pentagram Design*
DESIGNER: *Linda Hinrichs and Natalie Kitamura*
TEXT TYPEFACE: *Century Oldstyle*
CLIENT: *Pentagram Design*

99

JOHN CALLAWAY AND DAUGHTERS TALK ABOUT EACH OTHER ● ALTON MILLER ON THE MAYORAL MIRACLE
CLOTHES FOR WORKING WOMEN ● AEROBIC SHOPPING
July/August 1989
$3.00
CHICAGO TIMES
MAGAZINE
Letters of Advice to Mayor Richard M. Daley
Dear Richard:
Some of the more instructive experiences of my political life were my associations with your father.
In 1968 when I was briefly a candidate for the...
McGovern
George McGovern

100
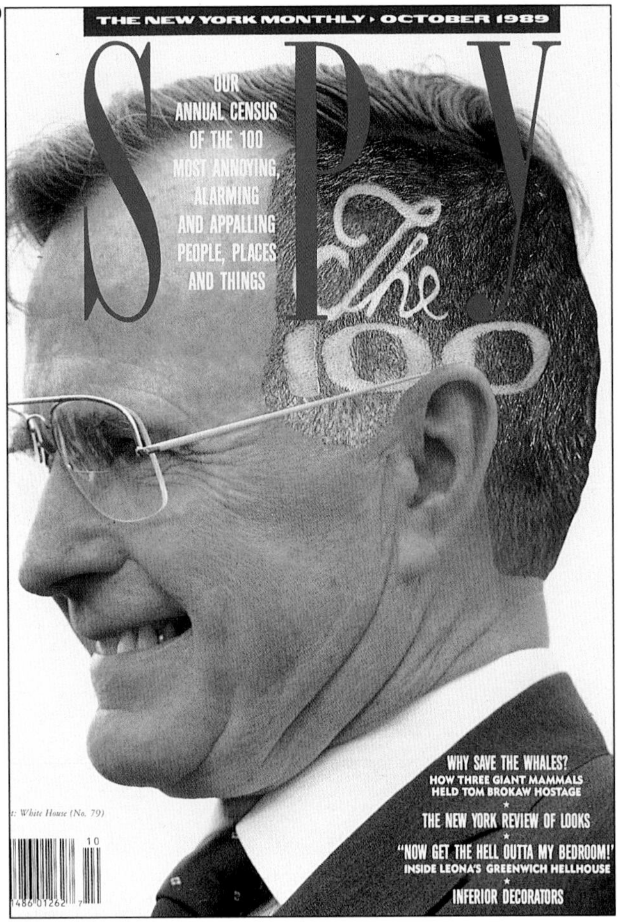
THE NEW YORK MONTHLY • OCTOBER 1989
SPY
OUR ANNUAL CENSUS OF THE 100 MOST ANNOYING, ALARMING AND APPALLING PEOPLE, PLACES AND THINGS
The 100
WHY SAVE THE WHALES?
HOW THREE GIANT MAMMALS HELD TOM BROKAW HOSTAGE
THE NEW YORK REVIEW OF LOOKS
"NOW GET THE HELL OUTTA MY BEDROOM!"
INSIDE LEONA'S GREENWICH HELLHOUSE
INFERIOR DECORATORS

101

PASTIMES

History tells us that you're safer on a sidewalk in Chicago than in a car.

walking's practical benefits by walking across the whole state into the governor's mansion. The spell did not last, however, and Walker was turned out of office after a single term by Chicagoan James R. Thompson, a pedestrian governor in every way but the way that counts. Statehouse insiders report that Thompson moved from the sprawling executive mansion in Springfield to his smaller North Side house in order to cut down the number of steps to the bathroom, with the result that the locus of political power in Illinois has shifted from Downstate to Chicago.

City hall is heir to the same tradition. (Why do you think they call them "sitting mayors"?) Aldermen were prepared to deal with a hands-on mayor when Richie Daley was elected, but a feet-on mayor? No move the new mayor made in the early days of his administration was as controversial as his decision to walk back to the office from a meeting at the Hyatt Regency. And making a city worker turn in his official car is like making a cowboy turn in his gun at the door of a saloon.

Is Daley yet another case of a politician out of step with the voters? Chicago's refusal to take to the streets seems impervious to reform, indeed even to explanation. These streets—all flat, and mostly paved—were made for walkin'. Weather? Montrealers walk in January, and Chicagoans don't walk on nice days either. Crime? History tells us that you're safer on a sidewalk in Chicago than in a car. Mayor Cermak, remember, was shot while riding in a car, and Bugs Moran's boys might have grown up to become

74 • JULY/AUGUST 1989

PASTIMES

The cynical Chicagoan sees too much wherever he turns, and grows weary of the world.

sports agents had they stayed out of garages and spent St. Valentine's Day in a shoe shop getting half-soles.

The most persuasive explanations come from those most arcane of specialists, the perceptual geographers. These students of the ways people perceive space remind us that walking down a flat, straight street is boring. You can see where you are going to be minutes before you get there, which robs the trip of those qualities that liven travel of all kinds. A walk needs adventure, serendipity, surprise. Europe's old city centers are like rat's mazes with cheese at the end of every passage. Even Manhattan's grid is full of surprises; the island is so dense with skyscrapers that much of it is dark at noon, with the result that turning from a sidestreet onto a sunlit avenue is like stumbling out a canyon onto one of the Lost Cities of Gold.

Build a city on a flat former lake bed and then lay out its streets on a regular grid, and you have provided for a pedestrian's ennui. See people sitting on benches? They aren't tired from a long slog. They're depressed, having glimpsed what life holds in store before they've had the chance to live it.

What Chicagoans need, in short, is cul-de-sacs, odd turnings, hills. Strollers on DuPage County's curvilinear boulevards move in a state of constant expectancy, filled with hope, the terrifying truth of their being in Naperville hidden by their inability to see more than a block or two of it at any one glance. The cynical Chicagoan, on the other hand, sees too much wherever he turns and grows weary of the world. ■

CHICAGO TIMES MAGAZINE • 75

99
DESIGN FIRM: *Essex Two*
DESIGNER: *Joseph Michael- Essex and Nancy Denney Essex*
LETTERER: *Joseph Michael- Essex*
HEADLINE TYPEFACE: *Franklin Gothic and Stemple Garamond*
TEXT TYPEFACE: *Franklin Gothic and Stemple Garamond*
CLIENT: *Chicago Time Magazine*

100
DESIGN FIRM: *Spy Magazine In-house*
DESIGNER: *B.W. Honeycutt*
LETTERER: *B.W. Honeycutt*
HEADLINE TYPEFACE: *Commercial Script and Spire*
TEXT TYPEFACE: *Antique Gothic Extended*
CLIENT: *Spy Corporation*

101
DESIGN FIRM: *Essex Two*
DESIGNER: *Joseph Michael- Essex and Nancy Denney Essex*
LETTERER: *Joseph Michael- Essex*
HEADLINE TYPEFACE: *Franklin Gothic and Stemple Garamond*
TEXT TYPEFACE: *Franklin Gothic and Stemple Garamond*
CLIENT: *Chicago Time Magazine*

102

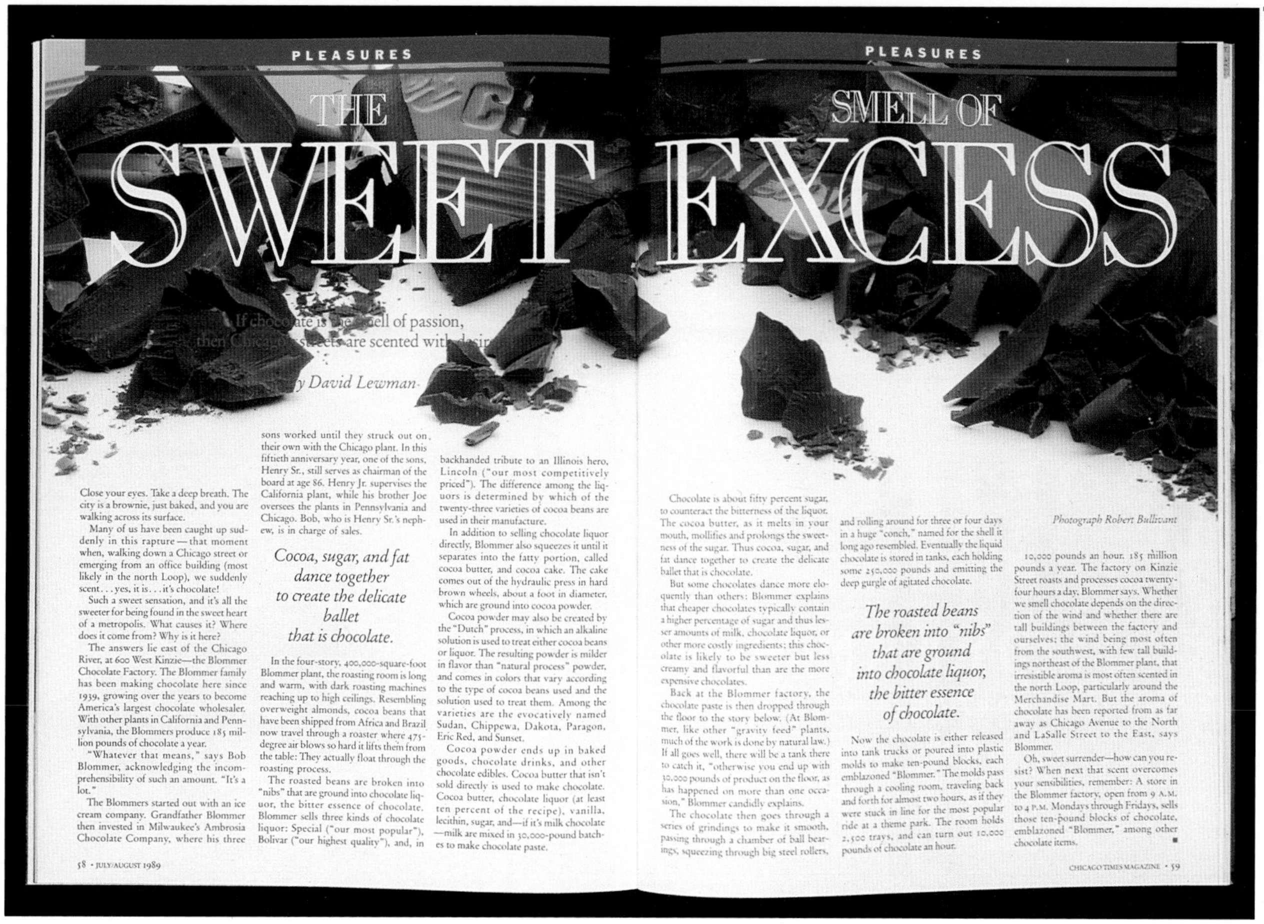

PLEASURES

THE SWEET SMELL OF EXCESS

If chocolate is the smell of passion, then Chicago's streets are scented with desire

By David Lewman

Close your eyes. Take a deep breath. The city is a brownie, just baked, and you are walking across its surface.

Many of us have been caught up suddenly in this rapture—that moment when, walking down a Chicago street or emerging from an office building (most likely in the north Loop), we suddenly scent. . . yes, it is. . . it's chocolate!

Such a sweet sensation, and it's all the sweeter for being found in the sweet heart of a metropolis. What causes it? Where does it come from? Why is it here?

The answers lie east of the Chicago River, at 600 West Kinzie—the Blommer Chocolate Factory. The Blommer family has been making chocolate here since 1939, growing over the years to become America's largest chocolate wholesaler. With other plants in California and Pennsylvania, the Blommers produce 185 million pounds of chocolate a year.

"Whatever that means," says Bob Blommer, acknowledging the incomprehensibility of such an amount. "It's a lot."

The Blommers started out with an ice cream company. Grandfather Blommer then invested in Milwaukee's Ambrosia Chocolate Company, where his three sons worked until they struck out on their own with the Chicago plant. In this fiftieth anniversary year, one of the sons, Henry Sr., still serves as chairman of the board at age 86. Henry Jr. supervises the California plant, while his brother Joe oversees the plants in Pennsylvania and Chicago. Bob, who is Henry Sr.'s nephew, is in charge of sales.

Cocoa, sugar, and fat dance together to create the delicate ballet that is chocolate.

In the four-story, 400,000-square-foot Blommer plant, the roasting room is long and warm, with dark roasting machines reaching up to high ceilings. Resembling overweight almonds, cocoa beans that have been shipped from Africa and Brazil now travel through a roaster where 475-degree air blows so hard it lifts them from the table: They actually float through the roasting process.

The roasted beans are broken into "nibs" that are ground into chocolate liquor, the bitter essence of chocolate. Blommer sells three kinds of chocolate liquor: Special ("our most popular"), Bolivar ("our highest quality"), and, in backhanded tribute to an Illinois hero, Lincoln ("our most competitively priced"). The difference among the liquors is determined by which of the twenty-three varieties of cocoa beans are used in their manufacture.

In addition to selling chocolate liquor directly, Blommer also squeezes it until it separates into the fatty portion, called cocoa butter, and cocoa cake. The cake comes out of the hydraulic press in hard brown wheels, about a foot in diameter, which are ground into cocoa powder.

Cocoa powder may also be created by the "Dutch" process, in which an alkaline solution is used to treat either cocoa beans or liquor. The resulting powder is milder in flavor than "natural process" powder, and comes in colors that vary according to the type of cocoa beans used and the solution used to treat them. Among the varieties are the evocatively named Sudan, Chippewa, Dakota, Paragon, Eric Red, and Sunset.

Cocoa powder ends up in baked goods, chocolate drinks, and other chocolate edibles. Cocoa butter that isn't sold directly is used to make chocolate. Cocoa butter, chocolate liquor (at least ten percent of the recipe), vanilla, lecithin, sugar, and—if it's milk chocolate—milk are mixed in 30,000-pound batches to make chocolate paste.

Chocolate is about fifty percent sugar, to counteract the bitterness of the liquor. The cocoa butter, as it melts in your mouth, mollifies and prolongs the sweetness of the sugar. Thus cocoa, sugar, and fat dance together to create the delicate ballet that is chocolate.

But some chocolates dance more eloquently than others: Blommer explains that cheaper chocolates typically contain a higher percentage of sugar and thus lesser amounts of milk, chocolate liquor, or other more costly ingredients; this chocolate is likely to be sweeter but less creamy and flavorful than are the more expensive chocolates.

Back at the Blommer factory, the chocolate paste is then dropped through the floor to the story below. (At Blommer, like other "gravity feed" plants, much of the work is done by natural law.) If all goes well, there will be a tank there to catch it, "otherwise you end up with 30,000 pounds of product on the floor, as has happened on more than one occasion," Blommer candidly explains.

The chocolate then goes through a series of grindings to make it smooth, passing through a chamber of ball bearings, squeezing through big steel rollers, and rolling around for three or four days in a huge "conch," named for the shell it long ago resembled. Eventually the liquid chocolate is stored in tanks, each holding some 250,000 pounds and emitting the deep gurgle of agitated chocolate.

The roasted beans are broken into "nibs" that are ground into chocolate liquor, the bitter essence of chocolate.

Now the chocolate is either released into tank trucks or poured into plastic molds to make ten-pound blocks, each emblazoned "Blommer." The molds pass through a cooling room, traveling back and forth for almost two hours, as if they were stuck in line for the most popular ride at a theme park. The room holds 2,500 trays, and can turn out 10,000 pounds of chocolate an hour.

Photograph Robert Bullivant

10,000 pounds an hour. 185 million pounds a year. The factory on Kinzie Street roasts and processes cocoa twenty-four hours a day, Blommer says. Whether we smell chocolate depends on the direction of the wind and whether there are tall buildings between the factory and ourselves; the wind being most often from the southwest, with few tall buildings northeast of the Blommer plant, that irresistible aroma is most often scented in the north Loop, particularly around the Merchandise Mart. But the aroma of chocolate has been reported from as far away as Chicago Avenue to the North and LaSalle Street to the East, says Blommer.

Oh, sweet surrender—how can you resist? When next that scent overcomes your sensibilities, remember: A store in the Blommer factory, open from 9 A.M. to 4 P.M. Mondays through Fridays, sells those ten-pound blocks of chocolate, emblazoned "Blommer," among other chocolate items. ■

103

FASHION

learn from me because I can't teach you." Firmly, but wisely, he pushed her away, into the direction she needed to go: off on her own. She found a backer and went to work, outgrowing the space in one loft after another as her clothing caught on and her operation grew. Her present 7,000-square-foot quarters on Erie Street can hardly contain her: "If we had to produce here," she says, "we'd need twice as much space." Only about three hundred units a week are produced here. The rest she sends out to three contractors who can produce eight times that.

"We would never sell it," says the Northbrook store manager whose chic gray hair is cut blunt. She is looking at a very smart chartreuse cowl. "It's Oak Brook. No, *Chicago*. It's urban, very Chicago."

Six buyers from local I. Magnin stores sit at a long white table in Kanae's loft like judges at a beauty contest, reviewing the new fall collection. Kanae shows the collection a few pieces at a time. Two jackets are at its core: a soft mannish one called the "boyfriend" jacket and a draped one called the "button-wrap"; they come in three colors and four patterns.

"This is not burgundy, Margot, it's brown," says one buyer to another. Kanae corrects her: "cordovan."

Margot ignores her: "Nothing in brown ever sells."

"But maybe now is the time," says someone gamely.

"Go for it then."

"We were thinking about last year's Anne Klein II in dark colors and how it sat and sat and sat," says a Northbrook buyer. "I'm going to do moss and blue. Moss more heavily."

"I think maybe Oak Brook gets cordovan," suggests Kanae.

"We're definitely an aware-enough store," says Oak Brook.

"We're doing cordovan and moss," announces Chicago boldly.

"That's very new," says Kanae. "Around here nobody else is buying cordovan."

"I took Kanae on a business trip to Boston, came back and hung the clothes up. When I returned to Boston, I took that same stuff—didn't press it or anything, just went out with it."

Elsa Rhoads, computer consultant, Rhoads Group

"When I wear Kanae I feel comfortable for one thing, for another, I feel quite chic."

La Engel, former chemistry and physics teacher

Ten years ago the store's Northbrook manager brought Kanae into I. Magnin. Today the designer does a million dollar business annually with the San Francisco-based chain. Bonwit Teller, Marshall Field's, and 350 specialty boutiques across the country also carry her clothes.

Kanae is in control, standing in the front of the loft near the desk and fax machine, in a white and slate top and billowy but neat pants from her spring collection. Rows of Singers and Consews (a Japanese machine) line the back portion of the loft. On another side, paper patterns hang on clothing racks. In between, still other racks hold clothing in various stages of progress. Bolts of fabric—cottons, wools, linens, and rayons—are piled everywhere and tomorrow 15,000 more yards will arrive from Japan, the first of two deliveries that will make up the fall lines. The shipment cleared customs earlier today.

Working with a Japanese color book, Kanae designs the fabric with a Japanese company. She then examines blanket samples for color and feel. When the order arrives, she checks it for damage. Then she has it cut and sent to her contractors. The clothing she designs in her head. The hard part, she says, is having to rely on so many outside sources and schedules.

In her own loft, she has a fifteen-person operation: about seven seamstresses, four pressers, a pattern maker, two cutters, and an assistant. By spring, she will have merchandisers and a business manager from a large Japanese corporation. She would also like to get help in design. "I personally can only do so much," she says. "This is a handful and I'm expanding every year. Everybody has certain talent. I'd prefer to bring in more assistant designers. I'd like to change someone else's idea to my look."

Two American companies have expressed interest in buying her stock, but she will sell stock to the gigantic Japanese company Renown, Inc., instead. "I want to be bigger, more popular. I have a big ego."

In the stores, you see her eyes peering out at you, unblinking from behind wire-rimmed glasses under dark bangs. Then they're gone, fluttering away as you rifle through the clothing on the rack. The designer has not only sewn her name onto the interfacings, but attached her face to the tags at the wrists. As she herself says, she has an ego.

"I talk straight," says Kanae. This upsets some customers: "They expect a very quiet little Japanese girl. People like me very much or not at all." ■

"I was an independent writer for seven years. I worked at home and wore jogging suits. Now I'm with clients every day. I wear Kanae because it's comfortable yet it looks pulled together."

Liz Mitchell, speech writer

"I have maybe forty pieces of Kanae. They're as comfortable as wearing sweats, but they're elegant. I wore this outfit driving to Lansing, Michigan, for a hearing. If I had been wearing a traditional suit, I would have had to take off the jacket."

Freddi Greenberg, attorney specializing in energy and corporate matters

102/103

DESIGN FIRM: *Essex Two*

DESIGNER: *Joseph Michael- Essex and Nancy Denney Essex*

LETTERER: *Joseph Michael- Essex*

HEADLINE TYPEFACE: *Franklin Gothic and Stemple Garamond*

TEXT TYPEFACE: *Franklin Gothic and Stemple Garamond*

CLIENT: *Chicago Time Magazine*

104
DESIGN FIRM: *Carson Design*
DESIGNER: *David Carson*
TEXT TYPEFACE: *Matrix*
CLIENT: *Beach Culture Magazine*

105
DESIGN FIRM: *Daniel Pelavin*
DESIGNER: *Daniel Pelavin*
LETTERER: *Daniel Pelavin*
HEADLINE TYPEFACE: *Handlettering*
CLIENT: *Adweek Magazine*

106
DESIGN FIRM: *Hess & Hess*
DESIGNER: *Richard Hess*
CLIENT: *Edward S. Gordon Company, Inc.*

104

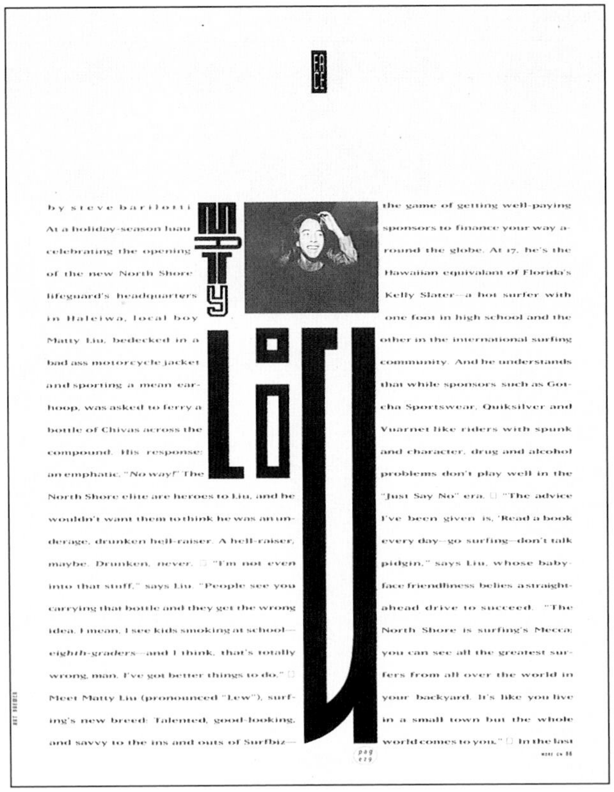
MATTY LIU

by steve barilotti

At a holiday-season luau celebrating the opening of the new North Shore lifeguard's headquarters in Haleiwa, local boy Matty Liu, bedecked in a bad ass motorcycle jacket and sporting a mean ear-hoop, was asked to ferry a bottle of Chivas across the compound. His response: an emphatic, "*No way!*" The North Shore elite are heroes to Liu, and he wouldn't want them to think he was an underage, drunken hell-raiser. A hell-raiser, maybe. Drunken, *never*. "I'm not even into that stuff," says Liu. "People see you carrying that bottle and they get the wrong idea. I mean, I see kids smoking at school—*eighth-graders*—and I think, that's totally wrong, man. I've got better things to do." Meet Matty Liu (pronounced "Lew"), surfing's new breed: Talented, good-looking, and savvy to the ins and outs of Surfbiz—the game of getting well-paying sponsors to finance your way around the globe. At 17, he's the Hawaiian equivalant of Florida's Kelly Slater—a hot surfer with one foot in high school and the other in the international surfing community. And he understands that while sponsors such as Gotcha Sportswear, Quiksilver and Vuarnet like riders with spunk and character, drug and alcohol problems don't play well in the "Just Say No" era. "The advice I've been given is, 'Read a book every day—go surfing—don't talk pidgin,'" says Liu, whose baby-face friendliness belies a straight-ahead drive to succeed. "The North Shore is surfing's Mecca; you can see all the greatest surfers from all over the world in your backyard. It's like you live in a small town but the whole world comes to you." In the last

105

106

NY SKYLINE

A New 'Golden Age' of Skyscrapers Draws on the Glories of Decades Past. Photography: Jay Maisel

Manhattan's ever-changing skyline, the product of successive building booms, is currently undergoing its most dramatic transformation since the first great wave of skyscraper construction more than half a century ago. And in what may be a nostalgic twist of fate, the latest tall buildings hark back not to the austere metal-and-glass towers that proliferated in the more recent decades following World War II, but rather to the romantic, even opulent designs of the Nineteen Twenties and Thirties — the so-called "Golden Age" of the skyscraper. A new generation of architects appears to have turned its back on the aggressive modernism that put an indelible stamp on the midtown and lower Manhattan office districts beginning in the Nineteen Forties, typified by the elongated, box-like structures that reached their epitome in the twin towers of the World Trade Center. Instead, the new form-givers bow to the sculptured textures of the Art Deco and Art Moderne schools that were rampant in the earlier boom, when the Jazz Age gave its exuberant blessing to the original skyline that made New York world-famous.

Perhaps the contrast is nowhere more striking than in the shadow of the gargantuan trade center, where Battery Park City, on landfill that has extended Manhattan Island into the Hudson River, is forming a new skyline that departs radically from that of its imposing neighbor and most of the other post-World War II towers downtown. In the new city-within-a-city, each of the three distinctive office buildings that make up the World Financial Center is shaped differently: one is topped with a dome, another with a pyramid and the third with a trapezoid — all a far cry from the flattop style that has become a New York commonplace.

GORDON'S NEW YORK 12

107

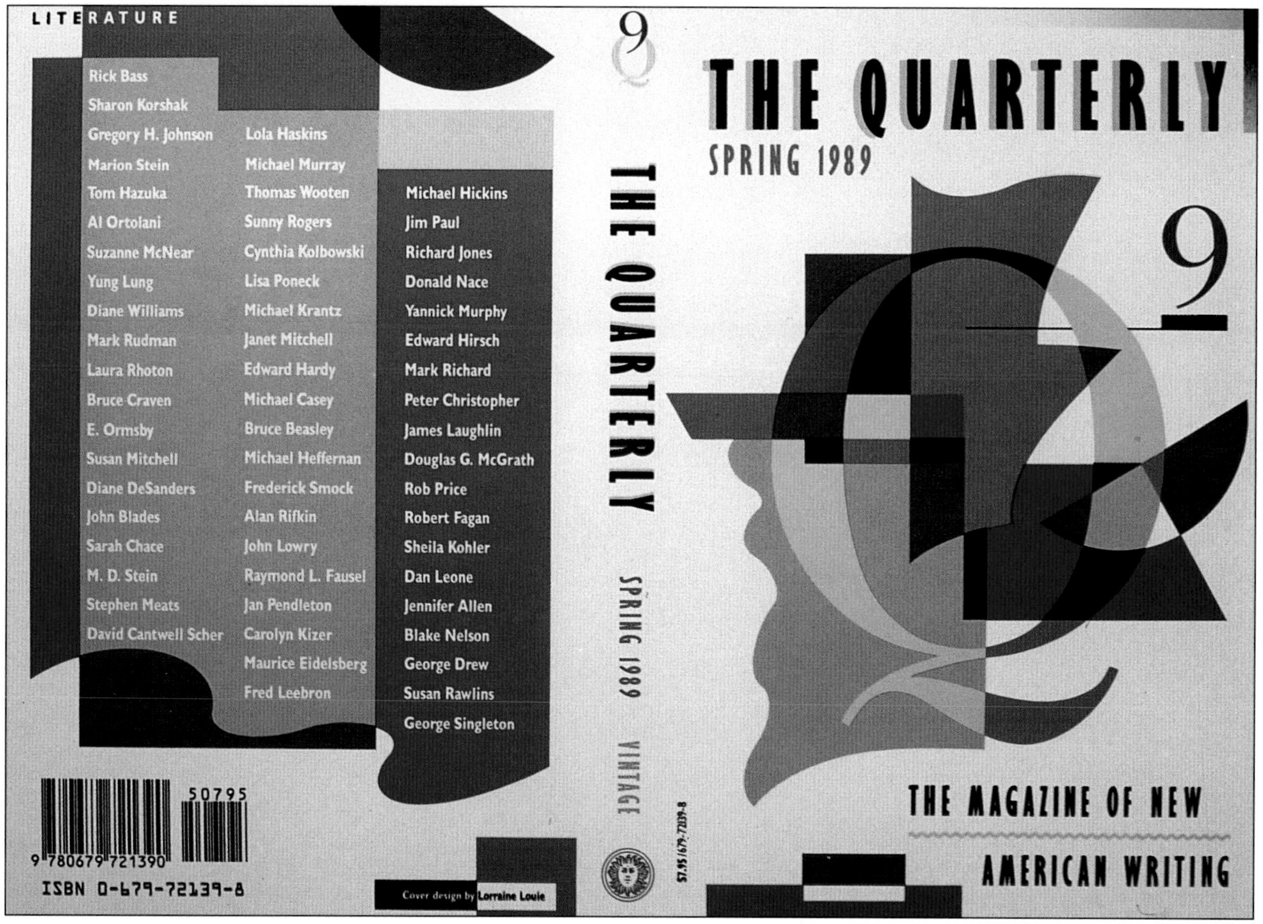

108

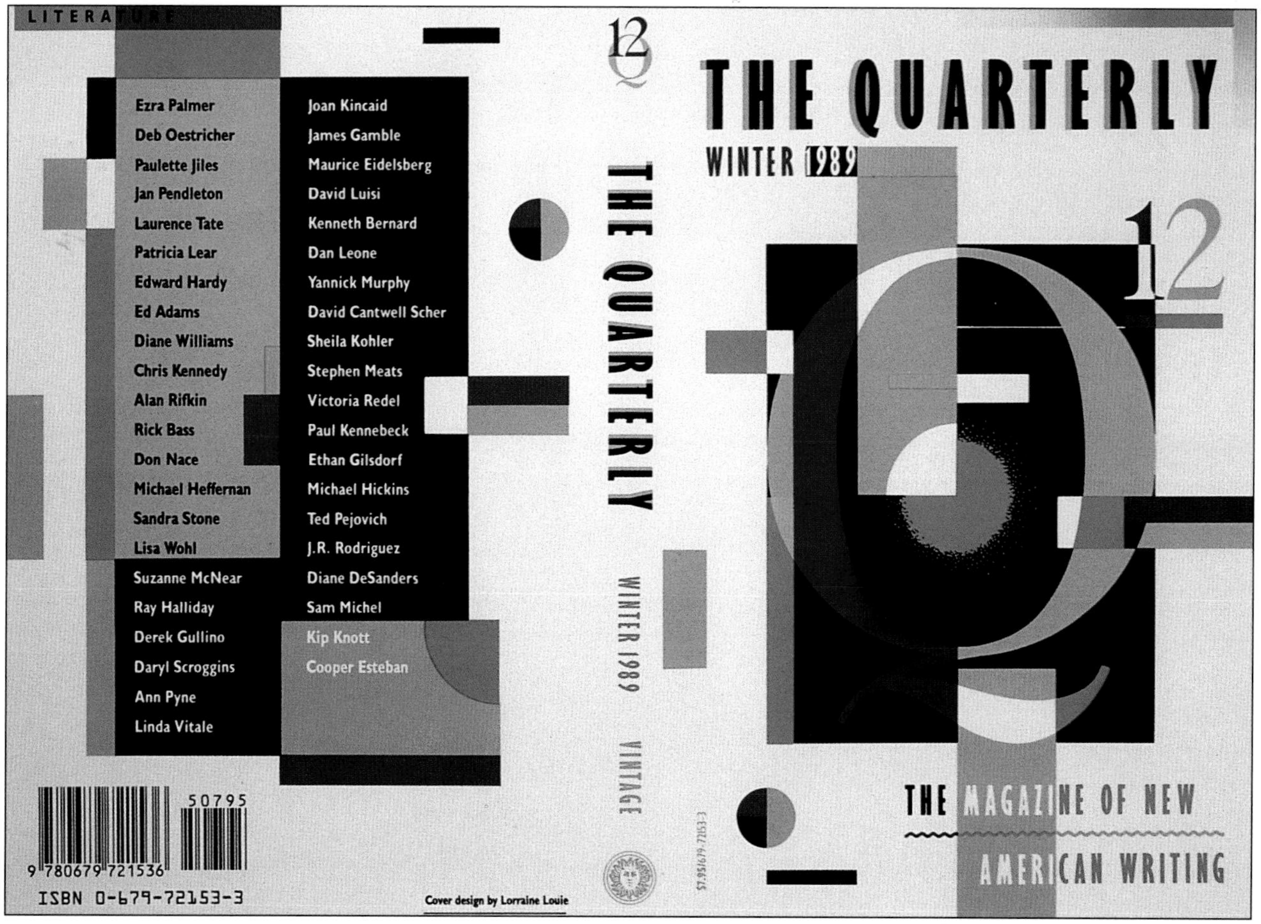

107
DESIGN FIRM: *Lorraine Louie Design*
DESIGNER: *Lorraine Louie*
HEADLINE TYPEFACE: *Gill Sans Extra Bold Condensed*
CLIENT: *Vintage Books, Random House*

108
DESIGN FIRM: *Lorraine Louie Design*
DESIGNER: *Lorraine Louie*
HEADLINE TYPEFACE: *Gill Sans Extra Bold Condensed*
CLIENT: *Vintage Books, Random House*

109

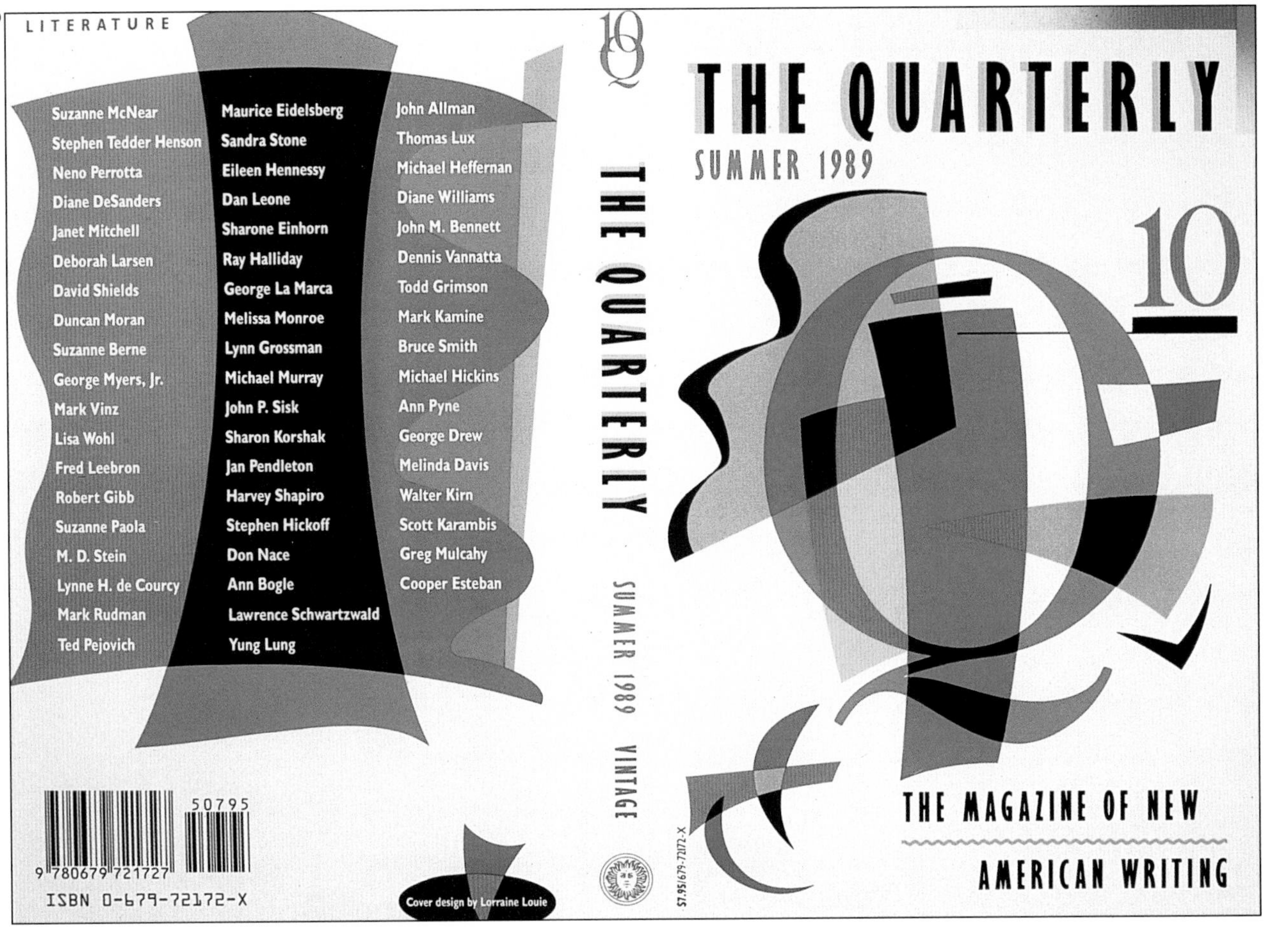

110

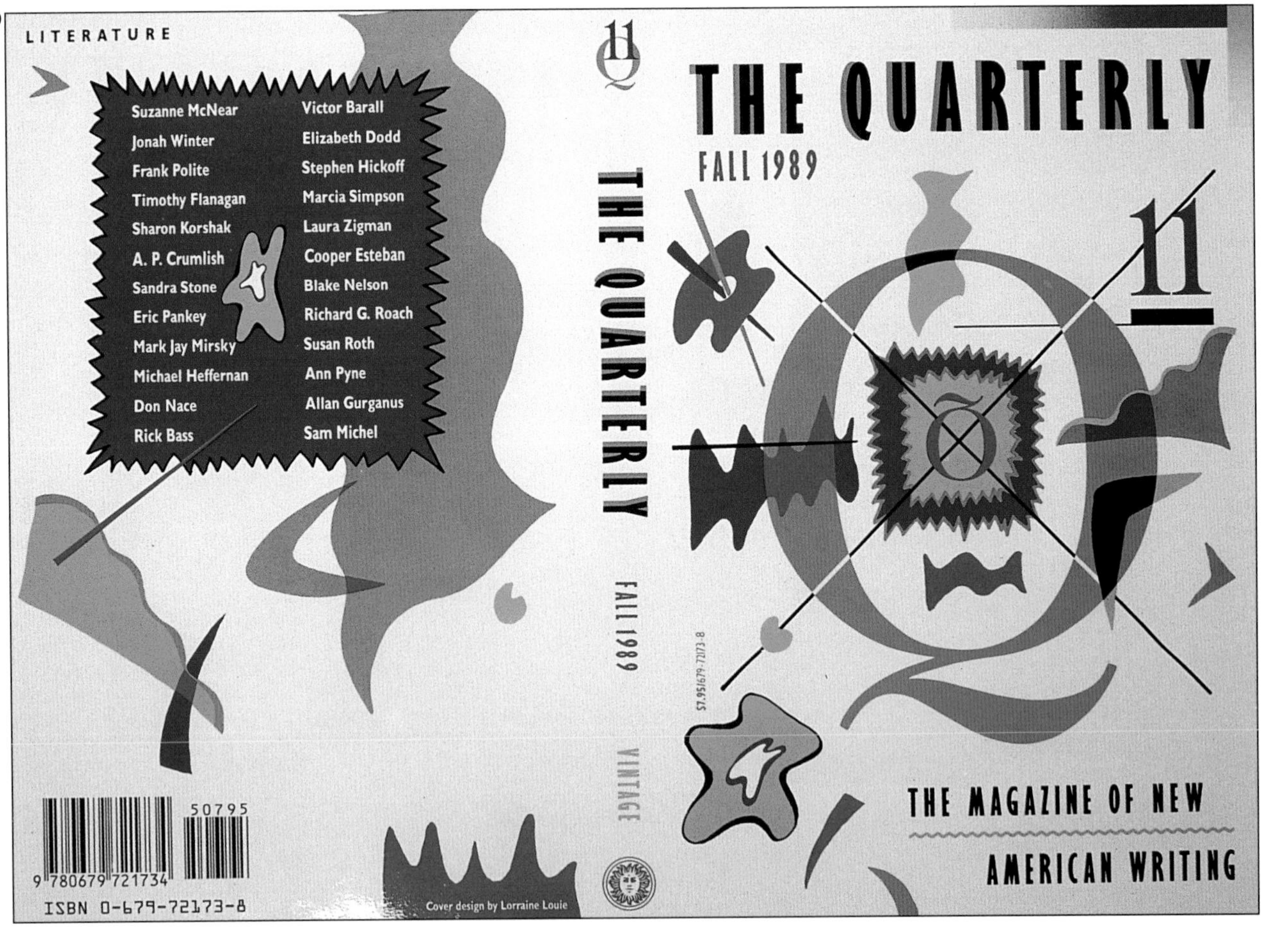

109
DESIGN FIRM: *Lorraine Louie Design*
DESIGNER: *Lorraine Louie*
HEADLINE TYPEFACE: *Gill Sans Extra Bold Condensed*
CLIENT: *Vintage Books, Random House*

110
DESIGN FIRM: *Lorraine Louie Design*
DESIGNER: *Lorraine Louie*
HEADLINE TYPEFACE: *Gill Sans Extra Bold Condensed*
CLIENT: *Vintage Books, Randon House*

111

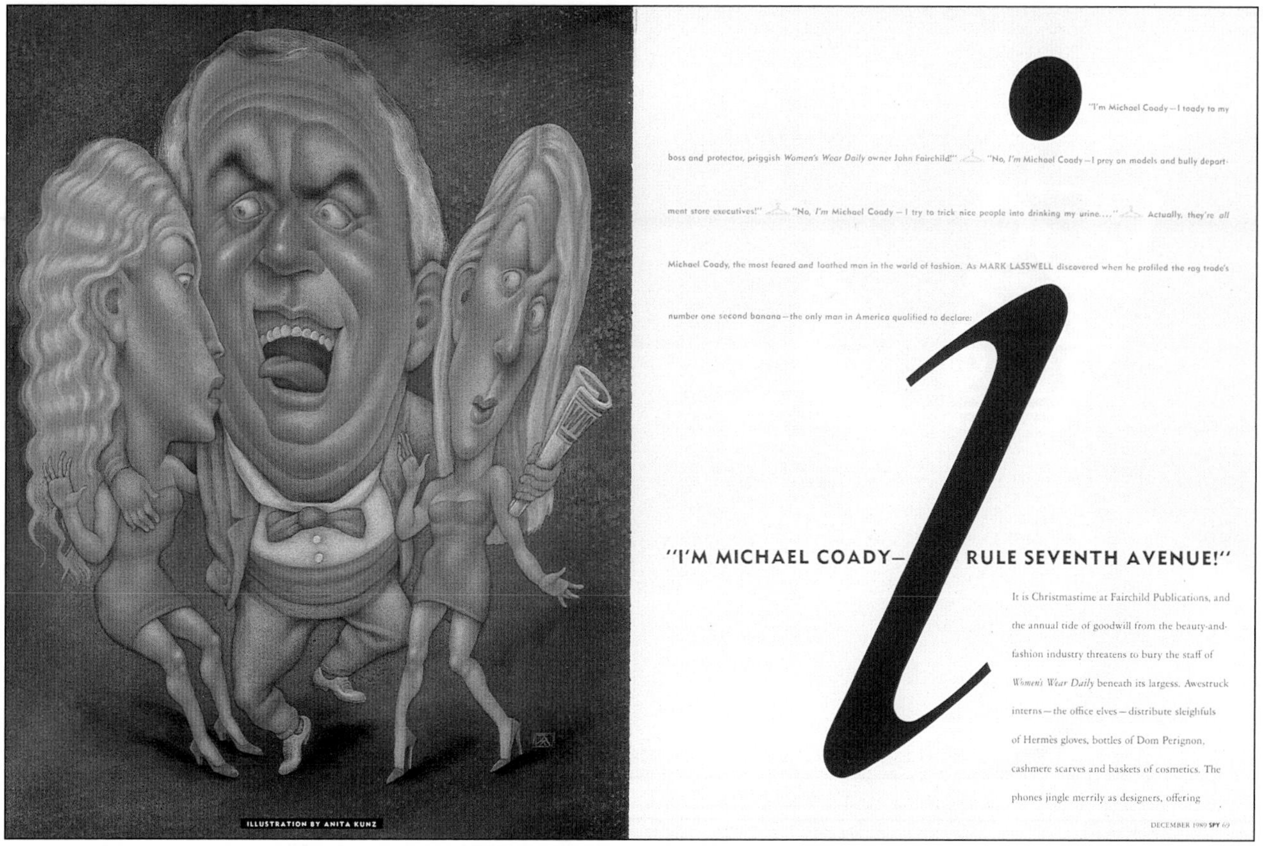

ILLUSTRATION BY ANITA KUNZ

"I'm Michael Coady—I toady to my boss and protector, priggish *Women's Wear Daily* owner John Fairchild!" "No, *I'm* Michael Coady—I prey on models and bully department store executives!" "No, *I'm* Michael Coady—I try to trick nice people into drinking my urine...." Actually, they're *all* Michael Coady, the most feared and loathed man in the world of fashion. As MARK LASSWELL discovered when he profiled the rag trade's number one second banana—the only man in America qualified to declare:

"I'M MICHAEL COADY—*i* RULE SEVENTH AVENUE!"

It is Christmastime at Fairchild Publications, and the annual tide of goodwill from the beauty-and-fashion industry threatens to bury the staff of *Women's Wear Daily* beneath its largess. Awestruck interns—the office elves—distribute sleighfuls of Hermès gloves, bottles of Dom Perignon, cashmere scarves and baskets of cosmetics. The phones jingle merrily as designers, offering

DECEMBER 1989 SPY 69

112

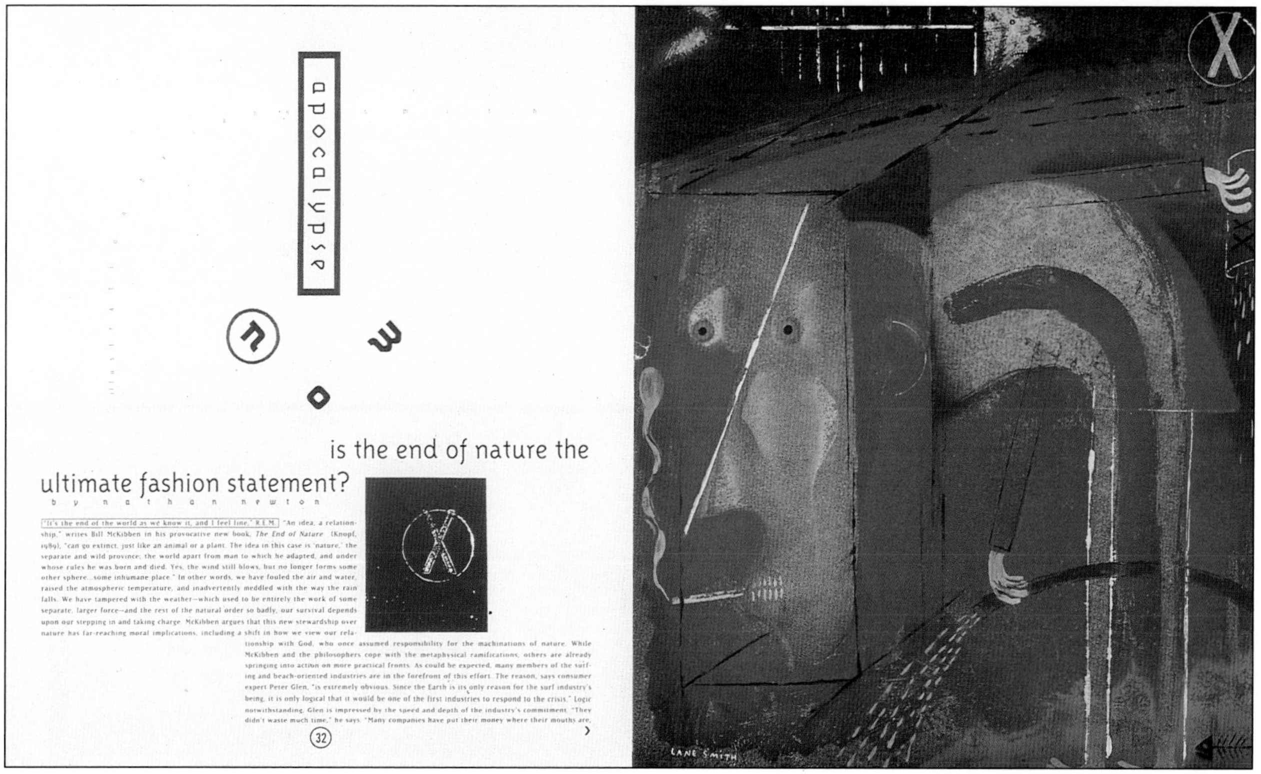

apocalypse

is the end of nature the ultimate fashion statement?

b y n a t h a n n e w t o n

"It's the end of the world as we know it, and I feel fine," R.E.M. "An idea, a relationship," writes Bill McKibben in his provocative new book, *The End of Nature* (Knopf, 1989), "can go extinct, just like an animal or a plant. The idea in this case is 'nature,' the separate and wild province; the world apart from man to which he adapted, and under whose rules he was born and died. Yes, the wind still blows, but no longer forms some other sphere...some inhumane place." In other words, we have fouled the air and water, raised the atmospheric temperature, and inadvertently meddled with the way the rain falls. We have tampered with the weather—which used to be entirely the work of some separate, larger force—and the rest of the natural order so badly, our survival depends upon our stepping in and taking charge. McKibben argues that this new stewardship over nature has far-reaching moral implications, including a shift in how we view our relationship with God, who once assumed responsibility for the machinations of nature. While McKibben and the philosophers cope with the metaphysical ramifications, others are already springing into action on more practical fronts. As could be expected, many members of the surfing and beach-oriented industries are in the forefront of this effort. The reason, says consumer expert Peter Glen, "is extremely obvious. Since the Earth is its only reason for the surf industry's being, it is only logical that it would be one of the first industries to respond to the crisis." Logic notwithstanding, Glen is impressed by the speed and depth of the industry's commitment. "They didn't waste much time," he says. "Many companies have put their money where their mouths are,

32

LANE SMITH

111
DESIGN FIRM: *Spy Magazine In-house*
DESIGNER: *B.W. Honeycutt*
HEADLINE TYPEFACE: *Metroblack and Garamond 3 Italic*
TEXT TYPEFACE: *Metro Black and Garamond 3*
CLIENT: *Spy Corporation*

112
DESIGN FIRM: *Carson Design*
DESIGNER: *David Carson*
HEADLINE TYPEFACE: *Lunatix*
TEXT TYPEFACE: *Matrix*
CLIENT: *Beach Culture Magazine*

118 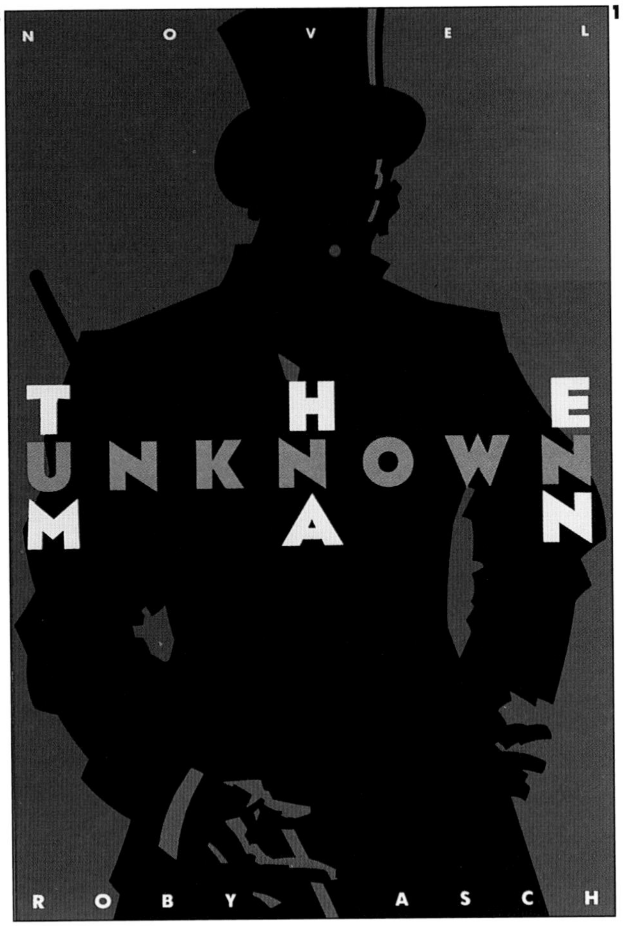

119 

120 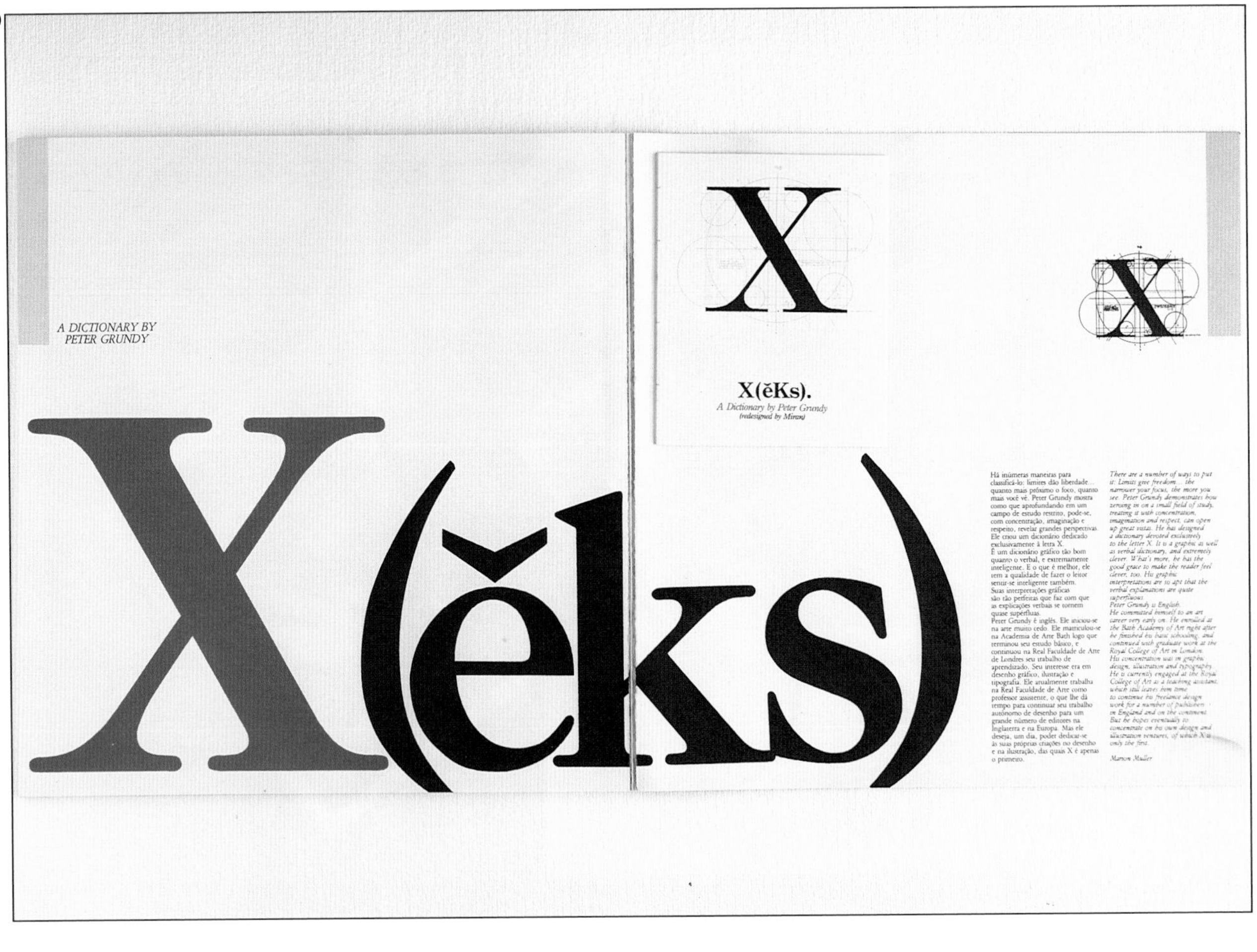

118
DESIGN FIRM: *Casa De Idéias*
DESIGNER: *Oswaldo Miranda*
HEADLINE TYPEFACE: *Eagle Type*
CLIENT: *Library of Paraná State*

119
DESIGN FIRM: *Casa De Idéias*
DESIGNER: *Oswaldo Miranda*
LETTERER: *Oswaldo Miranda*
HEADLINE TYPEFACE: *Neuland with Alteration*
CLIENT: *Library of Parana' State*

120
DESIGN FIRM: *Casa De Idéias*
DESIGNER: *Oswaldo Miranda*
HEADLINE TYPEFACE: *Art Deco Type*
CLIENT: *Library of Parana' State*

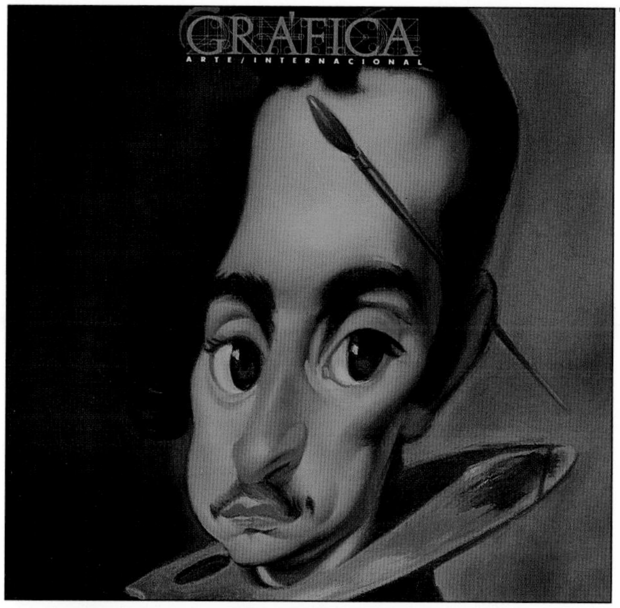

121

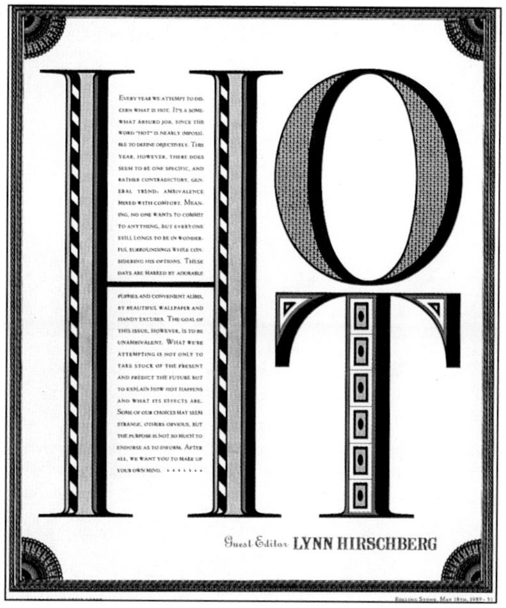

122

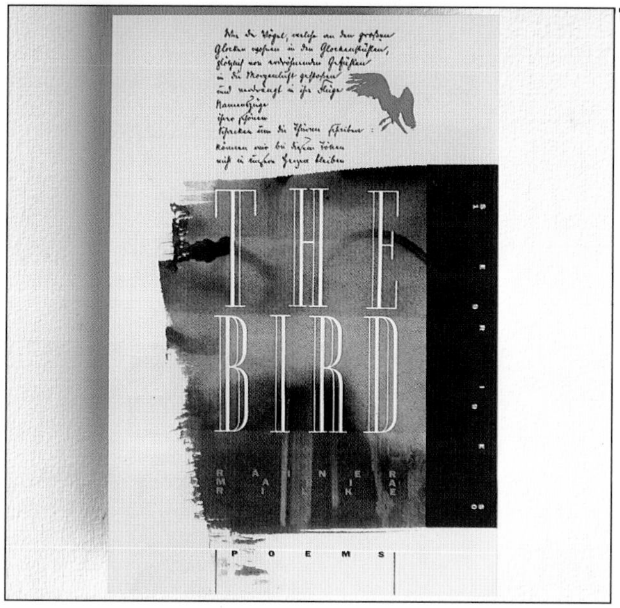

123

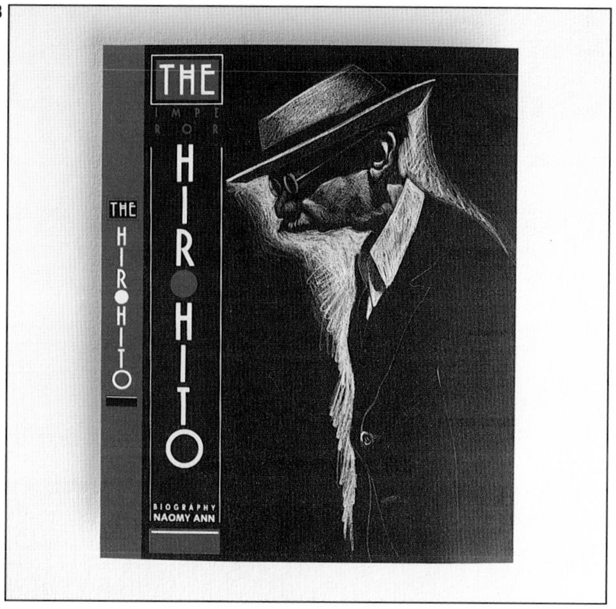

124

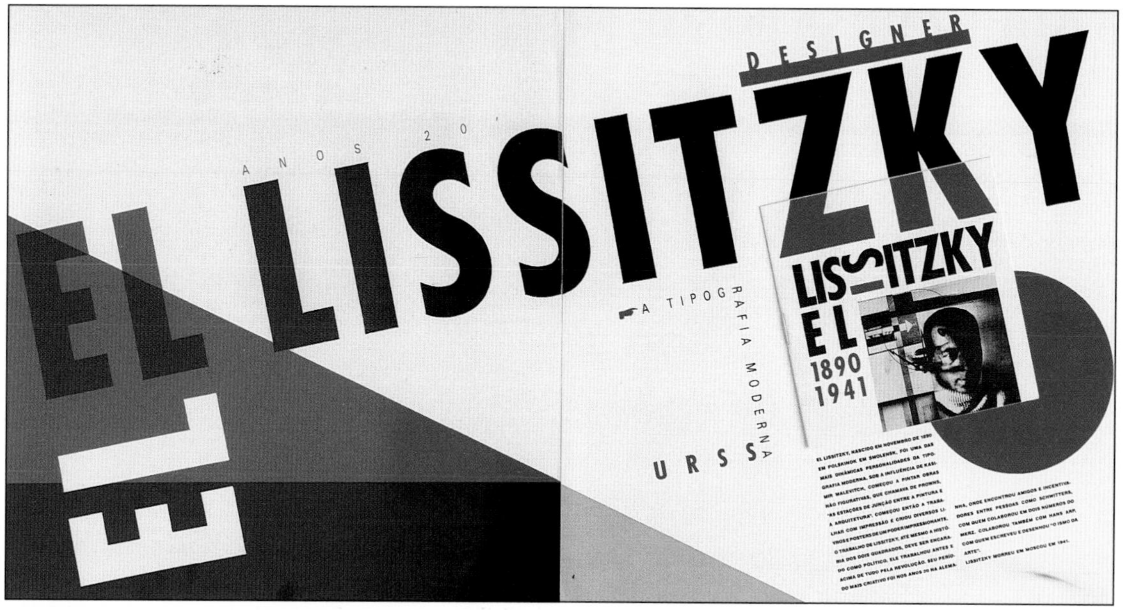

125

121
DESIGN FIRM: *Casa De Idéias*
DESIGNER: *Oswaldo Miranda*
LETTERER: *Oswaldo Miranda*
CLIENT: *Grafica Magazine*

122
DESIGN FIRM: *Rolling Stone Magazine In-house*
DESIGNER: *Fred Woodward and Gail Anderson*
LETTERER: *Dennis Ortiz-Lopez*
HEADLINE TYPEFACE: *Modern 20 Modified*
CLIENT: *Rolling Stone Magazine*

123
DESIGN FIRM: *Casa De Idéias*
DESIGNER: *Oswaldo Miranda*
HEADLINE TYPEFACE: *Onyx Outline Extra Condensed*
CLIENT: *Library of Paraná State*

124
DESIGN FIRM: *Casa De Idéias*
DESIGNER: *Oswaldo Miranda*
LETTERER: *Oswaldo Miranda*
HEADLINE TYPEFACE: *Art Deco Type*
CLIENT: *Library of Parana' State*

125
DESIGN FIRM: *Casa De Idéias*
DESIGNER: *Oswaldo Miranda*
LETTERER: *Oswaldo Miranda*
TEXT TYPEFACE: *Helvetica Condensed*
CLIENT: *Grafica Magazine*

126

DESIGN FIRM: *Rolling Stone Magazine In-house*

DESIGNER: *Catherine Gilmore-Barnes*

LETTERER: *Dennis Ortiz-Lopez*

HEADLINE TYPEFACE: *Handlettering*

TEXT TYPEFACE: *Cloister*

CLIENT: *Rolling Stone Magazine*

127

DESIGN FIRM: *Rolling Stone Magazine In-house*

DESIGNER: *Catherine Gilmore-Barnes*

LETTERER: *Dennis Ortiz-Lopez*

HEADLINE TYPEFACE: *Bauer Bodoni Title*

CLIENT: *Rolling Stone Magazine*

126

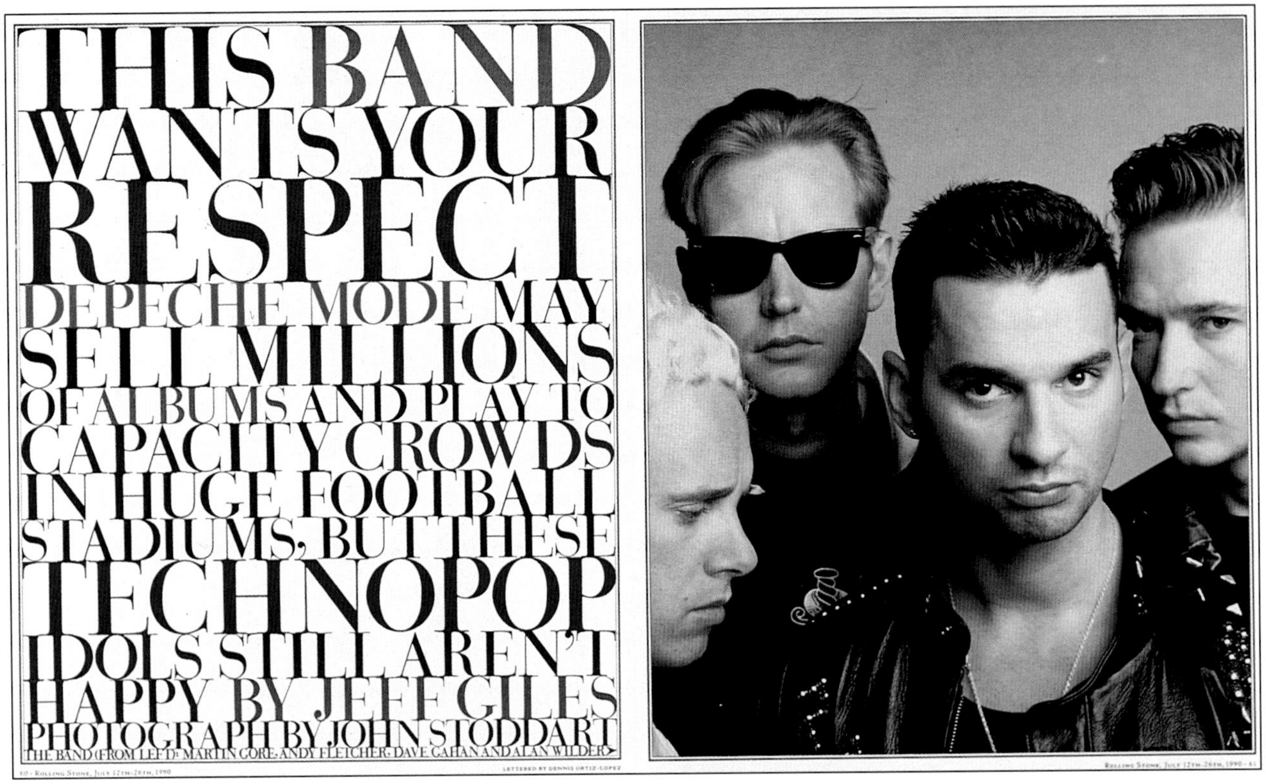

THIS BAND WANTS YOUR RESPECT
DEPECHE MODE MAY SELL MILLIONS OF ALBUMS AND PLAY TO CAPACITY CROWDS IN HUGE FOOTBALL STADIUMS, BUT THESE TECHNOPOP IDOLS STILL AREN'T HAPPY BY JEFF GILES
PHOTOGRAPH BY JOHN STODDART
THE BAND (FROM LEFT): MARTIN GORE, ANDY FLETCHER, DAVE GAHAN AND ALAN WILDER

127

VERY FEW PEOPLE ACTUALLY RECOGNIZE THE BAND MEMBERS, AND IF THEY DO, THEY TEND TO GET THE NAMES WRONG.

128

129

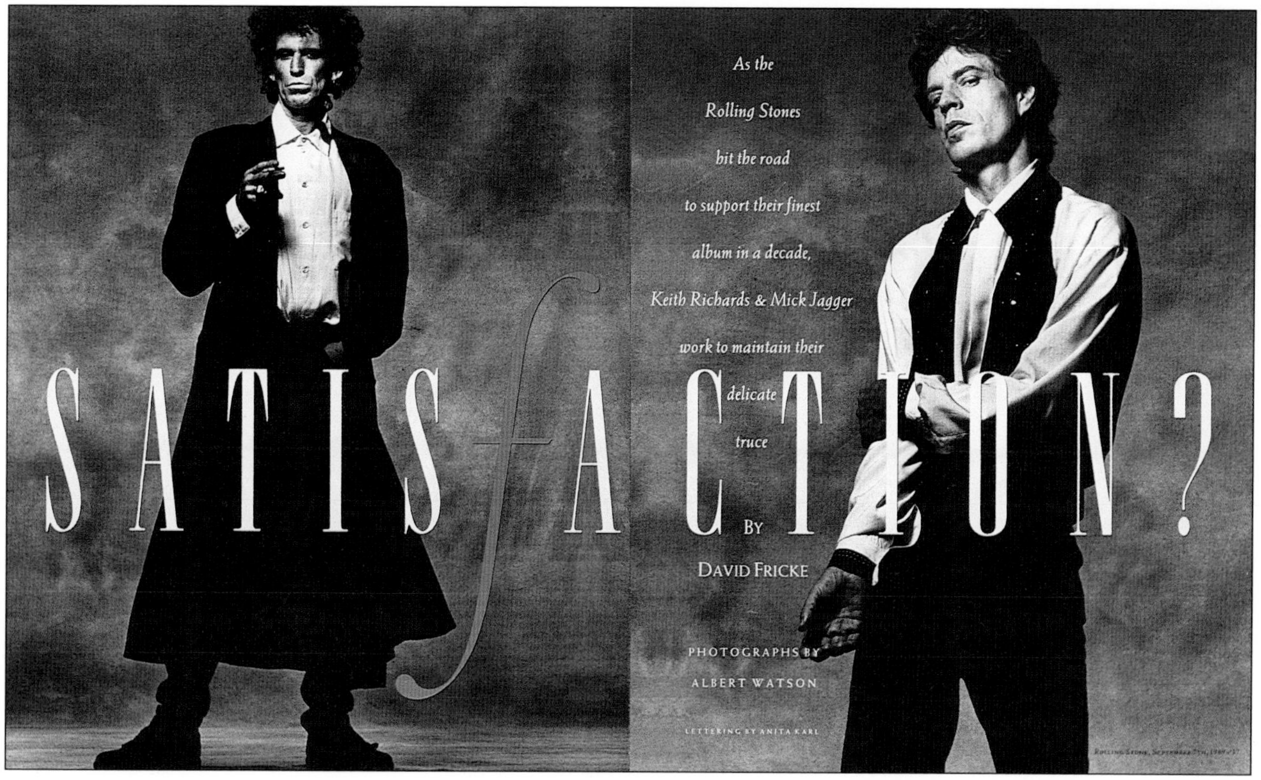

128
DESIGN FIRM: *Rolling Stone Magazine In-house*
DESIGNER: *Fred Woodward and Gail Anderson*
LETTERER: *Jonathan Hoefler*
HEADLINE TYPEFACE: *Marla*
TEXT TYPEFACE: *Cloister*
CLIENT: *Rolling Stone Magazine*

129
DESIGN FIRM: *Rolling Stone Magazine In-house*
DESIGNER: *Cathy Gilmore-Barnes*
LETTERER: *Anita Karl*
HEADLINE TYPEFACE: *Spire*
CLIENT: *Rolling Stone Magazine*

130
DESIGN FIRM: *Rolling Stone Magazine In-house*
DESIGNER: *Cathy Gilmore-Barnes*
LETTERER: *Anita Karl*
HEADLINE TYPEFACE: *Weiss Initials*
CLIENT: *Rolling Stone Magazine*

131
DESIGN FIRM: *Rolling Stone Magazine In-house*
DESIGNER: *Fred Woodward*
LETTERER: *Dennis Ortiz-Lopez*
HEADLINE TYPEFACE: *Grecian*
TEXT TYPEFACE: *Cloister*
CLIENT: *Rolling Stone Magazine*

130

131

132

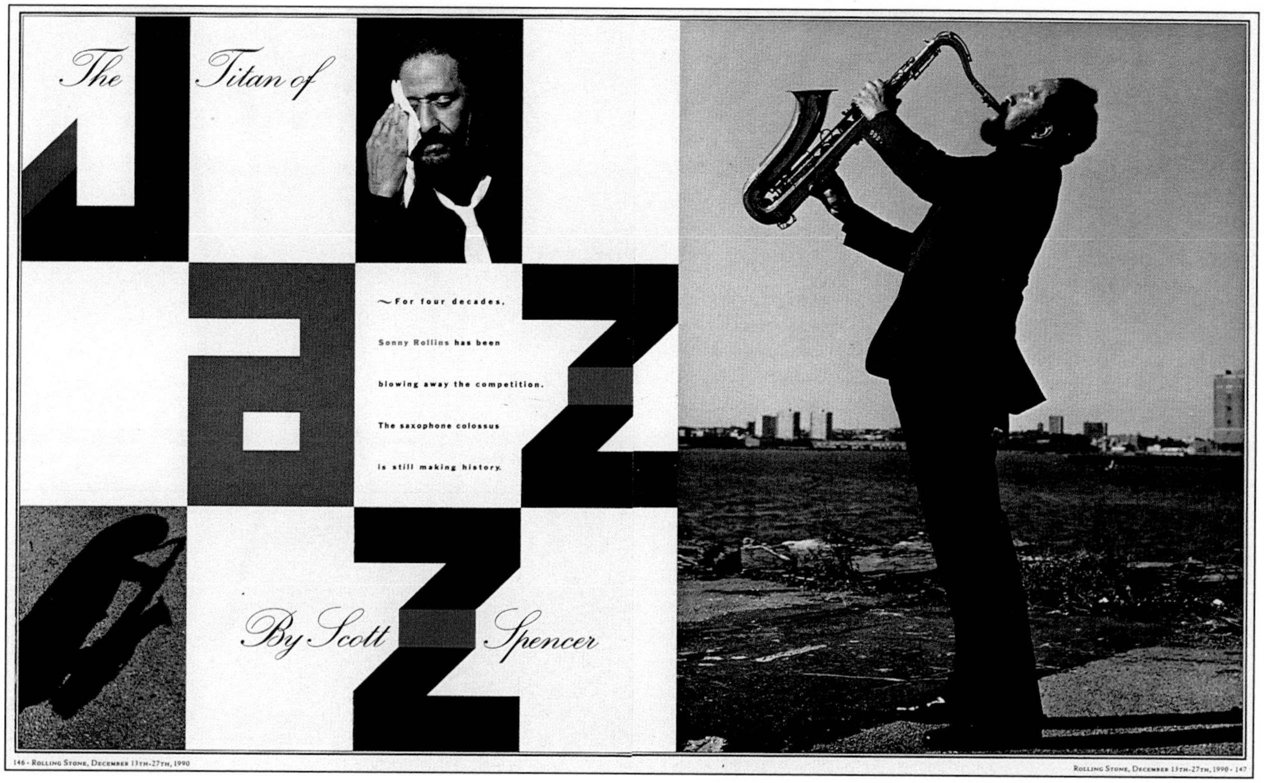

133

132
DESIGN FIRM: *Rolling Stone Magazine In-house*
DESIGNER: *Gail Anderson*
LETTERER: *Dennis Ortiz-Lopez*
HEADLINE TYPEFACE: *Poster Gothic*
TEXT TYPEFACE: *Cloister*
CLIENT: *Rolling Stone Magazine*

133
DESIGN FIRM: *Rolling Stone Magazine In-house*
DESIGNER: *Fred Woodward*
HEADLINE TYPEFACE: *Hand Cut and Excelsior*
CLIENT: *Rolling Stone Magazine*

134
DESIGN FIRM: *Rollling Stone Magazine In-house*
DESIGNER: *Geraldine Hessler*
LETTERER: *Anita Karl*
HEADLINE TYPEFACE: *Incised Gothic Capitals*
CLIENT: *Rolling Stone Magazine*

135
DESIGN FIRM: *Rolling Stone Magazine In-house*
DESIGNER: *Fred Woodward and Gail Anderson*
LETTERER: *Anita Karl*
HEADLINE TYPEFACE: *Handlettering and Oldstyle*
TEXT TYPEFACE: *Cloister*
CLIENT: *Rolling Stone Magazine*

136
DESIGN FIRM: *Rolling Stone Magazine In-house*
DESIGNER: *Fred Woodward and Gail Anderson*
LETTERER: *Josh Gosfield*
HEADLINE TYPEFACE: *Handlettering*
CLIENT: *Rolling Stone Magazine*

137
DESIGN FIRM: *Rolling Stone Magazine In-house*
DESIGNER: *Fred Woodward and Gail Anderson*
LETTERER: *Anita Karl*
HEADLINE TYPEFACE: *Handlettering and Oldstyle*
TEXT TYPEFACE: *Cloister*
CLIENT: *Rolling Stone Magazine*

134

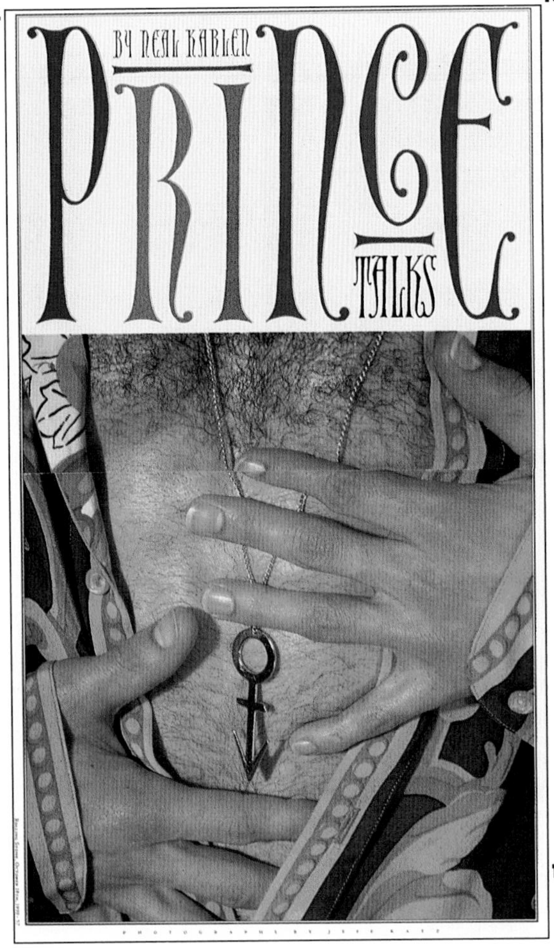

135

136

137

138

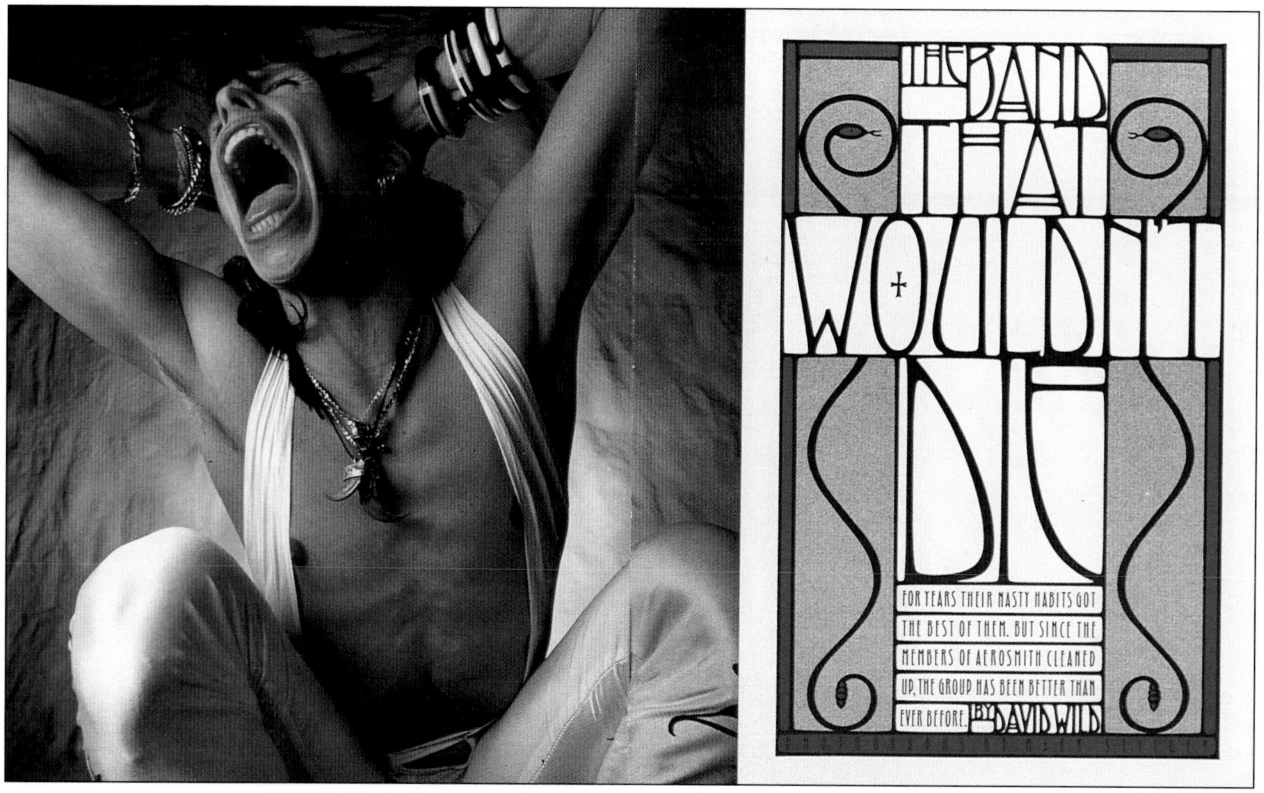

139

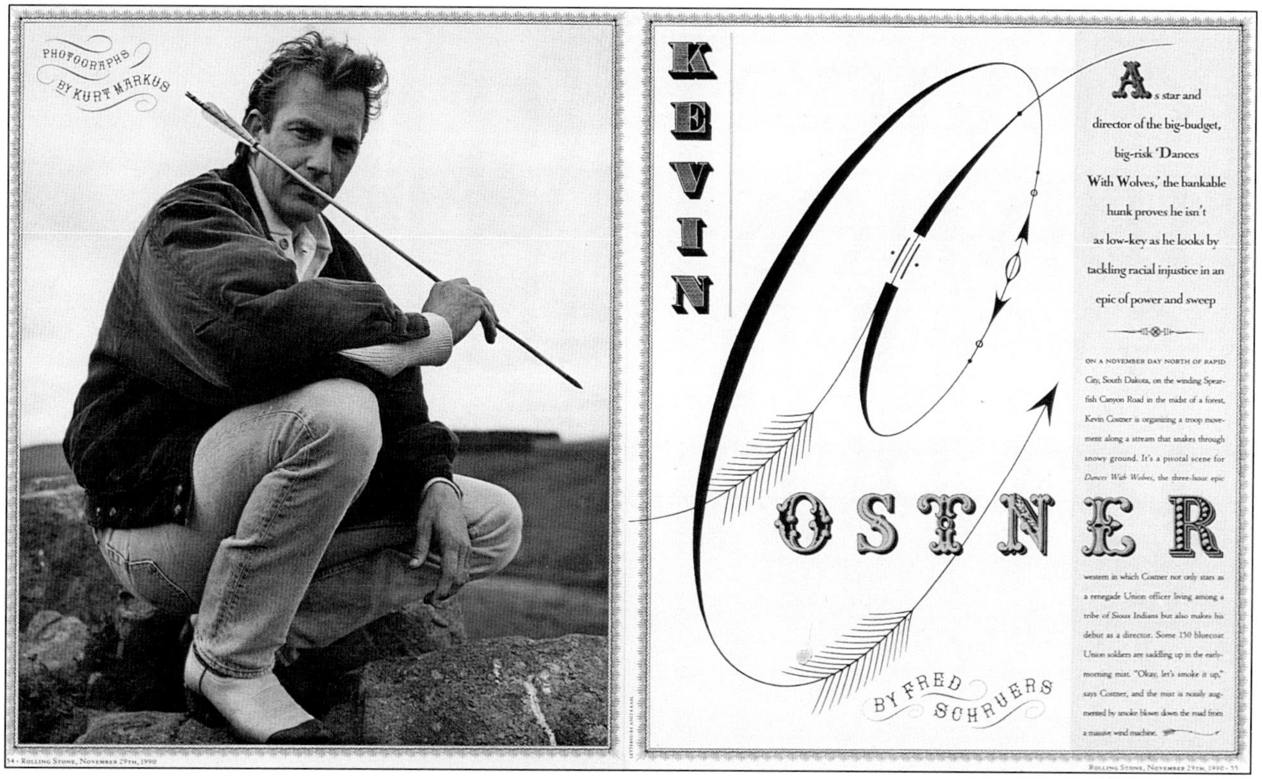

138
DESIGN FIRM: *Rolling Stone Magazine In-house*
DESIGNER: *Debra Bishop*
LETTERER: *Anita Karl*
HEADLINE TYPEFACE: *Shriften*
CLIENT: *Rolling Stone Magazine*

139
DESIGN FIRM: *Rolling Stone Magazine In-house*
DESIGNER: *Debra Bishop*
LETTERER: *Anita Karl*
HEADLINE TYPEFACE: *Wood Type*
TEXT TYPEFACE: *Cloister*
CLIENT: *Rolling Stone Magazine*

140
DESIGN FIRM: *Dennis Ortiz-Lopez*
DESIGNER: *Fred Woodward*
LETTERER: *Dennis Ortiz-Lopez*
HEADLINE TYPEFACE: *Handlettering*
CLIENT: *Rolling Stone Magazine*

141
DESIGN FIRM: *Dennis Ortiz-Lopez*
DESIGNER: *Fred Woodward and Dennis Ortiz-Lopez*
LETTERER: *Dennis Ortiz-Lopez*
HEADLINE TYPEFACE: *Handlettering*
CLIENT: *Rolling Stone Magazine*

142
DESIGN FIRM: *Dennis Ortiz-Lopez*
DESIGNER: *Gail Anderson and Fred Woodward*
LETTERER: *Dennis Ortiz-Lopez*
HEADLINE TYPEFACE: *Handlettering*
CLIENT: *Rolling Stone Magazine*

143
DESIGN FIRM: *Rolling Stone Magazine In-house*
DESIGNER: *Fred Woodward*
LETTERER: *Dennis Ortiz-Lopez*
HEADLINE TYPEFACE: *Empire Modified with Latin Serifs and Caslon 540 Italic with Swash*
CLIENT: *Rolling Stone Magazine*

140
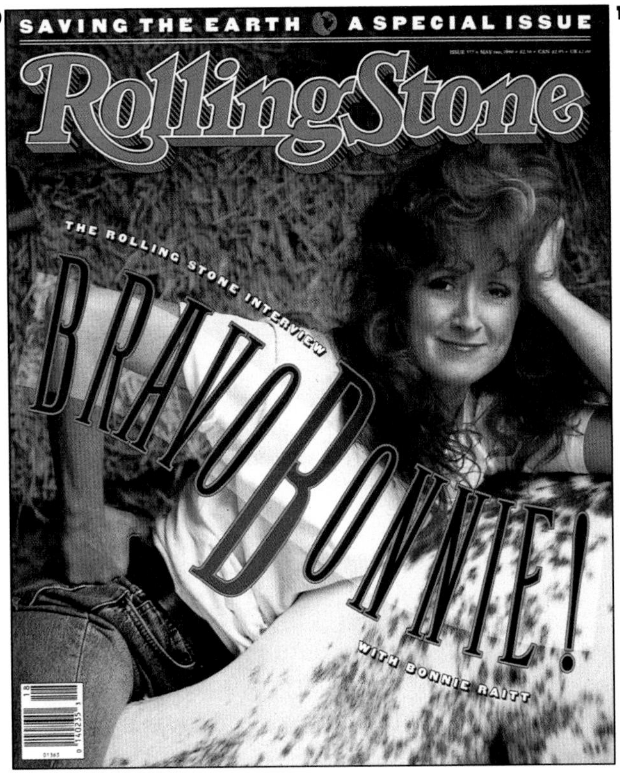

141
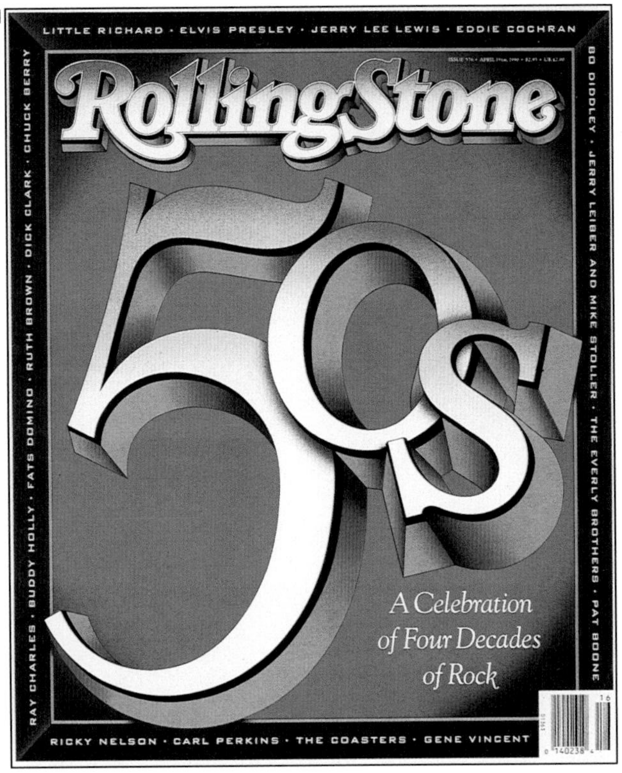

142
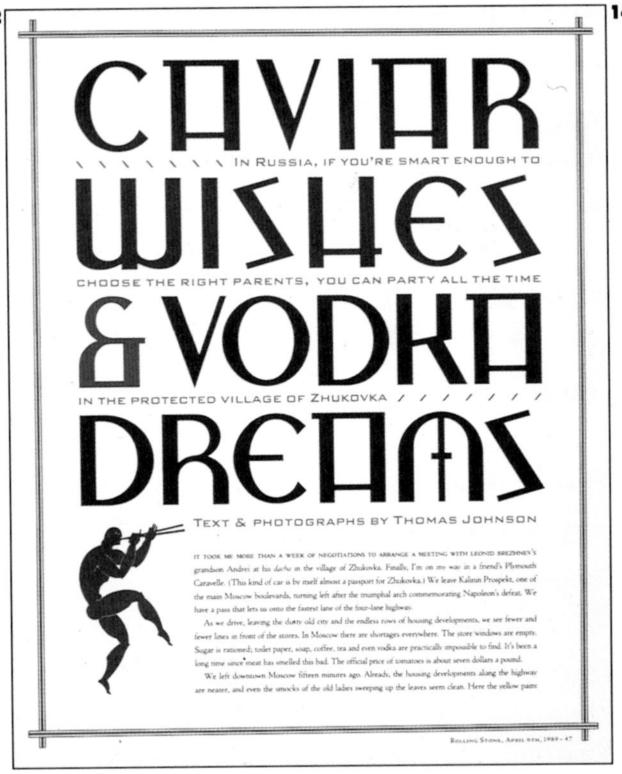

143

144

O'CON
NOR
O'Connor has emerged as the decade's first new superstar
44 • Rolling Stone, June 14th, 1990
PHOTOGRAPHS BY ANDREW MACPHERSON

145

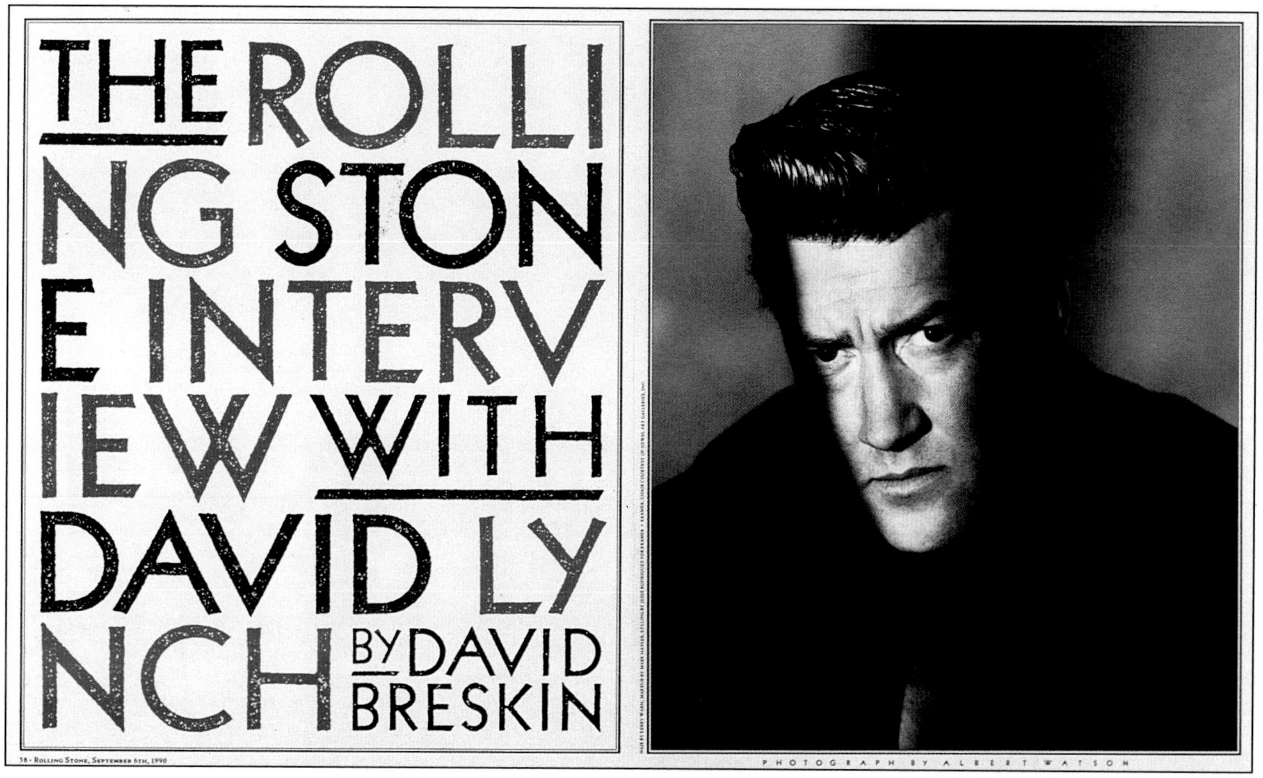

144
DESIGN FIRM: *Rolling Stone Magazine In-house*
DESIGNER: *Fred Woodward*
LETTERER: *Dennis Ortiz-Lopez*
HEADLINE TYPEFACE: *Empite Modified with Latin Serifs and Caslon 540 Italic with Swash*
CLIENT: *Rolling Stone Magazine*

145
DESIGN FIRM: *Rolling Stone Magazine In-house*
DESIGNER: *Fred Woodward*
HEADLINE TYPEFACE: *Kabel*
CLIENT: *Rolling Stone Magazine*

146

146
DESIGN FIRM: *Rolling Stone Magazine In-house*
DESIGNER: *Gail Anderson*
LETTERER: *Gail Anderson*
HEADLINE TYPEFACE: *Handlettering*
TEXT TYPEFACE: *Handlettering*
CLIENT: *Rolling Stone Magazine*

147

147
DESIGN FIRM: *Rolling Stone Magazine In-house*
DESIGNER: *Fred Woodward and Gail Anderson*
LETTERER: *Josh Gosfield*
HEADLINE TYPEFACE: *Handlettering*
CLIENT: *Rolling Stone Magazine*

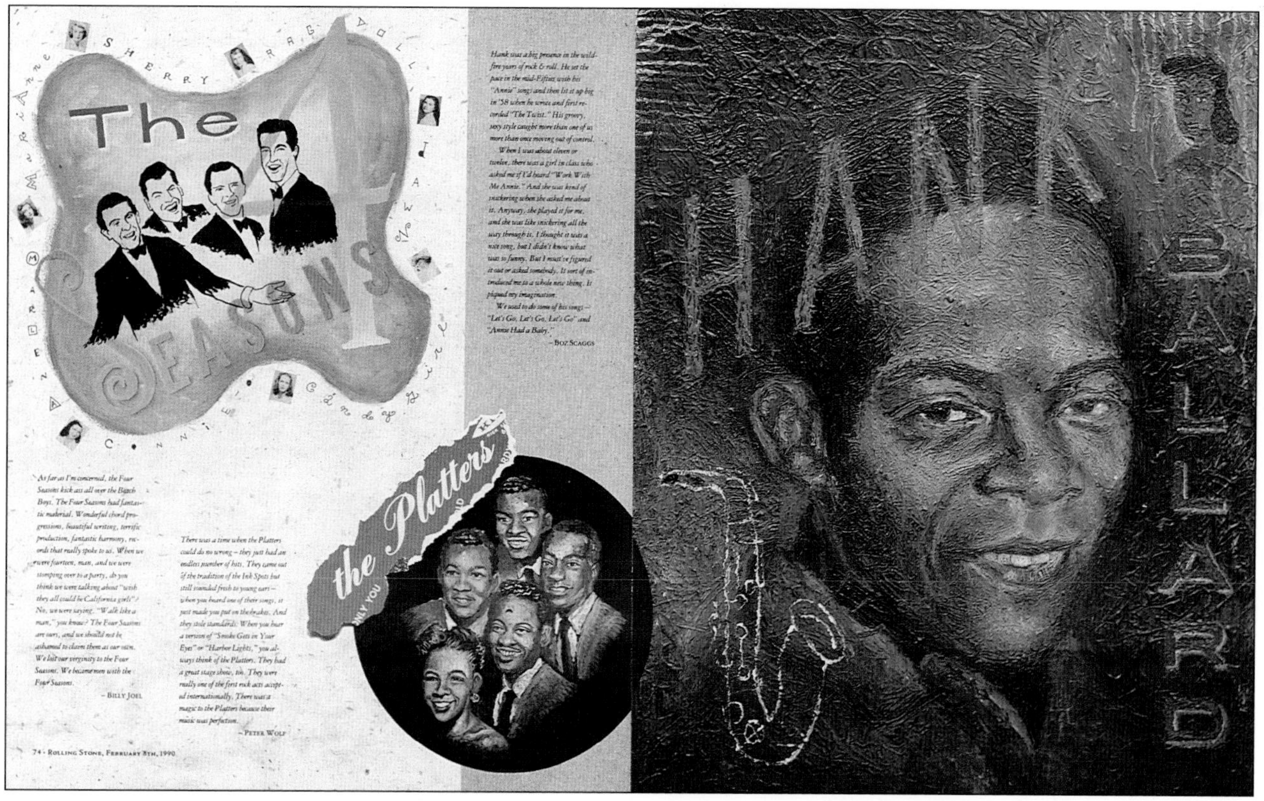

148

DESIGN FIRM: *Rolling Stone Magazine In-house*
DESIGNER: *Fred Woodward and Gail Anderson*
LETTERER: *Josh Gosfield*
HEADLINE TYPEFACE: *Handlettering*
CLIENT: *Rolling Stone Magazine*

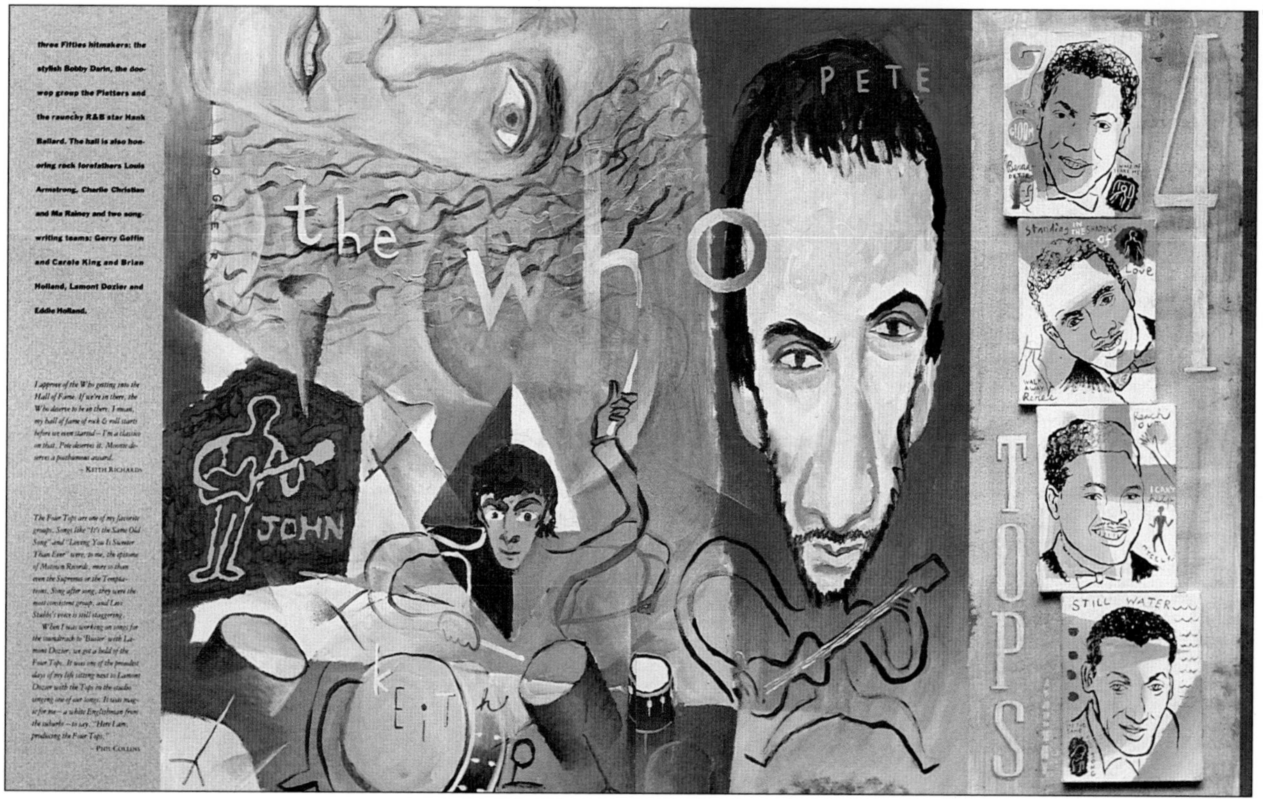

149

DESIGN FIRM: *Rolling Stone Magazine In-house*
DESIGNER: *Fred Woodward and Gail Anderson*
LETTERER: *Josh Gosfield*
HEADLINE TYPEFACE: *Handlettering*
CLIENT: *Rolling Stone Magazine*

150
DESIGN FIRM: *Dennis Ortez-Lopez*
DESIGNER: *Fred Woodward and Gail Anderson*
LETTERER: *Dennis Ortiz-Lopz*
HEADLINE TYPEFACE: *Handlettering*
TEXT TYPEFACE: *Cloister*
CLIENT: *Rolling Stone Magazine*

151
DESIGN FIRM: *Entertainment Weekly Magazine In-house*
DESIGNER: *Mark Michaelson*
HEADLINE TYPEFACE: *Bureau Grotesque 13*
TEXT TYPEFACE: *Century Expanded*
CLIENT: *Entertainment Weekly Magazine*

150

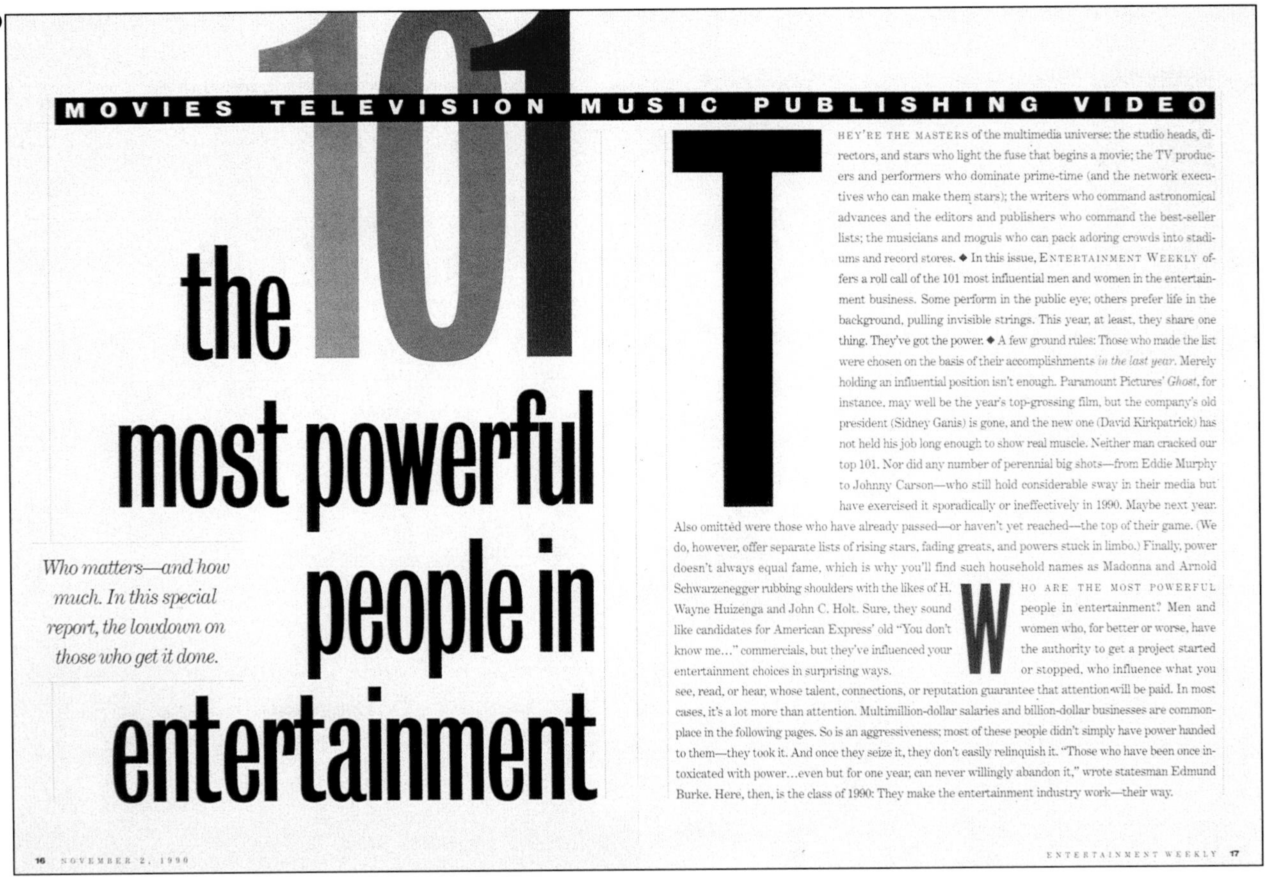
MOVIES TELEVISION MUSIC PUBLISHING VIDEO

the 101 most powerful people in entertainment

Who matters—and how much. In this special report, the lowdown on those who get it done.

THEY'RE THE MASTERS of the multimedia universe: the studio heads, directors, and stars who light the fuse that begins a movie; the TV producers and performers who dominate prime-time (and the network executives who can make them stars); the writers who command astronomical advances and the editors and publishers who command the best-seller lists; the musicians and moguls who can pack adoring crowds into stadiums and record stores. ◆ In this issue, ENTERTAINMENT WEEKLY offers a roll call of the 101 most influential men and women in the entertainment business. Some perform in the public eye; others prefer life in the background, pulling invisible strings. This year, at least, they share one thing. They've got the power. ◆ A few ground rules: Those who made the list were chosen on the basis of their accomplishments *in the last year*. Merely holding an influential position isn't enough. Paramount Pictures' *Ghost*, for instance, may well be the year's top-grossing film, but the company's old president (Sidney Ganis) is gone, and the new one (David Kirkpatrick) has not held his job long enough to show real muscle. Neither man cracked our top 101. Nor did any number of perennial big shots—from Eddie Murphy to Johnny Carson—who still hold considerable sway in their media but have exercised it sporadically or ineffectively in 1990. Maybe next year. Also omitted were those who have already passed—or haven't yet reached—the top of their game. (We do, however, offer separate lists of rising stars, fading greats, and powers stuck in limbo.) Finally, power doesn't always equal fame, which is why you'll find such household names as Madonna and Arnold Schwarzenegger rubbing shoulders with the likes of H. Wayne Huizenga and John C. Holt. Sure, they sound like candidates for American Express' old "You don't know me..." commercials, but they've influenced your entertainment choices in surprising ways.

WHO ARE THE MOST POWERFUL people in entertainment? Men and women who, for better or worse, have the authority to get a project started or stopped, who influence what you see, read, or hear, whose talent, connections, or reputation guarantee that attention will be paid. In most cases, it's a lot more than attention. Multimillion-dollar salaries and billion-dollar businesses are commonplace in the following pages. So is an aggressiveness; most of these people didn't simply have power handed to them—they took it. And once they seize it, they don't easily relinquish it. "Those who have been once intoxicated with power...even but for one year, can never willingly abandon it," wrote statesman Edmund Burke. Here, then, is the class of 1990: They make the entertainment industry work—their way.

16 NOVEMBER 2, 1990 ENTERTAINMENT WEEKLY 17

151

BY JEFF COPLON

SKINHEAD NATIONS

They love to party, they love to rock, they love to kick heads in with their steel-toed boots. They're the skinheads, the fastest-growing and scariest segment of the racist right.

AT BOB HEICK'S SPARE BACHELOR FLAT AT 312 PARNASSUS, just a few blocks up a hill from Haight Street, in San Francisco, four Nazi skinheads are about to listen to their favorite song.

"The bands I like and the bands we listen to are bands you guys don't say shit about, Mr. Music Journalist," Heick tells me, with a hauteur too thick to drip, as he fumbles through a stack of albums.

Then he finds it: "When the Boat Comes In," an early classic by Skrewdriver of England, the world's premier white-power skinhead band. The song is a simple pub sing-along, catchy and monotonous. But it is pushed for all it's worth by the raspy singer, Ian Stuart, who moonlights as an organizer for Britain's National Front, which is what you get when you cross a parliamentary party with a race riot.

Put up a fence,
Close down the borders,
They don't fit in
In our new order.

"It's fuckin' rad," Heick exclaims. "It's the fuckin' anthem for *years*."

All four are singing along with the cheap stereo: Heick, a solidly built twenty-year-old who manufactures rage ("That's *bullshit!*" he screams when I suggest that skinheads pick more fights than they admit) and has let his hair grow out a bit to land a day-shift job in a mail room; Dewey, also twenty, a shy smiler whose freshly shaven pink scalp gleams like a newborn gerbil; Rick, 19, lanky and self-contained, the son of a lawyer, with a blond fuzz clipped as short as a stuffed Pooh bear's; and Patty, 17, a chesty doctor's aide, who has come straight

BOB HEICK (LEFT) WITH STORMTROOP FIVE MEMBERS SPENCER (CENTER) AND DEWEY

PHOTOGRAPHS BY BRIAN SMALE

152

P O W E R 101 P E O P L E

1

MICHAEL
EISNER

CHAIRMAN/CEO, DISNEY

Michael Eisner, 48, chairman/CEO of the Walt Disney Company, has the touch. "If I do things I believe in, they tend to be good for the shareholders," he says. "If you try to outsmart any piece of the population, it never works. So you might as well do what you think is right. So far, it's worked out pretty well."

For Eisner's definition of "pretty well," see *Pretty Woman*, 1990's box-office Cinderella—complete with a last-minute happy ending and $175 million in nationwide ticket sales. Then add in Disney's more traditional fare—*The Little Mermaid* won two Oscars this year and made more than $250 million in theatrical and video releases. The list of successes goes on. Under Eisner, the Mickey Mouse business he took over in 1984 has increased its earnings sevenfold, to $703.3 million last year, on revenues of $4.59 billion.

Movies now occupy just one corner of Eisner's Magic Kingdom. The company's TV division produces *The Golden Girls* and a new Disney hour for NBC, and recent additions include Orlando's Disney–MGM Studios Theme Park, movie and music divisions Hollywood Pictures and Hollywood Records, and children's-book publisher Disney Press. Even Eisner's philanthropic ideas have synergistic fallout: The Disney Channel's *American Teacher Awards* (Nov. 4) will also serve as a nice plug for the cable series *The Disney Channel Salutes the American Teacher*. The result, says Eisner, is "good for the Disney Channel, good for our shareholders, good for everybody."

"It's very hard topping yourself," Eisner asserts. "To protect the sky from falling, you have to work harder to keep doing things that are innovative. I'm constantly nervous about finding that one good idea. That really is the pressure."

2

MICHAEL
OVITZ

CHAIRMAN, CREATIVE ARTISTS AGENCY

Michael Ovitz, 43, chairman of Creative Artists Agency, has signed 650 of Hollywood's biggest names by the simple expedient of making CAA's clients (including Tom Cruise, Madonna, Cher, and Sylvester Stallone) scandalously rich and unprecedentedly powerful. CAA squeezes unheard-of deals out of studios because, more than any talent agency in the U.S., it can combine stars, scripts and directors into big-name bankable talent "packages."

CAA has packaged 150 movies, including *Rain Man, Born On the Fourth of July* (which earned two Oscars and $69.7 million) and 1991's Peter Pan story *Hook*, involving CAA clients Steven Spielberg, Dustin Hoffman, and Robin Williams. At its best, Ovitz's strategy allows CAA to function as a mega-studio.

Last year, when Ovitz advised Sony in its $3.5 billion buyout of Columbia Pictures, it was rumored that he rejected Sony's request to run Columbia. Amazingly, Ovitz could actually *lose* power as a studio chief. He's currently setting up Matsushita's bid for MCA Inc., the biggest (an estimated $7 billion) potential deal in Hollywood history.

It's not surprising that Ovitz, who has reportedly taken Asian philosophy courses at UCLA, has been likened to a Zen master, a shogun, and a ninja warrior by those who study him. The labels enhance his growing mystique, and so does his careful avoidance of publicity.

Except for an acrimonious, embarrassingly public break with screenwriter Joe Eszterhas (*Jagged Edge*), who left CAA for rival ICM last year, Ovitz has kept his dealings out of the public eye. But the quieter he is, the louder his reputation roars. With a corporate philosophy direct from Japan Inc., Ovitz has brought the wisdom of the East to a business that runs like the Wild West.

POWER TEAM

The 101 Most Powerful issue was written by Tim Appelo, Giselle Benatar, Margot Dougherty, Mark Harris, Gregg Kilday, Kelli Pryor, and Benjamin Svetkey. It was reported by Michael Angeli, Martha Babcock, Meredith Berkman, Jess Cagle, David Craig, Steve Daly, Melina Gerosa, Roberta Grant, Kate Meyers, Jim Oberman, and Anne Thompson. The issue was edited by Steven Reddicliffe and Alison Gwinn.

ICON KEY

TELEVISION
MUSIC
MOVIES
VIDEO
PUBLISHING
KIDS

ICONS DESIGNED BY JONATHAN HOEFLER. EISNER: MARK HANAUER/ONYX. OVITZ: ANTHONY BARBOZA

18 NOVEMBER 2, 1990

ENTERTAINMENT WEEKLY 19

153

P O W E R 101 P E O P L E

3

BARRY
DILLER

CHAIRMAN/CEO, FOX

In his 20s, ABC programming executive Barry Diller invented the miniseries. In his 30s, he became chairman/CEO of Paramount Pictures Corporation and oversaw such megahits as *Saturday Night Fever* and *Raiders of the Lost Ark*. What happens when a wunderkind gets to his 40s? If you're Diller, you start your own TV network.

When Diller, chairman and CEO of Fox Inc., introduced Fox TV in 1986, he faced ridicule from his competitors—NBC's Brandon Tartikoff joked that Fox's TV stations had the power of a coat hanger. But Diller, 48, claims Fox has become "a player," and the numbers support him: great demographics, growing ratings, and, in *The Simpsons*, 1990's most successful new prime-time show. This year, Fox TV is even showing a $35 million profit—a number expected to double in 1991. Add to that Diller's other fiefdom, Twentieth Century Fox Film Corporation, which has stepped up production and will release up to 25 movies next year, and his entertainment empire's reach becomes vast.

Nicknamed "killer Diller" for his fiercely combative leadership style, Diller has fought aggressively to make Fox a contender. This year, he got an FCC waiver allowing Fox to produce and own 18½ hours of programming weekly (networks are generally barred from producing most of their shows). Even bolder was sending *The Simpsons* head-to-head against NBC's *Cosby Show*, a gamble that paid off when the cartoon clan's season premiere outdrew *Cosby* and scored its highest rating ever. Fox's growth isn't without bumps—its announced expansion to five nights has been temporarily cut to four—but few at the Big Three are laughing anymore. These days, Diller's plan to create a full-size, fourth prime-time network seems like an extremely possible dream.

4

STEVE
ROSS

CHAIRMAN/CO-CEO, TIME WARNER

In his first year sharing the helm of the world's largest media company, Steve Ross has been busy. In addition to working out the final details of the merger between Time Inc. and Warner Communications Inc., the new co-CEO (the other is Nicholas J. Nicholas Jr.) has helped keep the company on something of a roll. In television, Time Warner continues to score high ratings with such baby-boomer favorites as *Murphy Brown* and popular new shows for more youthful viewers, like *Tiny Toon Adventures*. Amid the summer's noisy, ultraviolent action films, the classy *Presumed Innocent* drew impressively well (grossing $83 million), and the company's fall movie line-up includes Martin Scorsese's *GoodFellas* and *Reversal of Fortune*, about the Claus von Bülow murder trial. Coming for Christmas: the film version of Tom Wolfe's best-selling novel *Bonfire of the Vanities*, with Tom Hanks and Bruce Willis. The corporation's music division had hits with Madonna and Prince, and its magazine division began publishing ENTERTAINMENT WEEKLY last February. The new Time Warner Enterprises president, former MTV chief Robert Pittman, plans to launch a cable-television legal channel early next year. Time Publishing Ventures, a new publishing unit of the company, will market the first issue of the magazine *Martha Stewart Living* this month.

In his new role Ross continues to concentrate on what he does best: the personal discovery, development and cultivation of entertainment talent. His stars are first and foremost his friends, and his empire is built on loyalty.

Ross, who started out in the 1950s as a funeral-home director, is a congenital optimist. *The Wall Street Journal* recently called him "the most bullish company chairman in the U.S." Despite the current depression of media and entertainment stocks, Ross' personal holdings of Time Warner shares, he vows, "are going to make me more money than I've ever made in my life." Considering the unprecedented stack of cash Ross has made so far, that is no small boast.

5

BRANDON
TARTIKOFF

CHAIRMAN, NBC ENTERTAINMENT GROUP

When Brandon Tartikoff moved up from president of NBC Entertainment to the new position of chairman last July, one reason was that there wasn't much left to achieve in his old job. As the man in charge of scheduling at NBC, he had guided the network from third place in 1984 to five straight seasons as No. 1, a position it narrowly retains this fall. Tartikoff's new role allows him even more authority in production and dealmaking, but he already misses life in the trenches.

"It's been ups and downs," admits the 41-year-old master programmer. "There are days when I feel frustrated because I've removed myself too far from the product, and other days when my clarity of focus has never been better, primarily because I'm not in every single pitch meeting. That part of it's been great. But I can't say it's been easy."

Tartikoff's touch remains evident in such programming strategies as October's successful use of Jackie Collins and Danielle Steel adaptations against CBS' baseball coverage. In addition, although his longtime No. 2 man, Warren Littlefield (see the Powers In Limbo list), has assumed his boss' former duties, some say Tartikoff himself is still rearranging the ever-changeable prime-time schedule.

In his new position, Tartikoff will oversee production of shows through NBC Productions. "We're just starting to bring to fruition some of the international co-production ventures we've been working on," he says. He won't be more specific about his next move, except jokingly. "If I had to guess," he muses, "I'll be at the Betty Ford Center for Nielsen Withdrawal."

6

THOMAS
POLLOCK

CHAIRMAN, UNIVERSAL PICTURES

When Thomas Pollock was named chairman of MCA's Universal Motion Picture Group in 1986, cynics scoffed at the idea of a lawyer, even an entertainment lawyer whose clients included George Lucas and Ron Howard, running a movie studio. Sure, Pollock knew how to make deals—which he quickly proved by persuading Arnold Schwarzenegger, Danny DeVito, and producer-director Ivan Reitman to forgo upfront salaries in favor of a bigger chunk of the box-office take so *Twins* could be made for a below-average $15 million. But how would he know *which* deals and *what* pictures to make?

What the critics didn't realize is that the 47-year-old Pollock is a longtime film buff with a genuine appreciation for movie talent. And his eclectic taste has served Universal well. Not only has he revived the studio's fortunes (from box-office grosses of $306 million in 1987 to $833 million in 1989) with commercial entertainments like *Twins* (which grossed $112 million), he has also bet on such iconoclastic filmmakers as Martin Scorsese (*The Last Temptation of Christ*) and Spike Lee (*Do the Right Thing*). In mixing mass with class, Pollock has demonstrated that success doesn't always stem from a pursuit of the lowest common denominator.

While Universal hasn't abandoned blockbusters—witness the forthcoming *Kindergarten Cop*, with Schwarzenegger—Pollock has demonstrated that aiming smaller movies at specific audiences can also be lucrative. "I wouldn't make a movie that I didn't believe would be profitable. But that doesn't mean that you always go into it believing it's going to be hugely profitable. It's all about the mix."

DILLER: JONATHAN LEVINE. ROSS: SMEAL/GALELLA LTD. TARTIKOFF: BONNIE SCHIFFMAN/ONYX. POLLOCK: MARK HANAUER/ONYX

20 NOVEMBER 2, 1990

ENTERTAINMENT WEEKLY 21

152/153

DESIGN FIRM: *Entertainment Weekly Magazine In-house*

DESIGNER: *Mark Michaelson*

HEADLINE TYPEFACE: *Bureau Grotesque 13*

TEXT TYPEFACE: *Century Expanded*

CLIENT: *Entertainment Weekly Magazine*

154

P O W E R 101 P E O P L E

7
SUMNER
REDSTONE

media conglomerates in the world. As chairman and 84 percent owner of Viacom Inc., he controls MTV Networks (which operates MTV, VH-1, Nickelodeon/Nick at Nite, and HA!), the Showtime and Movie Channel networks, Viacom Productions (which makes *Jake and the Fatman*, *Matlock*, and Perry Mason TV movies), and Viacom Enterprises (which syndicates thousands of hours of reruns, including *The Cosby Show* and *The Honeymooners*). Working for him are such high-powered executives as Frank Biondi (president and CEO, Viacom International) and Tom Freston (chairman and CEO, MTV Networks). Viacom also owns 5 TV stations, 14 radio stations, and 14 cable systems. Redstone's personal fortune has been estimated at $2.3 billion; Viacom's assets in June were estimated at $3.9 billion.

"I've never been motivated by money or power," says the Harvard Law School graduate. "I've just tried to do the best job I could, no matter what I was doing."

CHAIRMAN, VIACOM

One morning 11 years ago, Sumner Redstone awakened to find his Boston hotel room on fire. With no chance for escape, he climbed out a window, clung to the sill, and waited until help arrived. Severely burned, he underwent five operations lasting over 70 hours. "The doctors didn't think I'd live," the billionaire once recalled. "I sometimes think about that when I'm hitting a tennis ball."

This remarkable force of will has helped Redstone, 67, parlay two drive-in theaters inherited from his father into a 650-movie-screen operation and one of the largest

8
ARNOLD
SCHWARZENEGGER

Judgment Day. All this for a guy who might be described (from a safe distance) as muscle-bound, and whose Austrian-accented English does not always flow trippingly from his tongue. Not that it matters. From 1977's *Pumping Iron* to the amusing *Conan the Barbarian*, *The Terminator*, and *Predator*, he has made a career of flaunting his limitations and then surpassing them. To those who said he couldn't do comedy, he responded with the 1988 blockbuster *Twins*. In answer to those who said he was more brawn than brain, he built a real-estate empire and a reputation as one of Hollywood's shrewdest stars. The gap-toothed grin, deadpan jock humor, and agile bulk draws crowds from the Riviera to Lenin Square—his movies on video are expensive black-market items in the Soviet Union.

Ever since Schwarzenegger's marital merger with Shriver, there has been speculation that he may someday step into the political ring. "The joy in public office is a tremendous idea," he has said. "I think it could be the greatest challenge yet."

MOVIE ACTOR

One-time Mr. World, five-time Mr. Universe, seven-time Mr. Olympia, and full-time Mr. Maria Shriver, Arnold Schwarzenegger, 43, has been edging toward a new title in recent years: World's Biggest Movie Star.

In 1990, his box-office muscle nearly matched his gargantuan physique. *Total Recall* earned $8 million in one day, just a shade under his reported personal take of $11 million (plus 15 percent of the profits). The star will next flex his professional lats in this winter's *Kindergarten Cop*, and then appear next summer in *Terminator 2:*

9
H. WAYNE
HUIZENGA

CHAIRMAN/CEO,
BLOCKBUSTER
ENTERTAINMENT CORP.

He set out on the road to success riding a trash truck. In 1962, H. Wayne Huizenga started a waste disposal company; by 1971, when his firm merged with Waste Management Inc., Huizenga was hauling in $10 million a year—and he proceeded to guide the company into the billions. Having cleaned up in the garbage business, Huizenga retired and in 1987, with two associates, bought a major interest in Blockbuster. He has since expanded the chain from 19 stores to nearly 1,500 and expects revenues of more than $1 billion this year.

Blockbuster rents nearly 1 million tapes a day—one for every three people who buy movie tickets—giving Huizenga the power to turn a box-office flop into...well, a blockbuster. Hollywood movie companies pay their respects by wining and dining Blockbuster employees at conventions. But Huizenga, whose company is based in Fort Lauderdale, isn't impressed by his own impact. "I don't have time to think about it," he says. "We're too busy opening up new stores." Blockbuster is opening them at the rate of one a day. "We go through hundreds of low-budget movies a month" Huizenga says, "trying to decide on 60 or 70 new titles to stock." He won't carry X-rated tapes, and NC-17 movies will be approved case by case, though his blessing would give the new adults-only rating the kind of legitimacy it needs.

Huizenga proudly calls his company "the McDonald's of video stores." But unlike the burger business, Blockbuster doesn't have to take responsibility for the cuisine. "If someone rents a movie and doesn't like it," he once said, "they blame Hollywood, not us."

10
GENE & ROGER
SISKEL/EBERT

FILM CRITICS

Roger Ebert, 48, and Gene Siskel, 44, already the most powerful movie critics in history, reached the peak of their influence this year. Each reportedly earns more than $1 million annually for *Siskel & Ebert*, their movie-review show, watched by at least 3 million viewers a week. Siskel also appears on *CBS This Morning*, but this doesn't impress Ebert. "I reach more people than he does, because there's nobody watching TV at that hour," he says. "My column appears in more than 200 papers; he has about a third as many. My *Movie Home Companion* book has about a half-million copies in print. It's *facile* to put him first."

Though they snipe at each other, it is together that they carry the most clout. Eddie Murphy has credited them with the power to kill a film. They can certainly save one: 1981's *My Dinner With André* was about to close when their double-thumbs-up rave propelled it to a wider release and cult status.

Their thumbs pack so much wallop today that they can actually change the way films are made. Early on, "we contributed to the demise of the mad-slasher movie," Siskel boasts. Adds Ebert: "We were the first to do anything on TV about colorization. I feel we've won that battle." Their greatest triumph, though, is the new NC-17 rating. "We were the first on TV to deal with the ratings system," Ebert says. "We can take a certain amount of credit for the fact that the ratings system has been revised."

They have had a few setbacks—most of which seemed to have worked to their advantage. After panning *Nuns on the Run*, the pair were barred for a time from screenings of Fox movies. But Ebert says they've never missed a single Fox product. "We came out of that stronger than ever, because Fox was seen as firing from the hip and shooting themselves in the toe."

22 NOVEMBER 2, 1990 — ENTERTAINMENT WEEKLY 23

155

156

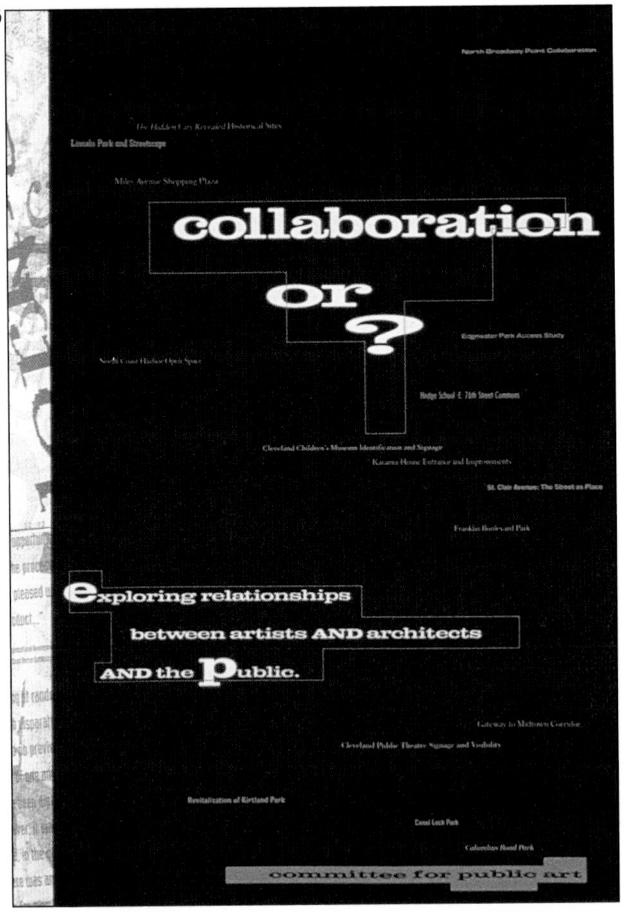

154
DESIGN FIRM: *Entertainment Weekly Magazine In-house*
DESIGNER: *Mark Michaelson*
HEADLINE TYPEFACE: *Bureau Grotesque 13*
TEXT TYPEFACE: *Century Expanded*
CLIENT: *Entertainment Weekly Magazine*

155
DESIGN FIRM: *Koepke Design*
DESIGNER: *Gary Koepke*
HEADLINE TYPEFACE: *Handlettering and Triplex*
TEXT TYPEFACE: *Bauer Bodoni and Futura*
CLIENT: *Bull H.N. Information*

156
DESIGN FIRM: *Pam Cerio Design*
DESIGNER: *Pam Cerio*
HEADLINE TYPEFACE: *Clarendon and Industria*
CLIENT: *Committee for Public Art*

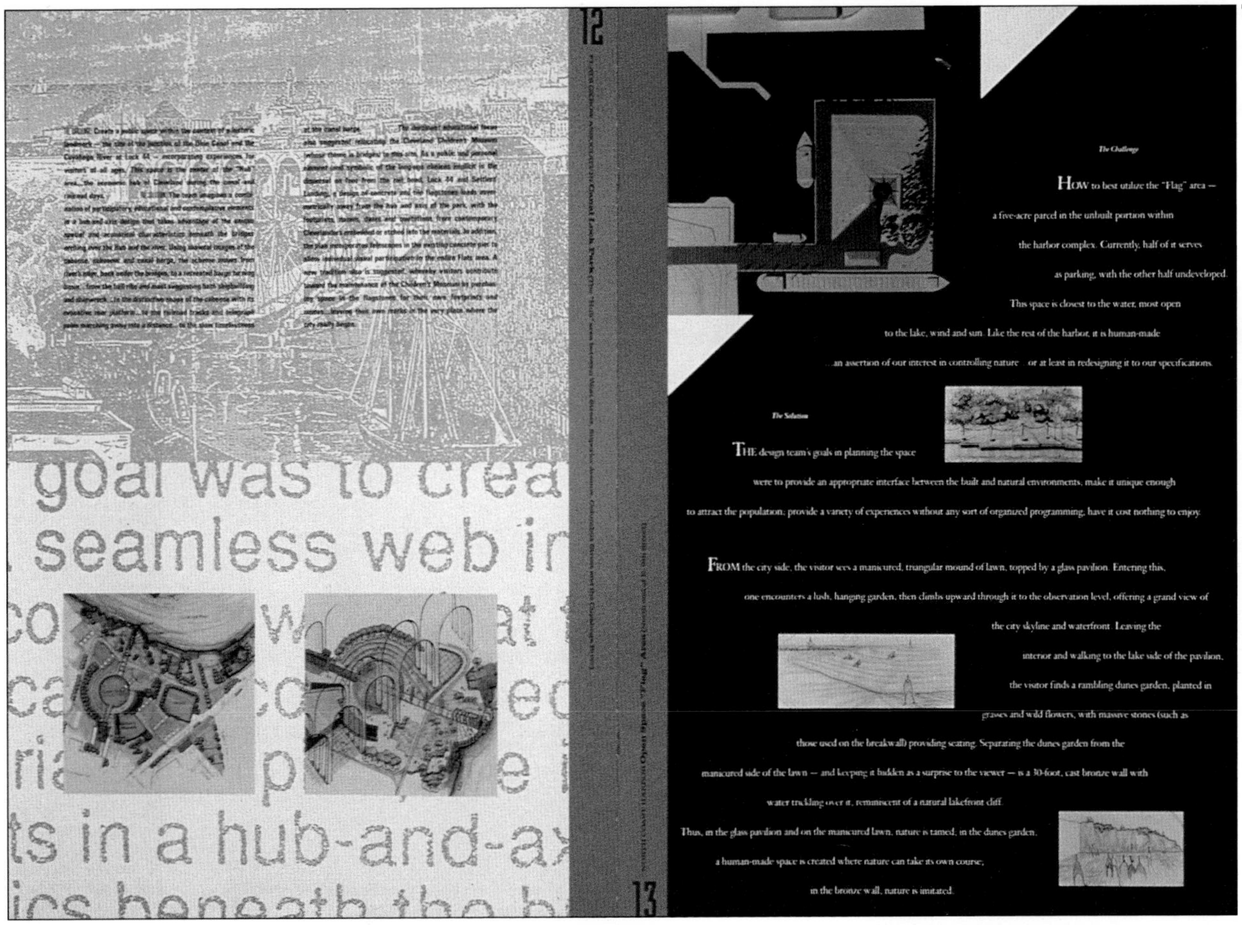

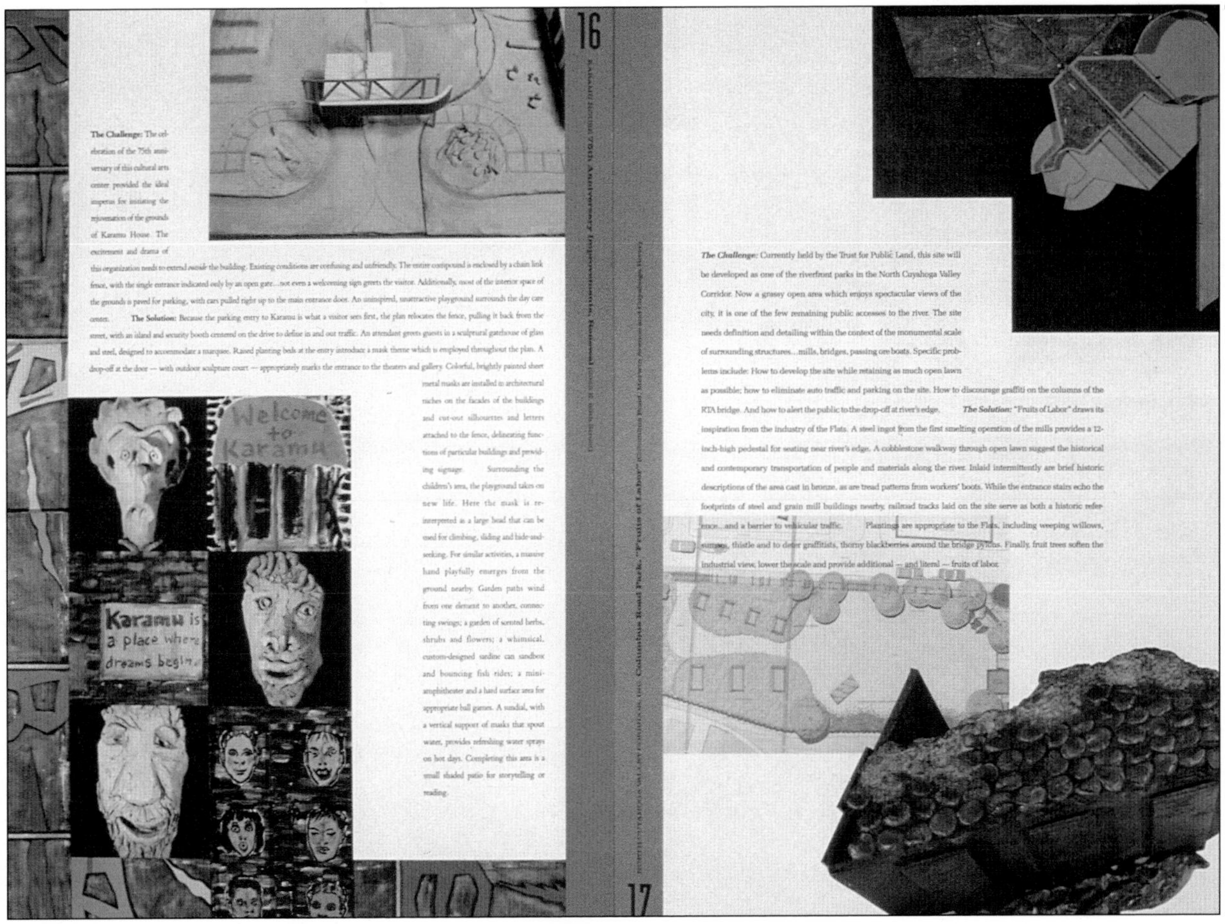

157/158
DESIGN FIRM: *Pam Cerio Design*
DESIGNER: *Pam Cerio*
HEADLINE TYPEFACE: *Clarendon and Industria*
CLIENT: *Committee for Public Art*

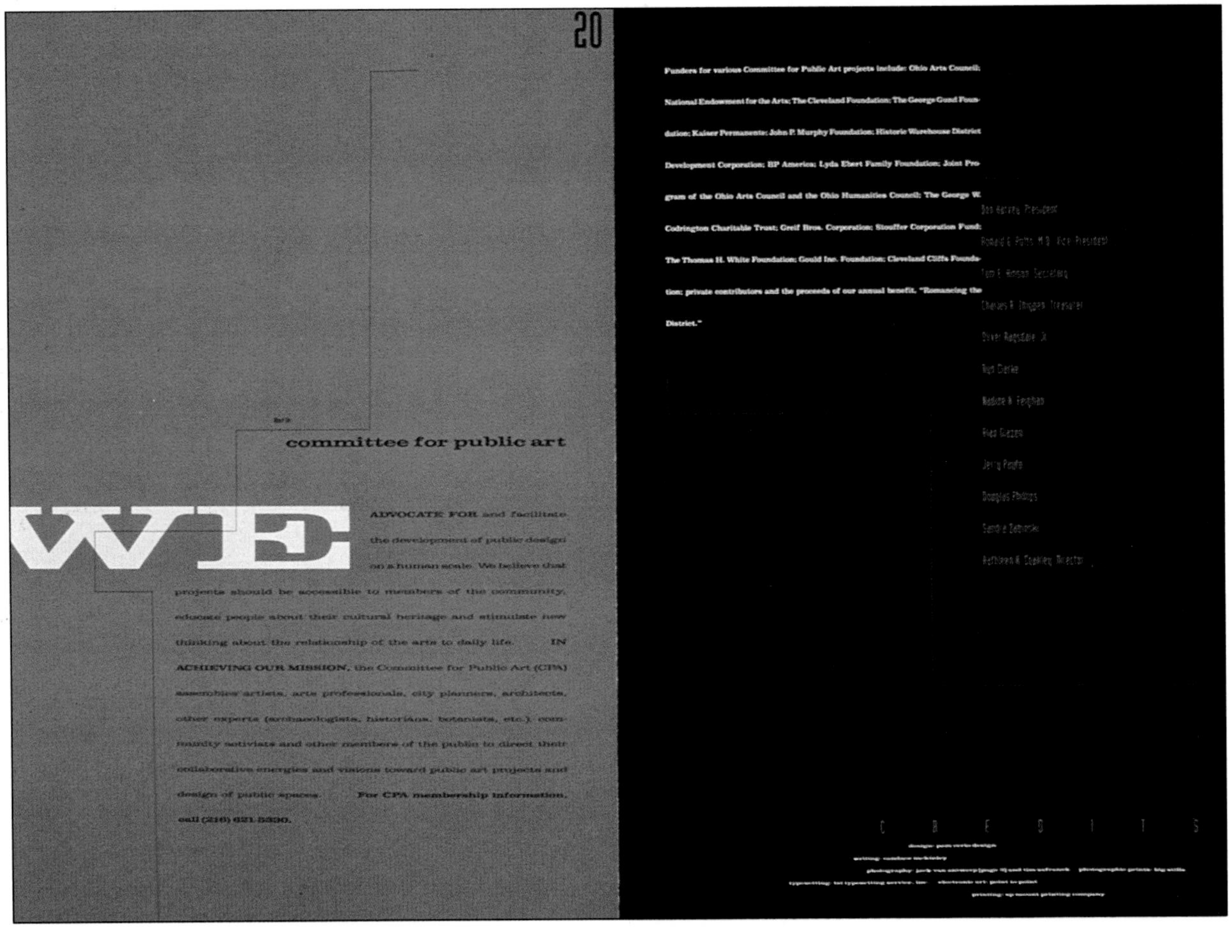

159
DESIGN FIRM: *Pam Cerio Design*
DESIGNER: *Pam Cerio*
HEADLINE TYPEFACE: *Clarendon and Industria*
CLIENT: *Committee for Public Art*

160
DESIGN FIRM: *Mike Salisbury Communications*
DESIGNER: *Damien Gallay*
HEADLINE TYPEFACE: *Helvetica Bodoni*
TEXT TYPEFACE: *Copperplate*
CLIENT: *Gotcha*

161

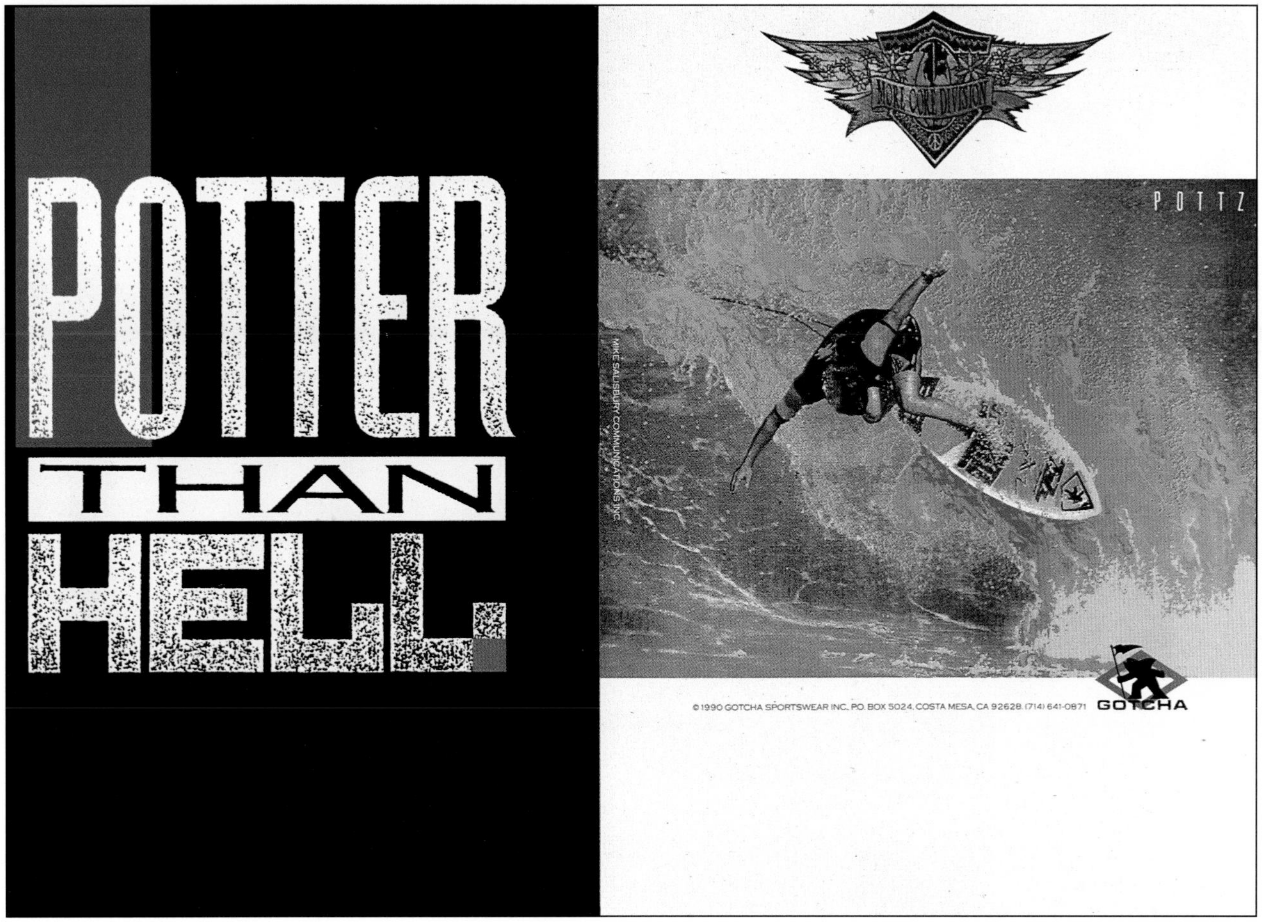

161
DESIGN FIRM: *Mike Salisbury Communications*
DESIGNER: *Damien Gallay*
LETTERER: *Damien Gallay*
HEADLINE TYPEFACE: *Handlettering*
CLIENT: *Gotcha*

162

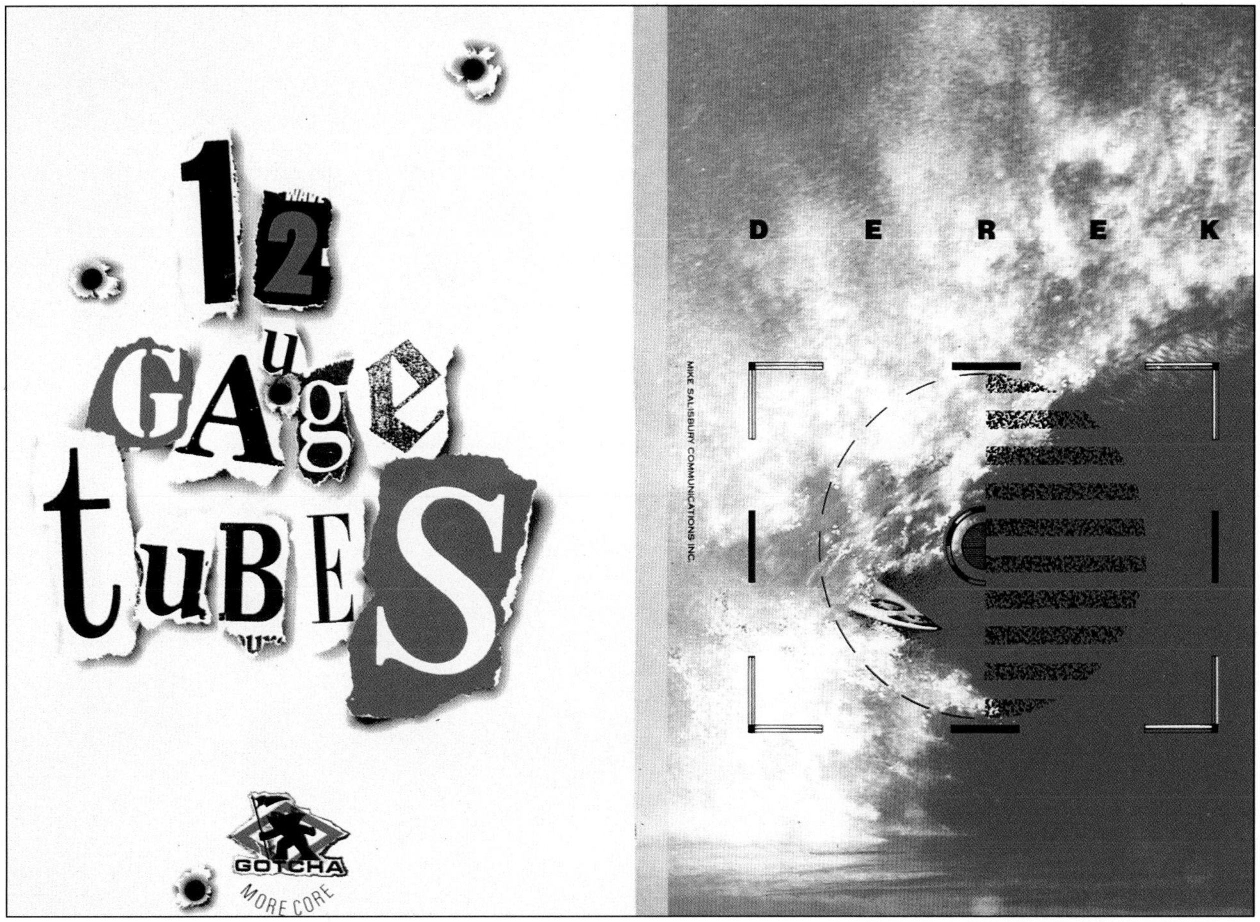

162
DESIGN FIRM: *Mike Salisbury Communications*
DESIGNER: *Damien Gallay*
LETTERER: *Damien Gallay*
HEADLINE TYPEFACE: *Various*
TEXT TYPEFACE: *Univers and Copperplate*
CLIENT: *Gotcha*

163
DESIGN FIRM: *Mike Salisbury Communications*
DESIGNER: *Damien Gallay*
HEADLINE TYPEFACE: *Helvetica and Futura*
TEXT TYPEFACE: *Copperplate*
CLIENT: *Gotcha*

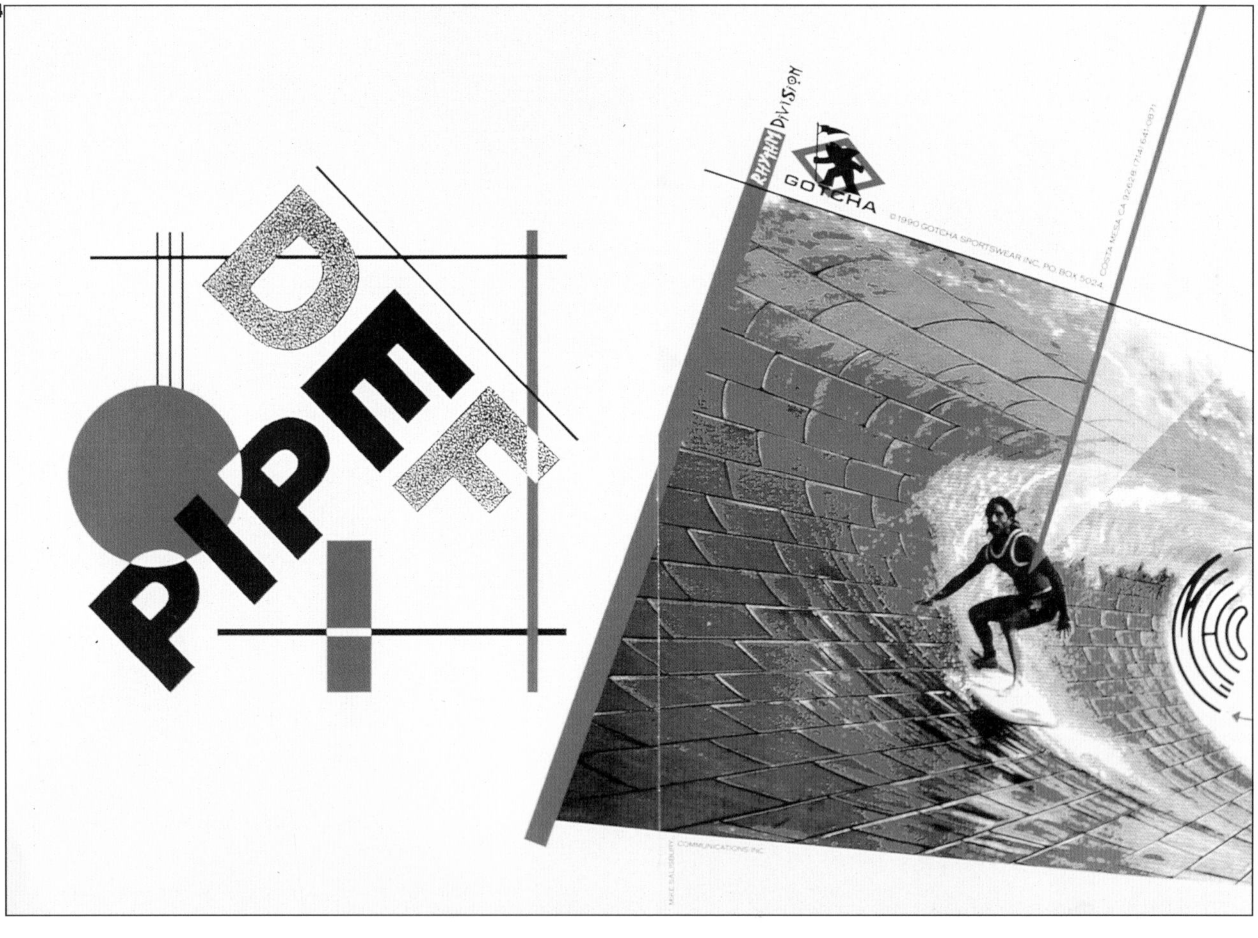

164
DESIGN FIRM: *Mike Salisbury Communications*
DESIGNER: *Damien Gallay*
HEADLINE TYPEFACE: *Helvetica*
TEXT TYPEFACE: *Copperplate*
CLIENT: *Gotcha*

165

166

165
DESIGN FIRM: *Mike Salisbury Communications*
DESIGNER: *Mike Salisbury and Damien Gallay*
LETTERER: *Damien Gallay*
HEADLINE TYPEFACE: *Franklin Gothic Extra Condensed*
TEXT TYPEFACE: *Helvetica*
CLIENT: *Gotcha*

166
DESIGN FIRM: *Mike Salisbury Communications*
DESIGNER: *Damien Gallay*
LETTERER: *Damien Gallay*
HEADLINE TYPEFACE: *Helvetica*
TEXT TYPEFACE: *Copperplate*
CLIENT: *Gotcha*

167
DESIGN FIRM: *Mike Salisbury Communications*
DESIGNER: *Damien Gallay*
LETTERER: *Damien Gallay*
HEADLINE TYPEFACE: *Helvetica and Handlettering*
TEXT TYPEFACE: *Univers and Copperplate*
CLIENT: *Gotcha*

168/169
DESIGN FIRM: *DBD International Ltd.*
DESIGNER: *David Brier*
LETTERER: *David Brier*
HEADLINE TYPEFACE: *Handlettering*
TEXT TYPEFACE: *Goudy Oldstyle*
CLIENT: *Graphic Relief/Studio Magazine*

167

168

169

170

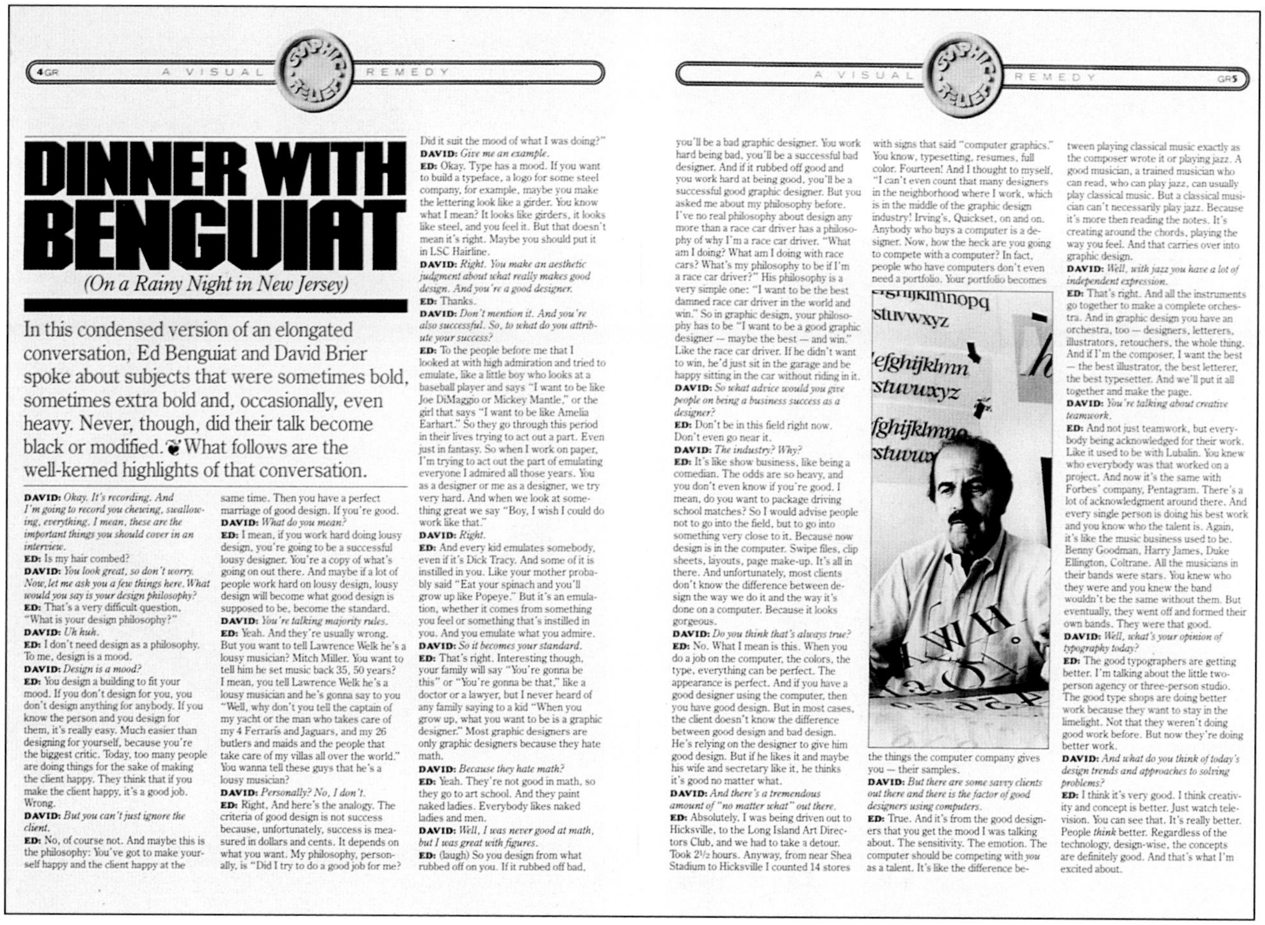

4GR A VISUAL REMEDY

DINNER WITH BENGUIAT

(On a Rainy Night in New Jersey)

In this condensed version of an elongated conversation, Ed Benguiat and David Brier spoke about subjects that were sometimes bold, sometimes extra bold and, occasionally, even heavy. Never, though, did their talk become black or modified. What follows are the well-kerned highlights of that conversation.

DAVID: *Okay. It's recording. And I'm going to record you chewing, swallowing, everything. I mean, these are the important things you should cover in an interview.*
ED: Is my hair combed?
DAVID: *You look great, so don't worry. Now, let me ask you a few things here. What would you say is your design philosophy?*
ED: That's a very difficult question. "What is your design philosophy?"
DAVID: *Uh huh.*
ED: I don't need design as a philosophy. To me, design is a mood.
DAVID: *Design is a mood?*
ED: You design a building to fit your mood. If you don't design for you, you don't design anything for anybody. If you know the person and you design for them, it's really easy. Much easier than designing for yourself, because you're the biggest critic. Today, too many people are doing things for the sake of making the client happy. They think that if you make the client happy, it's a good job. Wrong.
DAVID: *But you can't just ignore the client.*
ED: No, of course not. And maybe this is the philosophy: You've got to make yourself happy and the client happy at the same time. Then you have a perfect marriage of good design. If you're good.
DAVID: *What do you mean?*
ED: I mean, if you work hard doing lousy design, you're going to be a successful lousy designer. You're a copy of what's going on out there. And maybe if a lot of people work hard on lousy design, lousy design will become what good design is supposed to be, become the standard.
DAVID: *You're talking majority rules.*
ED: Yeah. And they're usually wrong. But you want to tell Lawrence Welk he's a lousy musician? Mitch Miller. You want to tell him he set music back 35, 50 years? I mean, you tell Lawrence Welk he's a lousy musician and he's gonna say to you "Well, why don't you tell the captain of my yacht or the man who takes care of my 4 Ferraris and Jaguars, and my 26 butlers and maids and the people that take care of my villas all over the world." You wanna tell these guys that he's a lousy musician?
DAVID: *Personally? No, I don't.*
ED: Right. And here's the analogy. The criteria of good design is not success because, unfortunately, success is measured in dollars and cents. It depends on what you want. My philosophy, personally, is "Did I try to do a good job for me? Did it suit the mood of what I was doing?"
DAVID: *Give me an example.*
ED: Okay. Type has a mood. If you want to build a typeface, a logo for some steel company, for example, maybe you make the lettering look like a girder. You know what I mean? It looks like girders, it looks like steel, and you feel it. But that doesn't mean it's right. Maybe you should put it in LSC Hairline.
DAVID: *Right. You make an aesthetic judgment about what really makes good design. And you're a good designer.*
ED: Thanks.
DAVID: *Don't mention it. And you're also successful. So, to what do you attribute your success?*
ED: To the people before me that I looked at with high admiration and tried to emulate, like a little boy who looks at a baseball player and says "I want to be like Joe DiMaggio or Mickey Mantle," or the girl that says "I want to be like Amelia Earhart." So they go through this period in their lives trying to act out a part. Even just in fantasy. So when I work on paper, I'm trying to act out the part of emulating everyone I admired all those years. You as a designer or me as a designer, we try very hard. And when we look at something great we say "Boy, I wish I could do work like that."
DAVID: *Right.*
ED: And every kid emulates somebody, even if it's Dick Tracy. And some of it is instilled in you. Like your mother probably said "Eat your spinach and you'll grow up like Popeye." But it's an emulation, whether it comes from something you feel or something that's instilled in you. And you emulate what you admire.
DAVID: *So it becomes your standard.*
ED: That's right. Interesting though, your family will say "You're gonna be this" or "You're gonna be that," like a doctor or a lawyer, but I never heard of any family saying to a kid "When you grow up, what you want to be is a graphic designer." Most graphic designers are only graphic designers because they hate math.
DAVID: *Because they hate math?*
ED: Yeah. They're not good in math, so they go to art school. And they paint naked ladies. Everybody likes naked ladies and men.
DAVID: *Well, I was never good at math, but I was great with figures.*
ED: (laugh) So you design from what rubbed off on you. If it rubbed off bad, you'll be a bad graphic designer. You work hard being bad, you'll be a successful bad designer. And if it rubbed off good and you work hard at being good, you'll be a successful good graphic designer. But you asked me about my philosophy before. I've no real philosophy about design any more than a race car driver has a philosophy of why I'm a race car driver. "What am I doing? What am I doing with race cars? What's my philosophy to be if I'm a race car driver?" His philosophy is a very simple one: "I want to be the best damned race car driver in the world and win." So in graphic design, your philosophy has to be "I want to be a good graphic designer — maybe the best — and win." Like the race car driver. If he didn't want to win, he'd just sit in the garage and be happy sitting in the car without riding in it.
DAVID: *So what advice would you give people on being a business success as a designer?*
ED: Don't be in this field right now. Don't even go near it.
DAVID: *The industry? Why?*
ED: It's like show business, like being a comedian. The odds are so heavy, and you don't even know if you're good. I mean, do you want to package driving school matches? So I would advise people not to go into the field, but to go into something very close to it. Because now design is in the computer. Swipe files, clip sheets, layouts, page make-up. It's all in there. And unfortunately, most clients don't know the difference between design the way we do it and the way it's done on a computer. Because it looks gorgeous.
DAVID: *Do you think that's always true?*
ED: No. What I mean is this. When you do a job on the computer, the colors, the type, everything can be perfect. The appearance is perfect. And if you have a good designer using the computer, then you have good design. But in most cases, the client doesn't know the difference between good design and bad design. He's relying on the designer to give him good design. But if he likes it and maybe his wife and secretary like it, he thinks it's good no matter what.
DAVID: *And there's a tremendous amount of "no matter what" out there.*
ED: Absolutely. I was being driven out to Hicksville, to the Long Island Art Directors Club, and we had to take a detour. Took 2½ hours. Anyway, from near Shea Stadium to Hicksville I counted 14 stores with signs that said "computer graphics." You know, typesetting, resumes, full color. Fourteen! And I thought to myself, "I can't even count that many designers in the neighborhood where I work, which is in the middle of the graphic design industry! Irving's, Quickset, on and on. Anybody who buys a computer is a designer. Now, how the heck are you going to compete with a computer? In fact, people who have computers don't even need a portfolio. Your portfolio becomes the things the computer company gives you — their samples.
DAVID: *But there are some savvy clients out there and there is the factor of good designers using computers.*
ED: True. And it's from the good designers that you get the mood I was talking about. The sensitivity. The emotion. The computer should be competing with *you* as a talent. It's like the difference between playing classical music exactly as the composer wrote it or playing jazz. A good musician, a trained musician who can read, who can play jazz, can usually play classical music. But a classical musician can't necessarily play jazz. Because it's more then reading the notes. It's creating around the chords, playing the way you feel. And that carries over into graphic design.
DAVID: *Well, with jazz you have a lot of independent expression.*
ED: That's right. And all the instruments go together to make a complete orchestra. And in graphic design you have an orchestra, too — designers, letterers, illustrators, retouchers, the whole thing. And if I'm the composer, I want the best — the best illustrator, the best letterer, the best typesetter. And we'll put it all together and make the page.
DAVID: *You're talking about creative teamwork.*
ED: And not just teamwork, but everybody being acknowledged for their work. Like it used to be with Lubalin. You knew who everybody was that worked on a project. And now it's the same with Forbes' company, Pentagram. There's a lot of acknowledgment around there. And every single person is doing his best work and you know who the talent is. Again, it's like the music business used to be. Benny Goodman, Harry James, Duke Ellington, Coltrane. All the musicians in their bands were stars. You knew who they were and you knew the band wouldn't be the same without them. But eventually, they went off and formed their own bands. They were that good.
DAVID: *Well, what's your opinion of typography today?*
ED: The good typographers are getting better. I'm talking about the little two-person agency or three-person studio. The good type shops are doing better work because they want to stay in the limelight. Not that they weren't doing good work before. But now they're doing better work.
DAVID: *And what do you think of today's design trends and approaches to solving problems?*
ED: I think it's very good. I think creativity and concept is better. Just watch television. You can see that. It's really better. People *think* better. Regardless of the technology, design-wise, the concepts are definitely good. And that's what I'm excited about.

A VISUAL REMEDY GR5

171

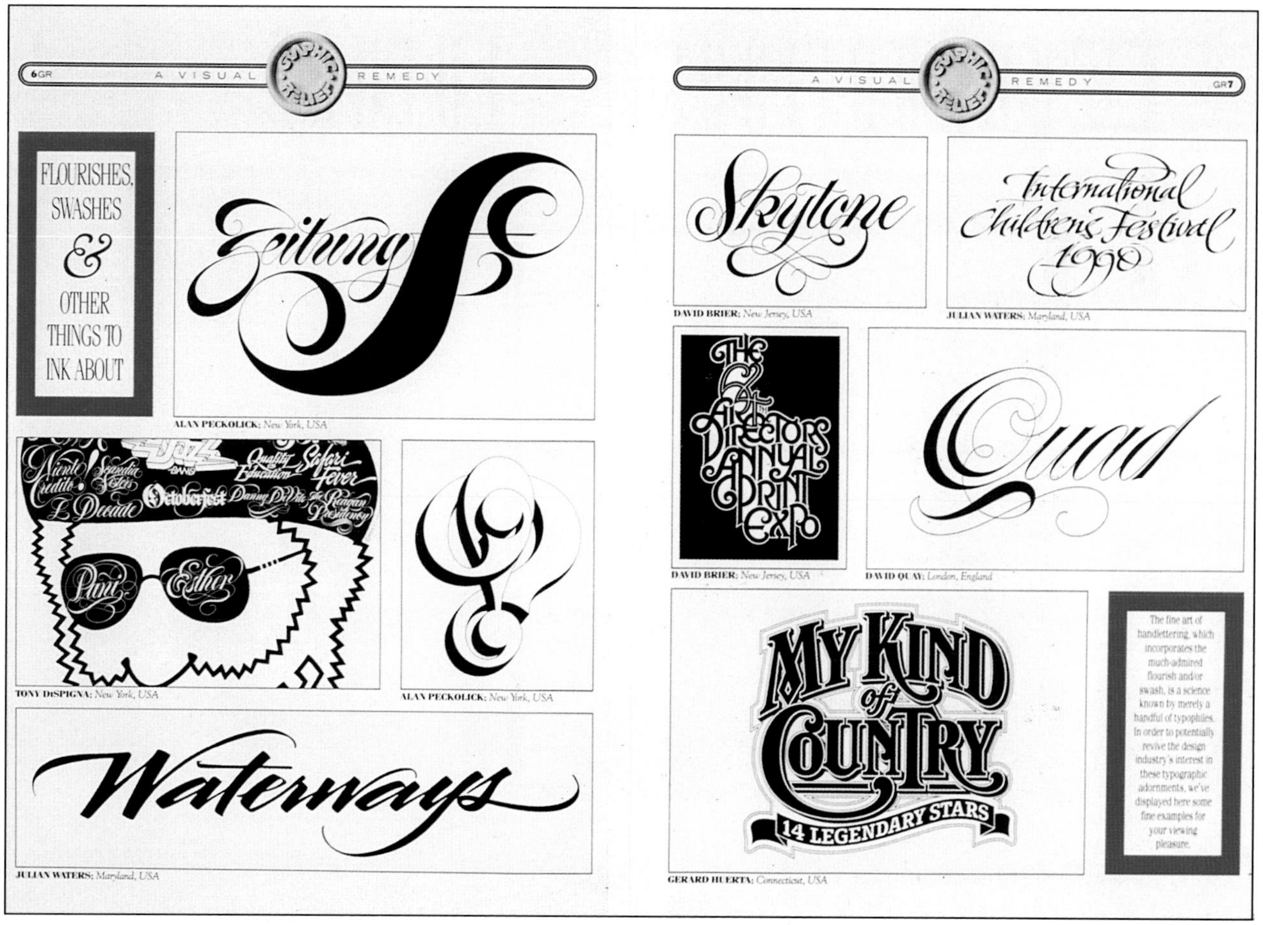

6GR A VISUAL REMEDY
FLOURISHES, SWASHES & OTHER THINGS TO INK ABOUT
Zeitung
ALAN PECKOLICK: New York, USA
Octoberfest
TONY DiSPIGNA: New York, USA
ALAN PECKOLICK: New York, USA
Waterways
JULIAN WATERS: Maryland, USA
A VISUAL REMEDY GR7
Skytone
DAVID BRIER: New Jersey, USA
International Children's Festival 1990
JULIAN WATERS: Maryland, USA
DAVID BRIER: New Jersey, USA
Quad
DAVID QUAY: London, England
MY KIND of COUNTRY
14 LEGENDARY STARS
GERARD HUERTA: Connecticut, USA
The fine art of handlettering, which incorporates the much-admired flourish and/or swash, is a science known by merely a handful of typophiles. In order to potentially revive the design industry's interest in these typographic adornments, we've displayed here some fine examples for your viewing pleasure.

170
DESIGN FIRM: *DBD International Ltd.*
DESIGNER: *David Brier*
LETTERER: *David Brier*
HEADLINE TYPEFACE: *Modified ITC Machine Bold*
TEXT TYPEFACE: *Century Oldstyle and Cooper Black*
CLIENT: *Graphic Relief*

171
DESIGN FIRM: *DBD International Ltd.*
DESIGNER: *David Brier*
HEADLINE TYPEFACE: *ITC Fenice and Goudy Italic*
TEXT TYPEFACE: *ITC Fenice*
CLIENT: *Graphic Relief*

172
DESIGN FIRM: *Carson Design*
DESIGNER: *David Carson*
HEADLINE TYPEFACE: *Helvetica*
TEXT TYPEFACE: *Matrix*
CLIENT: *Beach Culture Magazine*

172

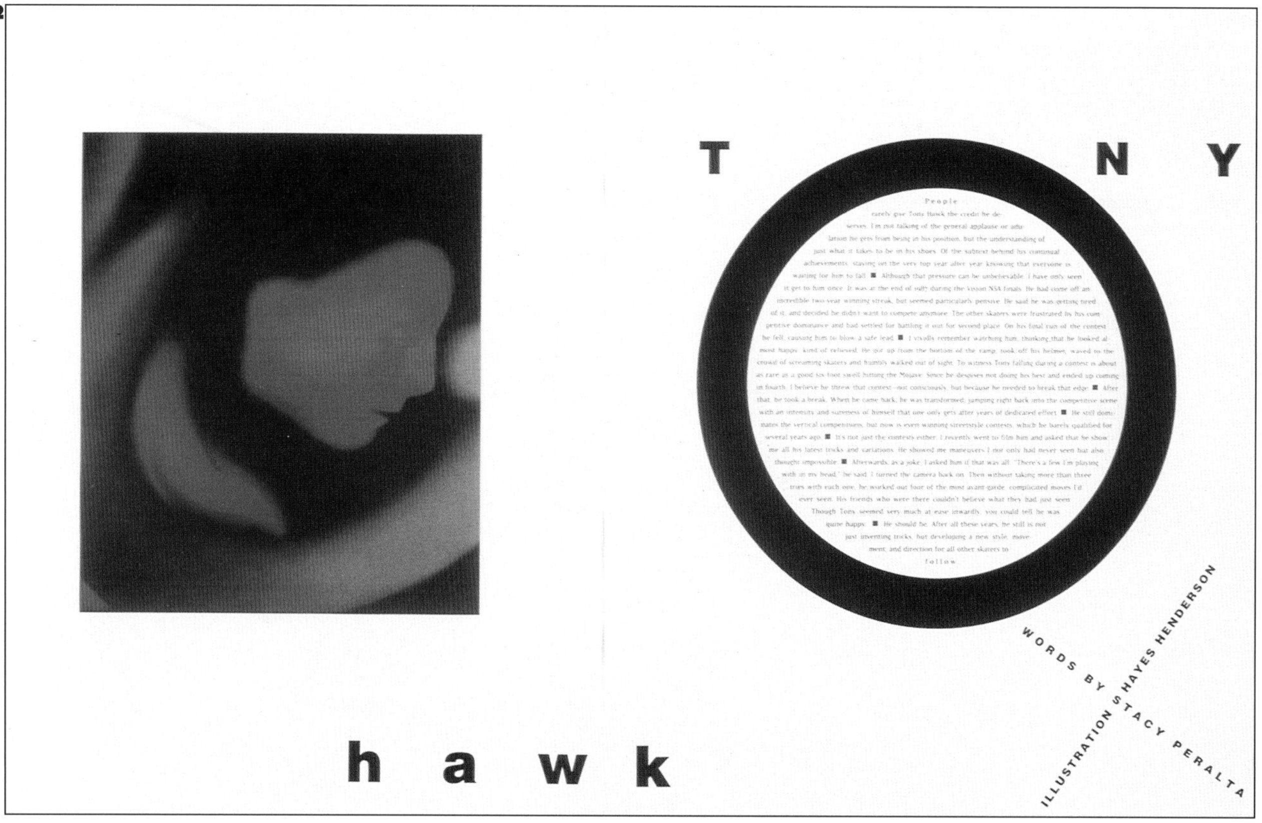

173
DESIGN FIRM: *Peterson & Company*
DESIGNER: *Scott Feaster*
TEXT TYPEFACE: *Bodoni*
CLIENT: *Southern Methodist University*

173

FOUNDATIONS *For The* FUTURE

THE UNIVERSITY REPORT 1989-90

The GRAND *Design*

EMBELLISHMENTS FOR A NEW CENTURY

By President A. Kenneth Pye

In 1911, when Robert S. Hyer looked across the expanse of Johnson grass that would become this prairie campus, he envisioned a grand design for learning that would give students a sound education embracing the values of Methodism and the liberal arts tradition. He gave us a founding vision and a foundation upon which to build.

Decades later, Willis M. Tate would reaffirm that tradition in his 1963 Master Plan, adding to it the establishment of selected graduate and professional programs to keep the founding mission vital and viable in a changing world.

In 1989-90 we have embellished the design once again, realizing a great sense of responsibility for the legacy we have inherited: to be true to SMU's past while planning for a future that will surprise the most astute of forecasters and pundits.

We do know, however, that the times will demand the best thinking of broadly educated individuals whose perspectives must be global, whose expertise must cross the artificial barriers of discipline, and whose cultural understanding must reflect the new diversity of demographics. They also must be capable of, and disposed toward, subjecting the personal and professional issues they face in life to the process of ethical reasoning.

Thus, our chief objective in 1989-90 was to set academic priorities for the next decade and century and to begin developing plans for implementation.

During the first semester, members of the campus community engaged in vigorous debate and discussion of the recommendations I issued in August, after I had studied the reports of four task forces: on Academic Priorities, Church Relatedness, Racial and Ethnic Diversity, and Financial Feasibility. In December the Academic Affairs Committee of the Board of Trustees and the full Board considered and approved the new academic priorities. For a complete description of the priorities, I refer you to the fall and winter issues of *SMU Magazine*, but I will summarize here the key elements of the new curriculum.

FORTIFYING THE FOUNDATION

As the first priority, we reaffirmed the centrality of an undergraduate liberal arts education in SMU's mission. For example, the core curriculum — liberal arts and interdisciplinary courses that form the base of every SMU student's education — has been strengthened. We are adding more courses in science and technology, a recognition that all citizens in the new century must be technologically literate to be civically responsible. Also, all students must study a

174

SAVE CBS
THE BIG SLIDE
SORRY SERIES AND JINXED NEWS SHOWS MEAN A TROUBLED NETWORK. HERE'S A RALLYING CRY FOR ITS RESCUE
BY MARK HARRIS
ILLUSTRATIONS BY TERRY ALLEN
32 MARCH 9, 1990
ENTERTAINMENT WEEKLY 33

175

LAST FALL, THE CBS LINEUP LOOKED LIKE A SUICIDE MISSION, NOT A STRATEGY
CBS NEWS CARRIES AN AIR OF FALLEN NOBILITY. ITS AGONIES HAVE BEEN VERY PUBLIC.
34 MARCH 9, 1990
ENTERTAINMENT WEEKLY 35

174/175

DESIGN FIRM: *Entertainment Weekly Magazine In-house*

DESIGNER: *Michael Grossman and Mark Michaelson*

HEADLINE TYPEFACE: *Monotype Grotesque Extra Condensed*

TEXT TYPEFACE: *Caslon 540*

CLIENT: *Entertainment Weekly Magazine*

176

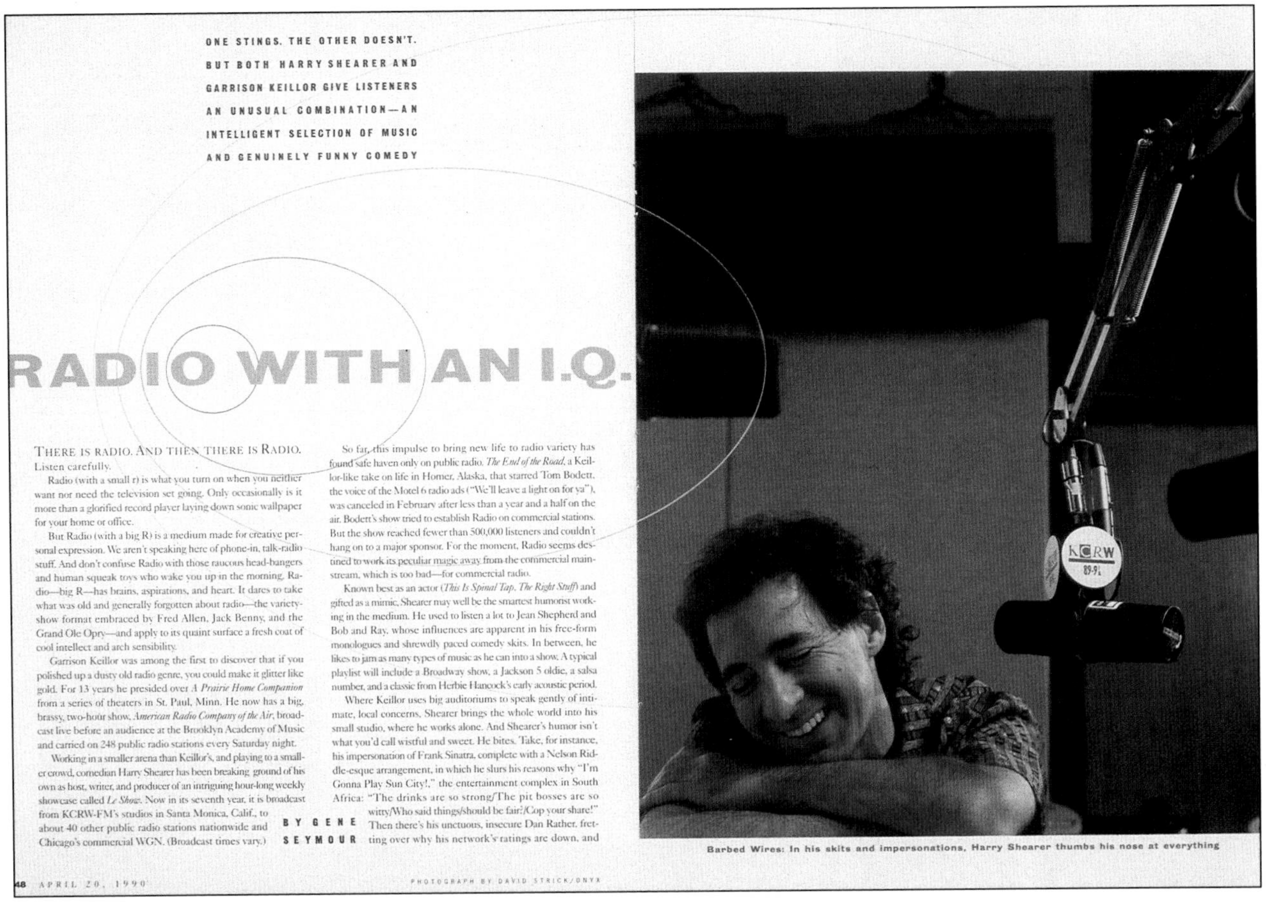

ONE STINGS. THE OTHER DOESN'T. BUT BOTH HARRY SHEARER AND GARRISON KEILLOR GIVE LISTENERS AN UNUSUAL COMBINATION—AN INTELLIGENT SELECTION OF MUSIC AND GENUINELY FUNNY COMEDY

RADIO WITH AN I.Q.

THERE IS RADIO. AND THEN THERE IS RADIO. Listen carefully.

Radio (with a small r) is what you turn on when you neither want nor need the television set going. Only occasionally is it more than a glorified record player laying down sonic wallpaper for your home or office.

But Radio (with a big R) is a medium made for creative personal expression. We aren't speaking here of phone-in, talk-radio stuff. And don't confuse Radio with those raucous head-bangers and human squeak toys who wake you up in the morning. Radio—big R—has brains, aspirations, and heart. It dares to take what was old and generally forgotten about radio—the variety-show format embraced by Fred Allen, Jack Benny, and the Grand Ole Opry—and apply to its quaint surface a fresh coat of cool intellect and arch sensibility.

Garrison Keillor was among the first to discover that if you polished up a dusty old radio genre, you could make it glitter like gold. For 13 years he presided over *A Prairie Home Companion* from a series of theaters in St. Paul, Minn. He now has a big, brassy, two-hour show, *American Radio Company of the Air*, broadcast live before an audience at the Brooklyn Academy of Music and carried on 248 public radio stations every Saturday night.

Working in a smaller arena than Keillor's, and playing to a smaller crowd, comedian Harry Shearer has been breaking ground of his own as host, writer, and producer of an intriguing hour-long weekly showcase called *Le Show*. Now in its seventh year, it is broadcast from KCRW-FM's studios in Santa Monica, Calif., to about 40 other public radio stations nationwide and Chicago's commercial WGN. (Broadcast times vary.)

BY GENE SEYMOUR

So far, this impulse to bring new life to radio variety has found safe haven only on public radio. *The End of the Road*, a Keillor-like take on life in Homer, Alaska, that starred Tom Bodett, the voice of the Motel 6 radio ads ("We'll leave a light on for ya"), was canceled in February after less than a year and a half on the air. Bodett's show tried to establish Radio on commercial stations. But the show reached fewer than 500,000 listeners and couldn't hang on to a major sponsor. For the moment, Radio seems destined to work its peculiar magic away from the commercial mainstream, which is too bad—for commercial radio.

Known best as an actor (*This Is Spinal Tap*, *The Right Stuff*) and gifted as a mimic, Shearer may well be the smartest humorist working in the medium. He used to listen a lot to Jean Shepherd and Bob and Ray, whose influences are apparent in his free-form monologues and shrewdly paced comedy skits. In between, he likes to jam as many types of music as he can into a show. A typical playlist will include a Broadway show, a Jackson 5 oldie, a salsa number, and a classic from Herbie Hancock's early acoustic period.

Where Keillor uses big auditoriums to speak gently of intimate, local concerns, Shearer brings the whole world into his small studio, where he works alone. And Shearer's humor isn't what you'd call wistful and sweet. He bites. Take, for instance, his impersonation of Frank Sinatra, complete with a Nelson Riddle-esque arrangement, in which he slurs his reasons why "I'm Gonna Play Sun City!," the entertainment complex in South Africa: "The drinks are so strong/The pit bosses are so witty/Who said things/should be fair?/Cop your share!" Then there's his unctuous, insecure Dan Rather, fretting over why his network's ratings are down, and

Barbed Wires: In his skits and impersonations, Harry Shearer thumbs his nose at everything

48 APRIL 20, 1990

PHOTOGRAPH BY DAVID STRICK/ONYX

176
DESIGN FIRM: *Entertainment Weekly Magazine In-house*
DESIGNER: *Paula Kelly*
HEADLINE TYPEFACE: *Bureau Grotesque 79*
TEXT TYPEFACE: *Caslon 540*
CLIENT: *Entertainment Weekly Magazine*

177
DESIGN FIRM: *Entertainment Weekly Magazine In-house*
DESIGNER: *Mark Michaelson*
HEADLINE TYPEFACE: *Monotype Condensed and Grotesque Extra Condensed*
TEXT TYPEFACE: *Caslon 540*
CLIENT: *Entertainment Weekly Magazine*

177

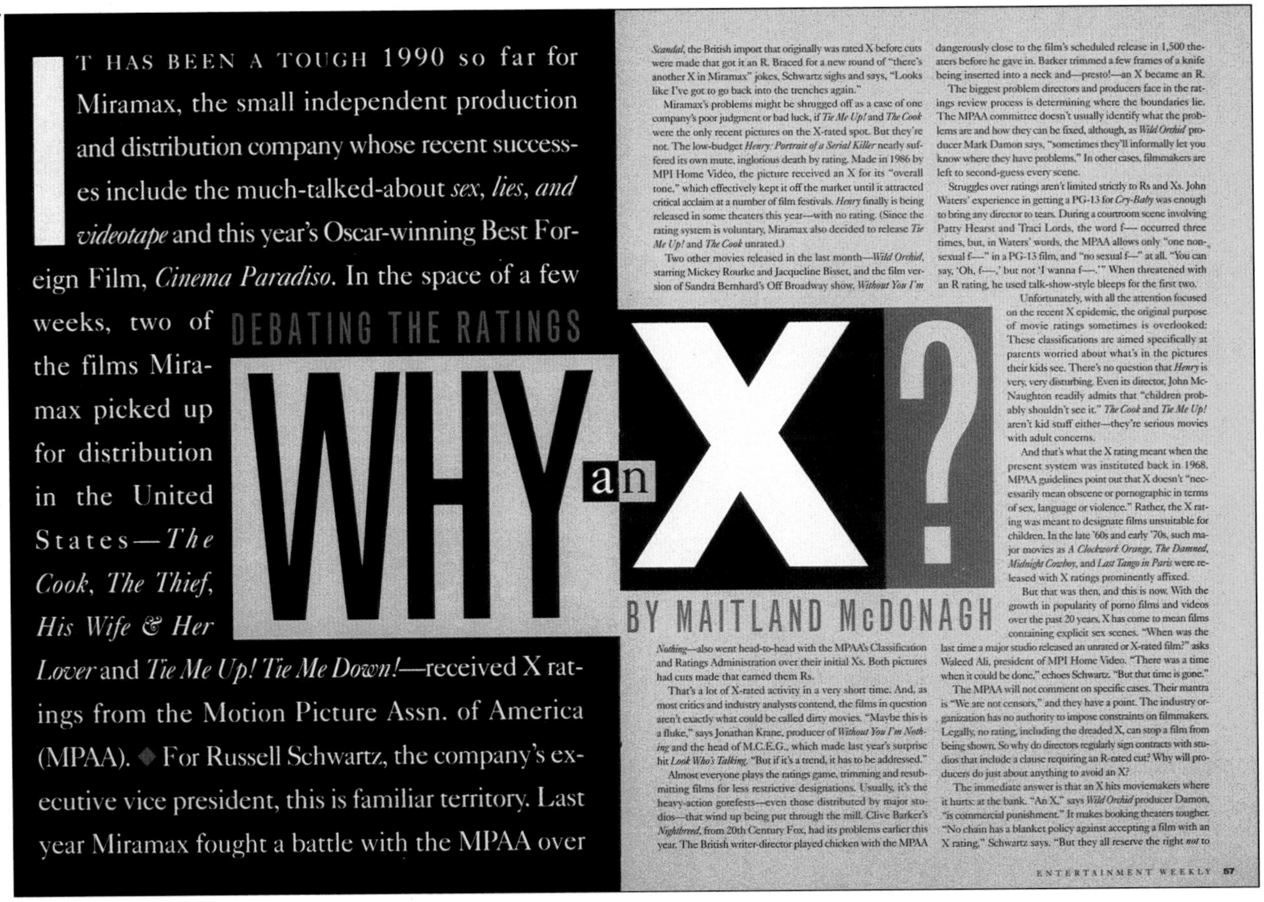

IT HAS BEEN A TOUGH 1990 so far for Miramax, the small independent production and distribution company whose recent successes include the much-talked-about *sex, lies, and videotape* and this year's Oscar-winning Best Foreign Film, *Cinema Paradiso*. In the space of a few weeks, two of the films Miramax picked up for distribution in the United States—*The Cook, The Thief, His Wife & Her Lover* and *Tie Me Up! Tie Me Down!*—received X ratings from the Motion Picture Assn. of America (MPAA). ◆ For Russell Schwartz, the company's executive vice president, this is familiar territory. Last year Miramax fought a battle with the MPAA over

DEBATING THE RATINGS

WHY an X?

BY MAITLAND McDONAGH

Scandal, the British import that originally was rated X before cuts were made that got it an R. Braced for a new round of "there's another X in Miramax" jokes, Schwartz sighs and says, "Looks like I've got to go back into the trenches again."

Miramax's problems might be shrugged off as a case of one company's poor judgment or bad luck, if *Tie Me Up!* and *The Cook* were the only recent pictures on the X-rated spot. But they're not. The low-budget *Henry: Portrait of a Serial Killer* nearly suffered its own mute, inglorious death by rating. Made in 1986 by MPI Home Video, the picture received an X for its "overall tone," which effectively kept it off the market until it attracted critical acclaim at a number of film festivals. *Henry* finally is being released in some theaters this year—with no rating. (Since the rating system is voluntary, Miramax also decided to release *Tie Me Up!* and *The Cook* unrated.)

Two other movies released in the last month—*Wild Orchid*, starring Mickey Rourke and Jacqueline Bisset, and the film version of Sandra Bernhard's Off Broadway show, *Without You I'm Nothing*—also went head-to-head with the MPAA's Classification and Ratings Administration over their initial Xs. Both pictures had cuts made that earned them Rs.

That's a lot of X-rated activity in a very short time. And, as most critics and industry analysts contend, the films in question aren't exactly what could be called dirty movies. "Maybe this is a fluke," says Jonathan Krane, producer of *Without You I'm Nothing* and the head of M.C.E.G., which made last year's surprise hit *Look Who's Talking*. "But if it's a trend, it has to be addressed."

Almost everyone plays the ratings game, trimming and resubmitting films for less restrictive designations. Usually, it's the heavy-action gorefests—even those distributed by major studios—that wind up being put through the mill. Clive Barker's *Nightbreed*, from 20th Century Fox, had its problems earlier this year. The British writer-director played chicken with the MPAA dangerously close to the film's scheduled release in 1,500 theaters before he gave in. Barker trimmed a few frames of a knife being inserted into a neck and—presto!—an X became an R.

The biggest problem directors and producers face in the ratings review process is determining where the boundaries lie. The MPAA committee doesn't usually identify what the problems are and how they can be fixed, although, as *Wild Orchid* producer Mark Damon says, "sometimes they'll informally let you know where they have problems." In other cases, filmmakers are left to second-guess every scene.

Struggles over ratings aren't limited strictly to Rs and Xs. John Waters' experience in getting a PG-13 for *Cry-Baby* was enough to bring any director to tears. During a courtroom scene involving Patty Hearst and Traci Lords, the word f— occurred three times, but, in Waters' words, the MPAA allows only "one non-sexual f—" in a PG-13 film, and "no sexual f—" at all. "You can say, 'Oh, f—,' but not 'I wanna f—.'" When threatened with an R rating, he used talk-show-style bleeps for the first two.

Unfortunately, with all the attention focused on the recent X epidemic, the original purpose of movie ratings sometimes is overlooked: These classifications are aimed specifically at parents worried about what's in the pictures their kids see. There's no question that *Henry* is very, very disturbing. Even its director, John McNaughton readily admits that "children probably shouldn't see it." *The Cook* and *Tie Me Up!* aren't kid stuff either—they're serious movies with adult concerns.

And that's what the X rating meant when the present system was instituted back in 1968. MPAA guidelines point out that X doesn't "necessarily mean obscene or pornographic in terms of sex, language or violence." Rather, the X rating was meant to designate films unsuitable for children. In the late '60s and early '70s, such major movies as *A Clockwork Orange*, *The Damned*, *Midnight Cowboy*, and *Last Tango in Paris* were released with X ratings prominently affixed.

But that was then, and this is now. With the growth in popularity of porno films and videos over the past 20 years, X has come to mean films containing explicit sex scenes. "When was the last time a major studio released an unrated or X-rated film?" asks Waleed Ali, president of MPI Home Video. "There was a time when it could be done," echoes Schwartz. "But that time is gone."

The MPAA will not comment on specific cases. Their mantra is "We are not censors," and they have a point. The industry organization has no authority to impose constraints on filmmakers. Legally, no rating, including the dreaded X, can stop a film from being shown. So why do directors regularly sign contracts with studios that include a clause requiring an R-rated cut? Why will producers do just about anything to avoid an X?

The immediate answer is that an X hits moviemakers where it hurts: at the bank. "An X," says *Wild Orchid* producer Damon, "is commercial punishment." It makes booking theaters tougher. "No chain has a blanket policy against accepting a film with an X rating," Schwartz says. "But they all reserve the right *not* to

ENTERTAINMENT WEEKLY 57

178

22 ENTERTAINMENT WEEKLY

TEEN HEARTTHROB JOHNNY DEPP IS CAST AGAINST TYPE AS *EDWARD SCISSORHANDS'* FREAKISH MISFIT

WITH 'EDWARD SCISSORHANDS,' 'BATMAN' DIRECTOR TIM BURTON UNLEASHES HIS DARKEST, SHARPEST CREATION YET

CUTTING EDGE

BY GISELLE BENATAR

PHOTOGRAPH BY FIROOZ ZAHEDI

179

Edward Scissorhands director Tim Burton is discussing the subtleties of scissors: "There's quite an interesting design to a pair of scissors, if you really look at them. How do they work? What do they do?" Burton punctuates his questions by furiously skewering the air with his large-knuckled hands. "They're both simple and complicated, creative and destructive," he concludes. "It's that feeling of being at odds with yourself."

On this day, the former animator who went on to startle critics and audiences with his artful visual dementia in *Pee-wee's Big Adventure* and *Beetlejuice*—then awed studio accountants with his megablockbuster, *Batman*—also seems more than a little at odds with himself. Holed up in a dimly lit hotel suite, just two weeks before *Scissorhands'* release, the 32-year-old director sips coffee, nibbles finger sandwiches, and contemplates the sprawl of rush-hour Manhattan. "I've had, uuhhh, too many of these today already," mutters Burton, pouring his fifth cup of coffee, or is it his sixth? "This is a tense time...a tough time," he says, drawing thin fingers through his tangled twist of black hair. After *Batman*'s success, the director suddenly had unmatched clout in Hollywood. He could have made almost any movie he chose, but instead of aiming for another surefire hit, he pursued a project that had obsessed him since he was a teenager: the strange story of a boy with scissors for hands. In Burton's warped fairy tale, Edward is a kind of teenage Frankenstein's monster, created by a half-mad inventor (played by Burton's lifelong idol Vincent Price) who dies before he can replace the boy's hedge-clipper hands with suitably human ones.

Though he claims not to worry about the box office, Burton has a lot riding on *Scissorhands*: If the movie is a hit, the director's status as Hollywood's weird wunderkind will be unassailable. But *Edward Scissorhands*—despite having the real-life teen-dream couple of Johnny Depp and Winona Ryder in the lead roles—is by no means guaranteed to warm the hearts of holiday moviegoers. With his spiked hair, ghoulish makeup, and grotesque scissorhands, Edward looks like a cross between Charlie Chaplin's Tramp and *A Nightmare on Elm Street*'s Freddy Krueger. Studio executives were so jittery that Edward's image would put audiences off they tried to keep pictures of Depp in his full regalia under wraps until the movie opened. And, though it has plenty of humor, *Scissorhands* is essentially a moody, somewhat forbidding fable. "I tend to, you know, see the dark side of things," Burton says.

Perhaps only someone of such a mindset could be so ambivalent about his own success. "I came up in a way that was very Hollywoodesque, which is, uh, kind of shocking to me," he says. "I have this natural reaction against it." In person, Burton seems to do all he can to undermine one's image of the powerful Hollywood film director. He wears his childish eccentricities—the frazzled hair, the deliberately obscure, fragmented speech, the wicked, rippling giggle—almost like a protective shield. Take his perverse insistence on dressing totally in black: black jeans, black T-shirt, black sneakers—Burton even drinks his coffee black. "I just don't feel good in bright colors, I don't feel that way," he insists. "I'm a human mood ring: I feel black."

In *Pee-wee's Big Adventure* and *Batman*, Burton built movies around characters conceived by others—Paul Reubens' Pee-wee Herman and cartoonist Bob Kane's superhero. But given the chance to film his own creation, Burton produced a character that resembles, more than anyone else, Tim Burton. The comparison sets the director on edge. "I wouldn't have been able to deal with it if I'd made that connection directly," he says. "It's dangerous to get that close to a character, especially when it's so, you know, weird-looking." But he admits that Edward was partly drawn from his own somewhat trou-

"I JUST DON'T FEEL GOOD IN BRIGHT COLORS," BURTON (ABOVE) SAYS. "I'M A HUMAN MOOD RING: I FEEL BLACK."

24 DECEMBER 14, 1990

PHOTOGRAPH BY MAX AGUILERA-HELLWEG

180

bled adolescence growing up in Burbank, Calif. Burton shared an uneasy relationship with both his father, who is retired from the parks and recreation department, and his mother, who operates a small gift shop. By the time he was 17, he claims, he couldn't wait to get out of the house. "Edward is a very teenage inspiration," says the director. "I think that's a time generally when you're at your most traumatic, in terms of feeling dark, operatic, melodramatic."

With his bizarre deformity and lunar ignorance of the ways of humans, Edward feels freakish, clumsy, and misunderstood—as would most any sensitive teen—after an intrepid Avon lady (Dianne Wiest) visits his castle and brings him down to the baffling world of suburbia. But he also discovers his creative genius, using his clippers to fashion delicate ice sculptures, surreal haircuts, and wild topiary confections. Though Burton prefers to downplay the connection, the similarity here to a director who has turned *his* sense of alienation into dazzling pop entertainment is obvious. *Edward Scissorhands* is a portrait of the artist as a young misfit.

Burton began working seriously—and somewhat secretively—on the picture two years ago, even before the release of *Batman*. Though Warner Bros. (the studio that also released his first two features) passed on the project, Burton found Twentieth Century Fox receptive to the idea. He hammered out a script with writer Caroline Thompson. "We kept it between ourselves, so that there weren't, you know, 15 executives telling us what we should write in the script," he says. Fox gave the project the go-ahead, and so began what Burton describes as a battle for creative control. Once *Batman* met with thunderous success, however, he was in a stronger position to demand and get that control. "I wouldn't have done the movie otherwise," he says.

Casting was the next major hurdle. Fox wanted a big name like Tom Cruise for the leading role. "They've always got their list," says Burton. "There they are, the top five, ding, ding, ding." He favored a lesser-known actor, but finally compromised and got Johnny Depp. When it came to control of the story and visuals, however, he stood firm. "I was very specific and said things to them like, 'I'm saying this right now, no matter what, the ending is not going to change,'" he says.

The job of physically translating Burton's fantasies to the screen fell to his tight-knit production crew, which included such Burton veterans as production designer Bo Welch and art director Tom Duffield (both worked on *Beetlejuice*), plus such newcomers to the group as Oscar-winning special effects designer Stan Winston (*Aliens, Predator*). According to members of Burton's inner circle, a prerequisite for being on his team was the ability to decipher his fragmented verbal instructions. Interestingly enough, almost everyone who works with Burton claims to communicate with him telepathically. "I don't believe in it, but that's how we connect," says Caroline Thompson. "He's so articulate, but he never talks." Bo Welch confirms that Burton's strongest communicative tool is his visual sensibility. "If you spend any time with Tim, you realize he does communicate verbally, but it's mostly through images."

One of Burton's main concerns in *Scissorhands* was to capture the exact mixture of surrealism and banality that—to him at least—represents life in the suburbs. Burton recalls feeling completely at odds with his Burbank environment as a child. "It had this very druglike, surreal feel about it," he says. "Everything was very textural, very tactile. You know, the shag carpeting, these white walls with those strange ceramic birds floating on them...and those resin grapes on the wall. Yeah, what are they for?" He wanted to recapture that disconnected feeling by viewing the setting through the eyes of his central character. "The idea was to treat it from Edward's point of view," he says. "We wanted the sense of, you know, the normalcy and the wonder."

Before filming could begin, Burton and production de-

UNDER THE INFLUENCE: Burton with his idol Vincent Price on the *Scissorhands* set; above, Winona Ryder, blond for this role, says, "I would do anything for Tim. I trust his vision completely."

"EDWARD IS A VERY TEENAGE INSPIRATION. I THINK THAT'S A TIME WHEN YOU'RE AT YOUR MOST MELODRAMATIC."

ZADE ROSENTHAL

ENTERTAINMENT WEEKLY 25

181

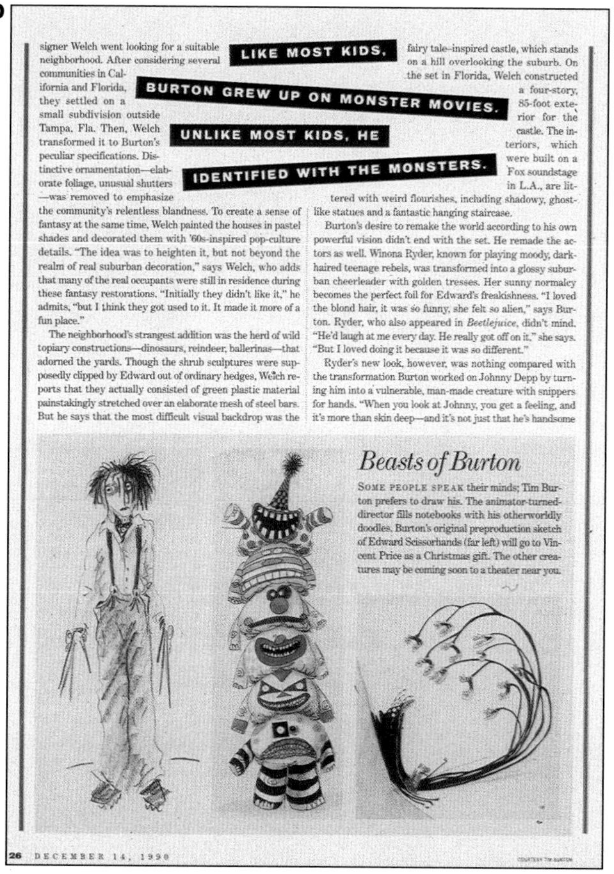

signer Welch went looking for a suitable neighborhood. After considering several communities in California and Florida, they settled on a small subdivision outside Tampa, Fla. Then, Welch transformed it to Burton's peculiar specifications. Distinctive ornamentation—elaborate foliage, unusual shutters—was removed to emphasize the community's relentless blandness. To create a sense of fantasy at the same time, Welch painted the houses in pastel shades and decorated them with '60s-inspired pop-culture details. "The idea was to heighten it, but not beyond the realm of real suburban decoration," says Welch, who adds that many of the real occupants were still in residence during these fantasy restorations. "Initially they didn't like it," he admits, "but I think they got used to it. It made it more of a fun place."

The neighborhood's strangest addition was the herd of wild topiary constructions—dinosaurs, reindeer, ballerinas—that adorned the yards. Though the shrub sculptures were supposedly clipped by Edward out of ordinary hedges, Welch reports that they actually consisted of green plastic material painstakingly stretched over an elaborate mesh of steel bars. But he says that the most difficult visual backdrop was the fairy tale–inspired castle, which stands on a hill overlooking the suburb. On the set in Florida, Welch constructed a four-story, 85-foot exterior for the castle. The interiors, which were built on a Fox soundstage in L.A., are littered with weird flourishes, including shadowy, ghostlike statues and a fantastic hanging staircase.

Burton's desire to remake the world according to his own powerful vision didn't end with the set. He remade the actors as well. Winona Ryder, known for playing moody, dark-haired teenage rebels, was transformed into a glossy suburban cheerleader with golden tresses. Her sunny normalcy becomes the perfect foil for Edward's freakishness. "I loved the blond hair, it was so funny, she felt so alien," says Burton. Ryder, who also appeared in *Beetlejuice*, didn't mind. "He'd laugh at me every day. He really got off on it," she says. "But I loved doing it because it was so different."

Ryder's new look, however, was nothing compared with the transformation Burton worked on Johnny Depp by turning him into a vulnerable, man-made creature with snippers for hands. "When you look at Johnny, you get a feeling, and it's more than skin deep—and it's not just that he's handsome

LIKE MOST KIDS, BURTON GREW UP ON MONSTER MOVIES. UNLIKE MOST KIDS, HE IDENTIFIED WITH THE MONSTERS.

Beasts of Burton

SOME PEOPLE SPEAK their minds; Tim Burton prefers to draw his. The animator-turned-director fills notebooks with his otherworldly doodles. Burton's original preproduction sketch of Edward Scissorhands (far left) will go to Vincent Price as a Christmas gift. The other creatures may be coming soon to a theater near you.

26 DECEMBER 14, 1990

COURTESY TIM BURTON

178/179/180/181

DESIGN FIRM: *Entertainment Weekly Magazine In-house*

DESIGNER: *Robert Newman and Elizabeth Betts*

HEADLINE TYPEFACE: *Bureau Grotesque 79 & 13*

TEXT TYPEFACE: *Century Expanded*

CLIENT: *Entertainment Weekly Magazine*

182

All Aboard the British

SOUL TRAIN

"THERE'S A *PAH-TEE?*" LISA STANSFIELD'S EYES POP WIDE OPEN. Sitting in the bar of a midtown-Manhattan hotel, hours before her New York debut at the Ritz nightclub last month, the British singer rouses herself. It has come to her attention that there will be a bash the following night at a downtown club in honor of Barry White.

Barry White? The R&B crooner best known for such '70s pillow-talk hits as "Never, Never Gonna Give Ya Up" and "You're the First, the Last, My Everything"? The least-hip musician anyone could idolize in 1990, despite his new album and summer comeback tour?

BARRY WHITE

"He could sing 'I'm just going to the toilet' and it would have been wonderful," Stansfield recalls wistfully between sips of coffee and puffs on a cigarette. "I used to be quite ashamed of [liking that music] when I was younger. When all my friends were into punk, I'd be singing versions of soul ballads. I thought, 'Oh my God, I don't want them to know I'm doing this.' But I really enjoyed singing those songs."

Stansfield's admiration for the flamboyant White may seem odd here. But back home in Britain, musicians and fans are breathing new life into a style of music Americans have either taken for granted or forgotten: the '70s R&B of Philly Soul (named for its base of operations) and the likes of Barry White, with its suave

BY DAVID BROWNE

DANCE DIVA LISA STANSFIELD (LEFT) GREW UP LISTENING TO BARRY WHITE (OPPOSITE PAGE). "IT'S QUITE CHEEKY WHAT WE'RE DOING—SELLING AMERICANS BACK THEIR OWN PRODUCT," SHE SAYS.

ENTERTAINMENT WEEKLY 29

183

"When we first heard Lisa's record, we freaked. It's classic Philly."

GAMBLE AND HUFF

LEADING WRITER-PRODUCERS OF THE PHILLY SOUND, THIS TEAM RECAST BLACK POP

rhythms, sweeping orchestration, and impeccable production. It's not unusual to hear 20-year-old songs by the Spinners, the O'Jays, or Lou Rawls in British clubs and restaurants. Or to turn on the radio—in the U.K. or the U.S.—and listen to what *Billboard* magazine calls the New British Invasion: records by Stansfield and such U.K. bands as Soul II Soul and the Chimes that are nothing if not high-tech updates of Philly Soul.

"[The revival] has a lot to do with when we were born and what we listened to," Stansfield, 23, says. "A lot of it's been influenced by Philadelphia and the '70s." Baby-boomers have their Motown records for memories, but for those who followed, the nostalgia of choice is the post-Woodstock, pre-disco sound of early '70s R&B. "We all grew up within that period of time, with that music and that feeling," Stansfield says.

The feeling is catching. Stansfield's debut album, *Affection*, and its hit "All Around the World" recently leapfrogged into the U.S. top 10. In 1989 Simply Red scored a comeback hit with its faithful remake of Harold Melvin & the Blue Notes' 1972 "If You Don't Know Me by Now." Soul II Soul—a combination group, clothing store, and overall enterprise organized by entrepreneur Jazzie B.—went platinum last year with *Keep on Movin'*, which fused Philly strings, rap, and disco. The group's second album, *Vol. II-1990-A New Decade*, covers much of the same ground. And Columbia Records is expecting big things from the Chimes, an interracial U.K. band powered by the funky vocals of lead singer Pauline Henry, who recalls peak-era Gladys Knight.

"Around Britain, a lot of people have the same attitude about music—that club music has really ruined everything," James Locke, the Chimes' drummer and keyboardist, says of the return to an older sound. "The typical kind of rock element, or the overproduced kind of dance and pop, has suddenly become boring."

"The Chimes are really like the Three Degrees, and there's a lot of Teddy Pendergrass in Lisa [Stansfield]," says Larry Gold, a longtime Philadelphia arranger and musician who worked on records by the O'Jays and other Philly Soul acts. "Maurice Starr [producer-songwriter behind New Kids on the Block and other teen pop acts] is copying the Philly Sound left and right. It comes down to the simpleness of the melody and the feel. Put those together with the right song, and you got it."

THE BLUE NOTES

TEDDY PENDERGRASS (RIGHT) WAS THE VOICE BEHIND SUCH HITS AS "THE LOVE I LOST"

THE "IT" WAS AN EFFERVESCENT COMBINATION of singer, song, and production flourishes, and nobody did it better than producer-songwriters Kenneth Gamble and Leon Huff, who redefined the sound of black music in the early '70s. During the '60s the two worked with the likes of ex-Impression Jerry Butler and the Soul Survivors ("Expressway to Your Heart"). By 1971 they decided to start their own label, Philadelphia International (PI), working out of a renovated Philly studio renamed Sigma Sound. A year later Gamble and Huff hit the ground running with the O'Jays' trailblazing "Back Stabbers"—all deft horn/string arrangement and neurotic lyrics—and didn't look back.

THE SPINNERS

THEIR '60S MOTOWN RECORDS BOMBED; THEIR '70S PHILLY SOUL FLOURISHED

Working mostly with down-on-their-luck veterans like the O'Jays, Gamble and Huff carved out a seductive new style of uptown pop-R&B. Elegant and supple, it used majestic singers like the Spinners' Phillippe Wynne, head O'Jay Eddie Levert, and Teddy Pendergrass, the voice behind Harold Melvin & the Blue Notes. Philly Soul records were also slicker and less overtly funky than Motown records, thanks to the 40-piece MFSB (for Mother, Father, Sister, Brother) orchestra. MFSB's pairing of veteran jazz musicians with classically trained string and horn players gave Gamble and Huff's records a gossamer-with-a-kick feel unlike anything heard in black music before.

The result was a virtually nonstop string of top 10 hits, and PI revenues neared $30 million a year. During Philly Soul's peak—roughly '72 through '78—David Bowie would record *Young Americans* at Sigma Sound, and Elton John would salute Gamble and Huff with "Philadelphia Freedom." Around the country, other producers and artists offered variations on the Philly theme. In L.A., a hefty, bejeweled arranger named Barry White took the sound to its extreme with 10-minute-plus tracks of lush string sections and let's-do-it lyrics. A Gamble and Huff protégé-turned-rival, pianist Thom Bell, carved out new careers for the Stylistics and the Spinners.

The music of this movement could be unabashedly romantic (the Spinners' "Could It Be I'm Falling in Love" and "I'll Be Around"), but it also tackled such themes as extramarital affairs (Billy Paul's "Me and Mrs. Jones"), brotherhood (the O'Jays' "Love Train"), social ills (the Blue Notes' "Wake Up Everybody"), and the evils of greed (the O'Jays' "For the Love of Money"). And, on MFSB's "TSOP (The Sound of Philadelphia)" and Archie Bell & the Drells' "Let's Groove," it simply, well, grooved.

"It was magic," Gamble and Huff arranger Gold recalls. "You'd come into the studio to play a song, and each one would be better than the one before it. John McFadden would come in with 'Back Stabbers,' and Gamble would hear it and say, 'That's a No. 1 song. I've got to try to top it.' And he would."

For a while, it seemed as if this genre of R&B and the team of Gamble and Huff in particular would go on forever, but the rise of disco, an increasing distance between Gamble and Huff, and the pair's reluctance to sign younger artists were all chinks in the armor. The indictment of Gamble and Huff in a 1975 payola investigation tarnished their reputation as well. (They were charged with attempting to influence radio stations in order to get airplay for their music; charges against Huff were dismissed, but Gamble was fined $2,500.) Barry White became a self-parody seemingly overnight, and star acts such as the Spinners and the O'Jays were consigned to the nightclub circuit.

The hits continued sporadically, among them "Use Ta Be My Girl" by the O'Jays (1978) and "Ain't No Stoppin' Us Now" (1979), written and recorded by Gene McFadden and John Whitehead, two of Gamble

MIDNIGHT TRAIN TO SCOTLAND: THE CHIMES ARE HIP-HOP MEETS SUPPER CLUB BY WAY OF PHILADELPHIA

30 JUNE 29, 1990

GAMBLE AND HUFF: BMI ARCHIVES; BLUE NOTES: MICHAEL OCHS ARCHIVES; SPINNERS: FRANK DRIGGS

DEBORAH FEINGOLD

ENTERTAINMENT WEEKLY 31

182/183
DESIGN FIRM: *Entertainment Weekly Magazine In-house*
DESIGNER: *Miriam Campiz*
CLIENT: *Entertainment Weekly Magazine*

184

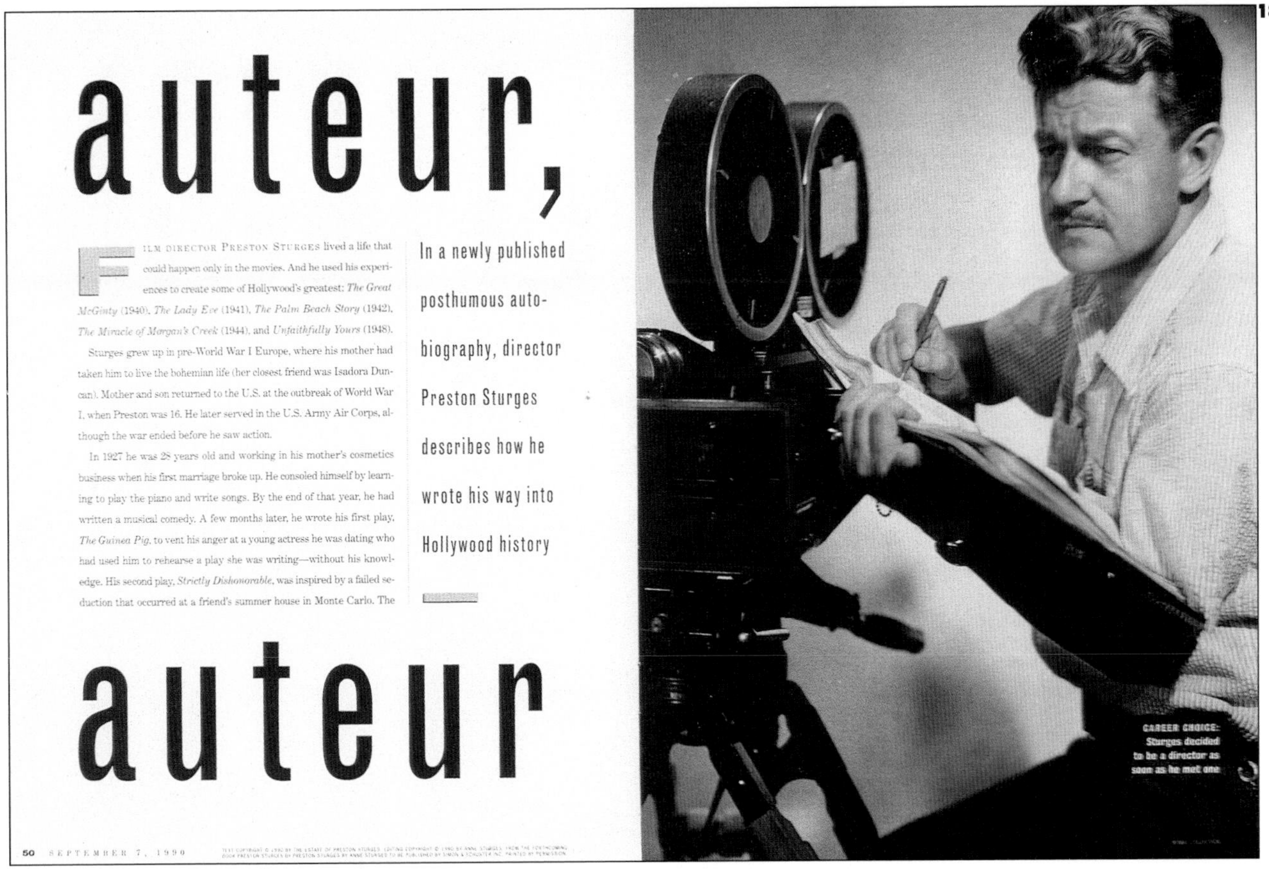

auteur, auteur

FILM DIRECTOR PRESTON STURGES lived a life that could happen only in the movies. And he used his experiences to create some of Hollywood's greatest: *The Great McGinty* (1940), *The Lady Eve* (1941), *The Palm Beach Story* (1942), *The Miracle of Morgan's Creek* (1944), and *Unfaithfully Yours* (1948).

Sturges grew up in pre-World War I Europe, where his mother had taken him to live the bohemian life (her closest friend was Isadora Duncan). Mother and son returned to the U.S. at the outbreak of World War I, when Preston was 16. He later served in the U.S. Army Air Corps, although the war ended before he saw action.

In 1927 he was 28 years old and working in his mother's cosmetics business when his first marriage broke up. He consoled himself by learning to play the piano and write songs. By the end of that year, he had written a musical comedy. A few months later, he wrote his first play, *The Guinea Pig*, to vent his anger at a young actress he was dating who had used him to rehearse a play she was writing—without his knowledge. His second play, *Strictly Dishonorable*, was inspired by a failed seduction that occurred at a friend's summer house in Monte Carlo. The

In a newly published posthumous autobiography, director Preston Sturges describes how he wrote his way into Hollywood history

CAREER CHOICE: Sturges decided to be a director as soon as he met one

50 SEPTEMBER 7, 1990

185

SHOWING THE WAY: Sturges discusses a scene with Veronica Lake and Joel McCrea during the filming of *Sullivan's Travels* in 1941

comedy was the hit of the 1929–30 Broadway season.

That winter, on the train to Palm Beach, he met Eleanor Hutton, the 20-year-old daughter of heiress Marjorie Merriweather Post and financier E.F. Hutton. Her parents objected, but the kids didn't listen: Eleanor and Preston eloped in April 1930. Their happiness was short-lived, however. His mother died on their first wedding anniversary; they separated on their second.

Looking for yet another new start at age 33, Sturges went to Hollywood to become a screenwriter. By the time he died in 1959, he had written 31 movies and directed 14 of them.

Sturges began to write his autobiography in 1959 but did not finish it. His fourth and last wife, Sandy, with whom he had two sons, took the manuscript as well as Preston's journals, diaries, and letters, and edited them into a book. *Preston Sturges* by Preston Sturges will be published in September by Simon & Schuster.

IN HOLLYWOOD I STARTED at the bottom: a bum by the name of Sturgeon who had once written a hit play called *Strictly Something-or-Other*. Carl Laemmle of Universal offered me a contract, with unilateral options exercisable by the studio, to join his team as a writer. My wife [Eleanor Hutton] had decamped, my fortune was depleted, and even though I was living on coffee and moonlight, my costs of living continued to cost. I did not have to wrestle with any principles to leap on Laemmle's offer. On Sept. 9, 1932, I arrived in Hollywood with my secretary, Bianca Gilchrist.

I was to write, offer suggestions, and make myself generally useful, and for this I was to get a nominal or beginning writer's salary of a thousand dollars a week. Junior writers got less, of course, but I *had* written *Strictly Something-or-Other*, and that made me a kind of senior beginner. I was charmed; it vindicated my contention that writing was my profession, and the money proved it.

There were a great many writers on the lot, and the reason for this was that at the time, writers worked in teams, like piano movers. It was generally believed by the powers down in front that a man who could write comedy could not write tragedy, that a man who could write forceful, virile stuff could not handle the tender passages, and that if the picture was not to taste all of the same cook, a multiplicity of writers was essential. Four writers were considered the rock-bottom minimum required. Six writers, with the sixth member a woman to puff up the lighter parts, was considered ideal. Many, many more writers have been used on a picture, of course; several writers have even been assigned the same story unbeknownst to each other.

Bianca and I were assigned beautiful offices in a little bungalow on the Universal lot affectionately known as the Bull Pen. It took me exactly two days on the job as a hired writer, or until I met my first director, to find out that I was in the wrong racket. I had expected my producer to be peculiar, of course, because the facts about Hollywood producers had been well publicized throughout the land. On meeting him, I was not disappointed. About directors, though, I knew very little, and it took me a few minutes to get the point.

It was not so much what the director said; it was the way he said it, especially the way he looked at me (a writer): coolly, confidently, courteously, but with a curious condescension. He was a perfectly polite and affable little man and did his best to put me at my ease, but one of my knees kept twitching and I had the uneasy feeling that instead of standing on my feet looking down at him, I should have been on one knee looking up at him. The man was obviously a prince of the blood.

The more directors I met, the more I realized that this was not an isolated case. They were all princes of the blood. Nobody ever had them directing pictures in teams with one of them handling the horseback scenes and another handling the bedroom interludes. The bungalows they lived in on the lot had fireplaces and private bathrooms and big soft couches. Nobody ever assigned them to pictures they didn't like; they were timidly *offered* pictures. Sometimes they graciously condescended to direct them, but if they said, no, a story was a piece of cheese, it was a piece of cheese.

This ennoblement, of course, had been conferred upon directors during the silent days, when the directors truly were the storytellers and the princes of the business. By the time I got to Hollywood, this aristocracy was merely a leftover from an earlier day. The reasons for it were no longer apparent, like the reasons for so many other aristocracies. Years later when I became a writer-director, actually the storyteller again, people said I was doing something new, but I was not; I was doing something old.

"When I became a writer-director, people said I was doing something new, but I was not"

SCREEN TEST: Sturges tries out a pogo-stick prop on the set of *Christmas in July*

As I had never written anything but comedies, my producer assigned me the job of writing the ninth script of a horror picture: an adaptation of H.G. Wells' book *The Invisible Man*. Hardly any of Wells' story was suited to a motion picture, so it actually meant coming up with an original story. Eight well-known writers had already been paid for adaptations which the studio said could not be used, and I thought that if mine were used, my future at Universal would be assured.

I hurried into the Bull Pen and came out 10 weeks later with 180 pages of stuff so chilling that it would cause the hair of a statue to stand on end and cold sweat to stream down its sculpted back. The director said it was a piece of cheese. The studio did not pick up its option on my services and I was fired without further ceremony.

I had just been assigned a rewrite of a continuity for Slim Summerville and Zasu Pitts when my contract was up, but I stayed on at the studio to finish the job and made them a present of a couple of weeks' work. For this they pronounced themselves grateful, and my hope was that this bread cast upon the waters would return as ham sandwiches.

Although off salary, I was not idle. Thoroughly displeased with the abysmal status of a Hollywood team writer, I considered the benefits of free-lancing, writing scripts on my own time and selling them to a studio later. I could then write anywhere I liked, spend the spring in Paris, for instance, the summer on my boat, the fall in New York, and the winter in Palm Beach, coming to California for a couple of days a year to sign contracts for the sale of the scripts.

Free-lancing to me was also a stab at raising the writer's status, if not to the level of prince of the blood, at least to the level of tender of the royal shaving paper or something of equal dignity; anything to get out of the cellar to which custom had assigned the Hollywood team writer.

Bianca got behind the typewriter and I got to work on *The Power and the Glory*, a story inspired by some incidents Eleanor had told me about her mother's father, C.W. Post, founder of the Postum Cereal Co., known today as the General Foods Corp. The fruits of inspiration bore no resemblance to the actual life and times of Eleanor's grandfather, of course, but I chose the nonchronological structure of the screenplay because I noticed that when Eleanor would recount adventures, the lack of chronology interfered not at all with one's pleasure in the stories and that, in fact, its absence often sharpened the impact of the tale.

The screenplay for *The Power and the Glory* had one thing that distinguished it from other scripts of the time. So far as I know, it was the first story conceived and written as a shooting script by its author on his own time and then sold to a moving picture company on a royalty basis, exactly as plays or novels are sold. It established a couple of other "firsts," too. It was the first script shot by a director almost exactly as written. It was also the first story to use what the publicity department dubbed *narratage*, that is, the narrator's, or author's, voice spoke the dialogue while the actors only moved their lips. Strangely enough, this was highly effective and the illusion was complete.

It was neither a silent film nor a talking film, but rather a combination of the two. It embodied the visual action of a silent picture, the sound of the narrator's voice, and the storytelling economy and the richness of characterization of a novel. The reason for trying this method was to see if some way could be devised to carry American films into foreign countries. It would be extremely easy to put a narrator's voice on the soundtrack in any language, because the narrator is heard but not seen. The further advantage of a narrator is that, like the author of a novel, he may describe not only what people do and say but also what they feel and what they think.

I sold the screenplay to Jesse Lasky at Fox in February

52 SEPTEMBER 7, 1990

ENTERTAINMENT WEEKLY 53

184/185
DESIGN FIRM: *Entertainment Weekly Magazine In-house*
DESIGNER: *Susan Levin*
HEADLINE TYPEFACE: *Monotype Grotesque Extra Condensed*
TEXT TYPEFACE: *Century Expanded*
CLIENT: *Entertainment Weekly Magazine*

186

ROCK & ROLL HERO

LENNON

John Lennon merged art with pop and redefined what it meant to be a rock star

ON THE 10TH ANNIVERSARY of his murder by Mark David Chapman, on December 8, 1980, it's time to remember why so many people loved John Lennon so much. Lennon wasn't the plaster saint Yoko Ono has tried to make him, nor the half-mad dope fiend palmed off by debunking biographer Albert Goldman, but someone far more lively and complex. He was funny, angry, smart, crazy, loving, grouchy, a sweet-voiced pop singer, a heroic inspiration, an avant-gardist with the common touch, and, at the same time, the bad boy down the block.

He was also the first of a new breed of rock stars: He seized the opportunity offered by the Beatles' unprecedented fame and refashioned stardom in his own image. We take it for granted today that rock stars have long careers, dabble in art as well as commerce, and get involved with social and political issues as well as messy divorces. When they do, they're operating within the large space between Big Beat and Big Ideas that John Lennon originally carved out.

He began whittling at that space in childhood. Born in 1940—he would have turned 50 this year—and abandoned by his parents in infancy, Lennon grew up rebellious in the comfortable home of his aunt and uncle in lower-middle-class Liverpool. In the mid-'50s, he was sent off to art school, the English education system's dumping ground for talented misfit adolescents. But even in such unconventional company, Lennon didn't really fit in. He hung around with slightly younger, working-class louts and—after meeting Paul McCartney at a church fair—even played in a band later called the Beatles. Both rockers and art students initially found his mixture of interests unfathomable.

Lennon didn't resolve the conflict—in his characteristic fashion, he managed to have it both ways. He found links between the art of Picasso and the rock & roll of Elvis, reveling in their mixture of manic energy, pure whimsy, personal expression, and social satire. And he didn't just demonstrate that these connections existed; he demonstrated them in a way that, as soon as his band got into a recording studio, proved seductive to an entire generation. From the minute the Beatles turned up, shaking their long hair, sporting their collarless jackets, snickering their way through press conferences, and generally goofing around—until *wham!* they slammed into a song that told you this brand of fun was serious business—they united art and entertainment, and joined the irresponsible with the visionary.

It was apparent to everyone that Lennon was the Beatles' leader. But he kept looking for a greater leader, a grander *(continued on page 16)*

BY DAVE MARSH

BOTH WITH THE BEATLES AND IN HIS SOLO CAREER, LENNON IMAGINED A WORLD IN WHICH MUSIC EMBRACED POLITICS—AND VICE VERSA. LEFT, RECORDING SESSION, JULY 1971; RIGHT, THE BACK OF THE 'TWO VIRGINS' ALBUM COVER, 1968

ENTERTAINMENT WEEKLY 13

187

It was apparent to everyone that Lennon was the Beatles' leader. But Lennon kept looking for a leader outside himself.

YOU SAY YOU WANT A REVOLUTION: BETWEEN THE TIME THE BEATLES FIRST APPEARED ON 'THE ED SULLIVAN SHOW' (LEFT, FEB. 1964) AND THE YEAR THEY RELEASED THEIR 'WHITE ALBUM' (RIGHT, 1968), LENNON REBELLED AGAINST THE CONFINES OF POP IN BOTH SONGWRITING AND APPEARANCE

ENTERTAINMENT WEEKLY 15

186/187
DESIGN FIRM: *Entertainment Weekly Magazine In-house*
DESIGNER: *Mark Michaelson*
HEADLINE TYPEFACE: *Bureau Grotesque 13*
TEXT TYPEFACE: *Century Expanded*
CLIENT: *Entertainment Weekly Magazine*

188

TOM DE HAVEN ON THE CLASSIC COMICS

STRIP MINING

THERE'S THAT LINE in a Paul Simon song: "It's every generation throws a hero up the pop charts." Yes, and a few comic-strip characters, too. It's Calvin and Hobbes this year. A decade ago it was Garfield and Opus. Before them? Zonker Harris and Duke. Hagar. Cathy. Miss Peach. Charlie Brown. Pogo. And on back for almost a century. Barney Google. Maggie and Jiggs. Mutt and Jeff. Buster Brown. The Katzenjammers. ◆ Some comic-strip characters stick around a long time, outliving their creators—the Wallets of *Gasoline Alley* have been in the papers every day since 1918. Others—like Andy Gump and Abie the Agent—are hot for a year, or 10, or 20, then vanish. And when they're gone, they're gone. ◆ Well, not quite. You won't find Rube Goldberg's Boob McNutt in your funnies this weekend, or Fred Opper's Happy Hooligan, or Crockett Johnson's Barnaby, but you can find them all, in the swell company of other rambunctious stars from yesteryear, in *The Smithsonian Collection of Newspaper Comics (Abrams, $24.95)*, a sumptuous treat that provides a full education about our liveliest branch of pop culture. For those after more than a generous sampling, a number of publishers have inaugurated ambitious projects that bring partial or complete runs of America's comic-strip "classics" back, this time on good paper and in book form. Here are the most interesting:

I WANNA PIECE OF CAKE:
The original Nancy in full cry

The Complete Little Nemo in Slumberland
(Remco–Fantagraphics Books, Volumes 1–3: $29.95 each; Volume 4: $35)

Winsor McCay's masterpiece about a dark-haired boy's dream adventures in a surreal metropolis populated by storybook royalty and flying whatchamacallits was published in the New York *Herald* from 1905 till 1911. A tour de force of design and draftsmanship, though often clunky in dialogue, *Little Nemo* remains one of the treasures of comic art.

The Komplete Kolor Krazy Kat
(Remco–Kitchen Sink, Volume 1, $34.95)

Krazy & Ignatz: The Komplete Kat Komics
(Eclipse, Volumes 1–6: $29.95 hardcover, $9.95 paperback; Volume 7: $35.95 hardcover, $14.95 paperback)

The premise was as simple as it was mad: dog loves cat, cat loves mouse, mouse loves...no one, but he sure does loathe that cat! George Herriman launched *Krazy Kat* in 1911, and from then till his death in 1944, he turned that simple, loony, unpromising premise into what's generally regarded as the greatest comic strip ever. Whimsy, poetry, pathos, masochism, and slapstick were all played out against the buttes, cacti, and ever-changing pastel mesas of a surreal Arizona desert.

The Complete Color Polly and Her Pals
(Remco–Kitchen Sink, Volume 1, $34.95)

Launched in 1913 to appeal to that era's "New Woman" (middle class and yearning to breathe free, or at least

Tom De Haven is the author of Funny Papers, *among other novels.*

ENTERTAINMENT WEEKLY 45

189

smoke a cigarette indoors), Cliff Sterrett's *Polly and Her Pals* quickly changed into something quite different: a gag strip full of Dickensian screwballs with cubist and Dada visuals borrowed from the Armory Show. In 1935, Sterrett abandoned the daily strip and devoted his energies to this Sunday *Polly*, which remains one of the most graphically innovative comics ever produced. Yeah, yeah, but is it funny? Very.

The Complete E.C. Segar Popeye
(Fantagraphics Books, 11 volumes, hardcover, $30 each; paperback, $14.95)

Elzie Crisler Segar's *Thimble Theatre*, a send-up of Victorian melodramas, had been running for 10 years in Hearst newspapers when a squinty-eyed sailor with forearms like provolones appeared one day in January 1929. Popeye proved such an instant hit with readers that Segar recast his strip, booting out most of the regular characters (except for a strident stringbean named Olive Oyl) and putting his gruff sailor man at the helm. From then until the creator's death nine years later, *Thimble Theatre* sizzled with antic invention and introduced a gallery of exuberant oddballs. Peerless.

Little Orphan Annie
(Fantagraphics, Volumes 1 and 2, $14.95 each)

The *real* Orphan Annie wouldn't have been caught dead trilling "Tomorrow" in FDR's Oval Office. The dime-eyed ward of a munitions billionaire spent most of the Depression selling apples, riding boxcars, and dodging busybodies from the social welfare agencies—when she wasn't helping her "Daddy" Warbucks outfox Wall Streeters, swarthy "foreign agents," and pinko union "racketeers." Creator Harold Gray used his strip to preach the 19th-century social gospel of American pluck and indegoldarn-pendence and caught hell for it. He was a writer's cartoonist and a serious man, and this is a very serious comic strip. The sun *never* comes out tomorrow—never!

Nancy Eats Food; How Sluggo Survives; Nancy Dreams & Schemes
(Kitchen Sink, paperback, $7.95 each)

Art Spiegelman, creator of *Maus*, claims it's harder *not* to read a *Nancy* strip than it is to read it, and therein lies the peculiar charm of Ernie Bushmiller's immortal creation. This is cartooning stripped to the basics. Sure, the gags are juvenile, but that was just the point—it was a kid's first comic strip. Grown-ups can admire the craft.

The Celebrated Cases of Dick Tracy
(Chartwell, $12.98)

Dick Tracy in the Thirties: Tommyguns and Hard Times
(Chartwell, $14.98)

On October 16, 1931, something brand-new entered newspaper comic strips: cold-blooded murder. With the slaying of old Pop Truehart on that Friday in the very first week of *Dick Tracy*, the violence

NOTIFY THE FBI THAT PIGGY BUTCHER IS NOW WANTED FOR MURDER!
2-WAY WRIST TV

taboo was swept away. Chester Gould did it first, and he always did it grislier. A weird, demented, and (no kidding) outrageously funny American Gothic.

Flash Gordon, Volume 1: Mongo, Planet of Doom
(Kitchen Sink Press, $34.95)

Comparing a *Flash Gordon* Sunday page to anything that's been around for the past several decades is like comparing the Andes to a speed bump. Inspired by the great magazine illustrators of the '20s, Alex Raymond aimed to boggle the eye—and succeeded. His science fiction, though, often tended to be stodgy and his characterizations as flat as, well, paper. For 50 years, comic-book artists have been swiping compositions from *Flash Gordon*. It set the standard.

OH, LI'L ABNER!— AH HAIN'T A RADDIO STAR NO MO'! BUT AH DON'T CARE— AH IS SO HAPPY THET YO' LOVES ME!!
AH LOVED "SORROWFUL SUE" THASS WHO!!

Li'l Abner, Volumes 1–10
(Kitchen Sink, $29.95 hardcover, $16.95 paperback)

When Al Capp retired *Li'l Abner* in 1977, after 43 years, he was better known as a strident misanthrope than as the man who'd created Dogpatch and Lower Slobovia, the Shmoos, the Kigmies, Fearless Fosdick, and Sadie Hawkins Day, and who'd once been called—by John Steinbeck, no less—the greatest satirist since Jonathan Swift. It was a sad end to one of the most brilliant careers in American cartooning. Kitchen Sink's gorgeously produced series should reestablish the Capp reputation. Maybe not Swift, but surely as good as Mark Twain.

The Phantom Sundays, Volumes 1–8
(Pioneer Books, $14.95 each)

The first masked adventurer in comics, Lee Falk's *Phantom* has been waging war against jungle pirates, poachers, and corrupt potentates since February 17, 1936. Pioneer's collections of Sunday episodes begin in March 1946 and continue chronologically, featuring the last several months of artist Ray Moore's work on the feature and the first few years of Wilson McCoy's. Slam-bang Saturday serial stuff—predictable, maybe, but fun. *The Phantom vs. The Sky Maidens* (Ken Pierce/Eclipse: $5.95) is a sampling of daily strips from the earlier, darker, pulpier days of the its run.

POW.
ZIP

The Complete Terry and the Pirates
(Remco–Fantagraphics, Volume 1, $34.95, available in November)

Terry and the Pirates
(Flying Buttress/NBM, Volumes 1–17, dailies and Sundays in black and white, paperback, $6.95 each)

Some comic strips are born great; others have greatness thrust upon them. Here was young Milton Caniff back in the late 1930s, turning out a solid adventure strip about a storybook China, when current events suddenly threw him one heck of a curve. When the Japanese invaded Manchuria, Caniff had to decide whether to ignore the news or incorporate it into his plots. To his everlasting credit, he threw out the river pirates and brought in the "invader," and *Terry and the Pirates* became *the* great strip of World War II. The *Casablanca* of comics.

Pogo, Volume 1
(Fantagraphics, $29.95 hardcover, $9.95 paperback, available Christmas)

Pogo & Albert: The Complete Pogo Comics
(Eclipse, $29.95 hardcover, $8.95 paperback)

Though Simon & Schuster regularly publishes Pogo collections, fans of Walt Kelly's Okefenokee menagerie have never had the chance—till now—to see this bona fide classic develop in sequence. Fantagraphics aims to reprint the complete *Pogo* comic strip, beginning with 1948, when it ran in only one newspaper, the short-lived *New York Star*, and continuing through 1973. Meanwhile, Eclipse has been reprinting the *original Pogo* (be warned, folks: He looks like a rat!) that Kelly created for comic books shortly after leaving the Disney studio in 1942.

SHUT UP! YOU HAD IT COMING!
LET ME GO! - I'LL TEAR THAT RITZY DAME TO PIECES..

Now that public libraries, and—to a degree—chain bookstores have shown some interest, the future of classic-comics reprinting looks good. *The Yellow Kid*, created by Richard Outcault in 1895 and considered the first real comic strip, is being published by Eclipse in time for Christmas. Also coming: *Alley Oop*, Frank Frazetta's *Johnny Comet*, several more full-color volumes of Harold Foster's majestic *Prince Valiant*, and—just maybe—Frank King's great *Gasoline Alley*.

We're not likely to see these kinds of strips again in our Sunday papers, but it's nice to know that what used to be hasn't been lost forever. And it's even nicer to lay on the floor with your ankles crossed and read 'em. ◆

Clockwise from far left: Chester Gould's Dick Tracy alerts headquarters on his two-way wrist TV; Li'l Abner during the heyday of his creator, Al Capp; Ignatz gets physical in *Krazy Kat*; the romance of World War II from *Terry and the Pirates*.

46 OCTOBER 5, 1990

ENTERTAINMENT WEEKLY 47

188/189
DESIGN FIRM: *Entertainment Weekly Magazine In-house*
DESIGNER: *Mark Michaelson*
HEADLINE TYPEFACE: *Bureau Grotesque 13*
TEXT TYPEFACE: *Century Expanded*
CLIENT: *Entertainment Weekly Magazine*

190/191
DESIGN FIRM: *Entertainment Weekly Magazine In-house*
DESIGNER: *Mark Michaelson*
HEADLINE TYPEFACE: *Caslon 540 Italic, Monotype Condensed and Grotesque Extra Condensed*
TEXT TYPEFACE: *Caslon 540*
CLIENT: *Entertainment Weekly Magazine*

190

AN EXCERPT FROM 'MO' BETTER BLUES'

Spike Lee Rides a
BLUE NOTE

AFTER THE SUCCESS of *Do the Right Thing*, his film about race and politics, Spike Lee has returned to romance with *Mo' Better Blues*, a film starring Denzel Washington as a horn player in love with two women. In the following excerpt from the movie's companion book, Lee—with the help of writer Lisa Jones—talks about his inspiration for this project.

HE MIGHT BE GIANT: Spike Lee (left) with cameraman John Newby between takes on the set of *Mo' Better Blues*. In addition to directing, Spike acts the role of flamboyant music manager Giant, a little guy with a big mouth. (Above) Behind the scenes with Jeff Watts (left) and Bill Nunn, who play jazz drummer and bassist, respectively. The musicians "emulate and dress like their heroes from other eras, especially bebop musicians of the '40s and '50s," Lee writes.

Copyright © 1990 by Spike Lee. From the forthcoming book *Mo' Better Blues*, published by Fireside/Simon & Schuster Inc. Printed by permission.

42 AUGUST 17, 1990 ENTERTAINMENT WEEKLY 43

191

I ALWAYS KNEW I would do a movie about the music. When I say the music, I'm talking about jazz, the music I grew up with. Jazz isn't the only type of music that I listen to but it's the music I feel closest to.

I saw *Bird*, Clint Eastwood's portrait of Charlie Parker, in the fall of '88. Bertrand Tavernier's *'Round Midnight*, which was released two years before, was a slightly better film, if only because of saxophonist Dexter Gordon's performance. Both were narrow depictions of the lives of black musicians, as seen through the eyes of white screenwriters and white directors.

Shortly after seeing *Bird*, I read that Woody Allen was planning a film about jazz. Now, wait a minute! First Clint Eastwood, and now Woody Allen! You know I couldn't let Woody Allen do a jazz film before I did. I was on a mission.

One look at *Bird* and *'Round Midnight* told me what not to do. I realized that any film based on Charlie Parker's life would be open season for criticism. Audiences bring excess baggage to films based on the lives of real people. Folks were bound to walk out of the theater saying, "I knew Bird, and he didn't hold his horn like that," or "He didn't wear his hat like that." I decided to stick with fictional characters, knowing it would give me more freedom.

In this day and age the idea of a jazz film almost always means a period piece. I knew that my film would take place in the present. I wanted to show that there are young jazz musicians out there today who are carrying on a tradition. At the same time, I didn't want to do a film that was exclusively about jazz, though I knew the script would center on characters who were jazz musicians.

Before I wrote one word of *Mo' Better Blues*, I knew I wanted Denzel Washington to play the lead. In the fall of '88, Denzel was starring on Broadway in *Checkmates* with Ruby Dee and Paul Winfield. I went to see the play a couple of times. The minute Denzel appeared on stage, the women in the audience started to scream. Not only was Denzel a great actor, he was a legitimate matinee idol. I wanted to write a role for Denzel that black women were waiting for him to play. He has done a number of important co-starring roles in films like *A Soldier's Story*, *Cry Freedom*, and *Glory*, and he has played a leading man in *The Mighty Quinn*. But he still hadn't done a bona fide romantic lead. *Mo' Better Blues* would be his chance.

So, I had my foundation. It would be a jazz film, set in a contemporary context, with fictional characters and Denzel Washington as the leading man. I took notes from Christmas '88 until early April '89, then wrote the first draft.

While taking notes for the script, I read *Beneath the Underdog*, the autobiography of jazz bassist/composer Charles Mingus. Though the book didn't influence the content of my film, I did like the title, so I gave that name to the jazz club. Around this time Malaika Adero, my editor at Simon & Schuster, passed me a copy of the advance galleys of *Miles: The Autobiography*, written with Quincy Troupe. The book helped put me in a jazz mode.

Mo' Better Blues is not a love story. I find love stories

Now, wait a minute! You know I couldn't let Woody Allen do a jazz film before I did. I was on a mission.

A LOVE SUPREME: Denzel Washington (left) plays Bleek, whose obsession makes him a great musician but a selfish man. Tragedy turns him around. Cynda Williams (above) plays Clarke, an aspiring singer. Bleek doesn't recognize her talent till it's too late. Bleek's band (below) performs at the club.

ENTERTAINMENT WEEKLY 45

192

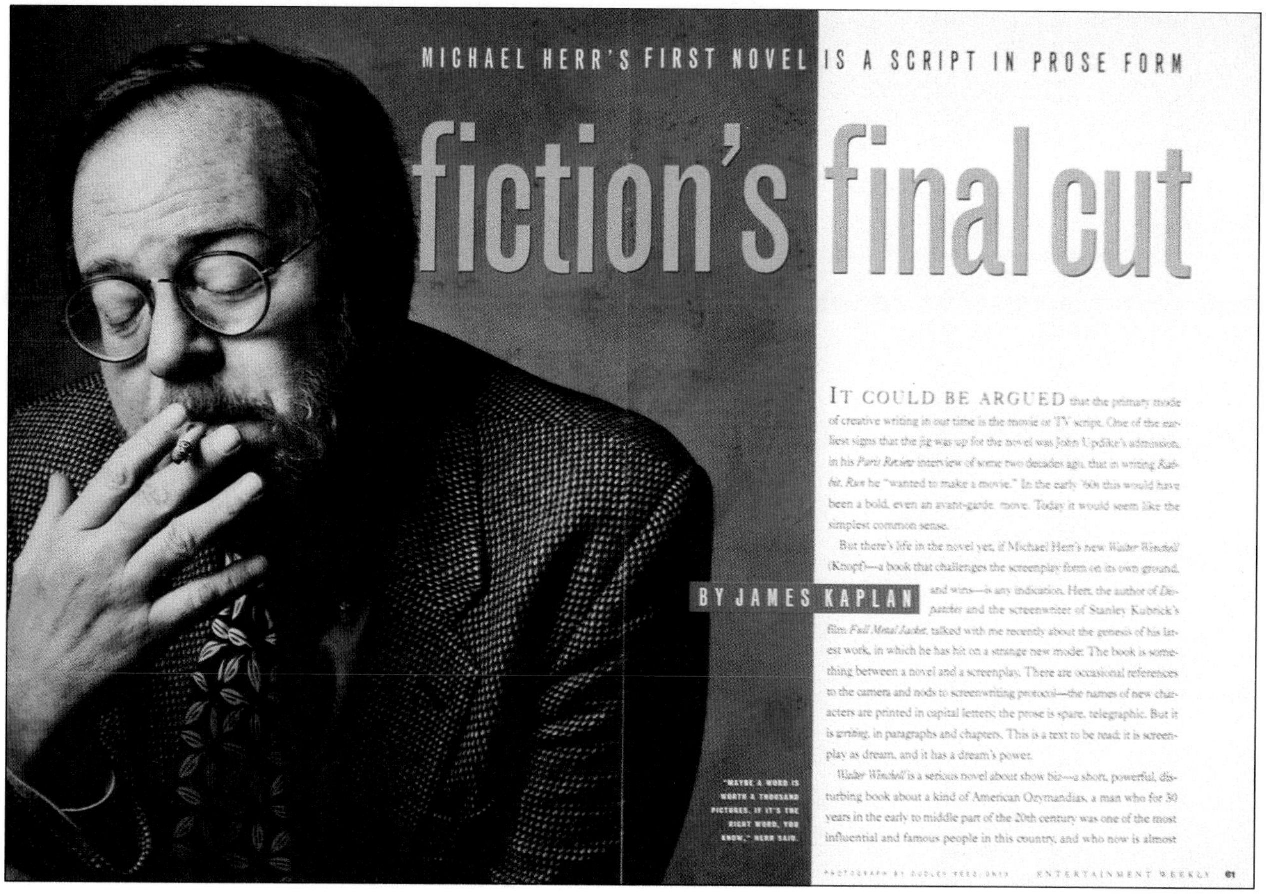
MICHAEL HERR'S FIRST NOVEL IS A SCRIPT IN PROSE FORM

fiction's final cut

BY JAMES KAPLAN

IT COULD BE ARGUED that the primary mode of creative writing in our time is the movie or TV script. One of the earliest signs that the jig was up for the novel was John Updike's admission, in his *Paris Review* interview of some two decades ago, that in writing *Rabbit, Run* he "wanted to make a movie." In the early '60s this would have been a bold, even an avant-garde, move. Today it would seem like the simplest common sense.

But there's life in the novel yet, if Michael Herr's new *Walter Winchell* (Knopf)—a book that challenges the screenplay form on its own ground, and wins—is any indication. Herr, the author of *Dispatches* and the screenwriter of Stanley Kubrick's film *Full Metal Jacket*, talked with me recently about the genesis of his latest work, in which he has hit on a strange new mode. The book is something between a novel and a screenplay. There are occasional references to the camera and nods to screenwriting protocol—the names of new characters are printed in capital letters; the prose is spare, telegraphic. But it is *writing*, in paragraphs and chapters. This is a text to be read: it is screenplay as dream, and it has a dream's power.

Walter Winchell is a serious novel about show biz—a short, powerful, disturbing book about a kind of American Ozymandias, a man who for 30 years in the early to middle part of the 20th century was one of the most influential and famous people in this country, and who now is almost

"MAYBE A WORD IS WORTH A THOUSAND PICTURES, IF IT'S THE RIGHT WORD, YOU KNOW," HERR SAID.

ENTERTAINMENT WEEKLY 61

192
DESIGN FIRM: *Entertainment Weekly Magazine In-house*
DESIGNER: *Mark Michaelson*
HEADLINE TYPEFACE: *Monotype Grotesque Extra Condensed*
TEXT TYPEFACE: *Caslon 540*
CLIENT: *Entertainment Weekly Magazine*

193

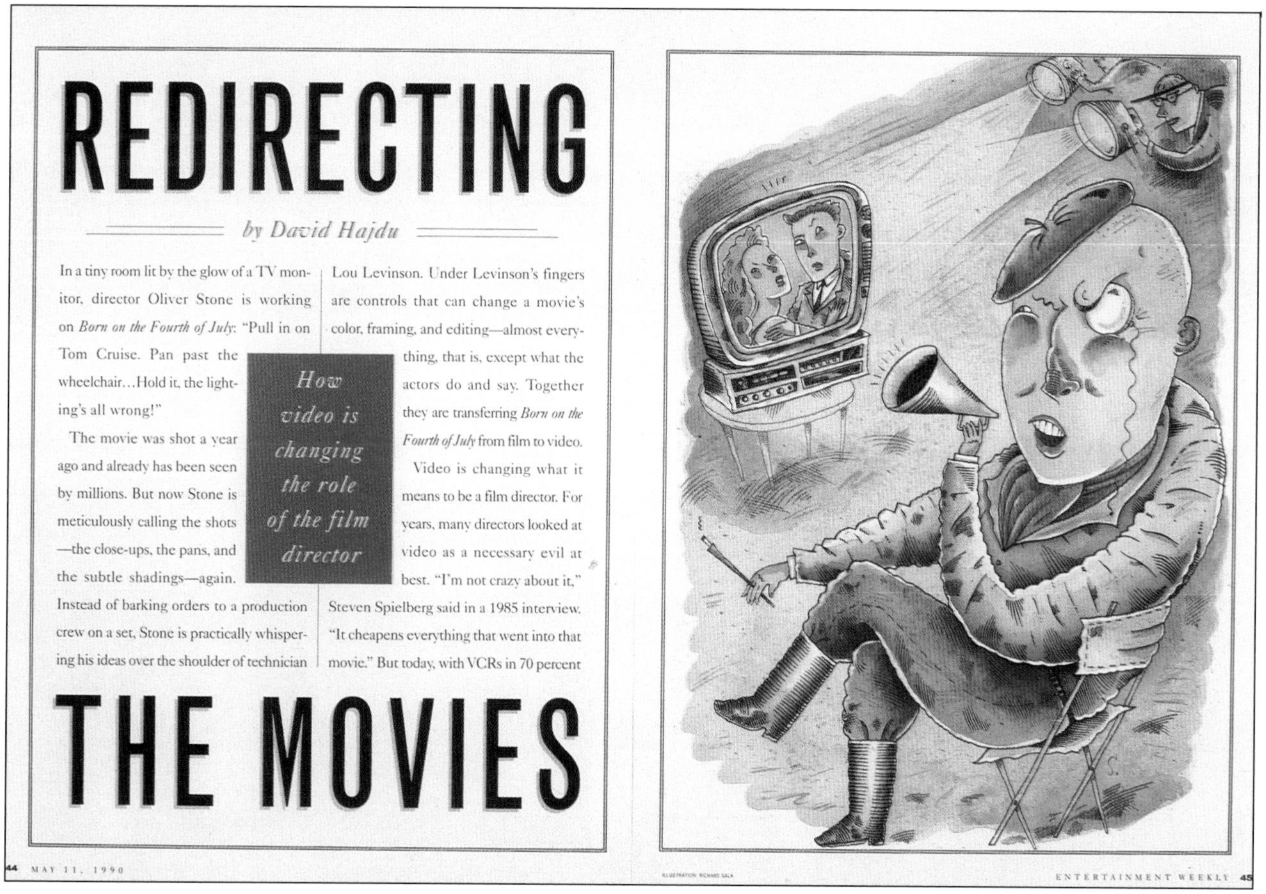
REDIRECTING THE MOVIES

by David Hajdu

How video is changing the role of the film director

In a tiny room lit by the glow of a TV monitor, director Oliver Stone is working on *Born on the Fourth of July*: "Pull in on Tom Cruise. Pan past the wheelchair...Hold it, the lighting's all wrong!"

The movie was shot a year ago and already has been seen by millions. But now Stone is meticulously calling the shots—the close-ups, the pans, and the subtle shadings—again. Instead of barking orders to a production crew on a set, Stone is practically whispering his ideas over the shoulder of technician Lou Levinson. Under Levinson's fingers are controls that can change a movie's color, framing, and editing—almost everything, that is, except what the actors do and say. Together they are transferring *Born on the Fourth of July* from film to video.

Video is changing what it means to be a film director. For years, many directors looked at video as a necessary evil at best. "I'm not crazy about it," Steven Spielberg said in a 1985 interview. "It cheapens everything that went into that movie." But today, with VCRs in 70 percent

44 MAY 11, 1990

ENTERTAINMENT WEEKLY 45

193
DESIGN FIRM: *Entertainment Weekly Magazine In-house*
DESIGNER: *Miriam Campiz*
HEADLINE TYPEFACE: *Monotype Grotesque Extra Condensed*
TEXT TYPEFACE: *Caslon 540*
CLIENT: *Entertainment Weekly Magazine*

194/195
DESIGN FIRM: *Entertainment Weekly Magazine In-house*
DESIGNER: *Mark Michaelson*
HEADLINE TYPEFACE: *Modern Extended*
TEXT TYPEFACE: *Century Expanded*
CLIENT: *Entertainment Weekly Magazine*

194

Schwarzenegger
A Hard Man Is Good to Film

Movie by movie, the former bodybuilding champ has transformed himself into the world's most popular action star. And now, with 'Total Recall,' Arnold is bigger than ever By Donald Chase

SCHWARZENEGGER: GREG GORMAN; IRON: MOVIE STILL ARCHIVES

ENTERTAINMENT WEEKLY 35

195

is important. If the character is very secure, you usually don't want to show him running at all, but walking, steady and determined, like the character in *The Terminator*. If in an emergency he has to run, you want him to dodge obstacles like a football player, with wrists tight and fists clenched."

It sounds simple enough, but veteran actor Michael Ironside, who plays a coldhearted thug in *Recall*, came away impressed with Schwarzenegger's "timing in action sequences...the way he turns and stares [shows he has] an incredible sense of what he looks like and

how he functions on camera. He helped me. In one sequence, he said, 'When you're running, some of the threat in your character drops. If you tightened up your arms here....'"

At the same time, Schwarzenegger, who recently tried his hand at directing an episode for HBO's *Tales From the Crypt*, picked up tips himself during the shooting. According to Schwarzenegger, Verhoeven purposely introduced uncertainty into the daily grind of filming. "His preparation is incredibly thorough and he's very precise about what he wants, so we feel we're in good hands. But because he has it in mind to throw the audience off all the time, he also throws the actors off all the time. Always at the last minute he will pretend he's changed his mind, that something will work better [than what has been discussed]."

For all that, Schwarzenegger was as responsible for the atmosphere on the set as Verhoeven. While working on a picture, Arnold usually creates a positive mood with his forthright style that's punctuated by bursts of locker-room humor and practical jokes.

"It's not just that he asks about you," Ticotin says. "It's that he remembers every last thing you told him." And asks for updates on that restaurant you were planning to eat at, that doctor's appointment, that family situation back in L.A. This is not a high-strung star who hides out in his trailer between takes or surrounds himself with an entourage of sycophants. This is a brand-new species: a 6' 2", 215-pound, cigar-smoking yenta.

Schwarzenegger accepts an obligation for the morale on the set because a bad mood on the part of a leading actor, the director, or a producer "will trickle down to the last guy in the company," he says. "But I don't [have to] make any effort, because I naturally am a happy guy. I like what I'm doing—I like the people I work with. I love finding out what everyone is up to, where they come from, what movies they've worked on. That way," he concludes with happy wonderment, "you can get a really good conversation going."

What excites Schwarzenegger even more are acts of stoicism and perseverance. He compliments his wife, Maria Shriver, for "joking about throwing up" during the pregnancy that ended with the birth of their daughter in December "instead of whining about it," and then praises costar Ticotin because "you can ask her to do something [physically arduous] a thousand times and

On the set, this is not a high-strung star; this is a 215-pound, cigar-smoking yenta

At left, searching for the bad guys who stole his identity, Schwarzenegger arrives in Venusville, the Red Planet's red-light district, a high-tech honky-tonk populated by rebel colonists and mutants.

she never complains."

All this pleasantness notwithstanding, Schwarzenegger has little patience with slackers and moaners. His good-natured imitation of costar Sharon Stone during a fight scene—"Don't touch my hair....Don't strangle me!"—is merciless.

He sits back and smiles, pleased at the laughs he's gotten from the small gathering of cast and crew members. And no wonder. The muscle-bound hunk with the heavy accent who the smart guys said would never make it in Hollywood has gone from pumping iron to pumping irony with the same impressive results. ◆

38 JUNE 8, 1990

DAVID JAMES

His Body of Work

The Complete Arnold Schwarzenegger: An Action Aficionado's Guide By Tom Soter

◆ NEWLY ARRIVED IN America, Arnold was a bulging Austrian babe in the woods when his bodybuilding mentor Joe Weider helped him land the title role in *Hercules Goes to New York* (1970), a low-budget oddity also known as *Hercules Goes Bananas*. The body is definitely Arnold's, but the unaccented voice isn't in this ridiculous adventure involving a toga-clad Herc on the loose in modern Manhattan. From this embarrassing beginning, Schwarzenegger worked his way up to muscularly mute bit parts to sword-and-sorcery epics to action and comedy to whatever else he wants to do. Here's a guide to Arnold's evolution as an actor.

HERCULES GOES TO NEW YORK

PUMPING IRON

CONAN THE BARBARIAN

STAY HUNGRY (1976)

◆ Arnold's big-screen "introduction" finds him playing the part of Joe Santo, a—what else?—bodybuilder competing for the Mr. Universe title. Also starring in Bob Rafelson's quirky comedy-drama are Sally Field, as Schwarzenegger's ex-sweetie, and Jeff Bridges, as the ne'er-do-well scion of an old Southern family. **B**

Charming moment: Arnold playing the fiddle with a hillbilly band.

Beefcake special: Arnold's choreographed posing at the bodybuilding contest.

Arnold as philosopher: "I don't like to be too comfortable. Once you get used to it, it's hard to give up. I like to stay hungry."

Arnold said it before Jane: "Make the thighs burn."

Must see: A herd of bikinied bodybuilders chasing the bad guys through the streets of Birmingham, Ala.

PUMPING IRON (1977)

◆ George Butler's documentary on bodybuilding liberated Arnold from the confines of his sport's limited appeal. Despite his heavy accent, Schwarzenegger's charm and wit were immediately apparent. Some of the best scenes feature Arnold needling rival Lou Ferrigno—making remarks that Arnold has recently shrugged off, claiming he was deliberately being outrageous simply to sell it. Whatever, his description of "the pump" remains a ribald classic:

"The most satisfying feeling you can get in the gym is the pump. Let's say you train your biceps. Blood is rushing into your muscles, and that's what we call the pump. Your muscles get a really tight feeling, like your skin is going to explode any minute, you know, it's really tight...it's like somebody blowing air into your muscle....It feels fantastic. [Arnold flexes.] It's as satisfying to me as, uh, coming is. You know, as, ah, having sex with a woman and coming. And so can you believe how much I am in heaven? I am like, uh, getting the feeling of coming in a gym; I'm getting the feeling of coming at home; I'm getting the feeling of coming backstage, when I pump up—when I pose out in front of 5,000 people, I get the same feeling. So I am coming day and night...." **A**

THE JAYNE MANSFIELD STORY (1980)

◆ Loni Anderson and Arnold team up in a simpleminded TV movie that portrays Marilyn Monroe–knockoff Mansfield as a tragic figure kept from the beefcake she loves, strongman Mickey Hargitay, by the evil studio. **C–**

Best line: "It's like my English...something gets lost in the translation."

Best scene: An angry Arnold smashing his free weights.

Arnold as analyst: "It really mattered to her to be a success. I always wondered what was it replacing in her life? What needs did it meet?"

CONAN THE BARBARIAN (1982)

◆ Schwarzenegger's breakthrough as an action hero found him battling the leader of a nasty snake cult (James Earl

HERCULES: SHOOTING STAR; PUMPING: MOVIE STILL ARCHIVES; CONAN: MICHAEL CHILDERS/SYGMA

ENTERTAINMENT WEEKLY 39

196

HE HAS BUILT his movie career the same way he once built his body—to Mr. Universe proportions. Programmatically. Relentlessly. Positively. Bulk up here, pare down there, round off this, square off that. And it has paid off.

With *Total Recall* now in theaters, the already incredibly successful Arnold Schwarzenegger has reached a new level of accomplishment. With a budget estimated at between $50 and $60 million, this futuristic thriller is his most expensive film to date. He has become the world's most popular action-movie star, surpassing Stallone and Eastwood, and reportedly is earning $11 million in salary for *Recall*. In a rapidly changing entertainment industry in which international revenues have become increasingly important, these achievements carry a lot of weight.

Forget all this business about the Austrian Oak who became the ambitious American, the Camelot crasher. The only thing to know about Schwarzenegger is that he works. He works hard. Just as you don't build biceps like Arnold's overnight, you don't become a movie icon with one picture. You start with a plan. You start small. You play to your strength. Then you can grow. And that's what he has done. From sword-and-sorcery adventures to action to comedy. Now, in *Total Recall*, Schwarzenegger even gets a love interest—two love interests, in fact.

"I've added new elements to my films," he says, "and cut back on old ones—but slowly, as I think it must be done. I hope to expand my range and win new audiences while keeping the old one."

This time out, Schwarzenegger has chosen to push himself by working with the highly regarded Dutch director Paul Verhoeven, who made *Soldier of Orange* and *The Fourth Man* in his native Holland before his smash U.S. hit *RoboCop*. Furthermore, Schwarzenegger is playing what may be his most complex role.

His Doug Quaid is a man caught in a reality-identity bind. Is he an average-Joe construction worker on Earth, with a knockout blond wife (Sharon Stone), content in every way except for strange recurring visions of life on Mars? Or is he the man of his own dreams, a heroic freedom fighter, with a knockout brunet sidekick (Rachel Ticotin), out to liberate an oxygen-starved Martian mining colony run by *RoboCop* villain Ronny Cox?

In the resolution of this conundrum, there are action and special effects aplenty, along with some of the humor that always enlivened Arnold's adventures. But sitting in the awning-shaded Astroturf "patio" outside his mobile trailer at Churubusco Studios in Mexico City, where the film was shot, Schwarzenegger explains how *Total Recall* offers a new and improved take on both action and humor.

"Sure, there are lines that are funny," he says. For example, he points a gun at his wife and she says, "You wouldn't kill me, I'm your wife"; and he, taking aim, replies, "Consider this a divorce." But, in general, he has moved away from his familiar signature lines, such as *Commando*'s "Let's party." Or *The Terminator*'s "I'll be back." In *Recall*, he says, "it's more the circumstances that make things funny."

Even though *Recall* has nonstop action, Schwarzenegger wanted to avoid the mega-body-count shoot-outs that ended his movies like *Predator* and *Commando*. This time the climax is more personal, as Quaid faces off with Cohaagen, the evil head of the Martian colonies, played by Cox. "It can be more powerful if there's only one guy you're going after and there are twists and a heightened mood or atmosphere, [rather] than mowing down a hundred guys," he says. That's why Arnold wanted to work with Verhoeven. "He doesn't just shoot the script; he brings some extra flavor to the material."

Part of that "flavor" is found in the sets that *RoboCop* production designer William Sandell has created for *Total Recall*. The scenes that take place on Earth use a number of the bulky, squat concrete buildings erected in Mexico City in the '80s, in a style architecture critics call the New Brutalism. Mars, consisting of 35 studio sets built at a cost of $100,000 to $300,000 apiece, is a metallic-modular, high-tech/honky-tonk nightmare. This is a big-budget, special-effects movie. No doubt about that.

But Schwarzenegger feels no sense of competition with the decor. "You don't have to always be the star, at the center of the screen. Every scene doesn't have to be a close-up. I can't sell the fact that we're on Mars, but the sets can—the machinery, those fire-red skies, the catacombs, the skeletons."

Schwarzenegger understands what makes a big picture work and can talk for hours on many aspects of the business. But when the subject turns to his own acting style and ability, he doesn't have a lot to say. No paeans to the "preparation" he goes through before a scene. No abstract discussion of a character's "emotional arc."

Action, however, is one subject he does discuss. "When you've done as many physical films as I've done, prehistoric or futuristic or in-between, you become aware that every single gesture

"You don't have to always be the star, at the center of the screen. Every scene doesn't have to be a close-up."

Clockwise from top: Quaid (Schwarzenegger) in Mars bar with Thumbelina (Debbie Lee Carrington) and rebel sidekick Melina (Rachel Ticotin); with director Paul Verhoeven; removing disguise; with mutant (Dean Norris) and Melina; and with earthly wife Lori (Sharon Stone)

CLOCKWISE FROM TOP: DAVID JAMES (2); DAVID APPLEBY; JAMES; APPLEBY

Arnoldspeak

◆ AMERICANS HAVE spent a lot of money buying books and exercise equipment guaranteed to pump them up like Arnold. But an increasingly popular—and much easier—avocation is parroting Schwarzenegger's famous movie lines in an accent as broad as the Austrian Oak's shoulders. So, for all would-be Hanses and Franzes, here are five easy steps to sounding like the world's most popular action-movie star.

STEP ONE: Muscle up *v*'s and *f*'s until they sound like double *f*'s, as in this memorable assertion from *Predator*: "Diss ting iss hunting us…all uff us." Or, from *Twins*: "In case uffa fy-a, I could haff giffen de alaam, ant safed all de odda offans."

STEP TWO: Double all *s*'s: Is becomes iss. He's rhymes with Meese. Ears rhymes with fierce. Deyah's lots of ecksemples.

STEP THREE: Change all *th*'s and double *t*'s to *d*'s. As in: "Sit offuh deyah." "Dat's right." Or, uttered in every Arnold movie, "Wadzemadda?"

STEP FOUR: Let no *ur* word escape umlautization. "He's been murdered!" becomes, "Heese been myurdered!" A driven man is properly called "a wyurgaholic." And any act of violence should be preceded with "I don't want to hyurt you."

STEP FIVE: Harden all soft *g*'s and *j*'s to *ch*, as in: "He iss probably chust like me." "I studied Biolochee." "I wass wyurking out at de chymnasium."

◆ TO BECOME REALLY good at aping Arnold, you've got to practice. Try 10 reps of this tantalizing tongue-twister from *Twins*: "It's chuss I haff neffer hyurd diss kynuff myussic befowah." And don't ever forget the Arnold ideal: A strong mind in a strong body—with a strong accent.

—Steve Daly

36 JUNE 8, 1990

ENTERTAINMENT WEEKLY 37

197

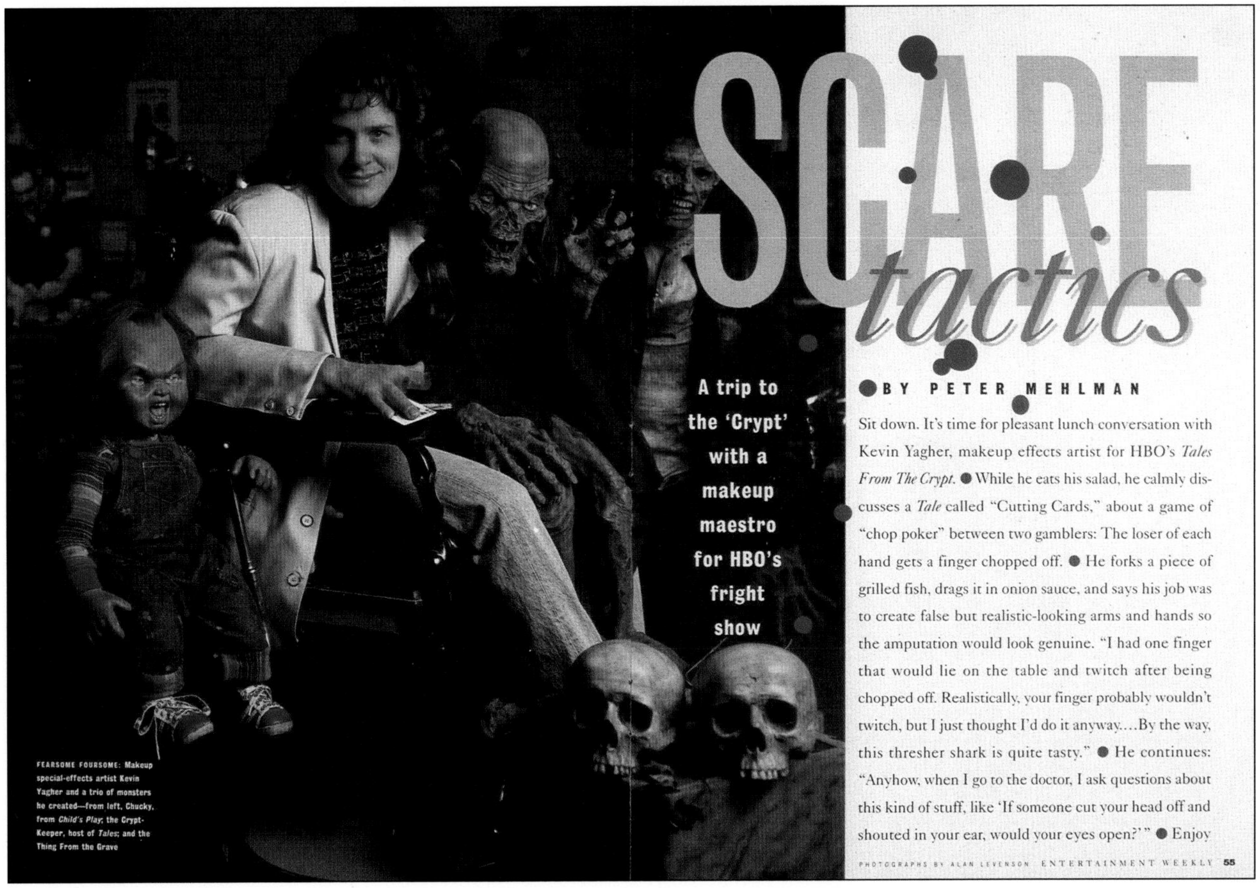

SCARE *tactics*

A trip to the 'Crypt' with a makeup maestro for HBO's fright show

BY PETER MEHLMAN

Sit down. It's time for pleasant lunch conversation with Kevin Yagher, makeup effects artist for HBO's *Tales From The Crypt*. ● While he eats his salad, he calmly discusses a *Tale* called "Cutting Cards," about a game of "chop poker" between two gamblers: The loser of each hand gets a finger chopped off. ● He forks a piece of grilled fish, drags it in onion sauce, and says his job was to create false but realistic-looking arms and hands so the amputation would look genuine. "I had one finger that would lie on the table and twitch after being chopped off. Realistically, your finger probably wouldn't twitch, but I just thought I'd do it anyway.…By the way, this thresher shark is quite tasty." ● He continues: "Anyhow, when I go to the doctor, I ask questions about this kind of stuff, like 'If someone cut your head off and shouted in your ear, would your eyes open?'" ● Enjoy

FEARSOME FOURSOME: Makeup special-effects artist Kevin Yagher and a trio of monsters he created—from left, Chucky, from *Child's Play*; the Crypt-Keeper, host of *Tales*; and the Thing From the Grave

PHOTOGRAPHS BY ALAN LEVENSON ENTERTAINMENT WEEKLY 55

196
DESIGN FIRM: *Entertainment Weekly Magazine In-house*
DESIGNER: *Mark Michaelson*
HEADLINE TYPEFACE: *Modern Extended*
TEXT TYPEFACE: *Century Expanded*
CLIENT: *Entertainment Weekly Magazine*

197
DESIGN FIRM: *Entertainment Weekly Magazine In-house*
DESIGNER: *Mark Michaelson*
HEADLINE TYPEFACE: *Monotype Grotesqu Extra Condensed and Caslon 540*
TEXT TYPEFACE: *Caslon 540*
CLIENT: *Entertainment Weekly Magazine*

198

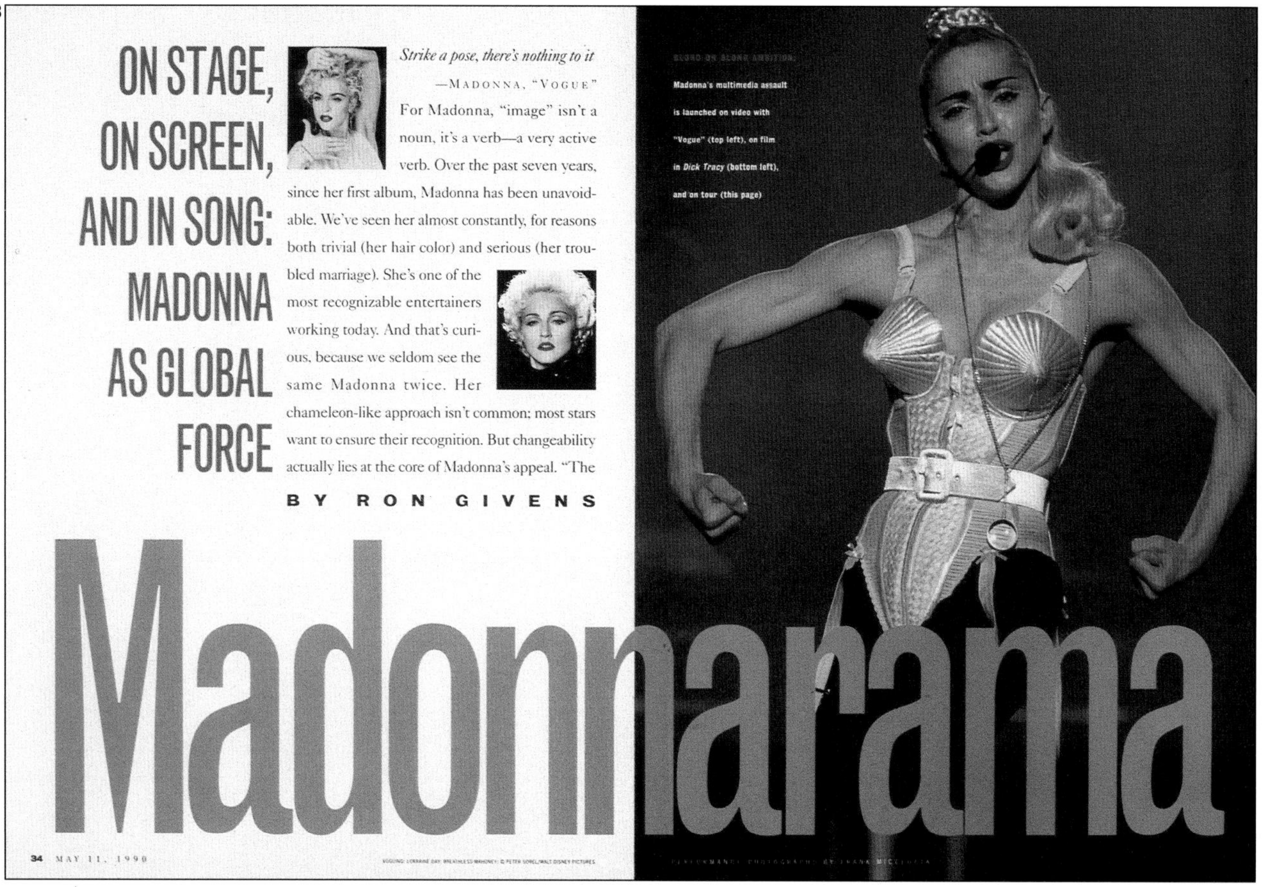

ON STAGE, ON SCREEN, AND IN SONG: MADONNA AS GLOBAL FORCE

Strike a pose, there's nothing to it

—MADONNA, "VOGUE"

For Madonna, "image" isn't a noun, it's a verb—a very active verb. Over the past seven years, since her first album, Madonna has been unavoidable. We've seen her almost constantly, for reasons both trivial (her hair color) and serious (her troubled marriage). She's one of the most recognizable entertainers working today. And that's curious, because we seldom see the same Madonna twice. Her chameleon-like approach isn't common; most stars want to ensure their recognition. But changeability actually lies at the core of Madonna's appeal. "The

BY RON GIVENS

Madonnarama

Madonna's multimedia assault is launched on video with "Vogue" (top left), on film in *Dick Tracy* (bottom left), and on tour (this page)

34 MAY 11, 1990

199

FROM 'VIRGIN' TO 'VOGUE': THE COMPLEAT MADONNA

ALBUMS

Madonna *(1983, Sire)* "Lucky Star," "Borderline," "Burning Up," "I Know It," "Holiday," "Think of Me," "Physical Attraction," "Everybody" ◆ A thin voice and even thinner arrangements: Madonna Lite. Only for dance fans. **C–**

Like a Virgin *(1984, Sire)* "Material Girl," "Angel," "Like a Virgin," "Over and Over," "Love Don't Live Here Anymore," "Dress You Up," "Shoo-Bee-Doo," "Pretender," "Stay" ◆ Is she learning how to sing, or are the backing tracks that much better? Still, only worth it for the hits. **B–**

True Blue *(1986, Sire)* "Papa Don't Preach," "Open Your Heart," "White Heat," "Live to Tell," "Where's the Party," "True Blue," "La Isla Bonita," "Jimmy Jimmy," "Love Makes the World Go Round" ◆ As much a pop record as a dance record. She's thinking some serious thoughts and singing some serious songs. Good when it's good and not that bad when it's bad. **B+**

You Can Dance *(1987, Sire)* "Spotlight," "Holiday," "Everybody," "Physical Attraction," "Spotlight (Dub Version)," "Holiday (Dub Version)," "Over and Over," "Into the Groove," "Where's the Party," "Over and Over (Dub Version)," "Into the Groove (Dub Version)" ◆ One new song, "Spotlight," and dance remixes of her hits. Includes an extended version of "Into the Groove," released as the B-side of "Angel" and not on any other album. Vocal tracks: **A**. Dub tracks (instrumental versions without Madonna's vocals): **D**

Like a Prayer *(1989, Sire)* "Like a Prayer," "Express Yourself," "Love Song," "Till Death Do Us Part," "Promise to Try," "Cherish," "Dear Jessie," "Oh Father," "Keep It Together," "Spanish Eyes," "Act of Contrition" ◆ Her most personal album yet, with songs about an abusive husband, a lost mother, and a distant father. But she remains true to her core audience as well, with songs you can dance to. A mature and accomplished effort. **A–**

I'm Breathless: Music From and Inspired by the Film Dick Tracy *(1990, Sire)* "He's a Man," "Sooner or Later," "Hanky Panky," "I'm Going Bananas," "Cry Baby," "Something to Remember," "Back in Business," "More," "What Can You Lose," "Now I'm Following You (Part I)," "Now I'm Following You (Part II)," "Vogue"

MAKING MUSIC AND MONEY: Madonna's *True Blue* album (top) produced two No. 1 singles; "Express Yourself" from *Like a Prayer* (above) went to No. 2

SINGLES
(not on Madonna albums)

"Crazy for You" *(1985, Geffen)* ◆ From the movie *Vision Quest*.

"Who's That Girl" *(1987, Sire)*
"Causing a Commotion" *(1987, Sire)* ◆ Both from the movie *Who's That Girl*.

MUSIC VIDEOS

Madonna *(1984, WEA, $16.98)* ◆ You'd think the Queen of Music Vid would have a major collection available, wouldn't you? But all we have is this paltry sampler—"Burning Up," "Borderline," and "Lucky Star" from the first album, and "Like a Virgin" from the second. **B**

Madonna Live: The Virgin Tour *(1985, WEA, $19.98)* ◆ Live from Detroit, her hometown. A lot of flat notes. Not much dancing. Maybe you had to be there. **C–**

Madonna Ciao Italia: Live From Italy *(1988, WEA, $19.98)* ◆ She has lost weight. She's hitting most of the notes. She's showing some good moves in the dance routines. Hey, she's back in the old country! **B+**

MOVIES

A Certain Sacrifice *(1980, Commtron, $49.95, R)* ◆ Is this rape-revenge film art or exploitation? You be the judge.

Vision Quest *(1985, Warner, $19.98, R)* ◆ A high-school-jock movie. Madonna is seen only briefly as a singer in a bar band.

Desperately Seeking Susan *(1985, HBO, $19.99, PG-13)* ◆ In this sly comedy of confused identities, a New Jersey housewife trades places with a shiftless Manhattan tart. Madonna plays the latter with a self-absorption that matches her own.

Shanghai Surprise *(1986, Vestron, $79.98, PG-13)* ◆ It's just as bad as you've heard, and maybe even worse. Madonna is a missionary in '30s China and Sean Penn is the ne'er-do-well who helps her out. This "mystery-suspense-romance" succeeds on none of its many levels. Madonna's performance is awkward and forced. Penn, then her husband, is equally bad.

Who's That Girl *(1987, Warner, $19.98, PG)* ◆ A screw-up of a screwball comedy. Madonna is an ex-con with a score to settle. Griffin Dunne is the stuffed-shirt lawyer who's mixed up in her shenanigans. Madonna isn't the worst thing in it, but that's not saying much.

Bloodhounds of Broadway *(1989, RCA/Columbia, $89.95, PG)* ◆ Did you miss this one about romance during the Roaring Twenties? So did everybody else.

Dick Tracy *(1990, Walt Disney Pictures)* ◆ The comic strip comes to life, costarring Madonna and Warren Beatty. Due June 15.

ACTING UP: Madonna received generally good reviews in Broadway's *Speed-the-Plow* (below); her role as *Dick Tracy*'s Breathless Mahoney (bottom) is being heavily hyped

THEATER

Speed-the-Plow *(1988)* ◆ Very respectable Broadway debut. Frank Rich of *The New York Times* praised her "intelligent, scrupulously disciplined comic acting."

COMMERCIAL

Like a Prayer *(Pepsi, 1989)* ◆ A rich little valentine to childhood dreams. Seen only once, during *The Cosby Show*, before controversy over the music video for "Like a Prayer" caused Pepsi to fizz over and pull the ad.

—Ron Givens

42 MAY 11, 1990 · EXPRESS YOURSELF: ALBERTO TOLOT/SNAP PHOTO

ENTERTAINMENT WEEKLY 43

198/199
DESIGN FIRM: *Entertainment Weekly Magazine In-house*
DESIGNER: *Michael Grossman*
HEADLINE TYPEFACE: *Monotype Grotesque Extra Condensed*
TEXT TYPEFACE: *Caslon 540*
CLIENT: *Entertainment Weekly Magazine*

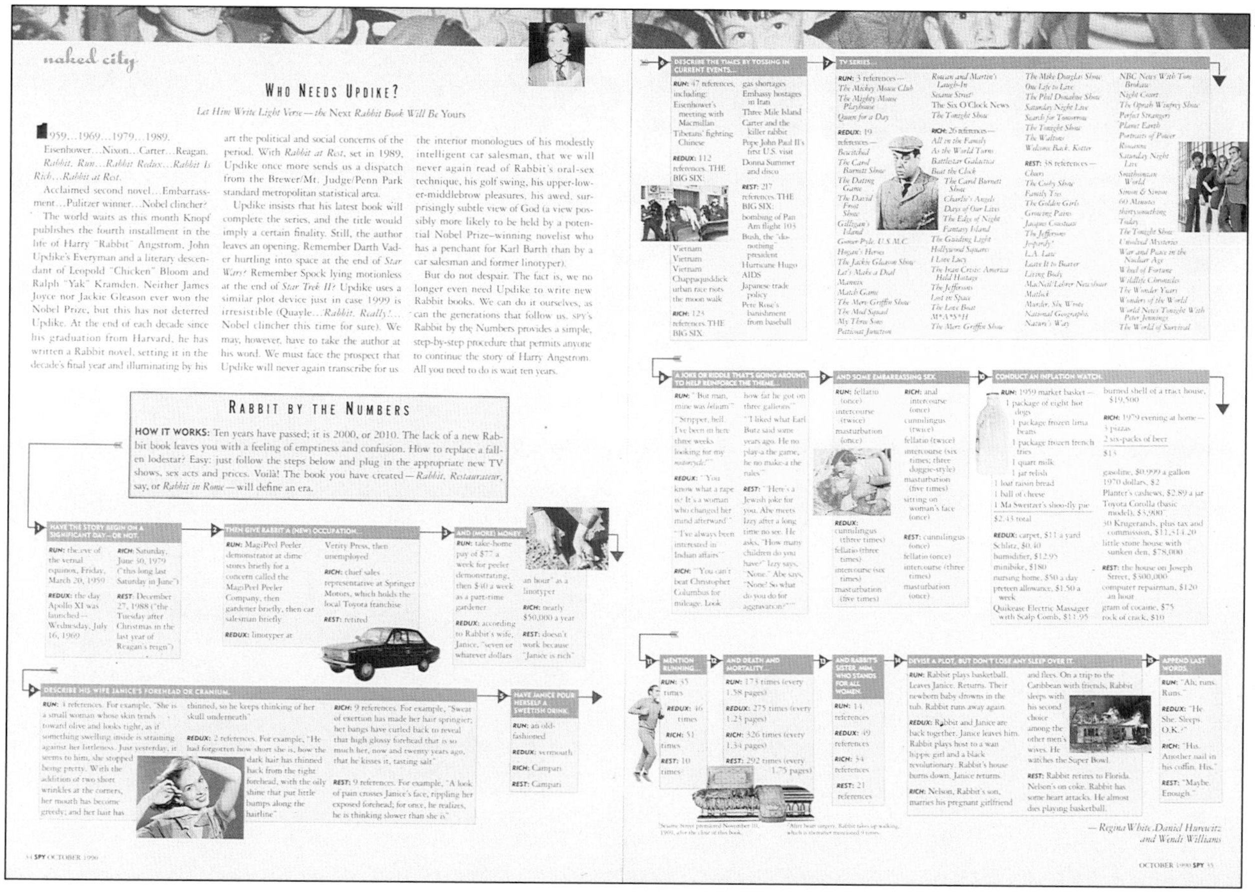

200

DESIGN FIRM: *Spy Magazine In-house*
DESIGNER: *Christiaan Kuypers*
LETTERER: *B.W. Honeycutt*
HEADLINE TYPEFACE: *Thompson Triple Condensed, Memphis Condensed and Cheltenham Bold & Italic.*
TEXT TYPEFACE: *Antique Gothic Extended, Garamond 3, Gazette and Dew Text*
CLIENT: *Spy Corporation*

201

DESIGN FIRM: *Spy Magazine In-house*
DESIGNER: *Erwin Gorostiza and Judy Simms*
HEADLINE TYPEFACE: *Alternate Gothic*
TEXT TYPEFACE: *Garamond 3 and Metro Black*
CLIENT: *Spy Corporation*

202

by Bruce Handy

the WORST of TIMES

SPLENDOR AND SQUALOR, PLUM-PUDDING RICHES AND *BLEAK HOUSE* HORRORS—VICTORIAN LONDON LIVES AGAIN IN OUR VERY OWN DICKENSIAN NEW YORK!

Hungry eyes wandered over the profusion.... Life and death went hand in hand; wealth and poverty stood side by side; repletion and starvation laid them down together. —NICHOLAS NICKLEBY

Sidewalk, midtown Manhattan ▸

"That's the state to live and die in!" said Mr. Boffin, in an unctuous manner. "R-r-rich!" —OUR MUTUAL FRIEND

◂ Private ball, Sheraton Centre

IN 1842, WHILE ON A FIVE-MONTH TOUR OF North America, Charles Dickens visited New York City, which offered much to which a celebrated English novelist could condescend. Among other things, he was amused to find packs of free-ranging pigs used for garbage removal ("Ugly brutes they are") and was repulsed by the particulars of certain nineteenth-century American habits: "I have twice seen gentlemen, at evening parties in New York, turn aside when they were not engaged in conversation, and spit upon the drawing-room carpet," he wrote to a friend back home. "And in every bar-room and hotel passage the stone floor looks as if it were paved with open oysters...."

By and large, though, Dickens was impressed by "the beautiful metropolis of America," as he referred to our city in his *American Notes for General Circulation*. Manhattan's streets, he wrote, were clean, sunny, quiet—even "cheerful." Its citizens he found to be good-looking, well dressed, generous and friendly. Cabs he found to be plentiful. Perhaps most noteworthy of all—especially for a passionate advocate of the poor and dispossessed such as Dickens—he realized one day that "we have seen no beggars on the streets by night or day."

No beggars? *In New York City?* Our town has clearly evolved during the intervening 148 years between Dickens's visit and this, the year in which our transit cops were directed to arrest subway panhandlers in a pathetic attempt to restore a veneer of civic well-being. In fact, late-twentieth-century New York has become rather like the mid-nineteenth-century London Dickens left, the London so richly and disturbingly chronicled in his novels and other writings. We suspect that, leaving aside his inevitable shock at such twentieth-century innovations as automobiles, television and overweight people in skintight bicycle shorts, Dickens would feel quite at home in contemporary New York, a city that has given new zip to musty adjectives like *wretched* and *ragged*, a city that is home to (as Dickens himself puts it in *Oliver Twist*) "every repulsive lineament of poverty, every loathsome indication of filth, rot, and garbage."

And that's not all:

Men and women sleeping in the open. Lung-burning air. Fetid streets. Hellish prisons. Nightmarish schools. Greed. Indifference. Profligate displays of wealth amid the squalor. A self-conscious fondness in certain precincts for rich fabrics, antique sporting gear and old framed prints of guardsmen with big whiskers.... These are only the more obvious parallels between Dickensian London and our own, Dickensian New York. Don't forget that tuberculosis is suddenly on the rise, as are circulation figures for *Victoria* magazine.

60 SPY DECEMBER 1990

DECEMBER 1990 SPY 61

202
DESIGN FIRM: *Spy Magazine In-house*
DESIGNER: *Christiaan Kuypers*
LETTERER: *B.W. Honeycutt*
HEADLINE TYPEFACE: *Holly Script and Antique Gothic Extended*
TEXT TYPEFACE: *Garamond 3*
CLIENT: *Spy Corporation*

203

203
DESIGN FIRM: *Carson Design*
DESIGNER: *David Carson*
HEADLINE TYPEFACE: *Franklin*
TEXT TYPEFACE: *Gothic*
CLIENT: *Beach Culture Magazine*

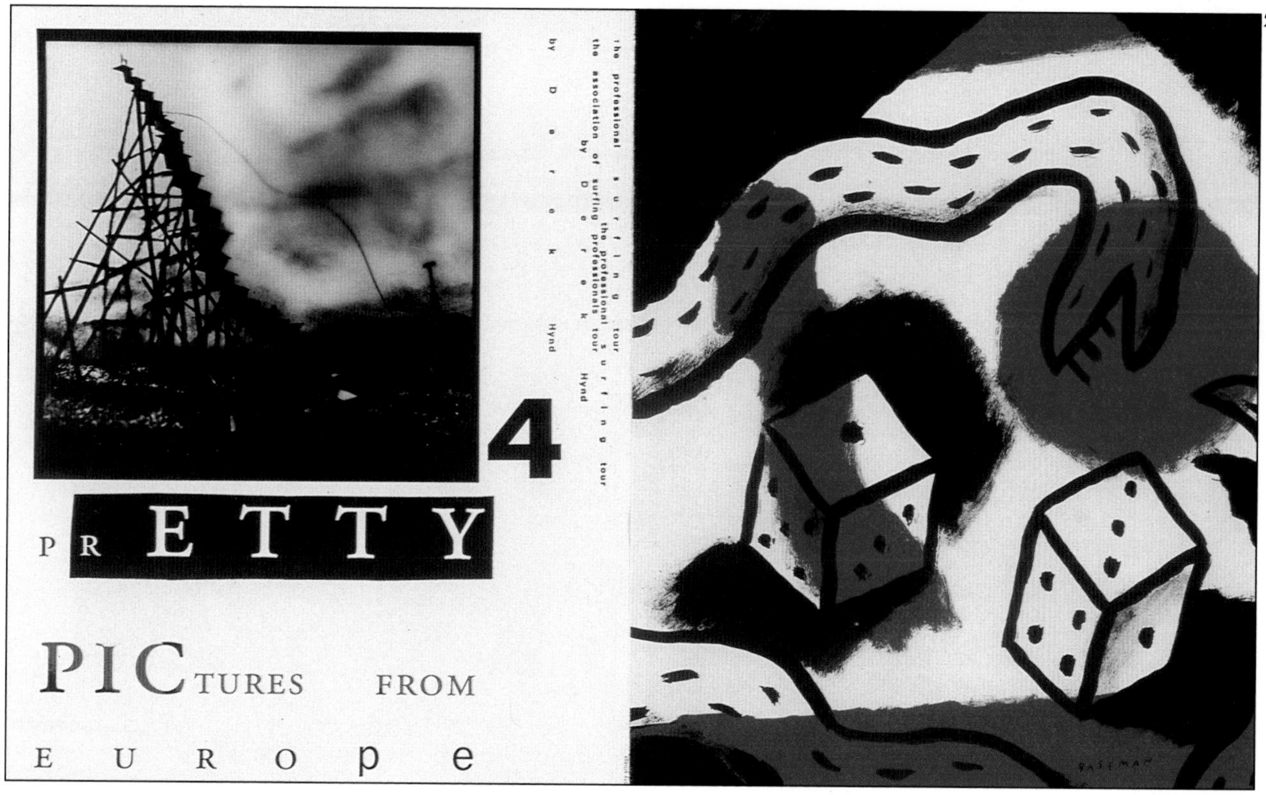

204
DESIGN FIRM: *Carson Design*
DESIGNER: *David Carson*
HEADLINE TYPEFACE: *Goudy*
CLIENT: *Beach Culture Magazine*

205
DESIGN FIRM: *Carson Design*
DESIGNER: *David Carson*
CLIENT: *Beach Culture Magazine*

206
DESIGN FIRM: *Casa De Idéias*
DESIGNER: *Oswaldo Miranda*
HEADLINE TYPEFACE: *Futura*
CLIENT: *Library of Paraná State*

207
DESIGN FIRM: *Casa De Idéias*
DESIGNER: *Oswaldo Miranda*
LETTERER: *Oswaldo Miranda*
HEADLINE TYPEFACE: *Art Deco Type*
CLIENT: *Library of Paraná State*

208
DESIGN FIRM: *Casa De Idéias*
DESIGNER: *Oswaldo Miranda*
HEADLINE TYPEFACE: *Futura*
CLIENT: *Library of Paraná State*

209
DESIGN FIRM: *Casa De Idéias*
DESIGNER: *Oswaldo Miranda*
LETTERER: *Oswaldo Miranda*
HEADLINE TYPEFACE: *Art Deco Type*
CLIENT: *Library of Paraná State*

206
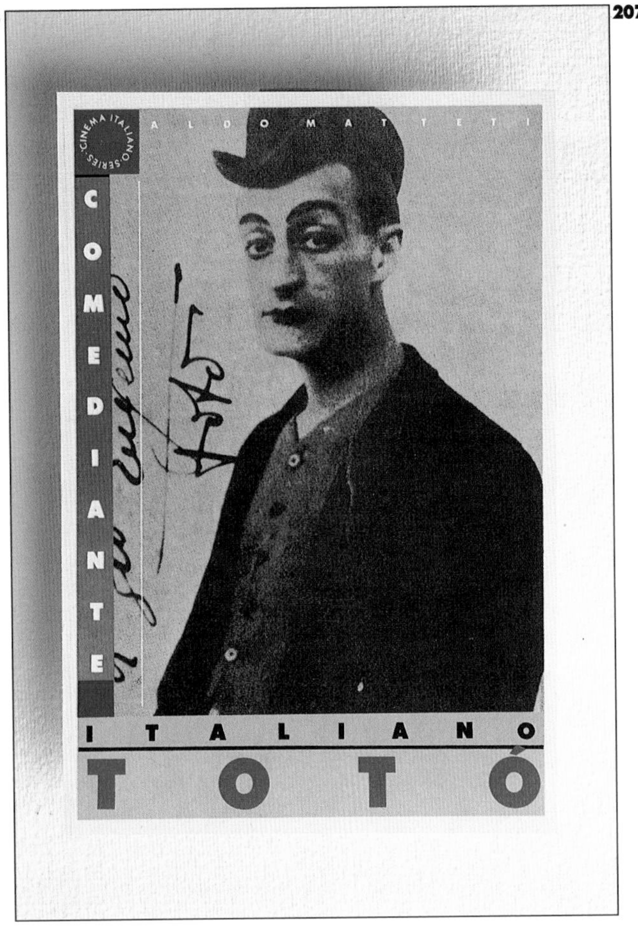

207

208
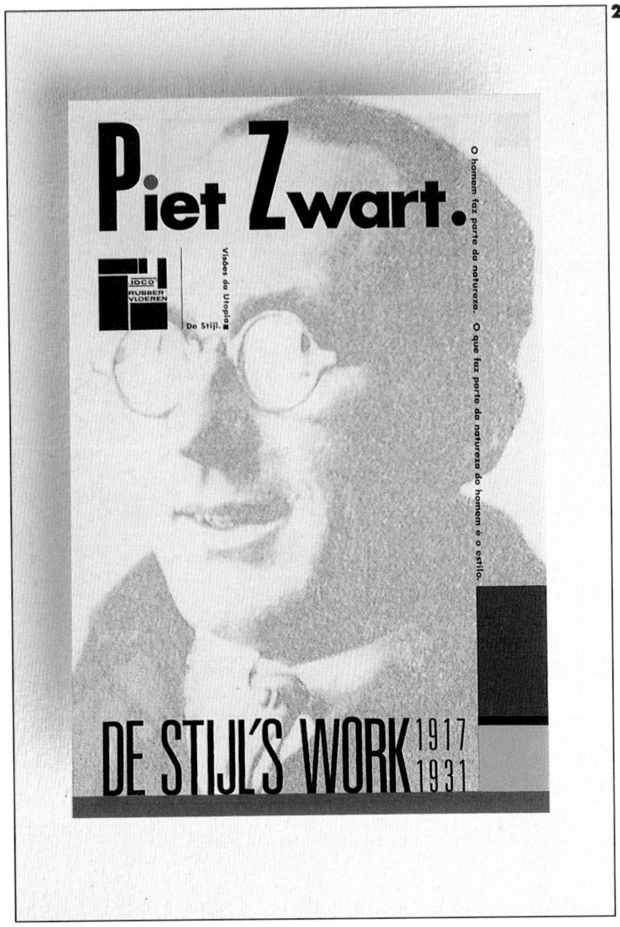

209
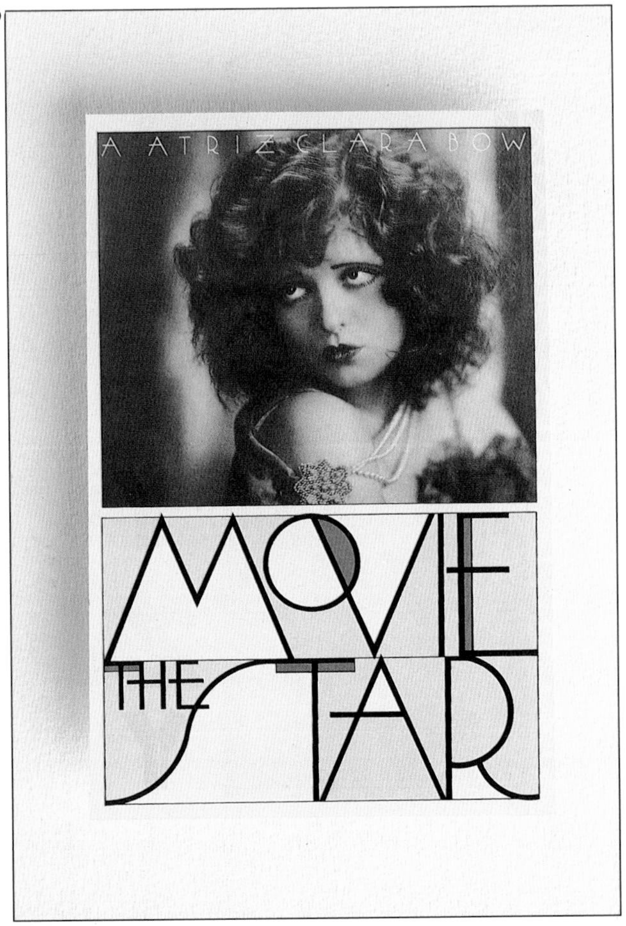

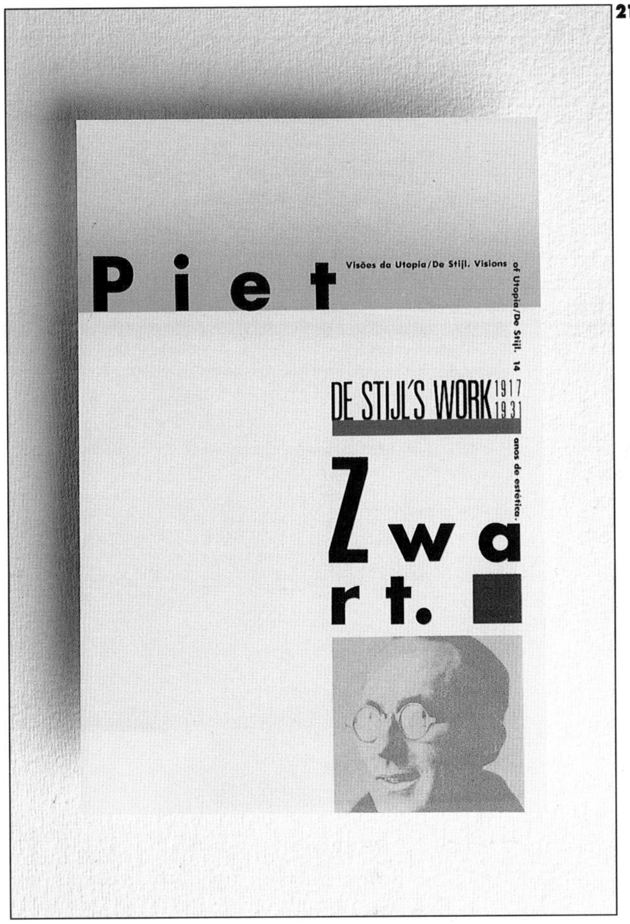

210

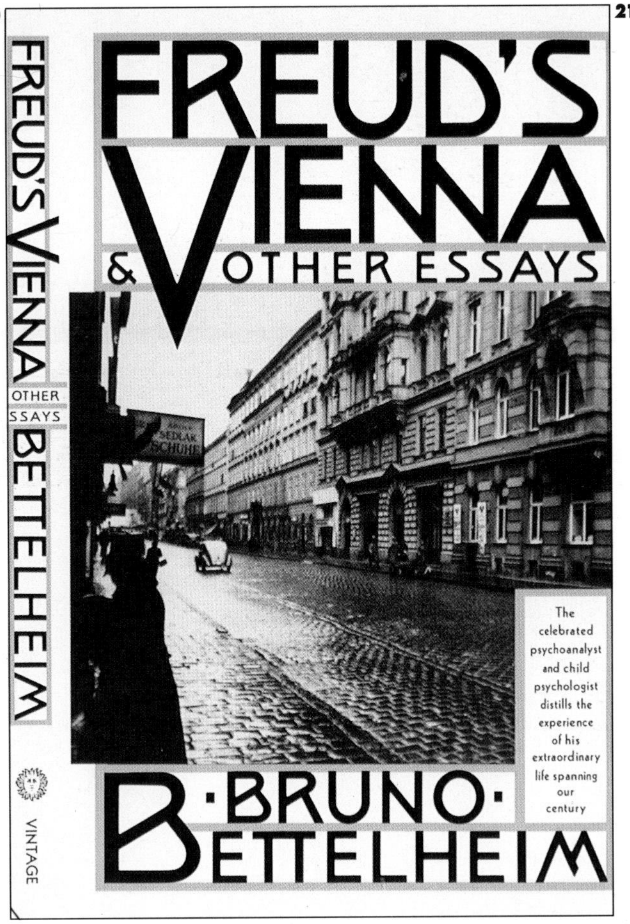

211

212

213

210
DESIGN FIRM: *Casa De Idéias*
DESIGNER: *Oswaldo Miranda*
HEADLINE TYPEFACE: *Futura*
CLIENT: *Library of Parana' State*

211
DESIGN FIRM: *Louise Fili Ltd.*
DESIGNER: *Louise Fili*
LETTERER: *Tony Di Spigna*
HEADLINE TYPEFACE: *Handlettering*
CLIENT: *Vintage Books*

212
DESIGN FIRM: *Casa De Idéias*
DESIGNER: *Oswaldo Miranda*
HEADLINE TYPEFACE: *Futura*
CLIENT: *Library of Parana' State*

213
DESIGN FIRM: *Carson Design*
DESIGNER: *David Carson*
HEADLINE TYPEFACE: *Franklin Gothic*
CLIENT: *Beach Culture Magazine*

P A C K A G I N G

1
DESIGN FIRM: *Gerard Huerta Design, Inc.*
DESIGNER: *Gerard Huerta*
LETTERER: *Gerard Huerta*
HEADLINE TYPEFACE: *Handlettering*
CLIENT: *CBS/John Berg*

2
DESIGN FIRM: *Bloomingdale's*
DESIGNER: *Laurie Rosenwald*
LETTERER: *Laurie Rosenwald*
CLIENT: *Bloomingdale's*

3
DESIGN FIRM: *Gerard Huerta Design, Inc.*
DESIGNER: *Gerard Huerta*
LETTERER: *Gerard Huerta*
HEADLINE TYPEFACE: *Handlettering*
CLIENT: *Gips/Balkind*

4
DESIGN FIRM: *Bloomingdale's*
DESIGNER: *Laurie Rosenwald*
LETTERER: *Laurie Rosenwald*
CLIENT: *Bloomingdale's*

1

2

3

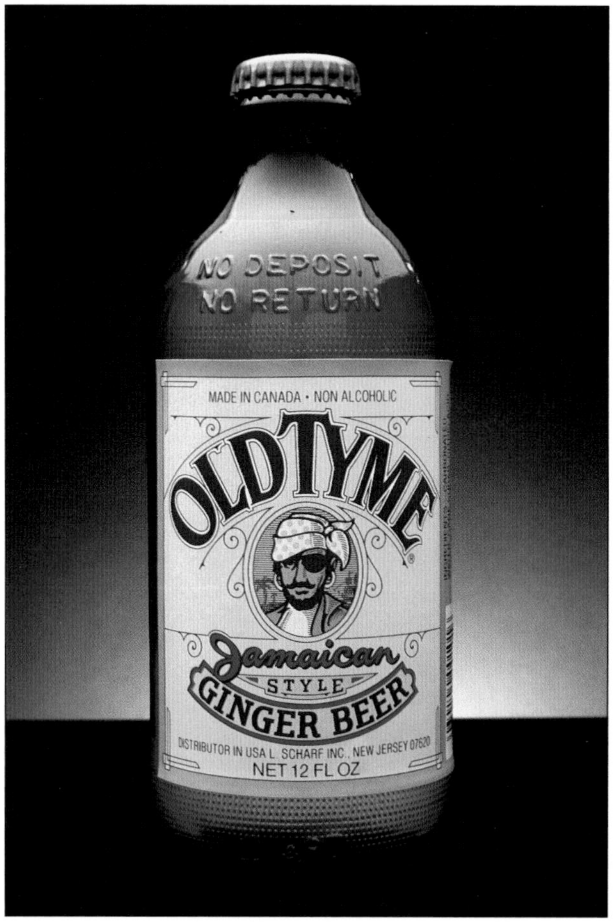

4

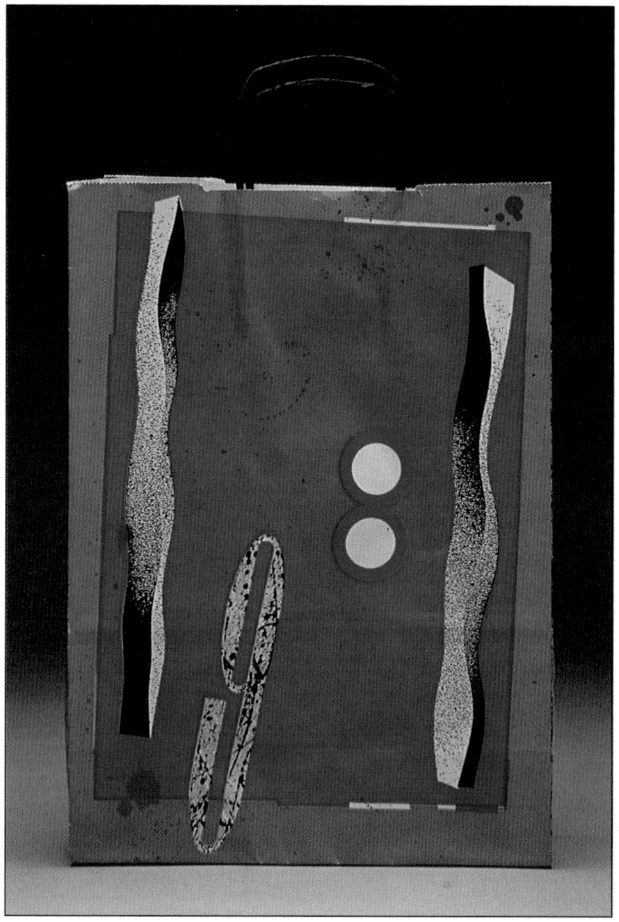

5

6

5
DESIGN FIRM: *Sam Payne & Associates*
DESIGNER: *Sam Payne*
LETTERER: *Tim Girvin*
HEADLINE TYPEFACE: *Calligraphy*
TEXT TYPEFACE: *Calligraphy*
CLIENT: *Specialty Seafoods*

6
DESIGN FIRM: *Dennard Creative, Inc.*
DESIGNER: *Rex Poteet and Bob Dennard*
LETTERER: *Rex Poteet*
TEXT TYPEFACE: *ITC Garamond*
CLIENT: *Bennigan Restaurants*

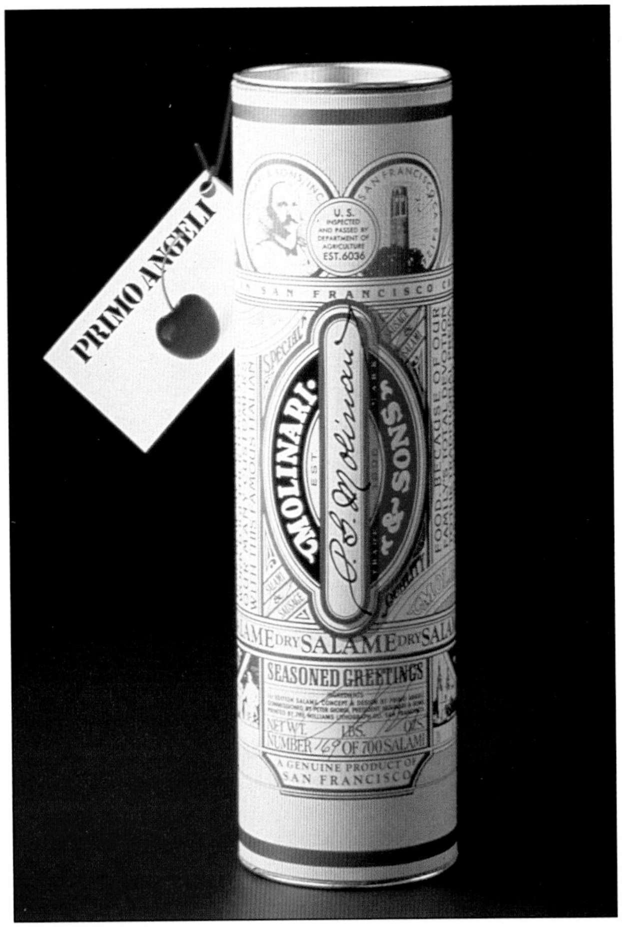

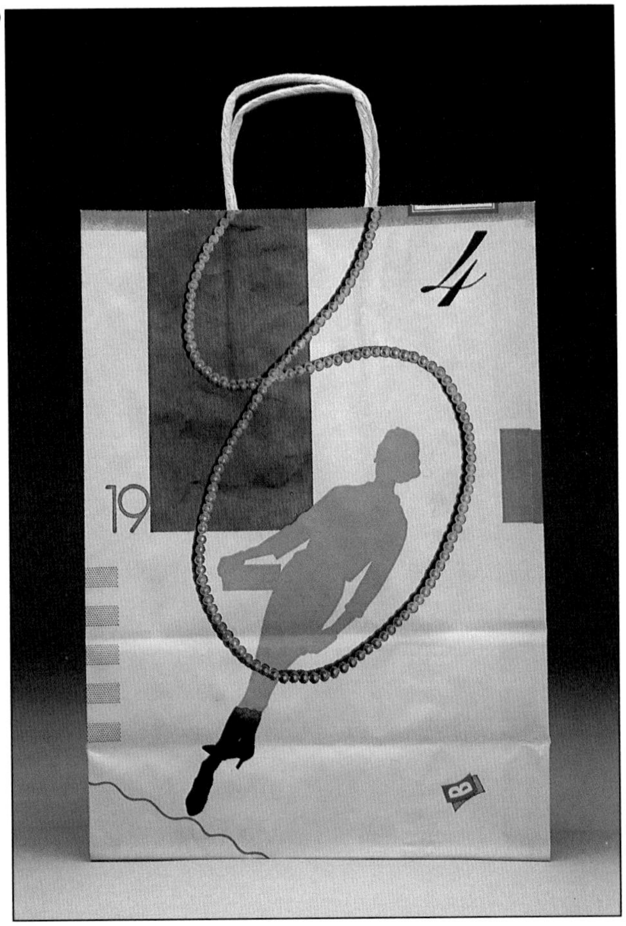

7
DESIGN FIRM: *Primo Angeli, Inc.*
DESIGNER: *Primo Angeli*
LETTERER: *Mark Jones*
TEXT TYPEFACE: *Korinna*
CLIENT: *Molinari & Sons*

8
DESIGN FIRM: *Bloomingdale's*
DESIGNER: *Melanie Parks*
LETTERER: *Melanie Parks*
CLIENT: *Bloomingdale's*

9
DESIGN FIRM: *Bloomingdale's*
DESIGNER: *Gene Greif*
LETTERER: *Gene Greif*
CLIENT: *Bloomingdale's*

10
DESIGN FIRM: *Bloomingdale's*
DESIGNER: *Anders Wenngren*
LETTERER: *Anders Wenngren*
CLIENT: *Bloomingdale's*

11

12

13

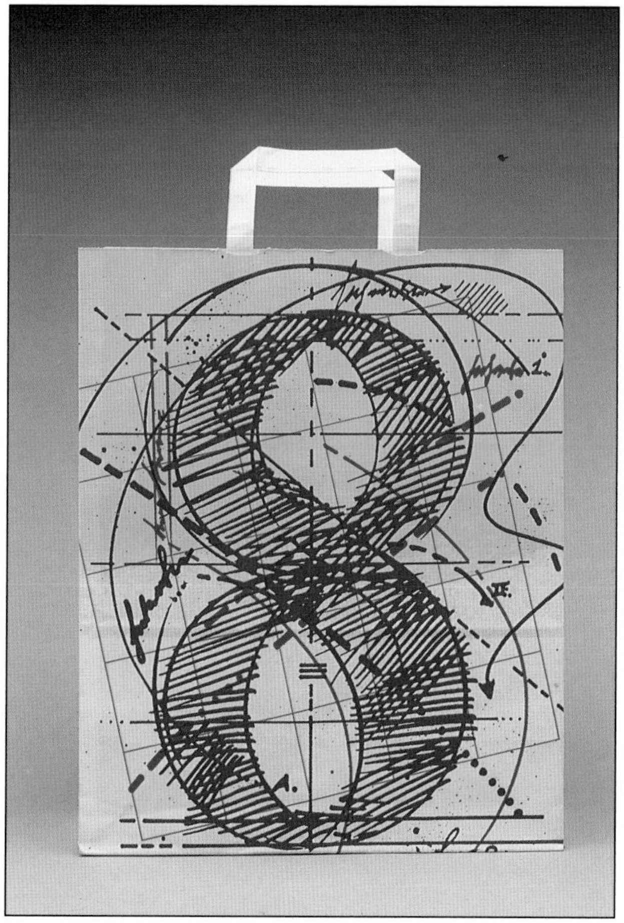

14

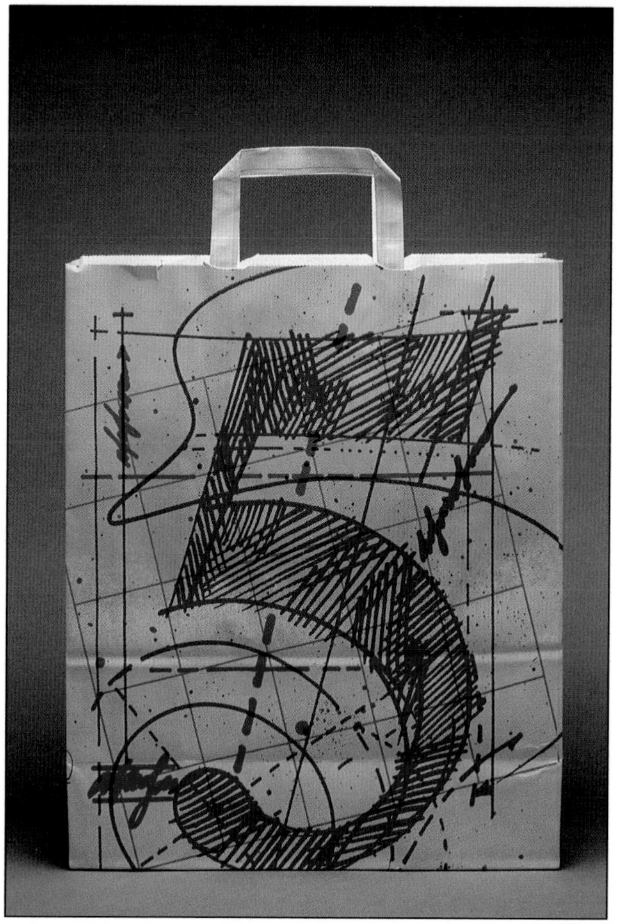

11
DESIGN FIRM: *Bruce Hale Design Studio*
DESIGNER: *Bruce Hale and Charles Finkel*
LETTERER: *Bruce Hale and Charles Finkel*
HEADLINE TYPEFACE: *Handlettering*
CLIENT: *August Schell Brewing Company*

12
DESIGN FIRM: *Hornall Anderson Design Works*
DESIGNER: *John Hornall*
HEADLINE TYPEFACE: *Times Roman*
TEXT TYPEFACE: *Times Roman*
CLIENT: *Tradewell*

13/14
DESIGN FIRM: *Bloomingdale's*
DESIGNER: *Tim Girvin*
LETTERER: *Tim Girvin*
CLIENT: *Bloomingdale's*

15
DESIGN FIRM: *Sam Payne & Associates*
DESIGNER: *Sam Payne*
LETTERER: *Tim Girvin*
HEADLINE TYPEFACE: *Calligraphy*
TEXT TYPEFACE: *Calligraphy*
CLIENT: *Specialty Seafoods*

16
DESIGN FIRM: *The Duffy Design Group*
DESIGNER: *Charles S. Anderson and Sara Ledgard*
HEADLINE TYPEFACE: *Bodoni*
CLIENT: *The Duffy Design Group*

17
DESIGN FIRM: *The Duffy Design Group*
DESIGNER: *Sharon Werner*
LETTERER: *Sharon Werner*
HEADLINE TYPEFACE: *Handlettering and Cheltenham*
CLIENT: *Sonny's Ice Cream*

15

16

17

18

19

20

18
DESIGN FIRM: *The Duffy Design Group*
DESIGNER: *Charles S. Anderson and Haley Johnson*
HEADLINE TYPEFACE: *Garamond, Franklin Gothic and Handlettering*
CLIENT: *Chaps-Ralph Lauren*

19
DESIGN FIRM: *The Duffy Design Group*
DESIGNER: *Joe Duffy and Sharon Werner*
LETTERER: *Lynn Schulte and Joe Duffy*
HEADLINE TYPEFACE: *Handlettering*
CLIENT: *Donaldsons*

20
DESIGN FIRM: *The Duffy Design Group*
DESIGNER: *Joe Duffy and Sara Ledgard*
HEADLINE TYPEFACE: *Garamond Bold and Helvetica Bold*
CLIENT: *Chaps-Ralph Lauren*

21
DESIGN FIRM: *Design/Art, Inc.*
DESIGNER: *Norman Moore*
HEADLINE TYPEFACE: *Franklin Gothic*
CLIENT: *Geffen Records*

22
DESIGN FIRM: *Payne & Associates*
DESIGNER: *Sam Payne*
LETTERER: *Bruce Hale*
HEADLINE TYPEFACE: *Calligraphy*
TEXT TYPEFACE: *Calligraphy*
CLIENT: *Specialty Seafoods*

23/24
DESIGN FIRM: *Bloomingdale's*
DESIGNER: *Mark Kostabi*
LETTERER: *Mark Kostabi*
CLIENT: *Bloomingdale's*

25
DESIGN FIRM: *Sullivan Perkins*
DESIGNER: *Art Garcia*
TEXT TYPEFACE: *Compacta Light*
CLIENT: *North Star Mall/The Rouse Company*

26
DESIGN FIRM: *Cipriani Kremer*
DESIGNER: *Rosemary Conroy*
LETTERER: *Larry Mc Entire*
TEXT TYPEFACE: *Garamond*
CLIENT: *Davidson Hubeny Brands*

21
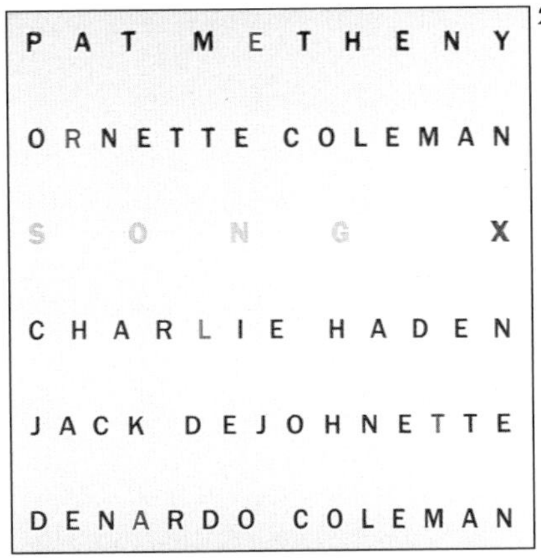

22

23
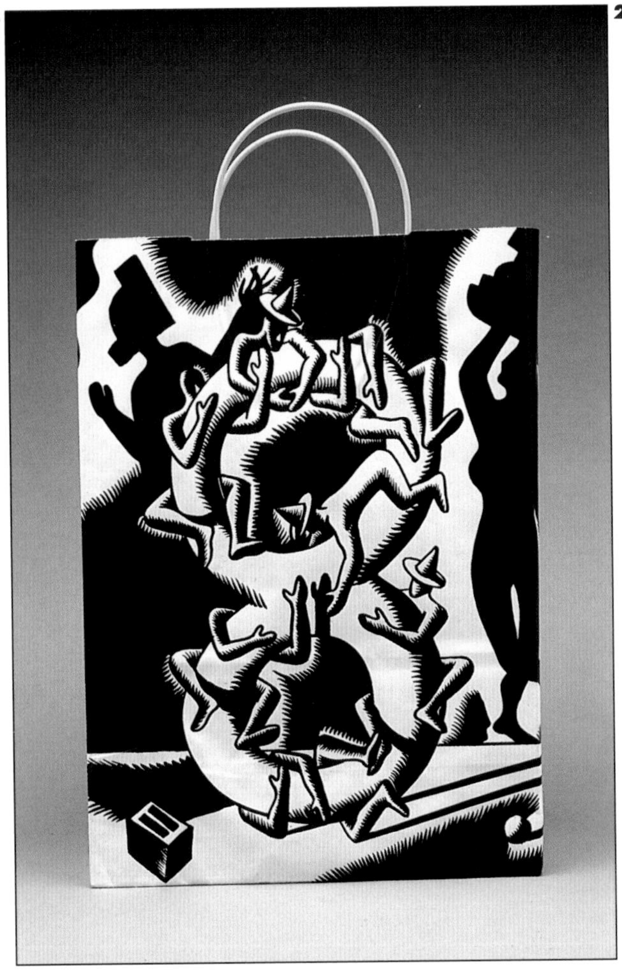

24

25

26

27

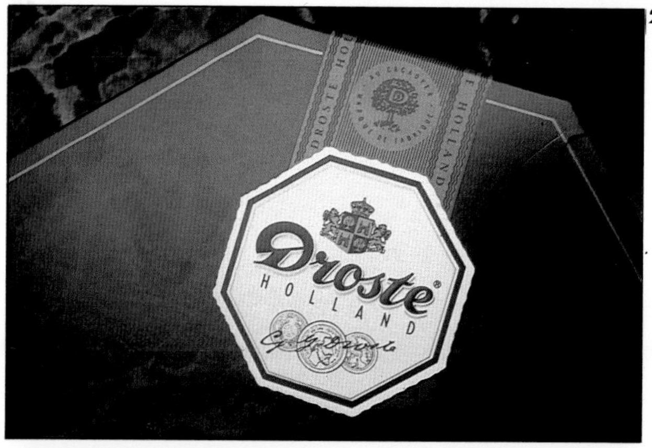

28

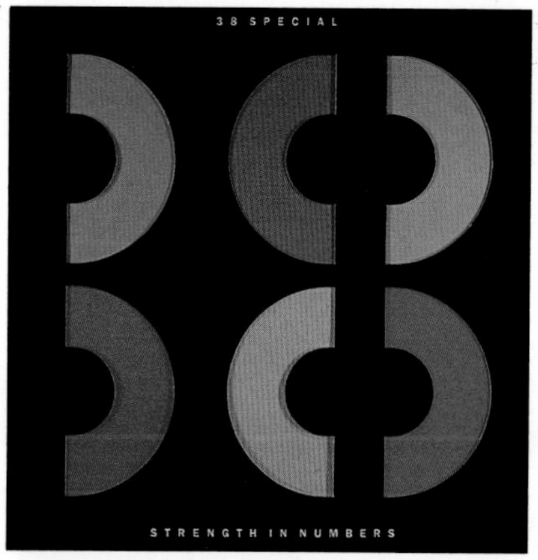

29

30

31

32

27
DESIGN FIRM: *Addison Design Consultants*
DESIGNER: *Addison Design Consultants*
TEXT TYPEFACE: *Helvetica Condensed*
CLIENT: *Droste Holland*

28
DESIGN FIRM: *Design/Art, Inc.*
DESIGNER: *Norman Moore*
HEADLINE TYPEFACE: *Franklin Gothic*
CLIENT: *Mark Spector/A&M Records*

29/30
DESIGN FIRM: *Bloomingdale's*
DESIGNER: *Neville Brody*
LETTERER: *Neville Brody*
CLIENT: *Bloomingdale's*

31/32
DESIGN FIRM: *Pentagram Design*
DESIGNER: *Paula Scher*
LETTERER: *Paula Scher*
HEADLINE TYPEFACE: *Handlettering*
TEXT TYPEFACE: *Handlettering*
CLIENT: *Oola Corporation*

33

34

35

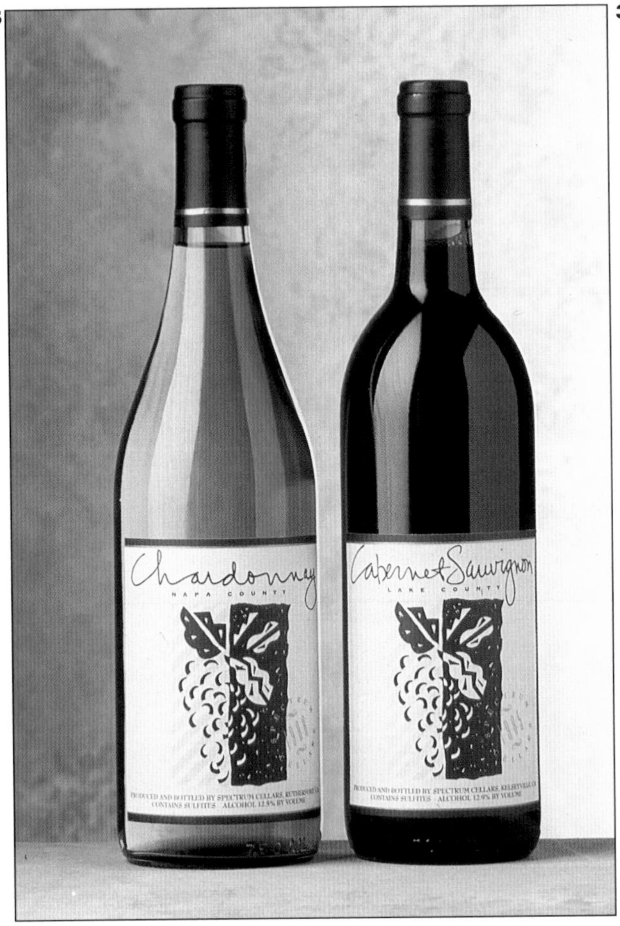

36

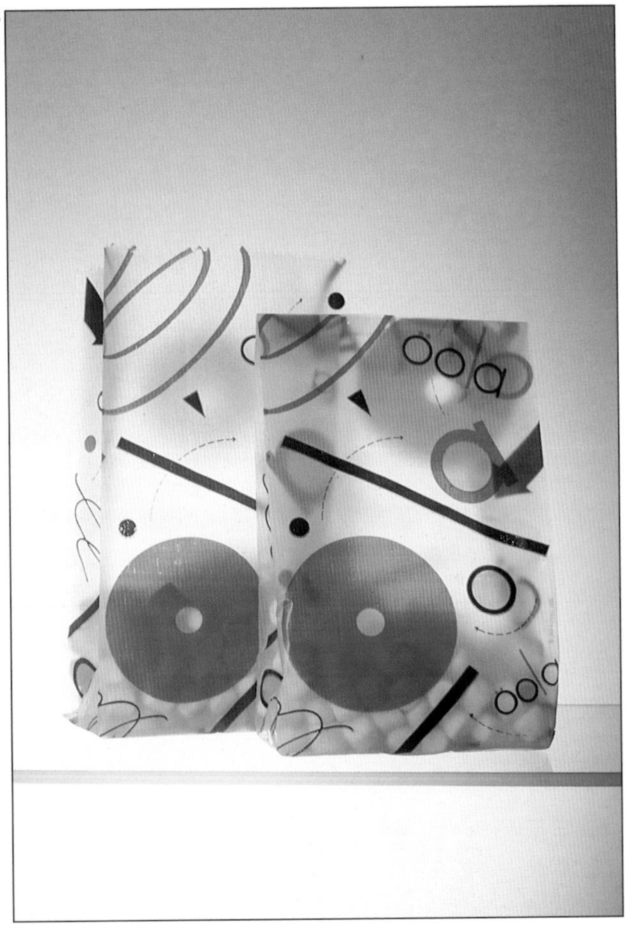

33
DESIGN FIRM: *The Duffy Design Group*
DESIGNER: *Sharon Werner*
LETTERER: *Lynn Schulte*
HEADLINE TYPEFACE: *Handlettering, Spartan Black, and Trade Gothic*
CLIENT: *Fallon Mc Elligott*

34
DESIGN FIRM: *The Duffy Design Group*
DESIGNER: *Joe Duffy, Sara Ledgard and Haley Johnson*
LETTERER: *Lynn Schulte and Joe Duffy*
HEADLINE TYPEFACE: *Helvetica Bold and Handlettering*
TEXT TYPEFACE: *Futura Bold Condensed*
CLIENT: *Wenger Corporation*

35
DESIGN FIRM: *Morla Design*
DESIGNER: *Jennifer Morla*
HEADLINE TYPEFACE: *Motion Picture B-2 and Copperplate Gothic*
TEXT TYPEFACE: *Bernhard Modern*
CLIENT: *Spectrum Foods, Inc.*

36
DESIGN FIRM: *Pentagram Design*
DESIGNER: *Paula Scher*
LETTERER: *Paula Scher*
HEADLINE TYPEFACE: *Handlettering*
TEXT TYPEFACE: *Handlettering*
CLIENT: *Oola Corporation*

37

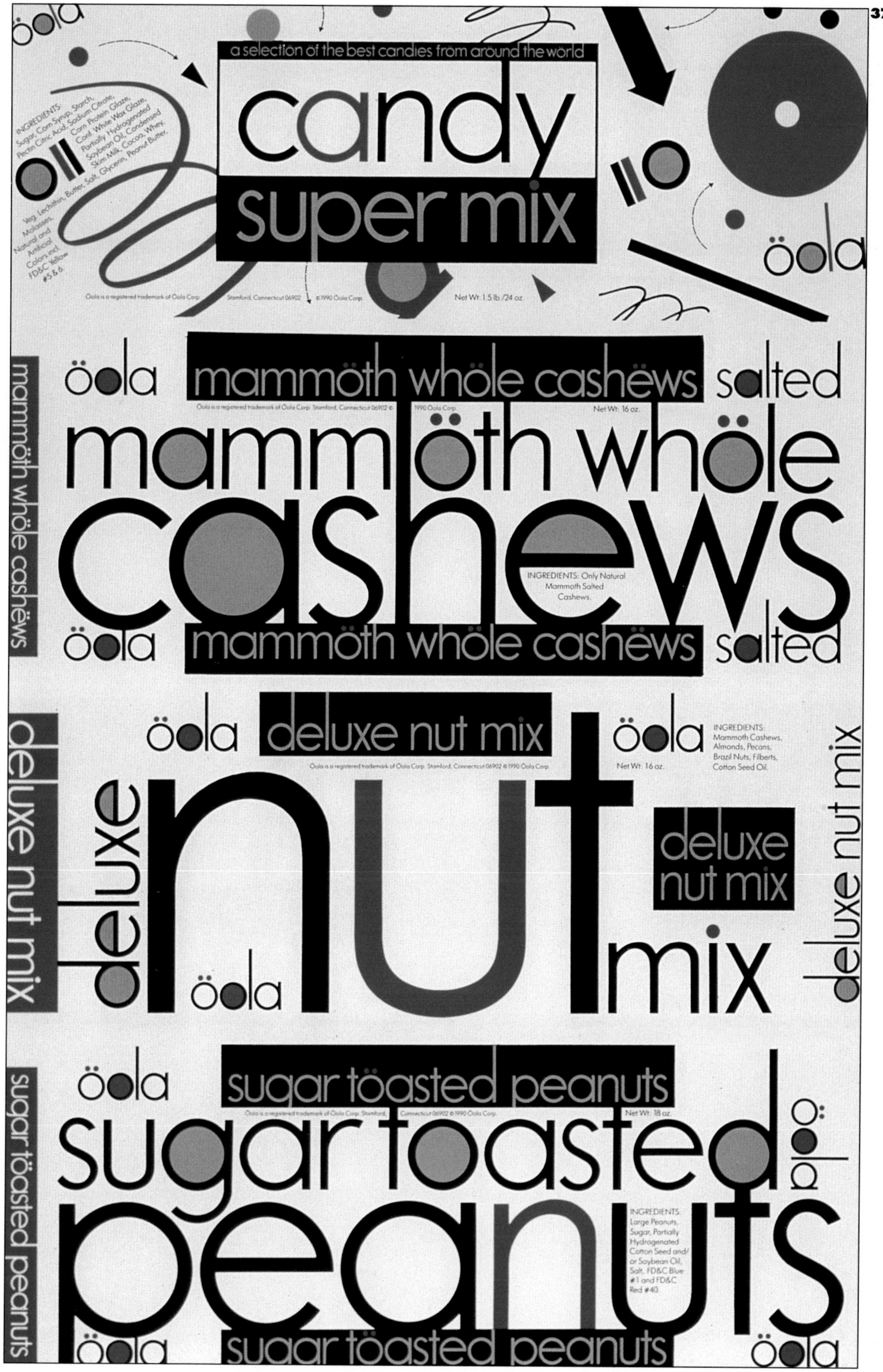

37
DESIGN FIRM: *Pentagram Design*
DESIGNER: *Paula Scher*
LETTERER: *Paula Scher*
HEADLINE TYPEFACE: *Handlettering*
TEXT TYPEFACE: *Handlettering*
CLIENT: *Oola Corporation*

38

39

38

DESIGN FIRM: *Pentagram Design*

DESIGNER: *Paula Scher*

LETTERER: *Paula Scher*

HEADLINE TYPEFACE: *Handlettering*

TEXT TYPEFACE: *Handlettering*

CLIENT: *Oola Corporation*

39

DESIGN FIRM: *Pentagram Design*

DESIGNER: *Paula Scher*

LETTERER: *Paula Scher*

HEADLINE TYPEFACE: *Handlettering*

TEXT TYPEFACE: *Handlettering*

CLIENT: *Oola Corporation*

40

41

42

43

40/41
DESIGN FIRM: *Bloomingdale's*
DESIGNER: *Robert Shadbolt*
LETTERER: *Robert Shadbolt*
CLIENT: *Bloomingdale's*

42
DESIGN FIRM: *Musser Design*
DESIGNER: *Jerry King Musser*
LETTERER: *Jerry King Musser*
HEADLINE TYPEFACE: *Univers*
TEXT TYPEFACE: *Univers*
CLIENT: *American Helix Technology*

43
DESIGN FIRM: *Cronan Design*
DESIGNER: *Michael Cronan*
TEXT TYPEFACE: *Palatino Italic*
CLIENT: *Electronic Arts*

44

44
DESIGN FIRM: *Yoichi Fujii*
DESIGNER: *Yoichi Fujii*
LETTERER: *Yoichi Fujii*
CLIENT: *CBS/Sony Group, Inc.*

45

46

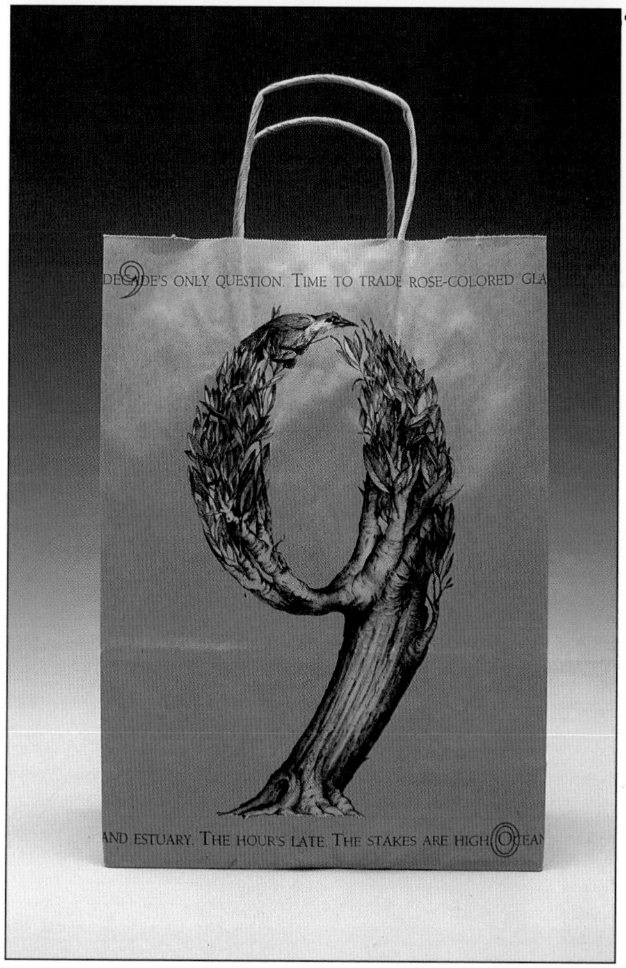

47

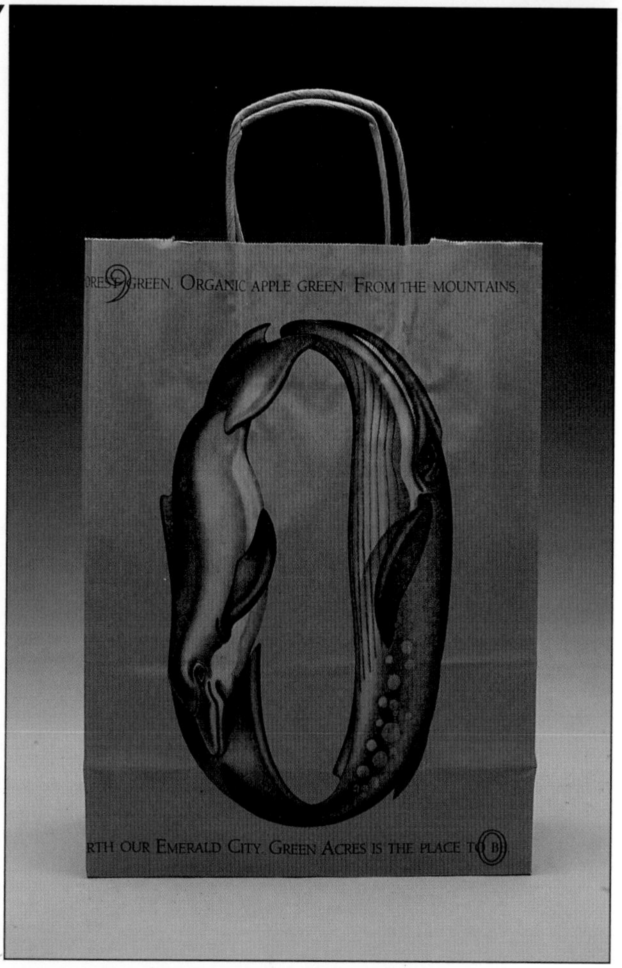

48

49

50

45
DESIGN FIRM: *Primo Angeli, Inc.*
DESIGNER: *Primo Angeli*
LETTERER: *Doug Hardenburgh*
CLIENT: *Pete's Brewing Company*

46
DESIGN FIRM: *Hornall Anderson Design Works*
DESIGNER: *John Hornall and Jack Anderson*
HEADLINE TYPEFACE: *Andrich Minerva*
TEXT TYPEFACE: *Times Italic*
CLIENT: *The Broadmoor Baker*

47/48
DESIGN FIRM: *Bloomingdale's*
DESIGNER: *Jözef Sumichrast*
LETTERER: *Jözef Sumichrast*
CLIENT: *Bloomingdale's*

49
DESIGN FIRM: *Sullivan Perkins*
DESIGNER: *Clark Richardson*
LETTERER: *Clark Richardson*
TEXT TYPEFACE: *Compacta Light*
CLIENT: *North Star Mall/The Rouse Company*

50
DESIGN FIRM: *246 Fifth Design Associates*
DESIGNER: *Terry Laurenzid and Greg Tudy*
LETTERER: *Terry Laurenzid*
TEXT TYPEFACE: *New Yorker and New Yorker Engraved*
CLIENT: *246 Fifth Design Associates*

51
DESIGN FIRM: *Design/Art, Inc.*
DESIGNER: *Norman Moore*
HEADLINE TYPEFACE: *Gill Extra Bold*
TEXT TYPEFACE: *Garamond Italic*
CLIENT: *Loot Unlimited/Adam Art*

52
DESIGN FIRM: *Capital Records*
DESIGNER: *Heather Van Haaften*
CLIENT: *C.P.O.*

53
DESIGN FIRM: *Capital Records*
DESIGNER: *Christina Haberstock*
LETTERER: *Heather Van Haaften*
CLIENT: *Melisa Morgan*

51

52

53

54

55

56

57

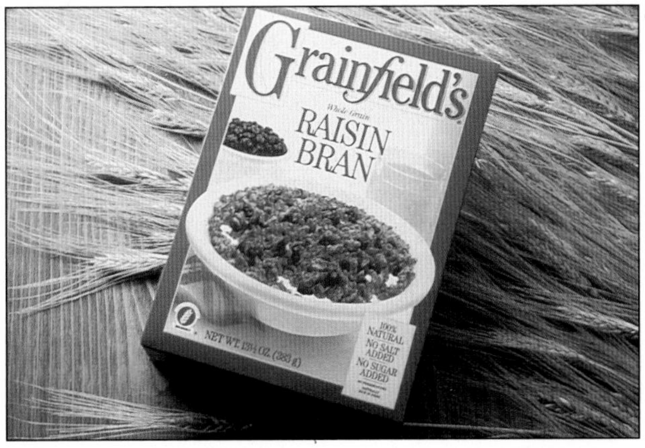

58

54
DESIGN FIRM: *SBG Partners*
DESIGNER: *Joanne Jones*
HEADLINE TYPEFACE: *Berling*
TEXT TYPEFACE: *Agency Gothic*
CLIENT: *Heritage Kitchen*

55/56
DESIGN FIRM: *SBG Partners*
DESIGNER: *Joanne Jones*
LETTERER: *Joanne Jones*
HEADLINE TYPEFACE: *Century*
TEXT TYPEFACE: *Century*
CLIENT: *Hills Bros. Coffee Company*

57
DESIGN FIRM: *SBG Partners*
DESIGNER: *Joanne Jones*
HEADLINE TYPEFACE: *Bembo*
TEXT TYPEFACE: *Bembo*
CLIENT: *Kraft General Foods Corporation*

58
DESIGN FIRM: *SBG Partners*
DESIGNER: *Joanne Jones*
HEADLINE TYPEFACE: *Century*
TEXT TYPEFACE: *Century*
CLIENT: *Weetabix*

59

59
DESIGN FIRM: *Hornall Anderson Design Works*
DESIGNER: *Jack Anderson and John Hornall*
HEADLINE TYPEFACE: *Bodoni and Goudy Open*
TEXT TYPEFACE: *Bernhard and Cochin Italic*
CLIENT: *The Broadmoor Baker*

60

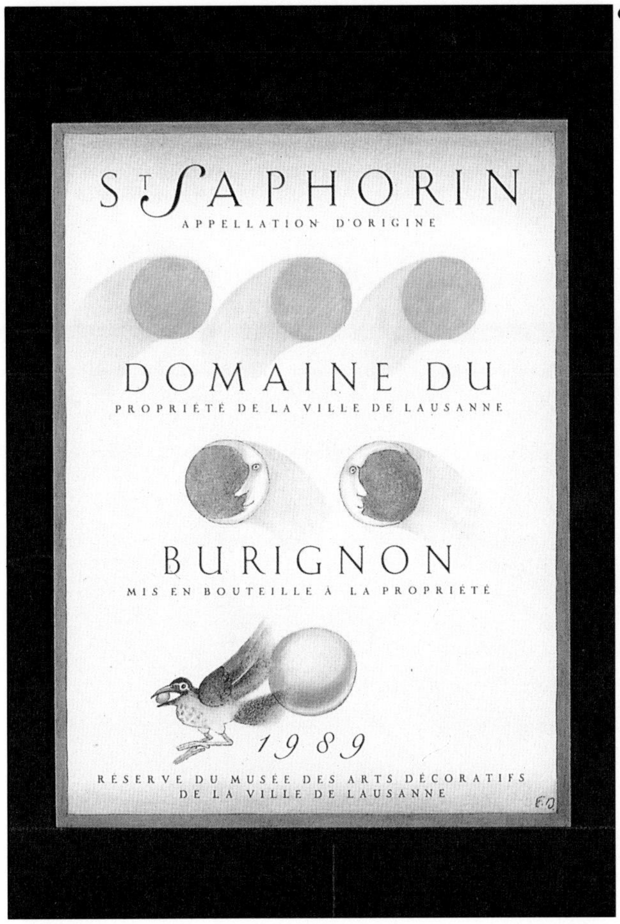

61

62

63

60
DESIGN FIRM: *Delessert & Marshall*
DESIGNER: *Rita Marshall*
HEADLINE TYPEFACE: *Bauer Text Initials*
TEXT TYPEFACE: *Nicholas Cochin*
CLIENT: *Musee Des Arts Décoratifs, Lausanne*

61
DESIGN FIRM: *Forsythe Design*
DESIGNER: *Kathleen Forsythe and Jane Cuthbertson*
HEADLINE TYPEFACE: *Serifa and Various*
TEXT TYPEFACE: *Caslon and Bitstream Zurich*
CLIENT: *Bitstream Inc.*

62
DESIGN FIRM: *Pentagram Design*
DESIGNER: *Paula Scher*
HEADLINE TYPEFACE: *Bodoni*
TEXT TYPEFACE: *Bodoni*
CLIENT: *The Rainforest Inc.*

63
DESIGN FIRM: *Sullivan Perkins*
DESIGNER: *Art Garcia*
LETTERER: *Art Garcia and Clark Richardson*
HEADLINE TYPEFACE: *Quorum Light*
TEXT TYPEFACE: *Quorum Light*
CLIENT: *Ham I Am*

64
DESIGN FIRM: *Sackett Design*
DESIGNER: *Mark Sackett*
LETTERER: *Mark Sackett and Steve Muller*
HEADLINE TYPEFACE: *Handlettering*
TEXT TYPEFACE: *Copperplate, Onyx and Bank Script*
CLIENT: *Levi Strauss & Company*

65
DESIGN FIRM: *Stan Evenson Design, Inc.*
DESIGNER: *Glenn Sakamoto*
CLIENT: *Stan Evenson Client Gift*

64

65

66

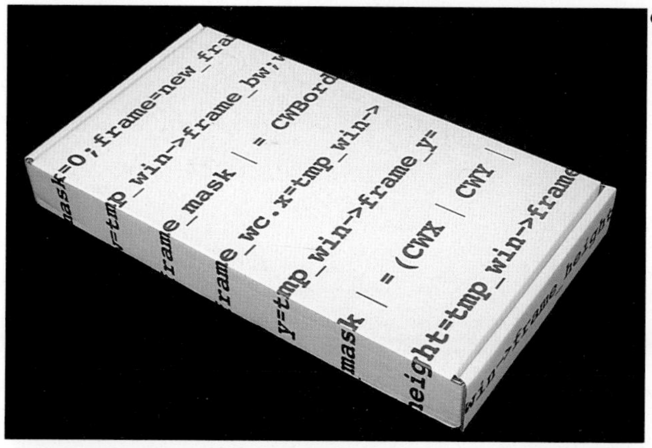

67

68

69

70

66
DESIGN FIRM: *Forsythe Design*
DESIGNER: *Kathleen Forsythe and Jane Cuthbertson*
HEADLINE TYPEFACE: *Courier*
CLIENT: *Saber Software, Inc.*

67
DESIGN FIRM: *Forsythe Design*
DESIGNER: *Kathleen Forsythe and Jane Cuthbertson*
HEADLINE TYPEFACE: *Caslon*
TEXT TYPEFACE: *Caslon and Bitstream Zurich*
CLIENT: *Bitstream, Inc.*

68
DESIGN FIRM: *Kan Tai-keung Design and Associates Ltd.*
DESIGNER: *Kan Tai-keung*
HEADLINE TYPEFACE: *Handlettering, Casablanca Light, World Class Denim and Latin Antique*
TEXT TYPEFACE: *World Class Denim and Various Type Faces*
CLIENT: *Lawman (Far East) Limited*

69
DESIGN FIRM: *Pentagram Design*
DESIGNER: *Paula Scher*
HEADLINE TYPEFACE: *Bodoni*
TEXT TYPEFACE: *Bodoni*
CLIENT: *The Rainforest Inc.*

70
DESIGN FIRM: *Wallace Church Associates, Incorporated*
DESIGNER: *Tom Carnase*
LETTERER: *Tom Carnase*
HEADLINE TYPEFACE: *Bauer Text Initials*
CLIENT: *Westpoint Pepperell*

P O S T E R S

1

1
DESIGN FIRM: *Pentagram Design*
DESIGNER: *Paula Scher*
HEADLINE TYPEFACE: *Various Wood Types*
TEXT TYPEFACE: *Various Wood Types*
CLIENT: *CBS Records*

2
DESIGN FIRM: *Container Corporation*
DESIGNER: *Tony Di Spigna*
LETTERER: *Tony Di Spigna*
CLIENT: *Container Corporation*

3

DESIGN FIRM: *Pentagram Design*
DESIGNER: *Paula Scher*
HEADLINE TYPEFACE: *Stymie*
CLIENT: *Columbia Records*

3

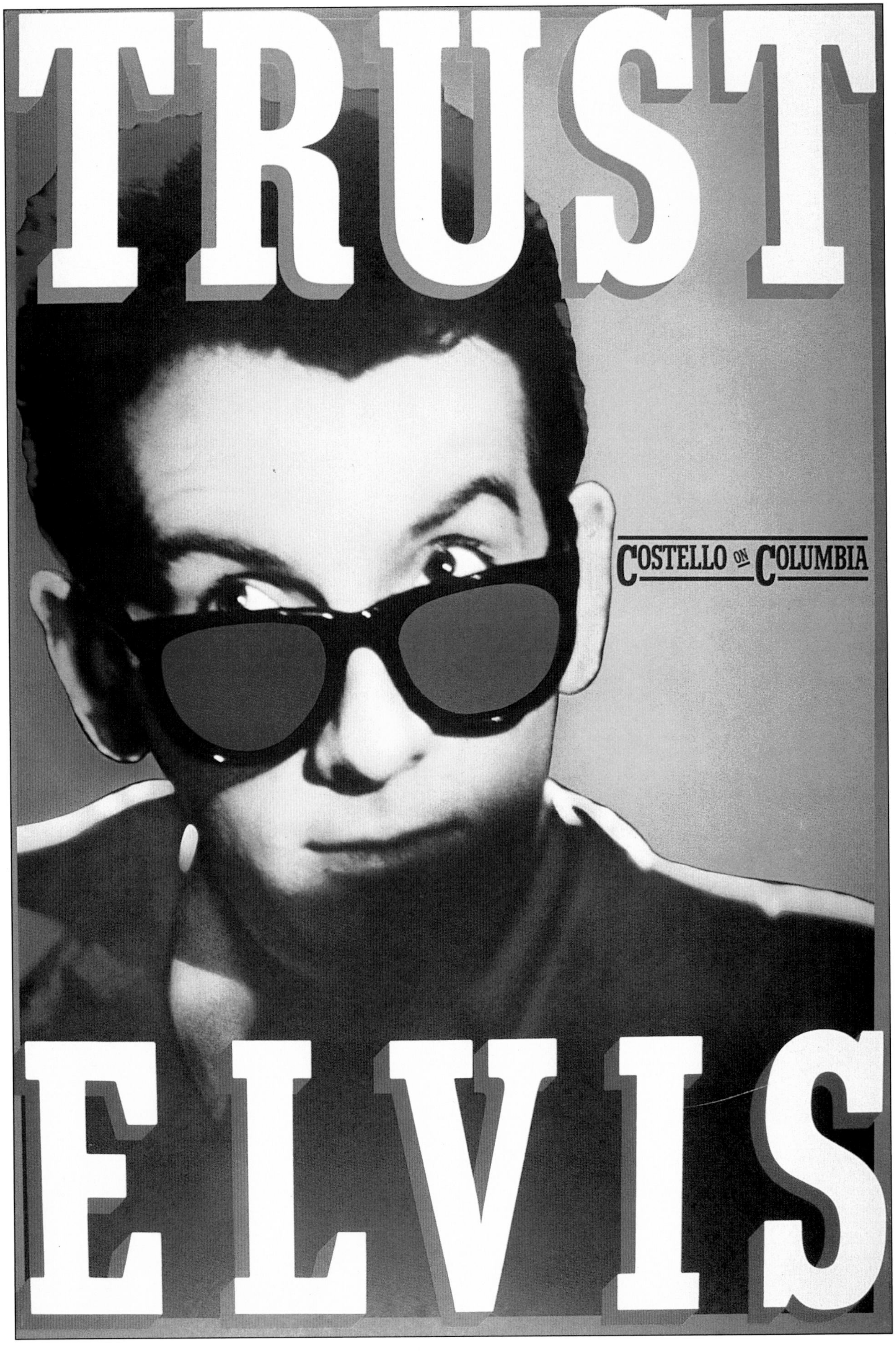

4

5

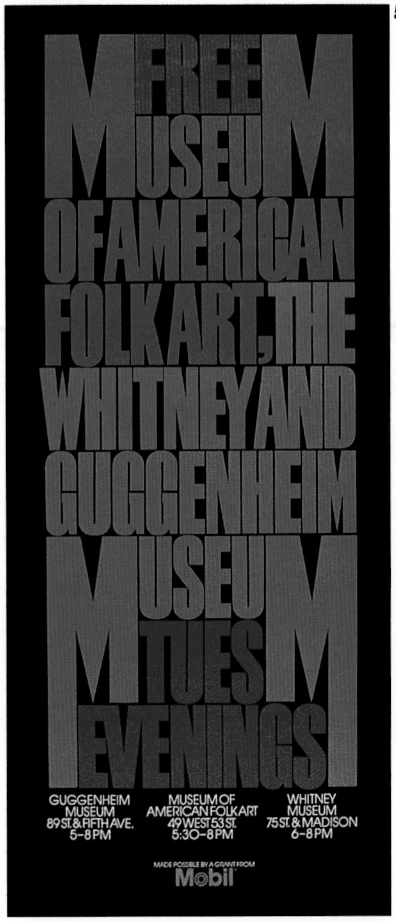

6

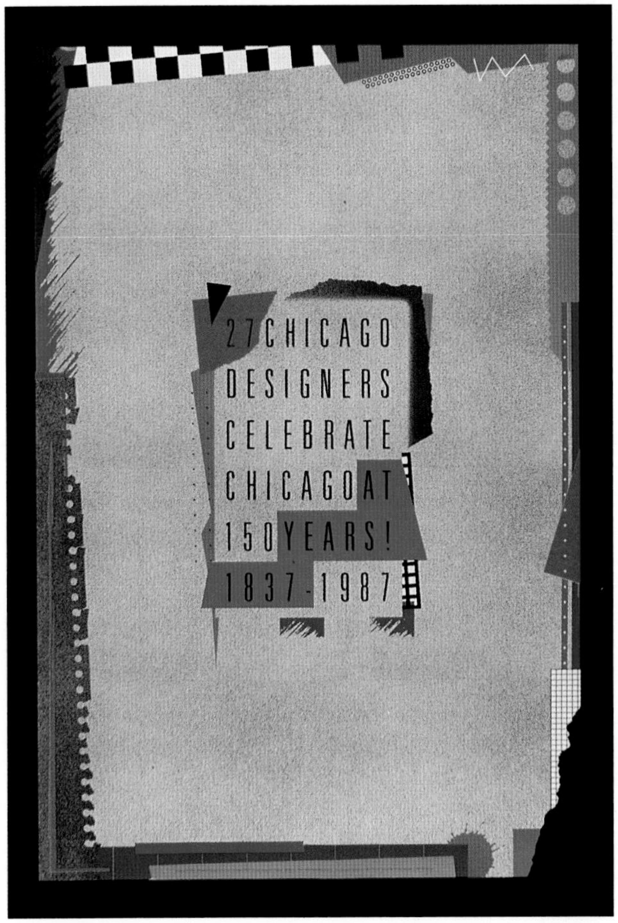

7

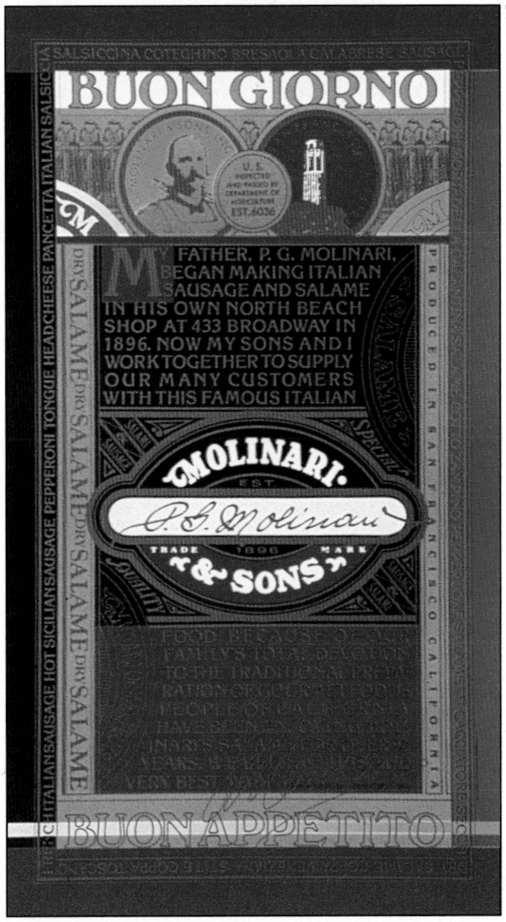

4
DESIGN FIRM: *M Plus M Inc.*
DESIGNER: *Michael McGinn*
HEADLINE TYPEFACE: *Goudy*
TEXT TYPEFACE: *Goudy*
CLIENT: *Pratt Institute*

5
DESIGN FIRM: *Peckolick & Partners*
DESIGNER: *Tony Di Spigna*
LETTERER: *Tony Di Spigna*
HEADLINE TYPEFACE: *Lettera Gothic*
CLIENT: *Mobil Corporation*

6
DESIGN FIRM: *Barnes Design Group*
DESIGNER: *Jeff Barnes*
LETTERER: *Jeff Barnes*
CLIENT: *Chiasso*

7
DESIGN FIRM: *Primo Angeli, Inc.*
DESIGNER: *Primo Angeli*
LETTERER: *Mark Jones*
TEXT TYPEFACE: *Korinna*
CLIENT: *Molinari & Sons*

8

WHOLE
AMOUNT
OR
QUANTITY
OF
Theatre
presents
FOR: USED AS A
FUNCTION WORD
TO INDICATE
PURPOSE
All For Love
LOVE: 1. STRONG
AFFECTION
FOR ANOTHER
ARISING OUT
OF KINSHIP OR
PERSONAL TIES
2. ATTRACTION
BASED ON SEX-
UAL DESIRE
3. AFFECTION BASED
ON ADMIRATION,
BENEVOLENCE, OR
COMMON INTERESTS
A SERIES OF FIVE PLAYS
BEGINS
ON SUNDAY, MAR. 31
STARRING
JOAN PLOWRIGHT,
ALEC McCOWEN
9 PM CHANNEL 13 PBS
HOST:
ALISTAIR COOKE
Mobil

8

DESIGN FIRM: *Peckolick & Partners*
DESIGNER: *Tony Di Spigna*
HEADLINE TYPEFACE: *ITC Benguiat*
TEXT TYPEFACE: *ITC Benguiat*
CLIENT: *Mobil Corporation*

9

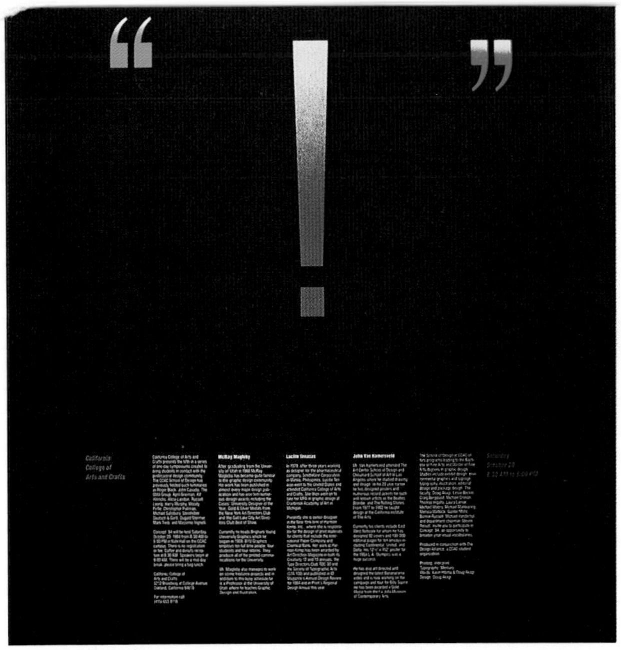

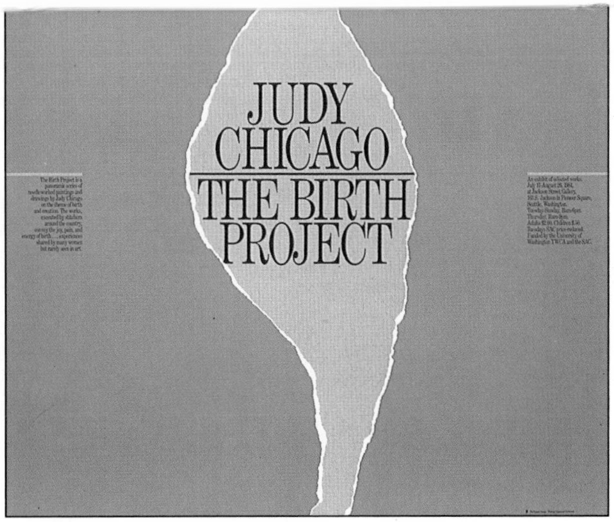

12

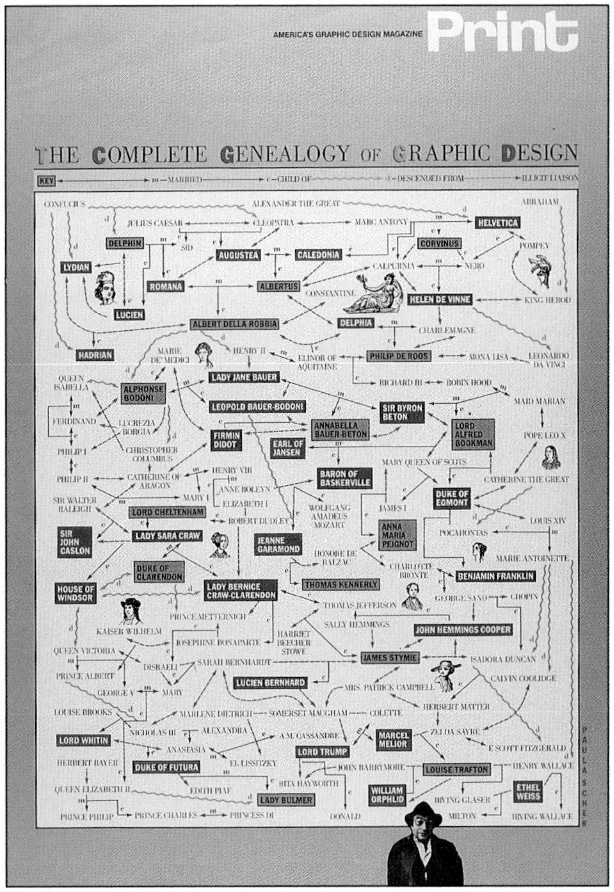

11

9
DESIGN FIRM: *Akagi Design*
DESIGNER: *Doug Akagi*
HEADLINE TYPEFACE: *Univers*
TEXT TYPEFACE: *Helvetica Condensed*
CLIENT: *California College of Arts & Crafts*

10
DESIGN FIRM: *Hansen Design Company*
DESIGNER: *Pat Hansen and Paula Richards*
HEADLINE TYPEFACE: *Century Light Condensed*
TEXT TYPEFACE: *Century Light Condensed*
CLIENT: *YWCA*

11
DESIGN FIRM: *Akagi Design*
DESIGNER: *Doug Akagi*
HEADLINE TYPEFACE: *Goudy Old Style*
TEXT TYPEFACE: *Goudy Old Style*
CLIENT: *Mercury Typography*

12
DESIGN FIRM: *Pentagram Design*
DESIGNER: *Paula Scher*
HEADLINE TYPEFACE: *Bodoni Book*
TEXT TYPEFACE: *Franklin Gothic and Bodoni Book*
CLIENT: *PRINT Magazine*

13

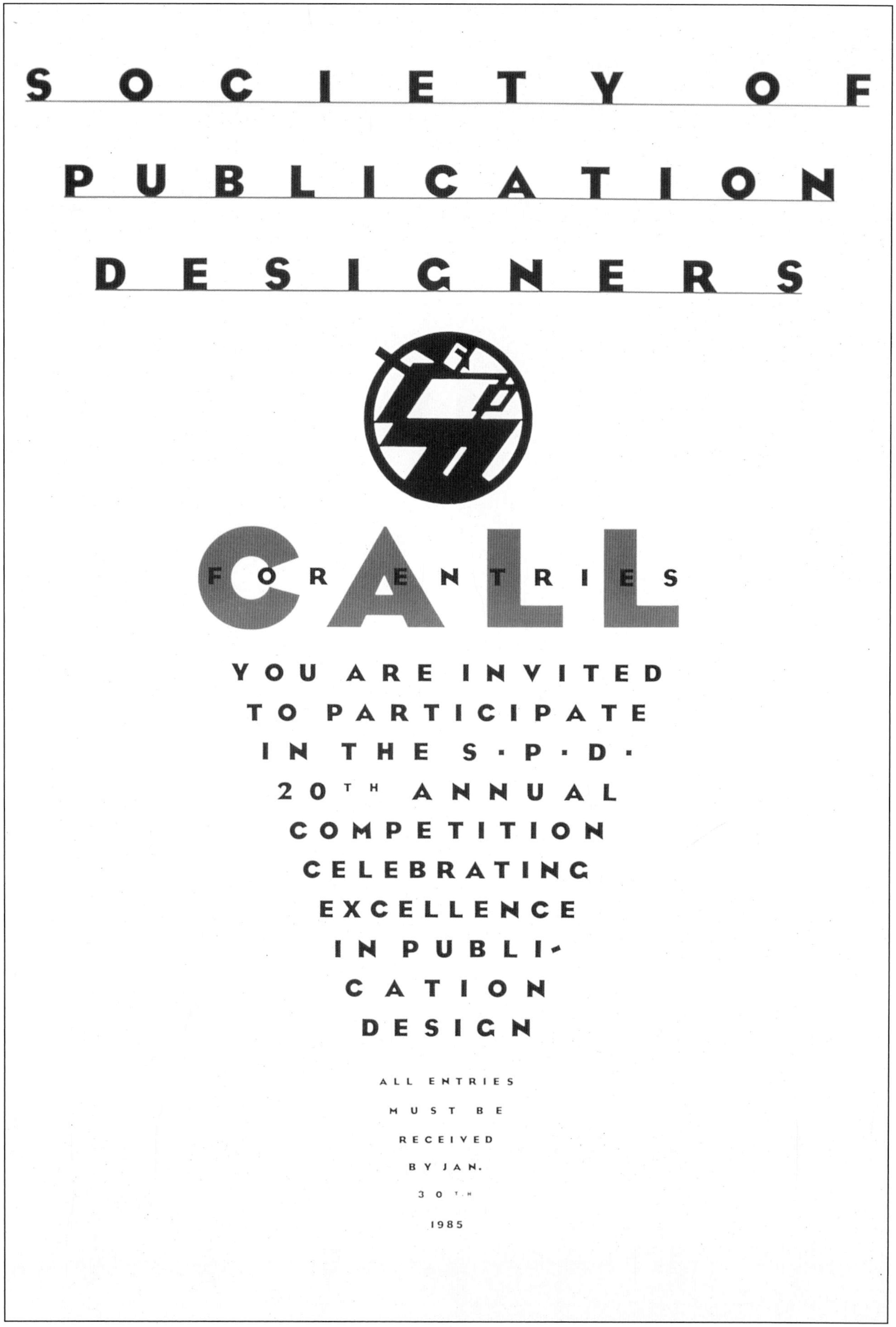
SOCIETY OF
PUBLICATION
DESIGNERS
CALL
FOR ENTRIES
YOU ARE INVITED
TO PARTICIPATE
IN THE S·P·D·
20TH ANNUAL
COMPETITION
CELEBRATING
EXCELLENCE
IN PUBLI-
CATION
DESIGN
ALL ENTRIES
MUST BE
RECEIVED
BY JAN.
30TH
1985

13
DESIGN FIRM: *Louise Fili Ltd.*
DESIGNER: *Louise Fili*
HEADLINE TYPEFACE: *Eagle Bold*
CLIENT: *Society of Publication Designers*

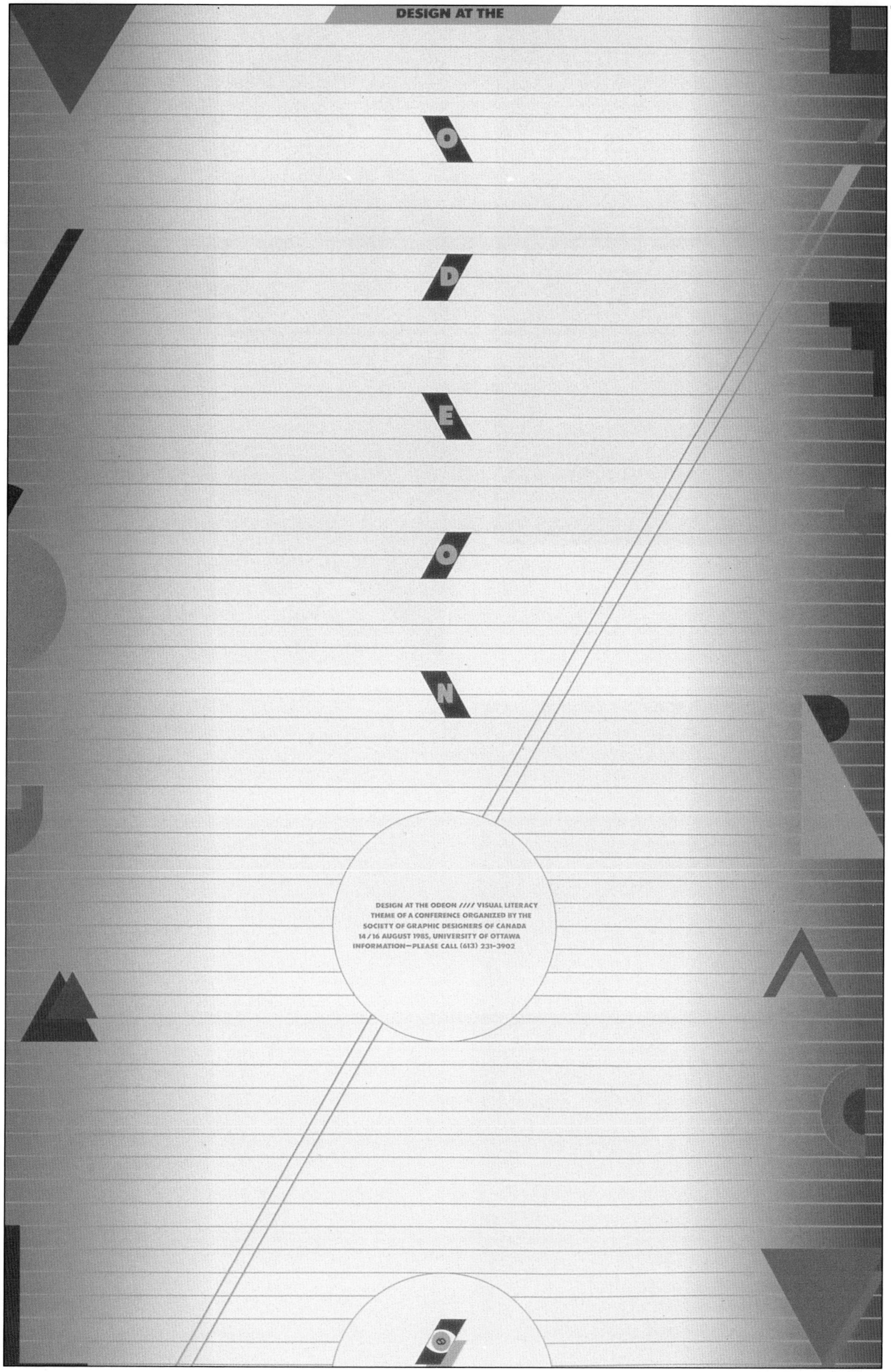

14

14
DESIGN FIRM: *Neville Smith Graphic Design*
DESIGNER: *Neville Smith*
LETTERER: *Neville Smith*
TEXT TYPEFACE: *Futura Bold and Letra Set*
CLIENT: *Society of Graphic Designers, Ottawa Chapter*

15
DESIGN FIRM: *The Duffy Design Group*
DESIGNER: *Joe Duffy*
HEADLINE TYPEFACE: *Glaser Stencil and Times Italic*
CLIENT: *Fallon McElligott*

16
DESIGN FIRM: *Pentagram Design*
DESIGNER: *Paula Scher*
CLIENT: *Swatch Watch*

17
DESIGN FIRM: *The Duffy Design Group*
DESIGNER: *Charles S. Anderson*
HEADLINE TYPEFACE: *Futura Bold Condensed*
TEXT TYPEFACE: *Bodoni*
CLIENT: *City of Minneapolis*

18
DESIGN FIRM: *Summerford Design, Inc.*
DESIGNER: *Jack Summerford*
HEADLINE TYPEFACE: *Garamond 3*
TEXT TYPEFACE: *Futura Bold*
CLIENT: *Heritage Press*

15

16

17

18

19

20

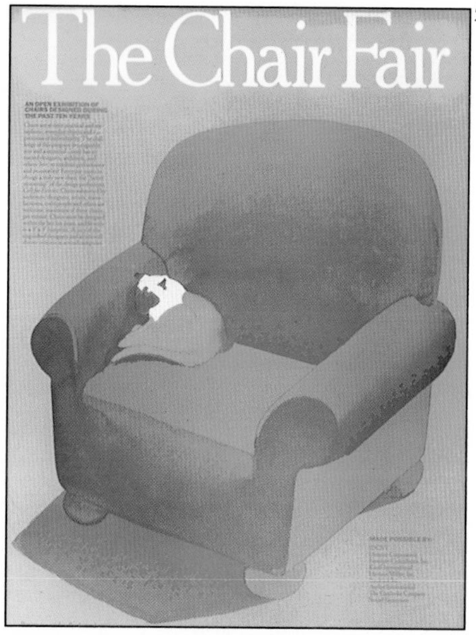

21

22

19
DESIGN FIRM: *The Duffy Design Group*
DESIGNER: *Joe Duffy*
HEADLINE TYPEFACE: *Spire*
CLIENT: *Gringolet Book Store*

20
DESIGN FIRM: *Milton Glaser, Inc.*
DESIGNER: *Milton Glaser*
HEADLINE TYPEFACE: *Cheltenham*
CLIENT: *Charvoz Artists' Materials*

21
DESIGN FIRM: *Milton Glaser, Inc.*
DESIGNER: *Milton Glaser*
HEADLINE TYPEFACE: *Cheltenham*
CLIENT: *International Design Center, NYC*

22
DESIGN FIRM: *Addison Design Consultants*
DESIGNER: *Adddison Design Consultants*
TEXT TYPEFACE: *Helvetica Conensed*
CLIENT: *Droste Holland*

23
DESIGN FIRM: *RBMM/The Richards Group*
DESIGNER: *David Beck*
HEADLINE TYPEFACE: *Bodoni Book*
TEXT TYPEFACE: *Bodoni Book*
CLIENT: *Northern Telecom*

24
DESIGN FIRM: *The Duffy Design Group*
DESIGNER: *Joe Duffy*
LETTERER: *Lynn Schulte and Joe Duffy*
HEADLINE TYPEFACE: *Handlettering*
CLIENT: *Donaldsons*

23

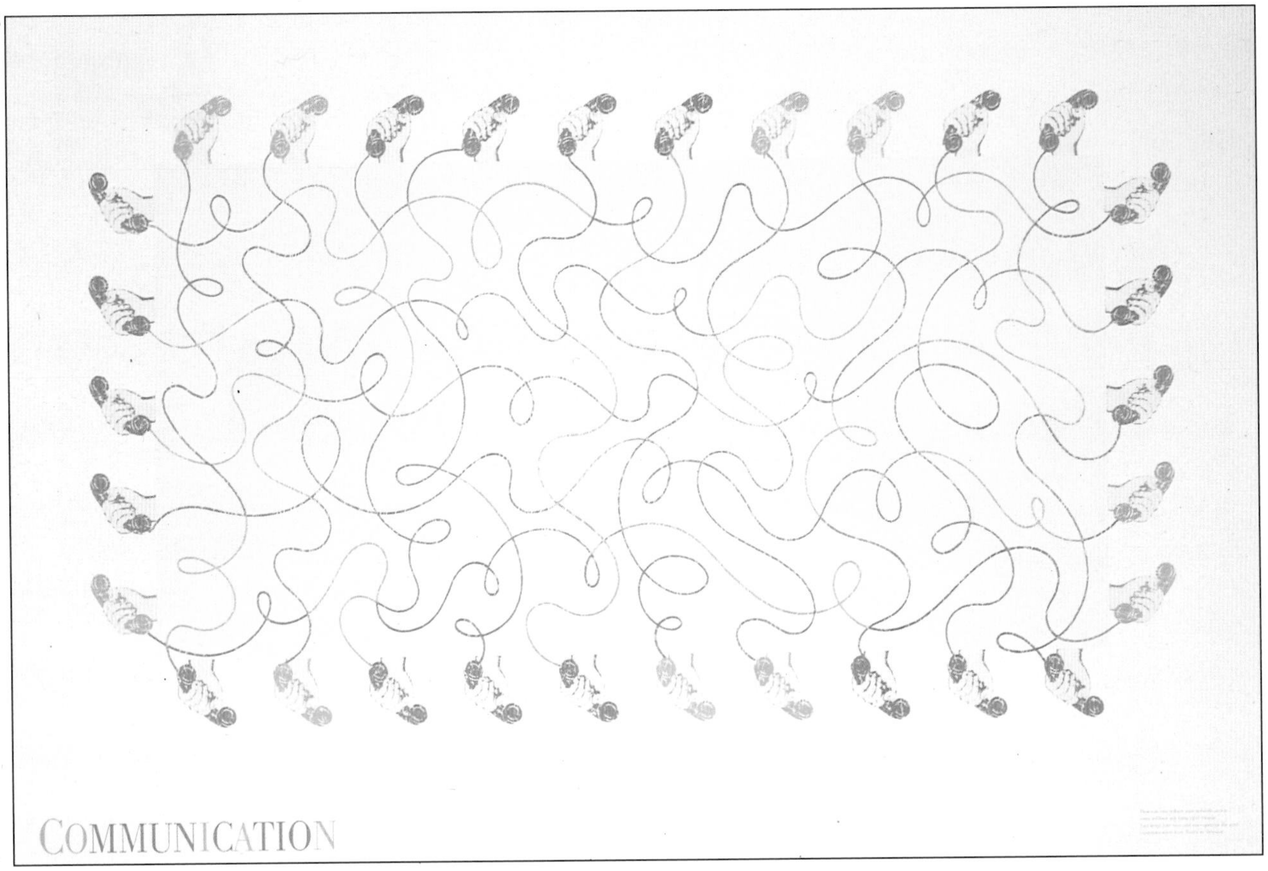

24

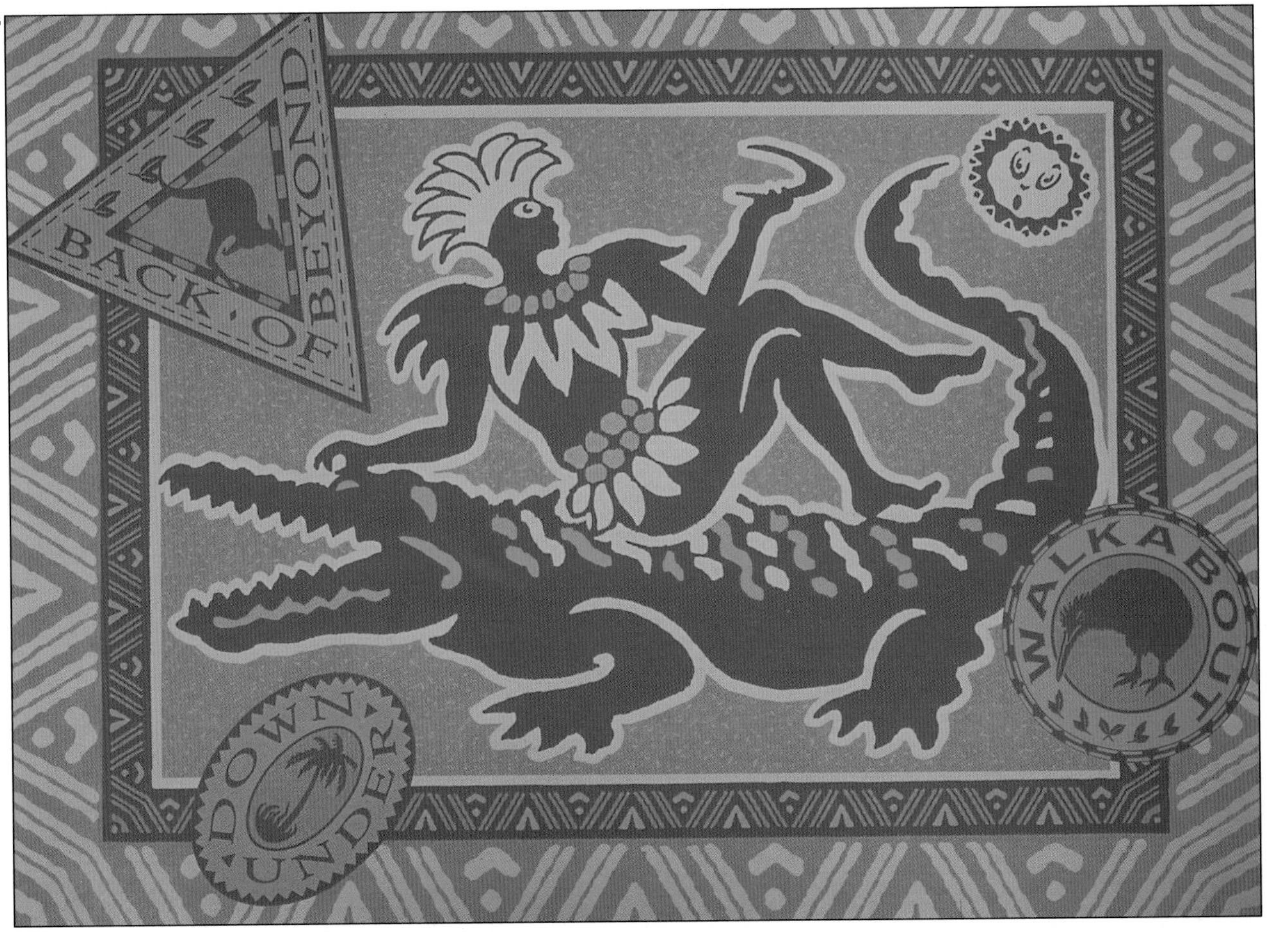

25

25
DESIGN FIRM: *The Duffy Design Group*
DESIGNER: *Charles S. Anderson*
LETTERER: *Lynn Schulte and Charles S. Anderson*
HEADLINE TYPEFACE: *Garamond, Franklin Gothic, and Handlettering*
CLIENT: *Chaps-Ralph Lauren*

26

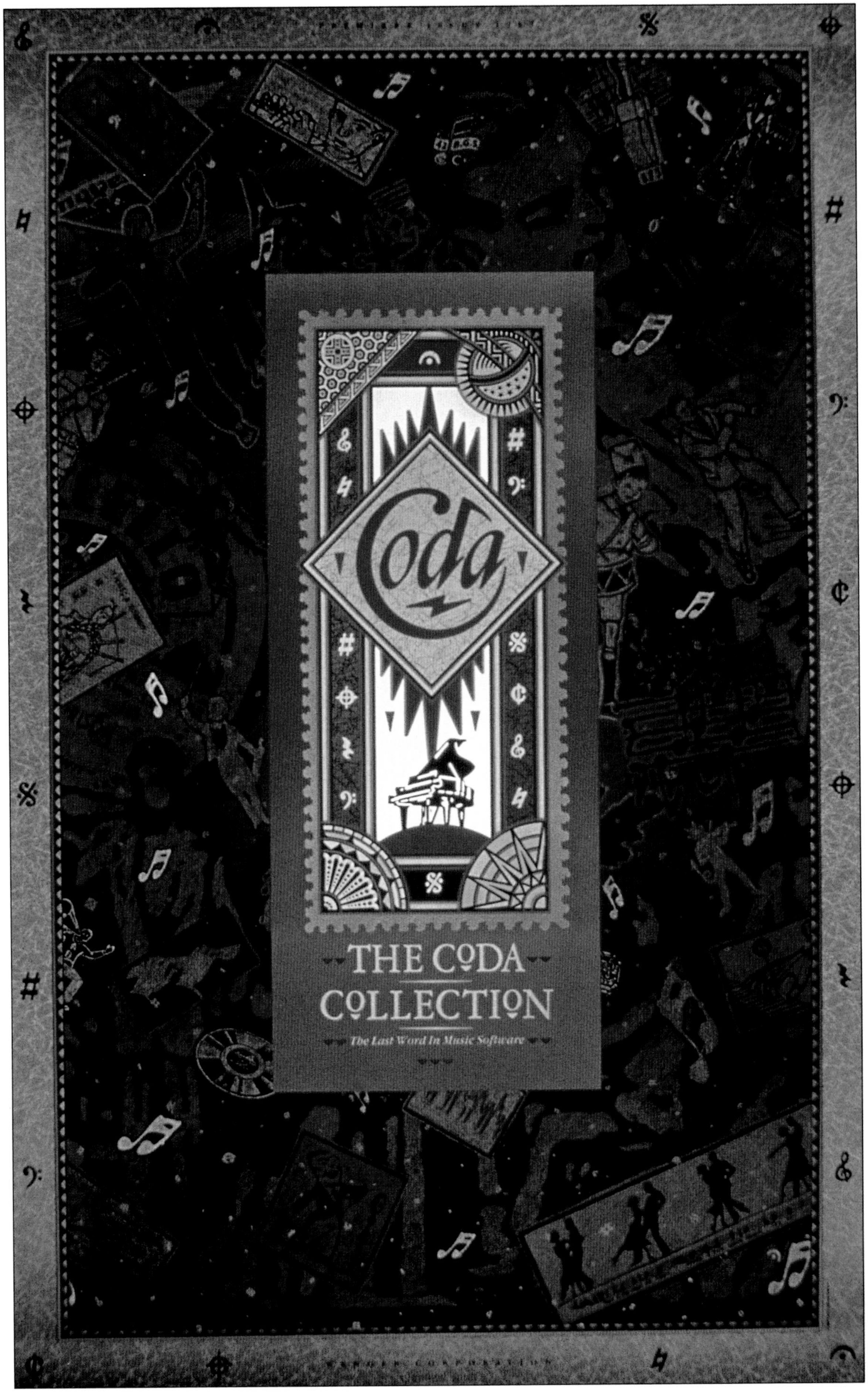

26
DESIGN FIRM: *The Duffy Design Group*
DESIGNER: *Charles S. Anderson*
LETTERER: *Lynn Schulte*
HEADLINE TYPEFACE: *Garamond and Handlettering*
CLIENT: *Wenger Corporation*

27

27
DESIGN FIRM: *The Duffy Design Group*
DESIGNER: *Charles S. Anderson*
LETTERER: *Charles S. Anderson and Lynn Schulte*
HEADLINE TYPEFACE: *Garamond, Handlettering, and Franklin Gothic*
CLIENT: *Chaps-Ralph Lauren*

28

28
DESIGN FIRM: *Grafik Communication, Ltd.*
DESIGNER: *Daniel Pelavin*
LETTERER: *Daniel Pelavin*
HEADLINE TYPEFACE: *Handlettering*
CLIENT: *Smithsonian Institution*

29

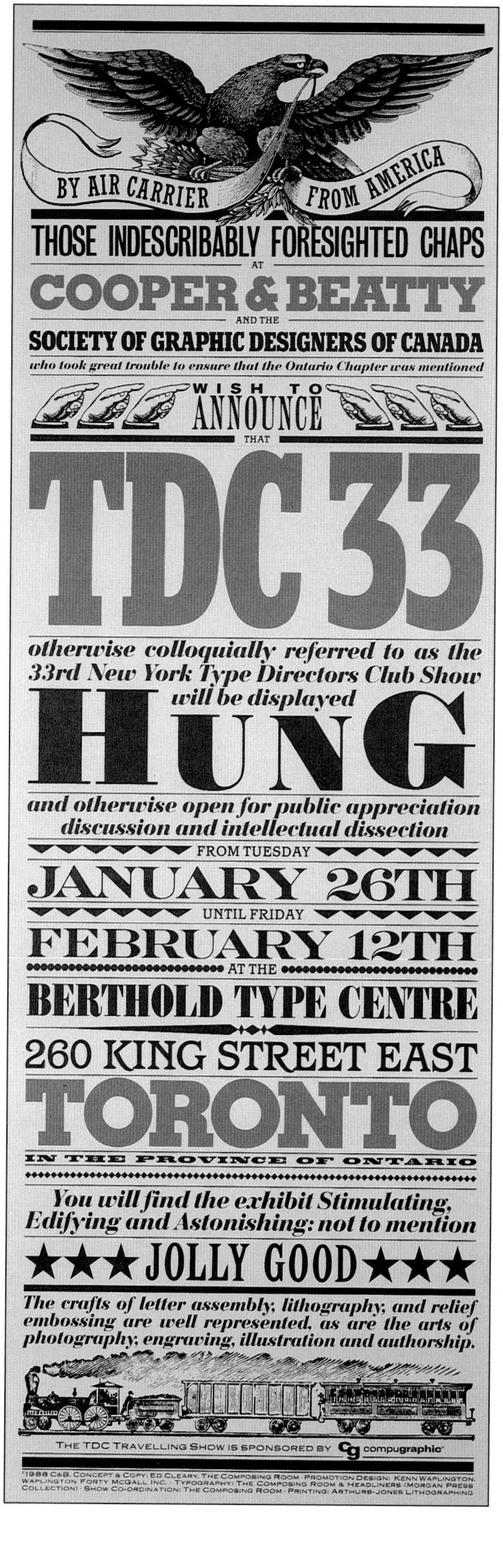

29
DESIGN FIRM: *Waplington Forty McGall*
DESIGNER: *K. Waplington*
CLIENT: *The Composing Room (Toronto)*

30

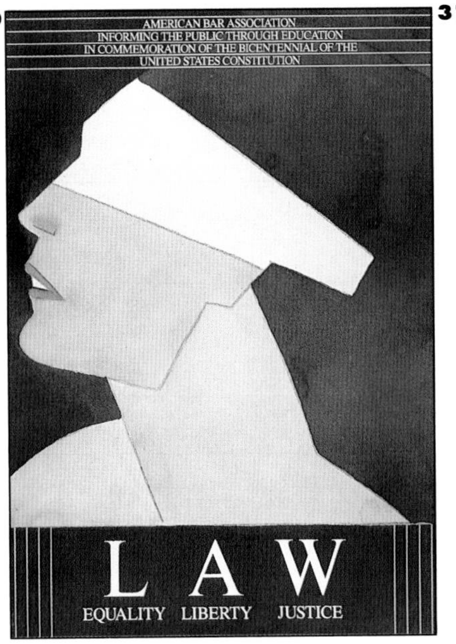

AMERICAN BAR ASSOCIATION
INFORMING THE PUBLIC THROUGH EDUCATION
IN COMMEMORATION OF THE BICENTENNIAL OF THE
UNITED STATES CONSTITUTION
LAW
EQUALITY LIBERTY JUSTICE

31

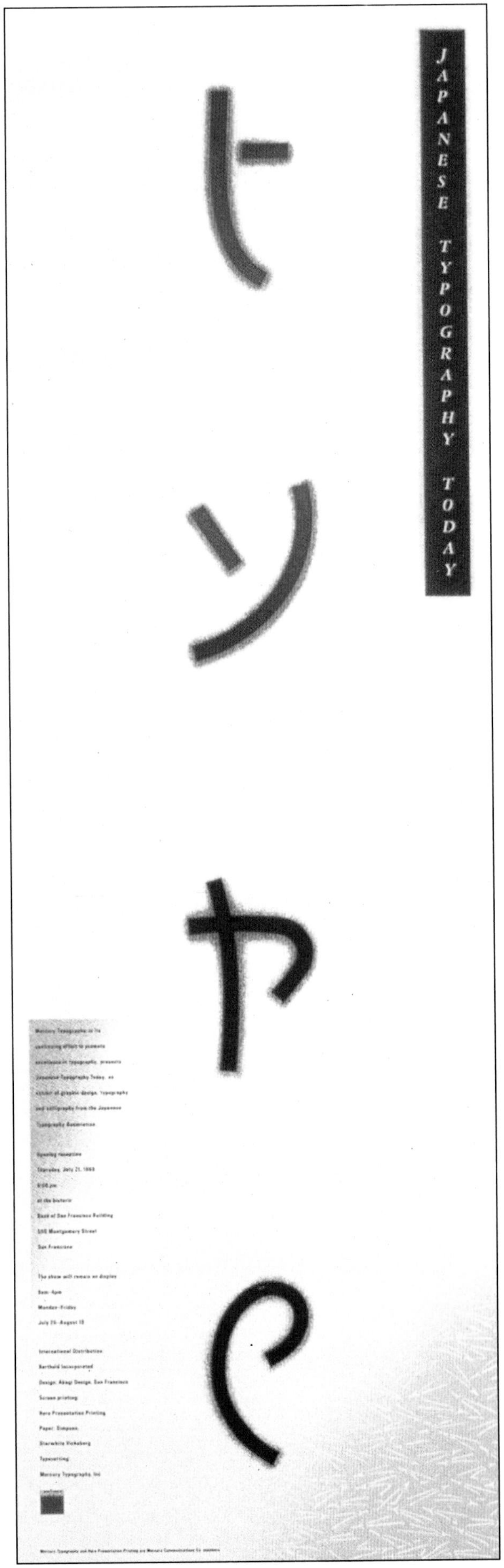

32

33

30
DESIGN FIRM: *Milton Glaser, Inc.*
DESIGNER: *Milton Glaser*
HEADLINE TYPEFACE: *Times Roman*
CLIENT: *American Bar Association*

31
DESIGN FIRM: *Akagi Design*
DESIGNER: *Doug Akagi*
LETTERER: *Sherri Brooks and Doug Akagi*
HEADLINE TYPEFACE: *Garamond Italic*
TEXT TYPEFACE: *Univers 67*
CLIENT: *Mercury Typography*

32
DESIGN FIRM: *Louise Fili Ltd.*
DESIGNER: *Louise Fili*
LETTERER: *Craig de Camps*
HEADLINE TYPEFACE: *Handlettering*
CLIENT: *Simon & Schuster*

33
DESIGN FIRM: *The Pushpin Group*
DESIGNER: *Seymor Chwast*
LETTERER: *Seymour Chwast*
CLIENT: *34 Festival International du Film*

34

PARTNERS PERFORM BETTER BY ACCEPTING, NOT ERASING, THEIR DIFFERENCES.
I DON'T KNOW THE KEY TO SUCCESS, BUT THE KEY TO FAILURE IS TRYING TO PLEASE EVERYONE.
BILL COSBY

35

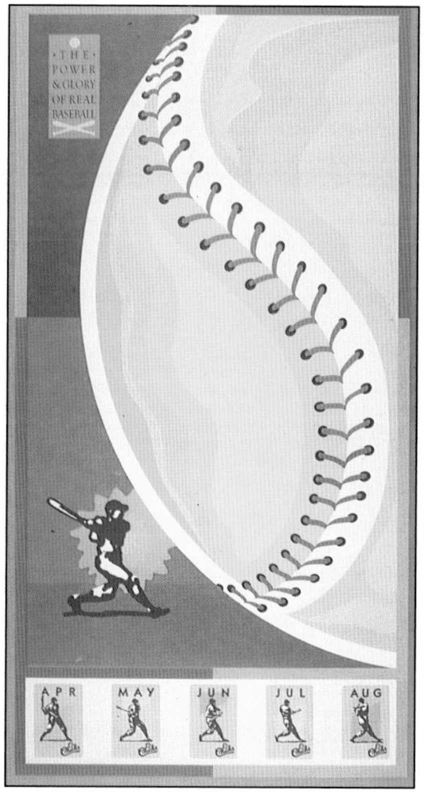

36

34
DESIGN FIRM: *The Duffy Design Group*
DESIGNER: *Charles S. Anderson*
HEADLINE TYPEFACE: *Eagle Bold*
CLIENT: *First Banks*

35
DESIGN FIRM: *The Duffy Design Group*
DESIGNER: *Joe Duffy*
HEADLINE TYPEFACE: *Motion Picture 4*
TEXT TYPEFACE: *Eagle Bold*
CLIENT: *First Tennessee Bank*

36
DESIGN FIRM: *Primo Angeli Inc.*
DESIGNER: *Primo Angeli*
LETTERER: *Mark Jones*
CLIENT: *The City of San Francisco*

37

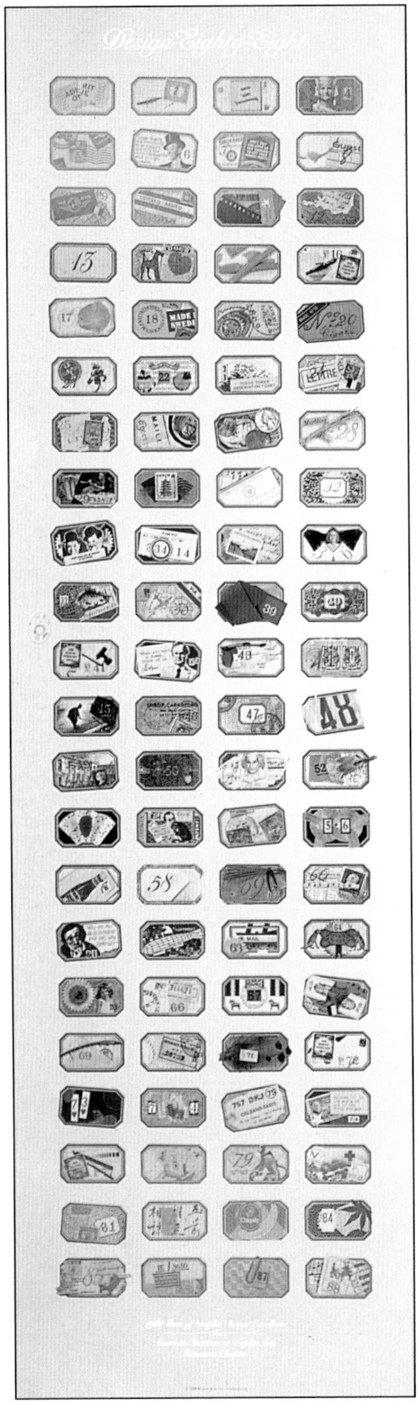

38

37
DESIGN FIRM: *Avchen & Associates, Inc.*
DESIGNER: *Leslee Avchen*
HEADLINE TYPEFACE: *Snell Roundhand*
TEXT TYPEFACE: *Copperplate*
CLIENT: *AIGA Minnesota*

38
DESIGN FIRM: *The Duffy Design Group*
DESIGNER: *Charles S. Anderson*
HEADLINE TYPEFACE: *Weiss Bold, Standard Condensed, and Helvetica Bold*
CLIENT: *French Paper Company*

39

40

39

DESIGN FIRM: *The Duffy Design Group*

DESIGNER: *Charles S. Anderson*

HEADLINE TYPEFACE: *Weiss Bold, Standard Condensed and Helvetica Bold*

CLIENT: *French Paper Company*

40

DESIGN FIRM: *Clifford Selbert Design, Incorporated*

DESIGNER: *Linda Murphy*

CLIENT: *Boston Society of Architects*

41
DESIGN FIRM: *McCool & Company*
DESIGNER: *Deb Miner*
HEADLINE TYPEFACE: *Letterworx*
TEXT TYPEFACE: *Carpenter*
CLIENT: *Donnalsons*

42
DESIGN FIRM: *Paul Davis Studio*
DESIGNER: *Paul Davis*
HEADLINE TYPEFACE: *Metro*
TEXT TYPEFACE: *Metro*
CLIENT: *New York Shakespeare Festival*

43
DESIGN FIRM: *Kan Tai-keung Design & Associates Ltd.*
DESIGNER: *Kan Tai-keung*
HEADLINE TYPEFACE: *Bodoni*
TEXT TYPEFACE: *Bodoni*
CLIENT: *Hong Kong Trade Development Council*

44
DESIGN FIRM: *Milton Glaser, Inc.*
DESIGNER: *Milton Glaser*
HEADLINE TYPEFACE: *Futura Light*
CLIENT: *Carnegie Hall*

41
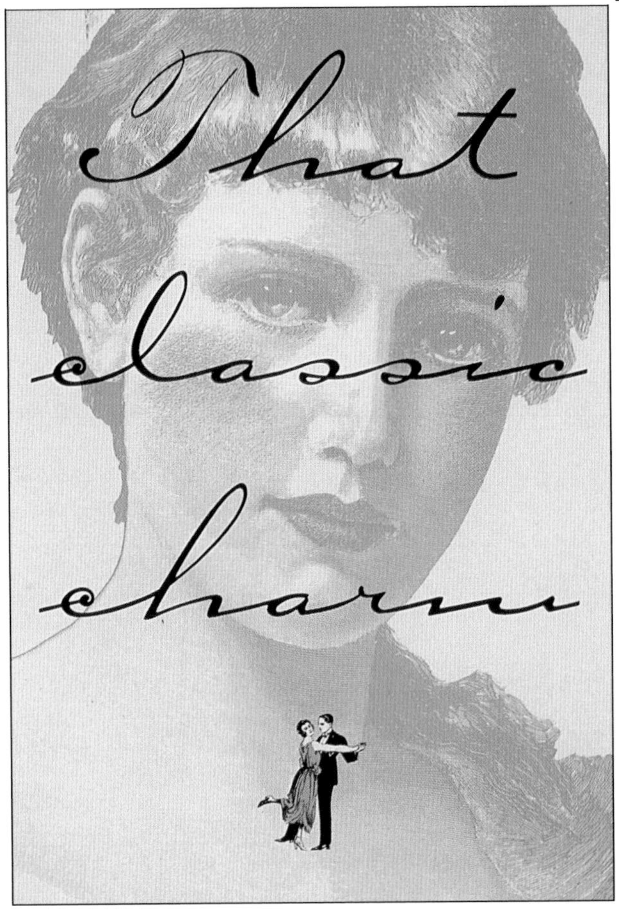

42
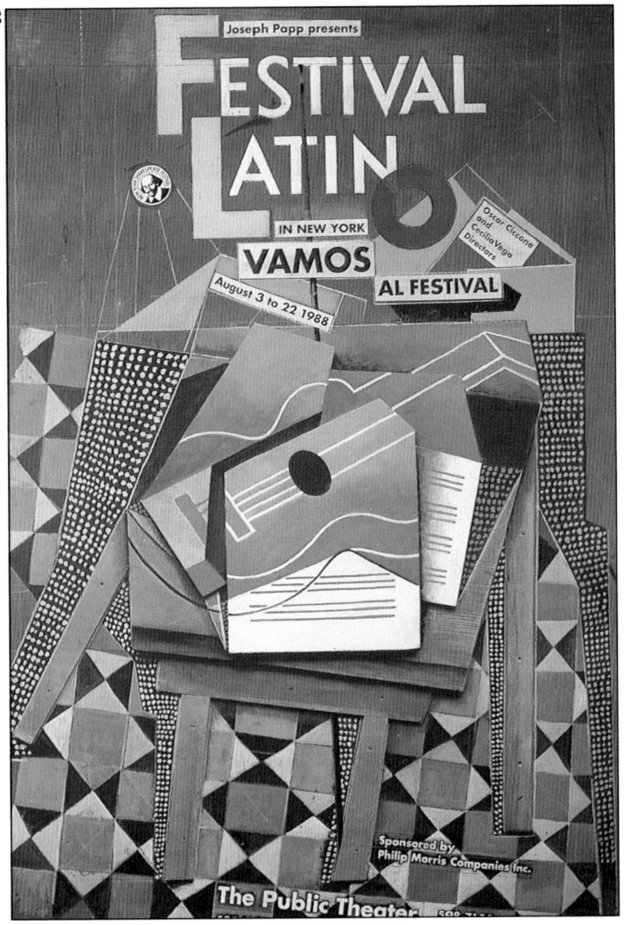

43

44

45

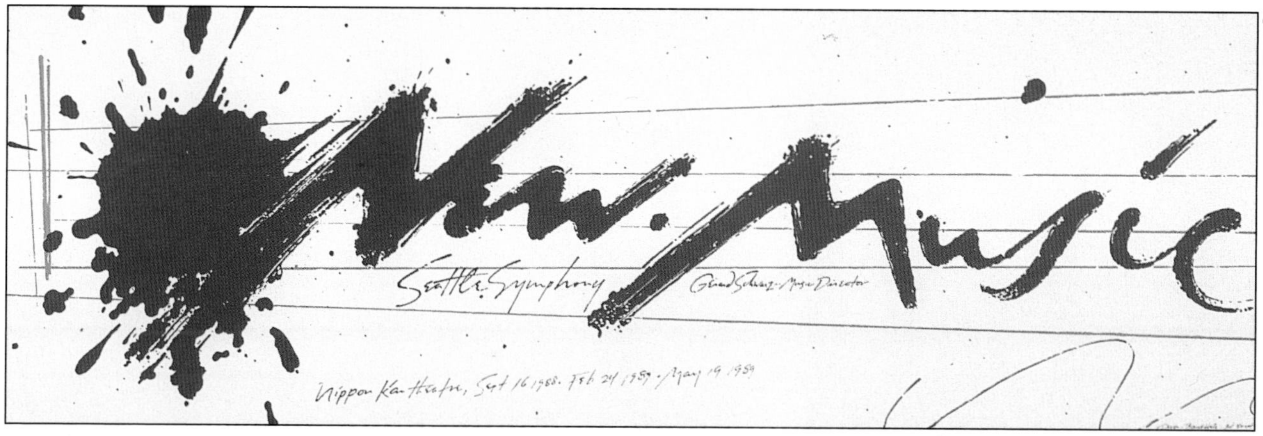

46

47

45
DESIGN FIRM: *Bruce Hale Design Studio*
DESIGNER: *Bruce Hale*
LETTERER: *Bruce Hale*
HEADLINE TYPEFACE: *Handlettering*
CLIENT: *Seattle Symphony*

46
DESIGN FIRM: *The Duffy Design Group*
DESIGNER: *Charles S. Anderson*
LETTERER: *Lynn Schulte*
HEADLINE TYPEFACE: *Handlettering and Franklin Gothic*
CLIENT: *Cincinnati Art Direction*

47
DESIGN FIRM: *Peterson & Company*
DESIGNER: *David Lerch and Scott Ray*
HEADLINE TYPEFACE: *Handlettering*
CLIENT: *International Association of Business Communications*

48
DESIGN FIRM: *Pentagram Design*
DESIGNER: *Paula Scher*
LETTERER: *Paula Scher*
HEADLINE TYPEFACE: *Handlettering*
TEXT TYPEFACE: *Handlettering*
CLIENT: *Oola Corporation*

49
DESIGN FIRM: *Muller & Company*
DESIGNER: *Patrice Eilts*
HEADLINE TYPEFACE: *Empire*
TEXT TYPEFACE: *Copperplate*
CLIENT: *KC Jazz Festival*

50
DESIGN FIRM: *The Duffy Design Group*
DESIGNER: *Charles S. Anderson*
HEADLINE TYPEFACE: *Eagle Bond*
CLIENT: *First Banks*

48
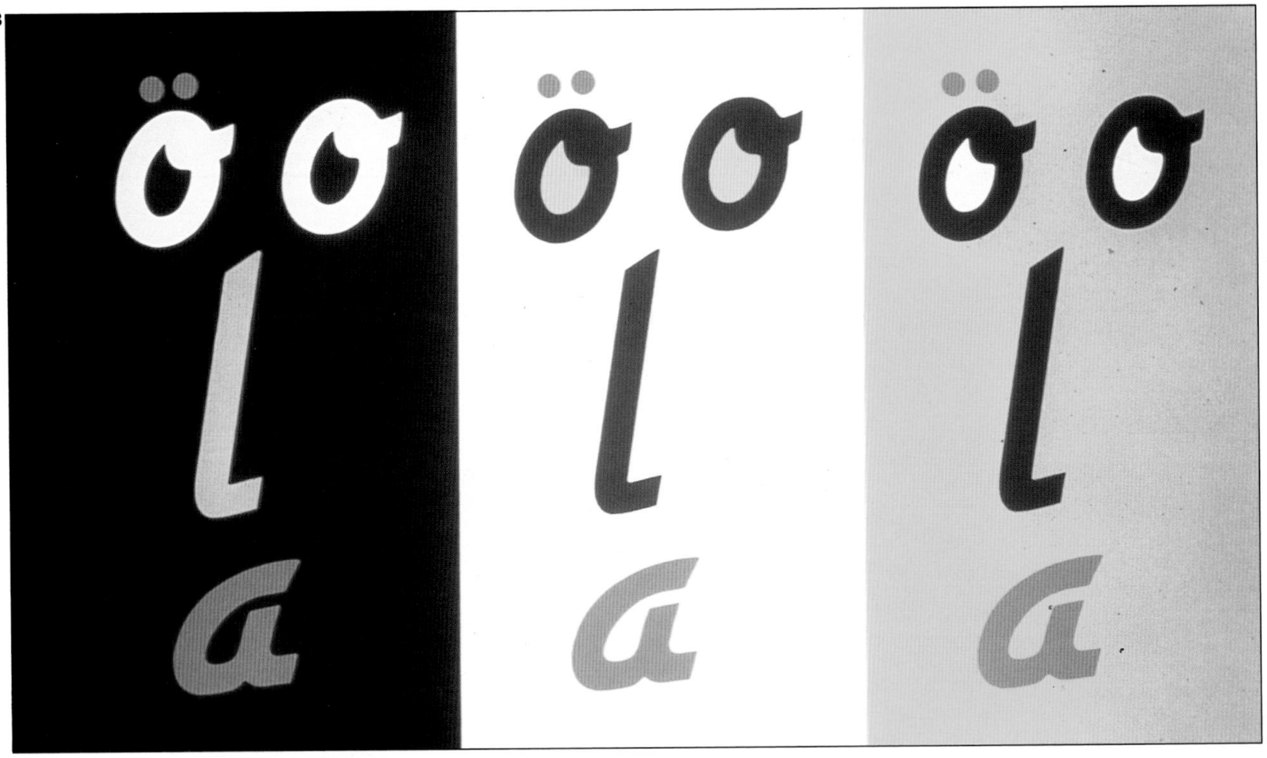
ööla
ööla
ööla

49
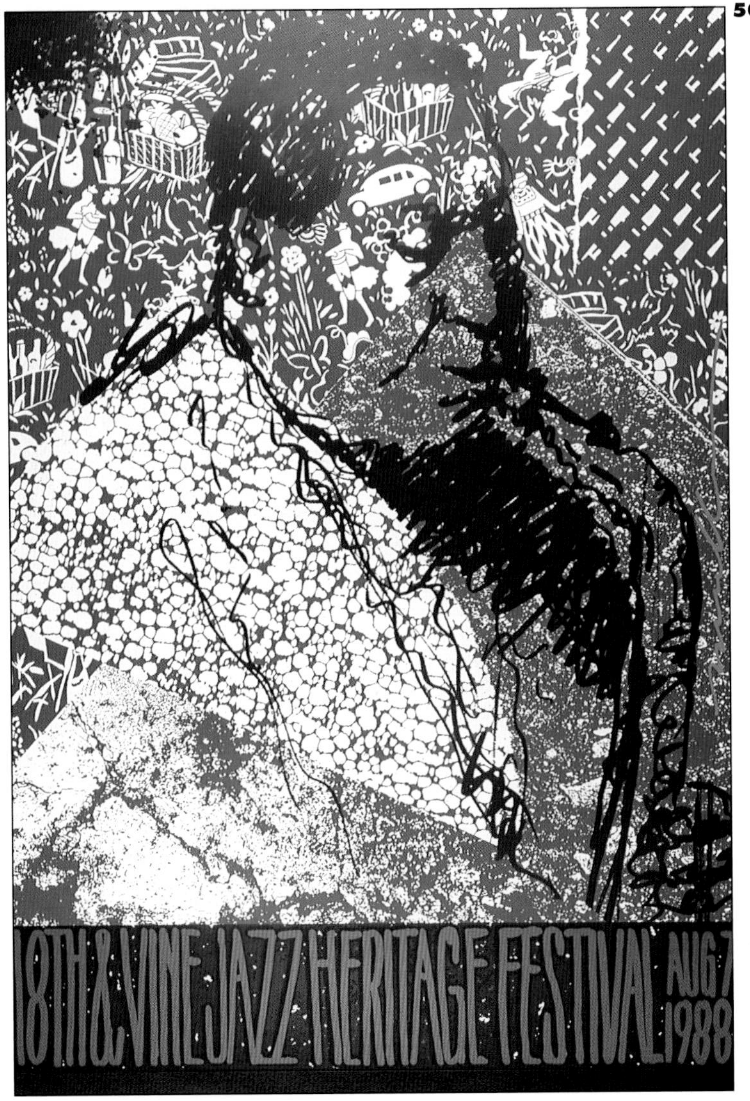
18TH & VINE JAZZ HERITAGE FESTIVAL AUG 7 1988

50

GOOD TEAMWORK
DOES NOT MEAN
LESS WORK •
JUST MORE PRO•
DUCTIVE WORK
EVEN IF YOU
ARE ON THE
RIGHT TRACK,
YOU WILL GET
RUN OVER
IF YOU JUST
SIT THERE •
WILL ROGERS

51
DESIGN FIRM: *Belk Mignogna Associates*
DESIGNER: *Howard Belk*
LETTERER: *Howard Belk*
HEADLINE TYPEFACE: *Univers 47*
TEXT TYPEFACE: *Bodoni*
CLIENT: *L.P. Thebault Company*

52

52
DESIGN FIRM: *Pentagram Design*
DESIGNER: *Paula Scher*
HEADLINE TYPEFACE: *Eagle Bold*
TEXT TYPEFACE: *Futura*
CLIENT: *School of Visual Arts*

53

53
DESIGN FIRM: *The Duffy Design Group*
DESIGNER: *Sharon Werner*
HEADLINE TYPEFACE: *Standard Bold Condensed*
CLIENT: *Donaldsons*

54
DESIGN FIRM: *RBMM/The Richards Group*
DESIGNER: *D.C. Stipp*
HEADLINE TYPEFACE: *Garamond*
TEXT TYPEFACE: *Garamond*
CLIENT: *Dallas Society of Visual Communications*

55
DESIGN FIRM: *Hal Riney Partners Inc.*
DESIGNER: *Lance Anderson*
LETTERER: *Lance Anderson*
CLIENT: *Spectrum Foods*

56
DESIGN FIRM: *Paul Davis Studio*
DESIGNER: *Paul Davis*
HEADLINE TYPEFACE: *Metro*
TEXT TYPEFACE: *Metro*
CLIENT: *New York Shakespeare Festival*

57
DESIGN FIRM: *M Plus M Incorporated*
DESIGNER: *Michael McGinn*
LETTERER: *Michael McGinn*
TEXT TYPEFACE: *Bodoni*
CLIENT: *Pratt Institute*

54

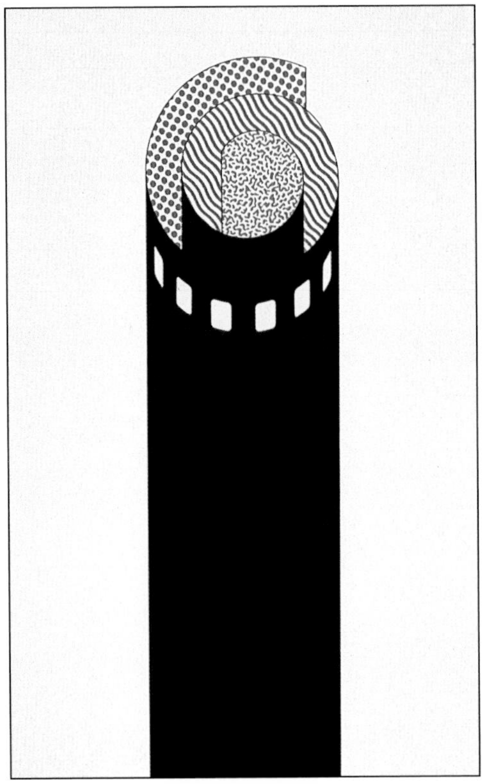

55

56

57

58
DESIGN FIRM: *The Pushpin Group*
DESIGNER: *Greg Simpson*
CLIENT: *Artis '89/Imaje International pour les droits de l'homme et du Citoyen*

59

59
DESIGN FIRM: *The Duffy Design Group*
DESIGNER: *Sharon Werner*
LETTERER: *Sharon Werner and Lynn Schulte*
HEADLINE TYPEFACE: *Handlettering*
CLIENT: *Lee Jeans*

60

61

62

63

60
DESIGN FIRM: *Peterson & Company*
DESIGNER: *Jan Wilson*
HEADLINE TYPEFACE: *Franklin Gothic*
CLIENT: *Dallas Society of Visual Communications*

61
DESIGN FIRM: *The Duffy Design Group*
DESIGNER: *Charles S. Anderson*
LETTERER: *Lynn Schulte and Charles S. Anderson*
HEADLINE TYPEFACE: *Bank Gothic*
CLIENT: *STA Chicago*

62/63
DESIGN FIRM: *Pentagram Design*
DESIGNER: *Paula Scher*
LETTERER: *Paula Scher*
HEADLINE TYPEFACE: *Handlettering*
TEXT TYPEFACE: *Handlettering*
CLIENT: *Oola Corporation*

64
DESIGN FIRM: *Yoichi Fujii*
DESIGNER: *Yoichi Fujii*
LETTERER: *Yoichi Fujii*
CLIENT: *CS Artists*

65
DESIGN FIRM: *Milton Glaser, Inc.*
DESIGNER: *Milton Glaser*
TEXT TYPEFACE: *Future Medium Condensed*
CLIENT: *Brooklyn College (NYC)*

66
DESIGN FIRM: *The Design Group, JRSK*
DESIGNER: *Paul Black*
LETTERER: *Paul Black*
HEADLINE TYPEFACE: *Futura Bold*
TEXT TYPEFACE: *Futura*
CLIENT: *EDS*

67
DESIGN FIRM: *Paul Davis Studio*
DESIGNER: *Paul Davis*
LETTERER: *H.C. Martin*
TEXT TYPEFACE: *Gill Sans Bold*
CLIENT: *Mobil Corporation*

64

65

66

67

68

68
DESIGN FIRM: *Hornall Anderson Design Works*
DESIGNER: *Glenn Yoshiyama*
LETTERER: *Glenn Yoshiyama*
TEXT TYPEFACE: *Palatino Italic*
CLIENT: *Hornall Anderson Design Works*

69
DESIGN FIRM: *Akagi Design*
DESIGNER: *Doug Akagi*
HEADLINE TYPEFACE: *Fenice*
TEXT TYPEFACE: *Fenice*
CLIENT: *Opcode Systems, Inc.*

70
DESIGN FIRM: *Kan Tai-keung Design & Associates Ltd.*
DESIGNER: *Kan Tai-keung*
HEADLINE TYPEFACE: *Univers 65*
TEXT TYPEFACE: *Univers 65*
CLIENT: *Alisan Fine Arts Limited*

69

70

71

The best things in life are free,
but you can give 'em to the birds and bees,
we want money, that's what we want.
There are many things to give us thrills,
There's only one thing gonna pay our bills,
And that's money, that's all we want.
there's lotsa things that we'd like to do,
and child, we want to do them with you,
It takes money, that's what we want,
that's what we want, want, want, want,
Yeah, that's what we want.
Check it out it's time for the 1st annual Texas AIGA Fun-Raising 919. And just what do you get for your 15 bucks? More shakin' and rattlin' at the Sons of Hermann Hall in Deep Ellum, more reelin' and rockin' with the "Fabulous and/or Dynamic" Reverb-Kings, more spinnin' times with all your friends, and gee, for your 15 bucks you can party till its 1999, So forget the fancy threads and come as you are Saturday night, March 26, 8pm to 1am, $15 a person, $25 a couple, in advance or at the door, cash bar, Sons of Hermann Hall, 3414 Elm Street in Dallas, for more info call (214) 855-5353.

72

71
DESIGN FIRM: *Peterson & Company*
DESIGNER: *Bryan L. Peterson*
LETTERER: *Bryan L. Peterson*
TEXT TYPEFACE: *Handlettering*
CLIENT: *American Institute for the Graphic Arts*

72
DESIGN FIRM: *RBMM/The Richards Group*
DESIGNER: *Brian Boyd*
LETTERER: *Brian Boyd*
HEADLINE TYPEFACE: *Serif Gothic*
CLIENT: *AIGA*

73
DESIGN FIRM: *Clifford Stoltze Design and Terry Swack Design*
DESIGNER: *Clifford Stoltze and Terry Swack*
HEADLINE TYPEFACE: *Handlettering*
TEXT TYPEFACE: *Handlettering*
CLIENT: *AIGA/Boston*

73

HOTLINE
LOUIS FISHAUF
SKOLOS · WEDELL · RAYNO
STEPHEN DOYLE
VAUGHAN OLIVER

74
DESIGN FIRM: *The Pushpin Group*
DESIGNER: *Seymour Chwast*
LETTERER: *Seymour Chwast*
CLIENT: *Mobil Corporation*

75
DESIGN FIRM: *Fuller Dyal & Stamper*
DESIGNER: *David Kampa*
LETTERER: *David Kampa*
TEXT TYPEFACE: *Caslon 540 Italic and Futura Bold*
CLIENT: *Texas Society of Architects*

76
DESIGN FIRM: *Hess & Hess*
DESIGNER: *Kathleen Hohl-Phillips*
CLIENT: *New York City Opera*

77
DESIGN FIRM: *Muller & Company*
DESIGNER: *Patrice Eilts*
LETTERER: *Patrice Eilts*
HEADLINE TYPEFACE: *Empire*
TEXT TYPEFACE: *Futura X-Bold*
CLIENT: *Crown Center*

74

75

76
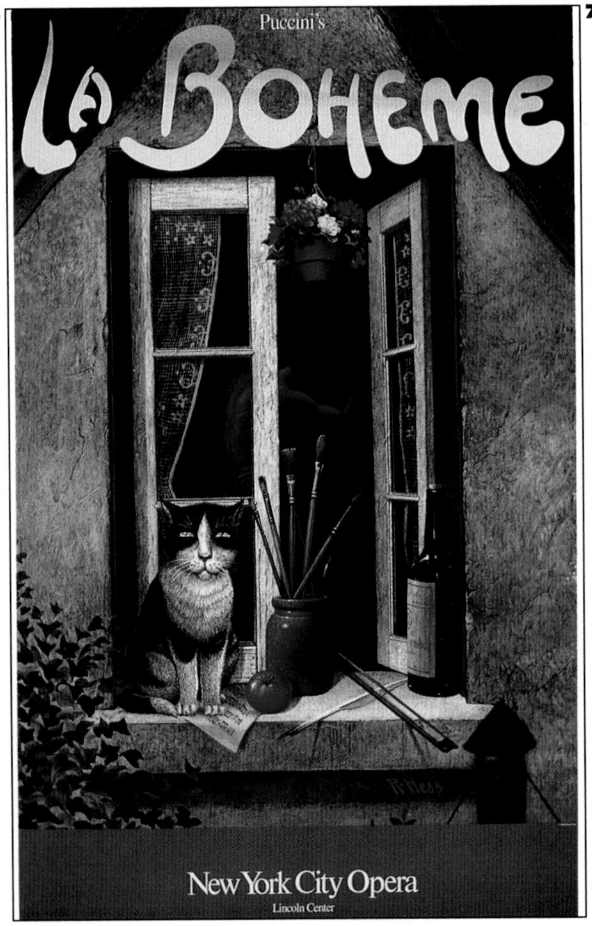

77
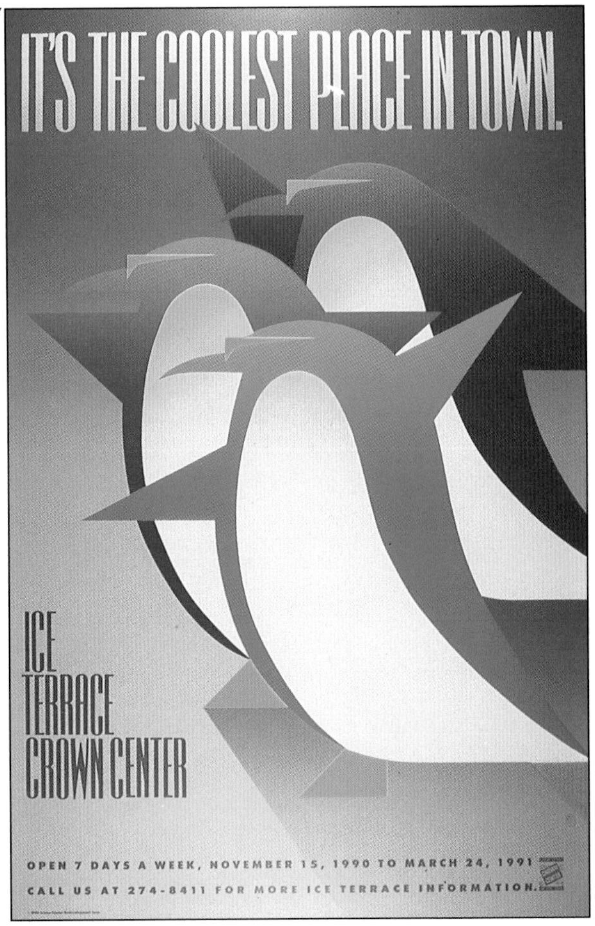

78

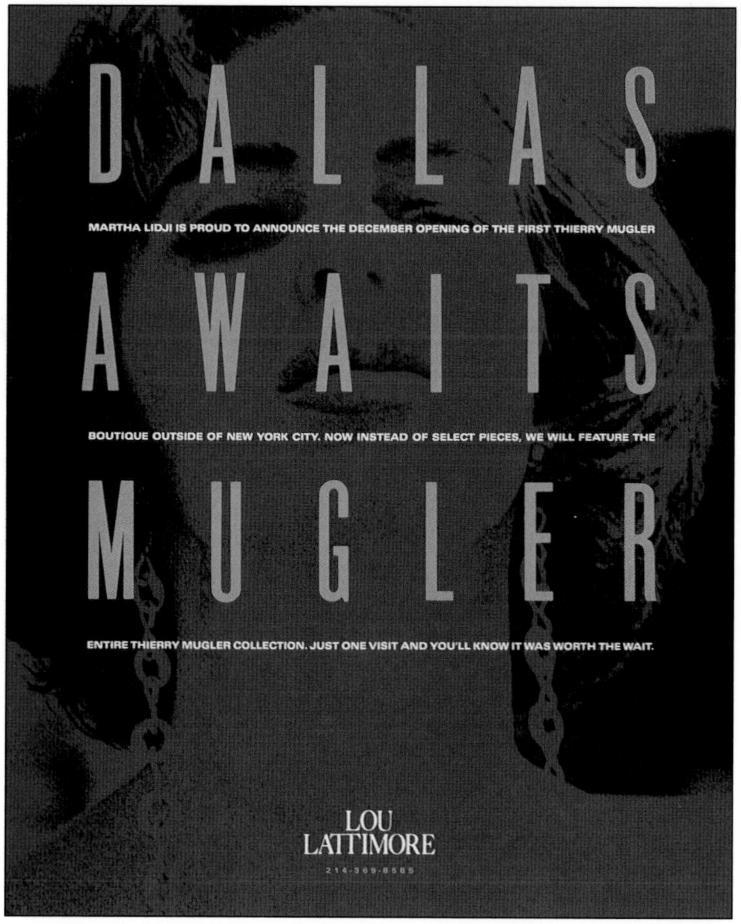

79

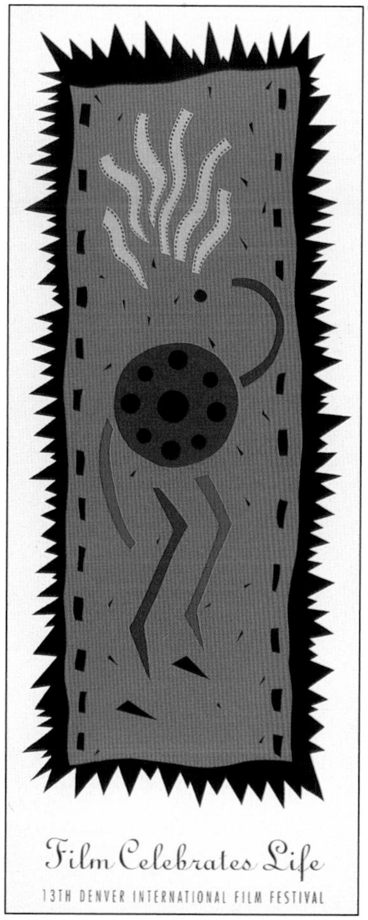

80

81

78
DESIGN FIRM: *Knape & Knape*
DESIGNER: *Michaels Connors*
LETTERER: *Michael Connors*
HEADLINE TYPEFACE: *Title Gothic Extra Condensed*
TEXT TYPEFACE: *Univers 73*
CLIENT: *Lou Lattimore*

79
DESIGN FIRM: *Merten Design Group*
DESIGNER: *Barry A. Merten and Steve Niemczura*
HEADLINE TYPEFACE: *Linoscript*
CLIENT: *Denver Film Society*

80
DESIGN FIRM: *Drenttel Doyle Partners*
DESIGNER: *Rosemarie Turk*
HEADLINE TYPEFACE: *New Barkerville and Franklin Gothic*
TEXT TYPEFACE: *New Barkerville and Franklin Gothic*
CLIENT: *Olympia & York, U.S.A.*

81
DESIGN FIRM: *Sibley/Peteet Design*
DESIGNER: *Don Sibley*
HEADLINE TYPEFACE: *Variex*
TEXT TYPEFACE: *Variex*
CLIENT: *Designers of Dallas*

82
DESIGN FIRM: *Pat Hansen Design Company*
DESIGNER: *Pat Hansen and Thomas Lehman*
HEADLINE TYPEFACE: *Empire and Handlettering*
TEXT TYPEFACE: *Univers Condensed*
CLIENT: *AIGA/Seattle*

83
DESIGN FIRM: *Sibley/Peteet Design*
DESIGNER: *Don Sibley*
HEADLINE TYPEFACE: *Bodoni and Futura Extra Bold*
TEXT TYPEFACE: *Futura Extra Bold*
CLIENT: *Dallas Society of Visual Communication*

84
DESIGN FIRM: *Fuller Dyal & Stamper*
DESIGNER: *David Kampa*
LETTERER: *David Kampa*
TEXT TYPEFACE: *Caslon 540 Italic and Futura Bold*
CLIENT: *Texas Society of Architects*

85
DESIGN FIRM: *Bruce Hale Design Studio*
DESIGNER: *Bruce Hale*
LETTERER: *Bruce Hale*
HEADLINE TYPEFACE: *Handlettering*
CLIENT: *Bruce Hale Design Studio*

82

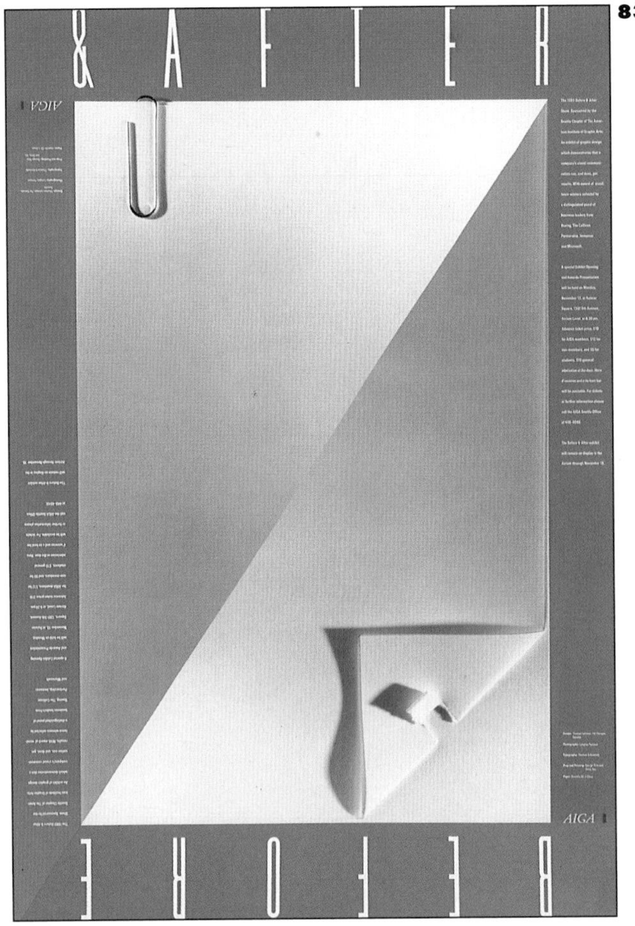

83

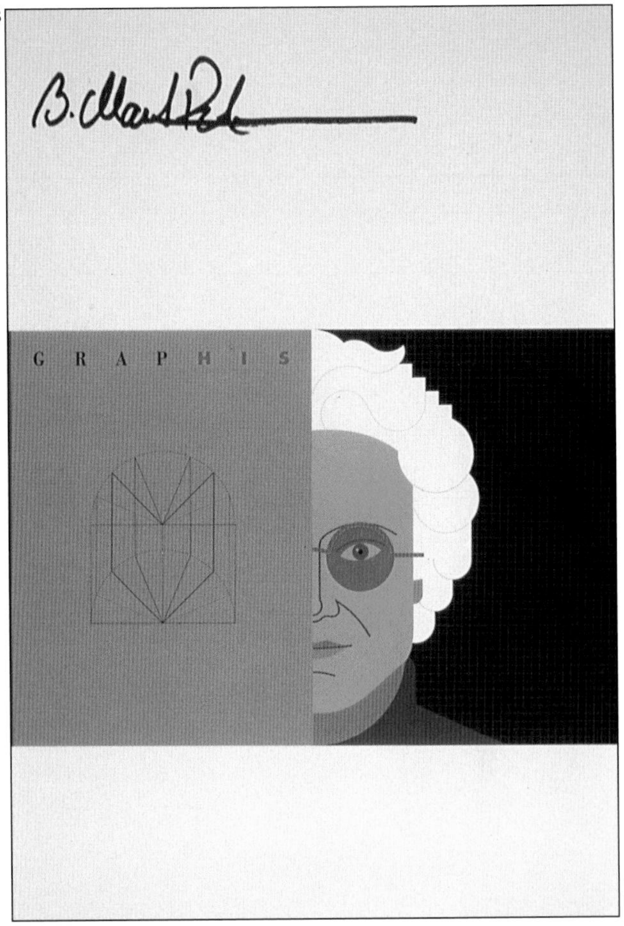

84

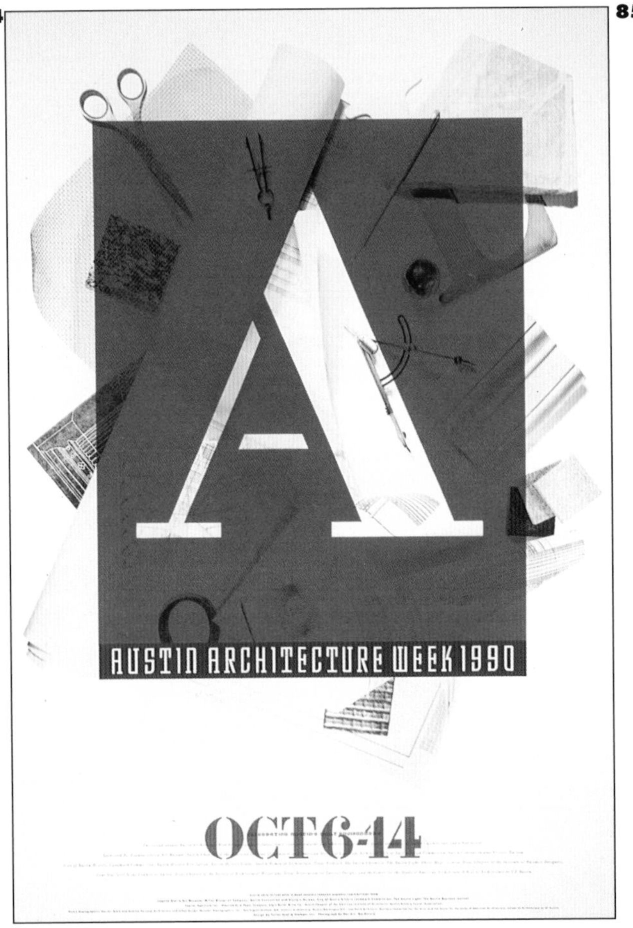

85

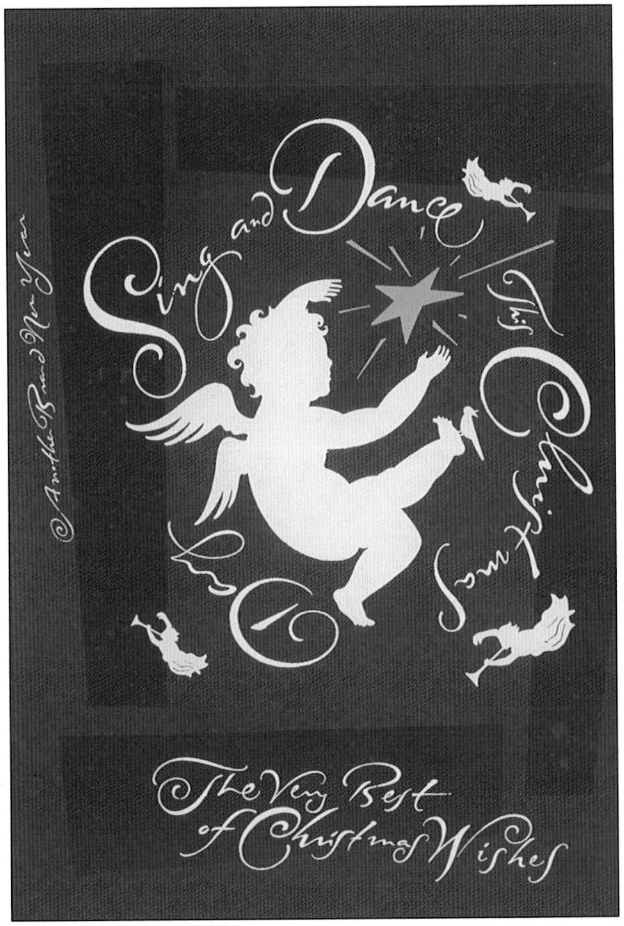

86
DESIGN FIRM: *Muller & Company*
DESIGNER: *John Muller*
LETTERER: *John Muller*
HEADLINE TYPEFACE: *Handlettering*
CLIENT: *KC Jazz Festival*

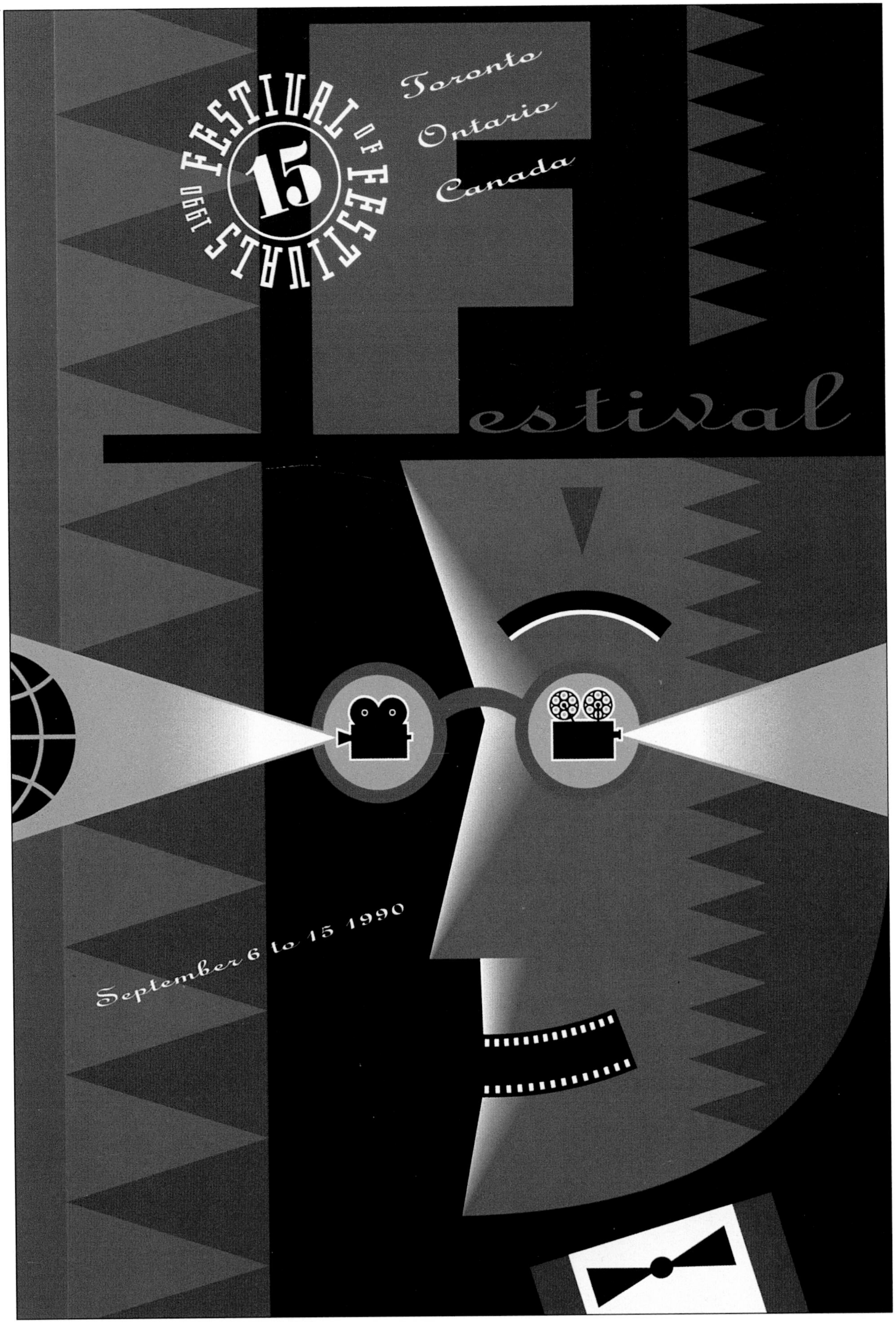

87
DESIGN FIRM: *Reactor Art & Design*
DESIGNER: *Louis Fishauf and Karen Cheeseman*
HEADLINE TYPEFACE: *Linoscript*
TEXT TYPEFACE: *Linoscript and Oblong*
CLIENT: *Festival of Festivals*

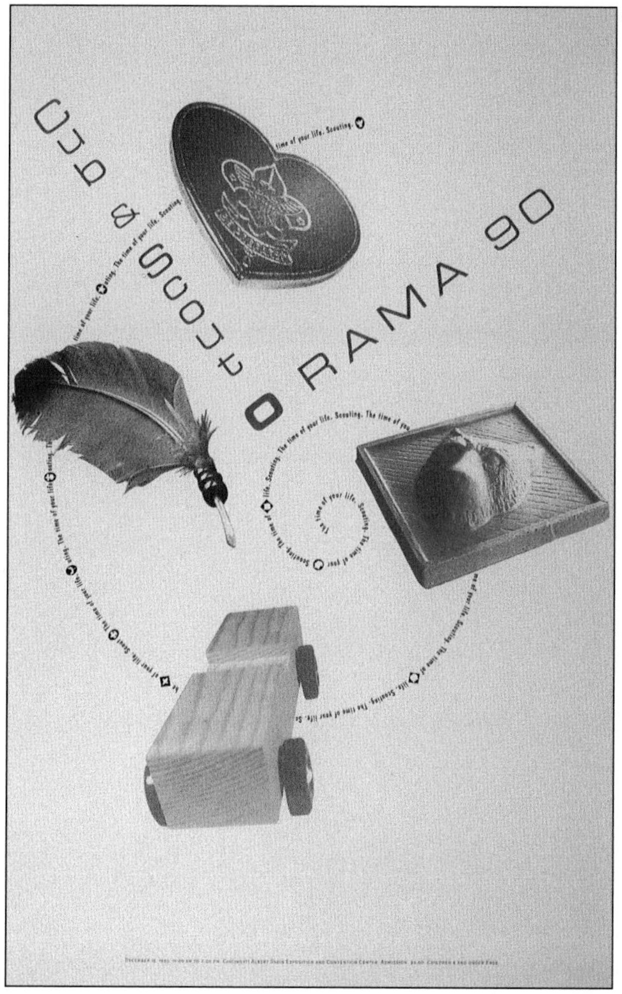

88

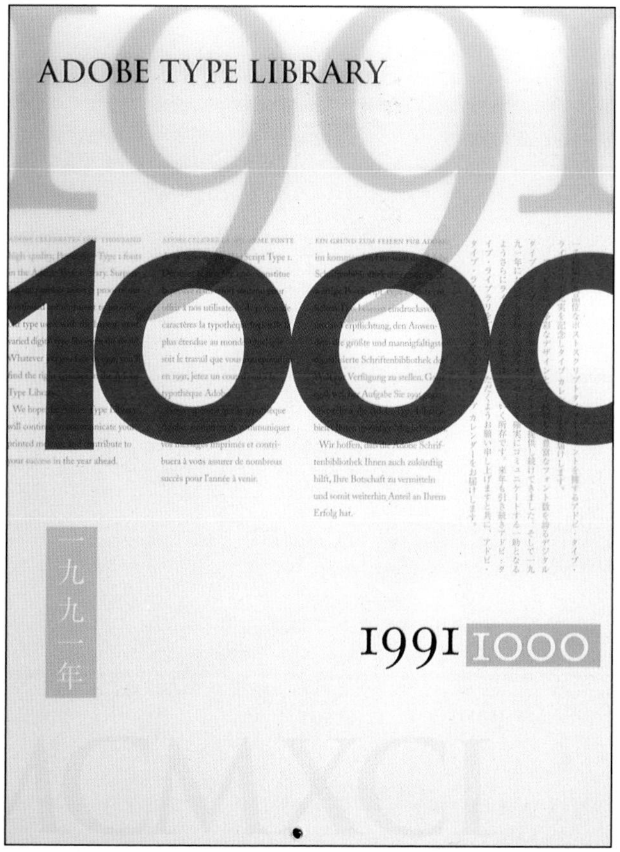

89

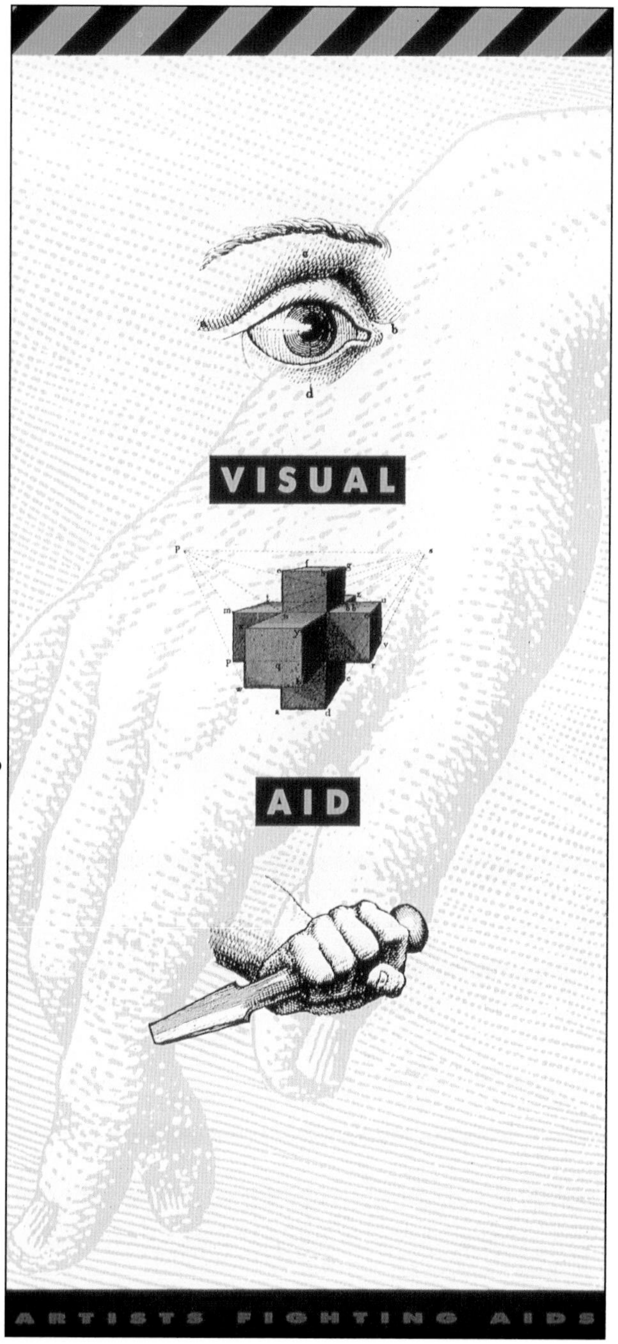

90

88
DESIGN FIRM: *Design Team One, Inc.*
DESIGNER: *Dan Bittman*
HEADLINE TYPEFACE: *Eurostyle Extended, Dom Casual, and Copperplate Engravers*
CLIENT: *Boy Scouts of America*

89
DESIGN FIRM: *Adobe*
DESIGNER: *Adobe MarCom Dept.*
CLIENT: *Adobe*

90
DESIGN FIRM: *Morla Design*
DESIGNER: *Jennifer Morla*
HEADLINE TYPEFACE: *Futura Bold*
CLIENT: *Artists for AIDS Relief: Visual Aid*

91
DESIGN FIRM: *The Duffy Design Group*
DESIGNER: *Sharon Werner*
LETTERER: *Lynn Schulte and Sharon Werner*
HEADLINE TYPEFACE: *Handlettering*
TEXT TYPEFACE: *Eurostyle Bold Extended and Brush Script*
CLIENT: *Fox River Paper Company*

92
DESIGN FIRM: *Blizzard Allen Creative Services*
DESIGNER: *Tony Coombes*
LETTERER: *Tony Coombes*
HEADLINE TYPEFACE: *Bodoni*
TEXT TYPEFACE: *Futura*
CLIENT: *Panorama Pictures PTY Ltd.*

93
DESIGN FIRM: *Art Center Design Office*
DESIGNER: *Rebecca Mendez*
LETTERER: *Rebecca Mendez*
HEADLINE TYPEFACE: *Handlettering*
TEXT TYPEFACE: *Courier*
CLIENT: *Art Center College of Design*

92

91

93

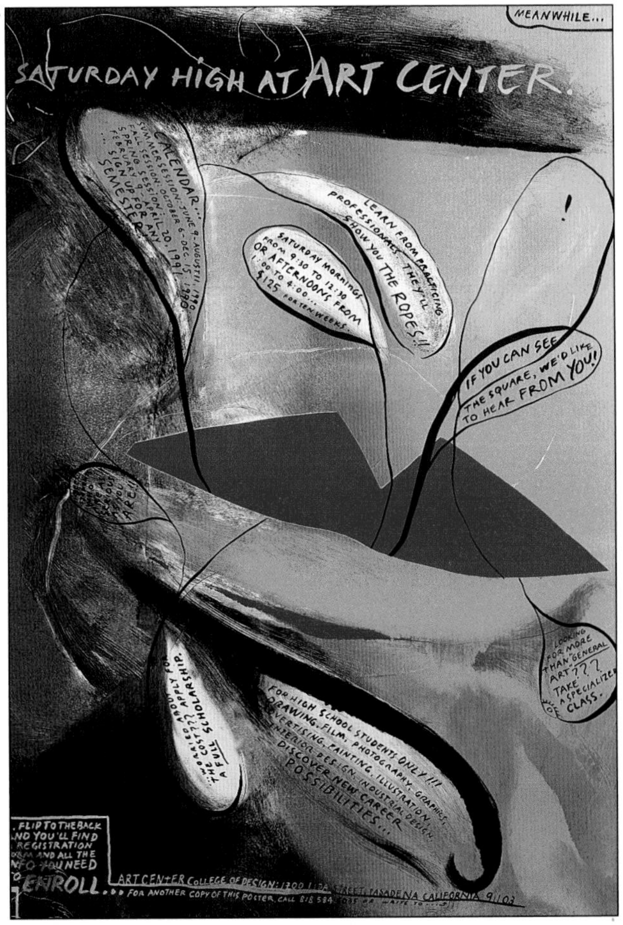

94

94
DESIGN FIRM: *Hess & Hess*
DESIGNER: *Kathleen Hohl-Phillips*
CLIENT: *New York City Opera/Franklin Typographers*

MISCELLANEOUS

240

1 In the beginning is the Word. Before Abraham was, the Word is. Before heaven and earth came into being, the Word is. This is true just as the beauty of the flower is present, but not yet radiant, in the seed; and as the power of the ocean is present, but unmoving, before it swells in tide; and as the wisdom of the messiah waits in silence before his flock is at hand. As it is written that before all things the Word is; it must also be written in the Book of the Times and the Timeless that during, and after, all things, the Word is. For if the beauty of the flower is present before the flower is in bloom, it most certainly is present while the flower is actually in bloom. And after the blossom falls, that same beauty must be said to be present in the next generation of seeds as well as in the blossoms of joy imparted to the hearts of all who knew the flower's glory. Similarly, if the power of the ocean is present before the tide, it is certainly present in the actual swelling of the tide; and after the tide has diminished, the power is also present as the sea concentrates itself in its motionless depths, in preparation to swell in tide again. And again, it is obvious that if the wisdom of the messiah precedes the arrival of his flock, then that same wisdom is present as it flows from the master's lips in waves of love-filled knowledge; and it is also true that that same wisdom is present when, after the master is departed, the flock is found drinking the waters of eternal life. The Word is with God and the Word is God. Being God, the Word is that One without any other. Being with God, he is between the One and the other...like the breath is between the singer and the song, and like the light is between the sun and the day. Being God, the Word is the Being, pre-being; the thought before it is thought; and, the action yet to be acting. He is everything which is yet to be made, but is unmade. The same is in the beginning with God. Being with God, he is the creativity of creation: that which changes no-thingness, or pre-thingness, into things. All things are made by him. This is so his own no-thingness can know thingness. He changes his no-thingness, his pre-thingness, his unmanifestness, into manifold thingness in order to know something; even to know everything. This is like an actor who wants to know what it is like to be a peasant, or a doctor, or a king. The actor just becomes whatever he wishes to know, for his own self is enough resource to play any role he desires. He needs nothing else. And like the actor who becomes something else while still remaining an actor, the Word becomes anything he wants and still retains his no-thingness, his status of infinite potentiality. His infinite potentiality is unaltered even though it becomes all things. Similarly, H_2O takes on the properties of ice, or water, or vapor; but it never loses its status as H_2O. Its essential nature as H_2O is independent of, and thus transcendent to, whatever physical properties it assumes as water, ice or vapor. Like this, the Word remains transcendent to the things it becomes. It remains the One even when it becomes the many. In becoming the many he not only retains his knowledge of himself from the vantage point of the One, but he also gains knowledge of himself (now him-selves) from the vantage points of the many. He knows himselves in and from the boundaries of space and of time and of change. He creates these boundaries with which to express his boundlessness: in space, his infinity is given somewhere to be; his eternity is given time, to enjoy itself; and, in change, his omnipotence is given something to do. Because each space and time and change, that is, each thing, retains within itself its transcendent source; and because that source is the same for all things; then all things are connected to each other by virtue of their omnipresent source, the Word. Even more, they are united in the Word. That which is become space is that which is become time is that which is become change. Each one is the other in him. The many are each other in the One. Space and time and change are just one set of unified differentiations of the Word; that is, they are just one way to consider the relationship of him to all things which are made by him. Another way to appreciate each of his creations is as the union of name and form. So united are the name and the form of each thing that from the original no-thingness, one automatically evokes the other. The form, when first introduced evokes automatically from no-thingness that by which it is known throughout creation: its name. And, conversely, the name evokes the form from the same unmanifest field of pure potential: the Word speaks the name within himself and the form automatically comes into being. Or, to look at creation from the converse side again, the Word creates a thing and thereby automatically assigns its name. To one he gives the name light; and to another, darkness. One he calls firmament and one he calls water. One he names heaven; and another, earth. One he calls flora and one, fauna. One, man; and one, woman. And one word he uses to describe them all, "Good." God good. All things which are made by the Word have his God goodness. And without him is not anything made that is made. So all creation is God good. Although the Word knows all things in his creation to be good, he does not create all things to be knowing each other's essential goodness. Being things, they have gained individual, rather than universal, vantage points; and, therefore, they see different amounts of creation and different values of creation. Even man, who on earth is given the greatest ability to see and to know, sometimes sees and knows only a small portion of his world and its environments. If man does not appreciate the fundamental, God good value of himself and his environment, he may ascribe to himself and to his neighbors in creation a full range of values, from good to evil. So that which is inherently good may be apparently not good. Naturally all inhabitants of creation act in accordance with their evaluations of each other and themselves, that is, in accordance with the amount of the original good they see or do not see in each other and within themselves. A rock doesn't perceive much difference between one neighbor and another: it treats all with the same indifference. An animal appreciates more than the rock in the world about him, but he may still run from that which he does not understand. And man, with the greatest vision, may either embrace his neighbors or wrestle them to submission. All things in creation are waves on the divine ocean. Deep within all waves is the boundless ocean, but not all waves see their own infinite source. Neither do all waves see that their own infinite source is also their neighbors' infinite source; and that their neighbors and themselves are one, indivisible, in that source. For while the waves bob up and down playing hide and seek with each other, they only occasionally think to look within themselves to find each other, and there to embrace one another in absolute union. And while they race each other across countless miles, they seldom consider that the race begins and ends in the same place, which is the infinite stillness waiting not far below the surface to announce that the winner of the race is that wave who will get there without leaving here: it is that wave who recognizes his deepest, truest nature as being the ocean and who can, therefore, go from this shore to that shore without leaving this shore. And if the waves climb each other's walls and jump on each other's crests in an effort to attain the greatest height, they rarely even dream that the ocean beneath is the only real foundation for their upward aspirations; and that they could by using their true ocean status rise to touch the moon. Yea, the ocean is the power and the substance of the waves: the very life and being of the waves. So it is with the Word and his creation. In him is life; and the life is the light of men. Indeed, he is the life. And the light. And the way. And the way treader. In addition to being his never changing self, God, he is that which he created out of his own no-thingness: he is that which does not know its own essential goodness, which is himself. In this form, if he is to know his own God goodness, he must tread the path back to himself. He is, then, the way treader. The way he treads is himself, for only he can connect himself to himself. He is the light which illumines the way, for only he shines steadfastly to light his path, which is himself. And when he rediscovers himself, he finds that he is the life which alone gives himself existence. It is a cyclical journey: he makes himself apparently apart from himself; then he treads himself by the light of himself back to himself. An analogy to this journey is the story of the adventures of the water. In this story the water is analogous to the life, the light, the way and the way treader. In its ocean form the water enjoys its infinite, omnipotent nature. Inasmuch as it (the water) can do whatever it wishes, it rises in the air to see what it can be and, for a time, it continues to see itself as a vapor extension of its own ocean self. But after a while in the air it (the water) becomes a cloud of ignorance, that is, it cannot see what it thinks is itself (the ocean), through itself (the cloud). Even though it can never lose itself (the water), it is destined to fall the moment it deems itself (the cloud) separated from itself (the infinite water of the ocean). And fall it does, sometimes to become streams and rivers which quickly carry itself back to itself (the ocean). But sometimes it (the cloud) falls to become lakes and puddles, and even stagnant pools and every form of mud imaginable. No matter what it becomes, it is still the water; but it may, nevertheless feel it most go somewhere to find itself. It may feel it must return to the ocean to find its source. If it is become a river or a stream, it hurrys itself back to the ocean where it discovers it always is that which the ocean is: the water. In this journey, the water in the form of a fallen cloud is the way treader; the water in the form of a river is the way; the water as the ocean is the light which in (re)union reveals to the water its true water nature, which is the life. In the following series of variations of the water adventures parable, the water finds various degrees of success in rediscovering its true water nature. In all cases it is seen that no matter what the results, the water is the way treader, the way, the light and the life. In the first variation, the water (as the cloud of ignorance) may fall to become a lake. It (the lake) may feel by virtue of its size and depth a sense of its former ocean self; and, it (the lake) may seek a river to carry itself back to itself (the ocean). Or it (the lake) may enjoy its lake state enough that it has little desire to find its original self. If the cloud falls to become mud, it may have no apparent desire to return to the ocean. It (the mud) may struggle in its murky darkness to become a pool or stream or anything but what it thinks it is. Or it may think it has no choice but to suffer its mudness. Deep within the mud (as well as within the lake, the pool and the stream) is the pure water (the life): the same pure water that originally rose to see what it could be. It (the pure water within) naturally whets its (the mud's) desire to be all that it can be and to know freedom from the bonds of mudness. And while it (the mud) longs for freedom to flow in fullness, it (the water within) continues to sparkle a hidden sparkle in its pure and original state. Of course the mud remains so unclear in its muddiness, it doesn't see that it (the water within) is sparkling. The light shineth in darkness; and the darkness comprehends it not. Although it (the mud) doesn't see its way clear to look within for a guiding light, it (the water within) knows out of love for itself that it must appear to itself (the mud) as a separate, fully enlightened water form: a manifestation of itself which brilliantly radiates the truth of itself, a veritable "sun of the water". This sun of the water can give the mud (and all other water forms) the freedom and the original source they seek. So it (the water within) summons itself (the sun of the water) to appear to itself (the mud). To the mud the sun of the water comes with the power and the authority of the ocean, yet it rides on the air of bliss. It speaks to the mud and the lake and the stream, saying, "Be joy-filled, for your fulfillment is at hand. You need go nowhere to find yourself. You are that which you were in the ocean. You are water, pure and simple. Therefore, you are what I am. Rise unto me and know that you and I are one just as I and the water are one. Rise by virtue of your true water nature and know that muddiness is past and forgotten. Forgiven. Rise and know the glory of the water in thyself and the glory of thyself in the water. Be perfect even as the water is perfect. Rise in perfection to accomplish your every desire: to sculpt the grandest canyons in the world; to cleanse the earth with thy pure water nature; and to carry every water form from the shores of suffering to the infinite bliss of thyself." Just as a silent tuning fork automatically joins in tonal union a vibrating tuning fork brought near, the water forgets its muddiness and rises to join the sun of the water in purity. To the mud which is darkness, the sun of the water is light. It is the true light which comes to radiate truth to all water forms and to give a rainbow of blessings. In addition to coming from without as the enlightened brother, this true light is now seen to reside as the original sparkle of water purity deep within the mud, the puddle, the lake and the stream. So it is with the Word. He is the true Light, which lighteth every man that cometh into the world. He lights every man from within by Being within, just as the sparkle of water purity resides in the innermost parts of the lake and even the mud. This light within every man is also like the light within every great piece of art. Truly fine art radiates the brilliance and fullness of the artist. Though the artist's brush may be long departed from the canvas, his timeless self has taken residence in his art to radiate the glory of his fullness in creation. But occasionally an artist not only illuminates his art from within but also from without. This occurs whenever the artist is called upon to explain his art or discuss its beauty. The artist is, then, shining his light on the art as well as in the art. Imagine a very great artist who shines his light both on and in his art. His creativity is so boundless it fills an enormous gallery. One of the marvelous things about his art in this gallery is that it is interactive. The various pieces of art respond in different ways to their viewers and even to each other. For instance, some of the paintings have been rendered in a special paint that seems to glow whenever a viewer smiles. Other pieces have sensors that respond to certain words of appreciation with a lovely light display or a soft, contented kind of hum. Some of the art is kinetic. It moves about the gallery smiling at the paintings and whispering, "Lovely, brilliant," as it stops before each piece of art. Now, even though the artist's timeless self resides within each marvelous piece of art in the gallery, it can happen that in time some of the pieces of art can miss their creator if they never see him in the gallery. If enough paintings and sculpture fail to see the artist shining within themselves, a great anxiety can develop within the gallery. The paintings may be so busy looking for the artist to appear, they may forget to glow at the smiles before them. And the kinetic sculpture may get so engrossed in discussing the lackluster of the paintings, that it may forget to whisper, "Lovely, brilliant." Innumerable things may appear to go wrong in this situation. This is the time for the artist to visit his gallery, which he naturally does. But with disarray prevailing in the gallery, few of the wondrous works of art recognize their creator. With their vision lowered to the level of seeing lackluster, the brilliance of the artist goes unseen. He is in the world, and the world is made by him, and the world knows him not. When the artist begins to comment on how beautifully the paintings glow and how wonderfully the sculptures can nurture each other's tender feelings with words of praise, some of art begins to scorn this stranger in the gallery. He comes unto his own, and his own receive him not. But, to the artist's delight, some of the art recognizes how he sees them in their best light, which they had forgotten. These fortunate works of art realize that he is their creator and that he is illuminating them from without so that they may behold the very same light within. Also, they see that the artist is showing them how to radiate the light and thereby enlighten the entire gallery. So it is with the Word. As many as receive him, to them gives he power to become the sons of God. Amen

1

DESIGN FIRM: *Siemsen Graphic Communications*
DESIGNER: *Paul Siemen*
TEXT TYPEFACE: *ITC Quorum*
CLIENT: *The Word/Form Corporation*

2

3

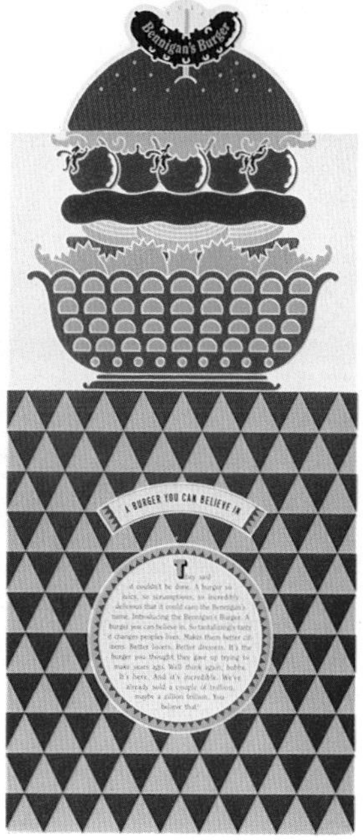

4

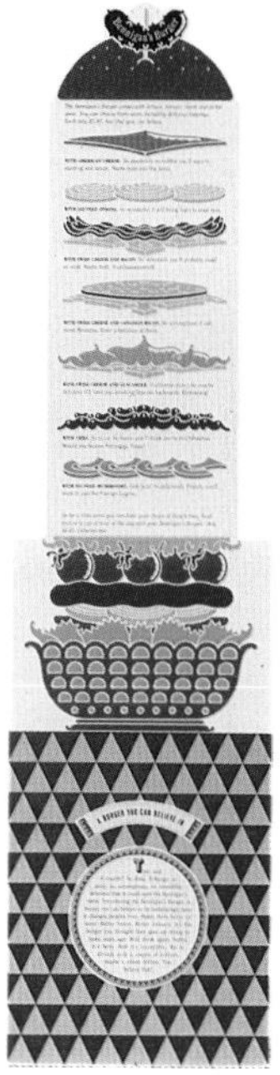

2
DESIGN FIRM: *Dennard Creative, Inc.*
DESIGNER: *Bob Dennard*
LETTERER: *Bob Dennard, Jan Wilson and Elyn Powell*
TEXT TYPEFACE: *ITC Cheltenbaum*
CLIENT: *Pizza Inn*

3/4
DESIGN FIRM: *Dennard Creative, Inc.*
DESIGNER: *Bob Dennard and Rex Peteet*
HEADLINE TYPEFACE: *ITG Garamond Bold Condensed*
TEXT TYPEFACE: *Clearface*
CLIENT: *Bennigan's Restaurants*

5

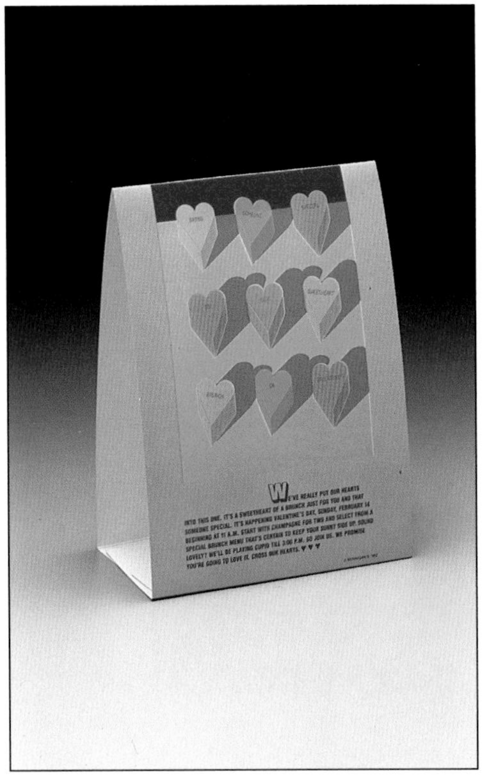

6

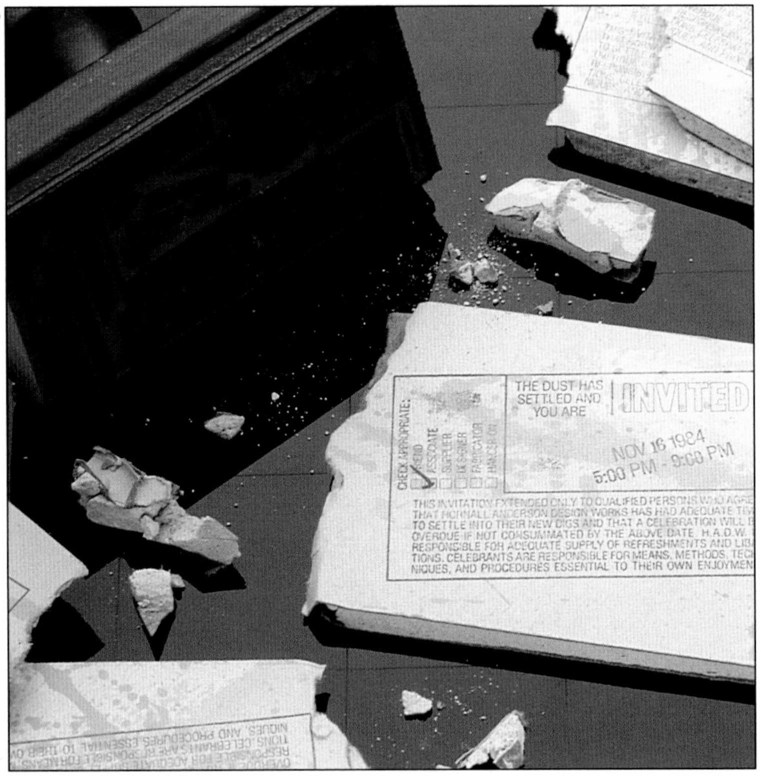

7

5
DESIGN FIRM: *Dennard Creative, Inc.*
DESIGNER: *Bob Dennard and Rex Peteet*
HEADLINE TYPEFACE: *ITC Garamond Ultra Condensed*
TEXT TYPEFACE: *ITC Garamond Book Condensed*
CLIENT: *Bennigan's Restaurants*

6
DESIGN FIRM: *Hornall Anderson Design Works*
DESIGNER: *John Hornall*
TEXT TYPEFACE: *Helvetica*
CLIENT: *Hornall Anderson Design Works*

7
DESIGN FIRM: *Sibley/Peteet Design*
DESIGNER: *Don Sibley*
HEADLINE TYPEFACE: *Fat Face and Latin Wide*
TEXT TYPEFACE: *Bodoni*
CLIENT: *West End Marketplace*

8

9

10

11

8
DESIGN FIRM: *The Duffy Design Group*
DESIGNER: *Joe Duffy*
HEADLINE TYPEFACE: *Standard Bold Condensed*
CLIENT: *Lee Jeans*

9
DESIGN FIRM: *David Carter Graphic Design Associates*
DESIGNER: *Gary Lobue, Jr.*
HEADLINE TYPEFACE: *Onyx*
TEXT TYPEFACE: *Garamond 3*
CLIENT: *Rosewood Hotels*

10
DESIGN FIRM: *The Duffy Design Group*
DESIGNER: *Charles S. Anderson and Sara Ledgard*
LETTERER: *Lynn Schulte*
HEADLINE TYPEFACE: *Garamond, Franklin Gothic, and Handlettering*
CLIENT: *Chaps–Ralph Lauren*

11
DESIGN FIRM: *The Duffy Design Group*
DESIGNER: *Charles S. Anderson*
LETTERER: *Lynn Schulte*
HEADLINE TYPEFACE: *Garamond, Franklin Gothic, and Handlettering*
CLIENT: *Chaps-Ralph Lauren*

12
DESIGN FIRM: *The Duffy Design Group*
DESIGNER: *Charles S. Anderson*
HEADLINE TYPEFACE: *Futura Bold Condensed*
TEXT TYPEFACE: *Bodoni*
CLIENT: *City of Minneapolis*

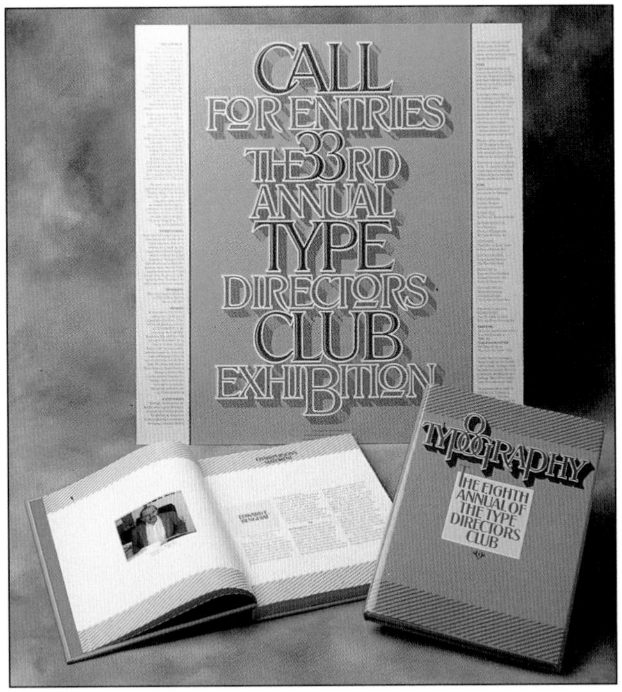

13
DESIGN FIRM: *David Brier Design Works, Incorporated*
DESIGNER: *David Brier*
LETTERER: *Ed Benguiat and David Brier*
HEADLINE TYPEFACE: *Handlettering*
TEXT TYPEFACE: *ITC Modern 216*
CLIENT: *Type Directors Club*

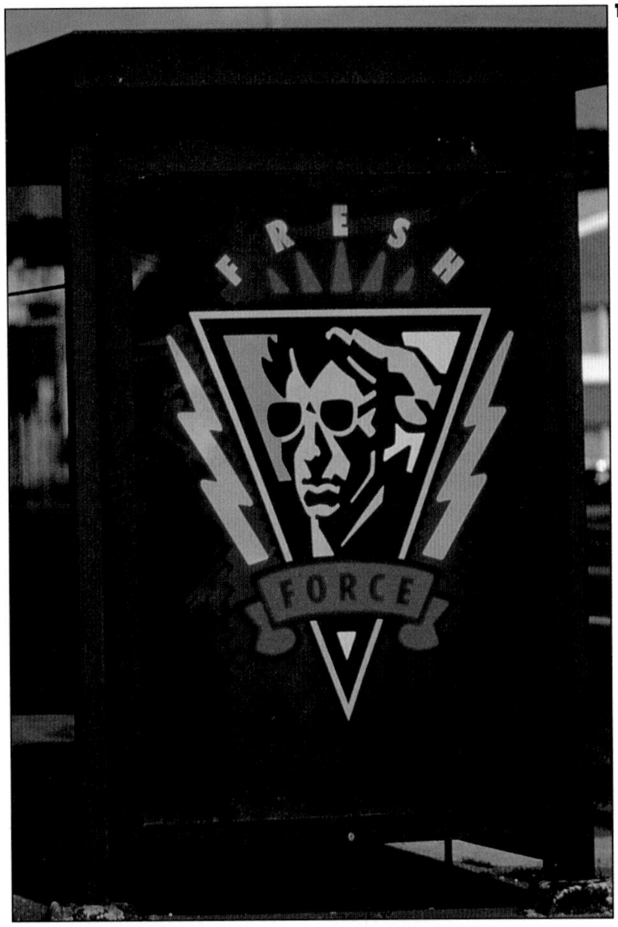

14
DESIGN FIRM: *The Duffy Design Group*
DESIGNER: *Charles S. Anderson*
HEADLINE TYPEFACE: *Futura Bold Condensed*
TEXT TYPEFACE: *Bodoni*
CLIENT: *City of Minneapolis*

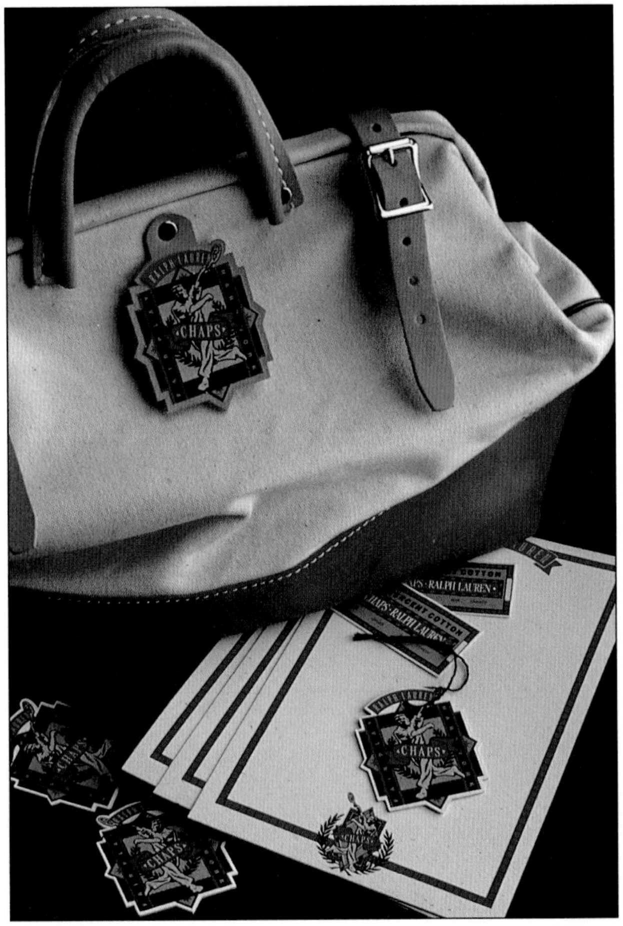

15
DESIGN FIRM: *The Duffy Design Group*
DESIGNER: *Joe Duffy and Sara Ledgard*
LETTERER: *Lynn Schulte*
HEADLINE TYPEFACE: *Garamond, Franklin Gothic and Handlettering*
CLIENT: *Chaps-Ralph Lauren*

16

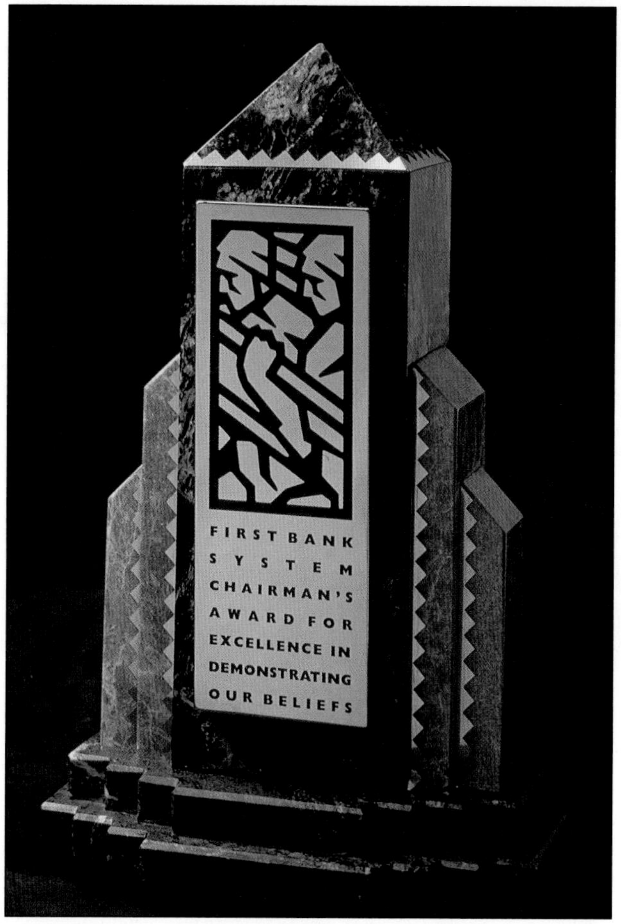

17

18

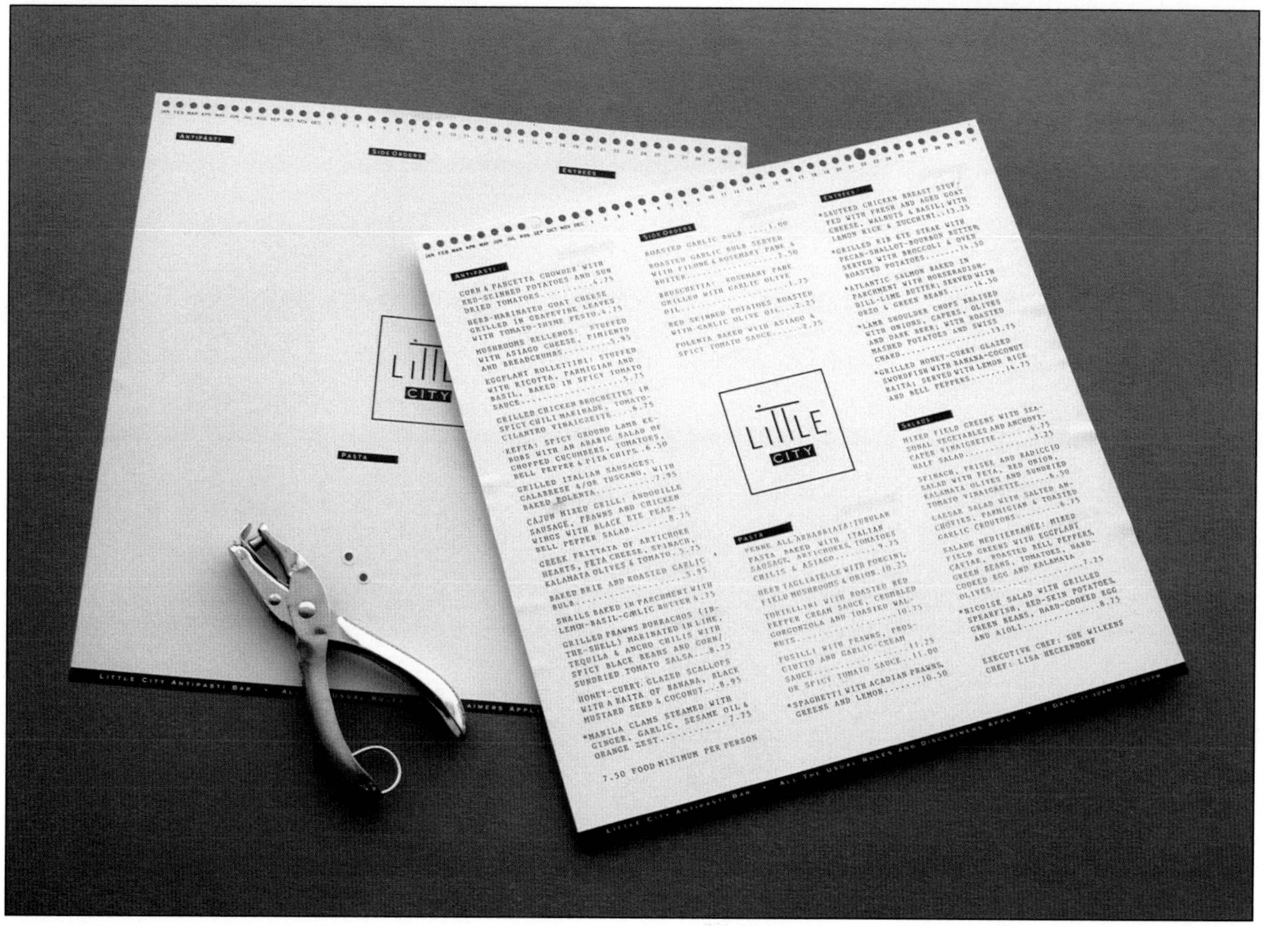

16
DESIGN FIRM: *The Duffy Design Group*
DESIGNER: *Charles S. Anderson*
HEADLINE TYPEFACE: *Eagle Bold*
CLIENT: *First Banks*

17
DESIGN FIRM: *Mark Anderson Design*
DESIGNER: *Mitchell Mauk*
LETTERER: *Mitchell Mauk*
HEADLINE TYPEFACE: *Univers 39*
CLIENT: *Z Typography*

18
DESIGN FIRM: *Bruce Yelaska*
DESIGNER: *Bruce Yelaska*
LETTERER: *Bruce Yelaska*
HEADLINE TYPEFACE: *Copperplate*
TEXT TYPEFACE: *Typewriter Imprint*
CLIENT: *Little City Restaurant & Antipasti Bar*

19

DESIGN FIRM: *David Brier Design Works, Incorporated*

DESIGNER: *David Brier*

LETTERER: *David Brier*

HEADLINE TYPEFACE: *Handlettering*

CLIENT: *David Brier Design Works, Inc.*

20

DESIGN FIRM: *Peterson & Company*

DESIGNER: *Scott Paramski*

CLIENT: *Kayren & Mark Schwandt*

19

20

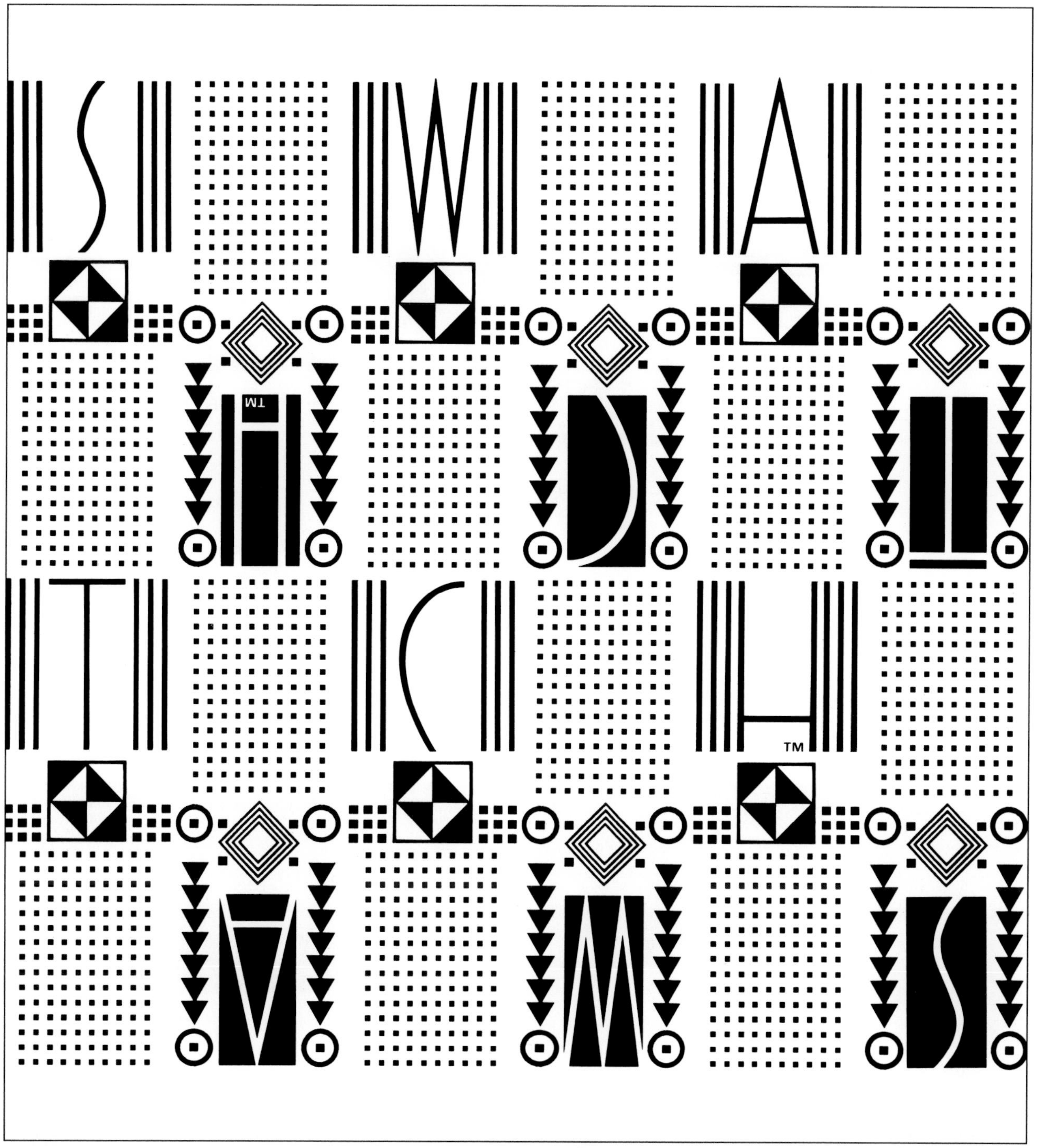

21

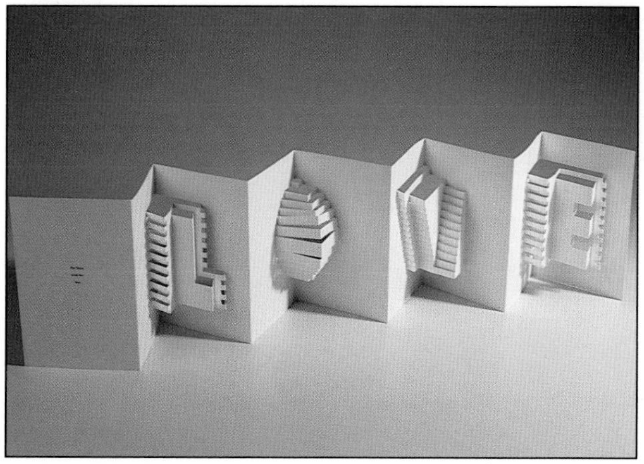

22

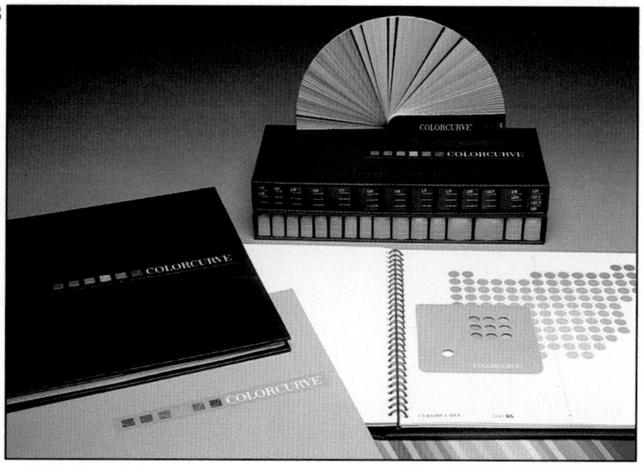

23

21
DESIGN FIRM: *Jeanne Greco/ Parham Santana Design*
DESIGNER: *Jeanne Greco*
LETTERER: *Jeanne Greco*
CLIENT: *Swatch Watch USA*

22
DESIGN FIRM: *Pat Sloan Design*
DESIGNER: *Pat Sloan*
LETTERER: *Pat Sloan*
TEXT TYPEFACE: *ITC New Baskerville Italic*
CLIENT: *Linotypographers*

23
DESIGN FIRM: *Designframe Inc.*
DESIGNER: *James A. Sebastian, John Plunkett and Frank Nichols*
HEADLINE TYPEFACE: *Bodoni*
TEXT TYPEFACE: *Univers Condensed*
CLIENT: *Colorcurve Systems Inc.*

24

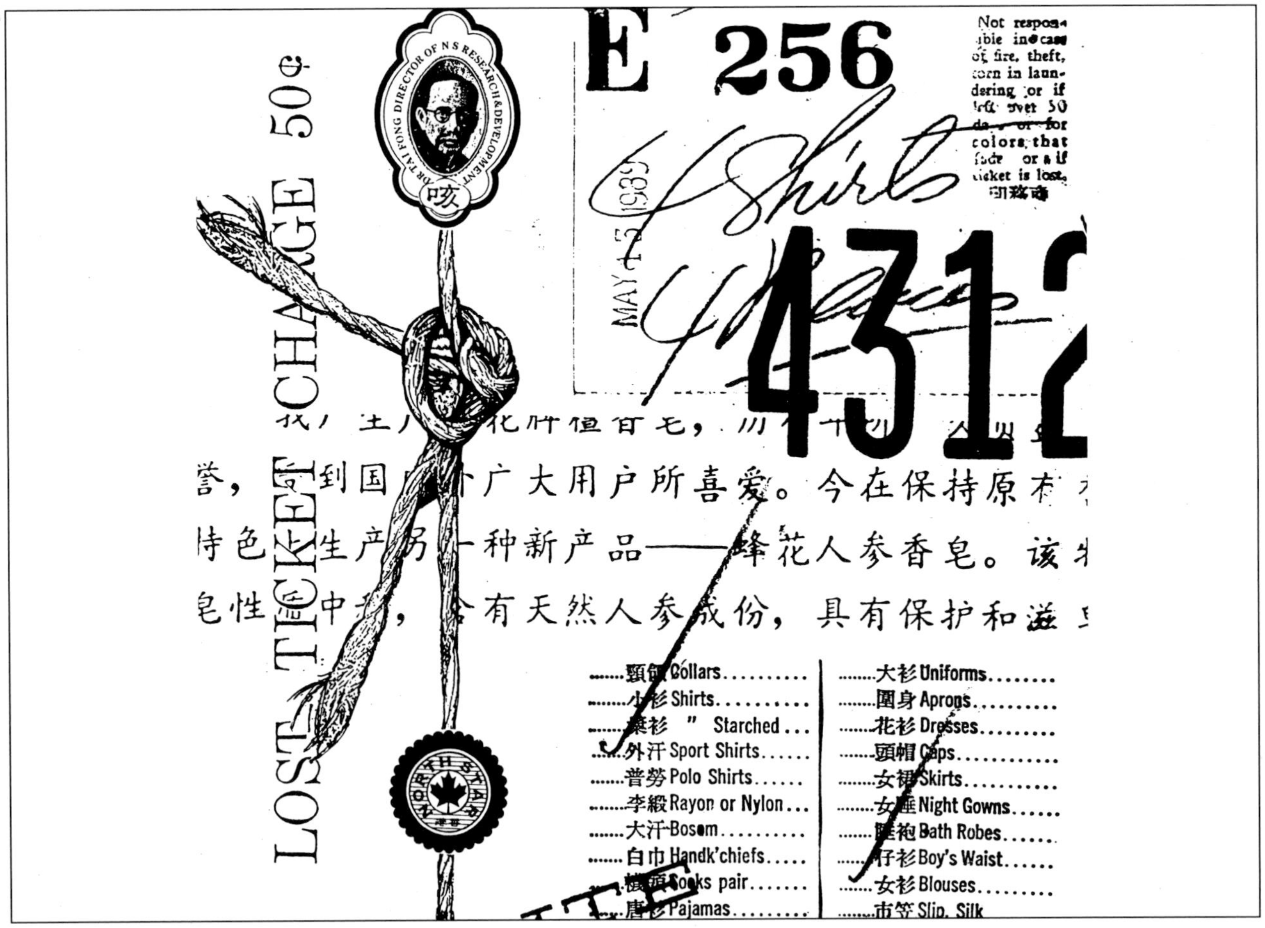

25

24
DESIGN FIRM: *Jeanne Greco/ Parham Santana Design*
DESIGNER: *Jeanne Greco*
CLIENT: *Murjani International, Ltd.*

25
DESIGN FIRM: *Donovan & Green*
DESIGNER: *Nancye Green and Clint Morgan*
HEADLINE TYPEFACE: *Helvetica Compressed*
TEXT TYPEFACE: *Garamond 3*
CLIENT: *Carol Groh and Associates*

26

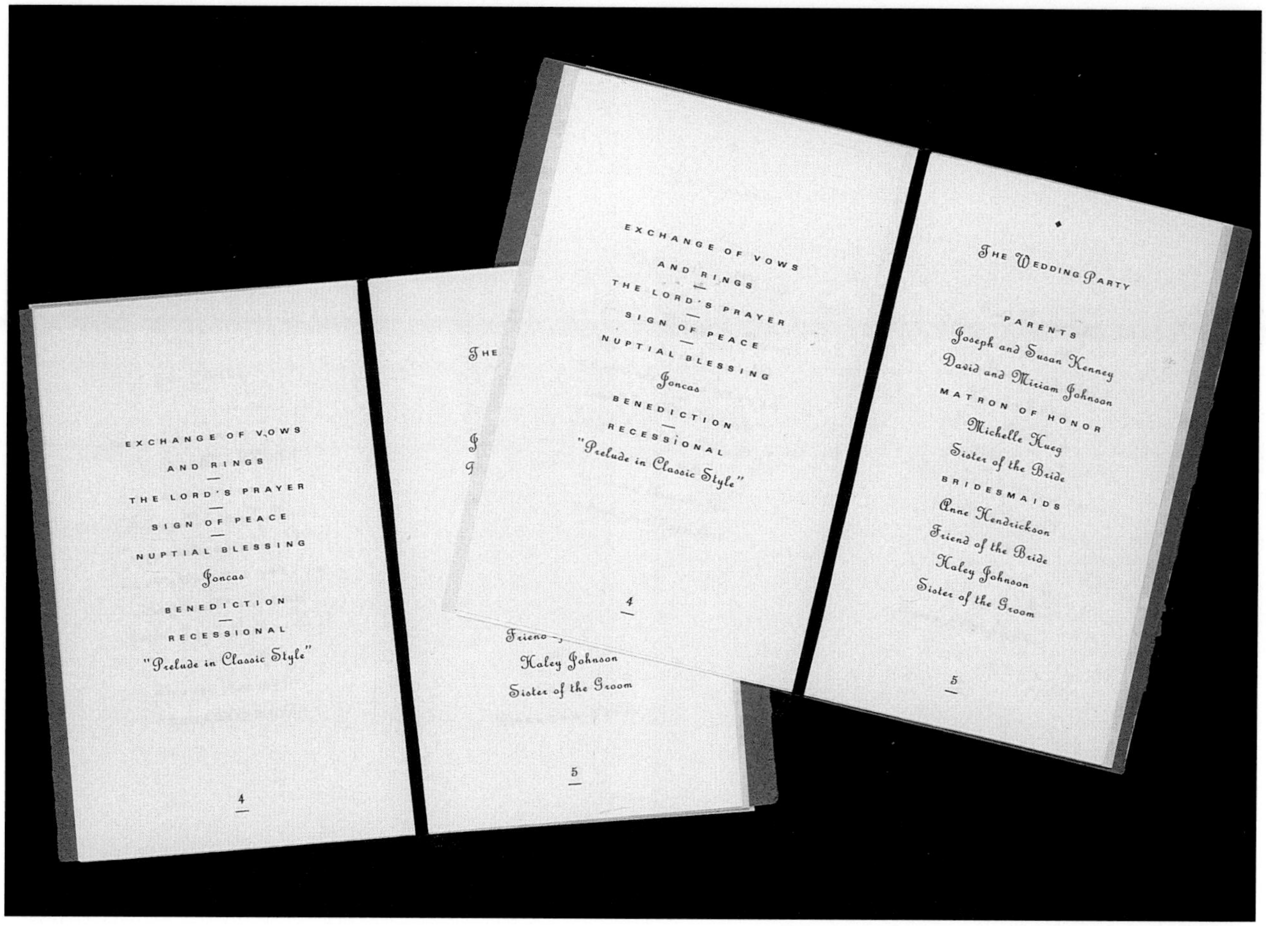

27

26
DESIGN FIRM: *The Duffy Design Group*
DESIGNER: *Haley Johnson*
HEADLINE TYPEFACE: *French Script and Venus Bold Extended*
CLIENT: *Darris Johnson*

27
DESIGN FIRM: *Grand Pre' and Whaley, Ltd.*
DESIGNER: *Kevin Whaley*
HEADLINE TYPEFACE: *Univers 49, 75, and 85*
CLIENT: *The Art Department/Chargo Printing, Incorporated*

28

29

30

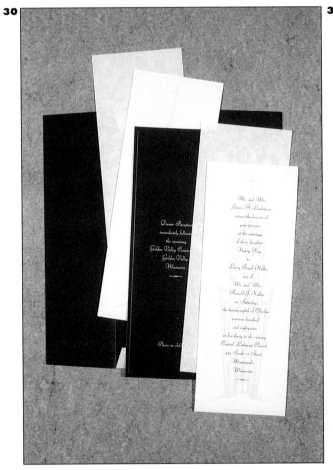

31

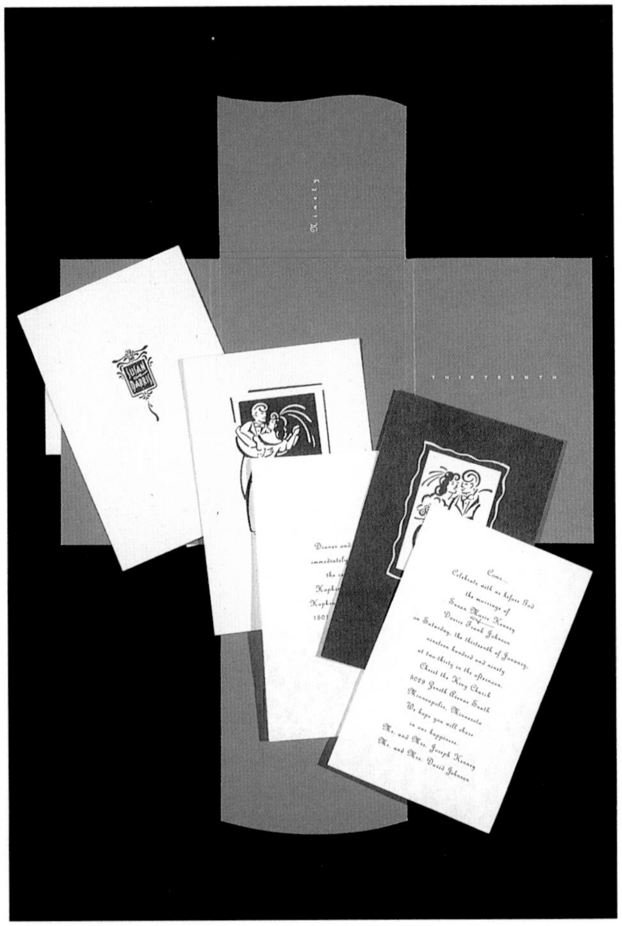

28
DESIGN FIRM: *The Duffy Design Group*
DESIGNER: *Sharon Werner*
LETTERER: *Sharon Werner and Lynn Schulte*
HEADLINE TYPEFACE: *Handlettering*
CLIENT: *Lee Jeans*

29
DESIGN FIRM: *Sackett Design*
DESIGNER: *Mark Sackett*
LETTERER: *Mark Sackett*
HEADLINE TYPEFACE: *Handlettering*
TEXT TYPEFACE: *Futura Book*
CLIENT: *Levi Strauss & Company*

30
DESIGN FIRM: *The Duffy Design Group*
DESIGNER: *Sharon Werner*
HEADLINE TYPEFACE: *Liberty*
CLIENT: *Nancy Kullas*

31
DESIGN FIRM: *The Duffy Design Group*
DESIGNER: *Haley Johnson*
LETTERER: *Haley Johnson*
HEADLINE TYPEFACE: *French Script and Venus Bold Extended*
CLIENT: *Darris Johnson*

32

33

34

32
DESIGN FIRM: *Summerford Design, Inc.*
DESIGNER: *Jack Summerford*
HEADLINE TYPEFACE: *ITC Garamond*
CLIENT: *Self-promotion and AIGA/Texas*

33
DESIGN FIRM: *Primo Angeli, Inc.*
DESIGNER: *Doug Hardenburgh and Phillippe Becker*
LETTERER: *Doug Hardenburgh*
CLIENT: *Matilda Bay Brewing Company*

34
DESIGN FIRM: *Brooks Champion, Inc.*
DESIGNER: *Alan Brooks*
LETTERER: *Alan Brooks*
HEADLINE TYPEFACE: *Characters Type*
TEXT TYPEFACE: *Characters Type*
CLIENT: *Heather & Alan Brooks*

35

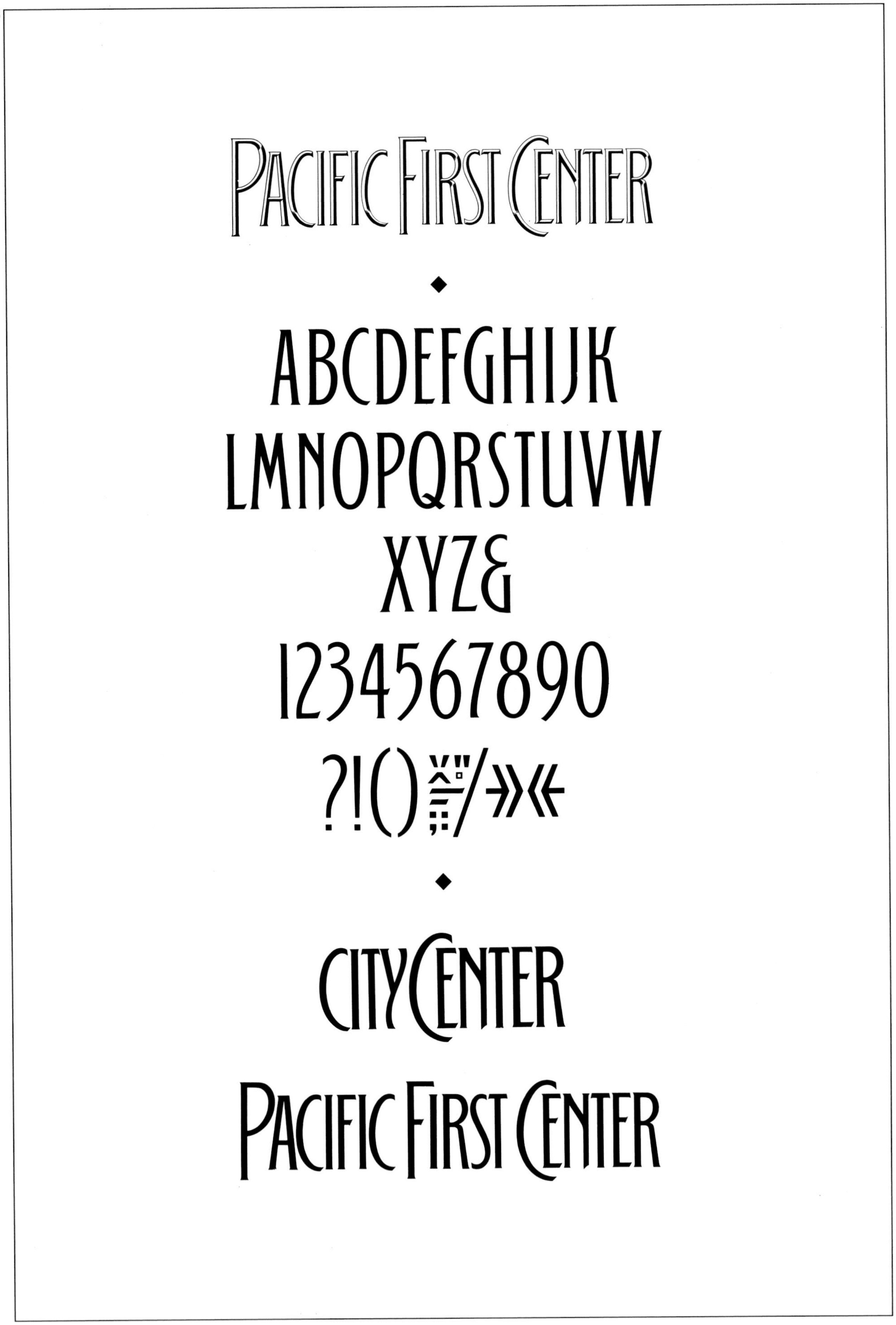

35
DESIGN FIRM: *Bruce Hale Design Studio/Rees. Thompson, Inc.*
DESIGNER: *Bruce Hale and Paula Rees*
LETTERER: *Bruce Hale and Paula Rees*
HEADLINE TYPEFACE: *Handlettering*
CLIENT: *Prescott*

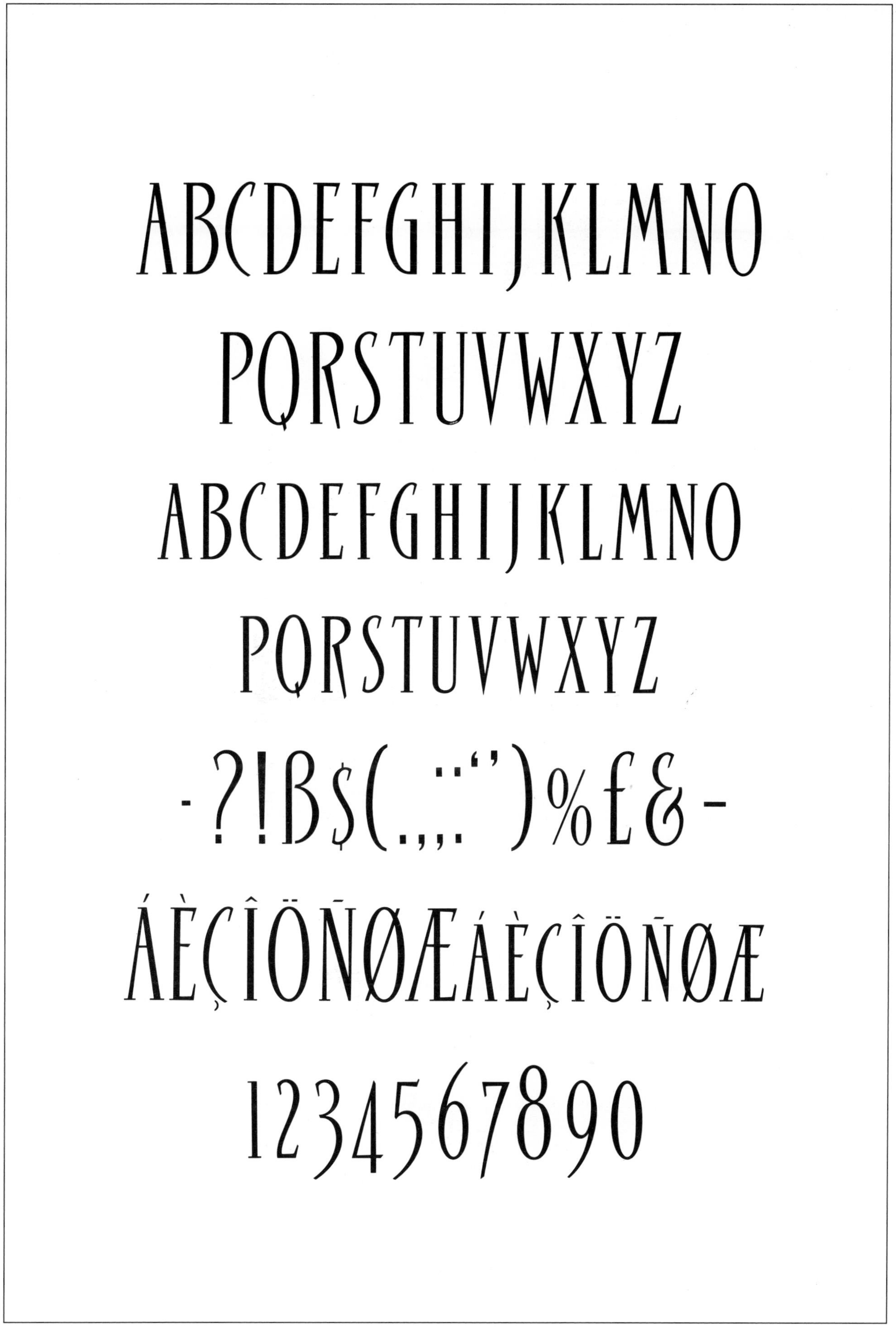

36
DESIGN FIRM: *Bruce Hale Design Studio/Rees. Thompson, Inc.*
DESIGNER: *Bruce Hale and Paula Rees*
LETTERER: *Bruce Hale and Paula Rees*
HEADLINE TYPEFACE: *Handlettering*
CLIENT: *Prescott*

37
DESIGN FIRM: *The Duffy Design Group*
DESIGNER: *Sharon Werner*
LETTERER: *Sharon Werner and Lynn Schulte*
HEADLINE TYPEFACE: *Handlettering*
TEXT TYPEFACE: *Eurostyle Bold Extended and Brush Script*
CLIENT: *Fox River Paper Company*

38
DESIGN FIRM: *The Duffy Design Group*
DESIGNER: *Todd Waterbury*
LETTERER: *Todd Waterbury*
HEADLINE TYPEFACE: *Venus Bold Extended, Uranus, and Futura Bold Condensed*
CLIENT: *D'Amico & Partners*

39
DESIGN FIRM: *The Duffy Design Group*
DESIGNER: *Joe Duffy*
LETTERER: *Lynn Schulte*
HEADLINE TYPEFACE: *Handlettering and Venus*
CLIENT: *Gorbachev Visit Committee*

40
DESIGN FIRM: *Julian Waters Letterforms*
DESIGNER: *Julian Waters*
LETTERER: *Julian Waters*
HEADLINE TYPEFACE: *Handlettering*
CLIENT: *Julian Waters*

37

38

39

40

41

A new year's wish for peace, happiness, and love.

42

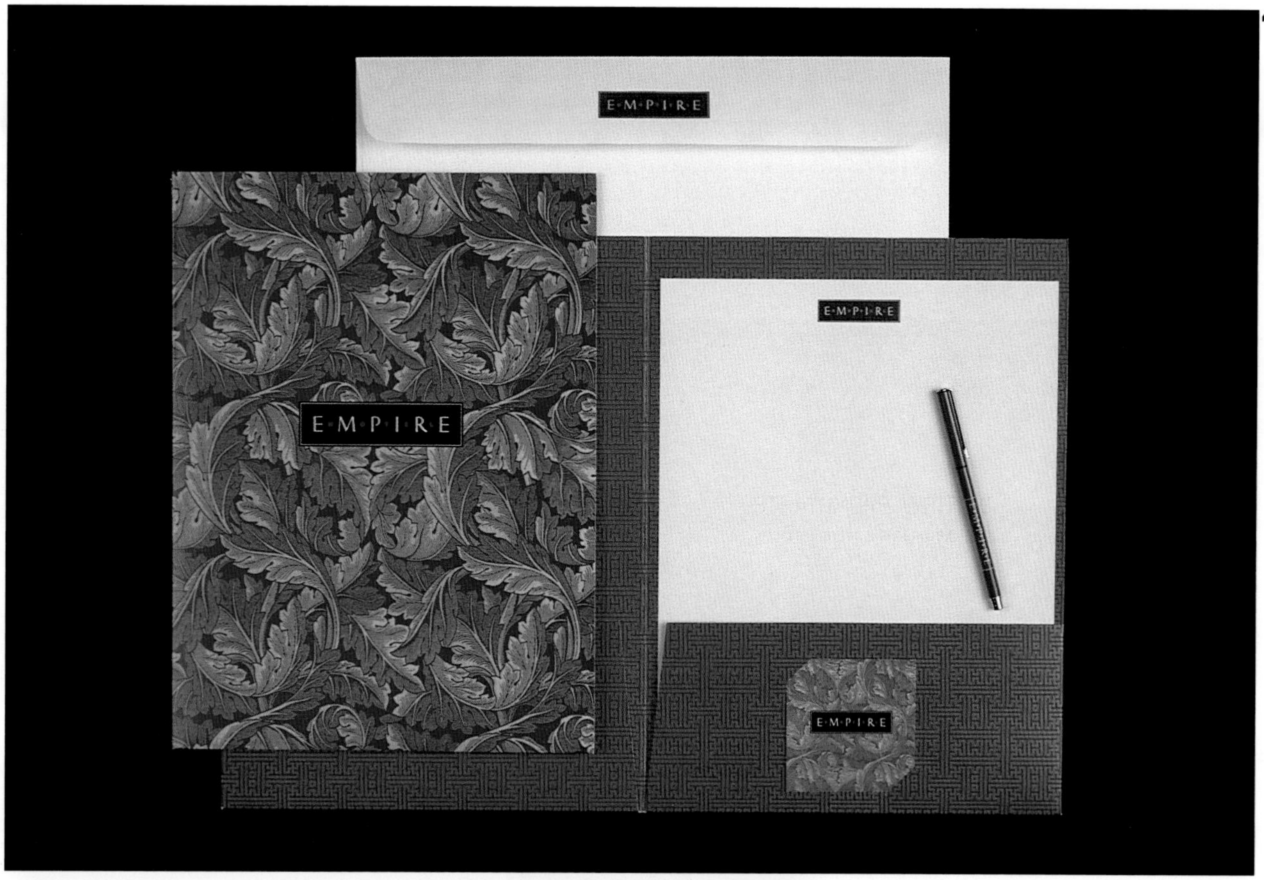

43

41
DESIGN FIRM: *Paul Shaw/Letter Design*
DESIGNER: *Paul Shaw*
HEADLINE TYPEFACE: *Caslon 540 (Foundry)*
TEXT TYPEFACE: *Sabon*
CLIENT: *Paul Shaw/Letter Design & Peter Kruty Editions*

42
DESIGN FIRM: *Pentagram Design*
DESIGNER: *Michael Gericke and Peter Harrison*
HEADLINE TYPEFACE: *Delphine and Futura Extra Bold*
TEXT TYPEFACE: *Bembo*
CLIENT: *Metromedia Company*

43
DESIGN FIRM: *Zimmermann Crowe Design*
DESIGNER: *Neal Zimmermann*
LETTERER: *John Pappas*
HEADLINE TYPEFACE: *Solotype*
TEXT TYPEFACE: *Eurotype*
CLIENT: *Levi Strauss & Company*

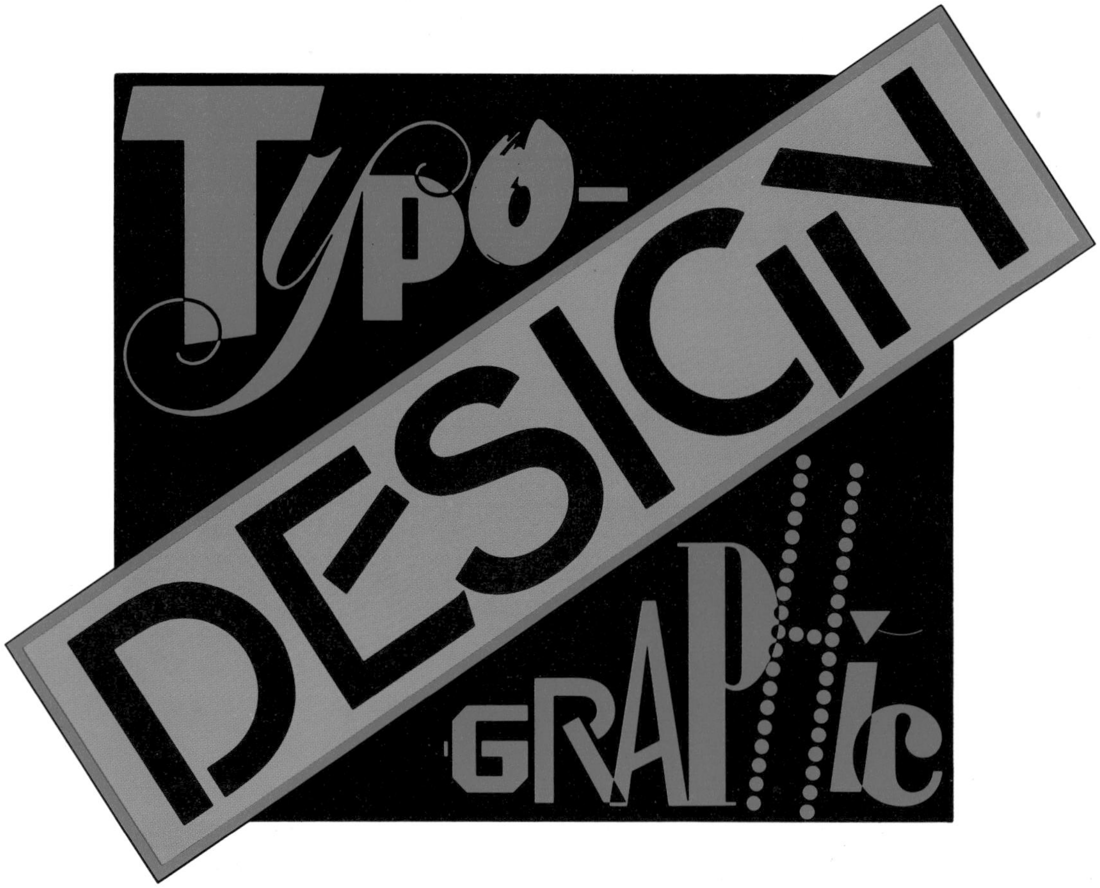

Typo-
DESIGN
GRAPHic

INDEX

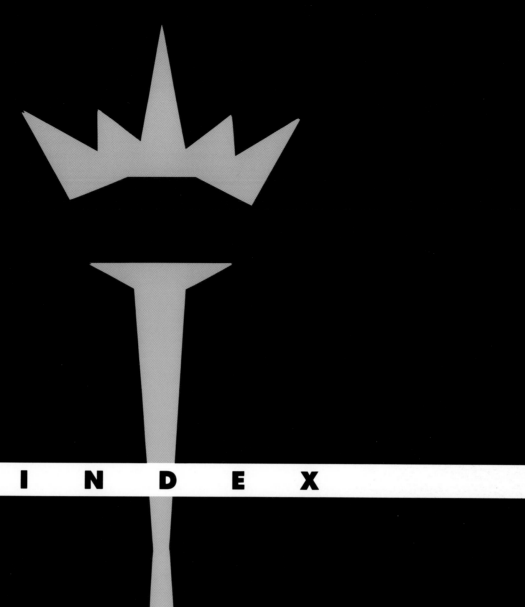

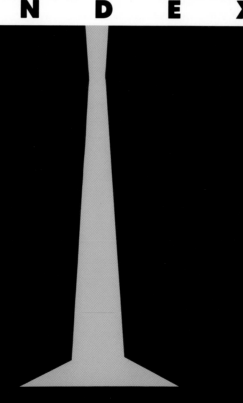

DESIGN FIRMS

DESIGNERS

LETTERERS

CLIENTS

DESIGN FIRM ADDRESSES

246 Fifth Design Associates
246 Fifth Avenue
Ottawa, Canada
KIS 2N3
CANADA
(613) 231-3000

Adobe Systems, Inc.
1585 Charleston
Mt. View, CA 94043 USA
(415) 962-2632

Addison Corporate Annual Reports, Inc.
112 East 31st Street
New York, NY 10016 USA
(212) 889-2450

Adrian Parry
1403 Linda Rosa Avenue
Salt Lake City, UT 84106 USA
(801) 272-2697

Akagi Design
632 Commercial Street
San Francisco, CA 94111 USA
(415) 397-4668

Altman & Manley/Eagle Advertising
1361 Elm Street
Suite 408
Manchester, NH 03101 USA
(603) 627-7469

Anton C. Kimball Graphic Design
820 S.E. Sandy Blvd.
Portland, OR 97214 USA
(503) 234-4777

Art Center Design Office
1700 Lida Street
Pasadena, CA 91103 USA
(818) 584-5191

Avchen and Associates, Incorporated
401 North Third Street
Suite 410
Minneapolis, MN 55401 USA
(212) 339-1206

The Bang Design Group
119 Danforth Avenue
Studio #1
Toronto, Canada M1W 1J1
CANADA
(416) 469-5128

Barnes Design Office
401 E. Illinois
Suite 528
Chicago, IL 60611 USA
(312) 527-0157

Barsuhn Design
420 N. 5th Street
Suite 1086
Minneapolis, MN 55401 USA
(612) 339-2146

Belk Mignogna Assoc.
296 Elizabeth Street
New York, NY 10012 USA
(212) 979-7060

Bennett Peji Design
1110 Torrey Pines Road
Suite B
San Diego, CA 92037
USA
(619) 456-8071

Blizzard Allen Creative Services Pty. Ltd.
179 Mont Albert Road
Canterbury, Melbourne
Australia VIC 3126 UK
(03) 836-8377

Bloomingdales
1000 Third Avenue
New York, NY 10022 USA
(212) 705-3472

Brooks Champion Inc.
9 East 40th Street
New York, NY USA
(212) 689-3620

Bruce Hale Design Studio
2916 5th Avenue West
Seattle, WA 98119 USA
(206) 282-1191

Bruce E. Morgan Graphic Design
4701 Connecticut Avenue
N.W. Suite 301
Washington, D.C. 20008
USA
(202) 244-5263

Bruce Yelaska Design
1546 Grant Avenue
San Francicso, CA 94133
USA
(415) 392-0717

Capital Records
1750 N. Vine Street
Hollywood, CA 90028
USA
(213) 871-5156

Carol Publishing
600 Madison Avenue
New York, NY 10022 USA
(212) 418-4067

Casa De Idéias
Av. Manoel Ribas, 445
Curitiba, Brazil
PR 80.510
BRAZIL
(041) 223-4240

CBS/Sony Communications, Inc.
2-16-1 Shibuya, Shibuya-ku
Tokyo, Japan 150
JAPAN
(03) 5485-2323

Cipriani Kremer Design
2 Copley Place
Boston, MA 02116 USA
(617) 236-1422

Clifford Selbert Design, Inc.
2067 Massachusetts
Avenue
Cambridge, MA 02140
USA
(617) 497-6605

Clifford Stoltze Design
49 Melcher Street
Boston, MA 02210 USA
(617) 350-7109

Concrete Communications, Inc.
2 Berkeley Street
Suite 206
Toronto, Ontario
M5A 2W3
CANADA
(416) 366-9908

Carlson Marketing Group
3415 Emerson Avenue So.
Suite 4
Minneapolis, MN 55408
USA
(612) 825-0538

The Consul
Commercial Wharf
6 Commercial Street
Manchester
M15 4PZ
ENGLAND
(061) 839-4799

Corey McPherson Nash
9 Galen Street
Watertown, MA 02172
USA
(617) 924-6050

Corporate Graphics International, Inc.
655 Third Avenue
New York, NY 10017
USA
(212) 599-1820

Cronan Design
One Zoe Street
San Francisco, CA 94107
USA
(415) 543-6745

Corning Incorporated
Corporate Design,
HP-AB-01-9
Corning, NY 14831 USA
(607) 974-8922

Cross Associates
3465 W. Sixth Street
Los Angeles, CA 90020
USA
(213) 389-1010

California State University Foundation, Northridge
18111 Nordhoff Street
Northridge, CA 91330
USA
(818) 885-2932

DBD International Ltd.
38 Park Avenue
Rutherford, NJ 07070
USA
(201) 896-8476

Daniel Pelavin
80 Varick Street
Suite 3B
New York, NY 10013
USA
(212) 941-7418

David Carson Design
128 1/2 Tenth Street
Delmar, CA 92104 USA
(714) 496-5922

David Carter Graphic Design Associates
4112 Swiss Avenue
Dalls, TX 75204
USA
(214) 826-4631

David Vogler Design
343 Fifteen Street
Suite 3A
Brooklyn, NY 11215
USA
(718) 499-1984

Delessert-Marshall
5 Lakeville Avenue
P.O. Box 1689
Lakeville, CT 06039
USA
(203) 435-0061

Dennard Creative, Inc.
13601 Preston Road
Carillon Plaza
Suite 814 East
Dallas, TX 75240 USA
(214) 233-0430

Dennis Ortiz-Lopez
267 West 70th Street
Suite 2C
New York, NY 10023
USA
(212) 877-6918

Design/Art, Inc.
6311 Romaine Street
Los Angeles, CA 90038
USA
(213) 467-2984

Designframe, Inc.
1 Union Square West
9th Floor
New York, NY 10003
USA
(212) 924-2426

Design Group JRSK
2305 Cedar Springs
Suite 450
Dallas, TX 75206 USA
(214) 871-2305

Design Studio of Steele Presson
3000 Carlisle
Suite 112
Dallas, TX 75204 USA
(214) 871-7587

Design Team One, Inc.
49 E. Fourth Street
10th Floor
Cincinnati, OH 45202
USA
(513) 381-4774

Donovan and Green
One Madison Avenue
39th Floor
New York, NY 10010
USA
(212) 725-2233

Drenttel Doyle Partners
1123 Broadway
New York, NY 10010
USA
(212) 463-8787

Duffy Design Group
311 First Avenue North
Suite 200
Minneapolis, MN 55401
USA
(612) 339-3247

Dunn and Rice Design, Inc.
16 North Goodman Street
Rochester, NY 14607
USA
(716) 473-2880

Earl Gee Design
501 Second Street
Suite 700
San Francisco, CA 94107
USA
(415) 543-1192

Emerson, Wajdowicz Studios, Inc.
1123 Broadway
New York, NY 10010
USA
(212) 807-8144

Eric Baker Design Associates, Inc.
156 Fifth Avenue
Suite 508
New York, NY 10010
USA
(212) 463-7094

Essex Two, Inc.
116 S. Michigan Avenue
Chicago, IL 60603 USA
(312) 630-4430

Forsythe Design
71 Newbury Street
Boston, MA 02116 USA
(617) 437-1023

Foster & Associates Design
201-20381 62nd Avenue
Langley BC, Canada U3A
5E6
CANADA
(604) 533-5113

Galarneau & Sinn, Ltd.
378 Cambridge Avenue
Palo Alto, CA 94306
USA
(415) 329-0110

Gerard Huerta Design, Inc.
45 Corbin Drive
Darien, CT 06820 USA
(203) 656-0505

Glass & Glass, Inc.
3286 M Street NW
Washington, DC 20007
USA
(202) 333-3993

GrandPré and Whaley, Ltd.
475 Cleveland Avenue
North
Suite 222
Saint Paul, MN 55109
USA
(612) 645-3463

Graverholz
89 Guilbault O.
Montreal, Quebec H2X
152
CANADA
(514) 499-9418

Hallmark, Inc.
P.O. Box 419580
Kansas City, MO 64141
USA
(816) 274-8083

Hansen Design Company
1809 Seventh Avenue
Suite 1709
Seattle, WA 98101
USA
(206) 467-9959

Hess & Hess
1 Coburn Road West
Sherman, CT 06784
USA
(203) 354-5261

H.M. + E. Incorporated
20 Maud St. Suite 501
Toronto, Ontario MSV
2M5
CANADA
(416) 368-6570

Hornall Anderson Design Works
1008 Western Avenue
6th Floor
Seattle, WA 98104 USA
(206) 467-5800

Ian Brignell Lettering Design
511 King Street W.
Suite 400
Toronto, Ontario M5V
1K4
CANADA
(416) 581-1075

Isley and/or Clark Design
8204 Canning Terrace
Greenbelt, MD 20770
USA
(301) 474-4955

Jeffrey Halcro
3444 Bannerhill Avenue
Mississauga, Ontario,
L4X1V1
CANADA
(416) 625-9888

Jessica Shaton
144 Seventh Avenue
Brooklyn, NY 11215
USA
(718) 788-6038

Jill H. Abbott Design
799 Bounty Drive
Suite 204
Foster City, CA 94404
USA
(415) 349-8463

Joseph Rattan Design
4445 Travis Street
Suie 104
Dallas, TX 75205 USA
(214) 520-3180

Julian Waters Letterform
9509 Aspenwood Pl.
Gaithersburg, MD 20879
USA
(301) 977-5314

Kampa Design
208 W. Fourth Street
Austin, TX 78701 USA
(512) 472-3145

Kan Tai-keung Design & Associates, Ltd.
28/F Washington Plaza
230 Wanchai Road
Wanchai, Hong Kong
HONG KONG
(852) 574-8399

Ken Shafer Design
13527 39th Avenue N.E.
Seattle, WA 98125 USA
(206) 364-5143

Kilfoy Design/Studio X
3301 S. Jefferson
St. Louis, MO 63118
USA
(314) 773-9989

Klaus Uhlig Design Group, Inc.
2490 Bloor Street West
Suite 401
Toronto, ON
M6S 1R4
CANADA
(416) 760-9125

Knape & Knape
3131 McKinney Avenue
Suite 800
Dallas, TX 75204 USA
(214) 871-2461

Koepke Design
P.O. Box 5360
Magnolia, MA 01930
USA
(508) 525-2229

Lance Anderson Design
22 Margrave Place
Suite 5
San Francisco, CA 94133
USA
(415) 788-5893

Landgraff Design Associtès, Ltd.
55 City Centre Drive
Mississauga, ON
L5B 1M3 CANADA
(416) 848-6768

Landor Associates Europe
18 Clerkenwell Green
London, UK
EC1R 0DP
ENGLAND
(71) 253-4226

Laura Coe Design Associtès
4918 N. Harbor Drive
Suite 206A
San Diego, CA 92106
USA
(619) 223-0909

Left Coast Press
81 Rock Lane
Berkeley, CA 94708 USA
(415) 527-6520

Letterform Design
501 N. Orange Drive
Los Angeles, CA 90036
USA
(213) 932-1875

Lisa Levin Design
2269 Chestnut Street
San Francisco, CA 94123
USA
(415) 332-9410

Little & Company
1010 South Seventh Street
Minneapolis, MN 55415
USA
(612) 375-0077

LLoyd Ziff Design Group, Inc.
55 Vandam Street
Suite 904
New York, NY 10013
USA
(212) 645-1949

Lorraine Louie Design
80 Varick Street
Suite 3B
New York, NY 10013
USA
(212) 941-7329

Louise Fili, Ltd.
22 West 19th Street
New York, NY 10011
USA
(212) 989-9153

M Plus M Incorporated
17 Cornelia Street
New York, NY 10014 USA
(212) 807-0248

Margo Chase Design
2255 Bancroft Avenue
Los Angeles, CA 90039
USA
(213) 668-1055

Maria Wang Design Studio
121 Second Street
2nd Floor
San Francisco, CA 94105
USA
(415) 957-0872

Mark Oldach Design
2138 W. Haddon Avenue
Chicago, IL 60622 USA
(612) 292-0717

Mark Palmer Design
41-995 Boardwalk
Suite A-1
Palm Street, CA 92260
USA
(619) 346-0772

Mauk Design
636 Fourth Street
San Francisco, CA 94107
USA
(415) 243-9277

McCool & Company
901 Marquette Avenue
Suite 2800
Minneapolis, MN 55402
USA
(612) 332-3993

Merten Design Group
3235 East Second Avenue
Denver, CO 80206 USA
(303) 322-1451

Michael Doret, Inc.
12 East 14th Street
Suite 4D
New York, NY 10003 USA
(212) 929-1688

Mike Salisbury Communications, Inc.
2200 Amapola Court
Torrance, CA 90501
USA
(213) 320-7660

Milton Glaser, Icn.
207 East 32nd Street
New York, NY 10016
USA
(212) 889-3161

Minoru Morita Graphic Design
192 Bible Street
Cos Cob, CT 06807
USA
(203) 869-5097

Morla Design
463 Bryant Street
San Francisco, CA 94107
USA
(415) 543-6548

Muller & Company
112 West 9th Street
Kansas City, MO 64105
USA
(816) 474-1983

Musser Design
558 Race Street
Harrisburg, PA 17104
USA
(717) 233-4411

Neville Smith Graphic Design
131 Mayburry Skyridge
Aylmer, Quebec J9H 5E1
CANADA
(819) 827-1832

The North Charles Design Organization
222 West Saratoga Street
Baltimore, MD 21201
USA
(301) 539-4040

Ostro Design
147 Fern Street
Hartford, CT 06105
USA
(203) 231-9698

Pam Cerio Design
7710 Wake Robin Drive
Cleveland, OH 44130
USA
(216) 845-3055

Parham Santana, Inc.
7 West 18th Street
New York, NY 10011
USA
(212) 645-7501

Pat Sloan Design
1933 Forest Blvd.
Fort Worth, TX 76110
USA
(817) 926-4769

Pat Taylor, Inc.
3540 S Street N.W.
Washington, D.C. 20007
USA
(202) 338-0962

Paul Davis Studio
14 East 4th Street
New York, NY 10012
USA
(212) 420-8789

Paul Shaw/ Letter Design
785 West End Avenue
New York, NY 10025
USA
(212) 666-3738

Peckolick & Partners
112 East 31st Street
New York, NY 10016
USA
(212) 532-6166

Pentagram Design
(New York)
212 Fifth Avenue
New York, NY 10010
USA
(212) 683-7000

Pentagram Design
(San Francisco)
620 Davis Street
San Francisco, CA 94111
USA
(415) 981-6612

Peter Nguyen
2676 Mayfield Road
Suite 7
Cleveland Heights, OH
44106 USA
(216) 321-2903

Peterson & Company
2200 N. Lamar
Suite 310
Dallas, TX 75202 USA
(214) 954-0522

Petro Graphic Design Associates
315 Falmouth Drive
Rockly River, OH 44116
USA
(216) 356-0429

Pinkhaus Design
2424 South Dixie Highway
Miami, FL 33133 USA
(305) 854-1000

Plus Design, Inc.
10 Thatcher Street
Suite 109
Boston, MA 02113 USA
(617) 367-9587

Ponzo & Company
188 Oakwood Avenue
Toronto, ON M6E 2T9
CANADA
(416) 653-5773

Porter/Matjasich & Associates
154 West Hubbard
Chicago, IL 60610 USA
(312) 670-4355

PrimaDonna
31771 Topper Court
Beverly Hills, MI 48010
USA
(313) 258-8714

Primo Angeli, Inc.
590 Folsom Street
San Francisco, CA 94105
USA
(415) 974-6100

Principia Graphica
2812 N.W. Thurman
Portland, OR 97210 USA
(503) 227-6343

The Pushpin Group
215 Park Avenue South
New York, NY 10003
USA
(212) 674-8080

RBMM/The Richards Group
7007 Twin Hills
Suite 200
Dallas, TX 75231
USA
(214) 987-4800

Reactor Art + Design
51 Camden Street
Toronto, ON
M5V 1V2
CANADA
(416) 362-1913

Richard Downer Limited
48B Grafton Road
London NW5 3AY
ENGLAND
(071) 485-6034

Rolling Stone Magazine
1290 Avenue of the Americas
New York, NY 10104
USA
(212) 484-1616

Ronn Campisi Design
118 Newbury Street
Boston, MA 02116 USA
(617) 236-1339

Rousso & Associates, Inc.
5881 Glenridge Drive
Suite 200
Atlanta, GA 30328
USA
(404) 255-7472

Sackett Design
864 Folsom Street
San Francisco, CA 94107-1123 USA
(415) 543-1590

Sage Design
351 South Fuller
Suite 9B
Los Angeles, CA 90036
USA
(213) 939-3011

Saint Hieronymus Press, Inc.
1703 Mlk Way
Berkeley, CA 94709 USA
(415) 549-1405

Samata Associates
101 South First Street
Dundee, IL 60118 USA
(708) 428-8600

Sam Payne & Associates
1471 Elliott Avenue West
Suite A
Seattle, WA 98119 USA
(206) 285-2009

Sarajo Frieden Studio
712 Grandview Street
Los Angeles, CA 90057
USA
(213) 388-7201

Sayles Graphic Design
308 Eighth Street
Des Moines, IO 50309
USA
(515) 243-2922

SBG Partners
1725 Montgomery Street
San Francisco, CA 94111
USA
(415) 391-9070

Schafer Studio
3405 Greenway
Suite 202
Baltimore, MD 21218
USA
(301) 366-5253

Shapiro Design Associates, Inc.
141 Fifth Avenue
New York, NY 10010
USA
(212) 460-8544

SHR Design Communications,
8700 E. Via De Ventura
Suite 100
Scottsdale, AZ 85258
USA
(602) 483-3700

Sibley/Peteet Design
965 Slocum
Dallas, TX 75207 USA
(214) 761-9400

Siemen Graphic Communications
P.O. Box 1325
Fairfield, IA 52556 USA
(515) 472-6965

Siquis, Ltd.
9 West 29th Street
Baltimore, MD 21218
USA
(301) 467-7300

Spy Magazine
5 Union Square West
New York, NY 10003
USA
(212) 633-6550

Stan Evenson Design, Inc.
4445 Overland Avenue
Culver City, CA 90230
USA
(213) 204-1995

Studio Guarnaccia
430 West 14th Street
Studio 508
New York, NY 10014 USA
(212) 645-9610

Stylism
307 East 6th Street
Suite 4B
New York, NY 10003 USA
(212) 420-0673

Summerford Design, Inc.
2706 Fairmount
Dallas, TX 75201 USA
(214) 748-4638

Supon Design Group, Inc.
2033 M Street N.W.
Suite 801
Washington, DC 20036
USA
(202) 822-6540

Sullivan Perkins
2311 McKinney
Suite 320 LB11
Dallas, TX 75204 USA
(214) 922-9080

Tenazas Design
605 Third Street
Suite 208
San Francisco, CA 94107
USA
(415) 957-1311

Tharp Did It
50 University Avenue
Suite 21
Los Gatos, CA 95030
USA
(408) 354-6726

Thirst
855 W. Blackhawk
Chicago, IL 60622 USA
(312) 951-5251

Tim Girvin Design, Inc.
1601 Second Avenue
5th Floor
Seattle, WA
98101-1575 USA
(206) 623-7808

Tom Lewis, Inc.
2190 Carmel Valley Road
Del Mar, CA 92014
USA
(619) 481-7600

Tyler Smith
127 Dorrance Street
Providence, RI 07903
USA
(401) 751-1220

TylerSmith Graphics, Inc.
33 South 7th Street
Allentown, PA 18101
USA
(215) 776-0556

Van Dyke Company Designers
611 Post Avenue
Suite 15
Seattle, WA 98104 USA
(206) 621-1235

Vrontikis Design Office
2707 Westwood Blvd.
Los Angeles, CA 90064
USA
(213) 470-2411

Wallace Church Associates, Inc.
330 East 48th Street
New York, NY 10017
USA
(212) 755-2903

Waplington Forty McGalling
40 Bathurst Street
Toronto, ON M5V 2P2
CANADA
(416) 366-0466

Warner Books
666 Fifth Avenue
9th Floor
New York, NY 10103
USA
(212) 484-3151

Zimmermann Crowe Design
90 Tehama Street
San Francisco, CA 94105
USA
(415) 777-5560

"Letters are

symbols

which turn

matter into

spirit!"

ALPHONSE DE LEMARTINE